COLLISION

Book Four of the
SECRET WORLD CHRONICLE

BAEN BOOKS by MERCEDES LACKEY

BARDIC VOICES
The Lark and the Wren
The Robin and the Kestrel
The Eagle and the Nightingales
The Free Bards
Four & Twenty Blackbirds
Bardic Choices: A Cast of Corbies (with Josepha Sherman)

The Fire Rose

The Wizard of Karres (with Eric Flint & Dave Freer)

Werehunter

Fiddler Fair

Brain Ships (with Anne McCaffrey & Margaret Ball)
The Sword of Knowledge (with C.J. Cherryh, Leslie Fish & Nancy Asire)

Bedlam's Bard (with Ellen Guon)
Beyond World's End (with Rosemary Edghill)
Spirits White as Lightning (with Rosemary Edghill)
Mad Maudlin (with Rosemary Edghill)
Music to My Sorrow (with Rosemary Edghill)
Bedlam's Edge (ed. with Rosemary Edghill)

THE SERRATED EDGE
Chrome Circle (with Larry Dixon)
The Chrome Borne (with Larry Dixon)
The Otherworld (with Larry Dixon & Mark Shepherd)

HISTORICAL FANTASIES WITH ROBERTA GELLIS
This Scepter'd Isle
Ill Met by Moonlight
By Slanderous Tongues
And Less Than Kind

HEIRS OF ALEXANDRIA SERIES
by Mercedes Lackey, Eric Flint & Dave Freer
The Shadow of the Lion
This Rough Magic
Much Fall of Blood

THE SECRET WORLD CHRONICLE
Invasion (with Steve Libbey, Cody Martin & Dennis Lee)
World Divided (with Cody Martin, Dennis Lee & Veronica Giguere)
Revolution (with Cody Martin, Dennis Lee & Veronica Giguere)
Collision (with Cody Martin, Dennis Lee & Veronica Giguere)

**To purchase these and all other Baen Book titles
in e-book format, please go to www.baen.com.**

COLLISION

Book Four of the
SECRET WORLD CHRONICLE

Created by *Mercedes Lackey* & *Steve Libbey*

Written by
MERCEDES LACKEY
with **Cody Martin, Dennis Lee** &
Veronica Giguere

Edited by *Mercedes Lackey* & *Larry Dixon*

Dedicated to the memory of Donald "Tre" Chipman,
known to his friends in Paragon City as "Ascendant"

Collision: Book Four of the Secret World Chronicle

A Baen Books Original

Baen Publishing Enterprises
P.O. Box 1403
Riverdale, NY 10471
www.baen.com

ISBN: 978-1-4767-3691-4

Cover art by Larry Dixon

First Baen printing, December 2014

Distributed by Simon & Schuster
1230 Avenue of the Americas
New York, NY 10020

Library of Congress Cataloging-in-Publication Data

Lackey, Mercedes.
  Collision : book four in the secret world chronicle / created by Mercedes Lackey
& Steve Libbey ; written by Mercedes Lackey with Cody Martin, Dennis Lee &
Veronica Giguere ; edited by Mercedes Lackey and Larry Dixon.
     pages cm. — (Secret world chronicle ; 4)
   ISBN 978-1-4767-3691-4 (hardback)
1. Science fiction. I. Martin, Cody, 1987– II. Lee, Dennis, 1939– III. Giguere,
Veronica. IV. Title.
   PS3562.A246C65 2014
   813'.54—dc23
                                                              2014032803

10 9 8 7 6 5 4 3 2 1

Pages by Joy Freeman (www.pagesbyjoy.com)
Printed in the United States of America

ACKNOWLEDGEMENTS

As usual, most (though not all) chapters were inspired by music. Here's the playlist, and a grateful acknowledgement to the musicians.

Don't Run Our Hearts Around (Black Mountain)

Here with Me (Dido)

Secrets (Strawberry Switchblade)

Hurricane (30 Seconds to Mars)

Holding On (Jeremih)

Man in the Mirror (Michael Jackson)

Danger Zone (Kenny Loggins)

Wounds (Raised Fist)

Dead Meat (Sean Lennon)

Hold Heart (Emiliana Torrini)

Cover Girl (Melody Club)

Beloved (VnV Nation)

Rubicon (VnV Nation)

Start Shootin' (Little People)

Collision (Disciple)

Soul of a Man (Beck)

Ablivion (Unkle)

INTRODUCTION

Victoria Victrix glanced at the clock. She was running out of time.
   Fortunately most of the rest of the story was self-explanatory. She wouldn't really need to preface anything.

   All right, O my supposed readers. Hang onto your hats. It's going to be one rough ride.

PROLOGUE

Penny

MERCEDES LACKEY AND DENNIS LEE

In the far corner of the cell, Penny lay curled up in a ball. She clamped her hands firmly over her ears and fought to keep those horrible voices out. They came at night, relentless, mixing together in a disjointed chorus of wailing agony and hate.

She kept her eyes shut tight now. She had made the mistake, that first night, and had watched the ghosts try in vain to torment the living, but to no avail. As eerie as they were, these luminescent figures that floated about, that winked in and out of existence and screamed their pain and loss, no one woke. The others barely stirred. No one believed in ghosts, not when you couldn't see or hear them, not even if they were wailing at you, their faces inches away from yours, their baleful glares betraying madness. Only she knew how real they were, all too well, and the folly of granting them audience. Penny had learned, long ago, that to acknowledge the dead was to invite their attentions. Now, she refused to even look, and spent each night, every night, all night, curled up and facing the wall, trying her best not to listen. It never made a difference; she heard it all and suffered as her cellmates should have suffered. These were not her ghosts; she should not have to bear them.

Screaming Girl was the loudest. Always so shrill, so persistent, Penny wondered how even a ghost could not go hoarse from that much caterwauling. Penny had caught a glimpse of her that first night. What was left of her hair was scorched, frayed, and hung in tatters, barely hiding the horribly burnt and scarred scalp beneath. She careened about in a frenzy of movement, her

3

limbs and skin crackling obscenely as they shook with pain. Faint tendrils of smoke seeped endlessly from her hair, eyes and hands, and faded in the dim fluorescent light that lit the cell from above. Every so often, she would stop and make a mad dash for Raphael, the nervous boy with the horrible stutter. Even in sleep his brow was fixed in a guilty furrow. Screaming Girl leapt, as she always did, her burning hands raging forwards to pierce his eyes, to sink into the flesh of his face, but stopped short, as they always did. She let her fingers caress his cheek, and she would murmur the only coherent words she seemed to know.

"Your lies were so sweet..."

Then she would be off again, dashing madly about the room, screaming.

Penny shrank away from her, from all of them. Screaming Girl was by far the loudest, but the others frightened her more. The Drunk Lady swayed about, moaning of lost loves and brandishing a broken glass that wept perpetual tears of blood from jagged shards. Awful Granny barely spoke above a whisper, but with each word she promised bloody retribution for even the slightest transgression against church, state and common decency. The Creepy Man was the worst. He never made a sound. He shifted about the room on sturdy legs that supported a twitching torso and shaking hands, glaring at them all in turn. His face, matted with long, damp and thinning hair, masked a pair of wide, luminous eyes that stole hateful looks about. His hands and feet were caught in irons, held together by short bits of chain, which seemed to catch the light. His feet, which would on occasion slam down with each agitated step, never made so much as a soft thud on the concrete. He would sometimes hunch over and convulse in coughing fits, without even a whisper escaping his lips. His chains, which dangled and slammed together during his odd patrols about the cell, did so in silence. Penny had once caught the full effect of his hateful glare. It burned into her, and it didn't seem enough to slam her eyes shut. She had burrowed deep under the thin shelter of her blanket, her shaking hands holding her head against her knees. She had done that for the rest of the night, silently praying for the sun to rise.

And so it would go, each and every night. The ghosts would rise, and Penny, at the tender age of twelve, would suffer them until daybreak.

"Not mine," Penny whispered, her voice muffled into her pillow. "You're not mine, go away..."

But a voice spoke in her ear. *"They're not, but I am, dear..."*

"You go away too," Penny groaned. "Stop bothering me. I didn't do anything to you. I hate you."

"Now, dearie," the voice purred, hovering just over her. *"I taught you better manners than that."*

Penny sobbed, and tightened up even more. "Just go away," she said, her tears seeping out and soaking her flat pillow. "I'm sorry you died, I'm sorry, but I didn't..."

"But you did, *dear."* The voice was impossibly close, and Penny could almost feel an icy breath on her neck. *"Didn't I always tell you? Tell me, what did I say?"*

"Go away..."

"Momma knows best, Momma knows all. And you believe Momma when she tells you..."

"No," Penny cried. "No no no no no no..."

"Momma died because you killed her."

Penny shrank away from her, pressed her hands tighter against her ears, and almost screamed when she felt the hand on her shoulder.

"Hey there, whoa, it's just me..."

Penny exhaled and turned to face her brother.

"She talking to you again?" He sat down on her cot and stretched out his legs to form a barrier between her and the rest of the group. When Penny nodded and buried her face in her pillow, he reached over to ruffle her hair with a gentle hand. "She's wrong. You can tell her that, too."

"You just did." Penny sniffled and shifted so that her head rested against his lap. "But she says—"

"Just because she's dead don't make her words true." He winced as she pushed against a particularly tender spot on his arm. She lifted her head, the skin around her eyes almost translucent from lack of sleep. "Aw, Penny. I'm okay. I told you, it doesn't hurt as much as before. Put your head down. Nobody's gonna come over while I'm here, okay?"

She did as he said, eyes closing while calloused hands patted her back in that awkward way of older brothers comforting younger siblings. It would work for a while, until Screaming Girl began a fresh tirade. His hands felt patronizing. He believed her about the ghosts, at least that's what he always said. He believed she heard them, that she saw them, how could he not? How many girls lay awake all night, pretending to shake with fright? But did he actually believe the ghosts existed, or did he think his sister was simply cracking up? She tried not to think about it. It was enough he was there, that he would always be there to protect her. It would have to be.

"How long?" she asked finally.

"'Til sunrise? Couple of hours. Then you can sleep, sis."

"Unless he takes you again," she said. "Unless he takes you away and makes you scream."

"He's been gone for weeks this time," he assured her, though his voice sounded far off, haunted. "Maybe he'll stay away for a while. Maybe he's dead."

Penny snorted. "You can't kill the devil, stupid. He just comes back, mad. He's always worse when he's mad."

He sighed, and patted her back again.

"Just hold on, Penny," Pike said. "I'll get us out of here."

CHAPTER ONE

Don't Run Our Hearts Around

MERCEDES LACKEY AND CODY MARTIN

There was light. There was peace. There was pain. Mostly, there was pain. At first the pain didn't have a name. It was abstract, as if it were happening outside of him. Then the name came to him. John. John Murdock. He was John Murdock and the pain was his. The pain suddenly became everything, it became him. He saw flashes that didn't make any sense through the haze of his anguish; shooting and fighting in a hangar, faces that he didn't recognize, blood and fire. It was all fire. As suddenly as it came crashing through him, it was over.

There was still pain, but it was the pain of someone dropped like a sack onto a hard surface in an exceedingly awkward position. John's shoulder hurt; his entire right side was lanced through with pain. More sensations. He was on a cement floor; it was cold and clean. It was dark around him, except for a slight electrical flickering coming from behind. Chairs in front of him, with something man-shaped sitting in one of them. He struggled, and then remembered how to talk. "Where...am... I?" He croaked out the last vowel before he lost consciousness.

The Soviet Bear stared dumbfounded at the naked man on the floor. It looked...it looked like Comrade Murdock. Except Comrade Murdock was supposed to be dying, or dead, and not appearing out of thin air, naked and healthy, into the middle of the break room. He looked at the bottle of "Worker's Companion" vodka in his hand. Looked at the naked man. Decided that the two had nothing to do with each other. Then he noticed that the break room's trusty television, a sturdy model nearly identical to the ones built in the Soviet Union and looking as if it was half as old as Bear, was cracked and smoking.

He decided that the naked man probably did have something to do with that.

He sighed. *"Borzhe moi.* Commissar will probably blame me." Then he looked at the naked man again. "On other hand, if this is Comrade Murdock, she will certainly blame *him* instead. Good thinking, Pavel." Much cheered, he shoved himself up out of the chair and headed for the briefing room.

At least a broken television set was not like a broken Ural. Many, many broken, burned, exploded, and mangled Urals.

Bella probably shouldn't have been here, but the ECHO debriefing wasn't until noon, so—hell with it. She was by-God going to sit in on the CCCP one, since she'd taken over for Vic at the tail end of the infiltration op. And anyway, this way she knew that Saviour would get everything.

Unter finished his debrief right up to the point where Vic had passed out. Bella picked it up from there. "...so when I got her conscious she told me she'd neutralized some sort of super-death-machine by pounding it into the ground. I dunno, I'm not inclined to send ECHO down there to look for it unless you're in favor, Nat."

Red Saviour shook her head. "Later maybe. Are being have enough on plate. We are having leads?"

"Da. But my people haven't got done with what the infil team extracted yet. Cross your fingers...I think we're going to have the location of their HQ when we're done."

Saviour let out a breath that she had clearly been holding in. "Then...*da.* Was worth ten times over, the co—"

Bella felt it. They *all* felt it. It wasn't physical, but whatever it was...it might as well have been. Like a body-blow that doesn't hurt. Except that in Bella's case—it did. She doubled over with the anguish of it, of something...vital...taken. And yet, it wasn't something that had been taken from *her.*

"...*Borzhe moi...*" She looked up with tears in her eyes from the crippling grief to see Red Saviour shaking her head as if someone had just hit her with a two-by-four. "...What?"

She choked down the tears. "I—I don't know, but—"

The clomping of heavy feet outside Saviour's briefing room heralded the arrival of Soviet Bear. "Commissar—comrades—" he whuffed. "Television is being broken. Also is naked man on floor, that maybe is Comrade Murdock. Not my doing, either of these things."

Bella suddenly was sure, instantly sure, that this was what she had felt. Or was at least part of it. Before Bear was halfway done, she was on her feet and pushing past him, headed for the break room, impelled by a growing urgency she couldn't even begin to explain.

John woke up again, slowly. It was brighter here; he could feel that he was in a different room. It smelled like antiseptic and rubber gloves. That was a familiar smell; it had been the same odor in nearly every Army sickbay he'd ever been in. The soft hum of monitors and someone moving around were the only sounds he could immediately pick up; slowly, other faraway sounds came through, but he couldn't recognize them right off.

That...was odd. Smells were more intense, nuanced. Sensations that should have hurt, didn't. The pain he'd awakened with was gone, leaving nothing behind but the memory of having hurt. The strangest feeling was that of being heavier; like he had gained mass, somehow. It was disorienting. John groaned weakly, trying to raise himself up and open his eyes.

"So, Comrade Murdock." The voice was too loud—but within a second, somehow, it had modulated down to normal levels. Almost as if he had some sort of amplifier hooked up to his ears so he could make out things that should have been too quiet to hear—and now he'd turned it down again since someone was speaking. "You are being make bad habit of waking up in my medbay, *da?*"

He struggled for the words, remembering how to speak again. "Where...my men. Where are my troops?" He still had to squint; his eyes hadn't adjusted to the bright light in the room yet; harsh halogens, they had left him half-blind.

"ECHO troops are being back at their own HQ. Comrades Untermensch, Mamona and old man Bear are here. You are being only casualty...well, *were* only real casualty of infil team. Pavel's arm has been replaced with a spare, and Mamona's fractured arm has been set. Angel took you and went poof. Then, you are being poof back into CCCP recreational room."

"What...? I don't know...any of those names. Who are you?" The shape was coming into focus now; obviously a woman from her voice. She was tall, with the classically beautiful features of a statue rather than a model or Hollywood starlet. Her black hair was cut in a severe style that was even with her jawline. She wore a white doctor's coat with a stethoscope poking out of one pocket, over what looked like a uniform; it differed from the coats Army docs wore only in the red star and Cyrillic name tag where an Army doc would have just the name tag, in English.

"*Shto?*" The woman blinked very blue eyes. "You are not being to remember? Not ECHO? Not CCCP? Not battle?" She muttered something in Russian. At least, he thought it was Russian.

"I've heard of ECHO, lady. Everyone has...where the hell am I?"

She held up an imperious hand. "Wait. What is last thing you remember?"

He paused. "I can't say, ma'am." He held up a hand, mirroring her. "I remember it, I'm just not allowed to say. Sorry."

She pursed her lips. "*Chert.* What is year? Month? Day? Who is being win World Series?"

"...It's 2006, August, thirty-first day, and I don't really follow baseball. I'm more of a football kind of guy."

The doctor's face froze for a moment. She licked her lips. "It is being 2014, Comrade Murdock. It seems you are missing more than your clothing."

Everything went very still for him for a moment. If he believed this woman—and he had no reason not to—he had lost eight years of his life. God only knew what had happened in that time. She mentioned ECHO, as if he had been working with them, which was impossible—something called CCCP, as if it was accepted he was a part of them. Commies obviously—so—whatever had happened, had been drastic. He was overcome with nausea and disorientation. "Ma'am, I've got one last question for you before I throw up."

"*Shto?*"

"Where *are* my pants?"

The group walked down the labyrinthine hallways of the CCCP HQ, heading for the Medical Bay. Jadwiga, callsign Soviette, was leading the way, and explaining while they walked, Bella and Saviour beside her. Vickie and Sera trailed behind. Vickie was not even sure she should have been there. Except—except that somehow she had gotten all tied up with this. Sera had materialized in *her* workroom, Bella was her dearest friend—the two of them were connected somehow, Vickie's mage-sight clearly showed the bond between them. Jadwiga was going on about trauma, transitory amnesia . . . Vickie wasn't paying much attention to it. Sera—well, Sera wasn't the Seraphym anymore, wings notwithstanding. She reminded Vickie of the description in the fairy tale of the Little Mermaid, how, once she got legs, she walked in pain as if every step was taken on the blades of knives. Bella reflected that pain. But how, or why this had happened—Vickie still wasn't sure. Sera hadn't said more than a dozen words so far.

As for what they were going to see, in the CCCP medbay . . . Vickie wasn't sure what that was going to be, either, at this point.

Hope and despair flickered over Sera's face by turns.

". . . so . . . here," Jadwiga said, opening the door to the medbay. "Here is being comrade patient."

The group entered the cramped medbay. Sitting upon a gurney in the center of the room, wearing only a hospital smock and a pair of skivvies, was John Murdock. But, at the same time, not. This John didn't have darkness under his eyes. The same quiet intensity, but none of the troubles which had seemed to weigh him down even before he knew of his own impending death. The scars were still there, but they seemed fainter, unimportant now. Not really a part of the man that was sitting in front of them. And he still had his same lopsided grin.

"Howdy, y'all." He regarded the group, still smiling. "Now, who exactly are you people, an' what the hell am I doin' here?"

Bella was hyperaware of Sera behind her. There were only two people in the whole world (as far as she knew) that knew anything at all about the angel. She was one. John Murdock was—or had been—the other.

Now? Well, Sera was no longer an angel. She no longer had that *feeling* of infinite power, infinite certainty and infinite control. Her wings were feathered, not fire. According to Jadwiga, John was back, but completely cured of what had been killing him—and Vickie had also said that Sera wasn't an angel anymore. Since the last time anyone had seen either of them, it had been together, it was pretty obvious that the one thing had to do with the other.

Right now, Sera was vibrating with mingled hope and despair, so much so it was making Bella's empathic shields hum.

According to Jadwiga, this *was* the same man, in every way but two. He was perfectly healthy, and the cellular disorder that had been killing him was now gone, as if every bit of damage had been instantly healed, the dysfunction removed. Jadwiga couldn't tell what had done that, and she was the more experienced healer of the two of them, and a full MD to boot. "Is being magic," she had said, and shrugged. *That* answer produced a derisive snort from Natalya.

And now, here was the man himself, sitting on an examination table, looking entirely like himself. Sera peered around Bella's shoulder, her wings trembling so hard that the feathers rustled.

"Who exactly are you people? I expect some answers, and right quick." he said, looking directly at Sera for a brief moment.

Bella had never actually seen someone's heart break before, but the change in Sera's expression showed that moment in agonizing detail. Bella's shields rang like a bell with the blow of grief and loss.

And then—Sera was gone. Literally *flying* from the room, and out an open hallway window. Bella was torn—follow Sera, or try and sort out Murdock? She'd never catch Sera; she couldn't fly, and certainly couldn't move that fast. Throttling down her own feelings, she turned to Murdock.

John only looked mildly surprised, but still expectant for an answer. "Well?"

Untermensch laid a hand on Natalya's shoulder. "Commissar..."

Saviour nodded. "*Da*. Comrade Murdock. You are seeming to be experiencing memory problem. For past year and more, you have been sturdy worker and operative for the *Super-Sobratiye Sovetskikh Revolutzionerov*. You Amerikanski are being know this as CCCP. This occurred after an invasion by an army of Nazi-affiliated metahumans and—" she paused.

"Oh, for God's sake, Nat, say it. Aliens. Big, ugly, aliens. ET, but not cute, not friendly, and as far as we can tell, planning to wipe us off the planet." Bella crossed her arms over her chest, trying to physically hold in her churning emotions.

"They attacked almost every major city on Earth a little more than a year ago in a coordinated strike, decimating much of the world and killing untold numbers. The attack was to soften up the governments of the world, and cripple ECHO, as well as other metahuman crime and logistics organizations. Since then, you have been helping us and ECHO fight these *fascista*. Questions, comrade?"

John's jaw didn't quite drop, but it was close. "This has to be bullshit. What happened to my troops?"

"I am not knowing which troops you are speaking of, Comrade Murdock," Saviour said crisply, "but if they are the ones in Costa Rica—"

Unter coughed. Nat's mouth snapped shut self-consciously. John stared at the two, his gaze going cold and dead for the barest second. Bella knew that look. She'd seen it before. It meant that John Murdock was considering every option he had... and a lot of those options included killing someone. The tension in the air was ready to snap like an icicle; Bella found herself holding her breath, waiting. It was Untermensch who broke it before things turned to the unfortunate.

"Comrade, my name is Georgi Vlasov. My callsign is 'Untermensch.'" He paused for a moment, to see if any recognition sparked in John. "You and I are being comrades in arms for the last year. During this time, we have killed many *fascista*, and struck hard blows against their efforts." He paused again; still, nothing but that expectant look from Murdock. At least the murder had gone out of his eyes. "Comrade, when you came to us, you were injured and were being on the run. It is our understanding from what you told us that you were the only survivor from your unit. I am sorry, comrade." Unter looked away briefly, then back to John.

Bella saw that John believed Unter; Murdock had a way of judging sincerity in people, and he always used to go with his gut. Emotions passed through John—no, they tore through him. Bella braced herself against them. Rage, despair, confusion— disbelief—the disbelief started to win. And who could blame him? Even in a world full of metahumans, this must sound like a bad science fiction movie. *Show, don't tell.* That would be the best way to cut through whatever walls he was already trying to put up between himself and reality.

She strode over to the medbay window and yanked up the ugly Soviet venetian blind. It clattered, and sunlight poured in the room. "Look for yourself," she said curtly. "That's Atlanta out there. What's left of it. What the Kriegers left us." John looked at her hard, then hopped off of the examining table. He strode quickly to the window, peering out of it.

Without looking away, he started to speak in harsh tones. "What the hell happened? Is everywhere like this?"

"We are being on edge of what *nekulturny* teevee calls 'destruction corridor.' Enemy marched war machines towards ECHO HQ and were not gentle about doing so. Many cities have them." Nat's jaw tightened. "Red Square is similarly...disrupted. My CCCP was there for a...meeting with officials. They came for us metahumans, we know this now—" She broke off. "I will to being get you briefing."

"Um," Vickie said softly from somewhere near Bella's elbow. "I can do that. I've got all the records and the hardware with me to make it happen; it won't take long. Heck, I can start on it now."

Nat nodded curtly. Bella took up where she had left off. "The world economy is devastated, but...coping. Relief efforts are going on everywhere. Cities are full of these corridors; the countryside was impacted the least or not at all, and it's hit or miss with manufacturing and industrial centers. The thing is, now we're finding out that the Kriegers had weapons cached damn near everywhere, and cells to activate them. Every time things seem to get a little better, they activate one, there's a helluva lot of fighting and death until we get it shut down, and governments go ballistic."

"Sorry, Kriegers?" John shook his head, uncomprehending.

Vickie ducked out from under Bella's elbow, her laptop open, typing away. "Here," she said, shoving the thing at him. "That's the enemy. We call them Kriegers, for 'Blitzkrieg.' They seem to be a combination of the aliens and a pile of Nazi metahumans and fanatics that escaped after the War. And recruits."

Light from the screen flickered on his eyes, mirroring the emotions that flitted through him. "So...y'all are fighting them? Stopping stuff like this," he gestured towards the ruined buildings outside, "from happening anymore?"

"*Nyet.* We are not doing so well as that. Trying to keep them from turning the world into giant labor camp," the Commissar said grimly. "Conventional forces—well, being to look at screen, comrade."

Bella sighed. "There are a handful—and only a handful—of

metas and special weapons that do anything but dent these guys and annoy them," she said, sensing that his first instinct was to head straight for the nearest Army base and volunteer. "Most of those aren't in the arsenals of most armies. Uh—and you happen to be one of the metahumans who can actively hurt them. Same for me, the Commissar here, most of CCCP...oh, yeah, I'm the head of ECHO...I guess you don't remember that."

John did a spit-take. "What? You said...that I'm metahuman?"

"Uh, yeah. You're some sort of fire-chucker. Plus..." She rubbed her temple. "Evidently you were in some kind of super-soldier program. You wouldn't tell us much. But you've got implants. And fire, which doesn't seem to have anything to do with the implants." She sighed again. "Conventional troops are good if we're the spearhead, Murdock. Without us...conventional troops are just a blunt stick against a hungry tiger."

"You're...what's your name again, ma'am?"

"Bella Dawn Parker, callsign Belladonna Blue, and acting head of ECHO. I'm not technically the CEO, that's Yankee Pride, but that's an administrative position and we're on a war footing. So sometimes they call me a CEO too."

"You're not feeding me a line about any of this, right? No BS?" John met her eyes. His were searching, looking for anything to latch onto. He *needed* someone to look to as an authority. That made sense; he was a soldier, after all...or at least, the *him* of eight years ago had been. And given he was US Army, he wasn't going to look to some commie foreigner as that authority, at least not yet. It had to be her.

Mutely, Bella fished her ID out of a pocket and handed it to him. As she touched his hand, she tried to send him a thread of reassurance, juggling her need to help him with the ethics of imposing anything on him.

John scanned the ID quickly before handing it back to Bella. "I need some time to think on this. And I'll be needin' some more information; hell, all of it." He looked to Natalya. "I'm guessin' from your charmin' Muscovite accent that you're in charge of this bunch?"

Saviour nodded. "I am being Commissar Red Saviour, second of that name, of CCCP. *Your* commander, Comrade Murdock."

Bella nodded. "Technically you should be in ECHO, but given that you clearly did not want your former...friends...to know you were even alive, this was the best place for you to go. You've also had Blacksnake sniffing at your heels...with guys with katanas. Who put holes in you. It's a long story. I'll cut to the chase. Until a few minutes ago, as far as I can tell, you were dying of whatever gave you that fire-chucking ability. And...something happened to you. Vick, scan him, would you?"

"You mean—" Vickie looked up at her, a little apprehensive.

"Yeah, I need to confirm my hunch. Make with the finger wiggling." John tensed as Vickie approached him, looking to Bella. "It's okay. She's a magician as well as a computer wizard." *Now that has to be a mind-screw, on top of everything else.*

Vickie paused about a foot away from him, and flexed her fingers. "All right. This won't hurt a—"

"—*YOW!*" Emanating from the center of John's chest, there was a pulse of white light, which hit Vickie squarely on her outstretched hand.

Vickie staggered back. Her short hair was literally standing straight up.

Bella grabbed Vickie's elbow and held her up. "*Vick!* Are you okay?" She did her own version of "scanning," making sure there was no damage. No physical damage, at least.

Vickie put shaking hands up to her head, smoothing down her hair. "Uh...yeah. Ever stick a fork in a light socket? Don't. But...yeah, he's...fixed, and the same, only different. And it's not 'magic' as I understand it. It's, well..." she waved her hands, vaguely. "Bigger. A lot bigger."

"Sera," Bella said flatly. Vickie nodded.

"What'd she just do to me?" Bella recognized John coiled and ready to spring into action. All of this was strange and new to him, and it must have been very frightening.

"She didn't do anything to you. You did it to her. She was trying to ID what it was that fixed you, it didn't want to be ID'd, and it bit back..." She shook her head. "Look, Vick, job one, get Murdock briefed. I'll try and find Sera, among everything else that's going on."

"Anyone gonna ask what the hell I wanna do, maybe?" John's back was against the glass window, his arms crossed.

Saviour snorted. "You are being registered member of CCCP and under my orders, Comrade. That was by your own—how you say—enlistment? So I am still your commanding officer, *nyet?*"

He bristled. "Lady, until about ten minutes ago, I didn't even know you existed. I'm slow on most days, so you're gonna have to be real slow with me now. Especially in telling me what the hell to do. Savvy?"

"*Lyuboi.* Your callsign is now being Slow Boy. So, Slow Boy, you are to being briefed on last eight years by ECHO OpThree Victoria Victrix. When you are to being caught up, then we talk. Daughter of Rasputin is also *bolshoi* computer wizard, anything you are needing to know, she can find. *Da*, Victrix?"

"*Da*, Commissar." Vickie tucked her laptop under her arm. "I've got it from here. Just one thing, Commissar?"

"*Shto?*" Saviour said, turning back.

"Can we *please* find him some pants?"

It's the same man. It's not the same man. Absolutely contradictory statements, yet somehow, both were true. Still... that could happen in magic and physics, which were more closely related than most people realized. *So... all right, first things first. Get him up to speed on current events, then hit him with the personal stuff.*

Fortunately, there was a crap-ton of media documentaries about the Invasion and subsequent events. Vickie just searched out the most unbiased accounts (BBC and a select mixture of online reporting, which was no big surprise for her), downloaded them and put JM in a chair and the laptop in his lap. Thankfully, he was dressed now; a spare CCCP coverall. He picked at the insignia now and again, clearly less than comfortable with it.

"There," she said. "That's about two hours. Pause it and ask questions if you want to." While he was watching, she was going to cobble up something showing him clips of himself in the CCCP. Maybe get other records. It was a good thing she carried a spare netbook; it was powerful enough for that task.

"Miss... Victrix, right?"

"Technically Nagy. Call me Vickie, or Vix," she said absently, using her PDA to access media files for the "Adventures of John Murdock" sequence.

"Right. Vickie. How the hell did I get mixed up in all of this? I mean," he shook his head, sighing, "last I remember, Nazis didn't run around blowing up things all that much, and aliens weren't exactly taken seriously as terrorists."

She ran a hand through her hair; she wasn't quite as prone to panic attacks as she used to be, but she could feel her nerves doing the jitterbug, and her hair was damp at the roots. This wasn't her room, her chair, her safe place. But this was Johnny, and they had done all those ops together with her as Overwatch. But...it wasn't. Dammit. "Look...watch the documentary first. What I am going to show you about yourself won't make any sense until you see what happened. Okay?"

"All right, ma'am. Do y'have any coffee or tea, since this seems like it'll take awhile?"

Tea. "Uh...it'll take a minute; the Russkis live on tea, but it's all black samovar tea, not green, and it doubles as paint-remover." Was it worth the effort to apport some from her kitchen?

John looked at her hard for a moment before turning his attention back to the laptop. *How did she know that I prefer green tea? This whole "being out of the loop" bit is getting old, fast.* This tiny woman...like a little blond pixie...she was making all of his internal alarms go off. Her body language said she was on the ragged edge of a panic—he could almost smell it on her—and yet her voice was steady, everything she said made sense, and she acted like an old friend. She wasn't faking it; this person *knew* him. It was disconcerting. All of his instincts told him to *run*; get distance, asses the situation, figure out what to do. He was fighting in the dark at the moment, however; he had been thrust into a world that seemed to have turned itself upside down. He was a *metahuman,* the world had been devastated, and now he was working with *commies.* It all seemed like too much to process. The only smart move he had to make, for now, was to wait and see. Learn what he could; these people seemed to want to help him, not play him, but he was still wary.

Then she said something that actually made no sense at all. "Um. Since I guess you've never seen real magic before, this might freak you. So, uh, you being special ops military and all, and military reactions tending to be a tad strong, uh—"

"Hold up, ma'am. Y'said 'magic,' right? We talkin' rabbits coming out of hats, sleight of hand, an' all of that?" He had heard the blue woman, Bella, and the commie leader, say that this Victrix was a magician before. He knew he hadn't misheard, but he hadn't exactly been ready to believe, either.

She sucked in her lower lip. "Uh, no. Magic. Real magic. Like...
oh, hell. Just don't freak."

"Metahumans exist. Broadcast energy exists; that much, ECHO
shit, I remember. Apparently, Nazis in power armor exist, along
with aliens. But...magic, ma'am? Color me an unbeliever; is this
just a schtick for your powers or somethin'?" He looked utterly
unimpressed.

"Just don't freak," she repeated. "Don't karate chop me, or grab
a scalpel, or...just don't freak."

She licked her finger, drew a circle in spit on the top of the
table, then drew inside the circle, and muttered...something.
Her eyes flicked back and forth in rapid fire while closed; she
was obviously concentrating extremely hard on something. There
was a little *bumpf* of displaced air. And where she'd drawn the
circle, the empty table now had...

A little stone figure inside it. No larger than an original G.I.
Joe action figure...but it was *moving*. The figure was lumpy and
prehistoric-looking. One "hand" clutched an electric teakettle.
The other held a wad of teabags to its chest.

John did his very best to keep his jaw from hitting the table;
he managed it, barely. After a few stupefied seconds, he regained
his words. "Ma'am...what is that?" He pointed at the stone figure.
This has gotta be some kinda trick.

"Oh, this's Herb." She turned her attention back to the ani-
mate rock. "Thanks sweets, you remembered the kettle, you are
a lifesaver," she said to the statue. Which squeaked, and moved,
holding the tea bags up to her.

John felt ill again. "This isn't a trick, is it? You're really doing this."

"It's my job," she said, dryly, taking the kettle, filling it from water
in the medbay sink, and plugging it in. "I'm a techno-shaman. A
mathemagician. I do cybermancy. My traditional magic is Earth
magic, primarily. Herb is an Earth Elemental."

"Techno-what? Your church give out pamphlets or have y'all shave
your heads or anything like that? I have no clue what you just said."

She sighed. "*Now* do you see what I mean by stuff not making
sense until you watch the film? So watch the film."

He nodded obediently, keeping his eyes on Herb for a few
more moments before turning to the laptop. When all of the BBC
recaps and Internet clips were over, he felt as if he were waking
up naked and disoriented all over again. *Jesus...eight years. I've*

been out of it for eight years. How did I get like this? John's head swam, and he felt sick to his stomach. He had to focus; he had to figure out what to do. If what these people were telling him was true—it seemed to be, so far—his troops were dead. He was out of the army, and a metahuman. And the world had been set on fire. What could he do?

She had been typing away madly at some smaller device while he had been watching, taking time out only to gulp tea herself. Now she looked up. "Okay. Sixty-four-dollar question. Do you want to know how you got into the CCCP first, or . . . or what you've been doing for the last eight years first?"

"If they're exclusive, I'd like t'hear where the hell I've been the last eight years. Ma'am."

She didn't answer him. She turned to the little stone creature. "Herb, remember the file cabinet in my Overwatch room? The file folder with the Solomon's Seal lock on it?"

The thing squeaked and nodded. She handed it a ring she took off her finger. "Unlock it with the ring and grab what you find in there, hold onto it and tell Grey to ping my PDA when you have it. Make sure you have every scrap of paper in that folder, 'kay?"

It squeaked and nodded more vigorously. She repeated the actions that had fetched the stone "elemental," tea, kettle and all, drawing a new circle around the thing. Then she clapped her hands, and it . . . vanished.

"Good help is priceless," she said to no one in particular, a bead of sweat running down her face. "This'll take a little bit. Tea?"

John shook himself out of a daze. "Um, yes please, ma'am." Magic was too weird. Even with strangeness such as metahumans and techno wonders that would boggle the mind, John figured that he had a fairly good handle on the world. Magic was different; it felt *wrong* to him. For some reason that sensation sparked something in him, like there was something he was forgetting that he ought not be. He dismissed it, staring at the laptop as Vickie made more tea, dumped what seemed like about a quarter cup of sugar in hers, and drank it down. He stared. That was a lot of sugar. "Uh . . . it's your body, but . . ."

"Right. I explained all this to you before, but . . . yeah. Uh, magic is like physics. No free lunch. Energy to move stuff has to come from somewhere, usually me. So figure I've been running up and down five flights of stairs to do this. A lot." She mopped her brow with a paper towel. "So while Herb gets what I need, I'm drinking sugar and I am taking a rest, here. But that's why I became a techno-shaman in the first place. I need a lot less energy to do stuff with computer assist. Like—well, keeping track of you, which was mostly my job. Is my job. Your techno-wizardry eye over your shoulder, called Overwatch." She blinked. "Huh. I wonder."

He leaned back in his seat. "That tone doesn't sound like somethin' I'll like, ma'am."

"Let me borrow that a second." She gestured to the laptop. When he handed it to her, she began typing furiously.

A moment later...a HUD appeared in front of him, seemingly about six inches in front of his eye. He swatted the air furiously for a moment before realizing that it was the projection of a heads-up display. "How did you do that?"

"In-eye implanted camera and projector, part magic, part mechanical. Also a subvocal pickup mic and a speaker in your ear. Still working...which proves that you are you, anyway." The other device made a chirping sound. She put the laptop down, took a deep, weary-sounding breath, and did her little ritual all over again. This time when the air displaced, the stone man was holding a fat file folder.

"Good job, Herb," she said with approval, and took it, then handed it to John. "This is your CCCP stuff, plus everything I have on you, as well as in regard to working with them. Read it. Then start asking questions." She was a little—no, a lot—pale. "I need to lie down and suck on some more sugar."

John hefted the folder; it was heavy. "What is it?"

"Your missing eight years. Part of it, anyway," she said, lying down on the examination table and sticking a lollipop in her mouth. "I'm still working on the video files to verify for you, but I need a break." *Curiouser and curiouser. I think I need to wake up, or somethin'.* He opened the file, and began to read.

John finished reading the thick folder some time later, standing up and walking to where Vickie was lying down. "All of this is legit?" He didn't look very impressed.

She cracked one eye open and looked at him sardonically. "Why in hell would I bother to fake up that much photoshopped material just to fool one guy? In case you hadn't noticed, hotshot, there's a war on, and I already need three of me just to keep up."

"Lady, I wake up and everyone is telling me the world is on fire, Nazi aliens exist, and that I'm eight years behind on all of my car payments. I'm not really takin' much for granted, 'kay?" He tapped the file. "According to this, I wandered in here, injured by some Blacksnake operatives who were trying to recruit me 'cause I'm a metahuman. I then became an operator for the CCCP, patrollin' this area of Atlanta and goin' out to blow Nazi stuff up regularly. Right?"

"When you weren't blowing up CCCP Urals, yeah, pretty much." She closed her eye.

"And you were part of my support crew. Just seems like stuff that, I dunno, I'd remember. How the hell did I lose my memory?"

"Wish I knew. You'll note at the end of your file that you were dying. As in, days to live. At the end of the last op, which was roughly yesterday, of which all I have at this moment is the recordings I made during it, not my notes, you had hours to live. Now you're bright-eyed and bushy-tailed and you don't remember eight years worth of living on the run, not to mention our last altercation with Hitler's stepchildren." Her eyes were still closed. "All I know is there was a big old mystical *bang,* and you turned up in the CCCP break room without either your clothing or your memory."

There was something about the set of her jaw, even with her eyes closed, that warned him she was not going to let things remain this uncertain.

"All right. I'll bite for now." He turned to start reading the files again, but looked back to Vickie before he sat down. "Who was that red-haired gal with the wings who ran outta here so fast? ECHO, like you and the smurf?"

Now she opened her eyes and sat up. "Now *that* is a very interesting question indeed. She used to be an angel. I mean that literally. Fiery sword, wings, Celestial powers, appearing and vanishing at will, speaking cryptically, the whole nine yards. I am not making this up, an angel."

John arched an eyebrow skeptically. "Ma'am, I wasn't much of a believer back before this craziness. I'm still not much of one now. An *angel*?"

"Verified by every magical and mystical authority that *I* trust." She shrugged. "And she seemed very attracted to you for some reason."

He paused for a few beats. "I'm not wholly sold on magic. But I'm not entirely unconvinced, either; I've never seen stuff like what you did earlier, an' I got the impression that it was all small-fry stuff. Nothin' metahuman I've heard of can do that, unless you're playin' with my head. But—angels?"

"Well, currently the most interesting thing is that she picked you up off the battlefield, coughing blood, and all my med-readouts said you had hours to live. None of our *our* people were able to heal or fix what was wrong with you. Then there was that mystical nuke going off somewhere nearby, and now here you are—and there she is, just a metahuman. Or...hmm, I'll say *mostly* a metahuman. Certainly mortal. I figure it's gotta be connected." She shook her head. "Anyway, let's bring you up to speed on you, first. You were a fire-chucker. So...make with the fire."

"Got a lighter or a couple of twigs? I'll get right on it."

"Okay, smart-ass..." she muttered. He saw her fingers twitch a moment.

He felt the movement; instincts kicked in. Something big behind him. John whirled around, the dropping feeling in the pit of his stomach telling him that it was going to be bad. He scanned it instantly, and everything seemed to move much slower than it should have. After reading the file Vickie gave him, and watching the recorded BBC broadcasts and CCCP archival footage, he instantly knew what he was looking at: one of the Nazi troopers, in full power armor.

There weren't any weapons nearby, beyond makeshift bludgeons and a few useless surgical implements; John had scanned the room the instant he'd been awake enough to be aware of his surroundings. He was as good as naked. Vickie was just some young gal, and worn out from whatever her magic was; he had to do something, give her time to get away, anything. He lunged towards the Nazi, thrusting his right hand forward—

—a large spit of flame blasted against the trooper, and it instantly disappeared.

"Nice shootin', Tex."

Where the trooper had been was a thin rock, tall as the trooper, now flame-scorched and partly melted.

"What the hell just happened?" John was still in a half-crouch, scanning the room for threats.

"You were a smart-ass, so I dropped a live-fire exercise on you." Vickie looked at her hands for a moment; they were shaking. "Think I can wait a little before I put that rock back out in the garden. I gave you a target with an illusion instead of just an illusion because I didn't want you to blast a hole in Sovie's med-bay. You're already down three Urals to the Commissar as it is."

He looked unbelievingly at his hands. "I could actually blast through the wall? Am I that powerful?" He glanced at her. "What are the ratings that metas use again? What am I?"

"You're an OpThree at least. Not a Four...yet. But a definite high Three. One of the few people who has anything that can actually get through the Krieger power armor." She gestured at the file folder. "There's recordings in there of you duking it out with one of their big shots, not once, but twice. Ubermensch II. Or you can wait for my director's-cut version."

John snapped his fingers, producing a lighter-size flame. "Fire weakens them, right? The suits. Makes 'em easier to take out?"

"That's it, in a nutshell. However, you can do more than produce fire, you can ramp up to plasma and cut through them. Even the Death Spheres, at full-on power." Again, she gestured at the folder. "I'd say go sit yourself down at a computer and watch my stuff. I've got all the feeds from the ops when I was Overwatch for you in there, including the last one. Eyes-only stuff, please. Don't want it showing up on the Internet."

"Uh, roger, ma'am." He closed his hand over the flame, extinguishing it.

"Oh, also? You have implants. Aside from mine, that is. Some sort of 'Super-Sekrit' implants. You wouldn't talk about them. At least not to me, probably not to Bell, and definitely not to Saviour. So if things seem to go all special-effects for you when you're ramped up, well, that's probably why."

"Everything is...enhanced. Things are too loud an' too bright sometimes, an' they got...'special effects,' as y'said, when I shot that rock. Is that the 'implants'?"

"Probably. You were faster than you should have been, and stronger, and a helluva lot harder to kill. Any human and most metahumans would have died from the gut-stab you had when you showed up here, long before you made it to the door." She watched him through narrowed eyes, face giving away nothing. He felt like he was going to throw up again, though he was trying very hard to hide it.

But her hands were still shaking.

✧   ✧   ✧

This was a gamble, a very high-stakes gamble. She was gambling that if he had the mindset of the Delta soldier she thought he had been those eight years ago—after working with all the ex-Forces guys who turned up in the FBI, she was pretty good at pegging people—he'd respond to her putting on the "command persona." Not someone in command of *him,* just someone who was used to calling some shots. It seemed to be working. It was giving her a chance to do a lot of fast observations.

This version of John was a lot less hardened, a lot less cynical, a lot kinder than the old one. He moved warily, as a combat soldier should, but without the paranoia. The old JM would have reduced her rock to a melted puddle if she had startled him that way; no hesitation, straight for the kill. Then he'd have yelled at her for pulling the stunt in the first place. This JM waited just that fraction of a second to ascertain *threat,* then responded with what should have worked to make that threat pause a moment. *Not* straight for the kill.

And when he wasn't under threat, he moved... easily. Without the tension Johnny carried around with him, always, like it was wired into him with the implants. There was a relaxed-but-ready air about him the Johnny she knew didn't have. The Johnny she knew was always ready, but it was the always-ready of someone who expects to lay down an arc-light attack at any moment with no survivors.

Then there was the fire....

It was different. It smelled of *Celestial.* Like the Seraphym's fire. She was beginning, she thought, to get the shape of this, and it made her itch to find out the details.

And last of all... this Johnny did not have that burden of sorrow and guilt that weighed the old John down, darkened his eyes, shadowed his features, as if the ghosts of a thousand victims walked behind him at all times. If she had to put a name to the difference, it would have been a name that both the old and new Johns would probably laugh at.

Innocence.

"Okay, sport," she said, hopping down off the bed. She apported the rock back to what had once been Fei Li's Zen garden. Steadied herself to make sure she wasn't going to pass out. "You've got my contact info. You've got a bunk, showers and three squares here. Get some food, watch the files, get some sleep, get hold of me when you're ready. Just say 'Overwatch: open: Vickie' and the system I installed in you will call me. I'd say get hold of Bell, because you two were tight, but she's sort of busy right now." She started out the door, then turned back. "You might want to pay close attention to the stuff about the Seraphym. I'm pretty sure you two have a major connection too."

"Right, ma'am. Vickie?"

"Yo?"

"Thanks. I realize that I'm not the easiest SOB to deal with on my good days, not to mention now. I appreciate you takin' the time for this."

She felt a wave of sadness pass over her. "Kiddo . . . I'll do more than that. You know, you were *my* friend too."

He smiled; it was the same carefree and lopsided grin that he always had. But—free of the shadow of hidden pain. "Were? I'm not dead yet, ma'am."

A little of the sadness passed. She mimed a blow at him. "Then for the love of Pete, stop calling me *ma'am*."

"Roger, ma'am."

John was used to thinking on his feet, adapting, getting out of tight spots in a hurry. But this entire situation was on a whole new level. These people didn't seem to be trying to feed him any lines; they were sincere, and expected him to believe them. They were telling the truth, as well as they knew it. His problem was that if it was the truth, it was almost too fantastical to believe. How could the entire world have gone to hell so quickly? Almost launched into an apocalypse, with millions upon millions dead. Governments battered to nearly the breaking point, and the citizenry of the world no better.

Even more maddening, he *couldn't* remember it. John needed more information to make sense of this mess. He knew a few things with certainty. He was now some sort of metahuman; his own senses and the incident with Vickie's stone proved that much. The world was in crisis; he'd been in war zones, but looking out the window of this compound, it appeared as if the entire world had become one. Finally, these people, the CCCP and ECHO, seemed to want to help him; they seemed to need his help, too, if the file he'd read was right.

Well, what are you gonna do now, moron? It was an interesting question. He was in a world of crap up to his neck, and the high-tide line was rising fast. He could go back to the military; almost immediately, he discounted that idea. John loved army life, but he also knew that since the early 70s the army had no great love of metahumans. There were some, of course, but by and large they were considered too unpredictable, and most of the best were already swallowed up by ECHO or, in recent years, PMCs; the pay and benefits were a lot better.

Then there were the implants. Where had *those* come from? Every time he thought about that, he got a cold, empty feeling in his gut, because there had been rumors...

He could also run; from the sparse information in the file he'd read, it seemed to have been what he'd been doing prior to the attacks. That wasn't any good either, though; these Nazis... they wanted the whole world. Nowhere was safe, not even here in this base.

That left one real option; it wasn't pretty, but it was the only hand he had to play. It was also the only one his conscience would let him take. He'd stay and help these people. Besides, it looked like he needed their help just as much as they needed his.

CHAPTER TWO

Here With Me

MERCEDES LACKEY AND CODY MARTIN

There was pain; terrible pain. The pain of *what she was* being reft from her, the pain of birth, and rebirth. It was pain so dreadful, so fundamental, that there were no words for it. There was *his* pain too; she was aware of every moment of it.

And then, worse than pain—the loss.

It was unfathomable. For every moment of her existence up to this point, she had always, always been submerged in the company of her Siblings. Humans said that the angels sang the praises of God; they even called it the "choir" of angels. That was only partly true, as were all things that humans thought they knew about the Siblings. The Siblings Sang, yes, but they Sang the great Song of all creation, echoing all that had been and all that was. Sera had been a part of that Song, had sung her thread of that Song, and it had been woven through her every thought for as long as she had been, along with the awareness of the Infinite—sharper and more defined than for a human, but still, even an angel could know only a fraction of what the Infinite was.

And now that was gone, and she was alone, terribly alone, in her own mind.

The pain of *that* loss was not one she had anticipated. The loss of her immortality, yes. Her invulnerability, of course. Her power, certainly. But not that. *Why would the Infinite take that from me? Why must I be removed from the solace of the Song?* It was not so much a *thought* as a cry of anguish.

She came to herself in the protected and sheltered bounds of a sacred circle, encased now in a heavy, mortal body, weighed down with loss that she thought she might die of it at that very moment of her birth, wracked by such grief that she could not even breathe.

It was the mage's circle; it was the little, perpetually terrified mage, and not her protégé, who found her there. It was the mage who coaxed her into that first breath, who clothed her in garments that smelled of incense and came from a hidden closet; a loose white tunic of the sort the Greeks had worn, which could be draped around her wings—long on the mage, knee-length on her. It was the mage who dried her tears and brought her to the CCCP HQ, making her understand that John *had* returned, reborn as had been promised. And that gave her the first lightening of her grief; she might not have the Song, but she would have his love . . . she might not have the knowledge of the futures, but together they would surely find the right path. As she had sustained him, his love would sustain her. She needed that love now, needed the bond between them more than she needed food and drink. She had lost her Siblings, but she had him. . . .

She vibrated with sorrow and anxiety and need of him as she followed the rest to where he had been taken. She peered around Bella's shoulder, the feathers of her wings rustling as they trembled with that need.

He looked—wonderful. Strong, sure, *clean,* none of the terrible guilt he had carried for as long as she had known him. No shadows. His soul was unscarred. Her heart leapt. This was as it should be—*now* he could help her see the way clear, and he could become all he had lost and more.

And then he looked straight at her—and did not know her.

She thought that she would die, in that moment. His look of blank unrecognition fell on her and nearly drove her to the ground. Unable to bear it, she fled, speeding away on wings that beat the air at the same frantic rate as her heart, tears pouring from her eyes, struck mute by this loss, this loss that was—oh yes, it was—as great and as terrible as the loss of heaven.

She knew, in that moment, *why* he had looked so unshadowed, so innocent. The soul that gazed from those eyes was not the John Murdock she knew. Literally. This was another John, a John from the time before the Program and all the things that had been done to him and with him. *That* John was gone. Perhaps *that* John was dead. This John did not know her, because he had never known her.

As she sped high above the city, she cried out her despair, in a wordless wail of agony and loneliness so profound, so unendurable, that those who heard even the faintest echo of it were rocked where they stood, and psions and sensitives across Atlanta suddenly found themselves, without warning, weeping for every grief, every loss they had ever felt.

She came to rest in the abandoned graveyard; it seemed fitting. She hid her head in her arms, propped on a gravestone, and wept soundlessly. *So . . . this is the rest of the price to be paid.* She accepted it. She had made her bargain; she would not repudiate it. Though she was in despair, this was still the only hope she had seen for the rest of this world. Duty as well as love had brought her to this; duty would hold her to whatever life she had left. And it would probably be short. Verdigris and Peoples' Blade would not cease to stalk her; never mind that what they wanted from her, she could no longer give them.

But without him . . . without the Song . . . life could not be short enough.

Everything was lost to her. Everything. She wept onto the headstone, and could find no comfort.

Bella followed the anguish. Sera had come to earth, but it had taken Bella this long to get a minute away from ECHO business. She'd managed—ironically, thanks to Sera's training—to wall off most of that terrible grief, but even walled off it was more than enough to follow.

"This is being bad idea, wandering about without bodyguard—" Saviour, however, looked as if she relished being out here in this wrecked neighborhood, heading for what looked like a jungle but which, according to the city map, was a city graveyard. Then again, right now there wasn't a lot of money to spare to maintain old graves; too, new ones had needed digging after the Invasion. "Verdigris would to be only too pleased to be finding you out here alone."

"I'm not alone. That's what you're for," Bella replied. "I figured if he sent his goons, or even Fei Li after me, you'd kill me if you didn't get a shot at them."

For answer, Saviour only bared her teeth. They gleamed whitely in the street lamp.

"She's in there," Bella continued, pointing at the graveyard.

She remembered, vaguely, that the Seraphym had been known to come here, before, when she wanted peace and quiet.

"Affirmative," Vickie seconded. "Whacking big magical energy source."

The three women hurried towards the graveyard, Vickie quivering like a hound on the scent, Bella trying to think of *anything* she could do when they found her angel, and Saviour looking hopefully around for something to break into tiny pieces. Verdigris didn't oblige, and the local thugs had learned better, finally. The only living thing they found was a winged woman in a crumpled heap on an old grave, shaking with silent sobs.

Saviour stopped first, frowning. *"Shto?"*

But it was Vickie who answered the many questions packed into that single word. "She's—exiled. Lost. She's human now, or mortal, at least. I think—I don't think she's Fallen, I think she sacrificed part of herself to save Johnny. That would account for why he's got Celestial fire now . . . maybe other things, I haven't dared test him after the zap I got the first time. But, Commissar—the Seraphym has just lost literally *everything*. Think about it. Home, friends, family, everything she's known, most of her powers—it's the loss of home, friends and family that's the worst, I think. She knows it's all still *there,* but as long as she lives, she can't speak to them, hear them, see them, feel them, not anything. It's all gone. It's as if you got exiled to the Moon with no way back and no way to speak to anyone; no matter how comfortable you were, it wouldn't matter if you were completely alone and isolated. Everything she ever knew is lost, and she doesn't know if it can be found again."

"Borzhe moi," Saviour muttered, but Bella and Vickie were already sprinting towards the prone figure.

Bella got there first, putting her arms around Sera's shaking shoulders, trying to get her to sit up. "Come on, sweetie," she murmured, as she would have murmured to one of her patients. "Come on, you can't lie here in the dirt. You have to stop crying sometime. Come on home."

"I have no home," came the heartbroken whisper. "I have nothing."

"Bah," Natalya replied brusquely. "You are having duty. That is not nothing." The Commissar stood next to them with her hands on her hips, looking down sternly. "In the Great War most in Stalingrad had lost home, family, friends, lovers—they fought on.

For Mother Russia. For duty. You are—we all are—being have duty to human race to fight these *svinya* to the last breath. *Da?*" Bella could tell that Natalya felt uncomfortable; she wasn't used to many situations that involved tears, and couldn't be solved with breaking something or an interrogation.

Bella felt the angel draw a long, shuddering breath. *"Da,"* she whispered.

"And you have us," Bella reminded her. "You still have us."

:I can't be the Song of your Siblings,: she said into Sera's mind, *:But I'm here. I'm with you, elder sister. Your heart isn't entirely empty.:*

She felt the fluttering wings of Sera's heartbreak, the brush of that last loss, when John didn't recognize her. But the reply came clearly, though sadly enough. *:Aye. You do well to remind me, younger sister. I am not entirely—alone.:*

Vickie joined Bella in urging the angel to her feet. "Come on, you can sleep in my workroom for a while. It's warded and sealed to a fare-thee-well. Nothing magical can track you in there."

Sera rose slowly to her feet, every movement graceful, the grace of someone dancing on bleeding feet and determined not to show it.

"Nat," Bella used the familiar name—one leader to another. "I think she needs to join CCCP."

"Shto? Nasrat. Nyet!" Saviour spluttered. "Marx would be to spin in his grave like sturdy industrial turbine! An *angel*—"

"She has to go somewhere, and ECHO's not safe," Bella said firmly. "I don't know how many more moles Verdigris has planted in my ranks. If she's going to fight like the rest of us, she *has* to have support around her."

"I must be told where and when to fight," Sera whispered humbly. "I can no longer see where I am needed."

"Marx said—"

"Marx said that *religion* is the opiate of the masses, Nat. I don't recall anything about angels. Sera, do you espouse any particular religion?"

Finally the angel raised her head. Her face was tear-streaked, tears still falling...and now Bella could see that her eyes were entirely human. Blue, in fact. "Names do not matter. Structures do not matter. Evil done in the name of Good is still Evil."

"There, you see?" Bella said, triumphantly.

Then Sera said something in Russian.

Bella and Vickie—who both spoke tolerably good Russian—stared at one another. Had they really heard that? Did it mean what Bella *thought* it meant? *Remember Worker's Paradise, Natalya. Remember what you saw. Who you saw there.*

Was Sera being absolutely literal? Because—Saviour *had* died under a building that Ubermensch toppled. Bella had brought her back, but only with Sera's help. . . .

Bella remembered something else Sera had told her. *When the Door is passed, mortals go to a heaven they expect. Or a hell. . . .*

Natalya Shostakovaya would certainly have expected a "Worker's Paradise."

"Bah," said Commissar Red Saviour, but the tone of her voice held resignation, and Bella knew she had won this round.

"Come on, sweetie," Bella said then, putting her arm around Sera's back, beneath those wings. Wracked with anguish though she was, Sera was human enough now; she needed to hydrate, to eat . . . eventually, to sleep. Right now, that was all that Bella was going to worry about. "Come on. Let's get you home."

It was into Vickie's care that Bella entrusted the—well, Vickie wasn't sure what to call the Seraphym. She wasn't an angel anymore. She wasn't human. Sera, then. That would have to do.

Vickie could tell that just being in Sera's proximity was straining Bella's strength, and she could certainly understand why. She could also understand why Bella needed to get some distance between them, some walls and shielding. There was only so much of that terrible grief that an empath could bear, and Vickie was very glad that *she* was not gifted—or cursed—with that particular power.

But as she made up a bed in her shielded workroom for Sera, wracking her brains to come up with something that was going to be moderately comfortable for a creature with wings, she found herself wishing there was something, anything she could offer besides a bed and the protection of her magic. Neither meant much in the light of that terrible pain—

It wasn't as if she had anything in common with—

—*wait*—

Then it hit her. The way in which they were all too alike.

So she came, bearing boxes of tissue, and sat gingerly beside the grieving creature and dared to cover one of Sera's delicate hands with her own. Sera looked up into her eyes, as tears coursed down her cheeks, slowly.

"I can't heal your heart," Vickie said, sadly. "I'm not an empath. I can't even guess about what it feels like to lose what you've been for—forever. But there is one thing I can offer you, Sera." She gently squeezed Sera's hand a moment. "This will always be a place where it's safe to cry."

And the beautiful creature put her head on Vickie's shoulder and shook with silent sobs.

After all, who could understand her pain like Vickie? Someone who worked every day with a man she loved with all her heart, whom she knew would never, ever love her back? The Seraphym had lost paradise. Vickie gazed on paradise from the wrong side of a locked gate.

Oh yes, she thought, giving the Seraphym another handful of tissues and surreptitiously wiping her own eyes. *Not so different except in degree.*

CHAPTER THREE

Secrets

MERCEDES LACKEY AND CODY MARTIN

In the hours that Vickie watched Sera weeping herself into utter exhaustion and only then, finally, into sleep—in the hours when she watched as she continued to weep even in sleep, Vickie had had an epiphany.

This...could not stand. This was an outrage. Vickie would not permit the Seraphym to languish in this kind of despair. Whatever it took to fix it, she was going to do. The Seraphym had terrified her, filled her with awe—but the Seraphym had also saved her life. Maybe more than once, it was hard to tell. Vickie owed her.

That John Murdock didn't recognize the angel—that she was now lessened—it all surely *had* to do with that meta-mystical moment when the universe had rung like a bell, and *that* could only be because the Seraphym had somehow sacrificed herself to save the dying man. There was no other possible explanation, as unlikely as this one seemed. Occam's Razor and all.

She didn't know *why* Johnny was—well, whatever he was. Rebooted? Maybe, it kind of made sense. Maybe it was the sheer trauma of whatever had happened to him. As for the Seraphym, well...

There was still Celestial energy about her. After nearly getting knocked on her keister just trying to examine Johnny, Vickie was not at all inclined to make a second trial on the Seraphym. But now, the Seraphym was more like a welding torch than the sun. And she had said in her own words she had lost everything that had made her angelic. Vickie had a vague notion of what that meant, and "bereft" didn't even begin to cover it, yet it looked

35

as if she had been holding herself together right up until Johnny had looked at her without recognition.

At that moment, seeing the Seraphym's reaction to John literally looking past her, Vickie'd had another idea of just what had linked the two, a crazy one, but—well, as a mage, she had heard crazier things. And the legends of the Nephilim, the alleged offspring of angels and humans, had had to come from somewhere...

Well, she needed confirmation, which the Seraphym, who was so silent on most subjects she might as well be mute, was not going to give her. And she needed to find some things out about Murdock—more than she had been able to get on her own. For it all came down to John Murdock and his past; from six years ago to—well, the moment he showed up starkers in the break room.

Time to research. Time to call in a few more of those favors she'd been earning. And work on some family ties....

She picked up the phone. "Mom? I need you to dig up things in some secret, dirty places..."

There was very little that the Nagys couldn't get their hands on. Whatever black-ops program John Murdock had been a part of...well, Vickie had learned a lot of her tricks in obtaining documents by means deep and arcane at the feet of her mother. Things like—getting just one little blank scrap of a piece of paper in a file in a locked file cabinet meant you could, with enough work, reproduce every single piece of paper in that file. Provided it wasn't warded. And even if it was...well, you could still get a lot. And things like "telling" a censored document to restore itself to the original, uncensored version. These were things that most government agencies were not aware of...

Well, maybe the Russians were. There had been plenty of talk of the Soviet Union experimenting with the occult to gain an upper hand during the Cold War. Most people took that to mean psionics...but it might have included magic. The very few Russian magicians she knew never spoke of anything of the sort, so all she actually knew about were the rumors of psionic experiments.

If there had been dabbling in magic, that would explain why Saviour initially wanted to burn her and Grey at the stake... Or maybe there was an easier explanation. Saviour kept calling her "Daughter of Rasputin," and one thing Vickie *did* know was that Rasputin had been *everything* he'd been rumored to be, and worse.

So... if Saviour knew all those dirty, dirty secrets from the last days of the Tsar, she'd have had plenty of reason to be wary of magicians.

Once the expert had done her work, and everything that could be dug up, had been, Vickie pondered her own next move.

Forensic magic at Murdock's squat, she decided.

Which made her more than a little nervous. She didn't like going out alone, particularly not to that neighborhood. On the other hand, who was free to go with her? CCCP and ECHO were both stretched thin, even though the elimination of the Thulian North American HQ seemed to have shut them down for at least a little while. All *that* meant was that all the rest of the cockroaches came boiling out to fill the vacuum; Reb activity had been on the rise again, several metacriminals were flexing their muscles for position, and so on down the chain. Everyone she could call on for backup was either sleeping the sleep of the exhausted or out on patrolling shifts...

Except... just maybe...

"Overwatch: open: private: Gamayun," she ordered aloud, as she began to suit up for this. Chainmail over nanoweave, and thank God it was late fall and kind of chilly. Glock and spare magazines. Mind, she wasn't going to risk driving or, gods forbid, walking. The ECHO jetpack came out of the closet, and with her magic kit in hand, she went out the window. She'd had a little faux balcony put out there since the Djinni came crashing through her window. It made a good launching pad. And this way, if he ever saw the need to come in that way again, at least now he could pick the window lock instead of leaving broken glass all over the living room.

"*Gamayun here, comrade,*" came the answer.

"Gamayun, is the Bear or Chug free?" she asked.

"*Borzhe moi. Bear is patrolling with Upyr. Chug is playing with paper dolls in break room.*"

"Spasibo. Is Sovie free to take him over to Murdock's old squat?" At this point she was about halfway there. The jetpacks were a literal dream come true for Vickie; she had always, always wanted to fly, but her levitation spells didn't work all that reliably on herself.

"*Is about time for her to take him to park, am thinking.*"

"You are a treasure. Overwatch out." She waited for the connection to drop and issued another command. "Overwatch: open:

Soviette: private." And as soon as the feed came up live, followed it with *"Privyet, sestra.* Are you about to take Chuggy for walkies?"

"Am thinking you are to be psychic as well as magic," came the amused reply. *"Shto?"*

"Could you take him over to Murdock's squat? I need some bodyguarding while I do some snooping into the mystery of why he doesn't remember anything. I'll walk him back for you. We'll visit his squirrels and I know a couple places where there's some snacks for him." At this point she was landing on the roof of Murdock's building, coming in like something from an old 1930s *Commander Cody* serial. If things hadn't been so serious, she would have been grinning from ear to ear. *Gods, this is fun . . .*

The locks on his door were no barrier to a techno-mage. One by one, they flipped open in response to her cajoling—and the bit of his hair she had. When the door opened, she found herself in what used to be the caretaker's apartment, back when this place was a factory. Now it was pretty much a concrete box with the basic amenities. She was a little surprised by how clean the place was—not that she expected Murdock to be a troll, but this was an old, dirty, industrial building and she had expected years of grime to have coated the walls. Instead, the place looked scoured.

Scoured, and baked into the walls was an aura of Celestial energy. *The plot thickens.*

As for the furnishings, they were pretty much as she had expected. A mattress on the floor made up as a military-style bed, blankets and sheets so tight she could easily have done the quarter-bounce on them. Makeshift bookcases with a selection of battered books in them. Scrounged things like lamps, a fan, a TV and a little fridge that looked as if it might have been pulled out of an RV.

Just as she had gotten done taking the basic inventory, she heard Chug thudding up the concrete staircase, followed by Sovie's lighter footsteps. She shucked off the jetpack and handed it to Soviette after Chug had squeezed in through the door. "Here, *sestra,* take this. You can take the short way home, then I can use it to jet home from CCCP HQ. Keeps us both off the street."

"Spasibo. I had rather not be walking without my bodyguard." The Russian healer patted Chug affectionately. "Chug, please to be staying with Vickie. She needs you."

Chug's eyes lit up. He always liked being told that someone

needed him. The poor thing was, in Vickie's opinion (and Soviette's as well, she suspected), too often treated as a large inconvenience. "Chug stay," he rumbled, and turned his craggy head towards Vickie. "What need?"

"I am going to be doing some pretty things, Chug, and I need you to make sure no bad people come bother me while I do them." One good way to keep Chug from being frightened and make him happy would be to add some harmless lights and music to her forensic magic. He always liked anything that looked like the pretty magic he saw in cartoons.

His brow stopped furrowing, and he smiled, though you would have to *know* Chug to know that he was smiling. "Chug watch for baddy bad mans," he said obediently.

"And when we are done, there will be Mr. Squirrel and ice cream," Vickie promised, and he rumble-chuckled with glee.

That settled, Sovie headed for the roof, Chug settled right in the door, and Vickie went to work.

Because if there was one single thing that the old Murdock was...it was introspective. He liked to pretend he was a simple country boy, but that was a load of baloney. Look at the books he read! All the standard anarchist tomes, poetry by Dylan Thomas and others, Kierkegaard...she would bet money he'd been keeping a journal of some sort all these years. And the secret of what tied him and the angel together was—had to be—in it.

She just had to find it.

Which, given Johnny's justifiable paranoia, could be a lot harder than it sounded.

She could almost hear Murdock in the back of her mind. *"Make with the finger-wiggling, Vix."* So she conjured up some pretty visual illusions for Chug, then held that strand of hair between her fingers and set up the equations.

In mathemagic, it was the equivalent of saying *show me what has the strongest connection to what I have in my hand.* And this was not going to be easy. This was the man's sanctum. *Everything* here had meant something to him. One by one, she was going to have to mathemagically eliminate items in the room from the answer to the equations—define things like *book* and *bed* and...well, she hoped it wasn't going to get any more intimate than that, but it might...and find the one thing she hoped she would find and thus, find the place where Murdock had hidden it. One thing that stood out was that the apartment was filled with weapons; rifles, pistols, and knives of all sorts. Not to mention the ammo, which looked like enough to start—or withstand—a prolonged siege. There was one handgun in particular that had a larger signature than the rest; a battered 1911. She didn't have to handle it long to recognize that it had had custom work done to it; she pocketed it for the moment, then resumed her search. This was tedious; eliminating variable after variable, and occasionally renewing Chug's viewing pleasures. Fortunately, like most "toddlers," he liked seeing the same thing over and over again.

It took two solid hours of work, but she finally not only found the battered journal in its hiding place, she managed to get it out without triggering the booby traps; one a decoy with some flash powder, the other a very real grenade. She'd been trained to deal with that sort of thing because of parents—you didn't partner with FBI Division 39 experts without picking up a lot of tricks—but there was a real pucker-moment when she spotted the live trap. *Jeezus, Johnny ... you* really *didn't want anyone getting at this thing. Or at least, if they got it, you wanted them to pay for it.*

The signature of faint Celestial magic was everywhere, including the hiding places, which by this point was making her *really* itch to read what was in that journal. She walked Chug back to the HQ, with two stops; one in his favorite park to feed the squirrels sandwich bits she made with the peanut butter and stale loaf of bread she found in the squat, and the other at the dumpster behind a newly reopened ice cream shop where Chug dove into the pile of discarded ice cream tubs with joyful abandon, topping it off with the full five-gallon tub of vanilla she bought him. With Chug returned to CCCP, she jetpacked back to her apartment, settled onto the couch with a meal-in-a-can and finally got to get into the guts of the journal.

Or, to be precise, the end. Just at the moment, she really didn't need to know about his life before Atlanta—just since the Invasion. Johnny's handwriting was tiny, neat and precise; the writing of someone who has to conserve paper. It was just barely larger than the type in a paperback book, in fact. But she wasn't here to marvel over penmanship. She was here to find out his secrets.

About two hours later, she finished, and closed the journal with wide eyes. "Bloody hell," she said aloud into the silent apartment. "I never saw *that* coming...."

"Overwatch: open: Murdock: private," she said after a few more moments. "Comrade fire-chucker, got a couple hours to spare? There's beer in it."

The comm crackled in response. "Murdock here. Anything would beat cleanin' up the garage bay again. Count me in."

"Come on up to my place. I have some more information on your 'lost time.'"

There was a pause on the other end of the line. "Roger that. You're gonna have to give me some directions to get to you; don't know where your place is, ma'am."

"Follow the yellow brick HUD," she told him, authorizing the Overwatch system to give him detailed guidance to the apartment. Then she dug out a blank journal-like book and a bottle of ink and while she waited, magically duplicated every page of the original over into it. She'd give him his own book back, but there was way too much in there that she was sure she needed to know. Maybe once she would have felt unease about jumping right into the guts of Johnny's private life, but not anymore. As she had told him when he'd first joined CCCP and she built Overwatch One, she was the poster-child for paranoia. There was no such thing as knowing too much about someone. The *only* downside was how they reacted if they found out what you knew.

Shortly after she finished, there was a cautious knock on her door. Glancing up at her security monitor, she made sure it was Murdock, and that there was no one with him, before letting him in. He looked nervous and a bit sheepish as he stepped through the doorway.

"Evenin', ma'am." He glanced around at the apartment. "Nice place y'have here."

"It's not home, but it's much," she replied, once again feeling her own nerves wind up tight at the presence of someone who wasn't Bella, Red or Grey in her space. "Have a seat and I'll get that beer." John nodded, taking up residence on one of the chairs in the main living room. He sat up straight; the old John would've probably stretched out a little more comfortably. He was still in the standard-issue CCCP overalls, with the sleeves rolled up. She noticed him tracing the scars on his arms with a finger, and looking at the tattoo on the back of his hand. *To wake up and have your body not be your own anymore...* Something they had in common, that. Although she had all-too-clear memories of how *that* had happened, there were still times when she woke from a dream of being her old, unscarred pain-free self to find herself once again imprisoned in her own scarred skin, and being completely disoriented.

She fetched a Guinness from the bottom of the fridge, and on second thought, added a double-shot of single malt for each of them. She handed him the shot and beer, sat down on the couch opposite him, and tossed her whiskey down without tasting it. "We've done some snooping," she said. "And by 'we,' I mean I had help. Some of your old files only exist on paper, the better to keep them 'eyes only.'"

"Snooping?" He downed the shot and chased it with a swig from the Guinness. "Snooping where, or do I not want to know?"

"You don't want to know, and you'll know why when you read through this." She shoved a file across the coffee table at him. "This starts where your memory ends." She considered a second double and decided against it for now. He was probably going to need another beer though, and soon.

John started reading through the file purposefully. He worked steadily on his beer as he went; Vickie didn't see his expression change, except for one moment when he lost his composure and a brief flash of anger, disgust and horror washed over his face. After that, though, he was ice. He had downed three beers by the time he finished the file, setting it down and closing it. There was a long silence before he turned to look at her. "Do you have any more of that whiskey? I think I need it right now."

She nodded, and got the bottle. This time she poured only for him. "Now, as you can tell, that's pretty explosive stuff. We can destroy it, you can keep it, or I can, and you can come look at it any time you want. Your choice."

He thought for a moment, choosing his words carefully. "You got this, so you know; people that have this sort of information when they aren't supposed to usually end up dead. You sure y'wanna hang on to it?"

She shrugged. "I've got other intel in here that is just as hot. That's off my digital copy anyway. Nobody gets that." Mom might not be a techno-shaman, but there were plenty of things she could do that worked with Vickie's magic. Like...she could load up the storage crystal she had, which was twinned crystal with one that

Vickie had, with the information she had gotten. That made use of the Law of Contagion and the Law of Similarity; what was loaded into one crystal duplicated itself into the other. Once Vickie had transferred the intel from the twinned crystal to her storage crystal, she'd wiped the twinned ones clean. There was now no evidence that the twins had ever held anything at all. Anybody who suspected what she had would have a damned hard time finding anyone who could ID the crystal she'd stored it in for what it was, and as for cracking a code to access it that was half magic and half bytes... well, good luck with that one. "So, what's your choice?"

"I'll hold onto this. There's... parts that I have to go over. A lot." From the look on his face, she hoped his liver would survive the amount of booze he'd be drinking while he did so. She knew exactly what was in the file, and could only imagine how he must have felt after finding out what had happened to him, and what he had done. Poor schmuck. How disorienting was that? Reading about yourself, reading about things you'd done and had been done to you, and not remembering one single moment of it?

"All right, that's just the part the government knows about," she continued, and now shoved his journal over to him across the table. "This covers the years you were on the run, until now."

He looked at her queerly, but accepted the journal and started leafing through it. "This... looks like my writing, that's for sure. An' y'said that this covers everything? From where my memory 'stops' up until that big raid?"

"I don't know about *everything*. It's your journal, for sure, I just don't know how *much* you wrote about. And it covers the time from when you had a breathing space after you went on the run, up until just before you woke up naked on the floor of the CCCP breakroom. Just before, because, the last time *I* saw you, you were clearly dying and probably not in any shape to be jotting anything down." She shrugged. "Something happened that didn't get written down, but it's easy enough to intuit from what *is* in there." The words he had set down about the Seraphym's offer were heart-rending, terrified and brutally honest. She felt as if they had been burned into her brain. This certainly explained the strong resonance of Celestial magic she'd felt baked into the walls of the squat. *I couldn't have written a sweeter and more heartbreaking romance if I had a hundred years to try.* "And after that... happened... you woke up *au naturel* for the benefit of The Bear."

John nodded, standing up with the journal and the file folder in his hand. He looked a little more steady; the booze didn't seem to have even touched him. "I'll read over this back at HQ. I've got the feeling it's going to take me a while to chew through it all." He started to leave, but turned back at the last second. "Vickie...thanks for this. I mean that."

"Hmm. Got something else for you." She pulled the 1911 out from the hiding place under the coffee table.

He looked at the pistol wearily. "I swear, ma'am, I didn't sleep with your husband. Or the cat."

She'd added a holster she happened to have around that fit tolerably well. "No husband, and Grey doesn't swing your way. No, this was yours, evidently. I found it where you've been living, where the journal was. It's had some custom work done to it, so I assumed it had some value to the old you."

John took the pistol, unloaded it, and did a quick function check. He cocked an eyebrow before reloading it and returning it to the holster, nodding approvingly. Apparently he was impressed. "This is much better'n the ol' Makarovs and such that the Commissar has issued." He looked at her soberly. "Now I owe you even more. This is gettin' to be an ugly habit, since I'm of a mind to always pay back my debts."

"You don't owe me a thing. You're a mystery. I hate mysteries. Mysteries have this habit of turning bad and biting you in the ass," she said, lightly. "And for the record, I loathe surprise parties, and I always read spoilers."

He grinned, lopsidedly as always. "I'll keep that in mind, ma'am. Thanks again for the brews and the whiskey. We'll have to do this again sometime, better circumstances an' such." With that he left, closing the door softly behind him.

For once, she expended the energy to throw the locks on the door magically rather than physically, and slumped back on the couch. She didn't envy him, not one bit. And yet, she wondered how he was going to take this all in, because for all intents and purposes, this had happened to a stranger. He had no memories of this. No memories of the girl in the Program, of incinerating up to a thousand people as he struggled to keep from being murdered. No memories of his life on the run. No memories of the Invasion.

No memories of...falling in love again. With an angel. Of

being taken to...what did they call it? The Infinite. No memories of the Seraphym in love with him....

He'd been remarkably delicate in what he had said. There was the makings of a real writer in that John Murdock. Each word had clearly been carefully chosen, and the whole was what *she* would have called a prose-poem. Beautiful. Tragic. Less prose, more a song...

Her kind didn't meddle with angels, and angels had very little to do with mages. She was sure, though, that there had been a greater motive to why the Seraphym had offered to sacrifice so much for John's rebirth than merely that she, personally, was in love with him. Angels were practically formed out of Duty and Responsibility, so there had to be something about John that made him important enough that the Seraphym would even be *allowed* to make the offer.

Still. It was also clear that at least one of her motives in doing so was love. And it was clear that she had counted on regaining that love when the great transformation was complete. After all, great sacrifice is supposed to be rewarded...right?

Except that it hadn't been.

It made Vickie want to weep for a year for her sake. Maybe for both of them.

She'd sensed it when she'd offered the Seraphym the shelter of her home. They *were* alike, far more than Vickie had ever realized until she read that journal. They were both in love with people who were hardly aware that they existed...and the odds of that changing for Vickie, at least, were worse than winning MegaBall. For the Seraphym?

I don't know. She put her head down in her hands, aching for herself and the Seraphym both, but knowing that if she was going to be forced into a choice of who would be the MegaBall winner—she'd choose the Seraphym over herself. No one who knew all the angel had sacrificed could choose otherwise and still call herself human. And damned be the consequences. *Heaven can go screw itself.*

John's fingers were itching to tear open the journal for the entire jog back to the CCCP's HQ. Every time he thought that he had this new life figured out, the ground got taken out from right under him. Nothing made much sense anymore. Even running, like he was now, was different; he didn't get tired or winded like he used to, despite being able to go *much* faster. Part of it was being a metahuman; something his old self had eight years to get used to, but he was still learning about. Part of it was the...other stuff. The things that had been done to him in the Program. John had kept it together when he read about his troop being slaughtered; he remembered the lead-up to that mission, but nothing about the actual op. In his mind, all of those guys were still alive when he had woken up. Men he had trained with, been trained by, lived with, fought with. He'd come up with a number of them through the Ranger Regiment. He had attended their weddings, been there for their divorces, and gone to the funerals with the rest of them when one of the team died. They were all what the public popularly called "Delta Force"; the best of the best in the special operations community. When you're that good, you're not just a unit; you're a family.

Now all of them were dead; even him, in a way.

Now he was surrounded by strangers, all of whom looked at him imploringly, asking him to remember. Remember things that seemed impossible to him. Remember things that couldn't *possibly* have happened to him. Things he didn't *want* to know had happened...especially not to him.

His parents were dead; he had learned that early on, while he was reading and watching reports about the Invasion. He still imagined his father fighting through crowds, trying to get to his mother as a destruction corridor crunched towards them, Kriegers marching and destroying everything before finally rolling over them. That had hit him hard; the feeling that he hadn't been there to protect them. Hell, if he had been on the run, he doubted that they even knew he was alive. Logically, he knew that was for their own safety; if the people after him were as bad as everything he had read, then not contacting them only made sense. But it didn't help him feeling like he had failed his parents as their son.

He was also out of the army. He had loved being a soldier; it had been his calling in life, and he had been good at it. After reading what had happened to his troop, and what had gone on in the Program...he was done with government work. You always read about black-bag projects and operations, government conspiracies and shady dealings that would always get the tinfoil-hat crowd going on tears. He'd never believed any of it; being a government employee, he had a pretty decent idea of how inept and bumbling the government could be. But there, in this folder the witch-gal had given him, was proof. *Pictures* of him, what they'd done to him, pictures taken during the surgery, the healing. Pictures of him training with the new abilities. Detailed, clinical reports. Too much to reasonably fake; anyway, why would the gal? There was no reason for her to that he could ascertain. He wondered if there was video, too, and if she could get it... then rebuked himself. There probably was, and why should he sit through hours of it, the way he'd sat through hours of Invasion footage? Punish himself for a decision he didn't remember?

There were also pictures of a woman. Jessica; her name had been Jessica. The reports didn't state it, but he could infer enough from the impersonal and cold notes that he had fallen in love with her. She had found out something, and they had killed her for it. Then they tried to kill him once he exploded into open rebellion. John, even back when he had been just a man, hadn't been easy to kill, what with the Ranger training and being a Delta operator. After what they had done to him, what they had unlocked from inside of him... He had slaughtered all of them; guilty, innocent, it didn't matter. He had let go; that was something else he had learned about his fires. It took concentration to keep them in check, once they had started; he had been practicing igniting his fires after Pavel had startled him on his way back from the HQ's laundry. Luckily, Bear's collection of politically incorrect T-shirts and a little paint from his chassis were the only casualties. But the power was there; it was terrible and vast and he was the only one that could control it. That time, in the Program, he hadn't.

That was all that he had gleaned from the file that Vickie had supplied him with. He would, without a doubt, go over it again and again, searching out each and every little detail until he memorized it. These were things he should have known; learning about them now, he knew he should never forget them again. There was still the journal. What horrors would that hold? What had he done while he was on the run?

What had he done since falling in with these Communists?

That was, oddly, a lot less of a worry for him. He had always been pretty good at reading people. Despite the dogma and rhetoric, the entire "Communism" bit seemed almost affected; caricatures from his father's era. They seemed like a good enough bunch; they were anachronistically hard-line in their ideology sometimes, but they were doing something about the Kriegers. The victory at the Thulian North American HQ seemed to be the first and real big victory against the enemy; but it was turning into a Pyrrhic one. While the United States military had participated, along with ECHO and the CCCP, the public and world governments seemed to be losing focus. The Thulians were *clearly* not done. In his opinion, at the very *best* interpretation, they were regrouping. That was their pattern in the past; hit or get hit, fall back, regroup, come back again. It was probably sheer dumb luck that the combined forces had managed to hit the North American HQ while the Thulians were actually still in the process of regrouping from the hit on their staging posts and Command and Control center in Kansas. He'd seen pictures of that massive Death Sphere that had gotten pounded into the ground like a tent peg. If that thing had been turned loose on a populated area—or come after a big strategic North American target—there would have been no way that the orbital launch platform for those projectiles could have gotten into position in time to take it out.

And yet, the public and the world governments were all acting as if it was all over. *Stupid.* "It's all better now, let's focus on rebuilding, not getting ready for another, bigger assault." All they were doing was providing *more* targets for the Kriegers when they came back. CCCP and ECHO seemed to be the only organizations that understood that. He didn't have the full picture, of course; stuff could be going on in the background, and almost certainly was. But he didn't like how it seemed to trickle down into the public consciousness. Everyone was relaxing.

Despite his reservations, staying with the CCCP was his best move for right now. To keep in the fight, to be doing something productive. And, of course, to find out who the hell he had become over the past eight years. He *sure* couldn't go back to the US Government now and ask politely, "I seem to be missing eight years, can you fill me in?" And despite interacting a bit with the ECHO head, that blue medic, Bella, he wasn't sure he trusted them not to turn him in. ECHO had always had a friendly relationship with the government, what with so many of their registered metas having law enforcement or military backgrounds at some point. CCCP was his best bet right now to find out who he'd been and what he'd done.

...Which led to another problem. When he did discover that—what if he didn't *like* that John Murdock? Sure, other people seemed to like the guy, fine, but...that didn't mean he would. And he was the one living inside this skin.

And then what? He was *not that guy*. He likely never would be that guy. He'd be a guy who knew what had happened to that guy, but it would just be information, not...the guy who had lived through all of that. Experience changed you, and he wasn't the one who had had those experiences.

All of this was flashing through his mind as he ran to CCCP HQ. He hadn't even broken a sweat, hardly; it wasn't just the cool weather, either. *Curiouser and curiouser, as that one gal said.* He was through the security door and about to jog to the barracks when Unter called after him from the front desk. "Another break in generator room. Duty roster is having you and..." He scanned down the list in front of him. "Bear. Tools are already there, *tovarisch*."

"Roger that," John sighed. The journal would have to wait until later; duty and Bear's off-color jokes were the order of the hour.

CHAPTER FOUR

Hurricane: Storm Warning

MERCEDES LACKEY AND DENNIS LEE

Bella felt a headache coming on at the back of her skull. Of course, the cause of the headache was sitting—or rather, slouching—on a seat across from her. Not across from her *desk*; Bella was trying to keep her identities of Bella Dawn Parker, Acting Head of ECHO, and Belladonna Blue, ECHO healer, separate. This exercise in futility was taking place in an exam room. Scope was sitting, slouched aggressively, on the exam table. Bella was in a chair whose hardness was only matched by Scope's scowl.

Bella put the chart down on her lap. It didn't matter if Scope could read it; it read the same as last time. "I can't clear you for duty when I know you aren't ready for it," she said, biting off the words a bit more than she had intended to. The last thing she wanted to project to a patient, especially this one, was aggression or aggravation of her own.

But there was a limit to the number of pointless appointments she wanted to keep when there was so much else that needed doing.

"If we weren't so deep in the kim-chee, Scope, I would recommend retiring you and cashiering you out," she continued, flipping through the most recent reports. "Another week and I'm going to need a file cabinet just for *you*. Here's a nice one. It isn't even from your superior officers, it's from the bunkhouse staff. 'Erratic behavior.' Not the sort of thing that bodes well in a meta." She waited for a response, but Scope only sniffed and shrugged.

"You aren't leaving here until you at least talk to me," Bella warned.

Scope sighed. "Yeah, I'm a little off, what of it?"

"The report continues that you stank of booze."

"What I do off duty is my own business," Scope growled.

"It seems to have flown under your radar, but this is a war. We're always on call. We're always on duty," Bella growled back. "Hey, I'm not about depriving people a little something to calm their nerves or blow off steam. God knows we can all use it. But from all reports you aren't just having a few to relax. You're drinking until you stagger out, barely able to walk. You're destroying yourself, girl. The Scope I would certify as ready for duty—the one who actually *wanted* to be certified as ready for duty—would know that and act accordingly." She leafed through another. "This is from your training exercises only yesterday. Failing scores."

"Yeah? Which ones?" She sounded indifferent.

"All of them," Bella said flatly.

"Bug going around, must've caught it."

"And that same 'bug' made you attempt to strike a superior officer?" Bella continued in a voice heavy with disbelief.

"He was being a *shit*!" Scope exploded. "Hell, *I* used to train *him*! Now the know-it-all bastard thinks he's got the goods when he still doesn't know a rope ladder from his own ass, just 'cause you all painted another stupid chevron on his arm!"

Bella took a long deep breath and reminded herself that *she* was the grown-up here. "Judging by the scores here—" she flapped the papers in one hand "—you're the one that doesn't have the goods. And as you should know, having been one, it's the job of a training officer to be a shit. From the attitude, I'd say someone's been hanging around the Djinni too much, but we both know it's something else, don't we?" She paged down to the next report, and sighed. "You've been asking for more meds."

Scope glared at her, defiantly, but averted her eyes at the last. For a moment, Bella thought she looked tired, defeated. This might be the opening she needed, and Bella took it. "Scope, the meds we can give metas that are even remotely effective are also damned dangerous. It's not just that they're addictive. It's that the longer you take them, the more unpredictable the side effects are."

Scope bared her teeth in a grimace. "Whatever, I can handle them..."

"Does that count going *permanently* blind?" As Scope's head finally came up, eyes wary, Bella pounced. "Look, Scope, I'm trying to work with you here. I'm not the bad guy. If it were anyone but you, you'd be gone, no matter how badly we need bodies. But it isn't a stranger, it's you, one of the Misfits. I know you're better than this. I want to give you a chance here." Bella hesitated. "Look, I know you've turned it down before, but frankly I don't see much choice here. Will you consider a psychic link? You know it's done a lot for others, for..."

"Oh, for the luva..." Scope sprang up from the table and headed for the door. "That's always your answer for anything! Ram your thoughts in where they're not wanted! Forget it, Bella! The answer was *no* before, and it's *no* now! You are not going to rummage around in my business! You want to bust me down to ECHO Support levels, then *fine*! But there's no *way*..."

The door opened outward before she could reach it; unable to stop herself, she bounced off a wall of chest in ECHO nanoweave.

"Session's going well, I take it?" Bulwark rumbled.

"Same ol', same ol'," Bella seethed, her hands flying up in exasperation. She stood up, flung Scope's reports on the desk next to the examination table and marched from the room. From the hall, they heard her bellow back. "Talk to her, Bull! Make her see some sense before I pop a vein. Or pop her in the eye and throw her out on her ass!"

Bulwark turned towards Scope, his expression deliberately unreadable. "Overwatch: command: off," he rumbled.

He heard the single tone that indicated his Overwatch rig had severed its comm link for now. For just a second, he considered the possibility that this was a ruse on Victrix's part; something to give him the *feeling* that she wasn't listening or recording when, in fact, she was. But he dismissed that idea immediately. No matter his quarrel with the little mage, he knew she was scrupulously honest with her Overwatch Mark Two subjects. If she said he could turn the system off, then he could, and she would not surreptitiously eavesdrop.

Scope slouched and glowered. If he hadn't known better, he would have considered the possibility that she'd been possessed by the spirit of a rebellious, sullen teenager. But he did know better. So he waited, patiently, with a patience that had been tested by more stubborn subjects than Scope, until she finally broke the silence.

"I'd be doing my goddamn job if Parker would just clear me for duty," she grumbled, unable to meet his eyes. "That pop-up two days ago—I could have shot out the oculars and—"

"I was the one that benched you, Paris," Bulwark interrupted.

Startled, her head came up, and she finally looked at him, as if she couldn't quite believe what she was hearing.

"Bella brought me the assessments, but I'm your team lead, and I benched you," he repeated.

"So put me back in the game, damn you!" she exploded, launching herself off the stool she had been sitting on. "If you benched me, you can just unbench me!" She stood there glaring at him the way she had glared at Bella, fists clenched at her sides, hands shaking ever so slightly.

He looked into her eyes until she dropped her gaze to the level of his chin, and shook his head slowly. "Not an option. You've lost your focus, girl. You're a hazard to yourself and everyone around you. I'm not putting you anywhere near field duty until you climb your way out of the hole you're in."

He really didn't expect her to react well to this statement, given her apparent state of mind, and he was unsurprised when she went tight-lipped and hot with anger. She didn't say anything, however, and reluctantly, he moved to goad her further.

"Bella was being generous when she said your scores were terrible. I've seen better marks from that last lot of Cub Scouts that came through on a tour." For a moment he felt a flash of nostalgia, and regret for what, in retrospect, had been the halcyon days before the Invasion. These days, no mother in her right mind would let her child anywhere near the ECHO campus. It would be like sending them on a field trip to Chernobyl.

He picked up the papers Bella had tossed on her desk, and made a show of leafing through them. In fact, he already knew the contents. "The *only* thing you've made your scores on is marksmanship," he continued, allowing himself a little frown. "Good lord, girl, *Victrix* has better times than you on the parkour course. You're late to everything, you leave early, and you haven't even got half your mind in the game when you're *there*. Not only are you not pushing yourself, you are not even trying in the least. You're phoning it in, then hanging up halfway through."

Bull leaned back against the examination table, his eyes fixed on Scope.

"You never quit," he said. "Of all the people I've ever trained, you were the one who pushed herself the furthest. Nothing you did, nothing your teammates did, no one, matched your standards, to the point where it got you passed over by every other training master until you came to me. They all closed the book on you. You didn't work well with others. You drove yourself past your own limits, made too many mistakes in the field. But then, something happened. You learned to rein that all in, to work with a team, to focus your energies on tough but attainable goals. And still, you never stopped pushing yourself, and it was finally getting you somewhere. You were on track to be the best field agent I've ever had the pleasure to command. Scope, where did that all go?"

He watched as a myriad of emotions played across her features. In the past, she had always tried so hard to keep her features stern, if not impassive. Bull knew it had been her attempt to emulate him. But Scope's past painted a picture of a young girl who could never escape a father's wish for a son, and whose ambitions and drive were only symptoms of an unrelenting need to break free of the bonds of a simple, rural existence. She hid within her a torrential sea of conflict, nothing that could be bottled up so long or so easily. Still, this disintegration went far beyond his preconceived notions. He could never have imagined she could let herself fall apart so completely. How could he have been so wrong? She was so different now, he could hardly believe she was that same raw recruit that had swaggered into his life, so full of herself and false bravado, years before.

Finally, she rose up and faced him, and whatever conflicting feelings had raged within her before coalesced into a snarl, a savage glare and wild fury.

"And what did all that pushing ever get me?" she shouted. "Pushing myself, pushing others . . . what did it get me? What did it get Bruno? *Dead!*" Her voice spiraled upwards. "I killed him, Bull! I made him promise me that we'd finish the job! Well, he *did* it, he kept his promise!" She was screaming now. "He kept his promise, just like I *pushed* him to! He kept it! *And now he's dead!*"

Abruptly, she . . . deflated. Whether the outburst had been something like the lancing of a boil, or she had simply run out of energy—or both—she collapsed back to her stool, her eyes dropping back to the floor.

Bulwark kept his face impassive, but mentally, he was trying to figure out his options. They had tried everything with Scope; first Einhorn's sweetly angelic "there, there;" less saccharine than it used to be, and a lot more genuine. But Scope had sneered at

Mary Ann and sent her away in tears. Then the ECHO Trainer Mike "Muscles" Grant—the one that Scope had, as she said, trained herself. He'd given her a dose of her own back, and she'd clocked him for it. Panacea had tried soothing, Gilead had tried "tough love," and neither got anything more than a rude demand for meds. And now Bella had tried every trick in her extensive arsenal, and to no avail. Bulwark knew he was Scope's only hope, because at this point, if he couldn't get her turned around, they would *have* to pension her out.

And on an ECHO disability pension, she could drink herself—or drug herself—to death, very quickly.

"Come with me," he ordered abruptly, and giving her no choice, seized her elbow and manhandled her out the door.

She shook herself out of his grip once they were in the hall, but she didn't, as he had half feared, stalk away. Her face still sullen, she matched his long strides as he led the way down to his office, by the new cells—the very special new cells—for high-powered meta prisoners. "Top Hold," they called it. When they reached the door, he opened it. Still staring at the ground, she slouched inside, and without invitation, dropped gracelessly into a chair.

"I want to show you something," he said, motioning to a wall of monitors beside his desk. There were easily two dozen small ones, surrounding one giant touch screen which served as a hub. They displayed short-circuit feeds of different prison cells, each specialized to house a specific type of meta inmate. She watched one display a cell in near darkness, its huddled captive only visible by infrared sensors. After a moment, the display flipped to another cell. This one seemed lit well enough, but was completely lined with heat units, forcing the cold-based meta to shy away from the walls to the center of the room. She watched as all the displays rotated through their set list of occupied cells, except for one. One display, top center, remained fixed on one cell. It was also brightly illuminated, and considerably larger than the others. One bare and Spartan cot in the middle of a large glass box, which was supported by reinforced metal pillars within another glass box, and so on. The refraction of light was blinding, and it was difficult to make out just how many layers the unique cell had. The figure inside, however, was immediately recognizable. She was sitting still on the cot, her legs crossed in lotus position, and Scope blanched as she realized who it was.

Harmony.

"She's been quiet, ever since we picked her up," Bull said. "She doesn't seem to eat, or sleep, or need to move at all, really. But our intel on her suggests that out in the world, she never *stops* moving."

"You got that right," Scope agreed. "Was hell for Bruno and me to keep up with her."

"Our intel suggests something else," Bull continued. "It seems that Alex Tesla was by no means Harmony's only target. We've been able to piece quite a bit together by seeing what plots fell apart since we took her in."

He stepped to the giant touch screen and keyed up the sequence of intended victims. As he described who these people were in a dispassionate tone, and not only who, but *what* and *why* they were important, while adding little details about their lives and their families, he watched Scope's face out of the corner of his eye. She feigned indifference, but her eyes never left Harmony.

"These are the people you and Bruno quite literally saved by apprehending Harmony," he concluded. "These are people who are alive today because you two saw the job through to the end."

Scope shrugged, barely noticing the parade of mugshots and stills that flowed over the screen. "If someone wanted those people bad enough to hire the likes of Harmony, all Bruno and I did was delay the inevitable. They'll find someone else, some other way."

"Perhaps," Bull agreed. "For a few. But the majority of people on this list are *very* well protected. There are likely few in Harmony's league to carry out their assassinations. I'm sure you noticed a few of them are under ECHO protection, openly or not."

Scope's eyes flickered to the large screen. Bull had stopped on a grainy picture of . . .

"That's President Shreeves," Scope murmured, sitting forward in her chair. "And behind him, the Secret Service goon, isn't that . . . ?"

"Jinx, undercover ECHO OpTwo," Bull nodded. "We wanted to make sure no assassin would ever get near him without . . ." He searched for the right phrase. ". . . endless pratfalls and fumbles. Sometimes it isn't enough to merely foil a plot. You have to leave it in a puddle of embarrassment. In any case, I don't see many besides Harmony who'd get close enough to present any real threat. Here's some more." He skipped from one still to another. Scope recognized a few of them. Another world leader, a few titans of industry, and . . .

She stood up, startled, and approached the bank of monitors.

Leaning forward, she touched the screen, her fingers shaking as she traced a familiar smile.

"Bella," she said.

"Sometimes we forget that the Thulians and Blacksnake aren't our only enemies," Bull said.

Both Bulwark and Scope jumped as they heard laughter erupt from a speaker above them. Looking up, they watched as Harmony rose from her bed and smirked into the camera. "Why, Gairdner," she said, in a faintly sardonic tone. "I had no idea that you'd managed to put so many twos and twos together. You're smarter than you look. But then, we always knew that, didn't we, Paris?"

Scope started. "The hell—" she croaked. "She can't—"

"Oh, yes I can," Harmony replied. "I can hear you quite well. I must say, Bull, it took all my self-control to avoid giving myself away when you and Bella were having your little trysts with the door locked." She sucked on her lower lip, thoughtfully. "I would have pegged her for a screamer, not a moaner. Interesting."

Scope watched as a red tinge crept up Bull's neck to his face. How long had it been since anyone had been able to make him blush? But he had picked up a pad and pencil from the desk, and while Harmony was speaking, he'd been writing. He turned the pad around so that Scope could read what he had written. He watched as Scope's eyes flickered back and forth.

Harmony's a mystery, he'd told her. *Unique kind of meta. We've tried everything. We can't read her. VV thinks there's magic at work. Enhanced hearing—that's new.*

Scope finished reading and nodded abruptly.

"You know, Gairdner, I think you and Bella deserve each other." One of Harmony's eyebrows raised slightly. "No, I'm serious. I really do. I've got nothing to gain *or* lose by being sincere about that. I hope it works out for you two."

Scope's mouth twitched and she gestured for the pad and pencil. Bulwark handed them to her, and she scribbled quickly and handed it back to him.

Better soundproof her cell block.

"Harmony," he said out loud, "Unless you want your cell to ramp up with another shock, you probably ought to keep the rest of your thoughts to yourself."

Harmony smirked again. "Do tell, *Silver Wolf.* I have to say I admire the stamina both of you have."

Bulwark's neck looked like it was on fire. That eliminated any shadow of doubt about her hearing. Bella had probably never called him that except in private. He scratched a few more words on the pad, handed it to Scope, and quietly left the room. Scope read the pad, and scowled.

Keep her talking. Calling Bella for a powers sweep. We might get lucky and find out how she's doing this while she's actively listening.

"Oh dear, was that a door?" Harmony sighed. "I didn't chase you both away, did I?"

"Only Bull," Scope said. "Just you and me now, you filthy piece of—"

"Language!" Harmony said. "Now now, Paris, you're a member of ECHO's elite meta force of high-octane do-gooders! You have all those lofty standards and moral quandaries to live up to. Not that Bull has any problems in that department, hmmm? He always knows the right thing to do. He's not like us."

"I'm nothing like you, you murderous bitch."

"Don't be so sure," Harmony laughed. "Anyway, it's good Bull left; thought he'd never leave. It was you I really wanted to talk to anyway."

"I'm surprised you even have enough in you to talk," Scope said. "How long have you been in there, without food or water?"

"I've been getting my daily bread in other ways," Harmony smirked. "Truth be told, I'm pretty juiced and have been for a while. Confined to this pretty, multilayered coffin, I haven't had much to spend it on either." She scowled. "Though I suspect my source might dry up soon. Didn't think that one through, I guess."

"Let's pretend I even know what you're talking about," Scope said. "You say you're telling the truth. Why should I believe you?"

"Why would I lie? Besides, isn't it common knowledge that us supervillains do more damage with the truth? Here's one that should make your head spin. I know you're not right. I could sense it the moment I felt you both coming. Wasn't sure who was walking with Bull. Imagine my surprise when I heard you speak."

"What are you talking about?"

"You're not Scope."

"Look, right now I'm painting a lovely mental image of having you drawn and quartered," Scope said, looking pained. "You're mucking it all up with this existential crap."

"I mean you're not the Scope I knew," Harmony said. "You're

all wrong, askew. That need to prove yourself, that's gone, and that's just the top layer. Overheard Bull and Bella talk about you, y'know . . . *afterwards* . . . when they stop being groiny. Sounds like you're on that long overdue vacation we always told you to take. Don't be so sure we're so different, you and I. I'm feeling closer to you than ever."

"Okay," Scope sighed. "I now officially want you to shut up."

"We're not so different," Harmony insisted. "We're not, because I've changed too."

"Well, considering that you spent years lying to us, telling me that you've changed doesn't mean a whole lot. I don't know what you've changed from, what you've changed into, and that whole lying thing doesn't make you very believable in the first place."

"I know," Harmony said with a smirk that somehow seemed less smarmy than . . . pensive. "This whole penance thing is a bitch. Probably why I've never tried it before."

"So why should I believe you?"

Harmony stood up and walked purposefully to the wall of her glass-lined cage. She stared intently into the camera.

"Paris," she said. "Do you really believe ECHO can hold me, if I don't want to be held?"

"No," Scope said, after a moment. "I guess not. So you're telling me—what, exactly?"

Harmony crossed her arms over her chest, in a move that made her look oddly vulnerable, and yet, nothing at all like the "Harmony" Scope used to know.

"Maybe I'm stealing a page out of the Djinni's playbook. Remember those weeks he was in solitary here? It gives you a lot of time to think, because that's all there is to do. I think that's what he wanted. But being in here now, myself, I think he wanted more."

"More?" Scope asked, perking up at the mention of Red. "Like what?"

"I think he wanted someone to punish him. I get that now." She let her hands fall, and softly rubbed them together. "I still feel it, y'know. I can't stop thinking about it."

"What?"

"His blood," Harmony said, her movements becoming frantic. "I still feel Bruno's blood on my hands."

"Well, that would be the nasty side effect of digging your claws into his chest!" Scope screamed, and turned away from the monitor. She let out the faintest of sobs, and clamped her hand to her mouth. After a few silent breaths, she steadied herself, and spoke without grief. "You're a killer, Harm. It's what you do. Why would it bother you now?"

"This was different," Harmony said. "I'm not going to blow smoke up your ass, Scope. I've also been a predator for a long time. And at that moment I was nothing *but* the predator. I had my prey in my hands and I was crazy with pain and starvation. I literally was not thinking. At all. All I was—was need. That was it. Need and hunger and pain and anger and at the end, I was desperate. You and Bull were too fast. Bruno won that fight, but not with his fists. It was something he said, near the end. He reminded me of something, something I haven't felt in a long time."

She paused, as if lost in thought, and looked at the camera again.

"Here, let me show you."

Scope gasped as her mind exploded with images. The Goldman Catacombs, and the sight of Acrobat diving off the ledge to catch her in mid-fall, before she went tumbling down into the pit of spikes. On the training field, dodging mechanical zombies as Bulwark and the Djinni rained down advice and criticism in equal measure. One of their first recruitment missions, and a mirthful sight of all of them, Bella and the Djinni included, doubled over in laughter and covered head-to-toe in mud, with Bulwark standing high above them at the edge of the pit, his face in his palm. A vast field of hay, and the odd spectacle of Bruno and Harmony prancing about in badger costumes, much to Red Djinni's dismay. Each mental picture told a story, a story she yearned to experience all over again. Each invoked a sense of friendship, trust...love? And it wasn't just images. She could *feel* them, and they all spoke of *family*. It came off of Harmony in empathic waves, powerful and enough to overwhelm her. She couldn't be lying, not about this. It felt too pure. It was enough to bring Scope to her knees.

"That's what he reminded me of," Harmony said as the images faded away, and the waves of love with them. "Before..."

"Before you ripped into him," Scope said.

"Before you and Bull showed up," Harmony said. "That cornered me, and I felt something else I haven't in a long, long while. Fear. Worse than that. Terror and panic. I had to escape, and the only way I was going to do that, was..."

"To rip into him."

"Yes," Harmony admitted. "I needed what he had. Desperately. Enough that it didn't matter that it would kill him. And I took it all, Paris. I took all of him. You ask why it bothers me? Because what I want now, is to give him back."

Scope rose to her feet, and struggled for the words. Finally, all she could manage was...

"Then show me again."

Harmony closed her eyes, and padded back to her cot.

"I will, later. All you need to do is return." She lay down beneath the covers, and turned her back to the camera. "And you will return, won't you?"

"Yes," Scope muttered, and left the room.

Bulwark was waiting outside. He held a couple of tablets, and handed one to her. Scope took one, grimly, and began the text conversation.

You get what you needed? she asked.

We managed to get a cursory sweep in place, Bull wrote. *But no, nothing registered above background noise.*

You overhear any of that?

Most of it.

And? You buy it?

I just don't know. I can't trust my instincts about her. She's proven more than adept at hiding the truth, even for years on end. What about you? Do you believe her?

Bull watched as Scope lowered her tablet. She was confused, her cheeks were flushed, with just a slight tremble in her fingertips.

"I don't know," she whispered, and rubbed at her eyes.

Bull watched her for a moment, then began typing on his tablet again.

She's speaking to you, he wrote. *She hasn't spoken a word to anyone until today. We want you to talk to her again. As long as she keeps talking, we want you to listen. Each time, we'll have the full array of sweeps and recorders up. Even if they pick up nothing, we're hoping she'll let something slip, some detail, anything. We've got nothing right now.*

Scope read the words as they flew across the screen.

Will you do it? he asked.

Yeah, she wrote. *I'll do it.*

CHAPTER FIVE

Holding On

MERCEDES LACKEY AND VERONICA GIGUERE

What had once been a sparse Zen garden now bloomed with a wealth of flowers. Even in the slight chill of the Atlanta night air, moonflowers and jasmine lined the path that led from the door to the edge. When Ramona couldn't sleep, she stole up the stairs and sat on one of the small benches. On a clear night, she could see almost all the way to Stone Mountain.

This evening, someone else sat on the small bench at the edge of the garden. Ramona paused, watching the slender shoulders tremble and the feather wings droop. The red and gold stood in sharp contrast to the darkness. Although she couldn't hear a sound from the bench, Ramona knew that the woman now called Sera was crying. Sera. Everyone had taken to shortening the Seraphym's name now. It was as if they had diminished her name to fit the diminished reality.

She considered turning around, but Ramona couldn't think to just leave her there in the dark without saying something. The Russians didn't have a middle ground when it came to dealing with people. If you were hurt, they smothered you with attention until you were better. After that, you were expected to hold your own. Ramona had been out of the infirmary for more than a week, and her contribution had consisted of paperwork. Considering the Seraphym's strange background, she couldn't conceive what the Commissar could have found for her to do.

Then again, Ramona thought as Sera passed a hand over her eyes, *the Commissar probably doesn't have any idea what to do with her.*

With a sigh and a quick check in her pocket for tissues, Ramona walked up to the edge of the roof. She made enough noise in the hope she wouldn't startle the woman, and she stood a few feet back rather than take a seat on the bench.

"I hear you, Ramona Ferrari," came the soft voice. "If you wish privacy I shall depart."

"No, that's okay. I just couldn't sleep, and staying inside just didn't feel right." She rubbed her hands together, the bits of metal that still covered the abrasions making an odd grating sound. "Did you want to be alone, or . . ."

"Being *alone* is . . . not what I wish. No. If you are desirous of company . . ." The words came haltingly. "I no longer may see inside another's heart. This is a handicap. Among others. You shall have to tell me what you want and need."

Ramona slid onto the concrete next to the woman who was hastily wiping tears from her face. "Well, I don't want or need anything, other than not staying downstairs and listening to that old television playing reruns of COPS. Coming up here seemed like the best way to sort out everything that's happened lately." She looked out over the quiet Atlanta rooftops, the damage of the destruction corridors muted in darkness. "You see all that? That's the world I had come to know, as sick and as twisted as that is. That was my reality, and I was dealing with it." She pointed to various ruined landmarks. "As least those are the same. Sitting up here is as close as I can get to feeling like I did before everything changed."

"Change . . . I said once to John that all things must change or die. I did not understand then how change can be so terrible." The woman let out a shuddering sigh. "I know it is wrong, but so many times I think, now, that death would have been . . . not so bad."

"Me too." Ramona leaned forward and hung her head. "At least once a day, sometimes more. Sovie says that it's normal, that any life-altering event resulting from an accident or illness carries the potential for depression and anxiety. And on a professional level, I know that."

"You are no longer the *you* that you have known all your life." Sera sighed. "Nor am I. And my life is—was—a little longer than yours."

"No one would take you for a day over twenty-nine." Ramona tried to offer a smile, but it was difficult. Part of her knew she could never compare her experience to that of the Seraphym, and to do so would be an insult. "And no," she agreed. "I'm not quite the same person, but there are still startling similarities. Changing the outside doesn't mean that you change the inside."

"I am glad you still recognize yourself," Sera said after a long pause. Left unspoken was the obvious corollary; that she did not. There was more silence. "The Commissar has sent me patrolling. 'Air support,' she calls it. But I do not know when to act. I do not know...what is...I have no guidance but that of the fallible mortal that commands the patrols! Is it right to act? These Russians are so...how do you live with such uncertainty?" The last had the tones of desperation.

Ramona let out a sigh. "Part of it is trusting the person guiding you. When that's not possible, you trust the people around you, and you trust your own judgment. As for what's right, that's..." She barked a short laugh. "I got into fights with the Jesuit priest teaching religion and philosophy in high school. That earned me a D, so I probably shouldn't be giving you advice. I slugged my boss in a freezer when he was in hysterics, and I scream at authority figures. I don't think those tendencies went away when I woke up." She sat back, chewing on her next question while she studied Sera. "I've always worked in situations where I didn't know if I would come back. I guess it's living in spite of uncertainty."

"I see." From the tone of Sera's voice, it sounded as if she had left quite a bit unspoken. Probably something like *well, that's all right for you mortals, but what about me?* "I mean repercussions. To yourself and to the world. I have always known what was and was not Permitted to me. I have always been able to see outcomes of my actions. Now I do not and cannot. I cannot rely on *I was just following orders* to protect me and the world."

"So, before you had choices, and now you don't?" Ramona struggled to understand the limitations of the woman's new world. "Because you can't see the result before the action, you can't trust the action in the moment?" Spoken aloud, the conundrum seemed almost silly, but metas with telepathy or any shred of emotional reception had struggled when their abilities were compromised. It was as much a part of them as an arm or a leg; Ramona could only assume that Sera's clairvoyant nature had similar qualities. "Well...how long have you been watching the Commissar? Like, really studying her and the way she treats her people here?"

"It is not the way she treats her people. It is the way she treats those outside of her sphere. I believe she has phrased it *kill them all and let Marx sort them out.* That is . . . not acceptable." The woman actually wrung her hands.

"And has she actually carried out those orders? Has anyone in the CCCP refused to act on those orders because they thought she was a few beets short of a pot of borscht?"

"I don't *know*. I cannot see the past anymore!"

Ramona sighed. There was a reason she'd chosen the detective route over the metahuman services counseling route. "You've said that her treatment of others isn't acceptable. Even though you can't see the past, you can still have an opinion based upon what you've observed before. You still have a choice. There are still things that are, uh, permitted, aren't there?"

"I do not know. I have never had Free Will." Sera shook her head. "Some things are obvious but most are not. I could make things so, so much worse. You, you look at—oh, say rescuing a child. But you do not know that child will grow to murder his playmates if he lives . . ." her voice broke. "That is a choice I made, not so long ago!"

She had no response to such an admission, other than to reach over and lay her metal-scarred hand over Sera's arm. How many seemingly right decisions had she made in her time with ECHO that had led to a more terrible outcome? Something as insignificant as a different parking space or the choice of one interrogation room over another might have made a difference, somewhere down the line of choices and consequences. Had she chosen the spot for breakfast, or was that Alex's decision? Why had she chosen the Varsity that day over NomKitteh, the sandwich shop by the ECHO campus? The possibilities were maddening. "And so . . . for every choice you ever made, you always knew the outcome? For every single person?"

"It would drive a mortal mad. It *did* drive Mathew March mad. Faced with too many choices to sort through, he chose to do nothing." She wiped away a tear. "And even that was too much for him, but at least he thought he minimized the damage."

"But you," Ramona pressed. "Did you always know every outcome? Where everyone would end up at the end of things?" She hated the finality in her words, but there was no other way to describe it.

"There was . . . a blank space. Now I know it is because I chose . . . *this*. I did not know that at the time. I only knew that on the other side of that expanse there were those who were present and those who were absent. The analogy of navigating a hole in a cave with a tiny flashlight comes to mind." Sera shrugged helplessly.

"And on the other side, are there..." Ramona stopped, uncertain if she wanted to ask or even know. Sera might have seen things far into the future, but she didn't know if she wanted a hint of tomorrow, next week or next year. "Never mind. I don't want to ask. I can't ask, if only because it would keep me from acting on what I see and know."

"I am—was—not Permitted to tell you, anyway." Another heavy sigh. "I must assume that edict stands."

"But you could see all of us, right? See and act upon, and choose?" Ramona sighed as well and stared out past the ledge. The woman nodded. "And did you ever not do something, even if it was, like you said, permitted?"

"It was...complicated," Sera faltered. "Things were Permitted, which I did, and things were Not Permitted, which I did not do, and there were things that were not Not-Permitted, which I did. And things that were not Not-Permitted, which I did not do, because I am not the Infinite and I could not be at all places at all times." Her voice dropped to a whisper. "I could not save the one called Devil, because I had to choose." The whisper broke on a sob.

Ramona's heart leapt in her throat. Poor Handsome Devil... who was it that Sera had chosen to save, so that she couldn't save Klaus? Had it been...her? She turned to face Sera before she could stop herself, unable to conceal the look of shock and sadness on her face. She hated the swell of gratitude and relief that accompanied the shock. Ramona squeezed her eyes shut and pressed her lips together, focusing on the words. "That... that choice. That's the uncertainty, and it does hurt. It does carry a ton of pain and regret with it. But we have to act in the moment," she added in a tearful whisper. "Acting and being able to seek forgiveness for our choice based on what we know in that moment...it's kind of all we've got. The flip side of Free Will."

Maybe it's a good thing Shakti and most of the others think that I'm dead. This isn't what I expected to learn, coming up here. Ramona stopped herself from wiping her face with her hand and resorted to the edge of her sleeve.

"But now I am...Lost," Sera continued, spreading her hands wide in a helpless gesture. "I do not know what is Permitted, what is Not Permitted, and what is not Not-Permitted. I am *in* the hole in the cave, and I cannot see the bottom nor the edges. Like Mathew, I fear to act. I could doom the world. I could damn myself."

Ramona hugged herself tightly, unable to focus on her own grief and loss. The woman sitting next to her had lost so much, to the point where the thought of acting on anything carried enormous consequences. Anything she said, any attempt to console or empathize seemed trite and almost inappropriate. Could Sera's choice to become human damn them all? Would her inaction force ECHO into a situation where nothing more could be done, other than wait for the inevitable day when the Thulians set fire to the Earth one last time?

Sera didn't know, and that not-knowing shook her to her very core. Ramona tried to grope her way towards some kind of answer. "Not-knowing is part of being human. Hell, acting in spite of not-knowing might be one of the hallmarks of humanity. That's sort of what Free Will encompasses, right? You're presented with the options, and based upon what you know and what you think you know, you act, and you live with the consequences."

Ramona lifted her head to see the stars above them. "And sometimes, the consequences aren't so bad. In fact, there's often joy in that ability to choose. Does following what's 'permitted' give any kind of happiness?"

"Of course." Sera looked at her as if she could not comprehend the possibility of the opposite. "We are not Fallen because we trust the Infinite over our finite selves. There is happiness in trust. This is unhappiness in mistrust. Mistrust brings—" she stopped. "I should not lecture on the nature of trust."

"But you know what it means to trust. That goes along with Free Will." Ramona seized the words, turning on the bench to face Sera. "Having Free Will means learning to trust your choices, based upon what you know, even when there's more that you don't know. Trust doesn't erase fear, but it can lessen it." She tilted her head and studied her companion. "Do you have trouble trusting the Commissar?"

The corners of Sera's mouth turned down. "Yes. She is inclined to extreme violence as her first choice. I know that she has on occasion turned to torture. Not recently, but . . . that could change at any moment."

"And because it's difficult to trust someone like that, you fear the choices that you could make when she's giving orders?" Ramona didn't try to sugarcoat her words, as the woman next to her wasn't a child and didn't deserve to be patronized. "If someone you trusted stood in her place, the choice wouldn't carry so much fear?"

Slowly, Sera nodded. "But it is not just that. There are so many other choices I face! Things that have nothing to do with the Commissar. Matters in which what *I* want may have terrible consequences, but all that I know is what *I* want!"

The former detective's mouth lifted in a faint smile. "Like?"

"There must be a reason why John does not remember. I want him to remember, but what I want may be..." She shook her head.

"Impossible?" Ramona asked. "Or maybe it's just that it might take a little longer and it's hard to trust an uncertain length of time?"

"No. There must be a reason. Which implies bringing back his memory could have terrible consequences." Sera was so tense now that the feathers of her wings trembled. "How can I make a choice when I cannot know this?"

"You trust yourself." The words came in a half-whisper, as Ramona glanced down at the small space between them on the bench and the wings draped down over the edge. "There could be terrible consequences or wonderful consequences, but you trust yourself. Go with your gut, that's the not-so-technical term for it. And really," she offered with a wistful smile, "it does work."

The look that Sera gave her practically dripped with skepticism and doubt. "For you, perhaps."

She shrugged. "For lots of people. Rumor has it that Bella and Bull didn't have a clue about each other, but one of them had to say something. Unless she read his mind, and that's not how she works. Somebody had to go with a gut decision, and there was a good, even great payoff. I'd say that it only happens in those goofy romance novels, except I'd be lying."

Sera shook her head. "I feel like—the one who walks a thin wire over a precipice. Around me all I see are the consequences of failure. How is that good?"

"You're surrounded by the consequences of whose failures?" Ramona scowled in the darkness, bothered that a creature this celestial in appearance could be so utterly pessimistic. "Yours? Mine? John's? Having Free Will might invite an opportunity for failure, but it doesn't guarantee it."

"The only potential for failure that I can affect—now—is my own. But the consequences are... terrifying. I cannot see any joy in this."

"You mean that you can't trust yourself that there could be joy in the consequences?"

Sera nodded, slowly. "All I can imagine is the pain of failure."

Ramona let out a long breath and shook her head. If the woman—angel, or whatever she thought of herself to be now—had never been able to make a choice and enjoy the outcome, then it was no wonder that the mere thought of choice paralyzed her. "You should spend some time with Bella. Part of her therapy for other metas includes this emotion-piggybacking. I hear it's done wonders for some of them. Sort of a vicarious walkthrough."

"Bella . . . has too much to handle now. I will not add my burden to hers. It would not be right." The tone of Sera's voice brooked no argument.

"No . . . no, I guess it wouldn't." Ramona stood and walked to the edge of the building. A broken beer bottle lay on the ground, bits of glass catching the faint light. She pressed her hands against the brick ledge and glanced back at Sera. "This might not be any of my business, but did you ever kiss him? Not one of those chaste little forehead deals, but a real curl-your-toes kiss?"

"Rather more than that." The Seraphym lifted an eyebrow. "Not that it is your business."

"So you didn't like it? Or you thought it was safe because you knew it would be, before it happened?"

"It was . . . love is always Permitted." Sera shut her mouth in a way that suggested that was all Ramona would get out of her.

It was enough for the detective to latch onto with a triumphant pointing of her finger in Sera's direction. "Always Permitted, whether or not you know the outcome. That's so screamingly close to trust, they might as well be cousins! And when you get that once, because of a choice that you made, you hold on to it. You remember that little bit of joy, even when the moment's passed." Ramona's mouth lifted in a smile, her eyes bright. "Even after weeks, months, or years, it's still there."

Sera hesitantly touched Ramona's arm for a moment, as if she was going to say something. But she never got the chance. Ramona found herself catapulted into memory.

They had come to try and find the Mountain, and the pair of them peered into the cavernous dark in search of the lone meta. Mercurye stood on the stone ledge and waited while she rummaged for her lighter. She held it out in front of her. "This will have to do."

"Just look for the giant made of stone. You can't miss him."

Mercurye flashed her that handsome smile that had made all of the girls at her table fall over themselves, and Ramona felt her heart leap into her throat. She found herself grinning back, closing the distance between them, and rising up on her toes until there were only inches between them. What would the proverbial damsel in distress say to the ridiculously good-looking heroic sort in this kind of situation? "Thanks for the ride, handsome." And before she could lose her nerve, she kissed him.

For a split second, Ramona questioned if it had been the right choice or if she had just made a terrible fool of herself. Was it too forward? Desperate? Unwanted? In that instant, Mercurye's arms wrapped around her and he returned the kiss with a fervor that made her knees grow weak and told her that the choice had been very much the right one. The horrors of the past hours, the utter destruction she had witnessed on the ECHO campus, and the excruciating pain that resonated in her entire body, they all ebbed as joy and passion flooded her entire body and provided an unexpected but much-needed respite. Time slowed around them and she allowed herself to enjoy that moment where for a brief time, everything felt so undeniably right.

When the kiss broke, Ramona took a deep breath and steadied herself. The guy even kissed like a movie star. "Wow," she managed. Her cheeks burned, and she noticed that Mercurye's face had a similar blush. "Okay, get going."

Ramona surfaced from the memory, not quite gulping for air but certainly surprised at the plunge. She choked and coughed, her cheeks flushed hotly from the thought of Mercurye's mouth crushed against hers like a scene out of a windswept romance novel. "Well," she managed after a minute. "I guess that's easier than just trying to explain things. But like I said, it's still there."

Sera shook her head. "I am unsure how this would apply to my situation." Then she looked off into the distance. "I think it is irrelevant to me, though very important to you. I must determine *why* things are as they are, and act from there. What I *want* is of no importance."

"But that's part of—" Ramona stopped herself as the explanation between Sera's *why* and *want* hit her like a sucker punch. Of course Rick was how-many-worlds away, but when she did manage to speak with him, Ramona knew that he hadn't changed. She couldn't say the same for Sera when it came to John; understanding

John's change and the circumstances surrounding it superseded the angel's desires. The freedom to want was so new, she could tuck it away for a little longer, but it didn't keep her from being miserable. "Oh."

"If I am to remain myself, it is duty and responsibility that must drive me," Sera continued, sadly. "There is no room in those things for *wanting*. Perhaps not even for Free Will. I am only here as an Instrument. If I forget that..." She did not add what the consequence would be.

"What if..." Ramona dragged her toe over the gravel, nudging rocks into a small pile as she considered her words. "What if there's a responsibility to love? What if somewhere down the line, you're supposed to be a, um, an instrument for that? Don't you have to leave that open, somehow?"

"I...don't know." Again, the uncertainty seemed to shake Sera. "I cannot help but feel that...what I *want* goes counter to duty." She paused in thought. "Or...perhaps my responsibility to love must come without being loved in return." She nodded, as if that had answered a question for her.

"Perhaps." Unrequited love wasn't a new concept for Ramona; the way that Sera had explained it made it seem noble. The way that the woman nodded after the statement made Ramona think that she had made at least one decision on how to approach the situation. Anything to reduce the uncertainty, she thought. "You said love is always permitted, so that makes sense. The duty and responsibility would be permitted, even if it's not returned."

Sera let out her breath, slowly, as if she had been holding it in all this time. "Yes. That answers the question. And also...this. John Murdock is no longer the same man. I must think of him always as someone else. Perhaps that will...help."

"It could." The former detective tilted her head and studied the angel next to her. "He changed more than you or I did. We're still the sums of our respective experiences, whereas he doesn't have that luxury...or burden," she added after a moment's consideration.

"I should be happy he is without that burden." Sera tried to smile but the effort fell flat. "Now..." Suddenly her face changed. Clearly she had had an epiphany. "Now he can become the man he would have been, had he not endured the last few terrible years. A different man. An unburdened man. I think, now, I understand."

Ramona smiled in the darkness. "Really? Understand what, exactly?"

"Why," Sera said, simply. "And as I thought, what I *want,* and my own wishes are irrelevant. I am still here as an Instrument. He is as he is because this is the answer. And as for me, my answer is, as it ever was, duty. In that, I am unchanged, and still myself."

It made perfect sense, out on the rooftop of the CCCP HQ. In spite of the addition or subtraction of abilities, the change of appearance, or the loss of a name, the person remained the same. Sera's loss of her powers had not lessened her role; the more Ramona considered the woman's simple declaration, the more she realized that her gaining abilities didn't change her role, either. She extended a finger and scratched at the exposed bit of metal that covered a healing scrape on her arm. Beneath the surface, she was still Ramona Ferrari.

"Yeah. Yeah, same here." Ramona pushed herself up from the bench and turned to face Sera. "Same, but different, I mean."

"So." Finally Sera actually met her gaze, solidly. "It seems we have answers. At last. And having answers gives us both direction. Also, at last."

"It does," Ramona agreed. "I can't promise that I won't question those answers half a dozen times between now and next week, but that's the human thing to do. Are you going to . . ." She frowned, trying to figure out how to phrase things properly. "Are you staying out here or coming inside?"

"I will remain here," Sera said. "If a call comes I—" And just like that, as if the alarm system had been waiting for the opening, the familiar three tones of the CCCP/Overwatch alert sounded over the earpiece Sera was wearing tucked into the collar of her tunic. "It seems," she said, wryly, "I am needed."

She put the earpiece on, ran a half dozen steps, and flung herself onto the wind. A few wingbeats, and she was out of sight. Ramona watched the woman soar on fire-red wings into the night sky, until Sera was a pinprick of light against the darkness. The voices chattered in her earpiece as the detective stood and crossed the rooftop. Meta or not, she would still be Ramona Ferrari, and she wouldn't sit idle. *Even,* she mused, *if that means doing paperwork.*

CHAPTER SIX

Penny: Tarnished

MERCEDES LACKEY AND DENNIS LEE

It was a cold morning when Penny heard the Devil again. He had been away for a long stretch this time, but he always returned, eventually. Some had taken to counting the days, but she didn't see the point of it. What did it matter, really? There was no pattern to it, no reason behind his visits as far as they could see. He came, he tortured, he left, and during the times between, his captives wondered which was worse—their turn in the chair or the terror of never knowing who was next, or when.

His roar was unmistakable. Mornings would often sound with whimpers as her cellmates woke, with the dying moans of the ghosts as they fled the sunlight, and with the muffled sobs from children from other cells nearby. Today was different. In the distance, a door slammed open, heavy boots pounded on the floor, the door slammed shut, and a great bellow woke the captive children from their slumber. He had returned, he was furious, and they all knew what that meant. Scores of them would bleed today.

On most days, while the others would wake in anguish to another day in hell, Penny would simply sigh in relief and lay her exhausted head down to sleep away the day. She didn't know why the Devil had only taken her away once, and never again. She didn't know why he hadn't simply killed her, if she was not useful to him. Maybe he kept her to use to manipulate her big brother. He had taken Pike often at first, but not so much of late. His interest seemed to have drifted to children in other cells. There was always that terrifying moment when the door to

73

their cell flew open. Would it be the Dark Man, dressed in black from head to toe, who would wordlessly stomp in and replace their food and sometimes bring more bedding? Or would it be the Devil himself, huge and faceless save for an enormous grinning mouth exploding with jagged teeth, come to drag one of them away? It seemed like so long ago that he had visited their cell. The shrill cries of terror from neighboring rooms on the odd morning suggested he had new, more interesting prey. But one could never tell. The last hiatus had left them feeling complacent, verging on an estranged sense of safety, when the door had flown open one morning and he had strode in, marched over to one girl's cot and had hauled her away, screaming. And *she* had never come back.

And on mornings like this, when he announced his presence with a blood-curdling roar, he would not take one, but many.

They began to scream, all of them, and it was at moments like this that Penny was struck by just how many of them there were. Not just the handful of children in this room, but others in nearby cells, unseen. The echo of his boots stomping down the hall grew louder, as did the screaming, until finally he kicked open a door.

Their door.

He appeared then, monstrous and misshapen as always, and as he strode in the children retreated from him. He didn't look at them, as he usually did. He didn't scan the room and select one or more of them seemingly at random and drag them screaming from the room. Instead, he marched to the far wall, the children scattering in his wake. Draped over his shoulder was a body.

Whoever it was, she was no child. She was clearly a woman, with wet and dirty blond hair that clung to her face. She was dressed in scrubs, as they all were, and her exposed arms and feet revealed many cuts, bruises and electrical burns that betrayed many long sessions with their captor. With a snarl, the Devil flung her against the wall, propped her into a sitting position and locked her wrists in shackles. She fell forward and snapped to a stop, her arms stretched behind her, her face inches from the ground.

"I won't be needing her for a while," the Devil rasped, turning back to the door. "But clean her up, and keep her alive. Force the food down her throat if you have to. She will need her strength if I am to continue my work." He looked about the room and snarled, causing the children to shrink away from him. "You are sure there is nowhere else?"

The Dark Man appeared at the door, and nodded. "The solitary cells still require... cleansing. I am lacking servants, so this will have to do for now. Perhaps if you had not butchered the last of my minions..."

The Devil chuckled, a horrible sound, and waved off the Dark Man's concerns. "Be patient, my old friend. The universe shall provide. It always does."

He turned back to the woman. "So be it, this will suffice for now." He turned and left without another word or a glance at any of them. The door slammed shut, and Penny heard them march away, their footsteps fading away until a final slam of a distant door.

The children exhaled in relief, and rose, shaking, from their points of retreat. There followed a chorus of whispers and tentative questions, which fell silent as one of the children began to approach the shackled woman. His name was Joey, and though he wasn't the oldest or strongest of them, the other children turned to him often for leadership. He had a quiet, yet sunny disposition about him, one that couldn't be touched even in a horrible place like this. He carried himself and spoke with a slight smile that suggested that everything would turn out fine. Joey, as far as Penny could see, wasn't plagued with ghosts.

"Ma'am?" Joey said, and took a small step forward. "Ma'am? Are you all right?"

The woman didn't answer, and simply swung in place, her chest rising and falling in time with her ragged breathing.

"Lady?" Joey said, inching forward. "Lady, you got a name?" He reached forward, and placed a hand on her arm.

The woman lunged for him, screaming, and Joey fell back on his hands with a cry as her chains snapped tight, holding her in place. Her matted hair fell away and for a moment they all saw her crazed eyes and bared teeth.

Joey scurried away from her, but waved off the concerns of others who came to his aid.

"S'alright, don't worry," he panted. "She just startled me is all."

"Keep away from her," another girl, Rachel, said. "She's batshit psycho."

"Can you blame her?" Pike said. "Looks like he worked her over harder than all of us combined."

"Lady?" Joey said, trying again. "Lady? You need water? A blanket?" They had both. One thing the Devil didn't deprive them of was food, water and basic comforts. "You got a name?"

But now she curled up in a fetal ball, huddling close to the wall. When Joey inched nearer, all she did was curl up more. "Lacey moan trankwill," she mumbled. "Lacey..."

"Lacey?" Joey prompted. "Is that your name?" He gestured to them to bring him a blanket, but only Penny dared.

"Lacey..." she groaned as he draped it carefully over her. But she didn't start up again, and she didn't thrust the blanket away. She just huddled it tightly around herself, or as well as she could with the chains on her wrists, and went into a fit of muttering and moaning.

CHAPTER SEVEN

Man in the Mirror

MERCEDES LACKEY, DENNIS LEE,
CODY MARTIN AND VERONICA GIGUERE

Mel leaned over the polished countertop and scowled. "This is a bar. People come here to drink."

Einhorn blinked at her. "Tea is a drink."

"No."

"But . . ."

"And if you're going to read a book, then find a table." She shook her head and walked to the corner where a far less talkative individual sat, hands curled around an amber bottle. The bar was meant for serious drinkers, those willing to either do shots in quick succession or maintain a strong and steady consumption of their tipple of choosing. There were those who would sit in the shadows, watching the action as they slowly nursed a single drink over the course of several hours. Some would unwind after a long day's work on the ECHO campus, and some would use the opportunity to push relationships that couldn't fit within the bounds of "normal" operations.

They were a diverse bunch, but one thing all her patrons held in common was power. The bar had no proper name. Situated approximately halfway between the main ECHO campus and the small headquarters of the CCCP in the downtown core, and owned by the Colt Brothers, it had become a speakeasy for metas. Some called it "Normality" while others referred to it as "No Heroics," while a select few had christened it "Mel Sent Me," a name that was quickly growing in popularity, since Mel was the most popular of the metas who volunteered as barkeeps. It was marked by a small sign on a plain, industrial metal door that read only "Private Club: Invitation Only." There were no windows in the brick exterior. Bella had seen to it that all of the proper licenses were obtained once she'd become aware of the existence of the place, which had operated since the Invasion under the quasi-legal facade of being a "social club."

Mel withdrew her trusty bottle opener and popped open two bottles, sliding them down to a pair of ECHO operatives who nodded their thanks and moved to join others congregated around a pool table. This would be the slowest time of the night; once the "comrades" of the CCCP showed up, she wouldn't get a moment's rest until closing time.

Untermensch always preferred the corner. For one thing, it was easier to keep an eye on the entire room. For another, it was easier to keep *away* from Pavel. Anyplace else, Natalya regarded *him*—or Murdock—as being responsible for Pavel's behavior. Well, Murdock wasn't an option, at this point. This . . . mind-wiped version hadn't the least idea of how to handle the Soviet Bear, at least not yet. Thus the responsibility fell squarely on Unter's shoulders. It wasn't that he resented the doddering old fool; Bear was his friend, his comrade. He could be counted on in a fight, and took his responsibilities seriously when he had to. The Bear was simply tiring; between his attempted philandering and the constant misunderstandings he got himself into, it took a lot of energy to look after Pavel.

Except, thanks be to Marx, here in this bar. Even Red Saviour would not ask him to babysit Pavel in the semi-private meta bar. Here, if Pavel insulted a pretty *devushka,* she could handle the situation herself—and would probably be equally infuriated to have someone else step in and interfere.

So Unter could, for a few hours at least, brood in relative peace over his vodka, merely *watch* Pavel, and enjoy the entertainment without being obligated to break it up.

Corbie was off in the corner. He had snuck in a gaggle of Georgia Tech coeds; they were all in ECHO personnel cosplay, which was the only reason he was able to get them past the bouncer.

One of them tugged at the edge of her pale blue skinsuit. Corbie playfully slapped her hand away. "Got to keep up appearances, love." All of the coeds swooned each time he talked; he hammed up his accent whenever he was trying to pick up American girls, and tonight he was in full form.

"I should have gotten better body paint," she lamented. "I mean, do you think this makes me look as cute as Doc Blue?"

"At least," Corbie smirked.

Her friend squealed at the compliment and patted the sparkly plastic horn she had pinned in her hair. "And me? Do I look as pretty as the real Einhorn? I think these shoes make me too tall," she drawled, extending a long leg for Corbie's approval. "What do you think?"

"Good enough to eat, m'love." He leaned in for a kiss . . . only to be bumped roughly aside by the Soviet Bear; Corbie cursed as his elbow dinged off of the Bear's metallic chest while the coed nearly lost her drink.

"Photo-grenade!" Pavel snapped a picture with a beat-up and ancient Polaroid camera; the over-bright flash blinded both Corbie and the coed. The Bear shook the picture, inspecting it. "*Da, da*, is good one." He clapped Corbie on the shoulder heavily. "So, comrade bird boy, how is rash? Or is molting? Always confusing the two." The coed that Corbie had been the most interested in, a disgusted look on her face, pranced over to her friends; the group of them started to crowd closer to Unter, who was seemingly ignoring them. Corbie was nonplussed.

"Thanks loads for that, mate."

"*Shto*? Am not good wing man?" He nudged one of Corbie's wings with his elbow. "Eh? Is proper *Amerikanski* term, nyet?" He switched his attention back to the retreating coeds. "Darlings, come to see dancing bear! My English is better than that sour old Ukrainian's!"

At the bar, two men in ECHO uniforms sat close together, hunched over their drinks. They were speaking quietly, furtively, breaking off whenever anyone came within five feet of them. They would have almost looked conspiratorial, if they weren't so painfully obvious. Mel had grown impatient with them, rolling her eyes at their pathetic (and failed) attempts to appear casual, and had chosen the expedient route of simply leaving the bottle next to them.

"I'm telling you, Matt, if Jensen doesn't give me that transfer request soon, I'm just going to call in sick for the next month." The man shuddered and reached for the bottle, pouring himself another shot.

"Christ, Dougie, you have to *relax*, man..."

"No, no..." Doug insisted, and raised the shot with a trembling hand. "You just don't know, man. No one does. I've logged more time in Top Hold, been closer to her than anyone. I'm telling you, everything about her is wrong. I haven't had a decent night's sleep in weeks. She's doing something to me, she's inside me somehow, I know it. I can't shake her eyes. Even now, it's like she's watching me."

"Doug," Matt said with a sigh. "I'll talk to Jensen, we'll get you transferred, but these things don't happen overnight. In the meantime, you have to pull it together—you're cracking up, dude. The lady's a prisoner. We're her guards. Just do your job, follow the rules..."

"Don't those rules bother you, man?" Doug interrupted. "She used to walk around, free, as one of us! How the hell did she pull that off? How'd she fool everyone? Don't we have, like, telepaths or something? And now, she's the sole prisoner in the highest security cell of Top Hold. They've got a strict fifty-foot-perimeter set up around her. Even we're not allowed to be within twenty feet of her, let alone touch her. They don't even want us to make eye contact. What is it about her? No one's saying dick about it. I tell you, man, she's just not *right*..."

"She was one of Bulwark's Misfits, wasn't she?" Matt mused. "Yeah, and she fooled Bull too. You ever try to pull the wool over Bull's eyes? Forget it, dude. Guy'll see you coming from a mile away. She's got game, sure. I mean, if even half of the rumors are true."

"What rumors?" Doug asked, pounding back another.

"Oh, you know, the usual crap. She's some sort of vampire ninja, or maybe a ninja vampire. They say that she can smell your thoughts. Some guy that saw Tesla's body said she must have scared him to death, because his face was all twisted up like he'd been screaming when he died. I heard tell she rose out of the ground, like mist, and punched her pinky into that Acrobat guy's ear, and just ripped his head off."

"You really believe that?"

"I dunno. The service was closed casket for a reason though, wasn't it? You hear what Scope did? Put a couple in her brainpan, point blank, and it didn't do much more than knock her out."

"I pity her," Doug said, shuddering.

"Who, Harmony?"

"No, Scope. You see her lately? She was all drive and Miss

Perfectionist before, but now? She reeks of booze, she's mouthing off to anyone who gets in her way, she's just a mess."

"That whole crew was messed up to begin with," Matt said with a shrug. "And Harmony was one of them, don't forget that. Just follow the rules. Watch the monitors, bring her dinner, and keep the hell away."

Doug nodded, his face gaunt and haunted. "You guys even got someone to take my shift? Reimer? Goodall? Bakersfield?"

Matt grunted a no. "Still on leave. Don't worry, we'll mix it up. There's got to be someone who can use the overtime."

Doug chuckled nervously. "Maybe you should get someone who knows her, can handle her. Like Bull himself."

"Yeah, like he'd bring himself down to guard duty," Matt scoffed. "Haven't you heard, he's been spending time with the boss lady herself. Don't think she'd like it, him spending time with his ex."

"You heard that too?" Doug exclaimed. "Man, Bull really got around, didn't he? Heh, then what about the Djinni?"

Matt laughed. Oh, the things he had heard about the Djinni, Bella and Bulwark. He motioned Doug to come closer, prepared to dish on all the interesting musings he had heard on his guard shifts, when the front door flew open with a bang and the occupants of the bar were presented with a truly astonishing sight.

Two men crashed through the open door. Both had been there before, though one had no recollection of it, and the other usually wore a friendlier face. No one could recall them entering together before, or even speaking to the other. More astonishing was the fact that one was riding piggyback, hanging on desperately by the red scarf caught in the other's teeth.

"Quit strugglin', goddamnit! I'm takin' you in, one way or another!" John was struggling to keep a hold on the scarf while simultaneously trying to put the other man's hands into a set of zip ties.

"Mmmmmmph! MMMMMMPH!" cried the Djinni, desperately trying to buck him off.

They bounced off the bar and careened towards the dance floor, scattering a few of the co-eds as they screamed and dove for cover. The Bear, dancing and oblivious to the sudden disruption, only noticed when his gaggle of young companions had chosen Untermensch as their new shield. He turned in dismay.

"Is too challenging?" Bear asked, his vodka sloshing over his chassis. "Is too suggestive? Bear would be happy to be having better suggestions for dancing! Perhaps we find pole...*AAIIIEEE!*"

The pair barreled towards Bear, Red bucking like a rodeo pony and John hanging on for all he was worth. John drove an elbow down into Red's side. The Djinni stumbled, and they collided with Pavel's armored legs. With a meaty *smack-clang* they bounced off, John losing his grip while Red fell to his hands and knees. The remaining rotgut in Pavel's bottle splashed out, completely drenching the three of them. Pavel looked forlornly at his bottle, shrugged, and then clomped nonchalantly up to the bar.

Red rolled away, came to his feet, and removed the scarf from his mouth. "Dammit, Johnny, for the last time, it's me, it's..."

John didn't let him finish. He dove forward, caught Red around the middle and hurled him back. They collided with a pool table, and Red screamed as the edge bit into his back. John jabbed Red once in the jaw, then drew his fist back, shaking it. "Sonofabitch, that hurt!"

Without missing a beat Red planted his right foot in the middle of John's chest, braced himself against the table, and kicked him off. John swung his arms to keep his balance. Both of them settled into fighting stances, and were about to start again when some of the patrons—not any of the serious drinkers, mind, who were watching the situation with bemused half-attention—restrained both of them.

"That's Draken, of the Rebs!" John screamed, trying to shake Unter off. "His power's in his speech! You can't let him talk!" One of his hands erupted in flame. "I found the bastard out on the street an' I'm tryin' to collar him!"

"No," Mel said dryly, her hands gently but firmly grasping the Djinni's shoulders. "That's Red Djinni, of ECHO. Any power in his speech is limited to cussing, sarcasm and poorly timed dick jokes. Ain't seen a rating on that yet. Now, both of you shut your mouths, stand down, an' maybe you'll get a beer out of this."

John relaxed after a moment's hesitation, and stepped forward as Unter let him go.

"Red Djinni?"

"Yeah," Red answered, wringing the vodka out of his scarf.

"Why the hell didn't y'just say so?" John was still nursing the hand he'd punched Red with. He was clearly more than a little annoyed.

Red paused, and gave him an exasperated look. He turned to Mel, and back to John, and back to Mel again. "Please let me hit him, just once more."

"If I do that, then he'll be buying you drinks and taking you home. Everybody knows what sorts of girls you favor." She winked at him and patted him lightly on the cheek. "Can't let him have all the fun, can I? And as for you," she called to John. "You're easy on the eyes from both sides, but don't think I won't send you out of here limping in a bad way if you pull that bullshit again. Understand?"

John extinguished his fires, then shrugged. "Your house, your rules," he said, a little angrier than he had intended. He looked to Red, motioning towards the bar. "Well, we're here. Drink?"

"Yeah," Red answered, massaging his jaw, and motioned to Mel. "The usual."

"Scotch an' a beer, plus whatever his usual is." John sidled up to the bar, still scowling a bit.

She poured two glasses of Laphroaig, setting one in front of each man alongside two ice-cold longnecks.

Red accepted his scotch, and favored Mel with thankful grimace. "I suppose I should've known better," he muttered. "Should've known the CCCP would have been after Draken too." He raised his glass up to John, who obliged the toast by raising his own.

Untermensch turned his face away so that neither of the two could read his lips. "Comrade Victrix," he muttered so that only Vickie's implanted mic could pick up what he was saying. "Why were you not informing Murdock that he was attempting to apprehend the Djinni?"

He was met with the sounds of brittle crunching; she was obviously munching on popcorn.

"What, and ruin the show?" she mumbled, and followed the statement with an audible gulp. *"And now I'm out of pop. Time to switch up to the hard stuff."*

"Y'know, you're okay, Djinni..." John said, leaning heavily against the bar. He hadn't started slurring his words yet, but his eyes had definitely taken a glassy shine to them. "I mean, y'know, for a rotten damned crook—"

"And you're just freakin' AWESOME!" Red exclaimed, throwing an arm around John's neck. "Man, we have to do this more!"

"Do what? Drink?"

"That's a great idea!" Red shouted. "More wine!"

"We're sippin' scotch."

"Whatever!" Red agreed.

Mel obligingly filled both of their glasses again without any further prompting. She favored John with a slight smile, but the look she flashed at Djinni was positively radiant. Both of them watched intently while she strutted away.

John was the first to shake himself out of it. "Scenery ain't that bad in this joint, it's got that much goin' for it."

"Mmmmm," Red agreed. Then he began to shake his head. Violently.

"If'n you're gonna puke, do it to your right." John said with mild alarm.

"No puking," Djinni said. "I just realized I'm drunk, the kind of bad things that happen when I get this way, and that I should *really* sober up."

"What? Walk out the door with your face upside down or somethin'?" This started John on a short giggling fit.

"No, but I can do that if it'd amuse you," Red sighed. "I meant that." He pointed at Mel with this chin. "Women."

John waved his hand, exasperated, finishing off his beer. "Don't even get me started on that, *comrade*."

"What? Like *you* could possibly have woman trouble!"

John grinned lopsidedly. "Well, I do all right. Like, fer example, there was this one gal, eyes as big as saucers, down in Bolivia..."

"So, Overwatch. My money is on Djinni to drink Murdock under table." Untermensch finished his vodka, and poured himself another.

"*My money is on you,*" Vickie replied. "*You've had more practice than either of them. Plus, you're Russian.*"

Untermensch barked a laugh. "Next one is on me, *tovarisch*."

"... and it turns out it wasn't her doing the licking. It was the badger."

John roared with laughter. "You ain't right, Red, I'm gonna say that right 'ere an' now."

"No argument here," Red shrugged.

The shouts came from around the bar.

"Or here!"

"You got that right, Murdock!"

"Djinni's about as right as a football bat."

"All right, all right!" Red barked. "Yeah, I see you, Doggy Man! At least my friends don't drink out of the toilet bowl!"

There was a pause.

"Except for Bear," everyone said in unison.

"*Shto?* Someone is wanting autograph?" Bear rose up from behind the bar, a bottle of Mel's best vodka in one hand. He tried unsuccessfully to hide it, but Mel snatched it back, smacked him in the head with his own hat, and chased him out to the front again.

The Bear was hooting with laughter. He settled the hat back on his head and waggled an admonishing finger at Mel. "Now, now, *devushka,* you must be to waitink your turn, my little *blini!*" He headed into the dance-floor. "The Bear is in demand tonight!" he trumpeted, as the cosplayers scattered.

Red watched him go with a grin. "Now see, Johnny, *there's* a guy who's got it wired."

"Well, I mean, he's got a lot of wirin', I can see that. More'n a few shorts, if'n ya ask me." John looked at the bottom of his scotch glass, swirling the drink slightly. "He sure as hell can drink, I'll say that much."

"He's my hero," Red said with wonder.

"Why, 'cause he's always pickled?" John chuckled.

"No, he's just so oblivious," Red said, dreamily. He motioned to the floor, as Bear sashayed up to yet another unsuspecting girl. She turned, found herself nose-to-nose with the grinning lecher, and screamed. "He has no clue the terror he's invoking in these girls. He just keeps on keepin' on. Thinks he's gifting them with his attention. There's no room to get hurt. Makes him invincible, in a way."

"Not to the Commissar's excoriations. Or whatever piece of crockery she feels like chucking around."

Red chuckled. "You saying Bear's made a play for your Commissar?"

John visibly shuddered. "Hell no. He wouldn't be among the livin' if he had. Everyone else seems to be fair game, though."

"Well, not like you have any shortage of cute girls at that old factory HQ of yours." Red gave him an oddly speculative look. "What about you? Any interests on the homefront?"

John shrugged. "Got a few prospective gals that seem interested. The Russians are a bit on the strange side, but that's all right every now an' again. Gamayun, little thing, is on the shy side; she's usually pulling double shifts using her radar stuff to keep an eye out around our area of operations. Mamona, she's an Atlanta native; I don't trust any gal that can throw knives better'n I can, though." He took a sip of his drink, thinking. "There's also that Sera gal. I really don't know what her deal is. She's . . . different; not just the wings, mind you. Always seems to be watchin' me, followin' me around. But a little scared, like." He finished his drink, elbowing Red. "You? I imagine that a campus would be a decent spot to pick up women. Any of 'em take a shine to you?"

Red chuckled. "Nah. I seem to have a bit of rep. People, not just girls, avoid me. Just as well. Like I said, bad things happen with me and women."

John looked at Mel. "What 'bout that one? She seems to have eyes only for you."

Red stole a look, and caught Mel casting furtive glances his way. "You noticed that, did you? I don't know, Johnny. I've worked with her before. She's never really given me the stare before. Something's changed with her."

"I heard she got shot in the head," John said with a shrug. "How's that for a change?"

"Could be," Red said. "Not the first time a severe head wound has gotten a girl to change her mind about me. I'm just getting a weird vibe from her. Like anything there would just start odd and end badly."

"Could be a fun middle though," John grinned.

"Could be," Red admitted.

"You ever get that feeling about a girl before?" John asked.

"Every freakin' time," Red muttered.

At the end of the bar, Untermensch shook his head. "Comrade Murdock is moron," he opined to Overwatch.

"What makes you say that?"

"All those stories of women, yet he has beautiful angel-creature sick in love with him still and cannot see it." Untermensch snorted. "Moron. Blind."

There as a long pause. Then, *"Yeah,"* came the soft reply.

In Untermench's corner, there was a puff of displaced air, right over something that looked for all the world like a stone drink-coaster set into the marble of the bar. There was a tracing of fine lines, like celtic knotwork, all around the rim of it, incised into whatever material it was.

And, at that moment, there was something that looked like a lumpy stone statue made by a kindergartener standing on top of the coaster. Unter nodded at it. It nodded back. Unter raised a finger to attract Mel, then pointed down at the little stone figure.

Mel reached under the bar and poured a double shot of single-malt into a small paper cup, and brought it over to the two. But rather than handing it to Unter, she gave it to the little statue, who took it, wrapping both arms around it to hold it. There was another puff of air and the statue, and its burden, were gone.

"Daughter of Rasputin is serious about drinking," Unter observed, and went back to his own tipple.

"Ain't no other proper way t'be," Mel answered as she sauntered back to her place at the bar.

From the corner closest to the door, Yankee Pride did his best to blend in with civilian clothing and a local brew that Mel had recommended for someone with "real hometown taste." Most of the younger patrons kept to themselves, casting suspicious glances as they avoided his table. Pride ignored the giggling group of non-ECHO ladies and focused on the latest report from the different groups in the city ready to lodge their complaints against the organization. It was a long list.

It came with being the face of the organization, the willingness to listen and nod in spite of half a dozen stuffed suits and their pet lawyers demanding compensation for what they felt were actions against the city. He had no problem going to those meetings and making the necessary concessions, but it didn't make him feel all that heroic. If anything, it just made him feel tired.

Pride knew that he was older than most of the metas in the establishment; if he was completely honest with himself, he was old enough to be a father to some of them. Instead of going home to a loving wife and a house full of kids, he sat in a dark corner of a bar, doing paperwork. He cast a furtive glance at the lone CCCP member across the room; even he wasn't doing paperwork, which was saying something for the Russian. Pride rubbed his face with one hand and let the slim tablet fall to the table.

"Not liking what you read, sir?" Mel stood at the table, a tray full of empty bottles and glasses balanced against her hip. "If you'd like,

I'll put on one of the evening's games. You root for the Bulldogs, or that other team?" she asked with a wink.

He couldn't resist the smile and answered with his own wink. "My momma warned me, some things are best kept a secret when you've got to be in charge. People form alliances over the strangest things."

"Ain't that the truth," she drawled. "But really, you want some company? If you squint hard enough, it looks like Parker, Mary Ann, and that CCCP woman are trying to tease Corbie out of all his feathers. I'm sure he could spare one of them."

That brought a laugh out of Pride. "I'll let him keep his feather-pluckers, as long as they don't pluck him bald."

"I'm betting he's happy getting plucked," Mel remarked dryly.

"And I'd bet that you'd be right." He took another pull on his bottle and nodded at the pair of Djinni and Murdock at the bar. "That seemed to go over well."

She nodded. "They ain't killing each other. You got a bet going?"

Pride frowned. "On?"

"Which one drinks the other under the table. Three to one on Murdock, although I personally think Djinni might hold his liquor better." Mel winked at him before patting him on the shoulder, her eyes quickly scanning the tablet. "And you might want to take it easy, sir."

He considered the advice as she weaved her way back to the bar. It would do him some real good to take it easy, she was right. Pride's gaze wandered back to the tablet and the reports, and he sighed. He knew he needed to take it easy, but he didn't have any clue where to begin.

The door flew open again, banging hard against the wall behind it, and didn't move. Of course the door didn't move. It wouldn't dare, considering who was standing in the doorframe.

A female was silhouetted against the night-shrouded street outside, arms akimbo, legs braced slightly apart, as she surveyed the interior of the bar. She looked exactly like a movie poster.

Or perhaps a propaganda poster for the CCCP, circa 1960, because she was wearing the "battle dress" version of the CCCP uniform; flack jacket and form-fitting pants of nanoweave (supplied via Bella's good offices), gold star in a red circle on her chest, belt supporting firearms and a short club around her waist—Red Saviour was always perfect happy to apply "non-lethal" force to various parts of thuggish bodies if the circumstances required she hold back on her powers.

Untermensch sighed into his vodka and slapped the shot-glass down on the counter, evoking a quick pour from Mel. If he was lucky, he might get one or two more before Saviour herded the cats home.

"Is being last call for comrades," Saviour announced into the silence, her voice deceptively mild and sweet. *"Davay!"*

Mel was already pouring three shots for her, as this was a nightly ritual. Saviour strode to the bar and tossed them back in rapid succession.

"Bah. Like water. When are you to being get proper wodka?" Saviour asked scornfully.

"I keep addin' diesel t' th' bottle," Mel drawled. "Guess I ain't got the mix up high enough yet."

Saviour barked a laugh, and her eyes lit on the CCCP member nearest her—which happened to be Murdock. He and the Djinni had their arms draped around each others' shoulders, obviously deep into their cups. They were performing a Johnny Cash song. "Ring of Fire," to be precise. What was absolutely terrifying was that they were actually doing a good job of attempted two-part harmony. Saviour had to grab the back of John's collar, dragging him away, though this didn't stop either of the two men from singing. Red got up, as if to follow, but was frozen in place by Saviour's cold stare. He sank back onto his stool.

"Aw c'mon, lady, can't Johnny stay out and play?"

Saviour's wordless glare could have lasered through steel plate. Red shrugged and raised a glass to her, grinning. "'Til next time then, darlin'. See you tomorrow, Johnny, see if we can follow up on that Draken lead..."

"Being try a little harder this time, Comrade Chameleon," she said dryly. "Is not to be found in bottom of bottle."

Her gaze next fastened on the cosplayer done up as Soviette. She did a double-take, frowned, and looked as if she might actually *do* something about the impersonator, before shaking her head and snorting. Her eyes moved on, catching Mamona, summoning her with a quirked finger, and sending her out the door without a single word regarding the fact that drinking age in Georgia was twenty-one and Mamona was two years shy of that. Another sweep of the bar—ignoring Unter for the moment, allowing him to signal Mel for a refill—and she caught sight of the little stone figure at Unter's elbow. She nodded briefly to it; the creature straightened, put down his paper cup, saluted her, and picked up the cup again before vanishing in a puff of air.

One by one, the Commissar gathered up her errant comrades, coming at the last to Unter, who sighed, drained the last drops of his last drink, and gave her a casual salute. "You missed Bear," he muttered, as he passed her.

"Am not missing Bear, tovarisch," he heard in his ear via the Overwatch system, as he joined the slightly weaving line of black-clad comrades heading on foot towards the base. *"Am not missing Bear at all."* There was a cruel chuckle. *"Is good to let Bear be run out by bartender. Better her arm wear out, beating him, than mine. Besides, we let him drink ECHO wodka instead of ours, are nyet having to clean up after, and also save all those many, many rubles."*

Bear burst through the bathroom door, a lighter in one hand and an empty tumbler in the other, screaming, "Free Bird! Play that funky music!" The Bear looked around, confused; the bar was empty and quiet, now. Beer bottles and dirty mugs littered the bar counter and the tables. He lowered the lighter and tumbler in his hands, sighing heavily. His shoulders slumped, and he seemed to collapse in on himself a little bit. He trudged towards the middle of the bar, looking wearier with each step. If anyone had been watching, they would have noticed that he looked smaller, diminished; if not for the metal chassis that comprised most of his body from the shoulders down, he would have just been another lonely old man at closing time. He looked up as he fumbled with one of his belt pouches to pay for his tab.

There was a battered and spotted mirror behind all of the drinks; polished metal, it looked like. Hard to break in case the patrons got a little rowdy. The mirror had small distortions and imperfections in it, but Pavel could see himself well enough in it. A battered and somewhat soiled WWII NCO's cap sat crookedly on his salt and pepper hair. *Almost all salt and no pepper, like bad* ukha, he thought wistfully. His mustache wasn't much better, framing his mouth and surrounded with deep furrows from age and fighting. The current song, some pop country garbage that was popular with the college crowd, ended. The one that followed it was somber, opening with muted piano.

"My body is a cage..."

Pavel listened quietly to the song, studying himself in the mirror. He was tired. His body had been destroyed in the Great Patriotic War, and remade using some of his own designs and what was then the cutting edge of Soviet engineering and scientific knowledge. It had left him frail, a shell of who he had once been. The son of a watchmaker and chemist, he had taken after his father before becoming a revolutionary. His experiments had led to the discovery of his own metahuman ability; generating energy blasts through specialized gauntlets that he wore. His research had taken him down dark paths to gain the knowledge to harness his abilities, but it had been in service to the People, or so he had always told himself.

That had been decades ago; his glory as a true hero was long since faded. He kept living, though, despite everything. He had seen the slow fall of his beloved Motherland, almost all of his friends dead, his name disgraced and then forgotten. Pavel had despaired for a time, before following even more selfish pursuits... but that was the past. That was what he thought about the most, when he was alone and vegetative in front of the television. Kept awake nights by the plasma heart chamber that whirred incessantly in his chest, with only vodka to somewhat dull his thoughts.

He sighed once more. The Commissar would be expecting him back at HQ, no doubt. Besides, there was a Matlock marathon tonight, and he didn't want to miss it. He finished fishing out money from his belt pouch, then added a little extra before leaning over the counter and grabbing another bottle of People's Choice. Pavel turned to leave, straightening up, puffing his chest out as much as the chassis would allow, and holding his chin high. He was halfway to the door when Mel emerged from the kitchen, polishing a glass and looking at him queerly.

"Why do you put on the act, old man?"

Bear turned, a little startled, before smiling sadly. *Hrm. Is something different about that* devushka. *Ah, bah, being shot in head would make anyone different.* "A man, a good *Bear*, is being what his comrades need him to be. If they are needing me to be jester, then that is what this Bear will be for them. *Spokoynoy nochi, tovarisch.*" Pavel glanced one last time at the mirror at the back of the bar, and with that he marched out, belting out a drunken and poorly done rendition of "Freebird."

CHAPTER EIGHT

Hurricane: Storm Flags Flying

MERCEDES LACKEY AND DENNIS LEE

"Her name is Emily."

Scope looked down at the timid girl who sat before them. She seemed to melt into the chair, determined not to be noticed, blanching each time she snuck a peek at any of them through her blond, tangled hair.

"No callsign yet?" Scope asked.

"She hasn't chosen one, no," Bull answered. "Jensen's getting antsy about it. He's on my case to pick one for her. It's playing havoc with his filing system."

"Jenson can sit and spin," Scope barked. "You can't just pin a callsign on someone. That shit will stay with you for a long time. To hell with his files. If he had his way, we'd all be numbers."

"You're just miffed that he still calls you Bulwark the Second."

"Been called worse things," she sniffed.

Bruno stepped forward, and offered his hand to the girl with a smile. "Hey, they call me Acrobat . . ."

He jumped back with a start as the girl slapped his hand away. "Get away from me!" she screamed, and disappeared again under her hair.

"Real winner you got this time, Bull," Scope said, shaking her head. "She makes Bruno look like an OpFour by comparison."

"Aw c'mon," Bruno said. "Give the girl a chance! She can't be that bad . . . hey!"

"She's not right in the head, sir," Scope continued, ignoring Acrobat. "Shouldn't she be going through Psych before us?"

Bulwark looked up from his tablet. Scope caught a glimpse of the girl's file scrolling down the backlit screen. He pursed his lips and shook his head.

"We're not there yet," he rumbled. "Bruno, I want you to show me those new maneuvers you've been working on. Scope, you stay with her." He gestured Acrobat to the door and turned to follow.

"Wait, what?" Scope said. "What do you want me to do here?"

"You could try talking to her," Bull said, and firmly closed the door behind him.

Scope swore. A lot. She turned towards the girl, and gestured helplessly.

"What am I supposed to do here?" she demanded, throwing her arms out in exasperation. No one answered. The girl, Emily, peered out once again through her hair. She fixed Scope with a glare that was far from trusting.

"Look," Scope said, her hands falling back to her sides. "I'm sorry, but I think you're stuck with me. Bull always does this. Dealing with people isn't exactly on my strong list of skillsets, and he's got a tendency to throw us in the deep end when we need to learn something. Sink or swim, y'know? So I'll tell you what. Me, I'm going to..."

Scope looked around. It was a bare staging area for the trainees, with little more than a few chairs and tables. She picked up a chair, planted it ten feet away from the girl, and sat down.

"I'm going to sit my ass down right over here. Okay? I'm going to sit here and not move or anything. Not until you're ready."

"You're going to be waiting a while," Emily said, looking away. "Don't have anywhere else to be."

"Why are you here?" Scope asked. "Doesn't look like you want to be."

"Don't have anywhere else to be," Emily repeated. To the casual observer, she might have sounded bored, if not for the faint tremor in her hands.

"Great," Scope sighed. "I was bitching that Bruno's too much of a hyperactive freak, so they send you to balance things out. Last time I ask for some harmony around here."

"Just leave me alone," Emily said. "I'm stuck here. They won't let me go. Just leave me alone and I won't make trouble."

"Not the way it works, rookie," Scope said grimly. "You're right about one thing, you're stuck here. You're stuck with me and Bruno and God help you, you're stuck with Bull. No way he's going to let

you sit out just because you've got your goth lever stuck in over-drive. As for me, I'm not buying it. I don't read people like Bull can, but I know when someone's covering up pain. Why don't you just tell me about it so we can go through the motions of getting all touchy-feely. Maybe Bull will leave us both alone after that."

Emily fixed Scope with a glare, but didn't answer.

"Nothing? Guy problems?" Scope prompted. "Sorry, don't mean to assume. Girl problems? You seem the sort. Romance crap, I mean, not the, uh...girl thing."

Emily continued to glare, and sighed as Scope continued to watch her.

"You're not going away, are you?" Emily said. "You want me to tell you things about me, things to make you cry and have us hug while the credits roll. Fine. I was ten when I discovered I wasn't your typical orphan child living in Surrey. My parents hadn't been killed in a car accident after all. They were wizards, you see..."

"Look," Scope interrupted. "I'm not asking for much. And unfortunately it'll have to be somewhat true. Bull has a way of knowing when you're not being straight with him."

"Can't bullshit the Bulwark, huh?"

"No," Scope replied. "He gets even a whiff of it, and he'll be all over you."

"Good to know," Emily said. "Thanks." She looked away, and appeared to be contemplating the floor when she finally spoke. "I don't have anyone. They're all gone now."

"That's a start," Scope said. "Where did they all go?"

"Not many to begin with," Emily shrugged. "Dad left before I was born. My older sister died when I was four in some freak accident. Never really had friends. People get uncomfortable around me. I think they're all stupid, never had much use for them. So it's just me." She shrugged again. "Better that way."

"Well, sister, you keep up that attitude around here and you won't have to worry about it. We might be metas, but we're still people, and people don't usually bother with emo chicks who think they're too good for the rest of us."

"You're one to talk!" Emily shot back. "Who are you to lecture me about dealing with people? God, I've seen better bedside manner in a morgue! Why don't you get off your high horse and cram it! Go tell your Bulwark whatever you want! I just want to be left alone! I don't want to join this piece of shit outfit and...and..."

She might have looked angry, she certainly sounded angry, but it was more than that. The way her lips quivered, the glassiness of her eyes, and her hands trembled more than shook—she seemed less angry than shaken. Something had stirred her up, something she was holding back. Her mouth closed, her lips pressing together in a strangled hold. She crossed her arms and looked away, her face disappearing once again beneath a tumbling mass of dirty hair.

"Thanks, Bull," Scope muttered, pressing a hand to her face in resignation. "Leave me with the mother of all—"

"Mother," Emily blurted, wincing, as if the word itself had stabbed her.

"Mother?" Scope said, and slowly came to her feet. She took a tentative step forward. "That's right, you didn't mention your mother." Scope took a few more steps. "You lost her, didn't you? And not long ago, I'm guessing."

Scope found herself kneeling before the girl, and before she knew it Emily had her in a desperate hug. Surprised, she forced herself to pat the girl gently on her back. Though acutely uncomfortable, she continued to hold her, and gently stroke the girl's hair.

"Cue credits, I guess," Scope said with a chuff, her expression one of panicked indecision. Still, she didn't let Emily go, and held her until Bull and Acrobat returned.

Then the room abruptly dissolved, and Scope was in another room; Bull's office. No longer kneeling beside the girl who would be given the callsign of "Harmony," but sitting in one of Bull's office chairs, staring at the monitor, staring at Harmony, who seemed to be staring back at her. It was uncanny, and Scope felt a chill.

"That's enough for now," Harmony said.

Scope felt the empathic bond slip away, drain away, a familiar hollow left in its wake.

She was in Top Hold specifically to see and talk to Harm again. Harmony had been asking about her, and Bulwark had obliged by sending Scope in. *Get her talking*, he had said. He was hoping she'd slip up, give herself away. Scope didn't share his optimism. Harmony was too careful, too *good*, to tell them something she didn't want to. Still, it mattered little to Scope. She was there for a different reason. What Harmony was offering was more important than glimpses into who or what she was.

She gave Scope glimpses of the past, a chance to re-experience things, as if she was really there.

"Why did you pick that?" Scope asked. "Our first meeting?"

"Some familiar ground," Harmony answered, her voice crisp and lively over the speaker in Bull's office. "To set the stage. Maybe remind you how we once were."

"That was some act you were selling," Scope exhaled. "If you're trying to convince me of a change of heart, you might not want to remind me of how good an actor you are."

"Unfortunate side effect," Harm said. "I was, in fact, shooting for nostalgic awakening of pathos for the poor, confused blond girl. You felt something that day, as much as you wanted to hide it. I remember, it came off you in waves. It coming back to you?"

"Sure," Scope said, shrugging it off. "Girl meets girl, girl falls for girl's sob story, they get ice cream, blah blah. Is that it?"

"Pity," Harmony said. "I'm not getting a fraction of what I'd hoped from you. You really felt nothing from that?" She looked hurt.

"It was a long time ago," Scope said. "The details are hazy. Watching it now, it's like watching it from the outside, and any feelings about it are being fed from you. It's weird, more than anything."

"You speak like you don't remember it at all," Harmony said, disappointed. "I suppose it was a long time ago. And we're different now, aren't we?"

"Very," Scope said.

"Perhaps something more recent then," Harmony mused. "Something with all of us . . ."

With ample warning from Victrix, the arriving EVAC crew had climbed high into the desert sky and shut down their systems midflight for twenty seconds, long enough to bypass the sudden EMP that would have normally torn through them and left them in helpless free fall. After a brief moment of powerless flight, the ECHO Swifts charged back up and righted themselves. As they touched down at their destination, just minutes before the land-based emergency vehicles, they were met by a strange sight—a large dune, roughly the shape of a man, disintegrating in the desert winds. From his chest cavity, figures emerged, some clearly unconscious and being carried by others. The Swift pilots wasted little time, popping open their carrier hatches and collecting their paramedic gear to attend to the wounded.

Of the fallen, the vital signs were strong, and each woke in turn before the arrival of wailing sirens and even more ECHO personnel in ambulances.

"Get this crap off of me, I said I'm fine!"

"Scope!" Bulwark barked, with difficulty. "Just lie back and let them do their jobs!"

"I'm blind!" Scope hissed, and swatted one paramedic's hand away. She pointed at her eyes. "Problems are up here, idiot, not here!" She cupped her breasts and shook them.

"I'm not feeling you up, moron, I'm getting your heart rate!"

"Here," Red Djinni said, kneeling down. "Check the blond one. I'll take Suzy Sunshine here."

"Gladly," the paramedic scowled and moved off. Acrobat squatted in his place and smiled at Scope while the Djinni continued to take her readings.

"It's blurry," Scope said, "but I can still see that stupid grin on your face, Bruno."

"Just thought you'd want to see a familiar face," Acrobat said. "I read somewhere that people who suffer from traumatic experiences do better when they can see a smiling loved one."

"Oh, gag me," Scope said. "You are a traumatic experience, you freak." She batted away a stethoscope and turned to look at Red. "And watch where you're pointing that thing, Djinni, you... WAH!"

"What?" Red said, then looked down at himself. "Oh, sorry." He closed his legs together, and repositioned Bella's jacket around his waist.

"I'M BLIND AGAIN!" Scope wailed. "WHY ARE YOU NAKED?"

"Long story," the Djinni said. "Maybe the medics brought an extra suit..."

"AGH!" Scope moaned. "DJINNI BALLS! RED, RED DJINNI BALLS!"

"Side effect of getting electrocuted," the Djinni said. "Still healing up. With that and the broken hand..."

He stopped, his brow furrowed in confusion. He brought his hand up and flexed his fingers. They were fine, healed, with no trace of broken bones.

"Well, that's just weird," he muttered.

"What is?" Bruno said.

"My hand," the Djinni said. "I cracked the hell out of it not ten minutes ago, riding that robot wolf. It healed up."

"That's...good, right?"

"It's...new. It's usually just my skin that heals quick. This is different."

"Well, that's just spiffy," Scope said. "Can you bottle whatever it is and pour it over my eyes?"

"Scope, relax," Acrobat said. "C'mon, this isn't the first time you've been blinded. Remember?"

Scope took a deep breath. "The Regatto Run," she said, finally.

"Right," Acrobat said. "They hit us with the strobes, and with the night-vision goggles you got hit the worst. Took you a few days to recover, but you were just fine. You remember what got you through it?"

"You promised me I could kick you around the sparring ring when I could see again," she said, her voice dreamy.

"And did I?"

"You did," Scope sighed. "You never saw that kidney punch coming..."

"And how did you get better?"

Scope grimaced. "I let you all bind my eyes shut behind a blindfold. Couldn't see for days. Crap, not again..."

"Yeah, again," Acrobat said. "But it'll be worth it. You know why?"

"Why?"

"This time, I'm going to let you wear the brass knuckles."

"Oh!" Scope said. "Oh, Bruno...that's the sweetest thing..."

"It'll be worth it," Acrobat said. "But only if you get better, Paris."

"That's...that's...BRUNO, ARE YOU STROKING MY HAIR?"

Acrobat jerked his hand away. "Sorry, got caught up in the moment."

"Oh, I'm going to enjoy pounding into you," Scope snarled, as the Djinni blindfolded her. "I'm going to...and what are you laughing at, Red?"

The Djinni suppressed a chortle as he knotted the blindfold.

"Nothing at all...Paris," he said, ducking as her fist lashed out. He caught it gently and led her to the waiting ambulance. "Let's get you back and healed up. I really want to see what you can do with brass knuckles."

❖   ❖   ❖

Scope gasped as Harmony broke the connection and fell back into her chair.

"There now," Harmony said. She smirked at the camera. "That's better, I definitely felt something from you that time. You saw something different this time around, didn't you? A revelation. It was Bruno, wasn't it? You really didn't know how much he cared about you, even then. For someone with piercing sight, you really are a blind one. So, am I right? Was it seeing Bruno in a new light? No, wait, don't answer. It's better this way. I felt confusion, elation, and yes...love. Delicious, like dark chocolate with a hint of spice."

"Yeah, whatever," Scope replied, scowling. "You were acting, even down there, even while we were fighting for our lives."

Harmony shrugged. "I don't think it would have made any difference. I might have been acting, but I was also working. And I don't think juicing Bella Dawn would have allowed her to heal your eyes fast enough to do any good. But regardless, I had faith in the team, and I was pretty sure I was going to be safe." She paused at that, and looked surprised. "Knowing that *I* was going to be safe used to be good enough. It's...not anymore...."

"Is that why you're doing this?" Scope asked sharply. "You really on a reparations kick?"

"Does it matter?" Harmony was back to her enigmatic self. Scope wasn't even sure now she'd seen that moment of shocked surprise on her face. "Aren't you getting something from these sessions?"

Scope grimaced.

"So, now, what do we say, Scope?" Harmony asked, her tone pitched *just* right so that Scope couldn't snarl at her.

"Thank you," Scope replied, the words pulled from her reluctantly.

CHAPTER NINE

Danger Zone

MERCEDES LACKEY, DENNIS LEE,
CODY MARTIN AND VERONICA GIGUERE

Soviet Bear, Untermensch and Upyr: CCCP

"Shut up, Old Bear," Untermensch said, wearily, for what felt like the hundredth time.

"But *LaVerne and Shirley* are to be sturdy workers!" the Bear protested.

"Less talking," Upyr replied, succinctly. "More shootings." Suiting her actions to her words, she raised her beaten-up AK-74M to her shoulder and managed to hit the target this time. Barely. "Bah. What am I to be doing wrong?" The trio were practicing marksmanship this afternoon. There was a stretch of destruction corridor behind the HQ that was close to two hundred meters long and blocked in on three sides by rubble. Getting some cheap fill was easy; there was plenty of torn-up ground where the reconstruction hadn't reached yet. With the fill piled at one end, the CCCP had its own private firing range. There had been one city council official who had tried to raise a fuss over it, but the Commissar had had . . . words with him. No one had bothered the CCCP after that; most of the neighborhood residents figured that the more practice the Reds had, the better. After all, they couldn't be worse shots than most cops.

Soviette, Mamona, Molotok and Rusalka were steadily working at their targets. As was Gamayun—who was still in contact with Vickie and the Overwatch system via her implanted Overwatch rig, and who occasionally put down her rifle to mutter into it. The rest were all on patrol or maintaining the HQ.

"If Sheriff Andy were here—" began Bear.

"Shut up, Old Bear!" came the chorus.

Red Saviour and Ramona Ferrari: CCCP

Red Saviour set a pile of papers in front of Ramona at the small desk. She offered her a wolfish grin. "Soviette has cleared you for administrative duties. You will not find CCCP to be plush office with secretaries. First duties is to be filing equipment requisition and damage forms."

"And let me guess, this isn't even half of it," Ramona remarked dryly. Exposed metal on her fingers grated against the thin paper. "A through F?"

"Through C. C is for Chug," the Commissar replied with a wag of her finger. "Many things are filed under Chug for damage. Some may be filed under Chug for disposal, but is different form. The two are not to be confused, *da?*"

"Da." Ramona wrinkled her nose and started to separate the pages. She noticed several pieces of office furniture as well as half of a tow truck categorized as damage, with notes mentioning Chug's insatiable appetite. Other pages described doors, tires and depleted uranium shells.

Chug would definitely need more than one folder.

Bulwark, Bella and Yankee Pride: ECHO Campus Training Course

Bella watched as Bull scanned his tablet, checked the time, and took in the sight of his new recruits struggling with the new obstacle course on the ECHO training grounds. His movements were slow and deliberate, but constant. She smothered a sudden urge to chuckle. He was a closed book, this tall, sturdy and beautiful man, but she liked to think that slowly she was beginning to understand him. It was very exciting for her to learn about someone at such a plodding and deliberate pace. Most men were so transparent, even without her ability to detect their every fleeting and often base thought. This time, she was doing things the old-fashioned way. Maybe it was love, maybe it wasn't, but time and tentative gestures and conversations would tell, and not be ruined by the abrupt mental readings she usually received by simply touching someone.

Bull's head swiveled slowly down to his tablet, and he grunted. Bella suppressed another laugh. It was rare to see him so restless.

"Well, Bull, what do you think?" Bella asked. "This lot up for some firearms training yet?"

"Are you insane?" Bulwark asked.

Bella smothered a smile. "Isn't that the Misfits' battle cry?" Here she was in what should have been a practically untenable position, de facto head of ECHO, an organization that was still reeling from what the Invasion, Tesla's death and Verdigris had done to it—and yet—she couldn't help but keep smiling. Because things were getting better. Insane or not, things were *better,* and one had to acknowledge that it was, in part, due to a certain level of deviousness and unpredictability that she and her rebels had shown since someone, someone insane perhaps, had placed her in a position of leadership.

"They're in terrible shape," Bull said, shaking his head. "Most of them are having trouble swinging on a simple rope over that mud pit. There's no way I'm putting lethal weapons in their hands. They're not even close."

Bella felt the urge to smile fade away. Bull wasn't just restless. He was pragmatic, to be sure, but this went beyond that. She actually felt something from him. It had a tinge of bile and disgust and it really didn't suit him.

"Something bothering you, big guy? They'll get there, I'm sure of it; just look at them, you can actually see them improving on the course while we watch. It's not like you to be overly hard on your recruits. What's got that tight butt of yours in an uproar?"

Bull exhaled and shook his head. "She's late," he muttered. "Again."

Aha, Bella thought. He was preoccupied with what seemed to be his favorite topic of conversation these days. *Scope.*

"I'm afraid she hasn't shown up for her last three appointments with Mary Ann," Bella offered. "All she did was call Gilead and ask for her scripts to get renewed." Callsign *Gilead* was one of the few full MDs among the ECHO metahealer ranks. "Gilead declined on the grounds that she has to actually see someone to renew that many restricted scripts."

"She is less herself every day," Bull sighed. "Would you believe that last week I found her firearms strewn about, unchecked and with the safety off? This is beyond troubling." He glanced again around the obstacle course.

"Rogers!" he barked, and waited patiently as a wiry young meta untangled himself from some netting and trotted over.

"Yessir?" Rogers asked, coming to a stop and saluting smartly.

"You need to pick up your feet more if you want to tackle that net trap. I want to see your knees up to your waist, son."

"Yessir!" Roger answered.

"Have you seen Operative Scope this morning?" Bull asked.

"No, sir!" Rogers said. "But we don't really expect to see her until this afternoon, sir!"

"And why's that, soldier?"

Rogers paused, clearly looking uncomfortable.

"Out with it!" Bulwark barked.

"She was at Normality with us last night, sir!" Rogers answered. "She was...she was tying one on, sir!"

Bull sighed, and glanced at Bella. "Looks like she's found an alternative for her meds."

John Murdock: CCCP

John Murdock was busy fixing the CCCP's fleet of Urals in the HQ's motor pool. Almost all of them were dinged up, with a few that were barely able to start. For some reason, the Commissar felt like this was the most appropriate job for him; he'd been slotted for it on the duty roster for a week solid, in addition to his substantial patrol schedule.

The particular Ural he was working on had a shot carburetor; he was in the process of rebuilding the entire damn thing, which was annoying and dirty work. All the same, he was thankful for the routine. It helped to keep his mind at least somewhat off of the whirlwind of information that he had been flooded with since "waking up." The world had been set on fire, and he was one of the few people that was trying to put it out again. Some days, it felt like they were using water pistols against a forest fire. These CCCP folks...they were underequipped, underfunded, and undermanned. There was some quiet support on those first two problems coming from contacts and friends they had in ECHO. Even still, it didn't seem like enough to John; he was used to being a part of one of the most well-equipped fighting forces on the face of the planet.

Despite that, these CCCP "comrades" were making it work, as well as they could. He had to remind himself; *it's not the arrow, it's the Indian.* Shiny toys and gadgets didn't matter for shit if you didn't have the skillsets and training to utilize them effectively. Back when he was still in the army, he'd had a few ops where he and his team were "running light"; civvie clothes, a backpack and an order to "procure on site." He didn't like doing things like that; too much left to chance, too many different things that could go wrong. Now, however, he was forced into that sort of situation quite regularly.

Perks of your new outfit, fella. John still wasn't sure that he liked the idea of taking orders from Commies, the Commissar in particular. He hadn't had the best impressions of women in combat positions from his time in the service; Ranger and Delta were both all-male units, after all. Still. She seemed to have good tactical sense, even if she was a bit overzealous. Time would tell. There's a big difference between being a cop, even one with metahuman powers, and fighting a war. John was eager to see how these Commies performed in a real, stand-up fight.

And if they can't make the grade, then this "comrade" is heading for greener pastures, John thought.

Red Djinni, Victoria Victrix and Mel: ECHO Campus, Parkour Course

Vickie frowned a little as she eavesdropped on the conversation between Bull and Bella. She'd known Scope was . . . turning into a loose cannon. But until now, since Scope had been regularly ditching her Overwatch Mark One rig, she hadn't known how bad it was getting.

She was preoccupied enough that she had paused halfway up the "bar climb" wall, which was made of lengths of rebar poking out at irregular intervals in a giant slab of concrete. Suddenly her train of thought was derailed by Djinni's upside-down face appearing in front of hers.

"Pardon me," he said, his voice only slightly muffled through his scarf. "Have you seen a tiny little waif of a mage around? She was *supposed* to meet me at the top of this here course thirty minutes ago . . ."

"Sorry. Shamelessly dropping eaves," Vickie apologized—without pointing out that it had only been about five minutes, not thirty. She made up for it by putting on some extra speed.

Red, of course, outpaced her. He was like a gibbon. How did he *do* that?

"How do you *do* that?" she asked, panting, as she paused at the top.

He flipped back into a handstand, balanced precariously on an exposed beam, and neatly toppled down to straddle the girder with his knees. "From what I'm told, my grandmother had a thing for chimpanzees."

Vickie pretended to consider this, then shook her head. "Not likely; you're not furry enough. From what I can tell, you don't have a hair on you."

"You don't know me!" Red objected. "I'll have you know shaving is a great ritual for me. Candlelight, some Sarah McLachlan playing in the background . . . wait, just how much of my hairless me have you seen?"

A lot more than you think, she reflected, and suppressed a grin. *Then again . . . privacy warring with vanity . . . I wonder if he forgets to turn off the camera feed on purpose?* She heard something below, and peered down. "Here comes Mel."

"Oh good, maybe she can give you a run for your money." Red paused as they watched Mel ascend. "You talk to her recently? She doing better?"

Vickie sighed, because to be honest, she wouldn't have been surprised if Mel was a wreck outside the bar. Mel had been in intensive care and rehab for weeks, completely missing the Big Push in New Mexico. Over the chaos of ousting Verdigris and capturing Harmony that day in the MARTA tunnels, she had become one of the many wounded that had almost been lost in the shuffle.

At least she still lived. They had lost a few to Blacksnake that day, including Paperback Rider and Frankentrain. She knew that Red still missed them, especially Rider, who could always carry the most interesting conversations on the most obscure topics. Vickie missed them, too. She still felt intense guilt over losing them—and even more guilt over losing Acrobat. She'd overruled Bull, and Acrobat had died. Of course, if she *hadn't* overruled Bull, Harmony would have gotten away. . . .

Mel had been shot in the head, by Harmony herself. A lot of ECHO personnel had to be treated in the field that day, and whoever had worked on Mel had at least done a first-class job.

She had arrived at ECHO Medical with strong vitals and a bullet-free wound, but had been unconscious for days. Chalk it up to metahealing that she had pulled through. Her rehab had proven remarkable, with no visible problems with motor control, memory or cognition. She was far from recovered, though. Whatever that bullet had done, whatever tissue it had burrowed into, it had cost her her talent. Mel could no longer summon her illusions.

"She's...coping," Vickie said. "As far as Einhorn can tell. She's putting up a brave front, I'll say that much. She's lost something vital, Red. It's got to be killing her, not to be what she once was."

"Well," Red sighed, and patted her hand. "It's a good thing you're here then. Might do her some good to talk to someone who's been through that."

She shuddered. That was something she never wanted to experience ever again. But Red was right. If there was anyone around who understood how it felt to lose an intangible part of yourself, to be walking wounded when the wound didn't show, it was her. "Yeah, I can do that," she said.

Red patted her hand again, and they watched as Mel continued to climb up to them. She moved with confidence. Vickie wondered if it was all for show. The girl had just recovered from a gunshot to the head, after all. One might have expected some signs of hesitation, even doubt, but Mel took each handhold and lift with ease. If she was in any way unsure of herself, she was hiding it well. As Mel crested the top, she hopped up to sit next to Red and favored them both with a grin.

"And they thought I should take things easy for a while," she scoffed. "It's not like I got shot in someplace that counted, *cher*, only my head!"

Caught off-guard by the unexpected joke, Vickie laughed uneasily. "I guess that could be said of a lot of us," she said awkwardly.

Mel blew a raspberry. "Don't go there. Last thing we need is to lose that pretty little brain of yours." Her lips curled as she glanced at the Djinni. "This one's another story. Don't know how much is rattlin' around upstairs, but I bet a bullet wouldn't hurt it none. Be a shame if he took one in the rump, though, and damage that fine property."

"You're too kind," Red said, dryly. "So they've cleared you for duty? Clean bill and all that?"

"Clean as a whistle," Mel said and flashed him a demure smile.

"But I might let you confirm their assessment, if you play your cards right."

Vickie fought down a pang of jealousy as Red's eyes lit up with surprise and interest. He recovered with a shrug and a flip comment on being years from proper medical accreditation, but she could feel the sudden heat between these two.

Yeah, right. What are you jealous of? It's not as if he's ever going to look at you the way he looks at any normal woman...

Her thoughts trailed off as a soft bell sounded off in her ear from Magic Eight Ball, part of her Overwatch suite back in the apartment. Eight Ball was a prognostication program; she'd started it to try and ID *who* was responsible for any given incident, but as with all things that were part magic and part tech, it had started taking on a life of its own. She was beginning to suspect it was... well, it was getting about as sentient as a parrot, and as eager to please as a puppy. Which meant it was trying to predict the future.

And right now, it was giving her tentative *pings* in her ear. Like a kid tugging on mom's pant-leg. Not exactly alarms, but...

Well, foretelling the future was always a crapshoot. No reason to think Eight Ball was any better at it than the average TV psychic, at least not yet.

She ignored it. There was still half the course to finish. "Hey, people. We're holding up traffic," she said, and swung herself over to the other side to start her way back down.

Soviet Bear, Untermensch and Upyr: CCCP

"I am remembering time in Stalingrad..." Bear was saying, as Upyr finished reloading her rifle. She hadn't had much more success with the last several shots, but she was beginning to suspect that was due as much—or more—to Soviet Bear's nonstop chatter as it was to her own faulty aim. It didn't help that he was hitting her target as much as his own, looking over his shoulder to chat with Untermensch, talking and shooting in equal amounts. "*Fascista* were yards away, we were having no food for week and a half, no vodka for two days—truly dark times, let me tell you—so Yuri was having bright idea—"

"If you are not shutting ever-flapping mouth," Untermensch interrupted, and paused, then got a sly look on his face. "If you are not shutting mouth, I am to being cutting off Waffle House privileges."

The Bear's normally stolid expression was transmuted into one of sheer horror. Upyr was fascinated. It appeared that Georgi had finally found a chink in the Bear's armor. She wondered what on earth it was that Bear wanted at the Waffle House. It couldn't possibly be the food, though she couldn't rule it out. The man had an iron stomach, almost literally, and seemed to subsist on a regular diet of rotgut vodka ("People's Choice") and canned pasta.

Whatever it was, Bear not only shut up but finally shouldered his own weapon and began taking methodical shots at his target. To Upyr's chagrin, they were all either in, or very near, the bullseye.

"*Blin,*" she muttered, and raised her own weapon. "What in name of Marx am I doing wrong?"

"Perhaps you just need the right motivation, as Bear does," Untermensch said, smirking.

"And his is...?"

"Her name is Paula," Georgi said. "Waitress at the Waffle House. She is...sturdy."

Aha, Upyr thought. *Not armor. A chink in the Bear's* amour.

Ramona Ferrari: CCCP

Near as Ramona could tell, the only difference between the paperwork that CCCP had to fill out and the paperwork ECHO had to do for the Feds was that the CCCP required two more copies. Other than that, it was pretty much the same, tedious stuff in the same excruciating detail. She was beginning to wonder about Chug, however. The rock-man had always seemed gentle and childlike around her—but some of the after-action reports showed an entirely different side to him. Situations involving hostages or direct threats to members of the the CCCP seemed to cause the man to become aggressive and unpredictable, with more than the usual number of cars being thrown. One report signed by Soviette had described not one but three separate trailers hurled at Blacksnake operatives who had tried to detain them during an afternoon stroll through the destruction corridor. Although Ramona could envision some of that behavior, she couldn't believe the level of rage that Soviette had detailed. The man fed squirrels and called them names like Pietr and Mischka. He wasn't the monster that some reports described.

Victoria Victrix: ECHO Campus, Parkour Course

The pings were getting persistent. Either there was something wrong with the Eight Ball program or Eight Ball *really* needed to be attended to. In either case...

"Overwatch: open: private: Red Djinni," she said. "Red, my computer suite is being obnoxious and I need to know why. Give me a minute."

She didn't wait to hear his answer. This could be done on her PDA; Eight Ball was a very simplistic little fellow. She unrolled her bluetooth keyboard on one leg, opened the screen on her PDA and strapped it to her arm, and logged in from the top of the bar-climb. "All right, you little bastard," she muttered, *"Now what do you want?"*

She had forgotten that her channel to Red was still open. *"I'll have you know my parents were married, Vix,"* came the snarky reply.

Before she could manage a snappy retort, Eight Ball was happily telling her why it was tugging on her pants-leg. "Oh...hell no..." she said aloud, and brought up her own HUD. "Overwatch: open: battlefield overlay: center: current position: max: fifty miles," she snapped out. And felt her heart stop.

"Overwatch: Priority One Alert!" she screamed.

John Murdock: CCCP

The carburetor was now completely disassembled, and ready for cleaning. The float bowl, the jets, the outer cover, the screws, the O-rings and gaskets had all been taken off. Now it was time to scrub the rotten thing down. *Another exciting day in the service of the people of Atlanta...*

If this and playing cops and robbers was all he was going to be doing, maybe he ought to check out ECHO instead. From his journal, he knew that they had tried to recruit him at one point; things hadn't turned out so well on that front. Were there *any* alternatives to ECHO and CCCP?

His train of thought was interrupted when he heard that little blond gal, Vickie, over the comms: *"Overwatch: Priority One Alert!"*

An instant later loud klaxons started blaring in the base, red warning lights accompanying them. John dropped the carburetor to the floor with a clank. *There's only one thing that alarm is supposed to mean.*

"It's a goddamned attack." John zipped up his issue coveralls and started sprinting towards the stairwell. They had drilled for this a number of times; Natalya had a penchant for surprise inspections and drills at odd hours. It was one bit of routine that he could truly appreciate; you could never be too ready for when the manure hit the fan. On the wall was a weapons locker; there was at least one in most rooms of the base. He stopped briefly, removing an AK-74M and as many mags as he could stuff into his pockets; depending on the threat, he'd primarily be using his powers, but a good rifle is always nice to have in a fight.

"Murdock," he heard in his ear. Vix again. *"I'm activating your HUD. We have Death Spheres incoming from the fifty-mile marker and closing. You're going to be front line for CCCP. Just like the drill. If the RPGs don't break on contact, you torch what they were supposed to hit."*

John's HUD lit up like a Christmas tree. "Copy, I'm on my way to the roof."

"You're being paired with Rusalka. She'll be busting one or more hydrants and directing the water. You two figure it out from there, I'll have my hands full here, and I'm handing CCCP off to Gamayun. Don't yell for me unless you have no other choice. I'm putting out an all-points and we aren't the only targets being hit."

All John could think of was the footage he had seen of the initial Invasion. The Death Spheres, the ranks of power-armor-clad troopers, and how they had shrugged off every attack. Well, almost every attack. Whatever sort of energy field they produced that made their armor nigh invincible, it was weakened by fire; heating up the suits made them vulnerable, even to small-arms fire if it was concentrated at the right points. *Time to earn my pay.*

He heard more people running up the stairs behind him; he chanced a look over his shoulder. Rusalka, like Vic had said, along with the local gal Mamona and a meta wearing an ECHO uniform and...black wings. Everyone was holding a rifle; Mamona and Rusalka each also had one of the new RPG systems slung over their shoulders, with the ECHO meta loaded down with ammo for them. After a few more flights of stairs, John burst through the door to the roof, followed by the others.

"Rusalka," he barked to the Russian, "you're on the Northwest corner with me." She nodded, then trotted over to her position, cocking her rifle as she went. John turned to the other pair.

"Mamona, you're going to be on the Southeast corner workin' as a rocket team with..." John looked at the winged meta.

"Callsign Corbie; I was on a walkabout in the ol' neighborhood when Vix shunted me over—"

"Handshakes and introductions later; you're going to be covering Mamona an' makin' sure her RPG keeps gettin' fed. Got it?" John started grabbing some of the ammo carriers from Corbie's arms; Rusalka would need them.

Corbie set his jaw, then nodded. "Roge-o. Let's burn some metal."

"Get to it, people. Just like the drills; keep an eye out for our people on the ground. Remember; anythin' worth shootin' once is worth shootin' three or four times." Corbie and Mamona had both already started towards their position; John moved to get ready next to Rusalka. She had the ability for water manipulation; any fires that he started, she was there to put out if they got out of control. It just wouldn't do to take out the Kriegers only to have half of Atlanta burn down. Again.

John made a final check to ensure that everyone was locked and loaded, and knew their responsibilities; they were spread thin at the moment, and the action would be happening before anyone on patrol was able to make it back. They had two things going for them: the strange, alien-looking woman called Gamayun and her ability to see things with almost perfect clarity through remote viewing, and Vix, with her frighteningly prescient Overwatch system. Those hadn't existed on the day of the Invasion, and they just might turn the tide today.

Seraphym: Airborne

The Seraphym found the microphone, earpiece and camera mildly irritating, but at least they were a substitute—a poor one, but a substitute nevertheless—for the senses she was now missing.

When the earpiece screeched at her, she knew better than to pluck it out and throw it to the ground; instead, she sorted through all of the confused shouting, as once she had sorted through the futures, until she heard the voice of the Colt Brother who was looking at the right screen at the right time. From that, she knew the direction from which the spheres heading for CCCP were coming; she arrowed upwards, knowing that she could no longer outfly the spheres and was no longer able to heal so fast she was figuratively invulnerable to their weapons. She would have to rely on fire and agility. She was at falcon-height when she spotted the spheres moving towards the CCCP HQ at a terrifying speed. She waited until they were just under her, called fires, and went into the classic peregrine-dive, beating her wings until she had gotten all the speed she could get from them, then folding them and turning herself into a projectile, yielding to gravity's embrace.

She caught up with the spheres just before they reached CCCP HQ. They, in their turn, must have seen her coming, and at least that pair of pilots was aware of what she had done to the Thulians in the past, and what her old powers had been. Instead of firing on the HQ, they unloaded their troops and sped away, with her in a full tail-chase, streaming flames.

Bulwark and Bella: ECHO Campus, Training Course

"Overwatch!" Vickie shouted over all channels. *"Priority One Alert!"*

Alarms were lighting up everyone's Overwatch rigs. For those with implants, this meant a flashing "red alert" light in the upper right of their field of vision, and a single, piercing klaxon before the channel cleared for human chatter and the HUD lit up. "What is it, Victrix?" Bull demanded. "What are you...?"

He stopped as he heard...it was a hum, but not like the background vibration of, say, an air-conditioning unit. This was a deep thrum that rattled your heart all the way inside your chest and gave you a sickening feeling in the pit of your stomach, a *hum* that you felt in every cell of your body. And if you were Bulwark, with half of your skeleton made of metal, it vibrated every bit of you to an unnerving extent. And more. He had felt this before.

"Never mind," he sighed, and turned to Bella. "Make the call."

"INCOMING!" Bella screamed, her voice amplified from long-ago operatic training. The recruits on the field, who did not yet have their Overwatch rigs, came to a surprised halt. Her cry startled some of them on the net-trap, who tripped and collided with each other and came to a tangled sprawl on the ground. Others dropped from their places around the scaling wall, while more paused during their race through a scaled-down, one-story parkour course. ECHO personnel, meta and non-meta alike, had been moving about the training field running courses, exercising or just socializing. They all stopped, and turned to her...

...to see three enormous Death Spheres rise above the canopy of the neighboring park and dozens of armored Kriegers emerge from the treeline.

"*RETREAT!*" Bella screamed again, then, using her Overwatch mic. "Overwatch: broadcast all. *BATTLE STATIONS!* Overwatch: open: Mark One Control: Boys, I'm online, do your stuff and route me command!"

There was a moment, just a moment, of surprise and fear, and then Bella watched her people scramble for the main campus. She bolted after them and heard Bulwark following her at a steady trot, the faint shimmer of his shield guarding them both. The field erupted around them with explosions, with sudden craters and scorched earth as the Kriegers began to lay down heavy fire with their energy cannons, and something new...

"Artillery!" Bull shouted, grunting as a shell reflected off his shield, bouncing up and exploding above them.

"And RPGs!" Bella shouted back, her hands flying up to cover her head as the ground erupted around her. "We need to get to the main campus!"

"Agreed," Bull rumbled, and hissed as he risked a glance back. "Bella! To me!"

"What?" she cried, and turned as he barreled into her and scooped her up in both arms. "*EEEP!*" She yelped as he launched himself up, his shield intensifying around them. Behind them, another artillery round crashed into the ground, and the blast suddenly hurled them forward. Bella felt Bull's arms tighten around her as she instinctively curled up, ducked her head down, and tried as best she could to replicate Harmony's ability to feed him energy. She felt like throwing up, and, disoriented, she didn't realize why until she opened her eyes.

They were bouncing.

Like a ground-serve on a tennis ball, they were bounding along the turf with way more forward momentum than height, his kinetic shield keeping them aloft. She caught a glimpse of some of her operatives sprinting for the main gate, their eyes wide as she and Bull flew past them. If she hadn't been so terrified, she might have laughed. She closed her eyes again; this was certainly an E-ticket ride but *not* one she would have willingly gotten on!

"Did you know you could do this?" she gasped.

"I had an inkling," Bull replied. "But I never thought to put it into practice."

"Why the hell not?"

"I'm still working out how to stop."

"Oh." She opened her eyes and stared up at him. It was times like this when she wished she *could* read him. Was he joking or what?

His eyes were narrowed in concentration, and she could feel all his muscles tensing. *Urk. Probably not joking.* All the one-liners about how "It's not the fall that gets you, it's the sudden stop" no longer seemed so funny.

She glanced up, and saw that they were hurtling towards the front gate of the main campus. "You, uh, might want to work that out fast. My stop's coming up."

"I think I've got something," he muttered.

"Good plan?"

"Stupid plan."

"Only plan?"

"Only plan. Go limp. Get ready to roll."

Her eyes went wide, but she obeyed, knowing he would feel her relax, and yelped as she felt the shield begin to catch on the ground, slowing them down but sending them into a violent spin. She risked a glance at Bull, who grimaced in concentration. She caught a glimpse of his shield, its odd translucent sheen usually uniform throughout, becoming patchy and even ragged in places.

"What are you doing?" she demanded.

"New trick," he gasped, his usual rumble now a bit forced and stuttering. "Haven't practiced much. Think of this as a field test."

"*Field test? ARE YOU INSANE?*" she demanded.

"No," he grunted. "Just out of options."

They collided with the gate, and Bella felt the wind knocked out of her as they were hurled back. She barely registered the shield fading away, but reacted instantly as she felt Bull's arms fall from her. She hit the ground in a near-perfect martial-arts shoulder-roll, relaxed but controlled, or as controlled as you could get under circumstances like this. But she knew she had too much momentum to get to her feet, so she kept rolling until enough speed had gotten scrubbed off to stop. She slapped the ground hard to finish the roll, leapt to her feet, struggled to regain her breath, and glanced up to see Bull lying sprawled on the ground just a few feet from her. He wasn't moving. With a cry, she scrambled over to him. The big, overly protective oaf had shielded her from most of the impact with his own body.

Of all the...

"Bull!" she cried, and laid her hands on him. He was still breathing, but she could sense torn muscles pretty much from neck to toes. At least his reinforced skeleton had kept his bones intact, but a quick scan confirmed a concussion. His poor brain had just taken a big hit. *I could sure use a jolt of angel-juice about now,* she thought grimly, took a deep breath, plunged into the Healing Gestalt and hit him with the equivalent of...

Holy—

She had been the equivalent of 220 volts, days ago, when the Seraphym had been an angel. Now she was 440. Not Seraphic strength, but certainly industrial strength. It was kind of euphoric. She resisted the impulse to shout, *"Be HEALED!"*

It took about a minute, because with power came speed, and she was already working with the benefit that he was a meta with fast-healing factor. She began with his head. Swelling that had started, reversed. Damaged cells knitted. She felt the healing waves pulse out through his body like soothing tides. Sixty timeless seconds, more or less, and all the damage was reversed.

—mother of pearl!

And as she opened her eyes, she realized something else. She was...a little winded. But not drained. A shot of glucose would be good right now, but not something she had to suck down like a starving vampire.

A movement caught her attention, and she cradled his head as he opened his eyes.

"Stupid plan," he whispered.

"Stupid plan," she agreed, then laughed as she held him tight. "Don't *ever* do that without me, you moron. Can you get up?"

"I'll be fine," he assured her, rising slowly to survey their surroundings. ECHO personnel from the training field were beginning to catch up with them, while others from within the compound had begun to take their stations both behind and in front of the gate. "Show time, leader lady. I'd say you've got about five minutes before they get here."

Time to be the boss of the outfit. "Overwatch: open: Mark One Control: Sam! Dean! Rally at the front gate. Deploy the Quartermaster Corps. Keep the sensors watching for reinforcements. Until Vix gets to her suite, you're running One and Two. Overwatch: broadcast all: ETA five minutes. Bring up blast shields.

Standard positions and rally point, front gate, take cover, priority cover for civvies."

At the command, Sam and Dean Colt activated the blast walls that rose up from the ground, along with half a dozen Jeeps with mounted Mk. 19 grenade launchers. She glanced back to confirm that the Q-Corps was on the way with the shoulder-mounted launchers. She couldn't make the vehicles run any faster by staring at them, so she turned her attention back to where it would do the most good; the people at the walls.

As she took her position next to Bulwark behind one of the central blast walls, she noticed a civilian dressed in a bright red jogging outfit cringing next to them. He sat with his back to the wall, his knees brought up tightly to his chest. He was hyperventilating.

"Breathe deeply, sir," she said, risking a look around the wall. She saw the tops of the Death Spheres growing over the horizon, and heard the steady march of the Krieger troops in the distance. Her HUD confirmed all of it. "Don't worry, we'll get through this."

The man struggled to answer, his words catching on his ragged breathing.

"Sir!" Bella dropped to one knee, and laid a hand on his shoulder. "Deep breaths. That's right, nice and slow..."

The man nodded frantically, and his breathing slowed and deepened.

"What's your name?" she asked.

"B-B-B-B-Bob..." he answered. "B-Bob McIntyre."

"Helluva morning for a jog, huh Bob?"

"My usual route," he gasped. "Figured ECHO campus would be...would be..." His voice trailed off.

"Safe?" Bella offered.

"Y-yeah."

"We're going to get through this, Bob," she repeated, and offered him a smile.

"H-how do you know?" he asked. "Do you have a plan?"

"Yes," Bella nodded. "Let us handle this. It's going to be a bit hairy at first, but we've got this, okay?" The Q-Corps had arrived and were distributing the RPG launchers and ammo.

"What are you going to do?"

"Well, Bob," Bella said, and let a soothing pulse of calm radiate out from her hand, "for starters, we're going to let them come in a bit closer."

The pulse wasn't quite enough.

"ARE YOU INSANE?" Bob demanded.

Bella stared at him for a moment. She chuckled. She couldn't help it, and soon she was chortling in helpless gales of laughter.

Victoria Victrix: ECHO Campus, Parkour Course

Vickie didn't remember coming down off the bar-climb. One minute she was shouting into her mic, the next she had a lump in her shirt that must be her keyboard, and she was on the ground, sprinting in a straight line for the ECHO Quartermaster Building. She couldn't manage everything from her HUD; it wasn't possible to get all the information she needed as fast as she needed it. Now all that parkour practice was paying off, even though her limbs were protesting mightily; she sped across the course without tripping once.

There were plenty of people who had orders to get into the sky, but the folks working with the Q-master knew Vix had priority, and he kept one jetpack with her name on it in readiness at all times. She was counting on that, as she tried to manage the battlefields, pass what she could off to the Colt brothers and Gamayun, and run at the same time. Somehow she managed to stay on her feet, though when she came bursting through the Quartermaster's door, she was staggering.

The racks where ECHO jetpacks were normally kept were empty. But as soon as the Q-master spotted her, panting and staring wildly, he hauled one out from under the counter, jumped *over* the counter, and got it on her back. She strapped in; he took care of what was needed at the back, and slapped the broadcast-energy engines when he was ready. And she was out the door, then in the air, heading for her apartment.

Flying *low*, below the rooftops. No point in making herself a target for the Death Spheres. She was pretty sure she was flying too fast—and weaving among the buildings—for ground troops to target her, but if she got up in the air, the spheres could and would take computer-guided shots at a lone flyer. She had to make this flight at top speed; at some point soon the ECHO Tesla-power broadcasters, hidden in structures all over the city, would shut off. Then she'd be down to the half-power mode of the onboard generator. Which would be just enough power to land. The broadcast power weakened Krieger armor, but the Kriegers knew that now and would make any broadcaster they could find a top priority for demolition. Shutting them off would hopefully keep the Kriegers from getting a solid fix on all of their locations.

She landed on the roof; punched in the code on the roof door and breathed a sigh of thanks that she'd managed to persuade the super to let her install a code-lock, because she would never have found the key in time. Then she staggered down the stairs, lurched to her door, shouted the keywords for the spell that flipped all the locks open at once, barreled through the door, dropped the jetpack in the living room, shouted the key to the spell that flipped the locks closed and pinballed into her Overwatch suite.

"Overwatch: Battle stations!" she cried as she tumbled into her chair. The monitors lit up, and she lost herself in the meld.

Ramona Ferrari: CCCP

The klaxons in the CCCP base came seconds after the cries of "Battle stations!" over the comms, and the occupants cleared the main areas as orders came through all possible channels. Ramona set the reports to the side and took off for the medical bay. With all of the battles she had witnessed with the Kriegers, she half-expected to scream, or panic, or rush to Soviette claiming that she didn't know the first thing about fighting the alien metal behemoths. Instead, she took the stairs from the basement office two at a time, her mouth set in a grim line.

The last time she had witnessed the full force of a Thulian attack, Ramona had had the terrifying yet frustrating task of keeping Alex Tesla company in a walk-in freezer while seated on a carton of tater tots. Although Vickie had chirped constantly in her ear, Ramona had remained an anxious and ineffective bystander, forced to wait and see if she would survive the attack. Now, she waited in the doorway for Soviette to point her in the proper direction. If nothing else, she could still fire a gun and provide cover for a field medic.

The Russian woman seemed to have the same idea as she raced through the doorway, combat nanoweave covering all but her hands and head. She carried a small kit on her back and threw another at Ramona before handing her one of the CCCP's standard issue PP-19 Bizons, Russian submachine guns with unique helical magazines. "Chug is waiting for us. You will not engage unless necessary, *da?* Is to be bringing others back for care, not requiring more care yourself. I would hate to be losing more scissors."

Ramona felt the butterflies in her stomach fade. *"Heads up, Detective, I'm activating your HUD,"* came the words in her ear that made the butterflies vanish. Suddenly she had information again; suddenly she wasn't alone. She was part of the whole. *Now* she felt everything settle into place. *"Okay, turning you over to the Colts. Sovie's your immediate in-command. I'll pick you up myself when I'm online. Vix out."*

It hadn't been fear, exactly, after all. It had been *disconnection.* She trotted in Soviette's wake as the CCCP's doctor collected her rocky protector. There was about to be a battle. She had a place in it. That was all she needed to know right now.

Bella, Bulwark, Red Djinni and Mel: ECHO Campus

"What kept you?" Bella asked, as the Red Djinni and Mel came hauling proverbial ass from the parkour course on the other side of the campus. "Stop for coffee? I've got stirrers if you take the SuperSize version." She gestured at the RPGs; there were still a few on the trucks but they were going fast. Red nodded and motioned to Mel with a curled finger. She flashed him a mischievous grin, slapped his ass, and followed him to one of the trucks.

"Overwatch Two online," came Vickie's voice in her ear, as her HUD lit up with a *lot* more information. She breathed a sigh of relief.

"Welcome to the party, Vix," Bella said. "I like feeling less blind."

"They're almost on you," Vickie said calmly.

"Can we get an accurate count?" Bull asked.

"Three Death Spheres, trailing..." Vickie paused. *"Jeezus Clooney...three hundred shock Kriegers. Atsa lotta Nazis."*

"That's a bit more than we anticipated in our simulations," the Djinni said as he and Mel joined them, toting their hardware. "We up for this?"

"Well?" Bull rumbled, and looked at Bella. "Are we?"

"As some famous guy at the Battle of the Bulge said, 'Nuts!'" She grimaced. "No, I can do better than that..."

Her muttering was drowned out by the thunder of the Krieger energy cannons, and the explosive rounds hitting the blast shields. A couple of the RPGs chattered as a few ECHO Ops returned fire.

"HOLD YOUR FIRE!" Bulwark roared. *"STAY BEHIND THE BLAST WALLS!"*

"What are you doing?" Bob screamed. "Why aren't you shooting them?"

"Sir, you need to calm down," Bull said. "Accuracy's limited at this range. We need them closer. They've got us a bit outgunned right now. Firing now won't mean jack if we run out of ammo."

"But won't it be easier for them to hit us?"

"Probably," Red grunted, as he charged his RPG up.

"Not helping, Red," Bella said. "Bob, you got a wife? Kids?"

Bob nodded. "Three," he said, and began to shake.

"You just think about your wife and kids, Bob. Think about how happy you'll be to see them again, and how much of that depends on you staying put and letting us work."

Bob stared at her. He whimpered, ducking his head under his arms and curling up into a ball as the Kriegers continued their assault. The energy-cannon fire ramped up, bombarding the shield walls until the steady barrage of noise and vibration drowned out everything. Bella stopped shouting orders, resorting to hand signals as she rallied her troops around her. Vickie's constant stream of audio cut out and was replaced by a scrolling mess of intel that streamed up the edge of Bella's HUD. Bull took occasional glimpses around the wall, each time looking back at Bella and shaking his head. Bella fretted. She wasn't the patient sort. Every nerve was screaming for action, but for this to work, they needed those murdering monsters closer...closer...

She chanced a look to her right. Mel knelt at the ready, her fingers locked firmly in place on her ordnance. Bella noticed she was shaking, ever so slightly. Mel had passed any test they had thrown at her and was declared fit for duty, but Bella still had her reservations about it. The girl had lost her powers, after all. Bella wondered how she would feel if she had lost her empath abilities. None too eager to jump into battle, perhaps. Mel caught her gaze, offered a smile and nodded. The girl had courage, Bella had to give her that. She glanced to Mel's right and noticed the Djinni beaming at her, his grin evident even through that stupid scarf of his.

She caught herself laughing again. In the thick of battle, under a barrage of enemy fire, and she was laughing. She felt an odd calm fall over her, an absurd sense of security, a certainty that they were going to be just fine.

Bull snuck another peek around the wall, glanced back at her, and nodded.

Bella flashed an open palm in front of her face, clenched her fingers into a tight fist, and pointed up. The stream of intel on her HUD came to a halt, and was replaced with a single word.

Roger.

No one heard the launchers rise up from their hidden nests; they couldn't, over the sounds of the Krieger onslaught, but as they rose by the dozens from behind the gate and from caches hidden in groves of trees that littered the landscape, the ground trembled, vibrating with the action of the huge gears raising the machinery. The Krieger energy-cannon barrage stuttered, then came to a halt, as the advancing army realized they were completely surrounded by giant launchers, fully loaded with rows of gleaming RPG warheads pointed directly at them.

Bella stepped around the blast shield and grinned at them. The launchers all began to fire at once; the air was filled with contrails and the shrill whine of the rocket motors as the ordnance flashed out to crash into the enemy. At first the Kriegers didn't seem to care; they were supposed to be invulnerable to damn near anything, after all. But these RPGs weren't conventional ordnance...and the Kriegers started to notice very quickly.

"*Yippie ki-yay, motherfuckers!*" she bellowed as her launchers began to tear into them. Over the sudden din of screaming rocket launchers and dying Kriegers, Bella winced and scratched at her head, annoyed. "No, can't pull that off. Maybe something from Tarantino..."

John Murdock: CCCP

"*Murdock!*" came the voice—disconcertingly, from inside his ear. "*Heads up! Two big birds incoming, your nine o'clock, fast and low.*" Also in his ear, but muted, was chatter from her Russian counterpart, Gamayun. Presumably she was saying the same thing in her native language. His HUD lit up, again with more information, just a little disorienting. He still hadn't gotten used to the fact that this stuff was all implants.

"Guns up! Here they come!" Everyone tensed in anticipation, staying low behind the short walls that topped the roof. John squinted in the direction that Vickie had told him the enemy was coming from; one moment, he saw what looked like two tiny dots in the distance. The next moment, there was a deep, thrumming hum that shook him to his bones, accompanied by a sick feeling in his gut. He'd read that whatever propulsion the Thulian Death Spheres used caused that, but this was his first time—that he could remember, at least—ever experiencing it. The spheres had skimmed over the roofs of buildings as they made their approach; one near the street in front of the HQ, and one directly over the destruction corridor behind it. Before anyone could track the spheres with their weapons, they had already gone. There was a flash of flame and wings following behind the spheres; not as fast, but definitely in pursuit. *The "angel"* was all that John had time to think. Less than a second later, however, there were very loud thumps and crunches coming from the ground.

"Air drop!" Mamona was pointing over her side of the building. John scanned the street in front of HQ and almost immediately spotted what had caused the noise; Krieger troops. Ten of them, all in powered armor. They were located approximately two blocks away from the HQ.

"Ten on this side," he called out, igniting fire around his hands after doing a final check on Rusalka's launcher to make sure it was loaded.

"Same here!" That was Corbie, the ECHO meta. *Let's see how this ECHO responds under pressure.*

"*This is Molotok. Ground units in position, rooftop is instructed to hold fire until after we engage. We will draw them in,* tovarischii. *Out.*"

"You heard the man. Wait until they're committed an' fire on my mark. We'll see if these new toys work."

The Krieger armored troops had reformed after touching down. Two squads, a modified wedge formation for each; all the troopers had line of sight to shoot past each other without much danger of friendly fire. Judging by the helmets, the team leaders were in front of each squad. *Suckers are looking to be real heroes, leading from the front. Good luck with that, boys.* The Kriegers weren't using cover, simply advancing down the street. John saw Rusalka lick her lips in anticipation; she was as eager for this as he was. The rest of the team looked just as ready; they'd need to be. He was going to be juggling coordinating all of them, firing at the Kriegers, spotting targets, and raising the temperature when the time came.

"Ground team, engage." Molotok again. His order was followed by loud and short barks from assault rifles on either side of the building. From John's vantage point, he could see where Molotok and Thea were hidden behind a hardened barrier; their shots were sparking off of the armor of the Kriegers, but had little other effect. The troops marched methodically down the street, still unconcerned. *They probably think that they're engaging all of what's left at HQ right now.* The squad was just over a block away when Thea popped up from behind the barrier; this time, she had a rocket launcher on her shoulder. The squad leader in front stopped, bringing his men up short behind him. Before he could give a command or raise a weapon, a rocket screamed towards him. It was a perfect shot.

The warhead hit the center of the Krieger's chest; crumpled, spraying thick gel everywhere before the pieces rained to the ground. The Krieger was stunned for a moment, then appeared to laugh; even from the roof, John could hear the amplified and ugly laughter, first from the squad leader, then from the rest of his men as he turned to face them. As soon as he had turned back around to face the CCCPers, another rocket impacted; the rockets themselves were only marginally accurate at distance, so this one struck him in the shoulder.

These rockets were new; a fusion of tech from ECHO along with one of the inventions left behind by the late "fire-breather," Zmey. He had been a tinkerer in the CCCP, and had died in the battle for the annihilation of the North American Thulian HQ. His legacy for destruction lived on, however. The second warhead exploded brilliantly; two different solutions, inert when separate, became extremely volatile when mixed. This happened in flight, so that when the warhead reached its target and ignited, it produced a super-heated conflagration. As with any new technology, it didn't always work as advertised, as evidenced by the first warhead.

The Krieger squad leader was fully engulfed, instantly. The heat generated by the warhead was designed specifically to be high enough to defeat whatever made the Krieger armor nigh invulnerable. As the Krieger was about to raise his arm cannons to punish his attackers, a very tight group of shots hit the face shield of his helmet. All of the rounds went through, killing the Thulian. Still on fire, the suit fell forward, hitting the ground with a loud crash. *One-two punch. Let's see you bastards deal with that.*

"All comrades, weapons proven to be effective. Open fire."

Ramona Ferrari: CCCP

Ramona watched the fiery behemoth topple face-first to the pavement. Molten metal flew toward her, fragments of Krieger armor ricocheting off concrete. She threw an arm up to shield her eyes and winced as her entire body squeezed inward. Bits of the broken face shield and earth hit her, making a hollow thud against her arms and torso. She heard Chug rumble behind her and she lowered her arm.

"Shiny," he offered, a finger pointing at the torn fabric of her shirt. The Krieger armor had embedded itself between black plates that covered her torso from ribcage to pelvis. He reached out a hand to grasp the shard, but his eyes grew round as it began to sink into the plates. Ramona drew a deep breath, and the jagged metal slipped into her skin before she could think to remove it. The skin and metal plating that remained bore no sign of damage, although an oily sheen covered the plates where she had absorbed the Krieger armor.

"Well, that's new. Helpful, too." She shared a quick grin with Chug before running back to provide cover for the rest of the CCCP as more of the warheads arced toward the stunned group of Thulians.

ECHO Campus

As one, the ECHO ground troops combined with the heavy support of the enormous MLRS—multiple launch rocket system—rained explosive fire down on the startled Krieger shock troops. Bella nodded in satisfaction as her people came out from hiding behind the blast shields, armed their launchers, and opened fire. RPGs flew, alone from shoulder-mounted units, or by the dozen from elevated launcher modules, trailing jets of smoke and slamming into the advancing force of metal warriors. Some Kriegers were knocked to the ground while others managed to stay on their feet. It hardly mattered. With the exception of a few duds, the

RPGs were doing their job. Fire erupted through the Krieger horde and began to decimate their ranks.

At the rear of the advancing column, the Death Spheres slowed to a halt. Their concentrated barrage of energy blasts on the shield walls faltered, paused, then began to pepper the ECHO forces seemingly at random. ECHO ground troops dove for cover as the blasts scorched the earth around them. In the midst of the Thulian ranks, shock troopers not yet covered with liquid fire began to break formation, scatter and look for cover. What had begun as a very one-sided assault on ECHO HQ had quickly degenerated into a chaotic free-for-all firefight.

Between firing and loading her own launcher behind cover, Bella noted that all the hours spent drilling her troops for just such an assault had paid off. She watched her ECHO Ops lead their squads around the battlefield with precision, gaining and losing ground to their advantage, maneuvering confused Kriegers into groups to douse with RPG-loaded infernos and bomb with impunity. The mounted launchers laid down a steady barrage of RPG salvos, each taking but moments to reload and swivel to fresh targets before unleashing their devastating arsenal.

At the perimeter of their advancing wave, the Thulian line crumpled and lay in screaming heaps on the scorched earth. The core of their advance came to a halt, like a wave hiccuping and dispersing upon itself. They scattered, caught off-guard in open territory, and returned fire. Bella signaled her advance troops to retreat. The ECHO squads fell back, behind the shelter of the shield walls, popping out only to unleash fresh volleys of explosive RPGs and heavy accompanying gunfire. With little else at their disposal, the Thulians resorted to using their own fallen for cover.

With the ECHO forces retreating behind cover, the Death Spheres renewed a concentrated attack on the shield walls, pinning their opponents down. The shoulder-mounted RPG fire slowed to a trickle, and with only the salvos from the automated launchers to deal with, the Krieger ground troops began a slow and disorganized retreat.

"Dean, we could use some uber fire!" Bella shouted into her comm.

"Affirmative, boss lady," Dean answered. Behind her, a new MLRS rose. Instead of the array of RPGs housed by its smaller counterparts, this unit only held two. In comparison to the

sleek-bodied missiles fired by the dozen, these missiles were considerably larger, sporting enormous warheads.

Bella glanced at Red Djinni. He gave the giant missiles a glance, caught her staring, and returned to reloading his launcher.

"What?" he said with a shrug. It was a good thing they had the Overwatch system; she never would have been able to hear him otherwise.

"No obligatory dick joke?" she asked, expectantly.

"Later," he grunted, aiming his launcher around the wall. "I'm working here."

"That's what she said," Mel chuckled.

"Firing, keep your heads down," Dean announced as one of the missiles flew past them, over the battlefield, and slammed into one of the Death Spheres. Over the deafening sounds of energy fire, explosions and screaming, they still heard the grotesque sound of a distant *splat* as the missile discharged enough persistent fire to cover the face of the sphere.

"Wow..." Bella said in awe. "Pie in the face. If the pie is *on fire*. And made of *more fire*."

"Now that's what I call a money shot." Mel nudged Red's shoulder and winked.

Red nodded in appreciation. "Needs an encore, though."

As if in response, the second missile flew overhead. This time, instead of a *splat*, there came a deafening boom as the payload exploded in the heart of the Death Sphere. The sphere flew back, its propulsion instantly shut off, and crashed to the ground in a heap of smoking and twisted metal.

"Yeah, that'll do," the Djinni said.

The barrage on the shield walls fell away as the two remaining Death Spheres retreated. They paused over the burning wreckage of their fallen ally, scooped it up with their tentacles, and fled, leaving the Thulian ground troops to fend for themselves.

"CHARGE!" Bella ordered, and the ECHO ground troops moved back on the offensive. *"Leeeroy! Jenkinsss!"*

As her troops began their attack, Bella heard those who were wired into Overwatch groan. Yep, the battle cry still needed some work. She ducked back under cover and hailed Vickie. "Overwatch: open: Vix: private. Vix, how are we doing?"

"Local or global?" Vickie sounded...reasonable. Bella couldn't hear excessive stress in her voice.

"Global?" she ventured.

"Nothing we can't handle. Needing to bring in the Supernauts in Moscow. Did NOT let Saviour know that. Had to bring in the local army in a couple of places. We're winning. Slowly in some places, with lighter casualties than anticipated."

"Local?"

"You and CCCP. Everyone else is mopping up small squads of suits. Linking you to Saviour now."

There was a very short pause. *"You are wanting update, ECHO Leader?"* There was a harsh laugh. *"They are no match for the comrades of the CCCP. We are obliterating them. The spheres are in retreat, and we are herding armor."*

That was far better than she had expected. "Uh—" Okay, better be a little formal about this. Saviour had given her the signal. "CCCP Leader, are you taking prisoners?" She paused again when Saviour didn't immediately respond. "They're soldiers, not rabid dogs—"

Saviour interrupted her with another laugh. *"Am thinking no one with swastika ever signed Geneva Convention. Are not entitled."*

Bella flushed. *"Dammit,* Saviour!"

Saviour interrupted her again as a volley of heavy fire from the Thulians hit the shield wall. *"Am hearing complications, ECHO Leader. Are YOU in position to be taking prisoners?"*

Bella peered around the shield wall and did a head count of the enemy, or tried. Lots. Too many. Far too many to be claiming victory, much less . . . taking prisoners. She blanked for a moment. *Dammit, what would Bull say?* "But you obviously *are,* Red Leader," she snapped. "Remember, we need intel, not a body count. Over and out."

The trap had been planned, implemented and practiced many times in the previous months. It was only a matter of time, after all, before the Thulians mounted another full-scale attack on ECHO HQ. Bella ducked back behind the blast shield to reload her launcher, and snuck a peek around at the remaining Kriegers. She swore. They had built and stocked the hidden MLRS machinery at a feverish pace, and in the end had wondered if they had perhaps committed an enormous act of overkill. It seemed they had not. Despite their best efforts, they had not anticipated the sheer concentrated numbers the Thulians would throw at them.

She fired off her last RPG, and fell back. Bulwark joined her.

"How many?" she asked. She had to use the Overwatch circuits to talk to him. Even though they were face to face, the noise was just that deafening.

"Too many," he grunted. "I'd say about a third left, a hundred, give or take. And we're running low on ammo. If they can get their act together, they'll probably have enough to overrun us."

"What do we have left?"

"Regular armaments and metapowers," Bull said. "Precious little in the way of firestarters. Best we've got is..."

"Overwatch! Open Jamaican Blaze! Blaze!" Bella barked over the Overwatch system. "What's your sitch?"

Bella's HUD lit up with a blinking fire icon where Jamaican Blaze was. It was green, signifying that Blaze was ready to work her power as soon as Bella needed it. Blaze had positioned herself well.

"Hit 'em and hit 'em hard, girl! We're between a rock and a hard place out here."

Blaze leaned back against the blast wall, took a deep breath to steady herself, and emerged to survey the battlefield. The RPGs had done a number on the Kriegers, but it wasn't enough. Most had been completely engulfed in fire and blown to pieces or simply shredded with explosive rounds, regular gunfire and every flavor of meta artillery you could think of. Unfortunately, many were still up and fighting. Worse, they were organizing a charge on the main gate. It was more than a little disconcerting how fast those suits could move when they wanted to. There were, however, a fair number of them covered in small patches of flame.

It was enough. It would have to be.

She studied the pockets of fire with both hands extended. The teenager gritted her teeth and shifted her focus to a sizable group that had clustered together in the center of the charge. She picked one shock trooper whose entire back was engulfed in fire, and stoked it.

You can do this, Willa Jean. The voice rang out in her head. It was a clear voice, one that had lifted her so many times in the past, and it was loving, oh yes, so loving...

The trooper screamed as the fire spread across his armor. His startled comrades leapt away from him. Blaze felt a sudden exhaustion as she willed the fire to burst, to spread, and soon the core group of Thulians were thrashing about in helpless agony as she willed the flames higher and brighter, as if she were conducting a blazing symphony among the burning Kriegers. The rapid jump from soldier to soldier generated a current, and the flames began to cycle counterclockwise of their own accord.

The whirling tongue of fire threatened to rise up and out of control; Jamaican Blaze cried out in pain. She had never truly tested her limits. She felt dizzy. Her knees began to buckle. Surely, this was it, she was at the brink, she was *past* it . . .

You can do this, Willa Jean.

In the past, Blaze had always found comfort and solace in her grandmother's voice. If there was ever anyone who could reach beyond the pain, to see it done through hell and high water, it was Dixie Belle. But her Gram was more than a role model for her, more than just guidance and wisdom and an shining example of true heroism. She was, simply, everything to her. Through it all, it was those six words that had always lifted her up. She was up to any task, to any ordeal, with those simple words of encouragement, and she would be damned before she let her Gram down.

I'll do this, Gram.

With nothing left except a sheer and desperate will, she brought both hands down, not to lessen the fires, but to widen their reach. The flames lashed out to drag the smoldering Thulians into the vortex. The remaining Kriegers on the fringe who had begun to join the assembled mass retreated instead, but to no avail, as they too were drawn inexorably into the swirling storm of fire and mayhem.

"Jamaican Blaze, your readings are starting to redline. Suggest you pull back." That was Sam Colt; Blaze was wired to Overwatch One, not the new system. She had the feeling that if it had been Vickie in her ear, there would have been some shouting and a lot of cussing.

Jamaican Blaze struggled to breathe in the superheated air, her hands shaking as she willed the vortex into a flaming whip that lashed furiously at the last of the Thulians. She gestured at the air with both hands, gripping and twisting an unseen line. The fiery tornado responded in kind, curling in on itself until the tip met the base and the loop weakened. She pushed both hands together, squeezing the remaining Thulians between the walls of fire until the wavering pillar erupted in a white-hot ball of molten metal.

It appeared that Vickie was paying attention anyway. Just when Blaze thought she was about to die, or fry, or both, a wall of earth and stone suddenly upthrust itself between her and the firestorm, and she was jarred to her knees by a waist-deep hole appearing under her. Suddenly, she could breathe again, damp, cool cave-like air soothing her lungs and cooling her burning skin. *"Breathe, girl. Good job,"* came the slightly hoarse voice in her ear. *"Yes, Overwatch and I are always here, and if we can help it, we will never let you fall."*

I did it, she thought in wonder, and even sobbed in relief as she slipped into unconsciousness. She was only barely aware of the earth folding around her like a pair of careful, sheltering hands, keeping her safe.

Willa Jean did it.

Victoria Victrix: Overwatch Suite

Frankfurt, Leipzig and Paris were all engaging. More of Zmey's RPGs had been shipped out to the EU than had been kept at ECHO HQ because there were fewer fire-chucking metas over there than there were here. Vienna had already beaten back the single squad of power-armored troopers that had been dropped there. Berlin had a pair of Death Spheres, but they were still on the approach. Every screen in the suite was live, and most were split in quadrants.

Vickie was coordinating the new Overwatch One controls in every city that was taking attacks, splitting the work with the Colt brothers. The drills had paid off, though; only Budapest and Praetoria had been caught with their pants down.

Vickie was keeping an ear out for a special little alert, however, because the last major attack—the Invasion—had included a cyber-attack, and she was grimly determined not to let a single Trojan slip past the ECHO defenses this time.

There was the sound of a doorbell. *"Candygram,"* chirped an animation-style voice in her implant. She spared one moment for a quick scan of all the screens; looked like Control could manage without her for a little. She cleared a screen by moving the pages over, and brought up the Honeytrap.

Sure enough... incursions being tried on systems all over the globe, but without the mutating FoF code, they were being blocked. That was good; the Thulians should have expected that after the last time. "So let's see which backdoors you're trying that you think we don't know about, you bastards," she muttered. She'd pulled in every white-, gray- and black-hat hacker she knew for this, besides people like ECHO's own Belgian geniuses from Toronto. They all *wanted* the Thulians to think they'd penetrated...and actually, they *would*. Just not what they thought they were penetrating.

It looked like the ECHO system, and it was connected superficially to the ECHO system. But it was a hollow shell, with Vickie's specialty, cybermancy, playing herd-dog. And there, there, there—there they were. The real attacks, the ones expected to succeed. She sketched the activation diagrams in the air, and turned loose her little semi-sentient guardians. They could do what no human could; chase after the code like sheepdogs herding sheep, and herd any strays into the Honeytrap. The viruses the Thulians had created were not semi-sentient; they did what viruses do—propagate, and hide themselves. Except they were propagating and hiding themselves inside a giant cage. When the last of them were in, she slammed the door.

And powered down the system.

And just for good luck, hit the system with a localized EMP. Nothing made of ones and zeroes would survive that.

"Byte me," she snarled.

John Murdock: CCCP

Three of the troopers, including the first squad leader, were down. The rest had wisened up fairly quickly, and had taken cover. Whenever he wasn't firing at a position, he was helping Rusalka to reload. They didn't have many rockets left, though; only three after this next shot. Once they were out—which would happen soon—it would be John's turn. His fires were extinguished for the moment. He popped up from behind the wall on the roof, took aim and fired a burst from his rifle at a Krieger that was crouching behind a newly overturned car. The rounds bounced harmlessly off of the trooper's armor, but he raised up to turn his cannons on John. The exposure was just enough for Rusalka to land a rocket directly on the trooper; combined rifle fire from John and Molotok finished the job.

From the sound of things, similar scenes were playing out

down in the destruction corridor. He could hear explosions, the chatter of assault rifles, and what he thought was Bear's manic laughter interspersed with Russian cursing. John had other things to focus on, for the moment. He set down his rifle and went to the business of reloading Rusalka's RPG launcher.

"Not being many left," she said, wiping a strand of hair out of her face. "Hope that you are holding up your end, *tovarisch.*"

"Don't worry 'bout me; just make sure whatever I start doesn't burn the rest of the neighborhood down. Property values are in the toilet already."

Soviet Bear and Untermensch : CCCP, Destruction Corridor

Soviet Bear and Untermensch had been forced to split up, taking different positions in order to spread out the Kriegers' return fire and give them more than one ground target to worry about. While that left Unter with the job of loading his own RPGs, it allowed Bear to do what he did best; create a spectacle. He was firing from the hip, one-handed, with his PPSh-41, sending blasts of plasma from the gauntlet on his free hand, and loudly cursing their enemies. Some of the insults were becoming quite poetic, even as they also became more vulgar.

"If you fired your weapon as much as you jabbered, there would be no Kriegers left, Old Bear," Unter grumbled as he finished reloading.

"But that would not being as much fun, *tovarisch!*" Bear ducked out of the way at the last moment as an actinic bolt screamed past his head, with several more impacting against the barrier he was using as cover. "They are getting a little more accurate."

Unter peeked around the corner of his barrier, nodded to Bear and then immediately raised the RPG tube. One Krieger who had been bounding forward to cover was out in the open; the warhead from Unter's weapon struck the Krieger in his midsection, igniting the armor. Less than a second later, and before the Krieger had reached safety, Bear had peppered the man's armor with bullets. Injured and dying, the Krieger kept crawling; he was finally put down by simultaneous shots from Bear's gauntlet and the ECHO meta Corbie on the roof.

"Six left." The troopers—deprived of their squad leaders, who had been targeted at the outset of the engagement—looked as if they were ready to bolt, perhaps to spread out and carry the fighting away from the CCCP HQ. Unter and Bear both recognized this immediately; it was their job to protect the people, and that meant keeping the fight here. "We must contain them." Unter keyed his comm unit. "Molotok; corridor unit is going to be triggering 'party favors.' On your command."

"Affirmative, tovarisch. *Murdock, Unter, on my signal, being prepared to fire. Ready? Three, two, one. Fire!"*

Immediately upon hearing the command, Unter retrieved and slammed the palm of his hand down on a firing device three times in quick succession. The "clacker" command detonated several flame fougasses that had been pre-positioned in the destruction corridor. This particular section of the corridor was closed off, and the firing device had remained disconnected until the attack was imminent for safety purposes. The flame fougasses themselves, which had been shown to be especially effective in the attack on the Thulian North American HQ, had been upgraded with the same mixture that Zmey had devised and had been incorporated into the new RPG warheads. The result of the detonation was that several large plumes of super-hot fire and burning compound engulfed almost all of the Kriegers.

"Let's hope the American Murdock is having same effect."

John Murdock: CCCP, Rooftop

Even from his position on the rooftop, John could feel the heat on the back of his neck from the buried explosives in the destruction corridor. *Looks like that training on improvised explosives is still paying itself off.* He focused back on the street. He had to do this exactly right, otherwise two of his teammates and potentially a lot of innocent people could end up dead. "No pressure." He had been reading and rereading the reports and the journal he had left for himself. He had been practicing, as well; igniting his fire, controlling it, manipulating the flames to do exactly what he wanted. There was something different from his old self, besides being healed. Control was much easier, and so was energy expenditure; he felt like he could burn, and burn, and burn until there was nothing left for him to destroy. The aspect that made it somewhat difficult was that he lacked experience with it; he had to be careful that he didn't get overenthusiastic.

Relaxing, he first let the fire ignite in his palm, then engulf his hand. Almost instantly, it seemed as if there was a white-hot flame-thrower belching hell out of his arm, as the flames swung down into the street. John could faintly feel what the fire was touching, as if he were a fireman at the end of a hose pouring out a stream of water, and he barely sensed the blowback of the stream hitting things. *There.* He knew that the troopers' armor was fully engulfed; he focused the flames on those points, intensifying it. Satisfied, he shut the fires off; everything dissipated immediately, save for some spot fires he had started. Rusalka immediately set to work on those, using water from a leaking fire hydrant on the street and rushing it to keep the fires from spreading. The entire process took less than ten seconds, from start to finish.

"*Ground units, move in to engage. Take the fight to the* fascista." The residual heat radiating from the ground still felt like an open furnace against John's face. He watched as Molotok vaulted over the barrier he had been stationed behind, and closed with the first Krieger. The Krieger was still dazed from the firestorm, and didn't see his attacker until it was too late. Molotok dodged the first clumsily swung arm, pushed aside the second and then uprooted the Krieger by lifting one of his legs out from underneath him. The Krieger fell flat on his back, and was trying to right himself when Molotok casually walked over and stomped on the Krieger's helmet, crushing it inward with a sickening crunch and shriek of tearing metal. The CCCPer shouted something in Russian before charging forward again. John had picked up his rifle, and was alternately shooting or blasting with fire at the remaining Kriegers.

"What'd he say to 'em?" He looked to Rusalka for a brief moment before scanning for more targets.

Rusalka grinned, keeping her eyes on the street. "He said, 'This pig died quick and easy. It will not being so for the rest of you bastards!'"

Seraphym: Airborne

Well, now I have the tiger . . . Sera had caught up with the Death Spheres, which had turned to evade her. Now they were all poised above the roof of the CCCP HQ, and Sera felt suddenly very naked and vulnerable indeed.

She didn't dare show that, however. If the Kriegers inside sensed even a moment of hesitation, they would strike, and she was no longer what she had been.

She arrowed for the nearest, aiming to engulf it in fire, and either use her spear on it, or hope that someone down below noticed that the spheres were above them and decided to try a weapon from below. With the tentacle-arms lashing at her like a nest of cobras, she landed on the top of it and surrounded herself with flame, concentrating to raise it to white-hot temperatures. She sensed the mental babble of the Kriegers inside; they knew this tactic, and knew what it meant, and their only hope was to get her off before she could fatally weaken the armor of the sphere.

The tentacles were not constructed in such a way that they could reach the top of the sphere they were installed on, so long as she crouched, but the operator of the sphere began all manner of gyrations trying to throw her off—or throw her into the path of one of the tentacles. She called her sword and hammered it into the skin of the sphere, desperately using it as a handle to hold on.

The second sphere was in trouble. While the one she rode bucked and spun, the CCCP had noticed the danger overhead. The CCCPers on the rooftop were firing RPGs at it—regular warheads, designed for penetrating tank armor, while those on the ground finished off the last of the armored troopers. John Murdock was also blasting it with fire, weakening sections of it. Despite this, the second sphere was coming to the aid of its comrade. Sera saw the tentacles stretching for her, and knew there was no way to avoid them without throwing herself into the reach of the tentacles on the sphere she was riding. The Kriegers were either taking the chance that she was vulnerable now—or had intuited it from her actions.

It was with a mingling of fear and relief that she watched Death reaching for her, and could not see a way to escape it. She closed her eyes.

There was a wash of heat that swept over her in an infernal wave, followed by the sound of a muffled explosion. She snapped her eyes open in time to see a lance of fire pouring into the second sphere. The sphere she rode stopped bucking for a moment, and she looked down to the roof. John Murdock had his eyes fixed on the sphere, and was filling the interior with scorching flame through a hole made by the RPGs. The sphere stopped its

forward motion, jerked a little in the air, and then partly burst at
the seams with gouts of fire spilling out and debris splitting the
air. The sphere started descending rapidly, clipping an abandoned
building before tumbling into a section of the destruction corridor. There was no way that anyone could have survived inside
the burning wreckage.

The sudden knowledge that she would live after all gave her a
burst of strength. She took advantage of the sphere's momentary
pause to assess where the pilot was inside. *There. Yes. Within
reach . . .* She summoned her lance of flame. *Forgive me.*

She leapt and tumbled along the top of the sphere until she
was just above the pilot, and without hesitation, slammed the
lance of fire down through the armor, impaling him and pinning
him to the control panel where he sat.

Then she leapt into the sky, beating her wings frantically to gain
distance, as the sphere shuddered, as though the death of the pilot
had struck a blow into its heart, and began to gyre wildly. It tumbled
out of control, canted over sideways, and followed its fellow down
into the destruction corridor. She lost sight of it behind a roofless
building, but the explosion and belch of flame and black smoke
that followed on the sound of the impact were more than enough
to tell her that the sphere was as finished as its fellow had been.

She glanced down, and again, caught sight of John Murdock.
As if her gaze had drawn his attention, he peered up, saw her
hovering above, and waved. Her heart contracted painfully. Did
he remember, at last—?

No. No, of course he didn't. She could see it in his face. She
was just another fellow fighter. It was a gesture of congratulations, nothing more. Her spirit plummeted.

Then she saw it—

One of the armored Kriegers had somehow escaped the fate of
his brothers and must have found a way to climb the blank back
wall of the CCCP firehouse. She spotted him just as he levered
his massive weight up onto the roof, the helmet optics centered
on John's back. The Krieger raised his arm cannon—

She called all her fires, and dove, fire-sword at the ready.

The Krieger never even saw her as she skimmed his shoulder.
A second later, his helmet, with his head in it, toppled from his
shoulders. Without direction, the armor shuddered into immobil-
ity, freezing in place like some grotesque martial statue.

Bulwark, Bella, Red Djinni and Mel: ECHO Campus

Bella hadn't really expected Armageddon to be unleashed when she'd asked Jamaican Blaze to do her thing. A lot more fire was what she'd had in mind, not a replay of the firebombing of freaking Dresden.

On the other hand, when the fire vortex roared up into life, she could not honestly say she was unhappy. Terrified, absolutely. Coming to an absolute blank when she tried to think of what she could do if it got out of control—you bet. Unhappy, however...no.

Not even though she could sense the blooming of panic, terror and pain coming from those armored troopers. She resolutely hardened her shields and told herself ruthlessly that they'd had a choice of whether or not to obey their commanders and attack. And tucked the "but what if they *hadn't?*" into the place she looked at deep in the night.

Now they were vulnerable to regular armaments and powers, and with Bull expanding his shield to cover everyone who wasn't on the offensive, she gave the order to pour it on. Too bad you couldn't fire from inside that shield, but at least he could cover the Medic Corps and give them, and whoever they'd dragged to safety, some protection.

Red Djinni watched as his allies advanced on the remaining Kriegers. There were perhaps only a few dozen left. The Kriegers had lost, though from their defiance it was clear they had yet to realize it. Or perhaps they simply didn't know that surrender was an option. Whatever drove them, it amounted to suicide as they threw themselves against the amassed ECHO troops, who had little option other than to shoot to kill.

Amidst the carnage, Red strode wearily to assess the fallen. It was an odd sight, seeing so many of the Kriegers in one place, often in piles, as they had resorted to using their dead as cover. Now they were strewn everywhere, lifeless. Would-be conquerors caught in a well-executed trap. He paused by a heap of dead soldiers, and a movement caught his eye. Trapped beneath the bodies of its fallen comrades, one of the Thulian troopers strained to free himself.

He stopped, looked up at Red, and snarled. He was in agony, but who wouldn't be with his entire head on fire? With a tremendous effort, the Thulian struggled to raise his arm cannon, only to scream in pain as Red drove his foot down, pinning the arm to the ground.

Casually, Red unlatched his sidearm, cocked it and aimed square between the Krieger's eyes.

The Thulian stopped struggling. His head fell back, and over the ringing sounds of gunfire and explosions, Red heard him choke out two words.

"Machst du."

The Djinni paused. He realized this was war. For all his time spent dodging bullets, fighting for his life and all that other fun stuff that seemed to crop up in a mercenary shithead's career, he had always enjoyed a certain emotional detachment when it came to ending someone's life. No, that wasn't entirely true. He remembered the Vault, when he had torn the life out of that kid, how it had tasted. Like ashes. And that wasn't the first time. Truth be told, he remembered them all, from the mob bosses to the heads of industry to those few unfortunate bystanders who had been in the wrong place at the wrong time. He had fooled himself for years. Some of them deserved it, didn't they? It had become a game of numbers—those who deserved it and those who didn't. As long as one column was longer than the next, it was all good. But it was a lie, something he told himself so that he could move on, to the next job. The next score.

The next hit.

Red felt the grip on his gun falter and shake. Was this it? Was this what Jack felt when he had emptied two entire magazines into him in the Vault? You stood your ground, you kept your gun on your target, and you went cold. But inside, inside the battle raged between your training and the mission and that part of you screaming to stop, to lower your weapon and find another way. Because there was always a cost when a life was snuffed out. On the same day, he had lived through one insane event after another, each trumping the last, and it had culminated with Amethist being blasted away in a torrent of blinding light. And here, lying at his feet, was one of the bastards that had taken her from him.

Red knelt down, his hand no longer shaking, and pressed the muzzle to the Krieger's head.

"MACHST DU!" the Thulian screamed. *"MACHST DU, UNTER-MENSCH SCHWEIN, DO IT!"*

Red stopped cold. He stared at the slits in the Krieger's helmet.

You couldn't see the eyes. You couldn't see anything human about whatever was in there. So why was it that he was reminded of that mob boss he'd taken out in Manhattan? He had given up a lot that day as well, and the years after, to become the man he was. It had cost him his love, an unborn child, his future. There was always a cost. Memories flashed in his head, images and scenes fired in a rhythmic, staccato picture show. A still, dark bedroom. A sudden slash of his claws. A young man, begging for his life, only to be silenced with a neat slip of a small wire around his throat. Him screaming at Vix. "I've killed people for this!" And he had. Why couldn't he do it now? Because there was always a cost. He had made many bad choices in his life, taken many questionable roads that offered little besides the thrill of the contest, of the hunt, immediate gratification. Sometimes the glory of the moment passed, and you were left with nothing but the void, and you stumbled along until you found another high. Sometimes, it took years for the scales to balance. Somewhere down the road, you really did pay for your sins. It had almost killed Vix, his anger and retreat from the bad choices he had made. He watched himself burst through the window of her apartment, spike her heart with adrenaline and force ipecac down her throat. He watched himself make a choice, to revoke an oath, to begin a long and arduous road to redemption. The only choices that ever seemed to actually pay off were the ones that were selfless. That, at his very core, seemed right for no other reason than they would protect others, give others what they needed, what they deserved, even if he was to suffer. Why was Bella with Bull? Because she deserved someone like him. The Seraphym had warned him of the consequences of choices. Ten years ago, hell, perhaps just months ago, he would have double-tapped this Krieger bastard through his flaming, vulnerable helmet. But he was better than this. Rather, he wanted to be. And if he wanted more, he would have to earn it.

"All right, angel lady, I get it. I do. So this is my choice. I don't need more needless bloodshed on my hands."

He lowered his gun.

"No one would blame you, y'know."

Red glanced to his side. Mel had joined him, her own sidearm trained on the helpless Krieger.

"Can't do it," he said. "I'm not that guy anymore."

She gave him a puzzled look, shrugged and cocked her pistol. She hesitated. He turned, and watched as the familiar conflict seemed to rage across her features.

"I get it," Mel agreed. "When you're a soldier, you have to turn it off. If you hesitate, you die. I heard that every day; they drilled it into you, 'cause you don't enlist ready to do any of this. At the beginning, I just wanted to help people. I didn't think I'd have to make decisions like this, or point a gun at an enemy and turn him into a stain on the battlefield. The girl they sent to war, she wouldn't have thought twice about this sort of thing."

She flashed Red a wry grin and lowered her weapon. "Guess I'm not that girl anymore."

He stared at her, startled, and finally nodded. He exhaled, and took in the field. The sounds of combat had ceased. They were surrounded by scores of dead Kriegers. He grimaced as he tallied the number of fallen ECHO soldiers. There weren't many, but even then, one was too many. He caught a glimpse of Bella as she instructed her troops to do a final sweep over the grounds.

"Yo, Boss Lady!" he shouted, ignoring his ECHO comm device. "We taking prisoners?"

Bella glanced over at him, and nodded, looking first surprised at the question, and then, almost irrationally happy.

"Bet your ass!" she shouted, and waved two of the ECHO Ops who were nearest her. "Bag him and tag him, boys."

"Stand down, Djinni," Bulwark rumbled, with an odd—was it approving?—look at Red. "I've got this." He joined the other two as Red backed off, and together they hauled the captured soldier away.

From behind the shield wall, Bob staggered into view. With shaking hands, he mopped the sweat from his brow with his jacket.

"Screw this noise," he shuddered. "From now on I'm jogging at the water works."

CHAPTER TEN

Wounds

MERCEDES LACKEY AND CODY MARTIN

John sipped his scotch and pondered the journal. If it had been a work of fiction, he probably would have thrown it across the room for being crap by the time he finished it.

The problem was . . . right up until the angel nonsense, he could relate to all of it. It was written in a voice he recognized. It sounded like something he might have written—maybe on some of the worst days of his life, but he could still recognize and relate to it. Then . . . well.

Snarky people with agendas say there "are no atheists in fox-holes." Which was bullshit, and he was living proof of that. So what had been written, well, it sounded like someone who was at the end of his rope and finally grasping at the straws he'd have rejected if he'd been in his right mind. John just wasn't sure if the chick herself was deluded or had been tricking "that guy." It'd be easy enough for a chick with mental powers to pick stuff out of that guy's brain, or shove illusions in there, right? And as desperate and beaten down as that guy had been . . . it'd be like a bottle of scotch in front of an alcoholic. Drink the Kool-Aid, and everything would be all better. Too many wounds, and a desperate search for redemption, especially after that death sentence.

Well, he wasn't that guy. He wasn't doomed to make the same mistakes; he didn't believe in destiny, and he sure as hell didn't believe that he was locked into this. This journal was a roadmap for him; the worst that could happen, if he let it. But he wouldn't. He couldn't say where that other guy was, mentally, after escaping the Program. John knew, however, that you didn't just run from your problems. You had to confront them, sometimes head-on, otherwise they'd plague you forever. Right now, the Kriegers had priority. After the war was over, though, it might very well be time for him to start digging into that piece of his past, no matter how bloody things got. He didn't much cotton to the idea of being on the run for the rest of his life.

There were a lot of things that made him different from that guy. He wasn't under a death sentence, for one thing. So far two different docs had given him a clean bill of health; whatever had been killing that guy wasn't killing *this* John Murdock anymore. So he didn't have that particular stick goading him into buying the ridiculous "angel" line.

Although...maybe...just maybe...that chick with the wings actually *had* cured him, somehow. Mind, he hadn't looked into every other possible explanation, but...

It still intrigued him. He didn't consider himself an easy mark. And even if he was at the end of his rope, from the journal entries, he figured that he'd been a pretty hard sell. Whatever this winged creature had, it must have been special. Did that "special" include actually being able to cure what ECHO and CCCP both said couldn't be cured? Was she just delusional about being an angel, but honest about everything else? Plenty of metas were batshit crazy in one way or another.

Even as unlikely as it seemed to him, the journal was pretty clear proof that he had fallen in love with her. That was another thing that just seemed incomprehensible to him, another instance where "that guy" was different from him. There had been women over the years, of course, but nothing that lasted more than a few months, a year at most when he was young and naive. John had been focused on his job, since at that level you had to be in order to simply stay alive. That didn't leave time for distractions; as lovely as they were, women and a family life could be a distraction. Some men were able to make it work; plenty couldn't. John always figured that, if he were to settle down, it would be "in the future"; a nebulous idea about when he wouldn't be a trigger-puller anymore.

In the middle of this war, however, "that guy" had found someone to connect with. Something John never had been able to do.

Even if she was crazy...it was still something. What had drawn the other guy in? She was pretty enough, certainly; gorgeous actually, with a sort of unearthly quality to her. But, there had been plenty of good-looking women in his life; looks only went so far with him. There had to be something going on upstairs to keep him around other than for temporary fun.

John had noticed her following him, always at a distance, and watching him while he was out on patrol. John figured it was just about time that they talked.

He pounded back the rest of his beer, setting the bottle down next to the empty scotch glass and gathering up his journal. He had first read the journal at the CCCP HQ, then reread it. And read it once more here at Mel's for good measure. It wasn't exactly light reading, and he wanted to analyze and absorb every single detail before accepting any of it as being true. Everyone had given him a pretty wide berth when they saw that he was occupied; Mel had dutifully kept the scotch and brews coming without a word. She was cleaning a glass and leaning against the bar when he started to get up, dropping a few bills to pay for his tab.

"Where are you off to, Murdock?"

John checked the bar one last time to make sure he had everything, then glanced over his shoulder at Mel as he walked away. "Gotta talk with an 'angel.' Keep the change, Mel."

"You want to watch that one. Careful you don't get burned." Mel gathered up the money and gave him a wink before taking his payment to the till.

How exactly did someone go about finding a supposed angel? John didn't have the first idea where to look; she certainly wasn't bunking at CCCP HQ, and going to the ECHO campus didn't seem like the best idea for him. He did have one friend who had a knack for finding things, though.

John keyed his comm for the Overwatch channel. "Murdock here. Y'awake, Vic?"

"*Hasn't anyone told you? I never sleep.*" He couldn't read her tone. Was she serious? Joking? Exhausted? He decided to take it at face value.

"My kind of gal. I need a favor from you, if'n you can swing it."

"*I have twenty-four-hour liquor stores that deliver on call. I know every good pizza parlor, Chinese takeout, taqueria, steak joint and rib crib. Hookers, you're on your own.*"

"Naw, nothin' like that; what do I look like, a politician? Naw,

I need you t'find someone; an 'angel' to be precise. I want to have words with her."

There was a long pause, pregnant with things unspoken. "*You finished the journal, I take it? The Seraphym's wired into Overwatch Mark One. I was not going to chance getting the crap fried out of me by wiring her into Mark Two. Just ask Overwatch from now on if you want to find her—or anyone else on the system. Use the 'Locate' command.*"

He thought for a moment. "Is that an automatic thing? The request just goes through and such? Or does it go through you first?"

"*I have a very sophisticated near-AI setup that doesn't route to me unless it's stumped. It's all automatic, and all voice-activated. Use the command 'Overwatch' to open a channel to the system, then give your command. In this case, 'Locate' followed by who you want.*" Another pause. "*I know you're a man, and men don't think they need to read the instructions, but reading the manual I gave you would save you a lot of hazing on my part.*"

John didn't feel comfortable having a computer tracking him day in and day out, but that was a discussion he'd have later. "Thanks, Vic. Murdock out." He cleared his throat and gave the commands that Vic had told him to. "Overwatch: locate 'Seraphym.'" A projection popped up in his in-eye HUD; that was still bugging the hell out of him, despite its obvious utility. Just another thing he'd have to get used to; he had the feeling if he asked Vickie to take it out, she'd refer him to the Commissar, and Red Saviour would give him one of those "excoriation" things and another round of duty scrubbing latrines. An estimated distance and mapped-out path appeared before him, pale and ghostly as it overlaid the sidewalk in front of him. *Time to get steppin', old man.*

The entire time that John was walking, he kept on hearing... something. He couldn't pin it down; even with his new and improved hearing, it was too faint and inconsistent. It sounded like someone talking to him, just out of range of his hearing. More than anything, it was getting annoying. As he neared his destination, he heard the faintest strains of some sort of music. It was like someone had left a window open while an orchestra tuned up, only miles away. Now *that* sounded interesting; he wanted to follow it and find out where it was coming from, but he had just arrived at his destination.

A cemetery.

The sun had started to set, so everything was cast in a slanting orange glow, with long shadows creeping over the tombstones. The cemetery was connected to an abandoned church, roofless and wrecked in the Invasion, though it looked as if it had been abandoned long before the Invasion had finished the job on it. Cut off on both sides by destruction corridors, it was isolated, off the beaten path. Once upon a time, this place had been prosperous, though. Under the enormous trees that featured huge swags of Spanish moss dripping from their branches, and between the overgrown bushes, were some graves with impressive statuary, and even some ornamented above-ground tombs or the entrances to crypts. Lots of marble and wrought iron.

There was one wall of the church building proper that was still standing. Set in it was a multicolored, almost fractal stained-glass window. The setting sun's light was spilling through it and bathing one particular grave in kaleidoscope colors. It took John a second, but he recognized Sera sitting on top of the headstone; she had been so still that he initially mistook her for one of the statues.

She didn't seem to realize that anyone was watching her. And she sat in a peculiar sort of posture—one that he recognized.

She sat as if she were mortally wounded.

He knew that look, that pose. He'd seen it before, in men who had thought they were invulnerable and suddenly had the shock of discovering they were not. There was a startled fragility about them, even if they had not yet felt the pain of their wounds, as though their bodies understood that they were dying. *This is getting awkward, fast.* John didn't enjoy seeing her like this; it made him vaguely uneasy for a variety of reasons.

"Excuse me? Ma'am?"

The woman looked up, eyes wide and pupils dilating; her wings immediately began to tremble, the feathers rustling against each other. For a moment, he was sure she was going to spring into the air and flee.

John held his hands up placatingly. "Sorry t'startle you. I don't think we've properly met. My name's John Murdock. And you're Sera, right?"

"I am." Her voice was soft and low. And that was all she said. It looked as if any attempt at conversation was going to have to come from him.

"Right." John didn't know exactly how to proceed; it seemed that after he saw her, he forgot everything he had planned on saying. "How are you?" He winced as he said it, realizing how dumb he sounded as the words were forming.

"I am...as I am," she replied. Not a lot of help. "If you seek... company, you should seek it elsewhere. The place of serving liquor, perhaps. I am not a good companion."

"Mel's? It's all right for a shot an' a brew, true enough. But I came here lookin' to talk with you, specifically." He took a couple of steps towards her, dropping his hands to his sides. "Kind of a grim spot, don't you think? Gotta admit, it's pretty this time of day."

"It suits me." No explanation. It sounded like he was going to have to pull words out of her with pliers. John's patience was wearing thin, but he knew that if he pushed too hard right now, she'd bolt and he'd have to start all over again. Time for a different tactic.

"I've noticed you 'round the neighborhood quite a bit. You've seemed to have helped out a lot of the folks there; kids especially seem to have good things t'say 'bout you."

She didn't rise to the bait. "What do you wish of me? You would not have come to me unless there was something you thought I could give you. I warn you, I am greatly lessened. There is much—too much—that I can no longer do."

He sighed, taking another cautious step forward. "You're right. I wanted to talk with you for a reason. I've read through this," he said, taking the journal out from a pocket. "You're a big part of this; it's a journal that the other—that I wrote. Before...well, before this."

Tears spilled out of her eyes. "You spoke truer when you said *the other*. You are not he. You do not know me. Possibly, you *should* not know me. But your face is *his* face, your voice is *his* voice, and the sight of you causes me pain like a knife to the heart."

"So why do you follow me? I'm not exactly the brightest bulb in the drawer, but I'm not dumb, either. I've noticed you when I'm out on patrol, or at the CCCP HQ. You follow me, Sera. There's got to be a reason to that, since y'don't strike me as the masochist sort."

"I suppose I hoped that...that he would awaken within you. And now you are here, and he has not. So it is not to be, and that is the end to it. Either you should go, or I will." She stood, and her wings trembled, unfolded and extended. They caught the colors of the stained glass. "As you say, I am not inclined to masochism, nor chasing after futility."

"Listen! Stop for just a second, okay? Please, ma'am?" He waited, gauging her.

She hesitated, then folded her wings, though she did not sit down. "I will hear you."

"We can't go on like this; you following me around, me tiptoeing around trying not to get in your way since it's plain that it hurts you to be... reminded. We need to come to some sort of peace, or something." John sighed, brushing his fingers through his hair. "We're on the same side; we're both in this fight together, against the Kriegers. That's the most important thing. I think it'd be better for everyone, not just us, if we could work together." He looked soberly into her eyes. "I'm not that guy, the one that fell in love with you. The one you cured. The one that you want. I know that. I'm not going to pretend that I ever will be that guy again; I don't know what you did that healed... him, or me, whatever. But I want you to give me a chance. I think you could use a friend, if'n nothin' else, ma'am."

Her eyes filled and spilled over again. "If only you had a different face," she said, her tone fragile and brittle. "If only you had another voice."

He reached out to lay a hand on her shoulder, thought better of it, and set it down on the headstone instead. "If only the Kriegers hadn't set the world on fire. If only... if only I hadn't been dying. We can't focus on *what if*; doin' that'll drive anybody crazy. We gotta focus on the here an' now. People are depending on us to keep this ball of dirt spinning without swastikas rulin' over everything."

She wiped her eyes with her hand and straightened. "You rightly remind me of responsibility and duty. But..." There was a long pause. "But I fail to see what is so vital that you and I undertake those together. I will cease to follow you. I will ask the Commissar to assign me to a different... shift? I will not trouble you again."

"That's the right word for it, shift. But that's not what I want. I've woken up to a whole new an' terrifyin' world here. Nazis and aliens in powered armor, bein' in a group of Commies, an' havin' superpowers; it's a lot for one fella to take in at once, y'know?" He chuckled, grinning lopsidedly before snapping his fingers, producing a single Zippo-sized flame. "This? This is crazy. There aren't any others in the CCCP that can do anythin' like this. I figure that you might know a thing or two 'bout fire an' how to control it." He snapped his fingers again, snuffing out the flame. "I could use a friend to help me figure out some of this craziness. Whaddya say?" He held out his hand. "Partners?"

Her face went blank. It looked as if she was hunting mentally for something, and not finding it. Answers, maybe. She didn't take his hand.

"I will consider this," she said. And before he could say anything further, she spread her wings, leapt into the air, and flew off into the gathering darkness.

But this time he could tell where she ended up—the top of a building that had a strange sort of fake Greek or Roman temple on it. Completely useless and only ornamental as far as he could tell. No purpose to it—no one these days would build a high-rise like that.

"Huh." *That could've gone worse. She could've set me on fire.* John started walking back to HQ. As he exited the cemetery, he glanced over his shoulder at the building that Sera was perched on. She blazed against the darkening sky, and looked perfect, like an ancient Roman goddess come to life. Wasn't the goddess of Victory the one that had wings? He felt strangely comforted, knowing that she was watching over them from above. *Time to find out where that music I heard was coming from.* With that, he set off in earnest.

CHAPTER ELEVEN

Lost Penny

MERCEDES LACKEY AND DENNIS LEE

"Moan is right," one of the girls said in weary disgust. "Can't she just shut up?"

The woman muttered and moaned and spoke, awake or asleep, and none of them could understand a word she said. The Dark Man had come in while she was asleep, given her a shot before she could wake up, and brought her back cleaned up. After that, the rest of the kids ignored her as best they could. The Dark Man kept giving her shots, which kept her from moving much, but didn't stop the moaning and mumbling.

He'd also ordered the kids to take care of her. Of them all, only Penny and Joey obeyed that order, squeezing paste from the food pouches they all got, and dribbling water into her mouth, though they left it to the Dark Man to carry her out and clean her up. He'd growled at them for not taking care of *that* part, but Joey, for once, had stood up to him, hands on hips, and looking up into that scowling face, said, "How're we supposed to do that, huh? We got nothin' to do that *with*." Because, of course, the only things they were allowed were the bedding and their clothing. There was the toilet in the corner, out in front of everyone. It had nearly paralyzed Penny at first, having to go out in the open like that, but now it was just one tiny indignity amid so much worse. There was a sink with a single tap that produced tepid water and had a pump for liquid soap, but how could they get a semiconscious woman over to either when she was chained to the wall? There was flimsy paper for the toilet and little paper cups for water that collapsed and melted so quickly

149

you had to be fast with your drinking; neither of those would be any help. So the Dark Man growled and carried Lacey out, bringing her back wearing a giant diaper. Twice a day, once in the morning and once at night, he hauled her out and brought her back cleaned and changed.

He must've just left her under a shower or something because she always came back with wet hair.

As Penny had figured, Lacey came with a ghost of her own, too. Most ghosts didn't show up right away, it was like they had to *find* the people they were haunting before they could settle in. Lacey's ghost was a young man, maybe two, three years older than Pike. He showed up midway through the third night she was there.

He was different, though. He just stood there, staring at Lacey, and not saying a word. It was an intent stare, as if he was trying to get something out of her, or maybe wake her up just by staring at her. He was strange and non-threatening enough that Penny felt safe to watch him, size him up. What could Lacey have done that would make a young man like *this* come to stare at her? All the other ghosts had obvious grievances, or were just plain crazy-acting, but this was different, and much more intense. Penny wondered and watched; it was easier to ignore the others when she had him to concentrate on.

It was only towards sunrise, when the others had started to fade, that he seemed to suddenly sense that Penny was watching him. Before she could glance away, he swiveled her head and *looked* at her, his stare going right *into* her, so hard she gasped under the impact of it, feeling her head reel as if he had actually struck her.

Then he was gone, like the others. But she knew he would be back.

Like the others. And now he knew she could see him.

CHAPTER TWELVE

Dead Meat

MERCEDES LACKEY AND CODY MARTIN

"... We are still getting details from reports coming in from around the world concerning last week's second Invasion by Krieger forces. Despite Krieger forces being estimated at matching—if not exceeding, in some areas—the numbers from the first attack, property damage and loss of life was unexpectedly minimal. Many credit the preparations made by national security forces, NATO, and meta-human police forces. Here in Atlanta the attack seemed centered on the ECHO campus and the 'CCCP' headquarters building. The bulk of the Kriegers were handled by ECHO personnel, while a smaller contingent was dispatched by the members of the 'CCCP.' On the scene we have Daryl Vickers, who spoke to the police commissioner early today. In the commissioner's own words, the collateral damage left by the Reds is 'deplorable,' and—"

"Bah!" Soviet Bear switched the television off. "They interrupt *Matlock* for this rubbish?"

John Murdock stood up from the battered couch he had been sitting on, zipping up the front panel of his coveralls. "If you're watchin' the news to get anythin' but entertainment, you're doin' it wrong, Pavel." He checked his watch. "Time for me to start on my patrol for the day. Y'need anythin' from the store on my way back?"

Bear thought for a moment, then held up a finger. "*Da!* Ravioli. And *TV Guide*. And ingredients to be making fluffernutter. And—"

"There is ravioli by caseful in storage, Old Bear," interrupted Untermensch. "And you are not to be eating flufferm—fluff—nasty

151

sandwich, by order of Red Saviour. Was to be a day getting sticky off where you left in couch."

John turned to Unter. "Are y'ready to head out, partner?" John and Untermensch had been paired up frequently lately; he suspected it was so that the older Russian could evaluate him, keeping an eye on him for the Commissar.

"*Nyet*. Check duty roster for assignment. I am being stuck with Old Bear today. The joys of service to the proletariat never cease." Untermensch waved at the bulletin board where a thin sheaf of papers—pinned to the cork with what looked like the broken tip of a knife—waved forlornly.

John walked a few steps over to the board, quickly scanning the duty roster. MURDOCK—SERAPHYM. *Huh*. After reading his journal, and the few encounters that he had had with the "angel," John was still rather curious about the woman. He had tried to keep it at that, a sort of detached interest, professional. That idea had not worked out so well; they kept on running into each other, and the interactions weren't always what he would call positive.

That she was curious about him had been another side of the coin. He'd been catching glimpses of her out of the corner of his eye for—well, since he'd woken up. She'd always flee if she thought he'd seen her, though. He wasn't sure what her motivation was. It probably should have felt creepy, as if she was stalking him, but for some reason, it didn't.

After their meeting in the graveyard and...well, when they had saved each other in turn during the second Invasion, it seemed they had reached a sort of truce. Or something. As much as he was intrigued by it—his past self's love for her, her nature, how she was acting now—he was also confused as hell as to what to do about it. He was pretty sure that he didn't love her. He just didn't know her; how could you fall in love with someone that you didn't know the first thing about? But then there was that little voice in the back of his head that always had an answer... *You've done it before, smart guy. Twice, by all accounts.* First "Jessica," the woman from the Program. Then this Sera. Even though she tried to hide it, he could see how much pain she was in, especially when he was around. *That just can't stand.*

With a sigh and a shrug, he started towards the locker room to change into his patrol uniform.

❖   ❖   ❖

It only took John five minutes to finish getting ready. Boots, nanoweave pants and jacket with the CCCP insignia, gloves, his duty belt with his battered 1911, spare pistol magazines, and a CCCP comm device for backup completed the picture. The nanoweave was lighter and less bulky than the old vests the CCCP had used; a "gift" from Bella, from a shipment that had fallen off of a truck at one point. He had expected to find Sera in the garage, but no luck. Thea, pale and quiet as ever, was busy cleaning her shotgun. "Away from Pavel's soaps," was the reason she gave for doing it in the garage. When asked about Sera, Thea explained that the "angel"—a term she used without a trace of irony or sarcasm—didn't like being indoors all that much anymore, and was waiting outside. The pale little Russian regarded John strangely while they talked; kind of like a cat, just studying him and watching to see what he would do.

John shrugged it off. He had enough to deal with without the expectations everyone seemed to have for him and Sera; there was a goddamned war on, wasn't there? Picking a Ural with a sidecar that he knew was in good repair—he'd spent three grease- and oil-soaked days making sure of that—John pulled out of the garage and into the thick and humid Atlanta air. There at the end of the sidewalk near the entrance of the HQ was Sera.

She wasn't wearing CCCP gear, and she wasn't wearing nanoweave. Instead, she sported a thin little tunic of some sort over tights, both in red. It didn't look very... protective. She was also wearing the earpiece and tiny throat-mic he recognized as being Overwatch Mark One gear. She was very hard to read, quite literally. Her face tended to remain in a state of mask-like inexpressiveness. But she did look surprised to see him, and blinked in what appeared to be confusion. "John Murdock," she said, carefully. "Is there a reason you are here?" She hadn't bolted immediately; an improvement.

"Yes, ma'am. We're partnered up for the day; on your patrol route, as per the duty roster." He waited a beat, then held up a hand. "Are y'alright with that, Sera?"

Her face remained without expression. "It is my duty to obey orders unless they violate... ethics," she said.

Kept your cool, but what was that right under the surface, huh?

"That isn't what I asked, ma'am. If you're not all right with this, I can take it up with the Commissar." He grinned lopsidedly.

"I'm pretty sure that she's gunnin' for me anyways, so it's no skin off of my teeth."

"Nose," Sera corrected. "What I *want* has no bearing. If the Commissar assigns me, it is my duty to obey. But..." She pointed at the sidecar. "...I cannot be in that...thing."

"How come?" John glanced at the sidecar sidelong. "Sure, the seat is a little on the lumpy side, but apart from that, she ain't that bad."

Now the woman finally had some expression. Annoyance. "And what do you suggest I do with my wings? They do not come off." As if to emphasize that, she spread them and pulled them back in again with a little irritated *flip*. They were a lot bigger than he had thought; they easily spanned twenty feet, fully extended.

"Y'got a point there; never really had to deal with wings before, aside from that limey outta ECHO. All right, stay here a second." John revved the engine, pulling around to take the bike back into the garage. When he came back, the sidecar had been detached. "We'll have to call the wagon if we nab anyone, but that's nothin' new. So, you fly an' I'll ride. Sound good?"

Her answer was to take a running leap into the air, wings beating so hard that the air thundered, and debris and paper flew everywhere. "Try and keep up," came the reply from the sky.

John grinned, throwing on a helmet quickly. "The gal has some style, I'll give her that." He pulled in the clutch, put the motorcycle into first gear, let out the clutch and gave it some throttle. After he was moving, he kicked it up a notch a couple of times just to keep up with Sera. *She sure as hell can move, too.* He opened an Overwatch comm link to her; using it was slowly becoming second nature, although it still sometimes freaked him out that what used to be a full headset and camera was somehow all parked inside his head. *Technology marches on.* This comm line was overlaid with the CCCP net, so HQ could hear and also respond; they were also patched in on the little mage's network, for security and redundancy. "This is your route, so I'm following your lead on this one. We're outside of my usual 'hood."

"*I shall restrain my speed,*" came the reply. He couldn't tell if it was meant sarcastically or not. "*The streets are less than salubrious.*"

A few seconds later, he got his answer. It was not meant sarcastically. The road...well, this part of Atlanta, being poorer, didn't see the upkeep that the more well-off areas did. With that being the case, a good portion of the damage from the initial Invasion had yet to be meaningfully dealt with. There just weren't enough people, not enough money to handle it. *Reminds me of Detroit* before *the Invasion.* He had to slow down to negotiate the many blockages in the road, from debris, burnt-out cars, trash, and other assorted obstacles. He could see why Sera had been assigned this area to patrol. It must be a *lot* easier from the air.

"*Unit* Pyat, *this is HQ. You have call to respond to.*" It was Gamayun, back at the comm station. *Doesn't that woman ever sleep? She's almost as bad as Vickie 'bout that.*

"*Thank you, Comrade Gamayun,*" Sera's voice said from the Overwatch mic in his ear. "*Location, please.*"

"*Residents report multiple gunshots followed by shouting and screaming, coming from former Piggly Wiggly store.*"

"*Thank you, Comrade. We are on the way.*" John's HUD lit up with a map, with his location and the store, and the fastest route plotted. The "angel" changed course abruptly and arrowed off; she was obviously taking the shortest route there, which was out of the question for him. *Time to play Frogger with debris and the crazies who still drive in this part of town.* It took John an extra few minutes, with some hair-raising close calls, but he finally arrived at the location of the disturbance. There were a few residents milling around across the street, some of them pointing and talking with each other. The grocery store was completely trashed. Several of the windows were broken, with only some of them boarded up. Graffiti covered everything, and there was a large pile of rubbish and debris blocking the main entrance. It looked off, for some reason; not quite out of place, but *new*, somehow. John drank in all of these details in the few seconds it took for him to bring the Ural to a shuddering stop.

He got there just in time to see Sera land, barely touching down before she started burning herself an entrance through the debris, and darting inside. Without waiting for him. "Shit!" John killed the bike's engine and dismounted, drawing his handgun and running after her. He ducked through the still-smoking doorway that Sera had created, still running, then came to a skidding stop several yards inside of the store. The shelves were bare, with only the occasional ruined and empty package dotting them. More trash and broken glass. And Sera, marching determinedly down one of the aisles.

"Sera, dammit!" John hissed out in a harsh whisper, knowing she could hear him through her Overwatch rig. She was wreathed in fire, somehow, which was going to make her a big, fat, literally flaming target. "The hell are you doing? Tryin' t'get yerself killed?"

She started, and tossed a glance over her shoulder at him. She looked completely taken off guard by what he'd just said. And was there just a tinge of guilt there as well? *Jesus, she really* might *be trying to buy the farm, get herself killed.* John softened a little, moving closer to her.

"Listen, if we're going to help anyone, we gotta be smart 'bout it. If we go in half-cocked and alone, might be that someone has to come save *our* asses. So, we do this together. Cool?" He flashed a smile at her, making sure that there was no edge in his words. After leading men in war, he'd learned that there were times to be a hard ass, and times when you needed to show some compassion. It wasn't hard to tell which this was.

"I would not wish to bring anyone else into danger," she said, a little too carefully. Then she winced a little, her brows furrowing. "There may be some toxin in the air, John Murdock."

John had noticed a fairly bad headache coming on quickly; it felt like someone was slowly driving a spike outward from the middle of his head. "Dammit, I think you're right. Whatever it is, we're already exposed. Let's make this quick." He looked down at Sera's body, still covered in flame. "I'll take lead; I'm wearin' armor, after all."

She merely nodded. But at least she wasn't charging ahead anymore. John took point, walking quickly but carefully with his 1911 out front. He scanned everywhere, looking for anything else that seemed out of place in this trash heap. The report they had received from Gamayun said that there had been screaming and gunshots; there certainly wasn't any screaming now. It took less than a minute for the two of them to clear the main floor; John motioned with his left hand for the back. That would be offices, restrooms, break room, stockroom and walk-in cooler and freezer. Plenty of places to hide. He figured that the offices would be the first place to check; if anyone was looking for a safe or some cash, they'd probably start there. The stockroom was next; food could be hard to find for some folks in the poorest parts of the city, and John had seen a lot of otherwise normal and good people turn ugly when they were hungry. It didn't look as if there was likely to be anything here to scavenge, but people got irrational when they were desperate.

There were two ways to clear a building; fast and loud, or slow and quiet. John was trying to split the difference between the two, staying as stealthy as possible when he was moving through the area while entering rooms dynamically and with calculated violence. The offices all were empty; no computers or other office equipment, just empty metal desks and filthy, graffiti-spattered walls. Looked like whoever had last been in here had done his best to wreck what little had been left; the entire place smelled rancid. John didn't want to think too hard about what they'd used as "paint" for some of the scrawled messages.

"Time for the storeroom," he whispered. Sera just nodded. John's headache had been getting worse the closer to the back they had gotten. They needed to hurry, now; whoever was in here was probably doing worse than they were, if it was some sort of toxin. The pain was starting to get between him and the ability to think. John and Sera were both outside of the door to the storeroom. With a final shared nod, John reared back, then kicked in the door. They both rushed through the opening, John in the lead, and stopped dead before they had gone more than a few steps inside.

There were two people, both obviously dead, lying on the floor. They were bound hand and foot, and had been shot in the legs, and then the back of the head. Before either he or Sera had time to react to that, two dozen men dressed in nearly identical tactical outfits simultaneously sprang from cover. *Blacksnake?* The mercs looked just as startled as John and Sera did, but it didn't last.

"Target is not alone! Capture the target, ice the other one!"

A volley of gunfire erupted from what seemed like everywhere. John answered in kind; he dropped at least three mercs that he could be sure of, maybe two more with his 1911. He had to spin and duck behind a metal rack while he reloaded after that; the gunfire was constant and deafening. Sera took a more direct approach, charging at her target, flaring her fire crucible hot to blind him, then striking with the butt of her spear, to disable rather than kill. The problem was . . . she was on fire. And as she left her target writhing on the floor, she left him fully engulfed. *Non-lethal doesn't work all that great for her . . .*

One of the mercs was armed with what looked like a net

launcher. Sera's head snapped over in his direction as he raised the launcher, aimed and fired. In what looked like one smooth motion, she transferred the spear to her left hand, generated what appeared to be a sword made of fire in her right hand, and brought it down in an arc directly in front of her, bisecting the launched net and leaving the two pieces smoldering on the ground. John had already emptied another magazine from his handgun; this time he only took out two mercs. They were using cover more effectively, now.

Time for us to find some cover of our own; we're too exposed here. "Sera, fall back! We've gotta get some help for this bunch!" John holstered his 1911, then focused for a half second. Fire coalesced in his hands, building into an orb. With a grunt, he threw it as hard as he could at the center of the room; it exploded brilliantly, splashing flame against everything—shelving and mercs, for the most part, and some on the ceiling—within twenty yards. *That oughta give them something to think about.* Sera retreated— reluctantly, it seemed to him—to his side. As they hurriedly backed out of the room, a huge chunk of ice exploded against the wall above John's head. *What the everlovin' hell?* No time to ponder it. He keyed his comm, transmitting on the Overwatch line and back to CCCP HQ. "This is Murdock, we're in a jam on our call. Lots of Blacksnake, we need backup to contain the area. Right now." John vaguely heard the affirmative come over the comm, but he was busy.

He winced as icicle shards pelted his head and shoulders. "What the hell was that?" Everything was happening very quickly. John had to consciously steady himself as he and Sera continued their retreat into the store.

They didn't have time to investigate any further; even with the fire, the Blacksnake mercs were starting to advance. John noticed that one was way ahead of the others; the second merc who had been armed with a net launcher. John swung around to the side of the doorframe, hiding himself against it. He waited a few heartbeats until he saw the muzzle of the net launcher come around the corner. Latching onto it with both hands, John pulled the merc in close, bumping their chests together. The man's eyes went wide behind the balaclava he was wearing. Before John could do anything, Sera was on the hired gun, clubbing him on the back of his head with her spear. Dazed, the merc went limp in

John's arms; igniting both hands, he set the merc ablaze, then spun around into the entrance to the storeroom.

"Catch, assholes!" Shoving as hard as he could with his augmented strength, he sent the fire-engulfed merc flying through the air directly at a clump of the oncoming Blacksnake. He didn't wait around to see what happened next; there was still a lot of gunfire, too much gunfire, coming his and Sera's way. He dashed back into cover, reaching out and grabbing Sera's arm and pulling her in with him. She was still exposing herself a lot more than he liked. They were hunkered down behind an open-top floor freezer; it wasn't the best cover, but it was something. "We need to keep this from spilling out into the street, if we can. We already know that these scumbags'll blast innocents." He reloaded his 1911; he had only three mags left.

"I shall not allow them to pass." The look on her face was stern and unyielding.

John smirked. "Let's earn our paychecks, then."

She lost the stern look. "We get paid?" she asked, bewildered for a moment.

John couldn't help it; he laughed. "If'n the Commissar had 'er way, she'd have us payin', what with the 'way *tovarischii* overeat!'"

The Blacksnake operatives had started to filter out of the storeroom; they were a little more cautious, now, and were spreading out into the store proper. How many of them were there? Had they been crammed into every bit of cover in the storeroom? *I'm already tired of these assholes coming after me, and I don' even remember the first time they tried.* John sprang from cover; he lit up three mercs with his pistol. Since they were wearing body armor, he was aiming primarily for their heads or at their pelvises; a cracked pelvis, not to mention whatever might be bleeding in that area, would stop damn near anyone. It was brutal, but effective; all three went down, two of them screaming. Return fire snapped and hissed all around him; he expended the last rounds in his gun while ducking down an aisle and running.

"Moving!" he barked.

There was another merc there; it looked like they were trying to flank around already. Reacting, John jabbed the hot barrel of the 1911 into the merc's right eye, and followed it by kicking the man's knee backwards, breaking and hyperextending it. The merc went down screaming, clutching his ruined eye. *He's out of the fight.*

John caught a glimpse of his partner as he was racing down the aisle; she was still wreathed in flame, looking for another target.

Sera fought like a wildcat; now that there was a bit more room, she darted around like a deadly dragonfly, using the spear like a staff. She still wasn't going for the kill, though, at least not deliberately. And that was a problem, because unless she accidentally set her victims on fire, they were going to get up eventually. These guys weren't paid to quit, after all. As she dashed back to John, he grabbed her elbow.

"Sera, these guys are playin' for keeps. If we don't stop 'em here, they're going to make it outside an' we'll have to deal with more dead civvies. Okay?" His tone was even, even slightly apologetic. But he had to get this point across. It hurt to tell her like that, but, goddamnit, it had to be done. Didn't it?

She looked stricken. Then her face changed. "Is this an order?" she asked.

John shook his head. *Never easy with this one.* "No, it's not. Your call; if you can take 'em down an' leave 'em breathin', do it. But keepin' yourself breathin', an' keepin' everyone out there breathin' is more important than these bastards."

She nodded. Then she took a deep breath, and dashed out again. This time, she wasn't holding back. But as she whirled and struck, with spear or with sword, he could see she was crying. John really felt for her; he was used to these sorts of decisions, as a soldier, but clearly she wasn't. *Nothing to be done for it, right now; our priority has to be to get out of here alive and to keep everyone outside alive.* She was still incredible; she was fighting everywhere that she needed to be, practiced and efficient with her weapons. If he hadn't been too busy with the ugly work that he had to do himself, he would have taken the time to be amazed.

A pair of mercs appeared at the end of the aisle that John was moving down; before either could train their guns on him, he fired off a burst of flame from his outstretched hand, engulfing both men. They went down, writhing on the ground as John leapt over them. He had to keep moving; otherwise, he'd get bogged down and surrounded. These Blacksnake were well trained, if nothing else. He also had to be careful about using his fires in here; he really didn't want to deal with a four-alarm blaze with these mercs breathing down his neck. Besides, he'd have to fill out more paperwork, which somehow worried him more.

Right now he wanted to hem the Blacksnake mercs in, keep them away from the entrance, at least until backup arrived. He had reached the cash registers and candy racks, blasting two more mercs with fire on the way. He noticed a single merc, just standing there. *Whatever; if you're too dumb to give up or take cover, that's on you, pal.* John launched a flamethrower blast at the merc, hitting him square on and covering him head to toe. Or at least, that was what he thought he'd done...

As the flames dispersed, John saw that the merc was still standing... and unharmed. Instead of being on fire, the merc was holding a head-to-toe shield in front of him. A shield made of what looked for all the world like solid ice. It took his mind a moment to process this; it couldn't be regular ice. *Another meta; this gig keeps getting better and better!*

The merc emerged from behind the ice shield, swinging it gradually to his side. John couldn't see the man's face underneath the balaclava, but he had the distinct impression that he was smirking. "I've heard about you, old man."

Old man? Goddamned punk oughta—

"You're the one that took out two of our best recruiters; Okagi and old 'Chuck Smith.'" The meta chuckled to himself. "They couldn't have been that tough. And honestly, I thought you would've been taller—"

John immediately raised and fired his pistol three times, all perfect shots at the meta's face. The merc was only saved by the proximity of his ice shield, which he brought up just in time to block the shots. John noted with satisfaction that the .45 ACP rounds were taking decent chunks out of the ice. *Smirk about that, asshole.*

As John took aim again, the merc emerged from behind his shield long enough to chuck several jagged and lethal-looking spears of ice at John; his next shot was thrown off, missing the merc wildly, but that was a small price to pay to keep from catching one of those frozen projectiles in his eye.

All right, shithead. Let's see if you like what I dish out. In a fluid motion John holstered his pistol, dodged under another ice spear and called the fire to his arm. It leapt from there at the merc as if bidden, three short blasts that splashed against the ice shield. As John concentrated, the fires on his outstretched arm intensified; the beam of fire was stronger this time. Punching a hole in the ice shield with a flash of steam, it narrowly missed the Blacksnake meta.

"Initiate protocol delta! We're blown here!" The merc screamed the command into his radio, tossing another spike of ice at John. It exploded against a shelf next to his head; by the time John looked up again, the meta was gone. Seconds later, a number of very loud bangs came from the back room. Almost immediately John's headache ceased; so suddenly that it nearly staggered him, and his thinking cleared miraculously. He didn't have time to think about the implications; four more mercs were heading his way. They started firing as soon as they saw him; two at a time, while the others advanced. Purely on instinct, he started blasting; in a moment, one went down with a smoking hole in his chest, but the others were being more careful.

Now all of them were firing. John darted behind cover; they'd spread out and try to get around behind him soon, pin him in place and then either start with the grenades or just shoot him. *Let's short-circuit that.* Instead of moving farther off, he waited just around the corner that he had ducked behind. The mercs continued to fire, but he knew what they were going to do; they wanted to close in for the kill, and they'd get anxious, over-excited that they had him on the run.

Or so they thought.

With his off hand John grabbed a broken soda bottle from a shelf, one of the thick-bottomed ones, while he was extinguishing his fires. The first merc rounded the corner, full of enthusiasm and ready to kill. Then the bottle came up under the merc's chin while the sling was pulled tight and away, bringing the rifle out of line with John. The bottle broke with the impact, shards digging into the soft part above the man's Adam's apple. The merc's blood poured down John's hand, but he kept ramming with the bottle until it shattered in his hand, cutting him. He'd been prepared for that; he was still getting used to how much stronger he was now than he remembered being.

The next two mercs rounded the corner. In the time it took them to drink in the scene, John spun the dead merc in his arms, grabbing the gear webbing on his back with one hand and try-ing to make himself as small as he could. The two living mercs opened up, firing full auto into the body. He felt the nanoweave stiffen on his abdomen and his left arm, but the dead man's body and armor absorbed most of the abuse. John fell backwards, dragging the body down on top of him and lying very still. The nanoweave protected him, of course, but they might not know that. They stepped forward, reloading. John flipped the dead man off to the side, drawing his pistol and firing twice. Both mercs caught the rounds in the face, dropping to the ground limply.

From the corner of his eye, he caught a flash of fire; it was Sera darting around the area, moving impossibly fast. *Even with my "enhancements," I don't think I could move that fast,* he thought. She disappeared around a shelf, but from the other side came gouts of flame, smoke and a lot of screaming. None of the mercs were going to get past her; when they tried, she intercepted them. It appeared she couldn't "throw" fire the way he could, but that spear and sword were plenty lethal, and anyone stupid enough to come close to her ended up engulfed in flame.

"Can't be too many more of 'em," he said under his breath. John scanned the area quickly, picking up the rifle—some sort of high-end M4 with all the bells and whistles—from the merc he had killed with the bottle. "Now t'find 'em—"

John spun around as a chunk of ice caught him in the left shoulder; the nanoweave stiffened so much under the blow that he momentarily couldn't move his arm. The next chunk hit him square in the chest, taking him off balance and partially knocking the wind out of him. Completely out of reflex, he brought the rifle up; the move saved his life. The Blacksnake meta brought what looked like a knife formed of ice down right at John's throat. Instead of nearly taking his head off, it split the rifle, passing between the upper and lower receiver with enough force to actually warp some of the metal. The ice was different this time; it had to be super-dense in order to do *that* to the billet receivers of the rifle. John, still off balance, had no leverage. He thought that the merc was grinning through the balaclava. Then he knew why; the ice knife was growing longer, the point driving towards John's unprotected throat. Centimeters away—

A wash of fire with a white-hot core in the shape of sword shattered the knife. Before the merc could react, he got the butt of a fiery spear in the gut, and as he bent over in pain, Sera hit him with the flat of her sword and flared all of her fires, sending him backwards, engulfed in flames. *Oh, shit. Some of that gear melts...* The merc shrieked in a high soprano, trying to roll to put the fire out, and only succeeding in spreading melting plastic and synthetic materials all over himself. The merc regained enough sense to use his metahuman power; a thick sheen of ice coated his body, extinguishing the burning materials and melting almost instantly. As his eyes fluttered open, John unholstered and pressed the barrel of his 1911 hard between the merc's eyebrows.

"Move and die, asshole," John growled. The merc, no longer grinning, surrendered.

With Sera's help, John secured the merc amidst the burnt man's cries of pain. John glanced at Sera as he easily dragged the Blacksnake meta up. "Any other survivors?"

"Two, John Murdock," she said, her aura of flame dying. She nodded her head towards the shelves. "There is one there, and one back in the larger room, whom you left wounded."

"Let's round them up," John replied. "Once we get 'em together, we gag 'em. I'll handle crowd control while you watch 'em." He thought for a moment. "I'll call HQ, let 'em know what the sitch is. Good?"

"As you will, John Murdock," she said, bowing her head a little and turning to go. John caught her arm lightly with his bleeding hand, still holding on to the merc.

"Sera," he breathed, his expression softening slightly. "I just wanted t'say. Thanks. For savin' me."

She caught her breath, and looked at him searchingly. What was she looking for?

Whatever it was, she didn't see it. She closed her eyes and let out her breath. "It is my duty, John Murdock," she said, and tugged her arm away. Then she paused, and gave him an earnest gaze. "But...you are welcome. I am pleased I could help."

By the time they had all three of the survivors trussed up and left together in a clear area at the front of the store, the reinforcements from CCCP had arrived. The usual assortment of cops, EMS personnel and firefighters all crowded around and busied themselves with their jobs; since CCCP had taken this call, ECHO was absent. Propriety was respected; you didn't come unless your help was asked for, and that cut both ways.

And last, after all of the others, came Red Saviour. Her first act was to order everyone out, save for Sera and John. Soviette stayed behind without prompting. That included the EMS people, who knew better by now than to object when Red Saviour issued an order. They'd already stabilized all three of the mercs, and Soviette was right there, qualified to take over responsibility. Truth to tell, John got the impression they were just as pleased to get out of there once Saviour showed up.

Saviour toed one of the mercs—hard—eliciting a groan. She grinned wolfishly, while Soviette frowned slightly. "I will be needing you to make sure this *svinya* can answer questions, Comrade Doctor," Saviour said, obviously savoring the chance to extract answers the hard way, if need be. "If any be living, we can pass them off to hospitals after."

Soviette frowned slightly. "Answers coming from pain are all but useless, Commissar," she protested. John nodded agreement as Saviour turned to face them. He had been through SERE training, and it was decidedly *not fun*. He had picked up a lot of useful knowledge there. One particular point being that people being physically tortured would do anything to make the pain stop; ask a guy if he killed Napoleon, or Jesus, or Batty Bunny, and he'd say *yes,* and tell you how. There were a lot of ways to make people talk; promise them pain, promise them favors, money, immunity from prosecution, protection for their families. But actual torture never got the job done. He'd seen it done. He'd never had the stomach to do it himself. *Not clean, like fighting a war. And I'll be damned if I stick with this bunch if this gets dirty.*

"True. So *svinya* are best to be answering before pain truly begins." Saviour stabbed each of the three in turn with her gaze, making sure they understood she meant exactly what she said. "You will be telling me why you were here, why you were killing two sturdy workers. You will be doing this quickly and to my satisfaction. You will be telling me who ordered you to do these things. If not, you will not live long enough to regret the consequences. But you will be *feeling* those consequences." She smiled, showing all her teeth. "I am to be having diplomatic immunity. And you are enemies of the State."

Sera stirred uneasily, looked as if she was going to say something, then looked at John and frowned a little.

The Blacksnake meta was the first to speak. "Any of you say anything, and you're dead men." He kept his eyes fixed on Saviour, sneering. Sera moved to interpose herself slightly, her fire-aura flaring a little. The merc recoiled from her, but then did his best to regain his composure.

"Oh. One of the dogs has a spine." Saviour casually stepped forward and backhanded the meta, hard enough to almost knock him over. "If you have anything other to say than answers to my questions, I will be most happy to break spine for you." She went back to where she had been standing, turning to face the other two wounded Blacksnake mercs. "Answer, please. You will go to hospital and will being tended to there."

The mercs looked to each other. Then the one in the middle— the worst hurt of the three, with a bullet wound to the pelvis courtesy of John—started talking in rapid-fire.

"It was a trap, it was a setup from the start—"

"Shut up!" The one on the left was trying to interrupt. "Stop fucking talking before you get us all killed!"

"I'm dying here! Screw you!" The middle one almost doubled over, then straightened up. "I'll tell you everything about the op, just get me to the goddamned hospital—"

The sound of ice breaking *did* interrupt the wounded merc this time. The ice chucker was up and moving. *Must've frozen the zip-tie handcuffs, made 'em brittle, snapped 'em—*

Everyone moved to stop him, get him back under control, but he had the element of surprise and they were just too far away. In a few swift motions he had formed an icicle as long as a yardstick, thrust it through the back of the nearest merc's skull, withdrawn it and planted it through the neck of the last merc. John felt sick in the pit of his stomach from the sound of the man's gurgling and the snap as the icicle broke on the floor. Sera's fires were ramped up. John, Saviour and Soviette all had their pistols drawn and trained on the merc. Sera was silent, but her fire sword was out again. Everyone else screamed for him to put his hands up, to get on his knees, and drop any weapons. Slowly, the merc dropped to his knees and raised his hands level with his head. Then the bastard grinned again. John already knew what the merc planned to do, knew he couldn't stop it but started forward anyway. Before he could take two steps, the merc formed a solid block of the super-dense ice around his own head, suiciding instantly. The body fell forward, the ice block slamming into the ground with a thud and sending skittering flecks of ice across the CCCPers' boots.

Sera started back, her eyes wide with alarm. So did Soviette. Saviour, however, only cursed. Loudly and colorfully, in Russian and English. She punctuated the final *"Nasrat!"* by kicking the block of ice around the dead meta's head.

She whirled and faced John. "You!" she spat, thrusting a finger at him. "Be writing full report." She glared at Sera and pointed at her as well. "You also! I want on desk in two hours."

By this time, the rest of the CCCP backup team had gathered, keeping one wary eye on their leader while they shook their heads over the ice-meta. "The rest of you!" she shouted. "Evidence! Be looking for anything out of ordinary! *Anything!*" Then she stormed off, and a moment later, the angry snarl of a Ural fired up and quickly faded into the distance.

John and Sera stood together silently as the rest of the comrades started to mill around them, looking for evidence amongst the wreckage and garbage in the store. Soviette was still next to the bodies of the last three mercs, shaking her head.

"Well," John said, "I think it's time for a beer. Or seven. And paperwork." He turned his head to look at Sera. "Walk you back to base? I'll have Bear or Unter ride my Ural back."

She looked at him askance. "Why would you choose to walk, John Murdock?"

He shrugged. "Clear my head, give me time to process this mess." He chuckled. "It'll give me more time before I have to face the Commissar again."

She looked a little past him. "If this is your wish, then we shall walk," she replied.

He grinned. "Let's walk, then." Three minutes later John had arranged for his motorcycle to be taken back to HQ, and they were both past the throng of official personnel and onlookers that had gathered around the front of the store.

"I am unsure why you wish my company, John Murdock," she said softly, wings moving restlessly as she walked. "Our patrol is effectively over."

"There's still the paperwork. Plus, I wanted to pick your brain, see what you thought was goin' on back there. That entire setup... it was goddamned strange. Don't y'think?"

"Very strange. And I cannot account for... for whatever it was that caused such head-pain," she said, looking thoughtful. "It cannot have been a toxin after all, can it?" She walked with her hands clasped behind her back, beneath the wings. The two of them were attracting a lot of curious glances.

He shook his head. "We would've been feeling the effects still, I would think. No way that they'd drop off all the sudden like that. An' Sovie cleared us when she arrived on the scene." He walked a few more steps, his thumbs hooked through the top of his belt. "It got worse the closer to the back that we got, where all of 'em were. Then it stopped real sudden-like, like it was... I dunno, shut off or something." He shrugged. "Could've been a meta? Someone like Mamona?"

"I do not know. I am not what I was," she replied, with both sadness and annoyance in her voice. "I suppose that is as good an explanation as any. I wonder why they wanted you, however."

"I was thinkin' 'bout that. I know they came for me..." John paused, looking slightly embarrassed. "They came for me before. Maybe they found out 'bout my memory, figure that they can give it another go." He shrugged again, then ruffled his hair. "Doesn't seem to fit, though. I'm just a trigger-puller with some extra tricks. That ain't enough to justify a high-profile operation like this one, especially with all of the heat that Blacksnake has already. There's gotta be something more to this, some bigger picture." He sighed heavily. "I'm just not smart enough an' don't have enough pieces of the puzzle to figure it out."

"You... were considerably more than someone with extra tricks," Sera replied carefully. "You have yet to utilize more than a fraction of your considerable power. I believe that you will discover your artificial enhancements also grant you far more than you are aware of. You should be testing your limits." Her feet made almost no sound on the pavement, as if she had no weight to speak of. "I have said this before. You should heed me. It is your duty to use every power at your disposal."

"All the same," he said, shifting the conversation, "This whole mess doesn't feel right. I hope that we get some sorta lead out of it. I just have a feelin' that there's somethin' bigger goin' on, and if we can figure it out we'll actually be makin' some headway."

The sun had set and twilight fallen while they were battling the ambush. By this point of their walk, they were in something that was clearly a neighborhood. People—old people mostly, but a few kids—were coming out to sit on their doorsteps and gossip. More kids were playing kickball in the street. When people saw John, they waved as if they knew him. He waved back; he had become "reacquainted" with some of them, and had been doing his homework with the journal. It'd take a while for that to become normal for him, though. The one real friendship with the neighborhood people that he had rekindled was with an elderly black shopkeeper named Jonas, who never wasted an opportunity to razz John about his "shit memory," especially when it came to his turn to bring the beer.

They passed by the community garden, which was flourishing. Kids were playing—carefully—in the rows between the plants. Or maybe they were weeding. Or both, really, they could weed and use the weeds they pulled up in whatever play they had going on. Despite the poverty of the surrounding area the people here were happy; struggling, but there was some spirit of togetherness that bound them together. John stopped in front of the entrance of the garden, watching the kids playing while their parents gossiped or worked on the garden or both.

"I helped make this." John's voice held equal measures of wonder and satisfaction. "Something good."

"Yes," Sera said softly. "You did. You gave them hope as well as food, and brought them together for each other." She sighed a little, but also smiled faintly. "Though you had help. It was—it is—a good thing."

John grinned, starting off again. "It's something we can both be proud of, then." His face screwed up for a second. "The reports we're going to have to turn in, though...how good are you at dodging ceramics?"

"Probably better than you," she replied, and smiled just a very little more. "I can fly."

He chuckled. "Maybe if we hurry back, we can get Chug t'eat the Commissar's supply of those horrible busts. Save everyone a lot of grief."

They walked easily through the neighborhood, and John realized that, despite the violence earlier...he felt pretty damned good.

CHAPTER THIRTEEN

Hold Heart

MERCEDES LACKEY AND CODY MARTIN

Although the days were growing colder, the Seraphym still resorted to her perch of choice, the faux Greek temple atop one of Atlanta's skyscrapers, for most of her waking hours. It was, despite being within eyeshot of the revolving restaurant atop the Westin hotel, the only place where she knew she was guaranteed privacy. It was much harder to think, in this physical body. She could not shut out the thoughts and emotions of people nearby as easily as she once could, and could not merely ignore someone who was trying to physically get her attention. Privacy, in the CCCP base, was nonexistent. She felt herself an intruder in Vickie's apartment. This was the only place that was solely hers.

Near at hand, the pillars and plinths showed the wear and abuse of pollution and weather much more than they did at a distance, which obscurely attracted her. Like her, they were not what they once had been.

All of the pieces had fallen together at last, and she could see what had only been a fragmented puzzle. She was still alive, and John Murdock had only half her powers, because holding all of her abilities too soon would have driven him mad, as Michael March had been driven mad. Only when he had mastered those abilities her sacrifice had given him would she be free. Free to die, and make him the synthesis of human and Celestial that he was meant to be, in order to find the way for humans to win against the Thulians without sacrificing what it meant to *be* human.

He would never be able to see *all* of the potential futures, she suspected. Nor have access to all of the collective memories of the past. That was still more information than a human brain was capable of processing. But he would have enough. And he would have what she did not; that spark of creativity that was able to look at two options and see a third.

The fact that he would never be "her" John, the man she had come to love so very deeply, was, in the larger view, irrelevant. It was, in fact, relevant only to her, and she was still an instrument, if not an *Instrument.* Her wishes, her longings, her loss... well, they meant nothing in the face of the reality that humanity was going to be obliterated and enslaved, the planet destroyed, and a vast swath of other worlds obliterated, if a way was not found to avert the Thulian conquest of this little globe. Averting it was why she was here in the first place. How criminal would she be if she allowed these human emotions to subvert her duty?

But she *was* human, or metahuman, now. And she had to reinforce her will against her emotions on a daily, sometimes hourly basis. And there was no denying that it hurt, it hurt, sometimes so much that she did not know how she was going to bear it; could not speak, could not think, could not breathe. Even at this very moment, the grief was building, and her throat and chest were so tight they hurt....

And, of course, as ever, in the midst of her own emotional maelstrom, her comm went off.

John didn't enjoy the quiet the way he used to. He couldn't appreciate it the same. In the past, downtime between missions had been when he could decompress, unwind and figure things out. He would find a quiet corner in the barracks, and lose himself in a book or some other menial task. It was the closest thing to what some folks called Zen that he had ever experienced. Since he had ... come back, he couldn't get to that spot anymore. John knew that it wasn't just the war; he'd been fighting for as long as he could remember, or getting ready to fight. He was a soldier through and through, so that wasn't what bothered him. While his new comrades were strange in ways he couldn't begin to describe, they weren't the cause of this unease either; he had become used to even Old Man Bear, or at least as used to the bastard as anyone could get.

What really had been bothering him were the noises in his head.

He knew he wasn't crazy—though people said the first sign of being crazy was that you thought you weren't. Despite that, John thought that he wasn't; although he had banged his head against plenty of surfaces in his time patrolling or running missions with the CCCP, not to mention his former career in the army, head trauma didn't usually make you crazy.

Besides, his symptoms didn't exactly match any mental illness he knew of. In truth, it had all started so small and innocuously that he couldn't place exactly when it had begun. Of course it had to have been after his "rebirth" or whatever you would call it; there had been no mention of the occurrences in his journal, and sounds in his head were definitely something he would have included.

It had started as breaths, whispers, things he could have put down to the echoes of his own thoughts. Little tricks of light and shadow in the corners of his vision. Then one day it had built up to the point that he couldn't help but notice it was there, and now it was only growing in intensity.

Sometimes it was a voice, murmuring too quietly for him to make out the words. Mostly it was music. Strains of something alien yet wholly familiar. The song was always distant, just out of reach; if he started to pay attention to it, it would slip away, a fading echo. The music came and went, but as of late it was coming more frequently. What could that mean? John could accept that there were aliens, that there were Nazis in powered armor with insanely advanced technology who were bent on world domination. He had awakened as a metahuman, missing several years of his memory; there were a lot of things he could accept after that. But this . . . he couldn't make sense of it. It was a problem he couldn't find a solution to; how could you find an answer to something if you didn't even know what the question was in the first place?

John was using one of his rare moments of down time to clean his weapons and sharpen his knives. It had been some time since he'd actually *had* any down time; luckily, it looked like the Commissar had found a new whipping boy, at least for the moment. Probably Bear. This exercise, something he could do without even thinking about it, had always been something that relaxed him, but now he was running into the same problem. Thinking about the music. It wasn't the music so much that bothered him, but rather when it seemed to pick up the most.

Namely, while he was around Sera.

He had been reaching out to her, trying to find a middle ground so that they could at least have some sort of dialogue about what had happened to him. He knew he was asking a lot of her, but what choice did he have? She was one more key to what had happened to him. Plus, they kept on getting paired together as the two "odd men out" within the CCCP; him for his memory loss, and her for . . . well, being her. She no longer fled when he came near, but she was still cold and distant. John didn't mind some people hating him; he could deal with that easily enough, since most anyone who hated him probably wasn't worth the time to think about. But with her it was different. He needed her to be okay with him; maybe not friends, but not however things were between them now. Especially with the music, and how it always seemed to pick up around her. . . .

John was sharpening the huge Bowie knife that a patrol he had been a part of had taken from a Reb called "Bad Bowie" when the call came.

"Comrade Murdock," Gamayun's voice came through John's internal comm with a burst of static, *"report to briefing room with Comrade Sera."* With a sigh John set down the knife and sharpening stone before gathering up the rest of his gear and setting off at a trot.

Sera was already there, sitting on a backless stool, wings pulled in so tightly to her body that it made his back muscles ache in sympathy. He'd noticed of late that her wings were a more accurate barometer of her emotional state than her face. Nervous, and she flicked them. Alarmed, and they half-spread and trembled, as if she was about to take off. Tense, and she pulled them in tightly to her body, the way she was doing now. Exhausted—or depressed?—and they drooped. He paused for a second at the entrance to the briefing room, shrugging on his vest over the nanoweave shirt.

"What'd I miss?" He glanced around; Saviour and Unter were absent, which was odd. It was just him and Sera.

"Nothing, sport," Victrix said in his ear. *"I needed a screen. Seraphym isn't wired up the way you are."*

"Oh. Well, fire away, comrade kiddo." John leaned against the back wall, folding his arms across his chest.

The large LCD screen—another piece of ECHO largesse—at

the business end of the briefing room lit up. *"Here's what I have. Some activity on Thulian freqs I triangulated here—"* The map showed a red spot. *"—combined with minor seismic disturbance. I think someone is excavating something. Maybe a buried sleeper cell, you know, the kind that produces a pop-up. It's in CCCP territory, and so far this is all new-new-new, like within the last twenty-four hours, so chances are it won't need more than the standard size patrol unit to squash. I passed on the info to RS; she nominated and assigned you two."*

"Pop-ups." That was the shorthand for attacks that just "popped up" in the middle of cities. A lot of them came from smallish units of Thulian armor that had been buried in place; presumably the operators infiltrated, looking like ordinary Joes, found the hatch or other access to the storage area, climbed into the armor and set out to make trouble. And they *did* make trouble, all out of proportion to their size, creating chaos and terror until they were taken down. The effect was that there were no safe areas, seemingly; everyone was kept on edge, because you never knew quite where or when the Kriegers would send one of their suicide squads.

More things came up on the screen; diagrams of Thulian power armor, Thulian Wolves, and Thulian Eagles with their vulnerable points helpfully indicated. *"Since you two are fire-powers, you're the logical choice, lucky you. We've never seen a Death Sphere with a pop-up, but if you get one, call for help pronto."*

"So, check it out, find out what we can, burn anything that looks at us sidelong. Got it. You op'ing for us on this one?"

"Ten-four. You two both speaka-da-English, makes it easier on Gamayun. Besides, I have my bag of tricks if you run into trouble; she doesn't."

John slapped a buckle on his boots, making sure it was tight. "Let's hope we don't need 'em." He looked to Sera. "Ready to roll out?"

The Seraphym nodded. "You must exert yourself, John Murdock," she said, with a very faint air of... what? Disappointment? Rebuke? Like she wanted this to be a bigger, more dangerous mission? Or something else? "You are not using a quarter of your abilities. You *must* master them. You should have done so by now."

Ah then. It was something else. *You're not living up to your full potential, Mister Murdock.* He was reminded of several of his teachers when he was in primary school.

"Do my best, ma'am. Don't wanna burn the whole 'hood down, though." He stood up from the wall, stretching. "Anythin' else, Vic?"

"Unter's already fixed you up with a Ural and a loadout. You get one of the new RPGs with the incendiary loads in case you get a sphere. Don't waste it, m'kay? You'll set fire to half a block with one if you aren't careful, and the charges each cost more to make than you're worth in parts. I'll guide you and Sera in."

"Roger that. Let's get on with it."

This had to be the most wrecked part of a destruction corridor that John had ever seen, and that was surely saying something given how badly Atlanta had been hit. He hoped that whoever had been in here during the first Invasion had been smart and run the hell away, because no one could have survived what had gone on here. Most destruction corridors were caused by one or two powered armor suits; unopposed or at least without effective resistance, they could carve entire swaths out of crowded cities. This one, though... at least a squad of Krieger armored troopers had to have moved through this area, with maybe a Death Sphere following. It was sickening and awe-inspiring at the same time that so few could wreak so much havoc.

"Vic, y'got any info on this area? This place is toast. What's the area like that we're going into?"

"The loc is what used to be Carver High School, built circa 1911. Closed down circa 1982 because it was too expensive to keep repaired. There used to be a fallout shelter in the basement. I'm betting that's where your targets are." In the upper left corner of his vision, a picture of what looked like a gigantic pile of brick and boards popped up. *"That's what the Kriegers left of it. No one knows why they bothered wrecking it since there's a ten-foot-tall fence around it. Cause, you know, Goddess forbid that homeless squatters get some shelter. Maybe they figured on keeping people out to keep what they had down there safe?"*

"What's this destruction corridor on track to? I didn't think that there were any ECHO transmitters in this part of town?"

"Negative. This is one of those cases where we don't know why they came through and leveled the place. From here, they joined the wrecking crew on the Ring."

"Roger." John swung off of the Ural. The RPG with the new

warhead was in a locked case that was bolted to the gear rack. He really didn't feel like going up against a Death Sphere today; if one showed up, it would've meant that he and Sera had really stepped into it, and back-up was minutes away. Minutes away, when seconds counted for everything.

There was a sound like thunder just behind him, and a wash of air hit him in the back. He turned to see Sera, wings beating furiously, touching down in a slightly clearer spot on the pavement, right foot extended. She folded her wings immediately as soon as both feet were on the ground, and sheathed herself in fire. John was aware that the music had started up again, but did his level best to ignore it. Not that it was easy; it seemed to invade his very thoughts, always coming back to Sera. And he didn't like it a single goddamned bit.

"We're probably going underground. Old Cold War fallout shelter, a bunker, forgotten an' sealed off. We're gonna want to watch the fires down there; not a lot of oxygen, also probably a lotta shit that can burn."

"Very well," she said, and the fire vanished. She looked very vulnerable without it. "If space is restricted I will be at a disadvantage. The wings occupy a great deal of space."

"If'n we get into any sort of trouble we can't handle with more conventional means, we'll back out an' take it outside. This destruction corridor stretches for a good long way; no need to worry 'bout civvies wanderin' into the crossfire."

"As you will," she said, without inflection.

"Heads up, chillun. I found the entrance. It will be of no surprise to you, given they either wanted out, or in, that although they have done a crackup job of hiding it, you can get to it. JM, it's on your HUD. Sera, follow him."

John started climbing through the rubble; it was rough going for certain parts. With this section abandoned, there wasn't as much of a rush for clean-up. They reached their destination a few dozen yards later; a large mound of rubble, supposedly the remnants of the school. Highlighted on the HUD were two large, weathered metal doors set into concrete recessed into the ground, with more rubble piled around it. It reminded John of tornado cellars that he had seen.

"Cellar doors. External access to the school cellar, probably used for bringing in coal for the furnace and boiler."

"Whew, you smell that?" John almost gagged, the scent was so strong.

"I don't get smell-o-vision, sport," Vickie quipped as Sera shook her head.

"Smells like burnt cinnamon and ass. That's being kind." He glanced over to Sera. "Definitely Kriegers, right?"

"I believe they have a particular scent that humans find faintly distasteful, yes," Sera replied, before Vickie could. "I am never aware of it, as my fire always purifies any air that reaches my nose." But she bent down and reached for the handle of the door nearest her.

John stopped her short. "Hey, lemme go first. I'm wearin' nanoweave an' the vest to boot. Plus, I've got my sidearm. If we need to go loud, it'll work out better that way. Gettin' baked to death or asphyxiated doesn't really strike me as a great way to go, kay?" He grinned lopsidedly to soften the rebuke.

"As you will," Sera said, stepping aside. *Baby steps, Murdock. Take it slow, like you would with a wounded animal.*

"You know it would help if you let me unlock it first. Although the sight of you heaving the door handle off would be highly amusing."

"An' here I thought that you were on top of it an' had unlocked it while we were walkin' up. Gotta catch up, Teen Witch."

"It's a mechanical lock, brainiac. Electronic I can do almost instantly, if I know the lock. Mechanical takes time." He thought he could hear her muttering under her breath; his ultra-sensitive hearing definitely picked up small sounds of metal moving, then the sound of something larger sliding. *"There. Unlocked and unbolted. Have at."*

"Makin' entry." John unholstered his 1911, doing a quick press check to make sure a round was chambered. Satisfied, he nodded to Sera, then lifted the left door of the entrance. He stepped through the threshold, moving down into the darkness. His eyes adjusted instantly due to his enhancements; there wasn't any illumination, initially, save for the low sunlight streaming in—which didn't actually help, as it illuminated everything in the entrance and made it hard to see what was still in shadow. The room was full of garbage mostly; piles of unidentifiable papers spilling out of disintegrated boxes and assorted trash, a few scattered and decaying desks. It was easy to see where the boiler and furnace had once been; it looked as if they must have been hauled out for salvage, leaving behind cut-off pipes that probably led to the restrooms and the steam radiators. John was surprised some enterprising soul hadn't gotten down here and started hauling out those copper pipes; they were worth a lot as far as scrap metal went. There were several Civil Defense posters adorning the walls; only the metal ones were vaguely readable past the rust and grime. The nearest end of the room had what appeared to be a collapsed stairwell, choked with rubble. On the far end, however, was a single metal door, with a painted sign that he could barely make out as saying SHELTER. He hadn't seen any obvious booby traps or intrusion detection devices; since Vickie hadn't said anything, he could only assume that there weren't any. Or, at least, any that either of them could detect. That uncertainty wasn't the most pleasant of feelings.

"That's our only way down. Stay behind me. If'n we have to move out in a hurry, we'll both start burnin' an' go for the surface. Sound good to you, Sera?"

"As you will," she repeated. John frowned a little. This was getting monotonous. Waiting for her to be ready to interact with him like a normal human being and not this current... funk that she was in was all well and good, but they were on the job right now.

"T'hell with that. We're partners on this, Sera. If'n you get a better idea 'bout something, I want you to voice your opinion. It could mean the difference between life an' death for us. I'm not always right, y'know. Okay?"

He glanced back. She just shrugged. "I have no knowledge."

"*Well, I do. There is a lot more void behind that door then there should be. Dammit, I knew I should have kept a piece of Krieger armor with me to help me ID stuff; there's also something alive in there but I can't tell how many or what, without getting eyes in there.*" John's HUD lit up; a spectral outline of the space beyond swam into his vision, a projection from Vic. There was something room-shaped beyond the door, then what looked like a corridor, then another, much larger space. "*That's what I have, and everything from that corridor on is NOT on the original plans.*"

"Someone's been expanding. Can't imagine that the foundations for this joint were all that great in the first place. If'n the Kriegers have been diggin' under 'em, no tellin' how they are now."

"*It's Germans, bonehead. They'll have reinforced anything they put in, and I'm assuming it's them. Shit coming down is going to be the last of your worries. Every bit of everything Krieger I've seen defines the word 'overbuilt.'"*

"Whatever. If it is Kriegers, then that'll hold. Whoever it is, they've gone to a little trouble to stay hidden, an' that means they've got to deal with us now. Be ready with your tricks, in any case."

"Victrix..." Sera began.

"Roger, Sera?"

"Can you count the number of feet on the ground, and divide by two? That will give you the number of Thulians." Sera glanced at John—for his approval? He grinned, nodding. *She's usin' her noggin, all right. Baby steps.*

"Brilliant, yes, I can even pick up armor, just takes a little longer. Stand by."

There was a pause. John thought he could hear faint noises on the other side of that door, but not *what* those noises were. That door must have been pretty damned thick to futz with his hearing. This might have been a genuine fallout shelter, not one of the "feel-good" models that wasn't going to do squat in the event of a nearby bomb. Something with filters on the air supply, and a real blast-door. *Wonder which muckity-muck lived nearby back then, that this shelter got upgraded?* he thought inconsequentially. *That, or the Kriegers have been doing some interior decorating.*

On the door itself, however... there was an extremely faint sound of metal sliding on metal.

"Okay. Door unlocked. I read seven sets of jackboots on the ground..." Vix began.

"Affirmative, seven JBTs inside—"

He was cut off by the wail of what was unmistakably a small child in distress. He and Sera shared a single alarmed glance before they both started moving. In one motion John threw the heavy door aside, his pistol already out, looking for a target. Sera manifested both her fire sword and spear, and followed right behind him, darting to his right as soon as there was room.

In front of them were the seven Kriegers. Along with a dozen more, all in trooper armor standing on catwalks... off the ground. And a single mechanical wolf at the far end of the room, apparently digging to expand the shelter. The child, undoubtedly one of the neighborhood kids, was on his knees on the floor, one of the unarmored Kriegers pointing a gun at his head. Everyone in the room turned to look at the pair, including the wolf.

"... *and smaller sign, a dozen troopers and something big.* Mia fasz?!"

The Krieger pointing the gun at the child's head grimaced and then tensed, looking back at his target. John and Sera moved almost simultaneously. John fired three quick rounds, all striking the Krieger with the ray gun in the upper neck and head, dropping the invader cold. He started moving forward, firing at the next threat nearest to the child. But Sera was moving too, diving with wings half-spread, to cover the child with her body.

"Get the boy clear!" John had already holstered his pistol. *Time to quit screwing around.* He ignited both of his arms, sheathing them in flame. Wherever he pointed, flame followed, alighting whatever it touched. He made especially sure that he was avoiding the area in the center with Sera and the child.

With her left arm, Sera had scooped the child up; her right still held her fire-sword, and since she was on her knees in mid-turn, she lopped a rushing Krieger off at the thigh as she pivoted. As soon as she was facing the door, she pushed off like a sprinter, wailing child bundled under her left arm like a parcel.

John brought up the rear; the Kriegers had started collecting themselves. Those who weren't dead or dying shot back; energy-gun fire for the most part, but one blast that went wild could only have been from a trooper arm cannon. He ran after Sera and the child, stopping at corners to send a few more blasts of flame to dissuade pursuit. The Kriegers were getting a little more cautious as they kept losing people. Finally they broke through the cellar door to the surface, the sunlight almost blinding after the near complete darkness. Both he and Sera turned, ready.

"John! Take him!" Sera cried out, simultaneously throwing the poor kid right at him. John grabbed the boy in his left arm, already knowing what Sera meant to do.

"Together! Now!"

John, shifting so that the child was further away from the entrance, concentrated for a split second, collecting fire on his right arm. Sera planted herself right in the side of the entrance and turned into a living torch, setting the entire entrance afire, while she swung at the supports with her sword.

It was as if she was able to read his mind. The instant he was ready to blast, she jumped clear. With a small grunt of effort he loosed the concentrated plasma right at the point that she had weakened. The fire drove the Thulians back into the basement, keeping them from piling out into the open. They were learning. Fire equals Bad.

"*Jump clear, you two!*"

The blast, in addition to driving the Kriegers back into the ground where they belonged, finished the job of collapsing the entrance. Sera extinguished her shielding fire, snatched the wailing child out of John's arms and took to the air, leaving John to scramble backwards towards the fence. His speed was the only thing that saved him. He was within two steps of it when the ground heaved and shook; he turned, grabbing for the fence with one hand, to see the entire mound of rubble that had been the high school cave inward. Vix had collapsed the first floor and the basement supports, bringing it all down on the Kriegers.

Sera set down outside the fence, putting the child down on his feet. She took his chin in her hand and looked him straight in the eyes.

"*Run,*" she ordered, forcefully.

The boy took off running, moving so fast John would have suspected metapower if he didn't have firsthand experience of how quickly a motivated child could move.

"Vic," John breathed, sharing a nod with Sera that they were both okay. "I'm hopin' you've scrambled the cavalry by this point. This ain't as small of a problem as we initially thought."

"*Az Isten faszat,*" she said, with feeling. "No lie. Yes, I have."

A very faint smile crossed Sera's face, and vanished as quickly as it had come.

John grinned, chuckling. "What's ticklin' ya, angel?"

"Nothing. Not really. Just Victrix's use of invective is—colorful—if—unlikely—"

Behind them, John heard the sound of bricks grating on each other. Then the ceramic *chink*s as they tumbled down the pile. Slowly, and with a growing sense of dread, he stepped out from behind the fence, facing the rubble where the school used to be.

"*Yebany v rot!*" That one he knew from hanging out with Pavel. She'd switched to Russian. The pile of bricks was moving.

"Hey, Vic...ETA on that backup?"

"*Not soon enough!*"

"That's what I figured." John ignited both of his hands, settling into an easy stance; light on his feet, ready to move. He looked over to Sera. "Well, you wanted me to push my limits, right? I'm thinkin' we're 'bout to find out what they are. You ready for this?"

She lofted back over the fence—half-flight, half-jump—landed beside him, lit up like a torch again, and nodded grimly.

The ground continued to tremble, shifting debris and rubble almost rhythmically. Without any warning, all of the vibration stopped. Three tense seconds later, the collapsed area where the school had been erupted in a fountain of bricks, dust and pieces of rebar. As the dust cleared, John and Sera saw the top half of the mechanical wolf exposed through a hole in the ground. It wriggled frantically in place before dislodging itself, dragging its lower half out of the ground. All twelve of the armored troopers followed it out of the hole, spreading out in a semicircle in front of the two CCCPers.

There was a steady stream of whispered curses in his ear. Some of it he recognized as Russian, from listening to Untermensch as he worked on the Urals.

"Your crystal ball sayin' we're screwed, blued an' tattooed?"

"Eight Ball doesn't work that way. Let's just say I do not care for the odds. But we've seen worse."

"Hey!" John shouted to the armored troopers, still ponderously moving into position. "Y'all pissed off that *Unteroffizer Affenschwanz* couldn't get his rocks off today by wasting a kid? The Master Race that easy to bend over a barrel?"

"Perfection. Pure poetry. Where'd you learn German?"

"I didn't. But I have been hangin' out with Red far too much."

The Kriegers didn't respond as positively as Vickie had. John could barely make out some guttural shouts that were undoubtedly curses. He was not making any fans among the Kriegers, which suited him just fine. This was going to be a fight, that much was for damn sure. Both he and Sera were on open ground; any scant cover they might've had could easily be evaporated by the weapons the troopers carried. Not to mention they had the inevitable risk of getting flanked by that damned mechanical wolf.

John and Sera did have a couple of advantages, though; John's speed and Sera's flight. Split the enemy's attention, whittle them down, and he and Sera had a chance. *Sounds great in theory, genius. But can you pull it off without getting schwacked?*

Sera's wings were half-spread and trembling. Clearly she wanted to be in the air, and from the look of her anxious expression, she wished it had been five minutes ago.

Wait for it...

John could feel something building, a sort of tension. He knew what to do, and he felt that Sera was ready for it too. The Kriegers were working up a full head of steam, and were going to try to make the first move. John had already keyed his enhancements. He envisioned exactly how it would go, what play he would make, where Sera would fly, who they would target first. It was all very clear to John; he'd used visualization techniques before missions in the past, but it had never had this sort of clarity. Maybe it was the enhancements, or the adrenaline, but he felt keyed up, ready for the perfect moment...

Now! The first Krieger on the far right had begun to raise his arm cannon. Sera vaulted into the air while John kicked hard against the ground and began sprinting for the Krieger. The shot from the arm cannon harmlessly obliterated the spot where Sera had been.

Sera had to close; she didn't have anything she could use at a distance, aside from throwing her spears. But close she did, fearlessly, *recklessly,* he would have said; despite all of that, her speed saved her. She came down behind the two Kriegers on the far left; since these were the ones in armor, she couldn't just cut off a leg the way she had the unarmored schmuck back in the cellar. And, in fact, she didn't use the sword at all; she grabbed the head of the one nearest her in both hands, and suddenly the fire around her went from yellow to blue-hot. She let go, and the Krieger dropped to the ground, thrashing, helmet looking like an ice sculpture that had just started to melt. Then she leapt straight up again, wings beating furiously.

John didn't waste any time with his first Krieger. He sent a quick blast of fire at the trooper's visor, blinding him momentarily. With his enhanced speed, he had crossed the distance and stopped behind the Nazi before he could react. John charged his fires for a moment, then sent three concentrated blasts into the armor; two at the knees to bring it down, and a final one at the base of the helmet, killing the trooper, who fell forward with a final spasm.

He turned to see that Sera was hovering just above another

left-hand Krieger, as if she were daring him to shoot her. Before he could shout, or even move, he heard the whine of an arm-cannon ramping up. That was when Sera dropped right out of the sky, fiery sword manifested, bringing all her weight and the momentum of the drop down on the sword.

She didn't just *slice* off the end of the arm cannon; it was more like taking a hot knife through a thick chunk of chocolate, melting as much as cutting. But it was relatively fast, too fast for the Krieger to react, and as soon as the end of the cannon dropped with a *clunk* to his feet, she was up in the air again, and *just* out of lethal distance when the cannon backfired into the Krieger's armor, shredding the right-hand side of his suit, and him inside it.

John grinned, turning back to face the next Krieger on his side of the fight. *She's good when she puts her mind to it.* There'd be time for back-slapping later, though; right now he had some killing to do. Vickie was keeping some of the Kriegers occupied by opening up holes underneath them, or thrusting up piles of dirt and concrete. As long as she could keep doing that, she would be keeping part of the horde off him and Sera. He snapped off another charged-up blast at the nearest Krieger, hitting the ground beneath its feet; the concrete super-heated in an instant, exploding and toppling the trooper. John continued blasting away, covering the trooper with fire, head to toe, weakening the armor. Before the Krieger could right itself, John ran to its side, scooping up a jagged length of rebar on the way. Sliding to a stop next to the downed armor, he brought the makeshift spear down as hard as he could, right through the Krieger's visor. He gave it a final twist, and the suit shuddered once, then lay still.

John looked up to see the nearest Kriegers visibly shaken. Obviously he couldn't see their expressions, but their body language told him all he needed to know. They'd thought they would be shooting fish in a barrel, and the joke was on them. They didn't have a lot of time to think about it; Vic was continually putting them off balance. John glanced to his left; Sera met his gaze in the same instant. They both seemed to already know what to do. John immediately started sprinting with everything he had towards the third Krieger on the left. Sera arced up and to the right, then plummeted straight down towards the first Krieger on the right-hand side, one who, in the same moment, got shaken to his knees by Vic. Sera's feet hitting his shoulder blades put him face-down into the dirt, and she crouched on his back and flared blue-white again.

As exciting as it was to watch Sera work, John didn't have the time at the moment. He had his own threats to focus on. The air was filled with bolts of actinic energy from the troopers' arm cannons; some of them were getting pretty close, leaving behind the smell of burnt ozone. He had almost reached the line of Kriegers on the left when he abruptly changed course, juking hard to the right at the last one in line and furthest from him. That would buy him a precious second. Concentrating as he ran, he thrust out his left arm, a solid beam of plasma arcing and hitting the Krieger he had initially been running at. The helmet was burned away, leaving the decapitated body taking another step before crashing forward. When he glanced over at Sera, or rather, where Sera had been, there was a suit of armor fused to the rubble, and she was already in the air again.

Three down for me, three to go for each of us. Let's rock an' roll! John reached the two he had juked towards. He enveloped both in a wide blast of flame; not too intense, but enough to keep them occupied and weaken them slightly. He killed it right before he reached them. Both troopers quickly scanned, reacquired and started tracking him with their arm cannons; they were well trained, at the very least. John took a chance, running to the middle of the pair. Another blast of flame at the visor of the one at the left while shouldering into the one on the right. He didn't budge it much, and the impact with the heated metal of the trooper armor left the shoulder of his jacket smoldering, but he was in close enough that it couldn't blast him now. The other one was starting to recover, while the trooper he was against was trying to give him a lethal bear hug. John took a step, and launched off of its knee hard enough to send him above the eye level of the leftmost Krieger. It looked up in time for another blast of flame, followed by a lance of concentrated plasma in a glancing hit to its left shoulder; a wound instead of a killing blow. John landed in front of it, crouched under, and then ran behind the still-blinded Krieger. Unable to see and in pain, the trooper's training failed, and he started firing wildly at the last spot it had seen John; directly in front of it. Two blasts from the arm cannon obliterated the Krieger across from it, leaving smoldering bits scattered for half the length of a football field. John didn't wait for the remaining Krieger to realize its mistake; he fired another weakening blast of flame at the back of its head, drew his pistol, and then emptied the magazine at the base of the helmet, punching a ragged and smoking hole through. John had to dodge out of the way to avoid being crushed by the falling armor.

Vic seemed to be working on the right now; screwing with the two Kriegers Sera was harassing. Rather than taking them straight on, Sera was waiting until one was off-balance, darting in to slash at him with the sword at one of the vulnerable spots, then darting away again. Every time she came in close, her fire flared up in the Krieger's visor, momentarily blinding him. Eventually she was going to manage to cut through *something*, he reckoned; and meanwhile, the creatures inside those suits must have been soiling themselves with fear.

Just as he thought that, she suddenly launched straight up into the air above and between them. She got up about a thousand feet, then dropped again, sword in her right hand, spear in the left.

Again, she was using her weight and the momentum of her fall, and she had flared to blue-white hot once more. He had just about enough time to take that in when she hit.

The white-hot spear transfixed the Krieger on her left, going in at the point where the neck met the shoulder, one of the vulnerable spots. The sword bisected the helmet of the one on the right. They were falling as she dissolved her weapons and sprang away. She headed up into the air again; her fires had faded, and her wingbeats looked labored.

The final two troopers had moved to the middle of the destruction corridor, standing back-to-back. *That won't save you, fellas.* John, his enhancements still keyed up, sprinted straight for the Krieger facing him. Just as the invader raised his arm cannons, John opened up with a large blast of flame, then jinked left. The trooper, armor weakening and temporarily unable to see, fired where John had been, sending up showers of rubble. John kept up the speed until he was right in front of the trooper, coming up short. He had a brainstorm; pausing, he ramped up the fires on his right arm, hotter than he could ever remember attempting before. He had to close his eyes and turn his head, the fires were so bright. Then he pushed his hand *through* the front of the trooper's armor, going in its chest and out its back. John staggered backwards, partially from the intense heat and partially because of the drain he felt from ramping up that much. His skin felt blistered and some of his hair smelled singed just from the residual heat, since he was protected from his own fires but not from what they might burn. Past the afterimage that was somewhat clouding his vision he could see the remains of the armor; the features were melted and the joints fused in place, leaving it standing in a horrid death rictus, the occupant very dead. The scene looked strikingly familiar, but he couldn't place where he knew it from.

Vic had been freed to concentrate on the remaining trooper, and had somehow managed to encase him to the waist in rubble. *Must be giving Sera a break.* As fast as the trooper struggled free, she piled more on him, and seemed to be opening up a hole underneath him at the same time, because he kept dropping lower. Or was she somehow turning the surface under him into a sort of quicksand?

"Just stay where you are, you rat bastard," Vickie snarled in John's ear, as the trooper sank a little more. *"I know where your air intakes are..."*

Suddenly, the trooper's movements got a lot more frantic. He was chest-deep now, and the rubble was...pulverizing, somehow. Getting finer. Neck deep, and his head was moving as if the suit was possessed.

Then there was nothing but a pile of fine sand about the height of John's waist. It was still moving as he watched...then...it wasn't.

"Not bad at all," John panted. He was doubled over, hands on his knees and trying to catch his breath. Still, he managed to give Sera a thumbs-up before wiping his brow of sweat and ash. Sera landed heavily beside him; she was panting too, and all of her fires were gone.

"You...achieved creditable success, John Murdock," she managed, between gasping breaths. *Better'n I've heard from her in... well, ever. Progress.*

"Thank ya, ma'am. Y'get some points for the assist, too, Teen Witch. Just remind me to have you on speed dial to handle sand traps if I ever take up golf."

"That's grounds *for an ass-whuppin', pinhead,"* she shot back. *"Uh...hey, aren't we forgetting something?"*

As if that had been a cue, the monstrous mechanical wolf burst out of hiding. It must have been lurking just inside the hole it had dug out, waiting while they finished off the troopers. It headed straight for the two of them. *Why the hell would it have been waiting?* John didn't have time to pursue that line of thought.

It was *fast*, much faster than the troopers had been. John tried to fire off a blast and completely missed it; he hardly *ever* missed with his fire. Sera tried a slash to its flank as they flung themselves to either side, and nearly got hit by a paw for her troubles.

While John recovered and tried to get some distance and figure out how to handle this monster, Sera moved in to distract it. She couldn't close with it, or it would certainly catch her. The most she could do was "dance" with it, a strange and deadly sort of ballet, half on the ground and half in the air, feinting, striking with sword or spear, before darting away out of reach again.

She can't keep that up forever; we're both flagging. With how fast the wolf was moving, he didn't have time to charge up a shot; he could only weaken it with flame, and even then he risked hitting Sera. But if she stopped her deadly distraction, it would focus on him, and probably get him. *Think!* He had to do something. John glanced frantically around. *The Ural! Oh, Saviour's going to have kittens over this one.* He ran for the Ural, jumping onto the seat and turning the ignition. His hands flew over the latches on the case holding the modified RPG and its warheads; he left them in the case, but went ahead and removed the safeties. The warheads themselves were impact detonated; even though they'd need to be shot from the launcher to actually arm, John figured that what he was about to do still had a decent chance of kicking off the payload.

"This is either a fuckin' genius move, or I'm a goddamned moron."

Sera seemed to be reading his mind again. Suddenly she shot off like an arrow, speeding along at barely head-height, with the wolf in hot pursuit, leading it down what passed for the road, away from John. He gunned the throttle, sending the Ural hurtling forward. He turned the handles sharply, bouncing and skidding over rubble as he pursued Sera. It only took him a few seconds before he reached the fastest he could safely go over the rubble; he gave it a little extra acceleration anyway.

Sera and the wolf had been pulling away from him. Now she

executed a hairpin turn by touching down, pulling her wings in tight, and somersaulting in the air like a gymnast, coming out pointed towards John. The wolf, caught off-guard by this, skidded for several yards before managing to reverse and pursue her again as she headed straight at John and the bike at full speed. She pulled up suddenly just at what John considered to be the *last* possible second—

He dove from the speeding motorcycle, twisting in the air. Time seemed to slow down as he took aim, charging his fires in the split second before the motorcycle impacted with the leading paw of the mechanical wolf. Snapping off the shot, he saw it hit perfectly on the warheads in the sidecar case; he had enough time to tuck and roll before the explosion completely engulfed the wolf. He hit the ground hard, and even with the jacket and the nanoweave he could feel the broken bits of brick and concrete biting into his arms, shoulders and back. *Confirm the kill, jackass; even if it hurts, you gotta get up.* Groaning, he peeled himself from the ground. The wolf was still there, but it wasn't doing well at all. The paw that the motorcycle had connected with was completely gone, jagged and sparking metal twisting up into the wolf's shoulder joint. The rest of it was still ablaze with the compound from the RPGs, thick and oily smoke rising into the air.

Sera touched down, as the remaining legs of the wolf suddenly stopped moving. Or rather, they were moving as if they were stuck in mud or quicksand.

"I'll hold it, you hit it!" Vic said in his ear, and Sera acted on the command by darting in and daring a slash at a rear leg, staying well clear of the jaws. The wolf was knee-deep in the ground now, and there Vic seemed to be stuck with her efforts, since it didn't sink any more.

"I hardened the ground like cement around the legs; that's the best I can do. It moves too fast and it's too strong even on three legs for me to manage anything other than a temporary hold."

John trotted over, centering himself in front of the wolf. Even damaged and immobilized, it was trying to thrash from side to side to free itself.

"Let's finish the bastard." John started charging up his fires, letting them build along both arms. Sera went airborne again; it was clear she was exhausted, but it was also clear she was grimly determined to do her part in killing this monster. Once she was in the air the wolf seemed to forget about her; it concentrated on John, optics glaring balefully at him. That gave Sera a chance to come in behind it, in its blind spot, while it was unaware she had returned.

With anyone else he would have counted down; somehow he knew he didn't have to with her. They were moving and acting like a single person. As he thought that, she manifested her spear, and dropped down onto the thing's back, ramming the fiery weapon through its spine at the join where shoulder blades would have been on a real wolf. At that same moment he released his fires, joining the concentrated blast on a single point at the back of the wolf's mechanical throat. Sera leapt off of the wolf's back, beating her wings furiously. The wolf shuddered once before its main body exploded in a too-loud *whump* that swatted John and Sera, the pressure wave washing over them. The mechanical beast finally settled to the ground, the optics dead and staring at nothing.

And only *then* did the snarl of approaching Urals signal that the "cavalry" was about to arrive.

"Right on time." John stood up to his full height, brushing off his uniform before standing at parade rest. Sera touched down to land beside him; as she stood there, at nothing like a military posture, her wings drooped with weariness.

Russian chatter came over the CCCP frequency, some Gamayun, but most of it was Red Saviour's barked orders. Urals rolled in from three directions in groups of three, one of the trios followed by the battered CCCP van. Saviour appeared in the sky a moment later, using whatever crazy-ass metapower she had for flying. She touched down in front of the Urals, still talking, as the CCCP troops spread out, taking cover.

But as soon as it became evident that the fight was over, they all broke cover and gathered behind Saviour. Untermensch looked put out—probably because he had missed an opportunity to kick Thulian teeth in. Bear was doing his best Golden Girls impression to try to comfort his friend.

Saviour stalked up to John, ignoring Sera. "How many? Why were you not waiting for backing up?" she barked, frowning. Looked like she was just as pissed as Untermensch at missing out on the fight.

John did his level best to resist smirking. Even though it had been a hairy fight, he'd had . . . fun. "After makin' entry into

the suspected Krieger outpost we had indications of an imminent threat to an innocent. We had to act right then an' there;
turned out to be a kid that had strayed a little too far into the
corridor." He glanced over at Sera. "There also turned out to be
seven unarmored personnel and then *twelve* troopers. Oh, an'
the wolf over there." He indicated towards the smoldering pile
of metal with his chin. "All destroyed. The outpost looks like it
was gettin' expanded by the wolf, but we won't know for sure
what they were doin' unless we excavate the entire mess. Vickie
helped bury the bastards while supportin' us."

The Commissar kept her expression neutral. She muttered a
moment, probably talking with Victrix. That was borne out by Saviour's next words as she speared him with her eyes. "Have consulted
with Daughter of Rasputin; she concurs with your numbers and
your conclusions." She paused, looking around at the destruction.
"Satisfactory work. For a couple of *Amerikanski*." That was fairly
high praise coming from Saviour. "*Horosho*," she added.

Then she looked around again, mouth moving as if she was
counting. She frowned faintly. "Where is being Ural?" she asked
sharply.

John shrugged. "Couldn't tell y'exactly where, Commissar. It
was a chaotic fight..." It wasn't technically a lie; the Ural was
spread around a lot of ground, to be certain. She got a brief
"listening" look on her face. Victrix again? Gamayun?

"*Yebat' vashu mat'*," she said with resignation. "Nevermind.
Excoriation, paperwork, you know what to do. Help clean up
mess, then report to HQ."

"I presume we walk," said Sera, wearily. "Of course, I could rest
here and then fly, while you return." She shrugged, as if it were
a matter of indifference to her. "I presume one of the comrades
would carry you double."

It had taken them three hours of hard work before they were
done helping with the clean up and cataloguing efforts at the crime
scene. They were both grimy with ash and dirt, and there were
still after action reports and other assorted paperwork to fill out.

"Naw, let's walk. Give us a chance to go over things, hash 'em
out 'fore we get back to HQ."

Her brow creased. "Why would we need to? All should be
clear in your mind."

John barked an exasperated laugh. "It is! But would it kill ya to chat for a few minutes, or are y'that eager to fill out more forms in triplicate?"

She shrugged again. "I speak to Vickie's machine. It does that."

"Well, I don't wanna get back in any sort of hurry. Besides, I'm starvin'. Let's see what we can rustle up on the way back. Okay?" He didn't want to let on how much he *needed* to talk with her. If past performance was any indicator, he knew that she'd be tempted to bolt if he got too serious with her this early. Best to soften things up first, keep it light, focus on the professional stuff a bit.

She pulled her wings in tight. "As you wish," she replied, making it perfectly clear without saying anything that she really would rather have been alone. Every other time, he had been willing to let her get away with that. Not this time.

Goddamnit, this isn't going to be easy. Like much of anything with her has been, save for that fight. Hell with it.

"Stick around, let's get a bite and talk a bit. Take that as an order if'n y'like, for your own good."

She nodded solemnly. "As you will."

They walked for a good fifteen minutes; the large destruction corridor eventually gave way to "John's hood"; people were out and about, going on with their lives. Many of them waved at him; he'd been spending more time away from the barracks, interacting with the people that he was responsible for protecting. It was occasionally awkward, as he didn't remember some of them from "before," but for the most part everyone was understanding. Having all of these people recognize him, and be happy to see him, took some getting used to. But he enjoyed it. He had always liked helping people; he loved serving in the military, and though the quasi-law enforcement gig that working with the CCCP had turned into wasn't the same, it had certain parallels to his old life that satisfied him.

John figured enough time had passed that he ought to start in. "Hey Vix, switch off eyes and ears on Overwatch for me, okay? Keep the loc data going on, just need some quiet time. Roger that?"

"That's a Roger. I'll turn off Sera's headset. Since you don't remember it, the command you programmed in is Overwatch: override: eyes and ears off."

"Thanks for the update. All right, switchin' off." He spoke the command, and walked several more paces, thumbs hooked into his duty belt. "Helluva fight, wasn't it?"

"It was very taxing," Sera said, carefully. "You finally have pushed your abilities. You must continue to do so. They will become greater the more you push at the limits. The next time, you likely will not require my aid."

"I don't know 'bout that." He shrugged. "I understand always pushin' the envelope, keepin' sharp an' lookin' for an edge. But I've almost always worked with a team; y'can't be awake all the time, an' y'can't see everywhere at once. Havin' teammates pushes you further, an' multiplies your effectiveness. Besides," he said, grinning as he looked at her. "We seemed to work pretty damned well together back there. I mean, really well. Didn't y'notice that?"

She turned to finally look him in the face, her brilliant blue eyes puzzled. "I had not noticed..." she let her voice trail off. "I suppose we did."

"I've been through a lot of shit in my time, Sera. An' I've worked with the best of the best. That fight was somethin' else. I mean, we took out twelve armored suits an' a wolf, with nary a scratch on either of us. I can't think of many other folks that could've done that with just the pair of 'em, no support."

She looked for a moment as if she might say something, but the moment passed as a group of preschool kids caught sight of her from a playground made of wood and metal salvaged out of the destruction and swarmed her. For the first time, at least in John's memory, she brightened and stopped to give every single one of them a moment of attention; a hug at least, a whispered word, a soft kiss on the top of the head. It didn't take long, but when they ran off again to their improvised playground, they were all smiling.

She looked after them for a moment, then back at him. "I am sorry. I let them interrupt what you were saying...."

"No worries, none at all. That was sweet of you t'do. It seems you've got some fans 'round here yourself."

"They should have come to you. You were the one who planned the playground and did the metalwork." She sighed. "But of course, that was not *you*...was it?"

"I suppose it depends on how y'look at it, Sera. Am I better or worse than I was? Do I fight for the same things? Do I help people for the same reasons?" He sighed, looking down. "I don't really think it matters, s'far as that. These folks need us, as much as we need them. The little things, the troubling things that we deal with . . . we just gotta deal with 'em. Gettin' the job done is what's important. That's how I've always looked at it. When you're on the mission, that's what you focus on. Y'know?"

"Yes . . . the mission. And when the mission is done . . ." She shrugged. "I, too, am a creature of duty."

John knew better by now than to have much physical contact with her; even with his "orders," he figured that she would bolt if he even came close to touching her. So instead of playfully bumping her elbow or anything like that, he just stopped walking.

"Y'wanna know the secret, Sera?"

She gave him a peculiar, puzzled look. "The secret of what?"

"What we do. It's that it's never going to be over. There's always another mission, another job, another gig. More people to help, more people to save, somethin' else to fight for." He looked around at the neighborhood for several long moments, taking it all in. "An' y'know what? I wouldn't want it any other way. It's a good thing that we can always find somethin' in this world to fight for, somethin' that's worth it." He hooked a thumb back at the playground. "I guarantee you that for the rest of their lives, those kids'll remember you, for instance. An' they're not the only ones."

She didn't say anything; just thinned her lips a little, as if he had struck some kind of nerve.

Oh hell, did I just screw this up?

"Let's keep walkin'; it's good for thinkin', almost as good as cleanin' guns, drinkin' or sharpenin' knives."

He got moving; obediently, she fell in beside him. The sky had grown overcast while they had been policing up the site of the battle; now thunder growled in the far distance—not unlike the hunger rumbling in John's belly. "It will rain soon, I think," she said carefully. "We should make certain we are back at CCCP before it does."

They turned a corner, and there, as if in answer to both his hunger and his wish to have *some* way to get something out of the "angel" other than pain or flight, was a line of three food trucks.

Their arrival seemed to be the occasion for a little street party among the residents. Someone had brought out an old-fashioned, gigantic boombox—well, *old-fashioned* to people around him, he supposed; by his recollection, boomboxes were as common as smartphones were now. Though it had been an age since he'd seen a fully tricked-out ghetto-blaster like the one on display. People had dragged out folding chairs, and with a wary eye on the sky, were buying foil-wrapped packages, setting up little groups to gossip and laugh, or dancing to the music.

These weren't some of the really high-end food trucks, like he'd seen once or twice down by the ECHO campus. One was a taco truck, one featured Cuban pressed sandwiches, and one was a Vietnamese *bahn-mi* truck. But their prices must have been reasonable, since all three were doing a brisk business.

The cloud cover—and maybe a cooler front coming in ahead of the storm—had dropped the temperature down to something pleasant. And the smells coming from the three trucks were good enough to raise the dead. It took him a good twenty minutes to get to the trucks and actually get enough food for him and Sera, between people coming up to talk, slap him on the back, offer him drinks, or just to BS about the 'hood. When he was done, John had managed to get something from each of the trucks; they had all tried to refuse his money, but he had insisted and eventually had his way in the end. When he was walking back through the impromptu block party, he saw that Sera had been similarly mobbed. He stopped a moment to just watch.

It was the children, mostly, who were occupying her. She had dropped down to sit on her heels in order not to tower over them. She had her wings cupped around four, who seemed too shy to talk, but were happy to be under the shelter of those feathers. When he first spotted her, she was listening with the grave intensity of someone listening to an epic poem while a little boy narrated—something—at the top of his lungs and the rest nodded at appropriate parts. At first, John thought it was real, until the kid got to "—and then—the *dragon*—jumped down on top of the *car*—and we all *ran*—" and he realized it was something they had all been playing at. Finally the kid came to the end, and Sera applauded.

"That was a wonderful story!" she said, actually smiling. "And you all made it up together?"

"Uh-*huh!*" the little boy said, beaming.

"I think you should all get together and make a book out of it," she said firmly. "You can go to the study center in CCCP and tell it to Miss Vickie or Miss Thea, and one of them will help you. And when you are all done, she can make real books of it for all of you to take home."

"And now y'all can stop botherin' Miss Sera so's she kin eat," called one of the mothers firmly from the sidelines. "And you kids need t'eat too. Right now." Obediently, if reluctantly, the kids separated from Sera and piled onto a clean but ratty old blanket spread out half on the ground and half on the sidewalk, and tucked into the food that was waiting there for them.

John strode up to Sera, arms full of bags with food. "Got some vittles, now that your adoring fans have to have dinner themselves."

"I am sure you are hungry," she said carefully, sitting down on a handy piece of concrete that looked as if it had once been part of a road barrier.

John sat down next to her, a respectful distance away. He opened up the bags and started laying out the food between the two of them, plastic forks and napkins enough for both. "Got enough for both of us. Dig in, 'fore it gets cold."

John ate ravenously. With his metabolism, not to mention the exertions of the day, he felt like he was starving. Even before he had become what he was now, he had always been a hearty eater; working out, running, fighting and such meant you went through a lot of calories. Occasionally some of the people from the party would approach them, usually with small talk or thanks or the like, but for the most part folks let them alone with their meal. John dug the vibe; this was a community, where everyone supported everyone else. He normally hated cities, since everything was disconnected and spread out, or horribly crowded and piled on top of itself. But he was starting to take a real shine to Atlanta, or at least this part of it.

Sera nibbled cautiously at a *bahn-mi*, then bit into it with more enthusiasm. "This is very satisfying," she said. "Vickie and I usually drink meals. Or sometimes Bella or Mel bring things, but they are often cold."

"I ought t'have lil' Thea bring ya some of her cookin'. It's great, if only 'cause it's fillin' an' it keeps forever."

"I...do not often go into headquarters," she confessed. "Red Saviour does not approve of me."

"Heh. She don't much approve of anyone that ain't a 'sturdy

Russian.' Especially us sorts that keep on destroyin' Urals, I'm told. I wouldn't think on it much. I've met her type plenty; she's got a rock-hard exterior, but she cares for her people way more than she'll ever show. Just ain't her style." John devoured two tacos, chasing them with an imported beer. "Y'ought to come by the soup kitchen that we run, too. Thea does a lot of work there, an' the grub ain't bad, at least s'far as Russian stuff goes."

"I do not think any of the comrades approve of me," she said, carefully, between bites. "I am not what they want in their ranks. I am not—I do not think correctly." She finished the sandwich and blinked at the other packets. "What is this?" She carefully put a finger on a stuffed burrito.

"That, ma'am, is what is commonly known as a burrito. I call it 'wonderful hangover food.'"

She examined it doubtfully. "I do not have a hangover."

John almost spewed his current mouthful of food out; he didn't know why what she had said was so funny to him. Choking down the last gulp, he gasped out, "S'alright, it's not required to be hung over."

She picked up the plump, foil-wrapped package and unwrapped it, then took a tentative bite. Then a not-so-tentative bite. "This is very healthy. You surprise me. I expect you to eat things that are not. But you have chosen two things that are very healthy."

"Doesn't hurt that they taste friggin' great, especially after a day like the one we had. Honestly, I'll eat pretty much anythin' if it stays still too long." He paused for a moment, eyed a cat that crossed in front of them, then looked at her soberly. "Not literally."

That surprised a little laugh from her, and a fleeting, tentative smile.

They ate the rest of their food in contented silence. The block party continued around them, but they were able to slip away easily enough when they were finished. *She looks better, healthier and happier, now.* It was a happy coincidence that they'd found the block party—or rather that it had found them. Being there had certainly seemed to have done Sera some good.

John waited until they had been walking and digesting for awhile, well away from the noise of the party, before he spoke again. "There's somethin' I've been wantin' to talk to you 'bout, Sera. Something I've been dealin' with for awhile, but didn't know how to bring up."

"I do not know how I could help you, John Murdock," she said hesitantly. "I am ... not very good at being a person. You should ask Vickie if you need some sort of advice."

"It ain't like that. For one, I think you're doin' a damn sight better'n a lot of folks at being a person. If'n you need an example, I refer y'back to those kids. You're really good with them," he said with a grin. "Two, it ... well, it directly concerns you. I know this isn't goin' t'be easy for you to hear or deal with, but I need you to promise me you're not gonna fly off. Okay?"

She looked visibly disturbed. "If ... that is your wish. I will promise."

John sighed heavily, looking her in the eyes as they walked. "I know it ain't easy for you. Any of this, since ... well, you know." *She needs to know, goddamnit. Just get it over with.* "It hasn't been easy for me, either. It's not the same, an' I'm not tryin' to say that it is. But I need to talk with you 'bout this. You're the only one I figure has any sort of way of helpin' me to figure it out."

"But I am as blind as you," she protested. "I only know that you *must* keep pushing your limits. Each time that you do, your abilities will become stronger. I have no other advice than that. I am not what I was. I no longer have the resources I had." From relaxed and even a little happy, she had gone to tense and pained again. "You were better off to ask Vickie."

"No." He stopped again, turning towards her. *Spit it out already, Murdock.* "It's not somethin' in her lane, as it were. I've been hearin' music, Sera. Like, when there's no music playin' or anythin'."

She stopped in her tracks, and went absolutely white. "Singing?" she whispered.

John felt his body go cold and he felt excited at the same time. "Yeah, but ... it ain't like any sort of singin' I've ever heard before. It's more than singin'. It's ... I don't have the words, Sera." He looked around, as if he was trying to find them. "It's intense, always on the edge of things. But it picks up sometimes, I can hear it more clearly."

She closed her eyes for a moment, and went completely still. It was as if she was fighting something inside herself.

But when she opened her eyes again ... something had changed. He couldn't put his finger on what it was, but *something* had changed.

"Listen to me, John Murdock," she said, her voice charged with intensity. "You must listen for that music. It is very, very important to you. You are not going mad, nor . . . nor is it going to harm you. On the contrary, it will help you. The more you push yourself, the more you will hear it. The more you listen for it, the more you will hear it. Eventually it will always be with you, and you . . . you will *know* things. Without being told. Things that will be important, important for this great battle. Do you understand me?"

John took a long time responding. "I think I do. But, y'gotta understand somethin', Sera. I only hear it really strong durin' certain times—"

"Then you must listen for it during *all* times," she said interrupting him. "There is nothing more important. Not the CCCP, not your comrades, not *anything*. This music is the key for you, the key to everything. Without it . . . without it, you *will fail*. And if you fail—"

She shook her head.

"You must not fail," she said, flatly.

And at the moment, the storm, which had held off this long, broke over them. She reacted by spreading her wings and taking to the sky.

John sighed heavily. "I hate it when she does that. I hadn't even gotten to the most important part yet." He kept walking towards HQ, mulling over everything. He'd made some progress with Sera; incremental, with levels of frustration that equated to pulling a croc's teeth. But, still, progress. He knew that it wasn't enough; she was still in a bad place, and would stay there unless he did something. And it had to be him, didn't it? It started and ended with him, at least where she was concerned. He owed it to her.

Sera curled up in a ball of misery up in the rooftop "temple," and let the rain pound down on her. She had not allowed herself to weep much, but now she was alone, and . . .

Oh, so very alone. *Why?* Why was the voice of the Infinite taken from her, and given to *him*? Why was that one source of comfort denied her?

Yes, he needed it, of course, but why wasn't she allowed to hear it too?

Thunder rolled, drowning her sobs, as the rain drowned her tears.

CHAPTER FOURTEEN

Cover Girl

MERCEDES LACKEY AND VERONICA GIGUERE

There were times when Bella was convinced she was running two separate ECHOs; hers and Spin Doctor's.

Spin had ambushed her just before she managed to escape the office to head to the CCCP and a visit to the quantator to have another little circular-argument-fest with Marconi and Tesla . . . she wondered if being ensconced as "machine intelligences" for so long meant that they had an established subroutine they had to run, like obsessive-compulsives, before they could divert to anything useful. In this case, it was always the argument about why Metis couldn't be persuaded to offer any material help, only what Marconi and Tesla themselves could give surreptitiously.

"We need another sexy spread," Spin had said, without any buildup at all. Then again, he knew she was immune to whatever power it was—some form of projective empathy?—he employed, so as often as not he cut straight to the chase with her. "Harpers wants a story, same format as before, an interview with the Head of ECHO—that'd be you—and two double-page photos, one with the models in whatever passes for a uniform or armor or something, and one in—"

"Not bikinis," she said flatly. "Never again. I swear to God every time I take a shower I feel fanbois eyes all over me."

"Fine, it's *Harpers*, it doesn't have to be bikinis. Anything *not* a uniform and reasonably sexy—"

"And not just women," Bella interrupted again. "Mixed sexes. This isn't a calendar shoot, right? This time we show that ECHO includes everyone."

That had stopped him with his mouth open, and he closed it with an audible snap. "Not bad," he had said, finally. "Not bad. I can work with that. I'll ping you via Victrix when I get a lineup."

He had turned on his heel and left at his usual fast walk. *"Uh...I'd apologize for telling him where you were, but I think it's a good idea,"* Vickie had said in her ear. *"We need some red meat to throw to the masses. You know, 'ECHO is your friend, not just the people who sometimes wreck your neighborhood.'"*

Bella had just shaken her head.

So, now she was coming out of the quantator room with, yet again, no material help, but at least *some* useful information and a handful of schematics.

Ramona waited down the hallway, the plastic coffee carafe and ceramic mugs safe in her hands. She raised the carafe in greeting. "Little bird mentioned that you might need a cup and a chat. I'm ahead of my paperwork duty. Did you know you can request two-ply in triplicate?"

"I'd be happier if that was single-malt," Bella half-sighed, half-growled. Then she shook her head. "Stupid. Last thing I need to do is turn into a lush. Thanks, sweetie."

"Least I can do." Ramona poured both cups only full enough so they could walk and talk. "Someone needs to look out for your caffeine levels, especially after dealing with the Metis Odd Couple. I guess they still don't want to do more than sit on their non-existent hands and wait?"

"That was pretty much a sure bet." Bella downed about a third of the cup. "Oh, want to hear the latest brain-fart from Spin? He wants us to do another photoshoot and interview. This time for *Harpers*." She rolled her eyes and then...stopped right there in the hallway. "I'll be damned. I wonder if *he* thought of that?"

"If who thought of what?"

Bella eyed Ramona without replying, then stood back a couple of paces and eyed her some more. "I will be going to freaking hell," she said out loud. "It could work. It could just—"

"I think he thought what you're thinking, Boss," piped Vickie in her ear and in Ramona's. *"The lineup he just sent me included 'Ramona Ferrari aka Steel Maiden.'"*

Ramona pursed her lips at the meta moniker, her mouth twisted as she tried not to laugh. "Points to Spin for an original name, but last I checked, Ramona Ferrari is dead."

"Listen, hear me out. Verd's been the original Invisible Man since we outed him. Which is logical; he's good at strategy and you can't fight a million shadows when you don't know which one he's hiding in. We need to draw him out, but not in such a way that he's *sure* it's you, so he has to start poking at us to try and find a chink in our intelligence armor." Bella smiled a little. "So, Vix, what's the lineup?"

"He says the theme is 'glasnost.' The lineup is you, Bull, Yank, Southwind—that's the girl, if you're forgetting—on one side, and Saviour, Unter, Chug and Upyr on the other, with Ramona in the middle, taking the place you *used to have as the liaison."*

Bella shook her head. "Freaking brilliant. Two strong female leaders, their backups, a couple rankers, two of whom are pretty weird looking. All-inclusive. Though we are never going to make Chug look sexy."

"Chug is Chug," Ramona pointed out. "And you'll have a better chance for sexy from him than Natalya. But getting me out there is..." She stopped, searching for the right word. "Questionable?"

In answer, Bella grabbed her wrist and pulled her along the corridor until they reached the door of the female comrades' changing room. She shoved the door open and pulled Ramona along until they came to the room's sole foggy full-length mirror, a narrow strip of glass that Ramona was sure wouldn't reflect all of her zaftig bulk.

"Look," Bella demanded. *"Look!"*

Ramona looked. Reluctantly, but looked. She'd avoided mirrors since—well, since she woke up with metal instead of epidermis.

A stranger stared back at her. And the mirror reflected all of her.

Bella stood behind her, one hand, and one coffee cup, atop her shoulders. "Do you see Detective Ramona Ferrari there?"

"I..." Ramona nodded slowly, then shook her head back and forth.

"Hear me out. We'll get you some kind of honest-to-God armor, with a helmet. Plastic, of course, so you don't absorb it, but it will look like real metal. Something that shows only your eyes and a little bit of your face. That'll be for the first shot. The second shot—that'll be where we do something to bring up the metal epidermis on your face. Scare your skin by threatening it with a needle or something. We'll put you in a silver lamé catsuit. That, and that new body of yours, will leave enough doubt that Verd is going to *have* to check this out personally."

Ramona tilted her head to the side. "And we want Verd to come out to see what's going on."

Bella nodded. "He won't trust this to just anybody. It will be him or someone he trusts, someone close to him."

"So we're betting on Khanjar first, and maybe Verdigris to follow." Ramona mused. She studied the reflection with a critical eye. "This is going to require stiletto heels. And no cutouts on the catsuit, if we can help it?"

"We can put in the request, but the best I can promise is that you'll never have to actually fight in the catsuit. One of the many perks of nanoweave is that, unlike lycra, it can breathe." Bella came around and held out her mug for a refill. "Verd might be a top competitor for hide-and-seek, but we've stayed a few steps ahead. With this kind of news, he'll have to peek out and see what's going on."

Ramona topped off both cups and turned away from the mirror. "And Verd being Verd, he's not going to be content with just peeking out. Once he sees something, it'll consume him."

"Exactly."

Karma, payback, cosmic order, whatever it was called, it had the strangest sense of humor. Not terribly long ago, Ramona had stood next to Bella and worked her charm to convince the healer to pose for the first ECHO photoshoot. Bella had warmed to the idea out of necessity, as had the chosen representatives in CCCP. Now, the roles had reversed and Bella watched while Ramona tugged and tweaked her own custom outfit in preparation for the camera.

Under the right circumstances, Ramona thought, *this could be a lot of fun.* The ECHO tailors had carried out Bella's promise for the first outfit to the letter. The "armor" resembled scales, thin polymer plates the size and color of half-dollar coins attached to a modified nanoweave undersuit. Something not unlike an overbust corset in a lighter shade of gray provided shape and support, the color matching the pale stiletto boots that Ramona had predicted. The mask to cover her face had covered everything but her eyes and mouth, and the effect had worked on those who knew she was alive. Even Spin, who did not surprise easily, had appeared suitably impressed.

The second half of the photos involved the sleeker outfits. Ramona could hear Natalya grumbling on the other side of the curtain while Bella cajoled and reasoned. Southwind had actually liked her outfit; Bella had a modified version of her first blue and white one-piece. Rather than be on the side of the whiners, Ramona took a deep breath and began to swap out her "nine-to-five" look for her "after-five" look. There wasn't enough fabric for a pillowcase, let alone decency, but complaining wouldn't make things better.

Taking a deep breath, Ramona—*Steel Maiden*, she reminded herself—slipped out of the changing area to wait for the photographer. The pale silver one-piece squeezed the more squishable areas into place. Parts of the outfit had enormous slashes for cutouts to allow her skin to come through; a quick dusting of iron filings over the skin triggered the metal carapace to show through. On her face, Ramona had used the same powder across her eyebrows, cheeks, and the bridge of her nose. Combined with a touch of white makeup, the effect was almost alien.

"*Damn.*" Vickie's approval came immediately as Ramona surveyed herself in the mirror. "*Serving extra-terrestrial realness.*"

"What can I say, I try." She poked at the metal patch on her cheek to make sure it would stay. "Everyone else is ready?"

"Almost." Bella poked her head out of the changing room. "Everyone else get in place, please."

Ramona could easily hear Bella continuing to talk to the one holdout—Red Saviour. "Look," the healer finally said, "it's propaganda of the most visceral kind!"

"*Shto?*" Although Ramona couldn't see Saviour, she could hear the sudden interest in the Commissar's voice. "Keep talking, blue girl."

"It's propaganda on three levels," Bella said. "Men first, and you know what these outfits will appeal to."

"*Da.*" That came out as almost a growl. Bella cut her off.

"That's on purpose," Bella continued. "I'm hitting back both at the meatheads here in the US *and* at the ones in Russia. When they see us parading around like supermodels, what will they think? We're shallow. Mindless. We've caved in to decadent pop culture. *They'll dismiss us as irrelevant.* Which means while they are ignoring us, *we* can run circles around them and actually get things done, which we *couldn't* do if they were eyeballing us all the time."

"Huhn." There was a long pause. "I wonder if this will fool my father and Boryets..."

"You know them better than I do." Bella let that sink in a moment, then moved on. "Then, propaganda to the women. I know you know women in the West dress more to impress other women than they do to impress men. Well, these outfits tell other women that we are powerful."

"In *these* shoes?" Saviour burst out. But Bella interrupted her again.

"Yes! Because we are not afraid to wear things like this! That we can *kick ass* no matter what we wear! The first shoot tells women we mean business and we are both the bosses of our respective organizations. The *second* one tells them we are *still* the bosses and can wear whatever we feel like." She must have been getting through to Saviour, because Ramona could hear the note of triumph in her voice.

"And this third level of propaganda?" Saviour prompted.

"Ramona." Bella practically purred. "She's the liaison, and as the metal woman, she looks the part. Tough as a Russian, slick as an American, and fronting for both of us. That tells anyone, whether or not they actually read the article, that when they mess with one of us, they mess with *all* of us."

"Huhn," Saviour said again. "All right. For propaganda I can wear ridiculous outfit. *Davay!* I wish to be climbing out of boots as soon as possible."

When the two emerged, Ramona could see why Saviour objected. Her outfit was another catsuit—a cut-out version of the CCCP dress uniform—with thigh-high boots with higher and more ridiculous stiletto heels than even Ramona's outfit sported. In contrast, Upyr's gothic-lolita version of the CCCP uniform looked positively Victorian.

The two respective heads of the organization took their places. The photographer made some . . . suggestions, rather than giving orders. He was the one from the calendar shoot, so presumably he remembered how unwise it was to give Red Saviour anything that sounded like an order.

About half an hour later, the shoot was over, and Ramona headed for the locker room to peel herself out of her outfit. But she stopped dead, hearing Saviour accosting Bella in there.

"I know what you did, blue girl," Saviour said, in mingled tones of admiration and irritation.

"That I manipulated you? I won't apologize. You've done the

same." Bella sounded calm rather than defiant. "Don't try to claim I used empathic projection on you, though. Upyr will be the first one to—"

"*Psssh*. I know you did not. No, but you did manipulate me. And it worked. *This* time. You won't be so lucky again, unless I choose to let you." Ramona heard the Commissar's footsteps heading towards the door and skittered a bit down the hall, so as to make it look as if she was just now approaching and hadn't overheard that exchange. The door flew open, and Saviour stalked out. She spared a glance for Ramona, and a harsh chuckle escaped her. "You are lookink like sex-bot," she said, and continued on her way.

Ramona edged inside the locker room. Bella was fastening the last snap on her ECHO uniform, and glanced at her. "Huh. She's right. Which, for that shoot, was not a bad thing."

"I want my sneakers," Ramona replied, and sat down on the nearest bench. "So, now what?"

"Now we wait for three days until the story hits the website." Bella heaved a long sigh and rubbed her forehead. "I'm glad we won't have to wait for the print version. I don't think I could stand the tension for a month."

"And then?" Ramona asked.

"Then we see what shakes down out of the trees."

Khanjar's intimate knowledge of the office building that ECHO was using for its headquarters—gained when it had belonged to Verdigris—had been of immense use in avoiding the guards and the traps. The ventilation ducts had been wired up to a fare-thee-well when Dom had installed himself here, and she was fairly certain Bella Parker had had that augmented, but she had discovered there was enough room in the areas between the ceilings and the floors *outside* the ducts to move in. You just had to know what parts would support a human's weight, and she had explored the entire building until she knew that intimately and in the dark.

So when she dropped down softly behind Parker's chair, she was not expecting to be addressed calmly.

"You could have just used the door, you know." Parker swiveled the chair to face her, cradling a gun in one hand.

"But that would have been so ... *déclassé*," Khanjar replied. "I assume those are armor-piercing bullets in there?"

"A little more than that, but I'm hoping I won't have to use them." Bella nodded slightly to the side. "Do have a seat. I was hoping my ploy with Steel Maiden would give you an excuse to show."

Khanjar glided gracefully to the offered seating; it was one of her favored chaise lounges, and she appreciated the effort. She arranged herself on it as Bella swiveled the chair to follow her movement. "What gave me away?"

"Now you really don't expect me to tell you *that*, do you?" Bella asked, with a hint of throaty chuckle. "I will tell you that you should never, ever expect to be able to sneak up on an empath unless you're wearing a psi-damper the size of a filing cabinet."

"I'll keep that in mind in the future." Khanjar was beginning to enjoy this. It was refreshing to be treated as an equal. Insofar as she could "like" anyone, she was starting to like Belladonna Blue. And she didn't think it was the blue woman's projective empathy at work, either. "Well. Obviously you got my message."

Bella nodded. "Obviously. And I'm very interested in why you decided to turn on your boss." She leaned forward a bit, and her demeanor turned... purposeful. "It's not an idle question. Before I can even begin to consider trusting you, I need to know your reasons. And I will be weighing them for truth, believe me."

Khanjar had no doubt that at this point Belladonna Blue was a walking lie detector. The only way anything would get past her was if the person in question actually believed the lie being told. And for all her self-control... *I am not that good.* Khanjar was many things, but that was not one of them.

"I have several reasons. Some are very personal, and I would rather not go into them. The one that is important to you is that I am a believer in reincarnation and karma, and I have no intentions of being reborn as a goat. Or worse." Khanjar raised her chin and looked Belladonna straight in the eyes. "Dom is... engaged in a matter which, if I continue to be a willing party to, will be impossible to counter in this lifetime."

Belladonna's face went cold. "You've murdered for him; you have helped him with the Bombay debacle. What could be worse than that?"

"It involves meddling with the Celestial." She licked her lips. "It is not wise. It is not even remotely wise. He has allied himself with a Chinese... creature."

Bella's eyes narrowed. "People's Blade?"

"Not anymore," Khanjar corrected. "Whatever is inhabiting that body calls itself Shen Xue. It is not mortal. I am of two minds whether it is demonic. It is certainly far more ruthless even than Dom imagines. I researched the name; it belonged to a great Chinese general who engineered massacres without turning a hair." She shook her head. "In order to gain its will, it would not hesitate to put half the world in flames." Of course, that was only part of the truth, but it was still the truth. Khanjar was not yet certain she wanted to reveal Dom's obsession with the Deva. It would be a good card to hold for a while.

This seemed to satisfy Belladonna. "All right, I can see how that's a motivator." She raised her voice. "Vix? Bring the Mac-Guffin in."

One of the doors into a side office opened, and a tiny woman dressed in head-to-toe nanoweave entered. Even her hands were covered. Khanjar recognized her immediately, of course, and was a little surprised. Victoria Victrix Nagy was supposed to be a minor operative, allegedly a magician—Dom didn't believe in magic, of course—and of no great importance except as a friend to the new Head of ECHO.

It appeared the intelligence on her was wrong.

The tiny blonde was carrying a small, hardened case with her. She set it down on the corner of the desk nearest Khanjar. Khanjar could smell the fear on her, and yet she managed to move without showing it.

"This is where I explain what you're going to have to agree to, if this association continues," Victrix said, her voice trembling only a little. "I assume, unlike Verdigris, you believe in magic."

Khanjar nodded brusquely. Of course she believed in magic. There was the Deva, of course, and that monstrous thing Shen Xue. That Dom didn't believe was a weakness on his part.

"I integrate magic and tech," Victrix continued. "And if you are going to work with us, you will have to agree to be implanted with something I've come up with. It will work as an undetectable way to communicate with us. It will also work as a way for us to keep track of you."

Khanjar felt her eyebrows shooting up in surprise. This . . . was completely unexpected. She had anticipated some form of "wire," perhaps a communicator of some sort. But an implant?

"It's not just for our benefit," Victrix pointed out. "If you get into trouble, we can pinpoint you and have a good chance of extracting you even if you are unconscious." Her little chin firmed in an expression that was remarkably like Belladonna's. "Unlike Verdigris, we take care of our own, even when they become inconvenient."

"As Harmony became inconvenient to Dom?" Khanjar said, after a moment. She pondered. "You have a point. A very good point." She thought a little more, but really, what choice did she have? It was this, or . . .

Or be reborn as a toad. I think not.

"I accept," she said, and then spent a very interesting fifteen minutes as the little magician implanted a camera in her left eye, a microphone in the roof of her mouth and a speaker and a sound-pickup in her ear. It was remarkably painless, all but the part where the camera-thing crawled around to the optic nerve. And that wasn't painful, just uncomfortable and rather unnerving.

Then Victrix walked her through the activation procedure. Interestingly, she called the system "Kali." Khanjar found that amusing, appropriate and convenient. "You can't turn it off, of course," Victrix said, matter-of-factly. "All you can really do is alert me by saying 'Kali, listen' to the fact that there is something you want to say to us, or to have us overhear. The rest of the time it will be on constant record."

Khanjar just shrugged.

"Dom and I have not been sharing much for several weeks now," she said with indifference. "I cannot say this matters to me, since he has not been taking any other partners. He goes through stages like this, where he devotes every waking moment to his projects. I don't expect this to change until the Thulian matter has been decided once and for all."

"Diplomatically put," Bella said dryly. "All right then, consider the bargain made." She stood up and reached over the desk with her hand extended. A little surprised by the gesture, Khanjar took it and shook it. The empath's handshake was firm . . . and surprisingly strong. The handshake of a truly honest person, Khanjar reflected, amused. But she noticed that Belladonna did *not* release her hold on the pistol, though she transferred it to her left hand. Khanjar had no doubt that the empath was an equally good shot with either hand.

"Now for my errand," Khanjar said delicately.

"Well, you can say that you know that Steel Maiden is the liaison between ECHO and CCCP," Belladonna said, sitting back down. Victrix retreated to behind Parker's chair. "What else, Vix?"

"Projector: Steel Maiden," the little mage said, and a half-height holographic image of the lady in question sprang up on the desk. It rotated. "Quick, answer without thinking. Does that look like Ramona Ferrari?"

"No," Khanjar answered, as ordered.

"Good. Hold that a moment. Bells?"

The empath's eyes narrowed and Khanjar felt a strange tickling sensation inside her skull for just a moment. She felt her eyes widen and she sprang to her feet. "What did you do?" she cried in alarm, fumbling for a weapon she wasn't wearing.

"Nothing unethical, sit down." The tone was that of an order, and to her shock, Khanjar felt herself obeying. The ECHO head continued. "I just grew a neural connection for you. Your very first response to that question will be, from now on, 'No, Steel Maiden does not look like Ramona Ferrari.' Not the best psion or the best lie detector will get anything other than that out of you."

"But—is it?" Khanjar asked. She was both appalled that Belladonna would *do* that to her, and . . . oddly comforted.

Belladonna shrugged. "Look for yourself."

Khanjar examined the hologram closely. And, truly, the more she looked at it, the less it looked like the presumably dead detective. Still . . .

"I . . . cannot be sure," she admitted.

"Good. We want doubt planted in Verdigris's mind. 'No, it doesn't' and 'But I can't be sure,' in equal measure." Khanjar noted that Belladonna was caressing the gun in her hand a little. She doubted it was an unconscious gesture. "Now you can say you have seen her and investigated. That's what we want. You *and* us. The more distractions he has, the better it is for our side."

Khanjar nodded. *The day that Dom made an enemy out of this woman was a very bad day for him, and he doesn't even realize it.* The thought made her oddly satisfied.

"Now, is there anything more we can do for you?" Belladonna said when Khanjar had been silent for several moments.

"This has been very satisfactory," Khanjar said, getting to her feet again. "Even if we are—what is the Western saying?—strange bedfellows."

"If we all survive this, I hope you'll consider coming over to us permanently," Parker replied, also getting to her feet. "ECHO could use someone of your talents. I can promise you there would be a vast improvement in your karmic balance."

Khanjar considered that for a moment. "I suspect my karmic balance may be in need of that," she said, thoughtfully. "I'll consider the offer, certainly." *If my bank balance is sufficiently weighted... it might be well to do just that.*

As the little magician cleared out of the way, Khanjar jumped and caught the edge of the ceiling panel, and pulled herself back up inside. Best to leave the way she had come in.

The last she saw of the two ECHO ops was of them watching her thoughtfully from below as she closed the panel again.

But that was not quite the last she heard from them.

"And remember. Kali is always watching," said a voice in her ear. *"Always."*

CHAPTER FIFTEEN

Eskimo

MERCEDES LACKEY AND VERONICA GIGUERE

The recent conversation with Sera had given Ramona Ferrari a lot to consider during her days at the CCCP headquarters. She spent much of her time doing paperwork, filling out forms stamped with the stylized hammer and sickle. Although she had felt odd writing requests in triplicate with the portrait of Marx scowling at her, Ramona had settled into a bit of a rhythm, managing Red Saviour's requests with a monotone *"Da, Commissar"* that walked the line between boredom and disrespect. The severe woman didn't argue with the detective's efficiency, and Ramona didn't argue with Natalya's demands for office supplies.

The Commissar didn't scare Ramona, which was something in and of itself. Most of the non-CCCP metahumans who encountered Natalya gave her plenty of space and didn't attempt to argue with her. Ramona had no problem pointing out the mistakes and fallacies in Natalya's arguments, but she did have the decency to do it when they were in the presence of a select few. Soviette and Bella were those select few, and Ramona had realized that Bella savored those moments where one of them could go toe-to-toe with Red Saviour.

At the moment, Bella stood with her arms folded across her chest, her blue lips pressed in a thin smile while Soviette held a hand to her own forehead in frustration. For her part, Ramona maintained a calm expression and tone as Red Saviour shook the upper half of a nanoweave suit inches from her face.

"This is CCCP standard uniform! This will go under the black and red if you are to be engaging in combat, and as you are no longer on medical leave, you will be engaging in combat exercises!" Red Saviour pointed a finger at Soviette. "She says you are no longer in infirmary. If you are not infirm, you will engage in duties other than paperwork!"

"Commissar, I'm not wearing that nanoweave. It's not an option," Ramona began for the sixth time. "My current physiology won't let me."

"You are no bigger than Chug, and we have standard uniform for him! Is not to be a fashion show on streets of Atlanta!" Red Saviour fumed and narrowed her eyes. "Is not ECHO and pin-up calendar time!"

Bella smothered a laugh. The noise prompted Saviour to fix her with a murderous glare, which only caused Bella to laugh even harder. A quick glance to Soviette told Ramona that she had gone from being frustrated to amused, the corners of her eyes crinkling even as tears streamed down Bella's face.

"Does this amuse you, blue girl? Is the demand for CCCP uniform and safety some kind of joke to ECHO now?" Red Saviour offered her own fierce wolfish grin in warning. "You find me funny?"

"Hysterical," Bella choked out. "Nat, this isn't about your uniform. This is about safety and support." The blue meta made a visible effort to restrain herself. "Bear will never be able to take his eyes off her boobs. You *really* want him drooling and shooting randomly in combat?"

Ramona had managed to keep a straight face in spite of the laughter. She cleared her throat and brought up both hands to gesture to her chest. "What Bella and Sovie are trying to tell you is that the nanoweave also isn't going to provide adequate combat support for someone of my proportions. The three of you don't have to contend with gravity in quite the same way that I do."

Natalya opened her mouth as if to argue again, but she stopped as Ramona continued to hold her hands level with her chest. "I need more than nanoweave or spandex up top, Commissar. Something that can provide protection without any metal alloy. Otherwise, that's going to disappear pretty quickly." In the weeks following her "death" and recuperation, Ramona had learned that any unprotected metal or metal covered with a layer of anything thin, like paint, could be absorbed into her skin. She had taken to wearing gloves while doing paperwork to ensure that staples didn't disappear. "Without that, I can't go on patrol."

Bella nodded in agreement. "She's right. Dolly's got it worse in the top-heavy department, but at least her skin won't eat her under-wires. If you want her out with the rest of the comrades, she'll have to wear something better than standard-issue CCCP." She studied Ramona's figure for a moment, her blue lips pursed in thought. "Something natural, maybe we could infuse it with nanoweave for structure. Kind of like a nanoweave mesh in between two layers. If we compact it enough, it could act like metal."

"Da. Would need a lot of support," Soviette offered. She stepped closer to Ramona and pulled at the baggy coveralls. "Here and here, especially in high combat situations."

Natalya scowled. "Mutation is metal, da? Why can you not to be making these supports on your own?"

Ramona scowled back at the Commissar. "It's not that simple. I'm still trying to figure out what to do. I haven't gotten to metal bikini level yet. And even if I do, is patrol really the best option? Is that all we're going to do, wait until the next wave of spheres and Kriegers descends upon the city? Sit and wait to react?"

"Is something better to do? You and blue girl are planning attack on metal alien *svinyas* over talks of fashion?" Natalya sniffed and crossed her arms. "More attack, less fashion. Keep talking."

The veiled bit of support from the Commissar was encouraging, and Ramona focused on Bella as she continued. "I'm serious. There's been some progress made in figuring out what they are, who's controlling them, how they attack, but we still don't have any more help. We're still no closer to getting the Metisians to help us."

Bella considered this and nodded. "They're a true democracy. They have to have the real majority in order to support us, but even then, we can't be sure of the kind of support."

Ramona pursed her lips thoughtfully. In any organization, strong lines of communication maintained some semblance of order when everything else crumbled. Leaders could change and locations could shift, but as long as someone kept the path of communication open and informative, life went on. It was why Overwatch was the backbone of the real ECHO and how they had managed to retain so much during the loss of Alex Tesla and the rise and fall of Dominic Verdigris. Everyone on the ground remained informed to some extent; some knew more than others, but the lines of communication stayed open and people knew the names and voices they could trust for the truth.

Because they hadn't been able to trust the Metisians, the leaders of ECHO had kept them out of the loop. They kept the talking heads informed, but Ramona knew that Tesla and even Marconi filtered the news that they passed to their caretakers and allies in the alien city. To make sure that Metis knew the whole story and what was at stake, they had to hear it from those who were in the thick of the fight and who understood the real odds against the Thulians.

"Eskimos," Ramona muttered, tapping her forefinger against her lower lip.

Bella caught both the word and gesture, and both eyebrows shot upward in surprise. "The iciest," she agreed in a heartbeat, "but I don't think we're there yet. We've got other options to speak with the Metisians. That's why we have the quantator and the blue heads and even Mercurye."

"And none of them really understand the scope of what's going on down here. Sure, Mercurye has seen the Kriegers and Death Spheres, but how long has he been stuck up there? How much news are they getting that isn't filtered through Tesla and Marconi?" Ramona glanced from Bella to the Commissar and Soviette. "Who else goes into that room to speak with them besides me on a semi-regular basis?"

Red Saviour wrinkled her nose at the question. "Is not more important than patrols and support of other initiatives. I have no desire to sit for tea and conversation with scared old men."

Ramona couldn't help but beam at the words. "Exactly," she said, triumphant. "It's a conversation with scared old men. They're adorable, they're smart, but they're lousy ambassadors for what needs to be done. They can't speak for you, Bella. They're not going to have the best interests of ECHO in mind when they present our case."

"They don't get it," Bella said, nodding slowly. "They can't. They've lost that human element, and they're terrified of mortality. Honestly, it makes me wonder if that isn't the main problem. They've had a good long taste of immortality and they are afraid to lose it."

"Exactly. We can only trust them so much, because they're not going to argue for something that could threaten their existence." The former detective flashed a wolfish grin that prompted the Commissar to snort in surprise. "Whereas I've already faced my end and come back with some interesting abilities. I'm fully invested in the cause, I know that we need real help, and I'm not afraid to go into whatever passes for their boardroom and make the case."

Bella had nodded throughout Ramona's little speech, her lips twisting in concentration while her eyes focused on the far wall. From the way the corner of her mouth twitched, Ramona wondered if Vickie was weighing in on the conversation from Overwatch. She glanced to the Commissar and found Natalya grinning back at her in what appeared to be enthusiastic approval. Soviette's expression wasn't as harsh, but she allowed a small nod of solidarity as Bella continued her private conversation with herself and whoever chimed in via her comm.

"You can't afford to send anyone else," Ramona added. "You need everyone else in the core group; Pride still needs to be your face, Bull needs to be right there in the mix, and I think we can all agree that the Djinni should not be allowed in any kind of public relations capacity. For all intents and purposes, I'm dead. No one's expecting me to show up anywhere. Steel Maiden doesn't need to be seen again now that I've made my appearance, and I can actually play bait a lot better if I am nowhere to be found."

"Maybe, but the question is, how do you get to Metis? We can't get you there," Bella pointed out.

Ramona drew a deep breath. "But if I find a way? If I buy my own ticket, so to speak, do I have your approval to speak on ECHO's behalf to get the Metisians in our corner and willing to help us?"

Bella glanced to Natalya. "You think she should go, don't you?"

"It would pain me to lose such efficient paperwork girl, but others will replace." The Commissar's eyes lit up in delight. "Would send this one to negotiate with Moscow, but Moscow would crumble too easily."

"Wow." High praise from Natalya was rare, and Bella didn't hide her surprise. "That settles it, then. You find a way, you can go, but you tell me first, you got it?"

Ramona bobbed her head in agreement. "Got it. Give me half a day and I'll know for sure. In the meantime, can we figure out a better clothing solution? If I'm going to head into the thick of battle, I'm going to need a real solution that won't be more than a cloth sausage casing, y'know?"

"Oh, I've got ideas." Bella's expression demonstrated her own wolflike grin, a testament to just how much the Commissar had rubbed off on the young metahuman leader. She grabbed one of the nanoweave suits and headed for the office door. "Sergei & Carson aren't officially part of ECHO, but they do a lot of custom solutions. I'll see what they can pull together for you." She left the room, chuckling to herself the entire way.

"You go nowhere until you eat." Soviette wagged a delicate finger at her patient and kept her voice stern. "You are getting too skinny, and you need to support your new metabolism. If you are wanting to speak with anyone else, you will eat first, *da?*"

"And if you are not to be choosing wisely, will send Pavel to share his canned ravioli and stories of Great Patriotic War." Natalya's smile was full of teeth and fierce delight. She rubbed her hands together. "Or will make you both share Waffle House."

Ramona crept through the hallway of the CCCP headquarters on her way to the room that held the quantator. She had made herself a pair of peanut butter sandwiches in the hope that would satisfy Soviette's requirement for eating, but the stern doctor had declared it a 'snack' and made Ramona promise to eat more later. That was...a big change from the life she had once led. But pictures didn't lie, and those pictures of Steel Maiden on the Harper's website had proven beyond a doubt that the "new" Ramona Ferrari was not going to have worry about weight ever again. Or—at least, not weight in the sense that normals thought about it. She had a different sort of "weight problem" now, one she shared with Bulwark. With plate in hand, Ramona approached the lounge that held the ancient television that Soviet Bear commandeered for much of the time when he didn't patrol. The theme from *Golden Girls* blared. Ramona heard a dirty chuckle, followed by a wolf whistle that ended in a rusty cough. She did her best to creep down the hallway, but her footsteps fell heavy and she heard the thick voice call from the other room.

"Is Bea Arthur! Best pin-up! Come, see!" He laughed but didn't get up. Ramona held her breath and waited for him to say something more. When she heard another cough, she continued down the hallway toward the closet that held the quantator.

Vickie's magic had locked the closet for most of the CCCP, but it still allowed Ramona to enter and pull up a chair in front of the desk. She froze as the chair creaked under her heavier frame.

She had already endured the embarrassment of a broken bed frame as well as bent doorknobs and cracked doorjambs. Having the chair break mid-conversation with Mercurye would be a level of mortifying she hadn't encountered since middle school.

Ramona felt her stomach twist and knot. She recognized it as hunger and attacked the first sandwich. Her metabolism had accelerated since the accident, requiring her to eat every three hours. She had asked Soviette if she could manage an IV, but Ramona's skin would not allow a needle to pass through the first layers. Both the Russian doctor and Bella had warned her that a metahuman metabolism required more calories, and that she needed to eat to heal from the accident.

"Paging Mr. Tesla," she said around a mouthful of sandwich. "Mr. Tesla, you're wanted in the lobby. Paging Mr. Tesla."

The blue electric field hummed around the slender antennae that extended from the desk. The image shuddered and flickered to show a different but equally familiar wireframe face. Mr. Marconi's expression registered nothing short of surprise when he recognized Ramona sitting at the desk.

"Signorina Ferrari? The reports, we received much of the information that was transmitted on the regular channels. The official reports all said that you were dead!" Marconi's eyes narrowed as he appeared to inspect her from head to toe. "But you are just too skinny. This is not good, Signorina."

"I'm supposed to be dead, sir," Ramona chirped. She chose to ignore the skinny comment. "Ramona Ferrari *is* dead, thanks to Dominic Verdigris and his flunkies. It's been an interesting experience, and I've not been able to talk with you and Mr. Tesla until now."

"You should not be concerned with the feelings of two old men. Your beau has been beside himself with the news." Marconi scowled at her. "And you wait until now to make this known?"

Ramona scowled back. "Security. Trust me, I nearly died. I'm not lying about that part, and we lost plenty of others. And that was just Dominic Verdigris trying to thin out the people he suspected of being malcontents. Attacks are happening on a more regular basis, Thulian attacks that are becoming more strategic. We've been a little busy, sir."

Marconi pursed his lips and studied her while she bit off a corner of her sandwich. "Well, you are quite alive, dear lady. The rest of this can be discussed later, after I reassure Nicola that you have not gone the way of his nephew. I have the feeling he will be as displeased with this charade as I am. For now, though..."

The image faded and the blue field shifted to show the little white room where the Metisians kept Mercurye.

"So, I wake up with the Russians and Parker staring at me like I'm at the bottom of a petri dish, and my tongue feels like someone's coated it with the stuff they use for dental fillings. Whatever she did to bring me back from the edge meant that she had to activate some meta-gene, and mine decided to go all heavy metal." Ramona sat back and offered a half-smile to the image in the quantator. Mercurye stared back, eyes red-rimmed without actually crying and an expression of utter disbelief on his face for most of her retelling. "It's got some interesting combat abilities, although I'm not completely cleared for active duty. They've already given me a callsign though. Steel Maiden."

Mercurye passed a hand over his face and looked away from the screen. He hadn't said much beyond a few half-sentences and a string of sailor-worthy swearing at the mention of Verdigris, and Ramona's story had seemed to drain the rest of the anger from him. He dropped his chin to his chest and heaved a huge sigh. "So you're alive, but since you're meta, they're going to put you on active patrol. I guess that makes sense, but how much training are you going to get?"

That question wasn't one that Ramona expected. She frowned at him. "Training? I went through years of training as an ECHO detective, Rick. I didn't spend a decade as a glorified paper-pusher while Alex was running things. I probably went through more firearms training than you did, come to think of it."

"Training to manage the mutation," he corrected, still not looking at her. "Training to make it work for you in combat, training so it doesn't control you when you don't want it to. And the psych evaluations..."

"Have already been done by two doctors," she finished. Ramona hadn't expected this sullen form of coddling, but she couldn't fault him for being angry. They had purposely kept the Metisians in the dark about the survivors of the accident, just in case those communications had somehow been compromised. "Look, I'm sorry you're upset..."

"Upset?" He whipped around to glare at her. "Upset doesn't even begin to describe it. I'm stuck here, unable to do anything but listen to those two argue about how the Metisians won't make a decision. When they heard about what happened at Five Corners, they kept putting things to votes! Votes!" Rick's voice echoed off the walls, exasperation in his words. "They're still voting!"

"Even your spaceship friends?"

He stopped and stared at her. "Who?"

"The pilots of that spaceship. You said they came to see you every so often. Purple hair, kind of grabby. One of them watched *Next Generation* because she had a crush on Riker?" Ramona saw him start to smile, finally. "Yeah, them. So they come over to watch TV with you?"

"Well, yeah. Trina mostly. She's nice enough," he said. "Why?"

Ramona took a deep breath. "What does she think of this whole voting thing?"

Rick snorted at the question. "She's one of the ones trying to convince them to send more help and get involved. They actually saw what happened down here, and they know that we need more help. There's more technology up here that she thinks could be shared without too many repercussions, but..."

"But," Ramona prompted. "What's the catch?"

"Prime directive," he answered. "That's half the argument."

She sat back and stared at the fuzzy blue outline surrounding the clear image. "You're kidding me. That's just... you're kidding me, right?"

"I wish. They call it something else and they have a bunch of other arguments about interference and influence, but a lot of the argument comes down to that. Influencing a 'lesser' species and civilization can be reason enough to not aid them in a time of war." Ramona started to open her mouth, but Rick must have seen it and rushed ahead. "Plenty of people here see that the war could come to them, but not enough believe that argument."

"Well, we'll just have to make them believe. Violate the Prime Directive first, as it were." She did her best Red Saviour grin; it had the desired effect as Rick leaned back from the screen with an uneasy smile. "You think Trina would be willing to pick me up sometime soon? Smuggle me up there?"

His eyes widened. "You... really? You're going to come here and talk to them?"

"You get me a ride, and I'll be there on behalf of ECHO. I talked Tesla into a magic solution," she answered with a hint of pride. "And if not, maybe I can at least get you home."

He let out a huge sigh, his shoulders sagging with the motion. "Home. Home would be amazing. Home would be color and sunlight and seasons and a chili cheese burger at the Varsity."

"With a frosted orange," Ramona teased.

"Chocolate shake."

"Chocolate shake, then." She ran both hands through her hair and leaned back. Eyes closed, Ramona thought through the plan out loud. "So, you talk to your contact and see what she can do about getting me a ride from here to there. Bella's given me permission to negotiate on her behalf, but we have to figure out what I can say that will get the Metisians to pull their enlightened heads out of their equally enlightened asses."

"Do the Thulians know that Metis has been sponsoring ECHO? All the technology and intelligence," Rick offered. "They have to know about the transport that got me here, and they have to wonder about where the body of their buddy Eisenfaust went."

Ramona pursed her lips. Did the Thulians have the intelligence to put two and two together? That hair-raising escapade at the diner had proven that they could track specific individuals, and they had been gunning for Alex Tesla. They hadn't managed to track the quantator, and Ramona suspected that they didn't know about that communication device. Given the history between the Thulians and the metas that had returned from the times of Nazi Germany, she figured that there must be some shared knowledge about the early days of ECHO and its founders. "If Metis is still ahead, they're not that far ahead," she said. "They won't be able to stay ahead if the Thulians keep picking at the defenses down here. Sooner or later, they're going to seek out better targets, and that's going to include Metis."

The figure on the other side of the quantator shook his head. "We've tried the defense strategy, remember? They don't think it's bad enough to get involved."

"But they think it's bad enough to indefinitely detain a metahuman who managed to accompany a body on an alien transport ship?" Ramona narrowed her eyes. "Did they ever give you a reason as to why you had to stay up there, or were they just looking for eye candy?"

Rick's cheeks flushed pink; whether it was from anger or embarrassment, Ramona couldn't tell. "I . . . well, no. No, they didn't, other than it was safer and that they couldn't let me go until they made a decision as to what to do with me."

"Sounds a like a bullshit answer to me," she snorted. "I think I can do better. You figure out a way to talk to your contacts there, see if they're up for a trip. I'll be back tomorrow to iron out the details. In the meantime, I need to get fitted for a suit."

"A suit?" For the first time, Rick seemed to study her more closely. "Because you went meta? But they can size nanoweave pretty easily. It's just the color you can't change."

"It's a long story. I'll tell you when I get there." Ramona winked at him and leaned forward. "Same time tomorrow. Don't let anyone talk you out of it, okay?"

"Like they could."

The next thirty-six hours went by in a blur of hurried subterfuge. Bella had returned to the CCCP headquarters with a fastidious Ukrainian gentleman dressed in a suit that he declared was aubergine when Ramona had tried to compliment the purple hue. Bella had introduced him as ECHO's personal tailor, a metahuman who made threads "speak" to each other much the same way she did with cells and neurochemicals. The three of them had taken over one of the offices as a fitting room for the evening. In less than six hours, Sergei had finished a silicone-reinforced version of the nanoweave suit, complete with a corset-like piece—the silicone reinforcement—that hugged Ramona's torso and provided both protection and support. He had declared it finished before asking Bella for a name.

"A name?" Bella eyed Ramona cautiously. "We're, uh, still working on that part."

"Steel Maiden," Ramona quipped dryly, flashing both hands with forefingers and pinkies extended. "I like the one Spin gave me, so let's keep it. So metal, dude!"

Bella had dissolved into a fit of giggles at that, but it satisfied Sergei and he jotted the name in a small notebook that he tucked into his jacket. He slipped out of the office, leaving the two women to discuss the final stage of the plan. Ramona waited until she heard the doors open and shut in the hallway before tugging on the sleeves and the underbust. She hadn't thought it

was possible to feel both completely covered yet exposed at the same time, but skintight silicone-nanoweave somehow made that possible. "Now that I've got an appropriate travel wardrobe, it's time to travel. I guess we should make the call, huh?"

Vickie chirped a reply. *"They're hee-eere. It's not the right time of year for reindeer, but it's something on the roof. Something big."*

Ramona and Bella shared a look of surprise. "I didn't think they'd show up that quickly. When I talked to Rick earlier today, he had said he was going to bring it up."

"Guess it was brought up, approved, and put into motion." Bella tilted her head toward the stairwell. "You got your toothbrush?"

"No. I'll pick one up when I get there." The two women climbed the back stairs to the roof, Ramona feeling the hairs on the back of her neck standing straight up as they pushed open the access door. The stars high above Atlanta shone bright, with the exception of a large blob of black that hummed and vibrated dangerously close to the rooftop. Ramona clutched at Bella's forearm as blue lines reminiscent of the quantator crisscrossed the sky.

"Jebus Cluny ..."

"Grown-up swear words, ma'am. This one rates at least a 'holy shit,' don't you think?" Ramona swallowed hard and watched the thin column of light pool on the rooftop. A ramp snaked through the light to grip the gravel-covered surface. "Victrix, are you sure you'll be able to keep an eye on me?"

"Magic's magic, across the street or halfway across the universe." Of the three of them, the technomancer's voice held the most calm.

A lone figure descended the spiraling ramp at a jog, dark purple hair swinging in a perfect chin bob. It stopped a few steps from the rooftop and waved frantically at the two women. "Well? One of you has to be Ramona Ferrari, because anyone else would be screaming. Please come aboard so we can close the aperture and depart!"

Bella nudged Ramona with her elbow. "That's your cue."

"Sounds like it." Ramona released the thin blue arm and exhaled slowly. "Here goes everything." She rolled her shoulders back and crossed to the light-filled staircase. As she stepped on the ramp, Ramona felt her entire body hum and resonate, and she realized that the translucent surface beneath her feet was bringing her up to the purple-haired figure. For a brief moment, she considered leaping back to the ground and asking Bella to find someone else to speak to Metis. By the time she realized that her new abilities would help her body accommodate the shock, Ramona stood face to face with the smiling Metisian pilot.

"Oh, brilliant. You managed to come up here the first time. Mercurye said that you wouldn't hesitate, but I admit that I had my doubts." The pilot beamed at her, showing perfectly straight teeth in a smile out of a chewing-gum commercial. "It's so delightful to be proven wrong. Are you ready to go?"

The whirlwind commentary and unfailingly polite address caught Ramona off guard. She bobbed her head in agreement, unable to find words to reply. The smile was so...bright. "Brilliant," the pilot repeated. "Have a seat. I can't wait to see his face when you finally arrive."

Ramona couldn't decide if the trip to Metis involved legitimate dimensional travel or if this genius race could break a half-dozen rules regarding the space-time continuum and just apologize afterward. She arrived at the hangar in Metis, only to be hurried down a long, white hallway and through a thin gelatinous barrier that clung to her skin. The pilot abandoned her just before the barrier, offering only a whispered "good luck" and a shove through the blue field. Ramona gasped at the alien sensation and gagged as her skin rejected the unwelcome coating by creating a thin shell of its own. The blue goo slid to the floor and she brought her hands up to her face to clear her vision.

The room, Ramona realized, was dark. She couldn't make out any walls or a ceiling, and the veil of blue disappeared in a electric zip that left the tang of ozone in its wake. Left in this expanse, Ramona wondered if she should expect the floor to give way and give her the opportunity to float. She tested the floor with one foot. The tap seemed solid enough. She tried with the other foot, and the entire floor hummed in response.

"Well, shit." The vibrations carried into her teeth. "Should have stayed still."

The vibrations intensified, the air around Ramona humming with energy. She blinked up to see tiny blue lines filling the space beneath what she hoped was the ceiling. The outline contained more and more details with each second, until Ramona realized that she stared straight into the larger-than-life-sized countenance of Marconi.

It grinned at her. Ramona was thankful for that much; she wasn't sure if she would have contained her bladder if the huge face had demonstrated anything but approval. She chanced a smile in return. *"Buon giorno, Signore Marconi.* I must say, you're a bit taller in person."

The wireframe laughed, a somewhat terrifying sight in the otherwise empty space. "Indeed, Ms. Ferrari. This is a surprise, although I should have expected it. Nicola, he will be surprised as well." The room hummed a second time, and Ramona was only slightly less surprised to find a second, more severe image hovering over the floor in blue wireframe. Unlike Marconi, Tesla did not appear amused at her presence.

"I see that you have found a way to leave the Russians," Tesla remarked, his tone dry and his words clipped. "You secured your own transport here?"

"I make friends easily." Ramona shrugged nonchalantly. "It's a gift."

"One of several, it seems." Marconi squinted, leaning uncomfortably close to her arm. "This is amazing. Nicola, did you notice—"

"Of course I noticed," Tesla snapped. "The manifestation of the meta ability is not easily ignored, especially in a case like this." The head swiveled to eye Ramona. "And this was a function of your accident? The events occurring after the unlocking of the charter?"

"Yes." Her voice did not waver. "The healer triggered the healing response, but the rest happened by accident when she took the chance that something else might get triggered as well. If she hadn't, I wouldn't be standing here."

The massive head spluttered, a terrifying display as the azure outlines buzzed and shifted. "The healer? ECHO has no healers able to function at the subcellular level, young lady. Not possible. Perhaps you are attributing the change to something else, given your limited exposure to—"

Ramona bristled at the condescending address and tone. Without stopping to consider protocol or politeness, she shook a metal-swathed finger at Tesla's enormous nose. "First of all, getting my own custom subcutaneous armor ability didn't take away my rank within the organization, so this 'young lady' nonsense can go the way of the dodo. It's 'Detective' or 'Ms. Ferrari' if you're going to pull that holier-than-thou bullshit with me. And second, you should stop presuming that you know everything about everyone in the organization, especially when it comes to Parker. If it weren't for her leadership and decisions, you'd probably be an app on Verd's phone by now. So how about you offer the little earthlings a bit of respect?" She paused to breathe and dropped her hand to her side. "Sir."

Marconi chuckled softly. "Amazing," he repeated.

Tesla drew his lips together tightly; if he had had hands, Ramona imagined that he would have pinched the bridge of his massive nose. "Detective."

"Thank you."

"The ability to deliberately engage the meta factor is not one that has been observed within other metahumans since the manifestations triggered by the Thulians." Tesla's eyes darted to Marconi. The other head offered a barely perceptible nod as if to agree with the line of explanation. "The surge of metahumans in the last century can be attributed to interference by the Thulians, not by Metis. The Metisians have devoted much of their time to studying the effects of the meta-factor manifestation and, when agreed upon by the populace, supporting those metahumans willing to counter the Thulians with technology and innovation."

Ramona couldn't have heard the last few sentences correctly. She shook her head, convinced that the odd journey from rooftop to conversation hangar had messed up her listening skills. "I'm not following. It sounds like you're saying that metahumans are a mistake caused by the Thulians screwing around with the human genome, and that they're able to willfully turn that gene on and off."

Marconi hummed, a base tone soon matched by overlaying harmonics. It made the exposed metal on her skin tingle. "Not a mistake, Signorina Ferrari. We have studied the Thulians for quite some time, and they engage in a purposeful sort of experimentation."

Ramona's mouth twisted in disgust. "Experimentation. I guess I should have expected that, given who they backed in the thirties and forties." She turned away from the two wireframes, her hands in her hair as she stared out into the darkness of the cavernous room.

"Perhaps, but they have perfected the ability to engage the metahuman factor. But once the initial wave was over, we believe that the genie, as they say, was out of the bottle. They could not control who they awakened or the expression of the metahuman talents." Tesla's crisp words cut through the air, clinical and cold. "And yet, we continue to see metahumans thrive."

Anger fought past confusion and Ramona shook while trying to control her voice. "So, what you're saying is that Metis has known about the Thulians since before the Invasion. They have known about metahumans and how metahumans came to exist, and they have known that the Thulians were involved." She ground her teeth together and pivoted on one heel. "And you're treating this like a fucking terrarium with a couple billion crickets and a few hungry lizards."

The two heads flinched at her use of language. Had Ramona not been so utterly enraged, she might have found the reaction funny. Instead, she saw an opening and moved in for the attack. "Has this all been some kind of joke, then? You both sit up here like a bunch of cranky assholes in the balcony of the theater and just offer commentary while everyone else in Metis watches like it's some kind of cutthroat reality show?"

Tesla opened his mouth, but Ramona rushed on. "You'd rather sit up here and watch your legacy go down the toilet because observation is good science? Really? Alex died because you wanted some more observations? Wow," she offered with thick sarcasm. "And here I thought all of my friends and coworkers got buried under a couple hundred tons of concrete on the ECHO campus because of some extraterrestrial threat. Now that I know it's for Metisian science, I feel so much better."

"Signorina Detective—"

"Shut up!" Her words did not ring in the dark, but both wire-frames ceased in their mumbling protest.

Marconi and Tesla were not her enemies. Metis... wasn't even her enemy. An adversary, at the moment, but not her enemy. *Think, Ferrari. Think. There has to be something you can tell these two that will get the Metisians off their chairs and into the game.* She couldn't threaten them. Lecturing them wasn't going to do any good. She needed to have a bargaining chip. There was nothing whatsoever that ECHO and the rest of the world could possibly offer to Metis that they didn't already have.

And probably better, she thought sourly.

She tried to remember what Bella and Mercurye had told her. No... it wasn't Bella. It had been Rick.

"They're scared, actually. They're afraid the Thulians will find them." He'd laughed ruefully. *"It's hard to negotiate with people who are afraid to come out of their bomb shelter."*

Yes, but... what if that bomb shelter might not shelter them anymore?

"So the Thulians can turn our powers on," she said out loud, looking from Marconi to Tesla and back again. "What is Metis going to do if they turn them *off* again?"

The wire-frame mouths dropped open. It would have been funny if the situation hadn't been so serious.

"If the Thulians did this to us in the first place, what's to stop them from undoing it?" she persisted. "And then what? Us metas are the only thing standing between you and them. Without us, the Thulians roll *right* over the rest of the world, and it will be only a matter of time before they find you. You can't hide forever. If they even *suspect* you exist, they'll find you."

The wire-frame eyes widened.

"After all, why should they care if they turn off their own metas?" She glared at them, hands on hips. "Ninety percent of what they threw at us wasn't metas anyway, it was... oh hell, alien science, I guess. They'll still have that. And what will we have? A few people with powered armor that they may, or may not, still be able to use, or even remember how to use, some incendiary shells and grenades... that's about it. We'll be toast, they'll have the world, and you'll be mice in a trap."

The two looked at each other, and the expressions of astonishment turned to glee. Tesla vanished. Marconi turned his gaze back to her.

"I think, Detective, you have given us exactly the... ah... *ammunition* we need to approach the Convocation. Tesla has gone to report this to the President. You will probably have to repeat your speech to him, and then to the Convocation as a whole, and it might take a little time, but—" his wire-frame lips stretched in a grin. "But I do not think this is something they will react to with... insouciance."

"Good," she said, and meant it.

"And while you are waiting..." A rectangle of white light opened in the wall behind him. "Please make yourself comfortable. Rick has been waiting a long time to finally see you again."

CHAPTER SIXTEEN

Found Penny

MERCEDES LACKEY AND DENNIS LEE

Penny hid in her bed. Lacey's ghost was back; he was the first to materialize, long before the others, just after they finished up the supper food-pouches. She hoped he didn't remember her; hoped, hard, that he didn't remember she could see him. Because that was always when the ghosts latched on to her, when they understood she could see them.

While she hid, with her head under the flat pillow with just enough of a gap so she could watch him without him knowing, he just stood staring at Lacey. He seemed so ordinary...he wasn't beaten up, or cut up, or dressed in tattered rags. His hair was short, and as far as Penny could tell, given that he was pretty see-through, he was wearing dark pants and a dark T-shirt, with dark high-top shoes or maybe lace-up boots. Back in the World, she wouldn't have looked twice at him.

But who knew what kind of craziness was behind those eyes? The fact that he hadn't done anything yet didn't mean anything.

Pike sat down on the side of her bed. He didn't look where she was looking. "So," he said, quietly, pitching his voice so only she could hear. "Lacey got a ghost too?"

"Uh huh," Penny whispered, shivering. "It's a guy. A young guy. He just stares at her."

"Well, that's different, isn't it?" Pike countered.

"Different's just different," she replied, trying to keep her teeth from chattering. "Don't mean it's good."

And right then was when Creepy Man faded in, homed in on her, and started shambling towards her. Then Screaming Girl and

Drunk Lady faded in, and headed straight for Penny too, led by Creepy Man. Screaming Girl started in moaning, working her way up to one of her howling rages.

And that was when Lacey's Guy whirled, as if he had not realized they were there until that moment, and leveled that intense stare on *them*.

They were oblivious to it, and kept coming towards Penny's bed. With a gasp of horror, she knew this was going to be one of the bad, bad nights, when all of the ghosts stood around her, screaming, babbling, saying terrible, terrible things. All of them trying to get her attention, all of them enraged.

She curled up in a tight, tight ball and started to sob under the pillow. And then the impossible happened.

Lacey's Guy charged at the Creepy Man, fists swinging purposefully. Belatedly the Creepy Man noticed he was coming, but too late to do anything but stumble back a couple of shambling paces. Lacey's Guy didn't say a word, not even a sound, not even a grunt, but in moments, he had somehow pummeled the Creepy Man right out of the air, right out of everything. It was kind of like he beat the Creepy Man into dust.

And then, as Screaming Girl started to shriek, he turned on her.

Drunk Lady had at least enough sense left to figure out what was happening after Screaming Girl got chased around the room a couple times, got cornered, and then was pummeled into nothing the same as Creepy Man. She disappeared on her own.

Lacey's Guy went back to stand over Lacey and stare at her, as Penny realized that about half way through that...performance...she had stopped shaking. But Pike sure noticed, and poked her shoulder. "What just happened?" he demanded, in a harsh whisper. "Something just happened, didn't it?"

"The...new one. The one with Lacey," she stammered, actually coming out from underneath the pillow a bit, like a turtle cautiously sticking its head out of its shell. "Creepy Man and Drunk Lady and Screaming Girl started coming over here, and he—he went after them. And he chased them and beat on them and now they're gone!"

Pike stared at her, as if he couldn't quite believe what she was saying. "They're gone?" he repeated. "How?"

"I dunno, just gone, he, like, beat them up and beat them into nothing." Well, she didn't quite believe it either. "And now he's back to staring at Lacey."

As if her talking about him alerted him again, he turned his head, abruptly, and stared at her. Stared at her so hard she felt as if she couldn't move. Like his eyes were pins, sticking her in place.

"What's he doing?" Pike asked, and poked her again when she didn't answer. "What's he doing?"

"He's looking at me," she squeaked.

Pike chewed on his lower lip, and then on a hangnail on his thumb for a while, as Lacey's Guy continued that intense, intense stare, without moving. "Well?" he said, after a long, long moment. "What's he doing?"

She gulped. Took a shuddering breath. "Still...staring," she said.

"Not coming after you?" Pike asked, putting the hand with the chewed thumb on her shoulder.

She shook her head.

"Just staring?" Pike asked.

She nodded. And to her shock, Pike began to chuckle.

"Well," her brother said. "Mebbe you got a boyfriend, then."

Before she could reply, he got up and sauntered back to his bed, laid himself down, and went to sleep.

Penny stared through the semi-dark at the young man, who stared back, eyes burning, burning, burning across the air between them.

And then, when she was afraid she would cry or scream or... well, she didn't know what, but the tension had almost become unbearable...he turned his head and went back to staring at Lacey.

Slowly, she put her head down on the pillow. She tried to keep her eyes open, tried to watch him, but for once, she was just too tired. Her eyes dropped shut, and for the first time since she had arrived in this terrible place, she slept the rest of the night through.

CHAPTER SEVENTEEN

Next to Normal

DENNIS LEE, CODY MARTIN, VERONICA
GIGUERE AND MERCEDES LACKEY

Tuesday evenings at Normality had become the preferred time for the ECHO regulars to relax and unwind. Fridays had their own sense of celebration, but Tuesdays brought a subdued crowd that was happy to cluster around tables with a few beers. Those who wanted more than that had to sit at the bar, and Mel kept that conversation going.

She enjoyed the back-and-forth, whiskey and scotch lubricating their words and bringing out their honest assessments of the current state of things. They hadn't seen the huge flying spheres and metal-suited Kriegers for a few weeks, but none of the regulars seemed complacent. Waiting usually meant there was something bigger, something scarier, on the horizon.

"And if it's not the Kriegers coming down Peachtree, it's Verdigris." Bella tossed back a shot of Glenlivet and turned her glass upside-down on the polished bartop. Next to her, Bulwark nursed his beer and nodded in agreement. "We can't count him out, especially with his personal assassin doing his dirty work."

"Think she's sleeping with him? Verd and his Girl Friday, I mean." Mel popped open two amber bottles and set one each in front of John Murdock and Red Djinni. Both men nodded their thanks, but her smile lingered on the Djinni for a little while longer. He wore his standard Clooney impersonation tonight, and he finally returned her smile with a smirk. She struck an impish pose, resting a hand lightly on her hip. "What? You don't think she would?"

"Couldn't tell you," Red shrugged. "Never met her, wouldn't want to, and I wouldn't presume to know her type. Maybe she likes crazy with a combover. Then again, he's probably too busy for romance. I'd bet on a pair of full-service mannequins."

"He steal your plans?" John asked dryly. He had become a fixture at Normality, just as much for the beer as for the company. Mel found him interesting, but he seemed too much of a soldier, and she had had her fill of those in her experiences. Next to him, Bella snorted and smothered a laugh with her hand. "Ya gotta stop puttin' those on the Internet."

"Nah, metal and polymers give me a rash. Besides, you're thinking of Pavel," Red answered.

"Oh, geez," Bella choked out. "Don't give him ideas. If Natalya found out…"

As if on cue, the door to the bar flew open and a Commissar-shaped silhouette filled the entry. Mel watched the theatrics of Red Saviour as she went from table to table, rounding up her charges and pushing them out the door. The severe Russian advanced on a group of college students surrounding Pavel, her fists suffused with a bright blue plasma. Squeals and shrieks erupted from the table before the coeds streamed out the door. Pavel stumbled after them with the Commissar on his heels, while Unter was left to pay the tab. He offered John an efficient nod in parting.

"Last call, comrade?" John indicated the empty seat between him and the Djinni. "One more for the night?"

Unter sniffed. "Last call went out the door. Another time, perhaps." He gave the same severe nod to Bella and Bulwark before leaving.

A small puff of dust erupted on the bar top. The little earth elemental hugged a small paper cup to his chest and he shook it back and forth in front of Mel. "Last call for you, too." She reached under the counter for the bottle that she kept separate for Vickie and Herb's custom delivery service. She poured two fingers' worth of the Ardbeg single-malt and cracked a smile in Bulwark's direction. "Djinni's got her clocking a good ten, fifteen seconds ahead of me on the parkour course. I gotta get some sleep before tomorrow's run or Victrix is gonna kick my ass."

Bull gave her one of his rare, wry smiles. "She's holding back, y'know," he said. "Doesn't want you to feel bad about the fact she might actually lap you now."

"I should have known," Mel laughed. "But if that were true, why doesn't she just let me overtake her?"

"It's still Victrix," the Djinni chuckled. "The lady plays to win."

"*I can heeeeeeaaar yooooooou,*" Vickie's voice came over the bar's sound system. "*And see you too.*" There was a laugh that sounded maybe just a touch tipsy. "*I am the fly on the wall! C'mon home, Herb. That stuff's not going to drink itself!*"

Herb gave them all a quick salute and disappeared with the paper cup. The others soon followed. John set his glass down on the bar with a flourish, rose and waved his good-byes. Bella and Bulwark started to do the same, although the Djinni didn't give any indication that he was leaving. Mel didn't mind, but Bulwark glared down the bar in Red's direction, and she caught the frown. Bella did, too, and she started to say something, but Mel interrupted.

"I'm a big girl, y'all. I've dealt with bigger and meaner in my day. I'm strong enough to haul his sorry carcass out to the alley if he passes out," she laughed.

"When," Bella corrected.

"If," Red shot back from his seat. "Go on, the two of you. Just make sure that you don't wear him out too much, Blue. It's a workday tomorrow."

"Every day is a workday," Bella corrected. Mel resisted the urge to smile when the young co-leader of ECHO laced her fingers with Bull's on their way out. The two made a perfectly matched couple, and the Djinni chuckled wryly as Bella led Bulwark through the door.

Mel followed them, turning the lock once the door shut. The Djinni regarded her with an odd expression that she chose to answer with a wink and smile. "Well, just you and me, *cher.* Considering that I hate to drink alone, mind keeping a girl company for a while longer?"

He didn't answer her immediately, but he didn't give any indication he wanted to leave. Mel took it as a sign that he would stay for one more drink, and she grabbed two glasses and the Laphroaig that he and John enjoyed with their occasional off-key serenades. She poured his glass before pouring her own. "So," she drawled. "How long has it been?"

Red stared at her. "How long has what been?"

"Since you've had a thing for her. Parker, I mean." Mel tilted her head at the front door. "Clearly, she's with the walking wall now, but either there's something there, or you wanted there to be something there. Not that I blame you. She's cute," she added with a half-smile.

He studied the bottom of his glass before answering. "Long enough. Long enough to know."

"Know what?"

He paused, and downed the rest of his drink. "She is not for me."

Mel's mouth twisted in a half-smile. "Well, I guess your princess is in another castle, then." She paused, a long pause. "Never mind. Granted, that might be the scotch talking, but I'd have to actually start drinking." She put back half her glass and winced. "There. Now it's the scotch talking. So, why not Parker?"

"I'm not drunk enough for that conversation," Red muttered.

"Amazingly enough, we are surrounded by alcohol, and you've got one of the finest bartenders from New Orleans at your disposal this evening." Mel slipped around the side of the bar and leaned against the barstool, one of her knees purposely touching his. "I can help you get drunk enough for that conversation, or for anything else that might require some liquid courage." She punctuated that promise by tossing back the rest of her scotch.

He stared at her, his eyes losing focus. "Yeah . . . now I'm thinking I'm *too* drunk for this conversation."

"Well, I'm not drunk at all," she said, promptly pouring herself a generous shot. "Law of averages say that we're only half-drunk."

"So, together we're not altogether drunk? Demi-drunk?" Red played with the words. "Semi-inebriated. Inter-inebriated. Half sheets to the wind. Partially pissed? Half-plastered?"

"I like that, half-plastered. Reminds me of the back wall," Mel answered.

Red's eyes began to wander, his gaze lingering on the worn ECHO symbol stretched across her chest, then at the wall, and back again. "You don't want to know what flashed through my mind just now."

"I got it," she said, snapping her fingers. "You an' me, we're not quite under the table."

"Not helping," he groaned, dropping his face into the palm of one hand.

"So, if not under the table, then maybe on the table?"

Both hands covered his face. "Still not helping. Really not helping."

Mel sighed and hopped up to sit on the bar. She pushed herself over until she sat with one leg on either side of him, the bottle in one hand. Mel reached forward and lifted his chin until his eyes met hers. "How 'bout now," she drawled. "This help?"

"Yeah," he muttered. "You're a real Samaritan." He raised his glass. "Give me another, and ask me again."

In his time, the Djinni had slipped past high-security measures of all flavors, shapes and sizes. On top of the usual tricks of the trade, he had an epidermal layer that he could expand to an odd spongiform texture to deaden his footsteps, and senses that allowed for a complete awareness of his surroundings. Taken together, he easily crossed the distance from the bed to Mel's window without a sound, handily avoiding creaks in the hardwood, dodging bits of clothing, shoes and armaments that had been hastily scattered about the night before. Pausing only to grab his scarf, he was ready to make his escape.

He hadn't counted on the alarm clock. Mel had yet to miss a morning at the parkour course, and the flat buzzing noise elicited a muffled "dammit" and a hand coming from out from under the covers to fumble for the snooze button. Red paused, his hands gently supporting the window he had halfway opened, one foot already climbing out onto the fire escape. He froze, but then relaxed as Mel's hand dove back under the sheets. In a moment, she appeared to be snoring.

Red watched her for a moment, and gave up. He climbed back in, crossed his arms and leaned back against the window.

"You're awake," he said, simply.

The rumpled mess of sheets moved and Mel lifted her head from the pillow. She stretched both hands above her head before rolling to her back and propping herself up on her elbows. A lazy yet satisfied half-smile accompanied her words. "Guess you found me out. What gave it away?"

"Your breathing wasn't quite right," he offered. "A bit exaggerated. Your acting needs a bit of work if you're going to fool me."

Mel chuckled, a throaty noise that he had heard multiple times the night before. "Well, the way you slid out of bed, it was artful. Didn't move the mattress or anything. I figured it would be poor taste to interrupt your getaway." She sat up a little more, the thin bedsheet tucked under both arms as if she meant to remind Red what he was escaping. "Not your first, I'm guessing."

"Don't mean to offend you, darlin'," Red apologized with a grandiose bow. "I've always found it easier on both parties to steal away in these situations. Keeps the awkward to a minimum."

"Oh, so this is you just being a gentleman for my sake," she drawled. "Chivalry in personal defenestration, right?"

He shrugged. "Call it a quirk. I'm the guy who likes to control when and how he leaves a building through a window."

"I'm guessing it helps when the window's open beforehand?"

"Like you said, not my first time. A few of the noisier goodbyes had memorable finales." He paused as she waited expectantly. "Yes," he confirmed. "I was thrown through closed windows."

Mel swung her legs around to the side of the bed and stood, pulling the top sheet with her in a makeshift robe. "My personal favorite was a drainpipe shimmy. Three stories to a muddy front lawn. All the dirt made up for the wet T-shirt." She winked at him. "You ever do a closed door?"

"Been slammed up against a few, I suppose," he murmured. His brow furrowed as he came to a startling conclusion. "It seems I've been with some really strong women."

"Apparently," she agreed. "Your retreat technique isn't bad, but I was in Special Ops, remember? Don't need to see or hear you moving to know it's happening." Mel took a few steps away from the bed, the sheet trailing behind her. "Think about it, though. Wherever you sleep," she said, air quotes and a wicked smile framing the word "sleep," "the setup stays the same. There's no real variation. There's something like a bed, something like clothes, and they ain't on either person in any presentable fashion. And," she finished with a Djinni-like flourish, "there's always one way out. It's that old saying, right?" Mel said with a wry smirk. "No matter where you go—"

"You're always alone," Red finished.

He knew the real saying, of course. Very Zen, very poignant, but he wasn't feeling it. It wasn't the same, he wasn't the same, and perhaps he was finally ready to acknowledge that some things just wouldn't be enough for him anymore. Moments before, caught in the act, he had fallen back to another line of defense. Mere words, said with a bow and with a nice flourish of charm and grace, could be a formidable weapon. He had many in his arsenal. But at their core, they were lies. Artful bits of deception with a lot of show and flash that did their job covering up a painful reality. And he was tired of lying. It just wasn't enough anymore. And so he had blurted a few words of truth, surprising himself with how deep the words cut through their little dance. And it *had* been a dance. Mel had been a willing partner, but the words had struck her as well, and in the shocked stillness he found himself lost in her face, her startled expression a mirror to his own.

She knows, he thought. *Well, sure. Not her first dance either.*

She looked away first. Gone were the flirtatious, knowing smiles, and when she moved away her steps were leaden, lifeless.

"I'll make coffee to go," she said quietly. "We've got a run start time in thirty minutes." She swapped the sheet for a robe and made a beeline for the bedroom door.

Red caught up to her, taking her hand firmly in his. She froze, not turning, her hand cold and lifeless in his. He tried to speak, but what was there to say? They stood there, still, neither quite sure what to do next. A moment of truth, naked honesty, and Red had effectively stripped away years of practiced subterfuge. For her, it might have been a first. For him, it had definitely been an age since the last. Since Victoria.

Finally, he felt her grasp his hand warmly as she brought it up to her shoulder. She took a few tentative steps and led him to the kitchen.

"No one has to be alone," she said, twining her fingers with his.

Bella always felt less alone when Mel was at the desk tucked into one corner of the far-too-spacious ECHO CEO office. Ever since shortly after Ramona Ferrari's "death," Mel had been occupying that seat, and the job of Bella's "assistant."

The conversation that led to the position had been interesting, to say the least.

"Well, you're cleared for work, according to Doctor Melbourne, Panacea and Gilead," Bella said, looking across her desk at Mel.

"Work," Mel repeated with a sigh. "I dunno what more there is to work with. After all that you did before—"

"Let's leave aside the little problem that you don't have your illusion powers for now," Bella said. "I'm not convinced they won't come back. They did for Fata Morgana. It took years, but they did. I'm more than willing to keep you in ECHO till they do."

Mel gave Bella a watery smile. "You sure? I mean, I've got plenty of training beyond those powers, but I don't know if I can trust myself out there. If you think there's something worth saving, well..." She trailed off and shook her head. "No wonder you two are fit for each other. I'll owe you both for my second chances."

"Depends on what you mean by 'out there.' There's plenty that Support Ops do. Some more cross-training and you could jump in as a detective. Trust, me it is a *lot* harder to cross-train someone who's had investigative training to learn the paramilitary and shooty side than it is the other way around. Or there's juggling paperwork, if you think you could stand that." Bella cued up the openings in ECHO Support Ops, got only half the ones she *knew* were there and sighed heavily. "Goddamnit. I miss Ramona. I feel like I'm operating with half a brain and only one hand."

"Bella, if having me file and sort and shuffle will bring you any bit of relief, then I'll do it. What part of 'I owe you three times over' don't you get? Want me to say it *en francais* to make it easier to understand?" The blonde gave her a lopsided smile, the one side of her head still buzzed shorter than the other after the attack at the MARTA station. "I ain't got a problem doing paperwork, and one of the secrets of running a bar off Bourbon Street is being able to make a cup of coffee that'll stand up and salute on its own. You want a secretary, you got one. I'm happy that you're still willing to keep me."

Bella stared at her for a long moment. "Sweetie," she said, slowly. "I don't need a secretary. Secretaries are easy to get. I have three. What I need is an *assistant,* and I'll be damned if I don't think you've got the chops for it." She began ticking things off on her fingers. "I need someone who can be the other set of eyes at my back when Bull can't—and can shoot to kill, and *will.* I need someone who can talk to people and get them to open up where they won't open up to me. I need someone better with the computers than I am when Vix can't do that—and you can learn that from Vix. I need someone who won't think because I ask them to run an errand that I'm exploiting them or something—because if I do that, the errand isn't 'just' an errand, it'll be something I need someone I can *trust* to do. There's a million little things that come up all the time, and I can only handle half a million. I need someone I can trust to handle the other half." She let out her breath in a long exhalation. "It's gonna involve a lot of learning shit. And tedium. And often as not, being charming to snakes and bastards. But if you're willing—"

"If you'll let me give it a go, I'll do my best. Learning doesn't scare me, as long as you don't mind questions now and then. The rest of it sounds just fine. Heck, a bit of learning and some familiar tasks might be what it takes to reset what got broken." Mel offered Bella a reassuring smile, her voice gentled and honeyed. "Just tell me where to begin, and we'll get a start on making this place a little more manageable."

Bella grinned with happiness and relief. A few clicks of the mouse and some typing and the deed was done. "Congratulations, Mel. You are now my assistant. Skirts optional. Oh, and the first secret you get entrusted with is this. Ramona isn't dead. Pull the chair closer and I'll tell you the whole story."

"Oh, crap," Bella said, her voice betraying dismay.

Mel swiveled in her chair, one hand on the most recent set of file folders procured from the ECHO vaults. The pair had worked together long enough that Mel reacted to the smallest changes in Bella's voice; each "oh crap" or "freakin' hell" could mean a dozen different things, but she had begun to predict them with surprising accuracy. "What's missing," she asked calmly. "What do you want me to get?"

"I intended to get Vix lunch. I promised I would about an hour ago, because if she doesn't get someone to bring her something she just microwaves something full of additives and crap calories or drinks a meal in a can. I wanted to bring her up to speed on the vault stuff Verd left there while we ate. But I have a meeting with Bull about Scope in five minutes and . . ." She threw her hands up in the air. "That's his only window and it'll probably take two hours."

"So let it take the two hours. I can come back to the files here if you think Vix would be all right with me bringing her some lunch. Herb's a cutie with his little cups at the bar, but he probably wouldn't handle more than that."

Bella pursed her lips. "Well, it's more like, 'Vix can't apport more than that without using up all the calories in the meal.'

Not *quite* as taxing and a little more complicated, but that's the 'too-long, didn't-read' version."

"Huh. Guess I get a magic lesson today," Mel grinned. "But really, I'm here for the errands. Tell me what you want, what she wants, and what Bull wants. I'll call in the order, pick up and deliver all around. That way, everybody gets a real lunch. Does she like that bento place as much as you do?"

"Sec," Bella said. "Overwatch: ping Vix." There was a pause. "Yeah, rerun the last three minutes of office chat." Another pause. "Great, it's a deal." She turned her attention back to Mel. "Bento boxes all around. Salmon for me, chicken for Bull, salmon and tuna for Vix, whatever you want, charge it on the ECHO account, and Vix's password will be *'Klaatu barada nicto.'* You say that in response to 'One small step for a man.' Oh, and make sure you have your Mark One headset on."

"Two if by sea, one if by land, ECHO plastic, and it's North in response to Armstrong." Mel popped open the desk drawer to retrieve her headset. "Anything else, boss?"

"Well...you're going to be next door to the Chinese joint. If they *don't* have a line, could you pop in and get a double order of veggie egg fu yong for her too? She didn't ask for it, but if it's in the fridge, she'll eat it instead of freezer-burned Minute Meals." Bella beamed at her. This was as good as having Ramona back.

"Can do. You want me to pick up their hot and sour for us? You said the next stack of folders was going to take us past dinner, and you've got to eat as much as the next person." Mel stood and winked at her. "Never mind, I'll grab it just in case. It can reheat for tomorrow's lunch, right?"

"Mel, you're a lifesaver. Make it so." Bella glanced at the time on her computer. "Gotta dash; it'll take me every bit of what I've got left to get to Bull's office. You know how he is about being on time."

Mel mock-groaned. "Do I ever. Go, cher. Meet you there."

Vickie studied the camera image for a good long time. Then she clicked over to the Overwatch scan...just to be sure. Only then did she finger the intercom button. "So, you look kind of burdened down there, Mel. Kind of a heavy load for just a couple of bento boxes. More than one small step for a man."

"Confucius say, *'Klaatu barada nicto.'* But Bella said that I needed to bring over some of the veggie egg fu yong so you wouldn't be scrounging from your freezer between now and tomorrow." Mel cracked a smile for the camera. "We're gonna have hot and sour tonight for dinner. It'll be a soup party."

"First time I've heard of soup as a party," Vickie replied, as she threw the locks and let Mel in. Then she took a long, deep appreciative breath. "Damn, I love egg fu... beats the hell out of Salisbury steak."

"Anything beats Salisbury steak." Mel stepped into the apartment and set the parcels on the nearest flat surface, which happened to be a table in the tiny foyer. "You sure that's enough? You want anything else?"

"I only ever think about food when it's in front of me," Vickie confessed, locking the door again. "Fridge is in and to the left in the kitchen. I'll set the bentos up in the living room and you can brief me. I'm dying to know what else Verd left in the vault." She picked up the white bag from the Japanese bento-box place and darted ahead of Mel, leaving Mel to get the heavier brown bag from the Chinese joint. As she set up the living room table with chopsticks, drinks and the bento boxes, she watched Mel stow the white styrofoam containers of Chinese takeout in the fridge. "You want chair or couch?" she called over the counter that separated the kitchen from the living room.

"Doesn't matter, I'm good with a chair if you want something comfy," Mel answered. The fridge door shut, the containers safely stored front and center so that Vickie would see them the next time she opened the door.

"Roger. You get the chair. I'm a sprawler. Tea okay?" Vickie was trying not to show it, by being the hostess, but having a new person in her space always made her nervous. So far, in the last year, she had had more new people in her space than in the previous eight. Bell, Ramona, Bull, the Djinni, Scope, Acrobat, JM, Sera, Mel. Of course the last time Mel had been here, it had been with the others, planning the Vault raid. This was the first time she was here alone. That made it harder, somehow.

"Tea's fine. You want to eat first and then talk shop, or would you rather multitask?"

Vickie snorted a little. "Mel... it's *me*. Multitask is my middle name."

"So's skipping lunch, according to Bella, but I figured it was your place and your rules." Mel rested her hand on her chopsticks, but didn't pick them up. "The way she talks, you'd think she was your Nana or something."

Vickie wondered how guilty she looked, and tried to cover it by picking up her box and chopsticks and fiddling with them. "She's a healer. She thinks I don't eat right, and she's probably right. But hell, even if I can force myself out to the store, when would I get the *time*? Overwatch is two full-time jobs, and then some."

Mel picked up her own box and chopsticks. "She's a healer, sure, but she's more than that. That caring about what you eat beyond lunchtime is being a friend, y'know?" She pushed some spicy chunks of tofu around before picking up a square. "She's trying to cut out the time part of that equation by having it here. You're important to her, Vickie."

Vickie flushed. "That's . . . new for me," she replied. "Bell's the first friend I had here. She's the one that got me out of the apartment. Hell, I think I probably put Overwatch together for *her*, not Tesla."

"You probably did. Helps her out a lot. Helps everyone, come to think of it," Mel commented around a mouthful. "If Bella's the glue of the organization, then you've got to be the nuts and bolts. More bolts, 'cause the rest of us are nuts."

Vickie sighed, but it was not a sigh of discontent or weariness. "It's the best thing I've ever done. It may very well be right up there in the top twenty of all major magical works put together by one person. I'm damn proud of it, Mel. And Mark One can run without me, which is even better; it'll outlive me. Most magicians can't say that." She chuckled. "Even Red Saviour approves of it, and getting her to approve of *anything* having to do with magic is harder than getting her to approve of anything created by a capitalist."

"She have a bad experience with it, or do you think she's just naturally suspicious? People who are violently opposed to something usually have a bones-deep reason for it.

"The one-word answer is 'Rasputin,' or so I have deduced. The longer response is that Rasputin evidently was up to a lot more government-meddling than the history books give him credit for, and yes, he was a magician." Vickie ate quickly and neatly, handling the chopsticks like a native. "How much bad he did, I don't know, and honestly, it is largely because I haven't bothered to research it. He's dead and gone, and I have more crap on my plate in the here and now than I can handle as it is. Saviour evidently has enough dirt on him to want to kill magicians on sight, and that's more than enough information for me." She paused for some tea. "If I live through all of this and actually have some leisure time, I intend to look into it, because I'm curious, but now is not the time. I can research, or I can build in more bells and whistles to Overwatch Mark Two while I do monitor duty. I know where my time is going to go."

"And there's always the parkour course," Mel said, with one side of her mouth quirking up.

Vickie groaned theatrically, although . . . now that there was less pain and less falling involved, she was getting to appreciate runs on the parkour course. Not *like,* but appreciate. "There's *always* the parkour course."

Mel laughed at the sentiment. "Five, six days a week. I thought about going out there in the evening when it got cooler since it's not my night for the late shift at the bar. Nobody's out there once first shift's done on ECHO campus, so there's less people to fight for a good corner." She stirred what was left of her noodles. "I'd like to be out there more often. Seems like you get in a fair amount of practice."

"I spent most of my time in a chair," Vickie pointed out. "I need all the exercise I can get. Though the Djinni seems to think I need more field work . . ." She shook her head. "Let's just say, when I've tried, things tend to go fifty-seven different kinds of bad."

"Really?"

She shrugged. "I may be a bad-luck magnet outside my four walls." She didn't see any need to elaborate. Mel had more than enough access to look at the AA reports if she wanted to. But she figured she would prompt. "It's all in the after-action reports. Unlike some people, I'm always on top of my paperwork."

That earned her a broad smile. "I know. About being on top of the paperwork, I mean. If everybody managed to be as thorough as you . . ." Mel set aside the remains of her lunch and leaned back. "Like I said before, Bella loves you, and not just for the paperwork. That's a bonus."

Vickie flushed a little. "Well, she loves me for Overwatch. We'd never have put Verdigris down without it. Hell, we couldn't have taken the New Mexico Thulian hideout without it."

"That was you first and Overwatch second. Bet that everyone else on that mission would have said the same thing." Mel leaned forward, her elbows on her knees. "Is it really so bad to think that Bella's valuing you for you, not just for the whiz-bang stuff that you're able to do?"

Vickie shrugged again. "Not used to having friends again," she said, and left it at that.

"Fair enough." Mel didn't appear the least bit offended by the admission, nor did she try to press the conversation. She picked up the empty boxes and stacked them. "If you want another one, or at least someone's ass to kick up and down the parkour course, I'm here. And if not, I'll be your own Cajun delivery service."

Vickie conjured up a half-smile. "I'll take you up on the parkour *and* the delivery, as long as it's not eating into your own time too much. Bella hates Nawlins food, so maybe you know. Any decent Cajun places that do carry-out around the campus?"

"How can something so dirt-cheap and simple be so good?" Vickie asked, halfway into her red beans and rice.

"Soul food is what people with no money learned to make taste good, *cher*," Mel replied, between spoonfuls of gumbo.

Vickie was about to say something when Overwatch gave her the *ping* that was associated with the Djinni opening his freq to her. She held up a hand to Mel to let her know she needed to concentrate. "Overwatch, go for Djinni," she said, before he could hail her.

"You psychic these days, Vix?"

"Nope, just made another improvement. Special people get a sign-on tone. And you're *special*," she quipped.

"That's what my teachers used to say," he replied. *"Got a situation here. Blacksnake poking around where they had no business to be; managed to find a pop-up site before it popped up. My inclination is to let them whittle each other down before we call in the troops to mop up the survivors."*

"Are *you* in a compromised position?" she asked quickly, grabbing a wireless keyboard off the coffee table and bringing up her enhanced HUD. "Overwatch: command: Maestro." That cued the motion sensors in the four corners of the room to follow her hand motions on her virtual monitors that were now seemingly floating in midair.

"*Ah, yeah, about that. I'm kinda pinned down...*"

"How badly, have you got any room to move, and do you need a hole?" She felt her heart racing with anxiety, the way it always did when *he* was in trouble. His life-sign monitors showed a lot of stress, and from the sounds his mics were picking up, the fighting was pretty close to him.

"*Any closer and they'd fall over me, enough, and yes.*"

She reached for the piece of his claw she'd strung on a thong around her neck, closed her eyes, and took a deep breath, bringing up the fractals that allowed her to manipulate and sense the earth and what was on it. Then she let go of the claw, connection established. "Hole coming in three...two...one." She clenched her hands around the "edges" of something that didn't exist, and pulled them "apart." She heard him grunt as the earth fell away beneath him and he dropped into the hole she had just made. "Six feet deep enough?"

"*Ah...make it ten?*"

She was sweating with the effort, but this was the Djinni. "Roger," she replied, and gave him another four feet. "You want me to call the cavalry, or do you want to?"

"*I'll do it. I'll just wait until the ruckus dies down, poke my head up like a gopher and see what's left.*"

"You didn't bring one of the eyes, did you?" she asked, not hiding her annoyance.

"*Makes an ugly bulge in my svelte outline.*"

"Moron. At least if they shoot you in the head, it won't hit anything vital."

"*Hardy har.*"

She brought up his eye-cam; as she expected, it showed the rough sides of the hole she had made for him. Lucky, this time. He'd been in a destruction corridor and she hadn't had to try and get through concrete. Just plain old red Georgia clay. Which was going to hold together well enough she didn't need to reinforce the walls to keep them from caving in on him. She typed rapidly on her keyboard, instructing the Colt Brother on duty to get ready to deploy a pop-up team on Djinni's signal, or hers.

With a gesture, she shoved a couple of the virtual monitors aside to get a look at Mel. She looked...tense. "Don't die," she said, shortly.

"*Awww, maaaaaa.*" The smart-ass retort relieved her, a little.

She had a good sense now of how he'd respond if he actually *was* in trouble. He had been when he'd called, for instance. She licked her lips, and only then realized they, and her mouth, had gone dry. She reached blindly for her coffee and swigged it down.

The combatants were moving too quickly and were clumped too closely together—and probably were on too much asphalt and cement—for her to get a good handle on how many there were. But the sounds of gunfire and energy weapons began to thin out. A sudden ramping up of the beam generators and a last burst, and then there was silence.

"Poking my nose up, Overwatch." There was absolutely no point in telling him not to, so she just rode that eye-cam like a cowboy on a bronco, and scanned what part of the area he could see before he had even begun to take it all in.

Nothing.

"Poking an arm up." He was going to use his skin-sense, amped up. She held her breath. As long as there was only powered armor there, and as long as they were still cooling down from the battle, he'd be able to tell how many of them there were...

"Four suits, which is more than I can handle. Send in the mop-up crew, Vix."

"Roger that," she replied, and then monitored the situation until the ECHO squad, equipped with those RPGs, of course, arrived. And then had another bad moment or three when the Djinni popped out of his hiding place to join them.

Finally it was over; the damn crazy fool had lived to tell another tall tale and was on his way back with the ECHO squad. She shut all the extraneous Overwatch stuff down and collapsed backwards on the couch, her eyes leaking tears of grateful relief. *He's okay. He's okay. He wasn't even nicked this time.* She'd forgotten she wasn't alone until Mel poked her with the plate of reheated food.

"Uh...thanks, Mel," she stammered, taking it with one hand and wiping her eyes with the other. "Men. Can't live with 'em, can't sell 'em for parts." She managed a laugh that sounded mostly genuine, and dug back into her food, pretty certain she hadn't let anything slip. *Don't let her guess. Don't let her guess. She's never seen me at work before, she can't know I don't react to everyone the way I just did to Red being in trouble....*

"If I could, reckon I know which part I'd sell first," Mel agreed.

Good. Dodged that bullet. She managed to get the food past the lump in her throat, helped by the fact that after all that magic and mayhem, she was *ravenous*. "You gonna eat all that?" she asked pointing with her spoon at the big box of fried calamari.

They were coming, and she was strapped to the table. Every time, the door would open and the men would file in, two by two, their faces hidden behind masks. They would move to surround her, and then they would begin.

And she would scream.

"Mel!"

It would never sate them. They kept digging. And she kept screaming.

"MEL!"

And screaming.

"WHAT IS WRONG WITH YOU, GIRL? STOP IT!"

His hands were on her, strong hands, grasping her by the arms. She expected him to shake her, perhaps hit her, until he got what he wanted. But she couldn't give him that. She was a soldier, and she had been trained to resist interrogation. Still, nothing had prepared her for this. It wasn't information they wanted, not something she could just tell them. No, they were after something else, and she had no idea what it was.

So they kept at her.

As far as torture went, they went to some exotic extremes. Sometimes she felt as if she were paralyzed, and slowly suffocating, and the suffering was less pain than helpless anguish. She couldn't move a muscle, she couldn't make a sound, her silent shrieks deafening only to herself. Other times it was nothing *but* pain, in every fiber of her being. They would turn it on, effortlessly, it seemed, and this time she was free to writhe and wail for all the good it did her. They were relentless. At first she thought them merely cruel. Now, it was clear they were far beyond that. They didn't see her as a person, only a subject. An artifact to calmly dissect, to take apart and examine. None of them held any enjoyment in debasing her. Except for one.

His hands were strong. They touched her knowingly. On rare occasions they were alone, and when they were, it was somehow worse.

She felt his hands on her again, and she cringed, and shuddered as her scream died away in her throat. Something was different.

His hands were firm, but gentle.

"Mel," he said again, but softly now. "Wherever you are, come back. Come back."

Her eyes opened to a dark room, the fog lifting from her mind. She was in bed. Her bed. She was sitting up, her shoulders and head hunched forward, her hair matted softly to her face. He knelt before her, his hands still on her arms, and as she looked up at him her expression became one of bewilderment. It made him laugh.

"New face," the Djinni said. "The most challenging one to date."

"God, I almost prefer the nightmare," she muttered, shuddering again. "When would you ever be called upon to impersonate Alfred E. Neuman?"

He repositioned himself beside her, and laid a tentative hand on her shoulder. "Nightmare," he nodded. "Yeah, I figured."

She glanced at him quickly, grimaced, and let her gaze fall back to her hands. They were shaking. "Was I screaming?"

"For about a minute," he said. "You bolted up from a dead sleep like a banshee, wringing your hands, hollerin'. Thought we were under attack at first, but nothing. You just kept going, didn't even seem to know I was here until I touched you."

She took that in, and finally nodded. "I say anything?"

"Nothing I could make out. But yeah, it was bad. You get these nightmares a lot?"

"Not for a long time," she exhaled. "Guess something woke it up in me."

"Need to talk about it?"

"Do *you*?" she snapped. "I don't see you volunteering intel on your nightmares!"

"What makes you think I have any?"

"Save it, Red," she growled. "You have nightmares all the time. Moaning, crying, fingers twitching. Difference is..."

"I don't wake up screaming from mine," he said.

She clenched up and withdrew from him. Finally, she reached for her robe and climbed out of bed.

"Yeah, I guess you don't," she muttered. She moved to the vanity, fumbled in the dark and managed to pour herself a stiff drink. "Want one?"

"Sure," he said, and in moments she was back in bed, handing him a tumbler of scotch. He raised it obligingly, they clinked glasses, and shot back their drinks in unison.

"Need to talk about it?" he asked again.

"No," she said, cringing inwardly at how quickly she responded, the sudden shrillness of her voice that betrayed an anxiety she had long thought forgotten. For the first time, she felt somewhat vulnerable around this man. That wasn't what she wanted. Of all the things the Djinni could be for her, confidant didn't top that list.

"Maybe it'd be more accurate to say that I might need to, in that psychobabbly sense, but I don't really want to." She studied the bottom of her tumbler. "No 'fense."

"Takes more than a little honesty to offend me, darlin'," he said. "As for what you need, you can't expect me to know if you don't give a little." He turned to her, his eyes boring into hers. "So give a little."

She frowned and looked away. "Yeah, right." What business was it of his? For the past few weeks there had been more banter and a few stolen moments away from their daily routines. And each night, they fell into bed and forgot about the rest of the world, for at least a little while. But he was not her boyfriend. That wasn't part of the deal.

"You want psychobabble?" he continued. "I can tell you what anyone with a psych degree would say about my nightmares. Survivor's guilt."

"Your dreams seem pretty agitated for that," she said.

"Well, it didn't help that she got atomized right in front of me," he sighed. "Anyway, they'd be wrong. Survivor's guilt is about living when someone else didn't. This goes a bit beyond that. She didn't just die. She died 'cause she pushed me out of the way."

"So...regular guilt. To the Nth degree. Was she someone close?"

"She was the One."

"The..." Mel sucked air through her teeth, realization hitting her hard. "You realize what you're telling me, don't you?"

"You read my file, didn't you?" Djinni scowled. "Or you just pay attention to the locker-room gossip that infects ECHO like a virulent strain of swine flu."

"I'm a bartender, you idiot," she hissed. "If they're talking, I hear it. Djinni, Bull's been after any concrete proof of his wife's death since it happened! You were there, you watched it happen, and you've obviously said *nothing* about it!"

"I know, I know...what *must* you think of me?"

"I think..." she paused as the enormity of his predicament became obvious to her. "I think it must be crazy what's going through your head, then, now...because you think of this man as your friend, and you loved the same woman. And that woman died, to save you. And the way I've seen you look at Bella, and seeing her and Bull...Shit, Djinni. That's a messed-up place you live in."

"*Mi casa es su casa.*" He shrugged, took her tumbler, and got up to freshen their drinks. He turned and gave her another penetrating look. "You gonna turn me in?"

"Can't," she said, and looked away. "Bartender's code. Long as you've got that glass in your hand, any and all secrets have to stay that way."

"The nightmares are pretty standard," he said, passing her tumbler back to her. "Y'know, for what they are. Sometimes, I freeze up completely. Other times, I manage to cry out. There are even a few where I'm fast enough to reach for her, maybe even enough to try to pull her down. I'm never fast enough. Each time, she's gone, but not without flashing me that damn serene look of hers. That goddamn look. She'd save it for special occasions, when she wanted to let me know that everything would work out, that we would get through it, that she..."

He stopped to take another shot, but remained silent, his fingers drumming a soft beat on his glass.

"You've come this far," Mel prompted him. "Might as well say it."

"That she still loved me," he muttered, and sank back into the bed. They sat in silence, until his tumbler slipped from his hand and fell to the floor. There followed a harsh rumble as it rolled away on the hardwood.

"I was tortured once," Mel said. "God, I can't believe I'm telling you this. I was part of an infiltration operation, but we were pinched. They worked us all up, but they singled me out. The others they used up, got what they wanted, and that was it for them. Me, I was different. I had something else they wanted. So they kept at me, and I fought, and I wouldn't give it up."

This was dangerous ground. She knew she shouldn't be telling him any of this. It was something she had kept bottled up for so long...and yet, she had so much more in common with Red Djinni than she had ever had with anyone else before. But she had known that, perhaps from the first time she had laid eyes on him. There was something that connected them, and it went deeper than she could have guessed. Maybe that was why it had all come pouring out. It was liberating.

She looked down to her hands and caught herself shaking again. With apprehension? No, not really. More with...

"You okay?" Red asked, noticing. Of course he noticed. Noticing everything was par for the course for him.

She laughed. "No. It's fine. Just letting go of some tension." It was oddly exhilarating, and definitely a release. As controlled as she was, the release was going to have some physical side effects, after all. "I'm not used to..."

"Talking?" he said with a wry grin. It looked extremely odd on the hideous caricature he had adopted. "I know, we usually skip the talking, don't we? Anything meaningful, anyway."

"That's how we roll," she sighed. She brought a hand to his face, her fingers delicately tracing the absurd lines and folds of his features. "And not just with each other. I see your veil, Red Djinni. And not just your mask, or the faces you use. The way you hide, I guess I relate."

"Yeah," he whispered. "You get it, I can tell. Hiding's what we do, and we've gotten good at it. Really good."

"Maybe too good," she said. "You hide from it for so long, it just becomes part of you. You don't expect to have to share it with anyone, but when you do..."

"... you hope they don't hate you for it."

She watched as his face softened, his eyes once again boring into hers. This time she didn't look away, and realized with a start that his smile came as a mirror to her own. She felt a flush rise in her cheeks, her breath catch in her throat, and for a moment she was lost in him. There were many reasons this couldn't work, but they didn't seem very important to her anymore. And then he was kissing her. It was different. Before, it was all a haze of lust and need. Now, it was simply... right.

After, he did something he never had before. He held her to him, and she marveled over the casual rush of sensation of his breath flowing over her shoulder.

"Can I ask you something?" he said.

"You can ask," she replied, burying her face deep into his neck.

"What were they after? Your captors, I mean."

She pulled away from him, startled. In the faint light, she

watched as his own expression shifted from surprise to comprehension and finally to guilt.

"Sorry," he said. "I didn't mean to..."

She stopped him with a gentle press of her fingers to his lips.

"Don't worry about it," she whispered.

He grinned, a full-on Alfred E. Neuman grin.

"What, me worry?" he said, and held her again and she smothered her laughter into his chest.

It would have been a complicated bit of programming if more
than half of it hadn't been spellcasting. *If Djinni's at Mel's place,
turn off Overwatch audio/visual. Unless*—and a complicated list of
biometric conditions. Because she didn't want to know, she truly
didn't want to know. Well, she *knew,* but she didn't want the
details. Didn't want the temptation of having a recording either,
because even though you don't want to know, there is still that
urge, like picking at a scab, to find out anyway.

It had all worked pretty well, until tonight, when Mel screamed
in her sleep, and not only triggered the Overwatch "wake up," it
triggered an alert that woke *her* up and fed the rest right into
her ear.

Stuck in a state that was half embarrassed shock and half sleep
fog, she stopped it right after *"I don't wake up screaming from
mine,"* and put Djinni's system back to "silent monitor." She sat
in her bed with her face buried in her hands, weeping quietly.

For what had been lost.

For what would never be.

Then, knowing that sleep would not be coming again soon,
she went to the bathroom, washed her face, and bundled up in
a heavy robe. Overwatch always needed additions, tweaking. Intel
needed sorting, looking over, analyzing. There was always work.

Until the day she died, there would always be work.

CHAPTER EIGHTEEN

Beloved

MERCEDES LACKEY AND CODY MARTIN

Oh, how Shen Xue despised this man, who bent over his desk, pointedly ignoring the one who had come to give him the news he so longed to hear. And yet . . . he had the means and resources to combat the Thulian menace, and the General did not. And the General knew that once Dominick Verdigris was no longer distracted by the Celestial and his need to obtain the creature, he would finally bend that formidable intellect on the *important* problem of how to defeat the Thulians. If only as a means to save his own gutless hide.

So the General would get him his toy. He would play with it, and get what he wanted from it, and then they would go to work. And eventually, when the Thulians were defeated, Shen Xue would end him. The Celestial would be a valuable tool for Shen Xue once Verdigris was removed.

There could only be *one* Emperor, after all.

And so the General made a perfunctory little bow to this thing he despised, and spoke the words Verdigris had been waiting for. "The trap is ready."

Verdigris's head came up, infernal fire in his eyes. "When?" he demanded.

But the General made a hushing motion with one hand. "The fewer that know, the better. But it will be soon."

"*Shto?*" Red Saviour stared at Untermensch in fury and astonishment. "What do you mean, there is no petrol?"

"There is no petrol, Commissar," Georgi repeated with a shrug.

254

"Is hazard of working with old equipment. Gauge reads full, tank is empty. Delivery will not be for four days. We are nyet petrol station, we do not get priority." With the entire world still in the midst of rebuilding, gasoline shortages were commonplace, unless you were part of an essential service, like the police, hospital ambulances, or the military. The CCCP fell somewhere along that spectrum, but also somehow short of it; some weeks it came down to how much threatening and cajoling Natalya could get away with being the only thing that kept the lights on and the gas tanks on the Urals full.

Natalya fumed, but what could she do? Not all the screaming or pounding a desk, or threatening boots to the head, would fill the empty tank. For the next four days, anywhere CCCP comrades needed to go, if they did not have some sort of power that enabled them to travel quickly, they would either have to walk, or...

Or call upon ECHO. Nyet! Saviour did *not* want to have to go to the blue girl—who should never have been put in charge—with cap in hand, begging for favors. Bella Parker was a good healer, a fine healer, but too timid to lead. Look what she was doing now! It was well past time to take the battle to the enemy, but she delayed and delayed, speaking words of caution. Words of cowardice? Maybe. She did not want to think such things of one that she had come to call *sestra*, but this was war. Natalya knew that she had to think dispassionately about the problem. It was never wise to put a healer in charge of an army. They thought too much of casualties, of losses, and not enough of victory at whatever cost was required. Natalya reflected for a moment on how much they had already lost; how many people, how many comrades... it was a stab of pain that she quickly locked away. Nyet, *must focus on the moment, not the past.*

And, of course, at just this moment there was an urgent delivery from Moscow waiting at the shipping depot. What it was, Saviour didn't know; she only knew there would be phone calls and shouting if it was not in her hands within an hour or two, because that was how her father and Boryets showed her that *they* were the ones in charge of CCCP, and not her. Petty tyrannies... well, Moscow had always worked by tyrannies, petty and not so petty, and right now, she needed Moscow's good will. And of course, the shipping company would not deliver *here*, oh no, it was too dangerous, they said. Which was why she had intended to send Untermensch, the best rider among the comrades, on a Ural.

"Bah," she said, then spat. "*Bah*. I will go myself!" She could fly, after all. It should not take more than half an hour, an hour at most, to go there and back. No wasted fuel that they didn't have, neat and tidy.

"Not advisable, Commissar," Untermensch objected. "You are needed here. Even with Overwatch and Gamayun, if something were to erupt, the Commissar must be in place to lead. How many times have you not shouted at the television, because *nekulturny* starship captain goes on away team?"

"Stupid *svinya* starship captain," she muttered, but as usual, Georgi was right. Who to send? The depot was across town, and across three separate destruction corridors. Impassible for anything other than the van and Urals, and a route which would take too long for one on foot. One would have to have wings—

"*Ha!*" she exclaimed, snapping her fingers. *Perfect.* "Overwatch," she ordered. "Open: Comrade Sera."

As Georgi tilted his head to the side, momentarily confused, the so-called "angel" answered the hail on her headset. "*Yes, Commissar, have you an order for me?*" came the infuriatingly calm and neutral voice. Natalya not only found the "angel" herself irritating, by virtue of simply existing, she found the woman herself doubly so because she was so impossible to read, or to intimidate. She did not like the business between the "angel" and Murdock, either. She needed all of her comrades to be at their best for the coming days, and right now the *Amerikanski* and the winged woman were certainly not, between his memory and her delusions. If nothing else, however, the "angel" knew how to take commands and carry them out, a trait that Natalya could certainly admire in a subordinate.

"Da, am having order for you. Important courier duty. You are being to fly with all haste to ExpressEx depot and pick up package for me."

At least the "angel" never argued with orders. "*At once, Commissar,*" she said, obediently, as Red Saviour replied to the email notice from ExpressEx with the reply that Comrade Seraphym—*nasrat*, even to type the word made her irritated!—was authorized to accept the parcel.

"There. That is sorted," she said to Georgi. "Now, what other crisis is there needing my attention?"

"Well, there is the matter of the Urals themselves, Commissar...."

Natalya let out an exasperated sigh. "How many *more* has that *Amerikanski* destroyed?"

It was winter now, and although Atlanta seldom was cold enough for snow, the world was still white and gray; the white of bleached concrete, the gray of stone, and bare or winter-dormant trees. The gray of leaden skies, through which the Seraphym flew. The bleakness of the still-shattered destruction corridors oppressed her, the skies oppressed her, the chill of the air oppressed her.

And yet, it seemed fitting. Fitting that the ground, the sky, be dressed in white and gray. It was winter's turn to dance in the skies where she had once danced, and where now she labored, heavy wingbeat after heavier wingbeat.

The cold had not mattered before; she had been indifferent to heat or cold. Now...now it seemed as if warmth never entered the core of her. Except when she was near John Murdock—and that was such a false and deceptive warmth. And a temptation, the temptation to see in him the man she had lost—no, not just that, to *make* him into the man she had lost, and that could not possibly be Permitted. She kept her distance from him as much as possible, which was exceedingly difficult given that the Commissar kept throwing the two of them together.

At least this assignment was one she had been given alone. It was better for them to be apart, no matter how much she missed the man he was now. That man was a good man, but he must become something she could not foresee. He must not bind himself to her in any way. He must not ask her for direction. He must grow.

And I must diminish. That is how it must be. My powers must become his. He must connect to the Infinite, and become something more than mortal, and less than seraph, with the understanding of the former and the vision of the latter. For that to happen, he must take what I have left, and I must dwindle and be gone.

The headset she wore chirped out its directions to her in a mechanical monotone as she flew. This landscape of alternately shattered and intact cityscape was not familiar to her, but the guidance of the computers that her headset was linked to was enough. Finally, she saw in the near distance a mathematical array of identical buildings, and the familiar orange and blue livery of ExpressEx trucks.

Odd. Something about this place seemed hauntingly familiar....

She landed on sudden impulse in a quiet spot, where there were no trucks, and no people; nothing moved in that gray landscape of faded asphalt and concrete and metal. It was a spot that she did not recognize until she turned a little, and then—oh then—she was struck dumb, and numb, with recognition.

This was where she had first seen him. This was where she had first encountered him; *spoken* to him. This was where she had met John Murdock.

It felt like a knife to the heart, that recognition. The memory overwhelmed her, blinded her, deafened and defeated her. *There* he had stood, over the body of the wounded driver he had saved, the man who had become the ECHO meta Speed Freak. *There* he had looked at her—actually seen her for what she *was*—without comprehension of what he was seeing. *There* was the scorched, vaguely man-shaped splotch on the pavement that was all he had left of the gang leader he had slain.

And there, there, there he had stood, the pain of his life standing clear in his eyes, the aching need for forgiveness a raw wound in his soul—

Without realizing it, she cried aloud, blinded, a cry of pain of her own, for *there she had stood, still at one with the Infinite, still at one with the Song* and now she was alone, alone, alone....

So it was, she did not see the furtive movement behind her. Did not sense the men around her. Did not know there was anything amiss until she heard a muffled sound, like an explosion, but nearer to hand, and she whirled, and saw the net in the air, the sparkling drops upon its weft like drops of black blood. Did not think to call her sword of fire until it was too late, and the net settled over her, each of those drops a focus of terrible pain that drove all thought from her, and the net flattened her to the cracked asphalt, afire with a fire that was not hers, until the sharp stab of a needle against her neck brought nothingness.

...how long had it been?

Minutes? Hours? Days?

Time was meaningless in the face of more pain than she had ever imagined it was possible to feel. She only knew the pain, and the voice of Dominick Verdigris, who asked the same questions, over and over.

How do I escape? How do I prevent becoming that brain in a box? How?

And over and over, because she could not lie, being what she was, she choked out words he would not understand. Refused to understand. *I do not know. I do not know.*

But you can see the futures! All the futures! How do I escape?

I do not know, she would wail, or scream, or whisper from cracked and bleeding lips, from a throat too raw to do more than whisper. *I do not know. I am not what I was. I do not know.*

And so her answer never varied, not when Shen Xue tortured her with means arcane and means mundane. Not when Verdigris ordered the men clad in black to inject strange drugs that made her veins cry and sent stranger visions than she had ever seen in all of her vast experience stream through her fevered mind.

Not when, in exasperation, they shattered her wings, first one, and then the other. She could only repeat the truth, for that was all that was left to her. *I do not know.*

And at length, Shen Xue finally said what she herself had been saying, in tones of detached disgust. "The creature is no longer Celestial. It truly does not know. We are wasting time."

She sensed the holographic image of Verdigris approaching the perimeter of the arcane circle inscribed on the floor, felt his eyes on her. Felt his anger. But he was silent for a very long time.

Then, at last, he spoke. "She doesn't know anything *new,* but there are still memories of the future in there. We'll take her to my psi lab and I'll have them out of her with a telepath. Even if we have to carve them out of her goddamned mind. At least we'll know what to avoid."

And then the footsteps, heavy and labored, light and indifferent, faded, and she was left alone with the pain of her shattered body.

But piercing through the blood-red curtain of the pain came... finally... a thought. *I am not what I was. But I can still will my own death.*

She knew death, knew all the ways there were to come to that door. She had passed in and out of it countless times, as escort to others, guiding them, sometimes carrying them. She had taken Mathew March through that door.

It had not been Permitted before, but surely it was now. She was no longer needed. John Murdock could hear the Song now, and the Song would guide him. The last of her powers would go to him when she died. And Verdigris—Verdigris must not extract what little she knew of the futures from her. Above all, he must *not* learn of John, and what John was poised to become! His psychics could, and would, pull that information from her mind, and then John would become his target.

Death was nothing in the face of that last possibility. Yes, death would be Permitted, she was sure of it.

Yes. Yes, at last it had been accomplished. Her work was done. She allowed herself to let go, to fall, to fall into deep and comforting darkness. Death was easy, it was living that was hard.

The pain fell away. Feelings faded. Moments were lost, though timeless time remained. From a distance, she saw the great things that burned within him, and was so proud, so proud of what they had been, of what he would be. And then that spun away into the darkness and was gone, and all she felt was the longing for her wings, to fly again, to fly into the darkness, to fly into Eternity.

And yet, she hesitated, for just a moment.

Then the wordless words came to her, the last thing she needed to do. One last word of farewell that she must send out, before she could be free.

With all of her heart, and her soul, and her fading strength, she sent it. A shout? A whisper? Both?

Oh, my Beloved . . . Beloved . . . goodbye. . . .

CHAPTER NINETEEN

Rubicon

MERCEDES LACKEY AND CODY MARTIN

The 'hood was quiet this afternoon. Well, it was cold, overcast, and what with the wind, pretty nasty out; not the time for kids to be out on the homemade playground. John liked this sort of weather, though; it was a welcome change from the usual boiling heat that defined the South, and Atlanta in particular. He had finished walking his beat for the day, and with nothing else immediate on the duty roster he had chosen to devote some of his free time to doing handyman work around the 'hood. He desperately needed some rack time, but the Commissar worked them all like "*nekulturny running dogs*," and he was no exception, so rather than having her "find" something for him to do, he'd opted for outside work. It beat the hell out of scrubbing the floor, or worse, babysitting the Bear. Despite John's weariness, keeping busy had the added benefit of keeping his mind off of things ... for the most part.

John Murdock certainly had a lot on his mind. The war, his new living situation, his past. More than any of that, however, today he was thinking most about Sera, and the music he had been hearing. What both of them meant to him, what he should do about it. Every time he seemed to find an inroad with either one of them, the path dwindled away before him, leaving him lost again. Sera was ... very, very good at evading him, especially since their last conversation. And chasing the music was like chasing a phantom. The more he chased after it, the faster it got away from him. Frustrating for a man that was used to solving problems, no matter what.

So, unable to make headway with that situation, today he chose to solve different kinds of problems, nice, easy, physical problems, hoping that working on them would quiet the chatter in the back of his mind.

Jonas, the elderly black shopkeeper who served as John's interface with the community, had met him at the playground after his patrol was over. "Got one of the boys watchin' shop for me;" the old man had said with a snort. "Kid needed somethin' to keep his dumb ass out of trouble."

Today's project was taking some of the scrap metal that residents of the 'hood had been salvaging and making a new set of monkey bars for the playground, bigger, more elaborate and better suited to the older kids. John and Jonas had selected the most suitable pieces of pipe, then designed the equipment. John would take care of welding everything together, since welding rigs were scarce in this part of town and prohibitively expensive on top of that—and that didn't even add in the cost for the generator to run an electric welder, or the gas bottles, for a gas welder. After that, Jonas would get some of the youths from the 'hood watch to sand everything down so it was safe and have the younger kids paint it however they liked. It'd be something everyone could be proud of and enjoy, that way. Little things like this served to bring the community that much closer together.

John was holding a pair of borrowed welder's goggles to his eyes; using a thin concentrated flame from his right hand, he was putting the finishing touches on the six-post frame that would make up the body of the monkey bars, when all the comm channels in his head seemed to erupt at once.

First a burst of confused words, none of them making sense. Then Gamayun. "...*but am getting ping from headset*—"

Vix interrupted. "*That's the headset ping, there's no life-signs ping! And she's dropped right off the magical radar!*"

"...*the hell just happened?*" That was ECHO CEO Bella Parker. "*I just got a...like a board upside my head, and it's Sera, only then she just vanished out of my skull!*"

"*I don't know, that's what I'm trying to find out!*" Vix shrilled. "*She's gone, Bells, I haven't got her live anywhere!*"

John shut off his fires, causing Jonas to cock his head to the side. "Hey! This is Murdock, what the hell is goin' on? One person tell me, not all of ya at once." John felt a block of ice slam into his gut. He didn't like the sound of the comm chatter, nor the panicked tones he was hearing from people he depended on to keep their cool when all hell was breaking loose. This had to be bad for any of them to sound like that.

"Gamayun, take him!" Vix snapped. *"I'm busy here!"*

The voice of Gamayun took over, as the others snapped off their links to him, for now, at least. *"Comrade Seraphym was to being sent by Commissar to ExpressEx Depot for courier duty,"* the Russian told him, her voice strained. *"She did not check in when arrived. I am having ping to headset there now, but Comrade Victrix says are no life signs, and that she cannot detect Comrade Seraphym by* nekulturny *magics either. Commissar Bella is to being say she has big empathic strike which is somehow linked to Comrade Seraphym. ECHO Corbie—is on way—"* There was a long pause. *"ECHO Corbie is to being on scene, this moment, following locator. He is finding . . . headset, camera and life-sign relay, all in pile. Nothing else."*

"So there's no body. She's not dead. I'm on my way." John turned to Jonas. "Emergency, man. I've gotta go. It's Sera."

Jonas slapped him upside the head. "Well, get the hell on then instead of jawin' at me, ya damn fool!"

John didn't need any more encouragement. He dropped the welder's goggles at his feet and took off running; Vix had already projected the path onto his HUD.

John's enhancements had been keyed up from the moment he had left the 'hood playground; it took almost no effort to do so, now, and he ran at incredible speeds, faster than any ordinary man and most metas could. When he skidded to a halt, sending up clouds of dust and bits of broken asphalt at the end of the path Vic had laid out for him on his HUD, Corbie was already working the scene, bending over an area marked off by crime-scene tape, and startled at his sudden arrival.

"God's balls, mate. You got here right quick." The winged meta held up bagged equipment; the Overwatch Mark One gear that John remembered Sera always wearing. Something about . . . Vix not being able to install the Mark Two internals on her. Sent her magic haywire or some such. "I got these. And I got this." He held up a smaller baggie, that seemed to hold a bit of broken . . . something. Crystal? Glass? It was a barely translucent black-red. "And this." This, at least, John recognized. A spent syringe.

Corbie seemed to be listening intently for a moment; probably to Vix. "Just a sec." The ECHO meta pulled something out of his pocket and unfolded it. It was a piece of paper with some sort of complicated diagram on it—it seemed to have been painted there in copper ink. He put it down carefully on the asphalt, and a moment later, there was a *piff* of displaced air, and Vix's little stone helper Herb appeared in the middle of it. Corbie handed off the baggie with the syringe and the other with the bit of crystal in it. Herb took both and clutched them to his chest. There was another *piff* and he was gone.

John started scanning the entire area, looking for anything that might have been missed. "Overwatch: command: open Vix. Vix, I need everythin' you can tell me 'bout what you just got sent."

"I don't know about the syringe yet. The rock is . . . it's anti-magic and anti-Celestial. I'll know more when I can analyze it."

"So this was specifically tailored for Sera. Someone who knows what she really is, an' was comin' after her only. This wasn't a random hit." John's mind was racing with possibilities, scenarios, suspects. Who could do this? Why? Kriegers looking to pick them off one by one?

"Comrade Murdock, answer." That was Untermensch, on the CCCP frequency.

"Murdock here. Go ahead."

"Am finding slow drain from main petrol tank into sewer, with sensor on it. Someone installed it, since last time we inspected. Comrade Angel was sent to make pickup because there was no fuel for Urals."

"A setup to give whoever did this the best chance to get Sera out an' alone. Snatch job. Someone's got her; there's no blood here, no body. They either wanted to disappear her, or whoever it is is takin' her for somethin' else. All of this is tailored for her. Am I off on this? Vic, Unter?"

"Ten-four, Johnny," Vix replied, her voice grim.

"Am seeing no other conclusion," Unter agreed. *"Only other comrade being able to fly is Commissar, and if it was Commissar they wanted, they would most likely nyet have taken Seraphym on whim. Nor would being use anti-magic device."*

"Murdock," the Commissar snapped on the same frequency. *"You are to be reporting to HQ now. We are not needing to lose two workers in same day. Let Comrade Witch do what is needed.*

CCCP must regroup and discover if this is attack only on Comrade Sera or on CCCP as a whole."

"Commissar, respectfully, I'm gonna request to stay on the scene." Before Saviour could answer, John snapped out an order of his own. "Overwatch: command: close CCCP channel." He breathed heavily for a moment, composing himself. Corbie had taken the cue and was busy on the perimeter. He knew he was probably going to get his ass kicked for disobeying the Commissar like that, but he didn't care at the moment. "Vic, I imagine you just heard all of that. I'm not quitting this. Okay?"

"Very okay. I'm keeping Gamayun from reopening your channel until I let her. Johnny, short of Bella, you're the one of us with the best chance of finding her. And I won't let Bella go hunting. I've got Bull sitting on her to make sure."

"That's 'bout the size of it. I'll get her back, Vic; count on it. What can you tell me from what Herb brought you?"

"The crystal is something really, really old, which makes me figure they used all or part of some artifact someone dug up. Like I said, anti-magic and anti-Celestial. The anti-magic part is pretty specific. Blocked the ability to be found by someone like me, and how the hell do they know about magic locators, and blocked her powers. That's why she dropped off my radar. Anti-Celestial... not sure what it would do to her. She's not an angel anymore, but she's also not just a metahuman."

"And the syringe? I'm guessin' somethin' to incapacitate her." John wasn't accustomed to praying, but if there was anything out there, he was praying to them that it wasn't anything immediately lethal.

"Just got the mass-spec readout from it. Matches propofol. That's a knock-out-an-elephant drug. Practically instantaneous." There was a pause, but with background whispers that suggested she wasn't done yet. *"Johnny... find her. You've got to find her. You're her only hope."*

"I'll find her, Vic. Or I'm goin' to die tryin'. Either way, I imagine that a lot of other folks are goin' to buy the farm on the way. Keep the Commissar an' ECHO off of my back. I need all the help I can get, but I don't need anyone gettin' in my way. Whoever grabbed her did it with a purpose. I can't imagine that purpose is goin' to be very comfortable for her, or have her long for this world." John was warring with a lot of emotions; fear, hate, rage, vengeance and the barest hope. He *had* to get Sera back. "Roger that?"

"Leaving your channel closed to everyone but me." Another pause. *"Shit."*

"What?" he snapped. Vickie cussed in probably more languages than John could count. When she did it in English, it usually meant something bad.

"Eight Ball gives it eighty-five percent probability it's Verd."

"We got any leads 'bout where he might be? I know he's gone to ground."

"In the wind. Bella had a plan to smoke him out, but it never went anywhere. Hell, he has more money than a lot of countries, he could be right under or on top of you and we probably wouldn't know until it was too late."

"So, that's a 'no.' Gotta be him using his faction that he split off from Blacksnake; that's a lot of manpower, but still nothin' concrete to go on."

"...look, I know you don't much like all that business that went on between you two ... before you woke up. And I know you don't like magic. But I was not saying you're her only hope lightly. You two are still connected, magically, spiritually. If you try, I am pretty sure you can sense that connection and follow it to her, and I am also pretty sure there is nothing that can block it, because it's not magic and it's not Celestial."

John waited a beat. "This isn't any hoodoo bullshit or anythin' like that, right? Cause ... there's somethin' I've only told Sera ... I've been hearin' music when I'm around her. Like, weird strains of stuff that I've never heard before. She said I had to listen to it. Does that track for you? Y'think it's that connection?"

"If it's not, I don't know what else to suggest."

"Then that's what we're going with."

As soon as John had finished the sentence, he was doubled over with the most incredible pain that he could ever remember feeling; it was from no cause he could fathom, either. It was as if all of his senses were on fire; he could feel a distant despair, a longing for release, almost insurmountable anguish. And it wasn't his, but he owned it all the same. He struggled to breathe through the pain, falling to his knees and fighting to stand again. The edges of his vision flashed between darkness, flaring white and deep red. *Sera's dying.* He didn't know how he knew, but he was certain of it all the same.

He felt hands on his shoulders, steadying him. He whirled

around defensively, hands up and immediately sheathed in fire until he saw it was Corbie. "Whoa there! What's wrong, mate?" the ECHO meta exclaimed.

"I've...I've gotta go. Right now. I'm sorry, but I can feel her. She's in pain. Goddamnit, she's dying!" John extinguished his fires with an effort. He felt himself retreat from the edge of panic, going cold, building his resolve. It was a practiced response, but one that took more will than ever before. "It's Sera. She's still alive. I know it."

Corbie stepped back. "Go!" he said, simply. "Get 'er back, mate."

John didn't waste any time. He ran. His enhancements keyed up already, he ran. He let the music guide him. It was fading in and out, and he stumbled and fell several times when jagged rays of pain lanced through his entire body; it felt like his core was being torn apart with rusty knives. He raced through the destruction corridors, breaching their barriers with a blast of fire when necessary, and crossing through the untouched neighborhoods and streets of Atlanta. He was almost a blur to anyone who happened to see him; weaving in and out of traffic, jumping over barriers, dodging pedestrians. He couldn't go fast enough, he knew he was losing her, losing Sera...she was growing further and further away with each passing second.

Then, as he tried to put on yet more speed...there came a whisper in his heart.

Oh, my Beloved...Beloved...goodbye....

John's entire being was on fire. Every fiber was alight, and how he *screamed* in that moment. He thought he was going to die. Instead, he ran harder, and kicked off the ground with all the force he could muster...and then he was in the air. Initially, he panicked. He was thirty feet above the ground, flailing his arms and legs, and was going as fast as a sports car when he touched down on the asphalt, rolling into an abandoned car and crumpling its rear panel completely with the impact.

It hurt like hell. And that didn't matter.

He didn't stop. He was up again, running, running, faster than he ever had before. His uniform was torn, tattered from the impact, scraped away by the friction, and then he kicked off again, instinctively...and he was in the air. He looked back for half a second, seeing a plume of roaring flame coming from his lower legs, as if he was some sort of missile or rocket, and his feet and calves were the motor. Since his head was turned, he careened off the side of an abandoned tenement building, a bloom of glass and shards of cement trailing from where his shoulder struck the structure; more pain.

Focus, focus, dammit!

The wind was so intense, he had to shut his eyes against it. Even opening them a sliver resulted in his eyes watering and stinging more than he could bear. All the same, he followed the music, the call, the urgent need to find the source of it. *Be just my luck if I splatter my brains against the side of a building or a plane.*

"Johnny, the hell, do you have a jetpack? What the—do you read?"

"Vic!" He called out unnecessarily against the wind; all of the Mark Two Overwatch rigs had subvocal mics, more literal technowizardry from Vic. "I'm going after her!"

"But you're flying!"

"Don't ask me how, goddamnit! Focus!"

"Okay. Okay. Your flight path will intersect with a C130 cargo plane. But it has the tail-numbers of an L1011 retired a month ago, and that ain't kosher. I'm betting that's your target."

"I don't care if it's a goddamn fighter jet! I can't stop, Vic!" John didn't dare turn his head, even though he could feel the wind scoring his face with its ferocity. "What is it over?"

"Swamp all the way to Athens and the coast."

"Whatever happens, I'm gettin' her out. If I don't, you know what to do, right?"

"No, but I'll think of something."

John gritted his teeth, shouting against the wind. "If I can't bring her out of where she is, you find some way to blow the fuckin' thing to kingdom come. I don't care how; I ain't leavin' without her, so if I'm not leavin', I'm dead. Got it?" If he was going to buy the farm on this, he sure as hell wanted whoever did it to catch a piece.

Vickie's voice turned . . . cold. Purposeful. *"Reprogramming ECHO intercept missile now."* A pause. *"But dammit, meathead, you better bring her back! Or I'll find a way to resurrect you and kill you all over again!"* Her voice broke on the last word.

John couldn't help but smile, and tried to laugh in the face of the wind. "I know, comrade. Just make sure that no matter what happens, the bad guys don't come out ahead. I'll catch you on the other side."

"With Sera." He felt a warmth wash over him that had nothing to do with his own fires. *"There. That's all the magical juju I've got to send you. Don't fucking waste it."*

John felt renewed; there was still the pain, underneath everything else, but he was able to put more of his energy into being fast, into finding Sera. The music, the Song—it was a dissonant choir that somehow harmonized, and the burden of the Song was agony. There was a single female voice atop it all, crying out, and yet fading at the same time. Longing for death, and yet longing for life. Willing to die and yet crying out for... something, something that was more precious than life itself. The closer he came to the blur that must be the airplane Vix had described to him, the louder, the more compelling the Song became. It towered over him, like a giant wave, and yet it hung there, it did not break.

All of his being vibrated like a bell struck on the right note. It was powerful, horrible, wonderful, all-consuming. As suddenly as it had come upon him, it ended. As he crashed through the back of the plane, ripping off the cargo ramp under the tail with his hands and fire, the wave of music broke over the top of him and made him part of it. He *saw* Sera; alight, flaming with glory and beauty and more *Song*. And pain, so much pain.

He landed in a crouch on the floor of the cargo section. A transparent man—a hologram?—stared at him from less than a foot away. Just as he recognized the man from pictures and video as Dominic Verdigris, the image flickered out and was gone.

And with a sort of double vision, he saw the Sera-in-Glory, reaching out to him, as if she was bestowing something upon him—and at the same time, he saw a crumpled, shattered, bloody thing in the forward part of the cargo-hold, caught. Captured. Debased and broken. No...not broken, not yet. Curled in on itself, but still holding out against all. Then John saw the ugliest reality of it all. Twelve men, armed and ready for him, weapons up. Behind all of them was People's Blade, cool and collected, sword still sheathed. She stood behind the chains and cage that Sera was trapped in.

"Anyone that doesn't want to die bloody needs to get off of this plane. Right now," John growled. It didn't matter to him whether these mercs were bad men, or guys just doing it for the money. At that moment, they were standing between him and

Sera, and that was *all* that mattered. If they didn't concede to his will, they didn't have a future.

People's Blade sniffed, then motioned with her left hand. "Kill him. We don't have the time to waste with such interference."

The first three rushed him, headlong. John somehow knew the angles they would be coming at, where they would attack, where they would try to land blows. Whether they would attack him with guns or knives or bare-handed, or some more esoteric weapon. It all flashed in his mind just before it happened; with his reflexes, he had all the time he needed. The first of the three squeezed off a burst from his rifle while the other two ran at him from the sides. John felt where the shots were going to go, and simply wasn't there when the bullets crossed that piece of space. He sent a flash of flame at the face of the one with the rifle, making the man reflexively flail backwards as his arms and head caught fire. John moved on the merc coming at him from the right; smoothly he sidestepped the merc's lunging knife, grabbing the man's outstretched arm. With a sharp tug he carried the man, knife first, into the third man, the one that was still rushing from the left, pistol in hand. The knife plunged through the third merc's chest. John ignited both of them, then sent the tangled pair skittering across the deck and out the destroyed cargo door with a backwards kick. They fell, screams vanishing into the distance.

The rest of the mercs were momentarily stunned.

"I said kill him! Now! Fire!" People's Blade stepped back as the remaining mercs raised their guns again. John dashed forward, juking first to the left, then committing to the right. The mercs all began firing at once, the noise deafening in the confined space. The rounds stitched holes in the fuselage, but none found their mark. They were all good shots, highly trained and used to working together; John was just too fast for them, anticipating where they were aiming and then *not being there.* John ducked under a burst from the closest mercenary, then unholstered his own 1911 and shot the man twice in the face, still moving. Instinctively, he knew he would have to use his fires sparingly. Nothing would be won if he set the entire plane ablaze. Time seemed slowed down, and he was moving faster than he ever had; it wasn't just his enhancements, but something more. Something from his connection to Sera. The next merc was in the center of the cargo hold, and had run his weapon's magazine dry. John slid next to him smoothly just as the man finished reloading. He jerked the submachine gun from the merc's grasp so hard that the strap broke, sending the merc to the floor face first. John finished the job by stomping on the back of the merc's head with a sickening crack; then he was moving again. He crouched behind a metal crate for half a beat before springing out from cover again; four quick bursts from the rifle, and four more mercs went down, dead or dying. The submachine gun was empty, so he threw it as hard as he could at one of the mercs at the back; the man caught the whirled hunk of metal and plastic full in the face, and was knocked out cold. John still had his pistol; he had to keep moving, otherwise they'd concentrate their fire and be able to pin him down.

The last two standing were spread out, on opposite sides of the cargo hold. John went for the one on the right first. He ran, ducking and weaving so that the merc couldn't get a clear shot. When he was next to the man, he grabbed the merc by his vest and planted the barrel of his 1911 under the man's chin. With a grunt, he pulled the trigger, and that was the end of that. The limp body still in his grasp, he spun it around so that it was between him and the other merc. The merc on the other side of the hold started firing, stitching his comrade's body and the surrounding fuselage with more holes. John felt a round impact with the shoulder of his nanoweave jacket; he knew the round would be slowed down going through the dead body, and thus the damage was minimal. John swung his pistol around the side of the dead merc's body, emptying the magazine into his target, starting at the pelvis and working his way up until the last round left a messy hole in the merc's skull.

The merc he had thrown the submachine gun at was now waking up. He dropped the dead merc he'd been holding—all of the bullets he had taken had left him less than intact—before holstering his 1911 again. Looking down at his feet, he saw the first merc who had shot at him, moaning from the burns on his arms and head. John hefted the man up by his belt and the drag handle on the back of his gear, and held him up between himself and the groggy merc. Both mercs screamed, one from fear, one from rage, as the final merc completely emptied his weapon into John's human shield. John dropped the burned and now very dead merc, the body crumpling to the floor. Very calmly, he walked up to the final merc. He could see the fear in the man's eyes as he reflexively continued pulling the trigger on his empty rifle. With his right hand, he grabbed the merc by the throat, and then *lifted* him off of the ground. John looked People's Blade in the eye as he ignited his hand, and the fire spread to the merc he was holding. His screams started low before building up into a high-pitched wail. When the man's entire body was covered in flame, John turned and threw him at the back of the plane, where he hit the edge of the ruined cargo door before falling into the darkening sky.

John felt as if he were holding a live wire. Everything he saw had a harder, cleaner edge to it. He noticed tiny details, like the headstamp on an empty shell casing, or the pattern the bullet holes in the fuselage made, the smell of blood and burned paint and metal, the cooked smell of burned flesh, the strangely crisp scent of scorched fabric, the acrid stench of melted plastic.

He drank in all of this instantaneously. His heart rate was steady and even. He had just brutally killed twelve men, and while that faintly disgusted him, he realized that, far from being repulsed by what he had done, he didn't care all that much. There was something much more important occupying his emotions. They were hurting *her*, and were trying to stop him. Sera was the only thing that mattered.

People's Blade drew her sword, although she did not otherwise move. Her eyes narrowed, and—John had the strangest feeling that there was something—alien—looking out at him from inside that tiny body.

"You would be well advised to leave now," the diminutive woman stated, in flat voice, and with a strange accent he didn't recognize. "This is Jade Emperor's Whisper, and not even a creature imbued with Celestial power can stand against it. We have this female, and we will keep her until we have no more use for her."

"I'm not leaving. An' you're not keepin' her. Let her go right this second, an' I won't kill you. What the Commissar will do, I can't vouch for, however." John paced slowly towards her, stopping about ten feet away. Sera was behind People's Blade now, still in her cage. She wasn't moving. John couldn't even tell if she was breathing.

The woman smiled slightly. "Hubris. How . . . American."

"It is what it is. Cut her loose, or get ready to die, *comrade.*" John put extra venom into the final word, spitting it out like a curse. John ignited both of his hands, his body relaxed but ready to spring into action.

Faster than he thought was possible, People's Blade charged him, sword raised high. Even with the wind screaming from the back of the plane and the noise of the engines, John's enhanced hearing should have picked up something. But she didn't make a single sound as she ran straight at him. He didn't have any time to blast her, draw his pistol or take any meaningful defensive action; she was just that quick, almost as fast as he was. He hadn't been expecting it, and, unlike with the mercs, he hadn't "seen" ahead of time what she was going to do. Reflexively, the threw his flaming hand up just as she was bringing the sword down to split him through the middle. John shut his eyes at the last second; he had failed, and now he and Sera were both dead. *Vic, you had better keep that promise . . .*

There was a too-loud crash, and John felt a flash of heat in front of his face. He opened his eyes . . . and found himself holding what looked like a large sword—a claymore, something in the back of his mind told him—composed entirely of flame. It held Jade Emperor's Whisper on its edge, away from both of them.

People's Blade looked up at her weapon and then at his, her eyes wide with genuine shock. "Impossible!"

John knew he had to end this, and end it quickly. For whatever reason, he couldn't anticipate what the little woman was going to do the way he had for the mercs. And he knew nothing about sword-fighting, where she was an expert. He had to take advantage of this moment of surprise. He shoved her hard with his free hand, then grasped his own sword with both hands. With his taller frame and longer sword, he had more reach. But she was just as fast as he was, and had experience to match. She immediately lunged at him, following with a flurry of blows that he was barely able to block. Her attacks were calculated, but there was an edge of fury behind them. She hadn't expected him to still be alive, or a challenge to her, and have the insolence to be fighting back, and that simply enraged her. He had the advantage that his "sword" weighed nothing; hers was solid steel and had weight and heft; he could move his weapon around faster than a comparable steel sword, his augmented strength making up for the lack of weight behind swings.

Just as People's Blade was about to make a cut at his thigh that he couldn't block in time, the entire cargo plane bucked violently. Both of them fell to the floor as the center of gravity shifted; the plane had abruptly gone into a dive. John looked at the cockpit; the door had slammed open, revealing that there weren't any pilots, only complicated apparatuses connected to the controls and panels. *Some kind of fly-by-wire drone?* Whoever held the controller must have figured that it was safer to crash the plane than risk John winning. Both he and People's Blade clambered to their feet, swords pointed at each other.

"You will not win, barbarian. You *cannot* win! I will not have you interfere with my destiny!" People's Blade was almost vibrating with rage now, seething through clenched teeth.

"Y'know, I don't have time for this shit." John lowered his sword, then held out his left hand. A pencil-thin bolt of super hot plasma lanced out, spearing Fei Li through the center of her chest, punching through her back before hitting a bulkhead and causing a small explosion. People's Blade looked down at her chest in confusion, then raised her eyes to meet his. Something behind them softened, and she smiled gratefully as she sank to her knees.

"Thank you," she whispered as the sword clattered to the floor beside her; her voice was different, nothing like it had been moments before. Finally she closed her eyes as she crumpled to the floor. John didn't have time to think about it. The plane was on fire now, and going down. He had to get Sera out of here. He ran to where she was caged. He recognized the construction of the restraints as very similar to something that the CCCP had recovered from a Blacksnake outpost that he had raided when the Commissar had first tasked him with hunting down People's Blade; not that he remembered this, of course, but he had seen the pictures in the AAR. It was covered in symbols; some of them seemed to be vibrating and glowing, and somehow he could read some of it. Powerful binding words. He didn't have the time to process it; he brought the sword, still in hand, down on the joints of the cage, then on the chains. Instinctively he knew it was meant to hold someone—an angel—in, not to keep someone out.

Sera... it lacerated his soul just to see her like this. Her wings were twisted into unnatural shapes, and he thought he saw bone-ends sticking through the feathers. She was cut, burned, bruised and bloody. She lay as if she had just been tossed into the cage and had not moved since. Was she even still breathing? She *couldn't* be conscious. John extinguished the flames on his hands as well as his sword. She felt like a doll in his arms as he scooped her off of the floor.

"C'mon, darlin', we're gettin' outta here. This isn't our flight." John ran towards the back of the cargo plane; more of it was on fire now, and some of the electrical systems were blowing out in showers of sparks. When John was at the exit of what was left of the ramp, he stopped short. "Fuckin' hell, I sure hope this works." With that, he took the final step off, and both of them were falling through the sky. The wind was blinding again, and he had to almost completely shut his eyes against it. John had been trained in parachute drops—but it helped if you actually had a chute for those. He was able to keep his body stable and was facing towards the Earth, which was starting to look much bigger. He chanced a look over his shoulder; the plane was even more fully engulfed than he had realized, and was continuing its nose dive. It looked like something else fell off of or out of the plane. *Hope it doesn't land on us.*

The ground was still rushing towards them, and John's flight hadn't "kicked in" again. *Think, think! How'd you do it before? Come on!*

Then again, that whisper in his mind. . . . *you must fly, Beloved. Fly.* The words were so loaded with agony . . . and yet, they were freighted with terrible, frightening power, power that rushed into him—as if he were trying to drink from a fire hose. They had to be less than one hundred feet from the ground when the plume of fire burst from his feet and legs with a jolt, and just like that, they were flying. John whooped, his voice lost in the rushing wind. He looked down at Sera, and immediately his smile vanished. *She* was dying; worse, she was giving up, no longer fighting against it. He had to hurry. Shielding her and his face, he closed his eyes and willed himself to go faster.

Long minutes seemed like an eternity to John, insulated from everything with his eyes closed and the wind making him deaf. He felt like he was getting close to where he wanted to go, so he slowed his speed and cracked open his eyes. They were back in Atlanta, and he was near his squat.

"Vic, are you on the line?" The frantic sound of his own voice came as a shock even to him.

"Here."

"I got her. She's in a bad way, and I can't move her any more. I'm takin' her to my squat. Send whatever you can. She's not goin' to make it for much longer without help."

"Scrambling ECHO Med now."

He landed with a flare of fire from his legs, like retro-rockets, scorching the asphalt of the roof. He wanted to lay Sera down on the roof, and at the same time, was afraid to, afraid if he let go of her, she would let go of the last bond she had to life. Afraid that only his raw will was keeping her tethered to her poor shattered body. So he stumbled forward, out of the overheated area where he'd landed, and knelt with her still in his arms, limp, bloodied and broken; so very, very broken.

"Sera!" he choked out, then, out of desperation, squeezed his eyes tight shut and tried that wordless communication she had just used with him. *Sera!* he thought at her, and fumbled for some sense of her.

His eyes were closed, and yet, it was as if he was looking down a long, dark tunnel, and she was at the end of it. She looked back at him, over her shoulder, then away from him, as if the mere sight of him brought her unbearable pain. And suddenly he was flooded with images, with . . . entire, whole thoughts. Visions of himself, but powerful, wise in a way he couldn't even fathom himself being. Images of himself wielding the fires as she had, as weapons, as protections, immensely powerful, infinitely precise. Images of himself somehow connected with . . . *everything* . . . past, present, future . . .

You are the man you should have been, before you were broken. Stronger. Great-hearted. No longer beset with guilt and grief. No longer plagued by doubt and self-loathing. You will become the Instrument of the Infinite, so much more suited than I ever was. You understand Free Will. It is a part of you, hammered into your soul. You know what it is to be mortal, as I did not. You will be both more and less than I was, and both are important. I give you the last of my power, my strength. You will see the way through the darkness of these days and into the light. And he suddenly *understood* what that was supposed to mean, understood everything she meant, what she had determined . . .

. . . what she was giving up. *Even now,* what she was sacrificing. Because she was no longer a Seraphym, or even an angel, because she had given all of that to *him,* selflessly, and she was going to the other side, not knowing what she would become or what she would find when she got there. Merely whatever it was a mortal became when she died? No longer able to hear the chorus of her Siblings? She didn't even know, not for certain, that she had done the right thing. She knew only that she would have sacrificed everything, and the only thing she dared to hope for was to hear the words, *well done, my faithful servant,* when she let go of life—

He reacted instantly to that thought. *No!* He couldn't let her do this!

He could taste her fear, and fear was something so very foreign to her. But there was nothing before her now but loneliness and uncertainty, and so, she feared.

She was sacrificing herself a second time to save the world, yes, but also to save him. Giving up her power, giving up that connection with whatever it was that was Beyond. And doing so without reward, as she had knowingly given up any hope of regaining the first and only mortal love she had ever known, so that he, he would be free to make unfettered choices.

Him. And he didn't even remember any of it...

He felt her, in his mind. She was drifting into darkness; he reached out for her, willing her to stay. She retreated from him and he pursued, pushing frantically through the dark, desperate to reach her before she was irrevocably out of reach. For a moment, she vanished, and he thought with a flare of terror that he had lost her—

But then he saw her again, poor broken wings dragging from her back like a tattered cloak, illuminated as if by a spotlight in the darkness, looking up. Yearning upwards. He hurried to her side and saw that she was staring upwards into a blinding light, with every fiber of her speaking how much she wanted to reach that light.

And yet...she couldn't. It was out of reach. She could no longer fly.

Still staring into the light, with soundless tears pouring from her eyes she sank to her knees. She seemed faded, her once-vivid colors muted, grayed out, as if she had lost everything that had made her vital and alive. Her hair, her tattered wings, now the color of dying roses, her eyes a pale gray, her skin like old paper. Everything about her posture spoke of pain and resignation. She was Moses gazing upon the Promised Land, yearning for it, and knowing it was being withheld from her. And he knew, without knowing how he knew, that if this was all that would be granted her, then this was what she would accept, with resignation and grace.

Go, he heard in his mind. *I have given you the last of what I held, I release you from any obligations. Go.*

For the briefest moment, some dark and self-centered, primordial part of him wanted to leave her there, to take the power that she offered for himself. What works could he accomplish with such power? Everyone that had ever wronged him would be punished, his will would be absolute...

As quickly as the thought came, he banished it from his mind. *No. I'm not going to leave you, Sera. I'm not going to let you fade.*

Though he could hear her thoughts, it seemed she could not hear his. *Why will you not leave?* There was an edge of anger to her thoughts, even though her face remained statue-blank, except for the tears pouring down her face. *You do not want to be the man you were. You do not wish to be obligated to me. I release you from both those things. Now, go, and leave me! You need not concern yourself any further!*

John saw in his mind as she started to fail, fading more and more. *She's letting go...* It felt as if every single fiber of his being were crying out at once, willing her not to give up, to stay alive. He had the vaguest sense that the outside world from whatever this place was had gone completely still, frozen. This was the moment, and everything had stopped until an outcome was decided.

John focused, digging deep, trying desperately to reach something, anything that would help. In the periphery of his mind, he heard the music pick up again, different and familiar. He grasped for it...no, that wasn't right. He *embraced* it. Sera had said... no, *Vickie* had said this was the thing that held them together. Whatever it was. So if this held them together, couldn't he use it to hold her to life?

In that moment John knew why Sera called it the Song as a proper noun, as if it was some sort of primal thing. It felt as if his whole consciousness was bombarded with every strain of music that had ever been or would ever be made, and even some that never could be. He saw things, felt things that he doubted any other mortal ever had; past, present and future all blended together, whipping through his mind at light-speed. It was terrifying, glorious and all-encompassing. He was almost overwhelmed to the point where he lost "sight" of Sera.

And then he *remembered*.

John reached down, taking her hand gently into his. Then he flew towards the light, carrying her lightly with him.

They did not so much reach the light, as the light reached them, opening up before them and then enveloping them; he sensed there was, somehow, an even *greater* Light somewhere ahead—"Light" in the sense of the "Song"—but he also sensed that it was time to stop, before they reached it.

So they came to rest, in a weightless state, cradled in the light. *Together.* He felt that he was made of light, as was Sera, and yet, somehow, they were also Sera and John, and his memories... his memories were returning. It didn't feel like he was changing, but rather like a fog was being lifted. It was disorienting for a moment, as his two different perspectives came back together... but he was still himself, he was still John Murdock. His old pain, his old guilt, were both muted. He had the memory of them, but he didn't feel their burden anymore. He breathed in and let it out in a great sigh before he realized his eyes were still closed. So he opened them.

Sera was—reviving. Like a flower that had been dying for lack of water, and now was waking up to blessed rain. Slowly, her wings unfolded, only they weren't broken things of shattered bone and feathers, they were fire that was somehow feathers at the same time. Color had come back to her—more than color. Her hair was like moving, living flame, she seemed to be clothed in flames, and as she opened her eyes, he saw they weren't that sad blue anymore. They were—they were exactly as he had known them, for most of the time he had known her. Golden as the Sun, without whites or pupils, glowing and enigmatic.

Exactly as he remembered her. Now that he actually *remembered*.

One hand went to her lips, as if something about him puzzled, perhaps even startled her. *What—?* he heard in his mind. *How—?*

John smiled lopsidedly, moving forward to take her hands into his. *Your guess is as good as mine... darlin'.*

Her eyes widened, and she was engulfed in fire and joy as she flung her arms about him. *Beloved!* she cried, and that was all that she said, but that was all she needed to say.

I'm back, love, he thought. It was strange, communicating just by thinking it, but it also seemed to come easily for him. *Sorry it took me so long; I guess I took the long way home.*

She rested her head on his chest, and they were quiet together for what could have been an age, and could have been no time at all. They just basked in the comfort of each other, needing nothing else.

It was only when a third ... presence ... spoke to them that they raised their heads, together. *Well done, my good and faithful servants,* the presence said, or rather, laughed. Not that it laughed at them, more ... it laughed for the pleasure of seeing a new creation, or that was the sense that John and Sera shared. They both went still at the same instant, listening attentively. For the moment, at least, there was no fire of rebellion in John Murdock.

And yet it was rebellion on both your parts that has created the unforeseen, the third way; neither up nor down, neither right nor left, but through. *This new thing that you have made together could not have been predicted, for it came from Free Will. And again, well done. By being willing to sacrifice all, you have gained all. You complete each other. Sibling, your experience as an immortal—Child, your experience as a mortal—you two will now be something more together. As you foresaw, Sibling, this is the melding that will continue to allow you both to evolve new ways, and* create *futures, rather than merely See them.*

John was the first to "speak up." *What do you mean by "create" futures?*

Only the mortal possess Free Will. The Siblings are obedient to the Will of the Infinite, and so they are blinded. They can only See the futures that branch from the actions of the present. They cannot, themselves, deduce new actions and predict new futures. You, as a mortal, always had that gift of Free Will. Now, you both do, and you both share some of the powers of the Siblings. There was a sense of a sigh. *It will be limited. You will never see the futures as she once did, for both of you are mortal, with only a fraction of the Celestial now. But be content; if you got but a glimpse of what she once did, it would drive you mad.*

John held up one of his hands. *That's fine by me, at least. I'm not sure I'd want to see the future like she did, even if I could.*

The Song... Sera faltered. *I hear it now but—*

It will never again, while you live, fill you as it once did. The voice turned tender. *You will never again lose it, either. You will have this . . . singular love . . . to fill you, as well, and I think you will find you do not need the Song as much as you once did. You two, and your love, are for each other the connection to the Song, and to this, the Heart of All Time.* Again, there was the sense of delighted laughter. *Love, oh yes, is always Permitted.*

So . . . what happens now? Where do we go from here? John couldn't help but feel an urgent need to get back to the world. This place was . . . wonderful, and beautiful. But he didn't belong here, not yet.

The futures are yours to decide. Free Will. Take your first steps into the new possibilities. Where do you want to go? Beside him, Sera was nodding, slowly, and he sensed a wonder in her that this precious gift of Free Will was now hers, as well.

He turned to look at Sera for a moment before facing forward again, towards where he thought that the "presence" was, even though it felt as if it surrounded them. *Back home, to Atlanta.* He felt a smile creep into his face. *We've got work to do.*

So let it be done.

And that was all there was to it. With no sense of shock, he felt himself in his body again, kneeling on a warm surface that smelled of scorched asphalt, and felt Sera still cradled in his arms. Sirens wailed in the distance as he opened his eyes. Sera was staring back into his eyes, smiling, beatific. Her eyes were blue again, but with gold glinting in the depths. And she was healed, whole.

"Hey there, darlin'. Nice t'see you back with us." John gently brushed a strand of her hair from her eyes.

Her arms tightened around his neck. "And I say the same, Beloved."

The sirens were growing closer. "I think we can call off the cavalry for now." John paused, looking off to the side. "Overwatch: reopen channel to Vix." Almost before the words were done leaving his mouth, the reply broke over the comms.

"Seggfej!" Vickie shouted into his ear. "Rosseb egye meg! *What the hell just happened? Why were you offline? Talk, you* fasz fej! *My head is ringing like the Liberty Bell and I'm going to be seeing stars for an* alattomos *week!*"

John winced; somehow the "volume" and her cussing were ramped up on his comms. "Take 'er easy, Vic. Call off the medical teams. Sera's gonna be all right. An'...I'm back. All the way back. Roger that?"

"Te fasz! *Bella nearly wiped out the ECHO ambulance when you...wait, what?*" There was a silence that practically was a sound in and of itself. "*You—what?*" Incredulity. "*Johnny? You're back? You mean—the old you? The hell you say!*"

"Not quite hell, but yeah, I'm back. You can commence cussin' again at yer leisure. Head over to CCCP HQ so I can get debriefed by everyone all at once?"

The sirens stopped abruptly. "*Vix, stay on-station. I'll divert to CCCP,*" Bella said, the relief in her voice so thick you could have cut it. "*Murdock, all I can say is, this had better be one hell of a story.*"

"It will be, kiddo. See ya at HQ in five." John looked down into Sera's eyes again, felt his mouth relaxing into a grin, a fit match for her joyous smile. "Better make that thirty. It's been a while since I've seen my wife."

CHAPTER TWENTY

Penny Saved

MERCEDES LACKEY AND DENNIS LEE

Penny had had three good nights, and she could scarcely believe it. Lacey's Guy had chased away every single other ghost that had dared show up, and by the third night they weren't even trying anymore. Not even Momma appeared last night.

When he wasn't chasing ghosts he just stood by Lacey and stared, as if, unlike some of the other ghosts, he already knew he couldn't touch her, so he was just touching her with his eyes. But it wasn't a creepy-sort-of touching, not like Creepy Man, whose eyes promised something Penny didn't really understand, but which she instinctively knew would be icky and horrible and scary. It was like he wanted to comfort her when she moaned. Every night he came earlier and stayed later. Today, the fourth day she'd awakened after a good night's sleep, he was there when she woke up.

He stayed there; through when the Dark Man brought the breakfast pouches and picked Lacey roughly up to take her away so he could clean her.

That was when he finally did something different.

He rushed at the Dark Man, fists and feet flying in a furious attempt to pummel the Devil's assistant in the same way he pummeled the ghosts.

He didn't manage to do anything, of course, though he tried all the way to the door, and only when the Dark Man had slammed and locked the door between them did he give up, sagging with a defeat that also seemed angry.

Finally, as Penny froze, the torn-off corner of her food-pouch

283

in her mouth, he whirled to stare at her. And then... then he came towards her.

She began to shake, the pouch dropping out of hands gone suddenly numb with terror.

His stare softened a little as he got closer, and when he got to where she was sitting cross-legged on the floor, he dropped down to sit balanced over his toes, not kneeling, but kind of squatting with his butt on his heels. "Hey," he said. It was the first word he had ever spoken. She hadn't even been sure he actually *could* talk.

The constant hum of the ventilation system tended to drown out anything but nearby conversations. Not that anyone would hear the ghost, but if she started to talk, they might hear her if she didn't keep her voice down.

She gulped, and looked around, to make sure the others weren't paying any attention. They already thought she was crazy; she didn't need them seeing her talking to empty air. "Hey," she whispered back, wondering how he was sitting like that. Okay, true, he was a ghost, but he sat as if this was the same way he would perch when he was alive. Balanced there, easily, comfortably, like a gymnast.

"So, you can see me, and you can hear me too?" he asked.

She nodded slightly, feeling odd about this whole conversation. This wasn't how things had always gone before. Ghosts realized she could see and hear them, and they'd come to attack her with the only weapons they had; sound, words and their own actions. Even if they couldn't actually *hurt* her, what they did was still scary. But this one wasn't attacking her.

But this one was here during the day. And this one had chased off the others....

"Those others—the ones I chased off—you could see and hear them, too?" he continued.

She felt herself on the verge of crying. Was he going to let them come back? "Y-yes," she replied, as a tear finally burned its way out of her left eye, making her vision blurry on that side. But she wasn't going to beg him to keep them away! She'd tried begging with the ghosts before, and nothing good had ever come of that!

But his expression softened, and he made an abortive little move, as if he wanted to brush that tear away and then realized he couldn't. "Hey, kiddo, don't cry," he said, his voice so *friendly* that it made her want to cry even harder. "I'm not gonna let those crazy things back here to scare ya. Okay? I thought only I could see and hear them, and they just annoyed me. I finally got tired of all the creepiness and the howling and got rid of them. If I'd known they were scaring *you,* I'd have run them off even quicker."

Pike had finished his breakfast, and clearly saw she was talking to something. With the ease of someone who has practiced *not being noticed* a lot, he ambled over to her without making it seem as if he was heading towards her. He stopped to talk to Joey, then Brit, then Tanya, before plopping down indifferently at the wall next to her.

"You talking to one of them?" he asked out of the corner of his mouth. Lacey's Guy turned to level that stare at Pike.

"Uh-huh," she said. "Lacey's Guy. He's the only one here. He chased all the others off and none of 'em come back."

"Can't he hear or see me?" the ghost asked before Pike could do more than nod.

She shook her head. Pike examined his ragged thumbnail critically. "Is he okay? Like . . . not bothering you? Cause it looked like you were gonna cry."

"He's . . . nice," she said, trying not to cry again. "It's . . . it makes me wanta cry 'cause he's nice."

Both of them reached for her at the same time. The ghost's hand went through her shoulder, as Pike's connected. "Hey," they both said at once. "It's okay." Then the ghost chuckled, a little uncomfortably, as Pike added, "Been a long time since anyone was nice to us," with a sad, sad look that made *her* reach for *him.*

The other kids looked deliberately away when they both broke down a little. You did that, here. There was no privacy, so you created artificial privacy when it looked as if someone needed some. It didn't last long; they both broke the embrace and wiped each others' faces after only a little bit. Then Pike smiled weakly and got to his feet.

"Guess he's your boyfriend after all, huh?" he said, and ambled off.

"Big brother?" the ghost asked. She nodded. The ghost sighed a little. "I never had any brothers or sisters. Not much family, actually. Maybe that's why—" Then he shrugged, not finishing the sentence. "—doesn't matter. Since you can see and hear me, you can help me."

"I—" she gulped. What was he going to ask her to do? Get Lacey out? How was she supposed to do that? And if she didn't help him, couldn't help him, would he let the other ghosts come back, and start screaming at her himself?

But he was already talking before she could say anything. "We need to get her awake. And . . . I need to talk to her. I mean, you talk to her and tell her I'm here and what I say."

Penny sighed with relief. At least that was something *possible*. "But . . . before you got here, all she did was cry and moan," Penny told him. "I don't—I don't think she's right in the head."

The ghost's expression darkened. "She looks like she's been tortured."

Penny nodded. "The Devil takes us away and hurts us. He hasn't been back since you came, but he does that. There's a bunch of rooms with more kids in them, and he comes and takes one, sometimes more than one in a day, and hurts us, then brings us back to our rooms. We don't know why, and we never know who he's going to take, or when he's coming. He's only taken her once, before you got here, but he could come back for her, or me, or anybody, any time."

The rage that came over his face scared her, but it passed quickly, and turned to determination. "Well, then—what's your name, kiddo?"

"Penny—" she offered.

He smiled at her. It was a funny, lopsided smile. Tentatively, she smiled back.

"Well then, Penny," he said. "You and I will just after to figure a way to make her sane again."

CHAPTER TWENTY-ONE

Hurricane: Storm Front

MERCEDES LACKEY AND DENNIS LEE

Strangely enough, there was part of Bella that intellectually understood Harmony. She'd gone over the recordings with Scope, and there was that part at the beginning, when Harmony talked about being desperate....

Bella was still linked, somehow, with the Seraphym; maybe some of her dispassionate compassion, even for people who were trying to murder her, had percolated over. Maybe it was a touch of the sort of... *alien* mind that could forgive anything... that gave Bella some understanding of alien thought now.

Maybe it was both of those things, or neither, and something else entirely. But Bella understood it; the desperation, being reduced to the state of a cornered animal, when you already were not human and didn't have the same concerns and mindset of a human. She could understand Harmony in that moment. Even, to a certain extent, accept it.

But she wasn't the Seraphym. She couldn't quite forgive.

But Harmony had suddenly asked for her, and Bull wanted her to come talk, on the chance that, up close, Bella might pick *something* up of the way Harmony was working. Bull didn't ask much of her, and she was guilty of asking so much from *him;* it would have been wrong not to do what he asked, even though she couldn't imagine what good it was going to do even if they found out how Harmony was doing what she did. It wasn't as if they were going to be able to replicate it....

So here she was in Top Hold. In Harm's cell, not in Bull's office; she was confident at least of Vickie's ability to shield her, and her ability to shield herself, to take the risk of getting this close. She entered the room carefully. Harmony watched her from inside her cube within a cube. Bella took a seat on the chair that someone had left there for her.

"Well," Bella said, after a long silence, and her mind always filled the silence. Always that terrible anxiety, that looming responsibility. *I never wanted to be a leader. And I know the Seraphym said... but I'm responsible, responsible for all of them... what if I make the wrong decisions? What if I don't ask for the right advice? How many could I kill...* "I'm not sure what to call you, anymore. None of the names you've used are you, are they?" *And you sure as hell aren't "Harmony."* "Maybe I should just call you 'Enigma.'"

"That's... better than what you *could* call me." Harmony gave Bella a long, level look. Bella thought her eyes looked cold. Reptilian, almost. Had they always looked that way? Had she just never noticed? "Stick with 'Harm.' After all, it fits."

Bella nodded, slightly. It did fit. *If I had touched her even though she told me not to, would I have known what she was in time to save Bruno? How many times have I slipped up like that? How many mistakes are still hidden, just waiting to surface?*

Harm regarded her calmly. "You worry too much."

Bella snorted. "In my position, there is no such thing as worrying too much."

"No, you worry too much about being a leader. Good leaders aren't always the obvious people to lead." She smirked. "Take politicians, for instance."

This time Bella rolled her eyes. "Anyone who *wants* to be a politician shouldn't be. And probably ought to be taken out and shot."

"It would probably do them a world of good," Harmony agreed. She pondered that, and smiled. "You know, I even know of someone, not unlike you. Here, let me show you."

There was no warning. Suddenly Bella was no longer sitting in that chair in Harm's peculiar prison cell. She was watching men in Redcoat uniforms at the bottom of a hill, with a river to one side of them. Someone in a fancy uniform had just been shot dead and was being carried off the battlefield.

But there was something more going on here. Not only could she *see* what appeared to be the middle of a battle between British and—American?—forces, she could feel everything that the men there were feeling. Despair, mostly. This was their beloved

General, shot down in front of them, and the enemy had superior numbers and, what was more, had the superior tactical position.

But then, one of the other officers stood on a rock and began speaking. She couldn't tell what his rank was; she wasn't familiar with the rank-markings of British colonial forces. An officer, was all she could tell for sure, as he addressed the eighty or so men around him. He was wounded. He held a lifeless arm to his side, a bloody bandage at the shoulder. The wound would have to be cleaned, but he paid it no mind as his voice rang out to the men, *his* men, now.

She was too far away to tell what he was saying, but she could *feel* what he was feeling, and what the men around him were feeling. He had never wanted to be a leader. He was a lawyer by trade, and a politician, and had joined the Militia out of a sense of obligation. He...he had been the aide-de-camp to the general who had just fallen, and was content in that position. But now, now the Yanks were on Canadian land, threatening to take the tiny town behind them, and the men were leaderless and afraid. Well, *he* was afraid, but someone had to lead them, and at least he knew what the General...General Brock?...had been planning.

She felt what the men were feeling. This man, this officer Macdonell...they knew him as a good man, as one of them. They knew him as someone who had always taken care of them, and maybe it had been the General who had sent him into the camp every night, seeing to it that their needs were met...but they thought it was more likely his own concern for their well-being. They also knew, absolutely, that he would never ask them to do something he was not willing to do himself.

They knew that Brock had been confident in him. They knew that Brock had shared the battle plans with him. They knew he was brave and intelligent, and unlikely to make stupid mistakes. And they knew that *he* believed in *them*.

He paused, for the briefest of moments, and glanced at his shoulder. They had removed the bullet, but the damage had been devastating. He would never use the arm again. It was likely that it would have to come off. Such things had terrified him, in all the days leading up to now. As he looked at his men, he felt such fears fade away. What was one arm, compared to the brave souls that stood with him? What was his fear, when there were soldiers to rally and lead against their foes?

He might not have wanted to be a leader—but he was a man who other men would follow, knowing that if they won, they would win together, but if anyone fell, he would place himself in the line of sacrifice first.

And as their confidence rose again, his voice rose enough to be heard from the distant place where Bella was. "No mair speeches, laddies!" he cried out in a rough Scots burr. "Let's take back the Heights!"

And then, as the men rallied behind Macdonell, chanting his name, the scene faded.

Bella blinked in shock at Harm. She had no idea how Harm had just done that. It had just . . . happened.

"Some of the best leaders never intended to be one," Harm said flatly. "What they had in common is a conviction that what they were doing was right. Not just that conviction, though. They cared about their people. Even when they were leading them into harm's way, they did their best to protect them."

Bella sucked on her lower lip a moment. People weren't following her because they had to, but because they wanted to. She knew that; hadn't they actually *voted* her in? And they could, at any point, vote her right out again.

That's their choice.

And Gairdner . . . he'd been an officer. He sometimes suggested something different than her ideas (and she usually took his suggestions) but never once had he ever said she should give up on being the CEO.

Hell, even Yank was following her lead, and if anyone had the right to be in the main seat, he did. And . . . why?

"They know you aren't a glory-hound, Bella. They know you don't want to be there, and they know you aren't the CEO because you want fame or attention. They know you won't put them out there as cannon fodder. They also know you always look for people who are experts to give you advice when you're not an expert. And you take it." Harm shrugged. "That doesn't kill confidence in what you're doing, that builds it, and it's confidence well placed. *I* think, anyway."

"Why are you . . . doing this?" she asked, finally, as she felt some of the weight of doubt slowly lifting from her shoulders. She didn't ask *how* Harm was doing this; she knew the woman—creature?—wouldn't answer that question. *It felt just like I was* there. *Was that a memory? If so...* But that was impossible. The figures looked to be from the early nineteenth century. If she had actually been there, Harmony would have to be at least two hundred years old. Bella shook her head. Just another piece to the Harmony puzzle. Well, maybe giving the images and feelings a good going-over would start to answer some questions. She typed into her PDA. *Bull, Harm just... did something with me. Explain more when I'm out. Give me the best third-degree you can, and we'll see if we can learn something.*

Harm smirked. "Why am I doing this? You wouldn't believe me if I told you. Let's just say I've got some history to work past before I can continue on my journey. For now, I can help you, as much as you will let me. So let me."

"Why wouldn't I believe you?" Bella asked.

"Bella," Harmony sighed. "Would you truly believe me when I say that when I'm not scurrying about in an effort to amuse myself, the things I do are for love? A sick and twisted love by your standards, I would suspect, perhaps muted, a shadow of what you might feel, but love nevertheless. No, I don't see how you could grasp that. But for the record, I'll say it. I can see a point within you that is sore and unnoticed and simply *begging* for attention, and I want to help you with that, out of love."

"Love for me?" Bella said.

"Yes," Harmony nodded.

"Bull told me you were planning on killing me."

Harmony spread her arms wide and rolled her head back in exasperation. "I *said* it was sick and twisted, didn't I?"

"You told him you loved *him*," Bella said. "Right before you sucked him dry."

"He told you about that, did he?" Harmony grinned. "You two really are the genuine article. Truthful, open... you don't even need safety words, do you?"

"He's never spoken about it," Bella said.

"Oh!" Harmony gasped, feigning surprise. "Then however did you manage to... ah, of course. The security feed. You watched it yourself, didn't you?"

"You told him you loved him..." Bella repeated.

Harmony chuckled and shook her head. "Yes, as I love you. You thought I meant something else. No, Bella, there was none of that between us. You want to pretend the thought doesn't bother you, but it does. I feel it rotting inside of you. I told you, I'm here to help, as much as it suits me to. So tell me, if I meant to hurt you, would I bother to tell you that nothing ever happened between me and your boy toy?"

Bella just looked back at her, speechless.

Harmony yawned.

"That should do it," she said curtly. "Interview's over."

Harmony lay down on her cot, turning her back to Bella and the door.

Bella left, her mind racing with what had just happened. Since inheriting a boost to her abilities from the Seraphym, Bella had struggled at times with the consequences of that boost. Her healing capabilities had grown much stronger, to be sure, but she was still adapting to how sensitive her empathic abilities had become. Some people were perhaps a little too open with their feelings. When she was around Mary Ann, Bella found she had to clamp down firmly, or be faced with an onslaught of whatever emotion Einhorn was wallowing in at the time. With Harmony, there was nothing. She had cranked it up, and felt nothing, nothing that Harmony didn't want her to. It begged the question again: *What are you, Harmony?*

She felt like she'd been played, that Harmony had led her by the nose and fed her answers to suit her own mysterious agenda. Still, despite her confusion, Bella couldn't help but feel . . . better. For once, this wasn't something that she could feel coming off someone in waves. Whether they were being truthful, whether they could be trusted. It came from her instincts, and her instincts told her that Harmony had showed her the truth. About leadership, about doing the job, and about Bull.

It felt as if a boil she hadn't even known was festering had been lanced. The relief was . . . considerable. There had never been anything between Harmony and Bulwark.

And she was right about something else, Bella thought. Together, Bella and Bulwark were open and truthful and . . . good. She was going to march back to her office to meet him and let him grill her mercilessly about her talk with Harmony. She would answer everything, completely and truthfully, and offer up anything he might miss, and then they were going to dissect everything Harmony said and did, in every which way they could.

They could do this, because that's just how they worked. They were that *good.*

CHAPTER TWENTY-TWO

Start Shootin'

MERCEDES LACKEY AND CODY MARTIN

Red Saviour lit up a cigarette and scowled as it went out. She knew better than to try again. That *nekulturny* meta that ECHO kept around to prevent her from smoking in the building was hard at work. All he could do was to detect and extinguish very small fires within a limited range, mere sparks or coals, really. If she ever found out which room they kept that person in, she'd have ... choice words to share with him.

Foiled of her ability to chain-smoke, she yanked open the door to Bella Parker's office, brushing past the receptionist and reaching for the door to the inner office with every intent to slam it open. But she was foiled in that, as well, as the door slid smoothly open at her approach. This did not improve her temper.

Nor did the fact that Parker finished whatever she was reading, and signed it, before looking up. "Commissar, so pleased you could drop in," she said dryly. "You know the door is always open to you."

"And you, Blue Girl. Too busy being petty bureaucrat with desk and papers as of late? I see more of Motherland here every day."

Her attempt to administer unto the head of ECHO an equal amount of the irritation she had received since entering the doors was met with yet more frustration. "Why, Commissar, I thought that Soviet bureaucracy was the height of modern efficiency," Bella drawled. "And actually, what I just finished signing was that requisition form for the CCCP—more of those incendiary shells your people designed and we are manufacturing. I took the liberty of doubling what you asked for, because as soon as we find the location of the Thulian HQ, I've always thought that 'too much ammunition is never enough.'"

Natalya sighed, pinching the bridge of her nose as she wished hard for a cigarette right then. "*Da, da*, fine. Is good. But you bring matter to table; finding the base of operations for *fascista*. What efforts are being made?"

Now Bella dropped the pretense of serenity and allowed Saviour to see the strain on her face. "Every effort. The problem is we have conflicting evidence for locations, and every damn one of them is even more inaccessible than the North American HQ was. The only place we *haven't* got a loc indicator for is, ironically enough, Siberia. Either you sturdy Russkis have always been damned good at keeping them out, or they were never there in the first place." She sighed. "We're trying to find them with satellites and spy planes, but so far, no joy."

"Why are you not sending physical scouting parties?" Saviour demanded.

"One—" Bella retorted, holding up a finger, "We don't have the personnel. If we send conventional troops, that means letting the country in question know we're wanting to go snooping, and that means a high potential for leaks. We can't send metas because we don't have enough. Two—" she held up a second finger, "Even if we could send metas, what happens if they just...stumble into the HQ? Then we've got an unholy mess on our hands, and who knows what the Thulians would do? No, our only option is to do this slowly and carefully, and I know it seems unduly cautious, but that is what *all* my advisors are telling me."

"Advisors," Natalya scoffed. "Unduly is not the word I would being using. Suicidally? Would being more fitting." She spread her arms wide, exasperated. "Every moment we waste with over-caution is another moment enemy is having to plan, to attack, to *kill*. It is what they do, these 'Kriegers'; it is all they do. We must be killing them first, and only way to do that is to devote resources to be finding them."

"ECHO *is* devoting resources to finding them," Bella retorted. "Just not boots on the ground." She visibly throttled down anger. "Look, we know this is an HQ. We know it has to be big. Something that big leaves signs. Even if they are disguising it somehow. Stuff has to enter and leave, the place needs to generate power, there are going to be tell-tales. We just haven't found the right ones to look for yet."

"Signs and tell-tales you cannot find, and have not been able to find, after all of this time." The Commissar shook her head. "The *fascista* must have counted on all governments of world hunting for them. Their technology is advanced, more so than almost anything known to us. So, you are thinking that spy planes and satellites, which they laugh at, are being answer? You were never fighter before Invasion, *sestra*. Nor part of law enforcement. When you have quarry who shuns places where there are being computers to track him, you do not keep typing into Gaggle browser to find him; you send men to places where he might being, and have them extract information from whomever they find there until you have quarry."

"Which means you increase your chances for a leak by a hundred-fold!" Bella snapped. "Not to mention that you'll be sending thugs to beat up perfectly innocent people in the mere *hope* of finding something! That'll go over well in the press," she added sarcastically.

Natalya snorted. "You are too soft. Press? World is close to being cinder. Would rather be vilified and alive than dead and well liked by newsman, who hate us 'Russkies' anyway. Let them print what they want. Results count, not opinion of soft-bodies that quiver in fear, unable and unwilling to fight for themselves."

"Enough bad press, and ECHO gets shut down. We've come damn close to that already," Bella said darkly, and shook her head. "No, it's got to be done this way. It's not just spy satellite photos. They have to be getting supplies from somewhere. Those supplies have to be moved somehow. They can't act in a vacuum. We—"

"Enough!" Natalya was fed up. This was becoming circular. Didn't her friend see that one couldn't count on anything from the Thulians? Not that there "must be" some sign, that there "must be" anything from them. They either came from out of nowhere on the day of the Invasion, which all evidence so far contradicted...or they had been here all along, behind the scenes, waiting and pre-paring. If over the course of sixty years they hadn't been detected as the world had shrunk due to the advance of technology and commerce, what would half-measures accomplish? They had leads; many contradicted each other, some of the intelligence gathered was "fresher" than other pieces. But every day they wasted in not acting, the greater the chance that the information they had would become even more dated, even more useless. That is one thing the healer didn't, maybe couldn't understand. "When you have stomach for what is needing doing, you know where we are."

Without another word, the Commissar turned on her heel and stormed out of the room, door swishing closed behind her.

Natalya chain-smoked in silence for the entire drive back to CCCP HQ. The more she thought about her exchange with Bella, the more furious she became. *Caution! Always caution! Never action!* When had the blue girl turned into such a coward?

When they made her ECHO head, Saviour decided sourly. That should have been the moment when she seized the reins and made it clear that *she* was the one in charge, and it was not some democratic nonsense with *advisors.*

Too much plotting, and scheming, and setting up pieces quietly. It was unbecoming; it reminded Natalya too much of the machinations of politicians and bureaucrats back home in Russia. In war, you were either advancing or you were not. Their enemy had declared the entirety of Earth as the battlefield; so they had no option *but* to advance, to push the invaders out. And to do that they had to find the heart of the beast, and kill it.

Few nations seemed to be doing much of anything, at least openly. With the devastation of the initial Invasion, and the destruction from the almost impossible to predict "pop-ups," most were comfortable with maintaining the status quo. "Let ECHO handle it," was the general response to attacks. Reconstruction was the word of the day. The militaries and police forces would put down individual attacks, almost always in support of the meta-humans of ECHO. But it was largely viewed as "someone else's" problem. Everywhere she looked, it seemed that people were being ruled by their fear; if they took a moment to acknowledge it, it would destroy everything they had built up around themselves, all of their mental and emotional armor. She had heard stories from her father and Boryets, even Unter once, about the Great Patriotic War, and how some people became hysterical, shutting out all reality when they couldn't cope. Natalya felt as if the entire world were in the grips of such hysteria, and she was in the minority of the sane.

All of it enraged her, and yet stiffened her resolve.

Mamona was her driver for this trip; she sat quietly, guiding the motor-pool van back to HQ through the maze of blocked streets and detours. That was just as well; Natalya's temper was liable to be taken out on the first thing that presented itself. She had to throttle herself just to keep from snapping at Mamona. If it had been Untermensch who was driving, she would have lashed out anyway; he was used to being her verbal whipping boy and thought no more of her outbursts than he would the wind blowing a swirl of leaves into his face. But there was no telling how Mamona would react, and Natalya did not want to alienate a useful comrade. The American, unlike her Russians, could always hand in a resignation and go to ECHO.

So she kept her temper barely in check all the way back to CCCP HQ; bit off an "efficient driving, comrade," to the American, and stalked back to her office. Word spread quickly when she was in a temper, even more quickly now that CCCP had its own version of Overwatch Mark One. Everyone kept out of her path, and she was free to storm through the halls to her office without interference. The satisfying *slam* of the metal door behind her released, briefly, a very little bit of her anger.

But then she sank down into the battered chair behind her desk and ran both hands through her hair with a tense exhalation of breath. She sat there for what seemed even to her like a very long time, breathing and thinking.

"Enough waiting," she said aloud into the silence of the room. "Overwatch: open: Gamayun." *Am beginning to think I like witch better than Blue Girl,* she thought sourly. *At least witch does not sit about twiddling fingers.*

"Da, Commissar," came the prompt reply.

"Status of Molotok and Untermensch. Report."

"Untermensch is returned from patrol, Commissar," said the CCCP comm officer. "Molotok is inspecting machine shop." Molotok, who was as much of a brother to her as a comrade, had only recently returned to the USA. As their official liaison to the main branch of the CCCP back in Russia, he often spent the majority of his time there helping the transition with the Supernaut Corps that were to be the primary defense for the Motherland. She missed him, though she would never say as much, and thought that he would be better put to use here in Atlanta. Such things were out of her control, for now at least.

"Alert both to come to my office," she said shortly. She knew Moji would be there quickly. He always came quickly when she asked for him. The two of them had almost been like brother and sister. Both of them were second-generation metahumans and

Soviet heroes. Both of them had been trained by Boryets, and looked on Worker's Champion as a second father. They had been born within a year of each other, and as children had called each other *brat* and *sestra*. And as for Untermensch, well, Georgi was always reliable. He was her sturdy right hand, as often as not.

She was not disappointed. The firm knock on the door was followed by the door opening before she could say the word "Enter."

Unter was first, brusque as ever in entering the room and finding his place within it. His once-dark hair and mustache had both gone salt-and-pepper at the edges this last year; seeing as how he had fought in the Great Patriotic War, he should have looked a great deal older than the fit, early-forty-year-old that he appeared to be. Once positioned, he stood at a sort of loose attention, awaiting Natalya's prompt.

Casually, Molotok strolled in, half-grinning like the cat who had just caught the mouse. He had strong Russian features; his face was severe, but not so much that he wasn't extremely handsome. Stark black hair, like Natalya's, and carefree eyes, not like Natalya's. He leaned against the wall next to the doorframe, his arms crossed in front of his chest.

"Here we are, *sestra*. What do you need?"

Natalya motioned with her chin towards the door. "Close it, *brat*."

Molotok reached out a long arm and closed the door. Quietly. The latch made scarcely a sound as it engaged.

"Overwatch: call Victrix. Are you there, daughter of Rasputin?"

"*At your service, Commissar.*" The reply came over Natalya's link and Natalya's alone. Moji cocked his head to one side. Unter nodded but lifted an eyebrow.

"*Horosho.* Please to add Moji and Untermensch." She waited while Vickie complied. "I have just come from meetink with head of ECHO concerning finding the next Krieger HQ. I would like if all of you took time to listen to it."

"*Roger. Playing back meeting recording now.*"

Moji and Unter were silent as the recording played over Unter's implant and Moji's headset.

Vickie switched to Russian. "*This'll be easier on all of us if we use the mother tongue, Commissar. I...I don't often disagree with Bells, but this time I do. You're right. You need boots on the ground. I have tried every damn detection method for this base that I have in my extensive arsenal, and yes, I used magic too. I've got nothing. These guys are . . . well, 'good' doesn't begin to describe it. I'm in, and I'll keep ECHO out of the loop."* Her tone turned dry. *"Fortunately, you of the CCCP do not have to answer to ECHO. Or the US Government."*

"Good," Natalya had switched over to speaking Russian as well. "It will be much easier than trying to deceive you and only have you go running to tell Belladonna." She looked at her two comrades in turn. "I propose that we begin sending reconnaissance teams out with the express purpose of uncovering the Krieger HQ. Spy planes and satellite imagery are all well and good; I will use every tool at my disposal in this war. But it is hard to do detective work thirty thousand feet above the ground. We need our people out there; we should have them out there already."

"Suggestion, Commissar."

"Yes, speak."

"You have possession of the Tesla quantator, and you are authorized to use it. Go excoriate Tesla, Marconi or both. They might just cough up information to you that they are withholding from ECHO. We sent them bucketloads of intel I pulled off the Thulian computers, and we've gotten dribbles back. I think they might be holding out on us. Or . . . well, you know how they are about only sending us what they are certain of. Rather than holding out on us, perhaps all they have is 'maybe the base is here or here, or here.' Methinks 'maybes' are enough to start a hunt right now."

This was turning out better than she had expected; if they hadn't had Vickie working with them, the series of operations that Natalya was planning on undertaking would have been . . . much more difficult, almost impossible to conceal, potentially. With her, especially with her Overwatch system, things would run much more smoothly.

"Once I have spoken with Tesla and Marconi, we will begin to draw up the general framework for these missions. I will need both of you to leverage your personnel and," she said, looking at Moji, "any influence you may have in the Motherland, still. We will be conducting covert operations, likely on foreign soil, and this is not apt to make us popular." She grinned wolfishly.

"I'm giving this op a codename so you can get my attention in a heartbeat. I'm coding Overwatch for it now. Just say 'Red Star,' and nothing else, and you'll have my ears and help in seconds, even if I'm asleep. It'll give me a priority alert and a direct feed."

"Good. Do any of you have any questions before I talk to the ghosts of two dead men?"

Molotok stepped forward, holding up a finger. "Just one; when we find these bastards and line them up against the wall, can I be the first to start shooting?"

The transport plane that John, Sera, Untermensch and Molotok were flying on was nothing short of a death trap. It was some variant of the Antonov AN-12. Originally produced in 1959, this thing looked like it had to have been one of the first ones off the assembly line, it was so ancient. The cramped storage hold barely had enough room for the team to wedge themselves into sitting positions; the rest of the space was filled with various crates and boxes, and incongruously, a brand new BMW. Besides the seating conditions, the plane itself was hardly what anyone could consider airworthy; various fluids leaked from seals and pipes, the interior lights had a tendency to flicker for seemingly inscrutable reasons, and John swore that he saw what looked like a Russian stop sign sloppily welded over a hole in the deck. Not to mention the multiple empty bottles of alcohol that served as glass tumbleweeds, rolling around between the crates.

"Darlin', remind me to book first-class next time; flyin' coach is for suckers."

Sera smiled at him. That smile warmed him deep inside and somehow calmed him at the same time. "Perhaps we could sit in the automobile?"

Molotok leaned over, grinning. "Would not advise to be doing that, *dorogoy*. Gypsy bastard flying this tub would likely shoot. Or crash plane." He glanced around looking at the plane. "On second thoughts, he may be doing that anyway."

Sera turned her intensely blue eyes on the Russian. "In that case, would you care to take the chance, after all?"

Molotok settled back in his seat, shrugging. John had only had a brief look at their pilot. Disheveled, furrowed face, slightly gray-ish complexion, clothing that looked as if he had slept in it for the past month, scraggly stubble and the stink of cheap vodka, body odor and engine grease completed the picture. He had gotten part of the story about the pilot from Unter before takeoff. His name was Vadim Barsukov; a notorious drunk, he had been kicked out of Russia's air force before he had graduated from the academy. He quickly fell in with gangsters, and eventually parlayed his meager flight skills into a semi-successful smuggling and gun-running operation. That is, until the Commissar caught him. Apparently he had ratted out all of his close associates for a reduced sentence, and had somehow managed to survive prison in spite of being a rat. John suspected that the Commissar might have had something to do with that, but he and Unter could only speculate. In any case, the man was smuggling them into India to check on one of the leads that Natalya had . . . convinced Tesla and Marconi to cough up. This was their second such mission together for that purpose; several other CCCP teams had already been similarly dispatched.

All done covertly, away from the prying eyes of ECHO, save for Victrix.

John agreed with the move, for the most part. They had to go after the Kriegers. To do that, you needed intelligence. And to get intelligence you needed boots on the ground, going out to gather it. Besides the infiltration he had done on the missile silo and what they had been able to steal from the Thulian North American HQ, there seemingly had not been any dedicated operations to obtain crucial intel on the Kriegers; for the most part, they were taking down pop-up cells or putting down random attacks. Never mind the bullshit they were still dealing with from Verdigris and his splinter group of Blacksnake.

He didn't know what Bella and ECHO were doing to find the next Krieger HQ, but it obviously either wasn't enough, or wasn't working.

"JM, deploy one of my eyeballs, will you? I want to be able to warn you if that miserable excuse for an airplane is about to go south and augur in."

"Yes, dear." John reached into one of his hip pouches, producing one of the techno-magical "eyes"; it hovered from his palm and then zipped away, weaving through the cargo compartment.

"Save the endearments for your wife. Which reminds me; when, exactly, did you two actually get hitched? Inquiring minds want to know."

"No real ceremony; didn't need one. I'll tell you all 'bout it once we get back." Sera rested a hand on John's forearm. Despite the world going to hell screaming, John felt happy. He could tell that she felt it too; it was something else he was starting to pick up from their connection. He could feel her emotions, even her thoughts. They both still worried about the war, how to fight the Kriegers, the safety of their friends and the 'hood. But there was a bit more peace that the two of them created within each other. There was a connection between them now, at a deep, deep level, that they had only begun to explore. There were implications to that connection they were just beginning to see.

And under everything was a new constant, part of the unbreakable bond that they had forged between them. Music. Faintly, but ever-present, that whisper of music that had nearly driven him to distraction when he'd first heard it. They both heard it now, and it was part of them both; Sera called it the Song, and now he knew what it was, and he knew now why being walled away from it had caused her such unbearable pain. Being able to hear it again, though it was a mere breath of what it must once have been for her, put a light in her eyes once more. Knowing what it was, and being able to hear it . . . well, was healing to his spirit in a way he had never expected to experience.

"You four want the good news, or the bad news?" This, in Russian, presumably being heard by the entire contingent.

John was the first to speak up. "You know me. Let's have the bad news."

"This heap is not getting off the ground again. Between the altitude and the cascading failures, she's gonna need an overhaul before she can fly again. So you better count on someone else for your ride out. Good news is, even though she's likely to blow a couple tires on landing and spring some more hydraulic leaks, she'll make it to the airstrip. Note, I said airstrip, *not* airport. *We're talking barely combed gravel. Better find some padding for those excuses for seats or your spines are gonna end up driven through your skulls."*

"Your optimism is always being appreciated, *tovarisch.*" John thought that Unter had been asleep; he guessed that the Russian was merely resting his eyes, listening and aware of everything. He was the team leader for this operation. John also suspected he was there to keep an eye on Sera and himself. Their . . . "return" had raised quite a few eyebrows, in both the CCCP and ECHO. Both of them had been prodded and tested and analyzed until they were completely cleared, body and mind. Still, they were an unknown quantity again, until they proved that they could hold it together once more.

"*I live to serve. And you are going into approach vector, so better find that padding in a hurry. Unter, you haven't got enough on that ass to cushion you through a* good *landing, much less the one you're about to get. JM, you better find some padding too; your brain isn't gonna be able to handle that much bouncing.*"

"Roger that. Speak to ya on the ground, one way or another."

John had been through worse rides in his life—though not worse *landings.* The plane had been airborne more often than it had had its wheels on the ground, at least until it came to a rattling, shrieking, screeching halt. The four of them had been out of the plane as soon as the cargo door was open; probably the same thing had been on all their minds, though Vix hadn't mentioned it. *What if this wreck catches fire?*

That the pilot had stumbled out of the cockpit, urging them to more speed in a slurred Russian dialect hadn't done anything to disabuse John of that thought.

The airstrip was barely passable as that; just a single shack and a battered windsock flopping limply on a pole denoted that planes were meant to be there at all. A group of locals were lounging around, drinking and smoking, until they finally jumped up and ran over to help with the unloading. There was an equally battered, abused and beaten-up Land Rover—which had to have been built in the 1960s—waiting for them. The pilot stood beside his plane supervising the off-loading of far more crates than that vehicle should have been able to hold, drinking from an unlabeled bottle. Once the cargo was off—which didn't take long—he clambered back into it, closed the hatch and turned the plane around. And to Vix's voluble astonishment, made it back into the sky.

Molotok just laughed at her. "Russian ingenuity, *tovarisch.* If it can be held together with bailing wire and drunken hope, it will fly."

The four of them crammed themselves and their packs into the two bench seats in the Rover, which was not easy, since the "packs" included two purloined jetpacks for the two Russians, who couldn't fly on their own. By the time the luggage had been piled in around them, John was buried, and couldn't see anything but a sliver outside the filthy window on his side. The locals piled on the boxes on the top of the vehicle, secured them with enough rope to scale Everest with, and then the team was off.

✧   ✧   ✧

The Rover dropped them, their gear, and the cargo they had hitched a ride with off in a little Indian village. The cargo vanished almost as soon as it hit the ground. They were met by a villainous-looking fellow who could have stepped out of a B movie featuring Himalayan bandits, but who, surprisingly, turned out to have tolerable Russian and be quite personable. He had organized a string of ponies that Unter regarded dubiously, and which all the men looked...well...ridiculous on. Sera perched on hers as if she had always been a rider; Moji and Unter looked awkward as hell. John felt awkward at first, but then he caught Sera's gaze for just a moment, the music strengthened within him for about thirty seconds...and his body began to adjust without him thinking about it, and in a few moments, he was sitting in the saddle as easily as Sera, even if he *did* feel a little like a grown man on a kid's tricycle. But the ponies were a lot stronger than they looked and their guide—who only gave them his first name, Jagat—turned out to have been a polo player, who certainly knew how to pick his mounts.

Jagat got them as far into the mountains as he would let the ponies go, which was a lot farther than John had expected. Then he helped them unload their gear. "This is where I leave you, my friends," he said, as Moji paid him in gold. "When you come back out, use your satellite phone and call me. I will bring the ponies up to get you. If you don't come back out, I will pray for your next incarnation." It wouldn't be a sat-phone that called him, of course, it would be Vix. But he wouldn't know that. Spoofing a phone was less than trivial for her.

The next leg of the journey would require something more... exotic, in order to get the team around.

The jetpacks were conversion models that ran on something like a power cell. Mad-scientist stuff, literally, it was one of the latest things to come from Tesla and Marconi, because Vix'd had some words with them. Seemed she hadn't fancied dropping out of the Atlanta sky if there was need to turn the power broadcasters off.

And speaking of Vix... "Overwatch: command: open Vix," John said, as Moji helped Under into his jetpack.

"*Vix here. I read you five by five.*" There was a yawn; of course, it was the middle of the night in Atlanta. "*System recalibrating. Your maps should be updated with your position now.*"

Vix had installed one of the last of her "internal" sets on Moji just before they left. Now John heard him utter a low whistle. *"Borzhe moi!"* he exclaimed. "If this is magic doing, little witch, I am very much liking it!"

"I live to serve," Vix replied. *"You didn't have time to read the manual, so I'm just repeating to your set whatever JM calls up on his. If you'd rather I keyed to Georgi..."*

"Nyet, Murdock will be a-hokay. Target is being . . . twenty kilometers, roughly? And mostly up."

"Da. That puts it in that big valley just the other side of those mountains. Very much of nothing all around it. Watch those jetpacks; I'm not sure they're going to have sufficient oxygen to operate once you start climbing. And don't forget to wear your oxy concentrator masks."

"John and I won't need them," Sera said serenely, and exchanged another look with John. Once again, he heard the Song strengthen and fill him, then felt something . . . adjusting. This time, inside him. And where a moment before he had been straining to get breaths, now . . . he was breathing as easily as a Sherpa.

Huh.

"I'll take your word for it; Moji and Unter, however, make sure you have your concentrators on."

"Yes, Little Mother," Moji said with amusement, but put on the mask anyway.

Sera spread her wings wide and was the first into the air. Untermensch was the second. John relaxed and concentrated at the same time, then began to run. When he'd reached what he *felt* was the right speed, he pushed off . . . and that rocket-like fire erupted from his feet and lower legs. He still had no idea how he was doing that . . . but it felt damned *good.* He had invested in a pair of goggles since his last attempt at flying; polarized, the wind and sun didn't bother him now.

In a moment he had caught up to Sera, and they flew under the bright Himalayan sun, side by side.

The jetpacks were not equal to the altitude. They gave out just below the pass that was going to take them into the valley. John was grateful that at least they were still below the snow line; they weren't equipped for snow-trekking, and they would have been hideously *visible* trudging across the pristine face of a glacier.

There had not been a single sign of life, not even a village or a herdsman, in all the time they'd been flying under Vix's guidance. Then again, she would have been routing them to avoid detection.

"Well, comrades," Moji said with resignation, peering up at the pass above them, "It looks as if we are walking."

"Ditch the packs; hide them in the bushes or... wait, JM, put your hand on the ground for me."

He knew what was coming, pulled off one of his gloves, and knelt to do so. This was the first time he had acted as a channel for Victrix since his re-awakening—and this was—different. He *felt* it; felt something warm and deep coming from somewhere outside of himself, going *through* him, and into the earth. There was some vibration, and two mounds of earth heaved up, and parted in the middle, leaving a cavity just big enough to hold the jetpacks. Moji and Unter didn't need to be told what to do; they pulled ultra-thin, ultra-strong nanofiber tarps out of their backpacks, wrapped the jetpacks in them and set them side by side in the hole. The earth moved to cover them, evening itself out and settling until John himself would never have known the packs were there.

"That should do it. When you come back down, I'll dig 'em out for you. Meanwhile, nobody's going to find them."

"Roger that, Vic. We're proceedin' along the course. It's all shank's mare from here."

"Just follow the yellow-brick HUD. Put two eyeballs up for me, please. I'll be your fore-and-aft scout."

The route that Vickie had plotted out for the team avoided as much of the harsh country as it could, but it still wasn't easy going. It was going to be an almost entirely uphill trek, over rough terrain that had a habit of giving way underfoot unexpectedly. It wasn't long before all of them, even with the concentrators and John and Sera's altered metabolism, were breathing hard from the exertion. Though the view was rather stunning if one of them paused long enough to look back along the path they had taken, there wasn't much else that stood out about this place. Just untouched, mountainous wilderness for miles and miles, with the glaciers and snow-capped peaks high above them. Well, the snow was covering considerably more than just the "peaks" of these mountains. It came down about halfway, and John was just glad that they weren't going to get near it.

"Are we being sure about intelligence on this area from electric dead men? Expense of this trip alone, not to mention wasted time..." Untermensch eyed the slope above them with disfavor.

"Only being one way to find out, *dedushka*. And that is to go there and look, with own eyes." Moji shrugged his pack into a better position before marching forward.

"I...have a feeling, beloved," Sera whispered. Sera had slowed so that John was abreast of her, with both of them being several paces behind their Russian comrades.

"A feelin'? 'bout the mission?" Ever since their "connection" had been made, John was able to sense Sera's feelings as if they were his own. It was a new sensation, but it didn't feel altogether alien for him. He had settled into it comfortably almost immediately, and hardly thought about it consciously anymore.

"Perhaps...I don't know. I sense...lives. Many living things, nearby." She looked at him uncertainly.

John concentrated for a moment, then nodded. "I can feel it, too." Now *this* was alien to him. It felt as if there were "shapes" on the edge of his perception, shifting and mingling. He knew, though he didn't know how, that they were alive. "Moji, hold up for a second." The two Russians stopped and turned to face the couple as they caught up. "Sera is gettin' a sense that there's a lot of...someone, up ahead. I can confirm it. I think this lead might not be a bust after all."

Molotok raised an eyebrow, trading a look with Untermensch. "A 'sense'?"

"It's not somethin' I can really quantify. But I'm not bullshittin' you, comrade."

Untermensch clicked his tongue in exasperation. "And our tactical doctrine is supposed to do what with these feelings? Eh?"

"Comrades, you don't argue with Soviette when she senses something, do you?" John knew that Vix had hit on exactly the right analogy when he saw the exasperation start to fade from both of the Russians' faces. *"I don't know exactly what Johnny and Sera have now, but I'm pretty sure part of it is like Sovie's psionics. Only neither of them have the right language yet to describe what they're picking up, or the experience to know what it is, exactly, that they're sensing. Hell, it's like learning to use a HUD when you've never seen one before."*

"Da, point made. So, we proceed with caution. Spread out formation, send 'eyes' forward to scout. Mission being to observe and report back any activity, with detail." Molotok nodded to the group. "Murdock, you will be on point. Lead us in direction of this sense of yours. Weapons out, all." With that, the big Russian unslung his rifle, press checked to make sure it had a round chambered, and then set off for the left flank. Unter did the same before setting off to the right.

"I strongly feel I should not be flying," Sera said firmly, and manifested the spear of fire. "I shall cover the rear."

"Roger that, love. Mute the brightness on yer spear if'n y'can; don't want to give away our position."

She frowned with concentration for a moment, and in her hands, the spear seemed to take on the color of old, hot coals.

As she turned to leave, John caught her by the elbow. "Oh, an' love?"

"Aye, beloved?"

"Be careful." He pecked her on the cheek, then winked at her as he grinned lopsidedly. Unbidden, he felt himself feeding reassurance and his love for her into their connection, and felt it returned in kind.

"And you as well." She smiled impishly. "You would be much less attractive with bullet holes in you." Then she was off to her area of responsibility, leaving John alone at the middle and front of the team's formation. *Time to get on with it.*

"And put up the other two eyes. I want all four quadrants covered from the air."

John fished two more of Vickie's technomagical "eyes" from the pouch on his load bearing equipment, tossing them up into the air; they disappeared almost immediately, off on their errands for the mage. John checked his own rifle, making sure the suppressor was affixed properly, that he had a full magazine, and that there was a round chambered. Satisfied, he set off at a careful trot; the ground had leveled out a little bit, and thus the going was easier.

They were trekking through upland forest, evergreens of some kind, tall and thin. Above them was alpine meadow, and further above that, the snow. And ahead of them, towering impossibly above the slope they were climbing—probably the tallest mountains John had ever seen, so tall it was hard to wrap his mind around how big they were. Steep, craggy, snow-crusted and utterly unforgiving. No wonder the people here considered those peaks sacred. It didn't seem possible that anything *mortal* could climb those near-perpendicular slopes. And as for living there...no. They were the essence of frozen death.

This was John's kind of country; he could easily see himself spending his days living in these kind of woods. It was also the kind of terrain that he was born, bred and trained to make war in. There wasn't much in the way of underbrush beneath these trees. This was a hard land, and an unforgiving one. Everything that lived here had to fight to exist.

And now, to complicate matters, they were moving into an area of heavy fog—or maybe it was clouds, they were certainly high enough for the thick mist to *be* clouds. It obscured everything, shutting down their range of vision to a few yards ahead at times, and rendering the entire landscape into a scene that could have been pulled from the opening to a horror movie.

John felt the Krieger's presence before he saw the man. John immediately signaled for the rest of the group to drop, go prone and still. And a few moments after his feeling of a *presence* alerted him, Vix confirmed it. *"Heads up! Bogie at eleven o'clock! Five hundred twenty-one meters."* John shifted slightly from his prone position, bringing up his rifle to look through the Trijicon ACOG scope. He could see the tiny figure clearly, when he wasn't moving in and out of fog. Definitely a Krieger, and one who was trying to be sneaky for whatever reason. At this range, the Krieger was just inside of John's engagement envelope for his rifle...but it would have to be a perfect shot. Better not to chance it.

"Molotok, I've got eyes on the Krieger. He's alone, armed. No signs of any other enemy presence; this guy's alone out there in Injun country. He's tryin' to sneak around, it looks like. What's the call?"

There was a short pause on the comm. "We need to find out what that *fascista* is doing out here; if your 'feelings' are correct, he isn't going to be alone for long. Intercept him. Victrix, can you block his communications once we are getting close?"

"Da, comrade." He could hear the glee in Vix's voice. *"Moron is broadcasting a carrier wave. Making my job easier. Jamming in three...two...one...engage. He probably won't notice he's jammed until he tries to call home."*

"Intercept and record any transmissions the *svinya* attempts. Murdock, move in and engage the target. Team, keep dispersion, and hold on Murdock's signal."

John waited a few moments, observing the Krieger's movements and the likely paths that he would take based upon his direction of travel. Studying the terrain, John quickly outlined in his mind the way he would go, where he would take cover, likely positions that ambush could come from and so forth. The mist would help to conceal the team; with Vickie's "eye" and his "sense" of where the Krieger was, he'd be able to track the Thulian without needing to maintain a visual. The Krieger was further down in the valley from them; John would need to be particularly careful that they didn't get caught on the slope of the mountain, since they'd be exposed to any sort of counterattack.

It was slow going, since John paused often to do a listening check, but he was still able to close the distance to the Krieger. When the team was roughly fifty meters away from their target, John signaled for everyone to hunker down. Looking over his shoulder to confirm that everyone was in good cover, he continued forward, alternately crawling or in a low crouch, using the mist, trees, rocks and vegetation to keep himself concealed. As he got closer, his sensitive nose picked up the burnt cinnamon, musk and rancid oranges scent that characterized Thulians. Peeking out from behind a large boulder roughly ten meters away from the Krieger, John saw that he had stopped and was fiddling with a device, muttering occasionally. *Finally noticed that Victrix broke his walkie-talkie.* John took the time to sling his rifle, unholstering his pistol and checking its suppressor; the supersonic crack from the rifle, even suppressed, would travel a lot further in this valley than that of the pistol.

Crouched low, with his pistol trained on the back of the Krieger's head, John moved forward in complete silence. He was rolling his feet with each step, going from the ball of the foot to the outside edge, keeping his movements deliberate and smooth. Despite his approach being as near to perfect as was possible, dumb luck had the Krieger turn his head at the last moment. His enhancements already keyed up, John made a snap decision; he holstered his pistol, took a step while unsheathing his knife, then clasped a hand over the Krieger's mouth as he stabbed the man underneath the solar plexus with the blade angled upward. With a sharp tug to the right, he bisected the Krieger's heart, killing him almost instantly. As the light faded from the Thulian's eyes, John set him down softly, scanning the immediate area for any other threats. There was something... else. He felt the Krieger's presence fade as the being died, and he knew that Sera could feel it, too.

It was...uncomfortable for John. He had never liked killing, and still didn't. He saw the necessity of it, sometimes, in his job; before, when he was in the military, and now, in his role as a metahuman fighting against a genocidal menace. But this...this felt like a dissonance in the Song. Something needed, but wrong at the same time. He didn't shake the feeling, but he didn't have time to process it at the moment, either.

"This is Murdock; Krieger neutralized. Move everyone up, slow."

"Bugger, that's a complication. Johnny; ground, bare hand, please. We don't want anyone finding the dead rat."

"Had to be done. Gonna strip him of gear and any intel."

"Roger that, but I need to make a big enough hole so no one is going to find him, and that takes time and energy. Give me the loc with your hand and I can take it from there while you search him."

John stripped off one of his gloves, placing it against the ground. As before, two mounds of earth heaved up and parted, as if someone was digging up from below. This was going to be a deep one, though; Vix would have to bury the body deeper than, say, a dog could find it. Just in case the Kriegers had something like a body-sniffing dog. Of course, once the body began to decay, that bet was off, but they should be well gone before that happened.

"One thing's for sure." Vix sighed. *"I'm burning energy like a fiend and I'm never gonna gain weight as long as you keep this kind of thing up."*

"So, this will make you less-sturdy comrade?" Molotok quipped. "If you grow any smaller, we will never be finding you!"

John had already begun stripping the Krieger down to his clothing. One of their energy pistols, the comm device he'd been fiddling with, some assorted kit that wasn't particularly interesting, a couple of devices that he didn't recognize and an honest-to-God Hitler Youth knife. John piled all of the regular gear together, and separated out the Thulian tech. Once that was done, he rolled the body into the hole that Vickie had created; almost immediately the earth that she had moved started to roll on top of the body, burying it. Once again, the earth packed itself down, and what little had been displaced, scattered itself. Then the detritus of the forest floor rearranged itself until there was no sign that the earth had ever been dug up.

Vickie's four "eyes" came back into visibility, hovering above the pile of Thulian tech. They quivered and rotated as Vickie worked her techno-shamanism.

"Johnnie, separate out this thing, will you?" One of the "eyes" landed gently on the top of a rhomboid-shaped object that had odd dimples in it, as if it was some sort of dingus to exercise your hand with.

John obliged, turning it over and around at Vickie's direction. "Done. Whatcha think it is?" The others on the team had spread out around John, keeping a watch on the perimeter while Vickie performed her magic show.

"I think I'll know in a minute..." The thing popped its top, right in John's hand. Inside were what looked like a couple of tiny gauges with a button between them. *"I think it's a key. Like, I am eighty percent sure it's a key. You're supposed to go where he was going, and when both those gauges redline, you push the button, Max. The indentations are so you get a better grip on it. I think having a good grip on it...means you're alive or something."*

John turned the device over in his hands, then looked at the other two. "What 'bout those gizmos?"

"One's his comm. You're too far from me to get a good read on the other. Maybe a storage device? Get your mind out of the gutter, but I don't have the right equipment out there to stick into it to find out. I wasn't anticipating having to do a remote access and debug." Her voice turned a little grim. *"Besides which, I know they have viruses that can infect our stuff, and I don't want to find out they put JIC booby traps on their equipment the hard way."*

"Right. Let's just hope that this gizmo doesn't blow up in my hand, then, Miss Eighty Percent." John stood up, grasping the Thulian device as Vickie had instructed him to. "All right folks. I guess we're followin' wherever this thing leads us." Molotok adjusted the team so that he was covering John, freeing John up to operate the device. Untermensch and Sera were set to guard the flanks and rear, alternately. As soon as they started moving again, the gauges became active. It took John a few minutes before he found just the right way to hold the device and to find the proper heading, but they were soon on their way to...whatever that Krieger had been trying to find.

They had come to top of a pass looking down into the next valley that gave the team a good vantage point for the rest of it when the device's gauges redlined just as Vickie had predicted, and the device itself started vibrating in pulses.

"I think this is it. Y'all ready?"

"The presences are very, very strong, beloved." Sera's voice trembled just a little. "They are all ahead of us."

"I am seeing nothing but an empty valley full of trees," Molotok said doubtfully. "Perhaps is large population of monkeys?"

"I doubt it, but let's be prepared for anythin' once I push this button. Vic, you recordin' this?"

"Continuous since you hit the ground."

"Roger. Let's rock an' roll." Everyone tensed, bringing their weapons to the ready. John pushed the button...and everyone collectively gasped, Vickie included.

In the center of the pass, the air...solidified in a circle. Then a kind of portal irised out of the center of that circle. And what showed in that circle was *nothing* like the empty, tree-filled valley that *seemed* to be there if you looked outside the circle.

"*Svyatoye der'mo*..." It was one of the few times John had seen Unter lose his composure. He felt that it was a rather appropriate moment for it.

"*Comrades, I have the distinct feeling it would be extremely unhealthy for anyone to try and go over this pass anywhere but through that doorway. Someone chuck a rock to one side of it, would you?*"

Molotok picked up a small round stone and obliged the mage. The stone sailed through the air to a point just past the portal... then slowed...then stopped in midair. John noticed that there was a slight distortion in the air around the stone a split second before the piece of rock disintegrated in a fizzle.

"*Uh yeah. Not particularly fussy about collateral damage, are our Nazi friends. And I know I have seen those buildings before.*"

As Vickie had said, the valley was *filled* with buildings. Not just "buildings," but monumental structures. Romanesque in design, impossible in scale. John, too, had a disconcerting sense of familiarity, as if he had seen this urban landscape somewhere before. *Did they actually flatten the valley floor to build that?* It certainly looked as if they had, because John couldn't see anything that looked as if the Thulians had built to follow the contour of the land. The entire...city, it had to be a city...was laid out with precision. Somehow, he *knew* that if he measured anything in there, it wouldn't be off by a micron. The centerpiece of the city was a huge domed structure that was so far away that more of the wisps of mist, or floating cloud, obscured it. And every single structure was pure marble. Or at least, some white substance that looked from this distance like marble.

"I knew I'd seen that before." In place of one of the information screens in the upper right of John's HUD, was a picture. It matched the city he saw before him almost perfectly, with one exception. Instead of the arena, it looked as if the builders had substituted a giant parade-ground.

"What—" Molotok asked, hesitantly.

"Germania. Albert Speer's planned supercity for the Reich. What was going to take the place of Berlin when the Nazis won the war. Some bright young things found the plans and did a digital mock-up of it. There was even a television program about it. That's where I saw this."

"Question now is . . . do we go in? If'n nothin' else, we probably ought to send some eyes in there. Start mappin', cataloging . . . I mean, just look at this goddamned place." John was awed by the spectacle of it. But not so much that he lost sense of purpose; they had a job to do here, and time was of the essence.

"We don't need to map it. Near as I can tell from where you are, it's an exact copy except for that parade ground," Vickie pointed out. *"I think you need to GTFO as fast as your feet will take you."*

"Nyet." Molotok's gaze was hard. "We will go inside. This is what we came for. The more intelligence we gather now, the better."

"It's official. You are freaking insane. You do realize I cannot do much of anything for you in there, right? Other than what I'm doing now. No giant rock man, no escape tunnels, not much in the way of rock barriers between you and Very Bad Fatal Things. You are a long, long way away from me, and the farther you are, the harder it is to do the earth-magic stuff that keeps your asses intact."

"Understood, Victrix. We will make do."

John saw the logic behind it, but even he had some doubts about the course of action. He knew through his connection that Sera felt the same. He *thought* he heard Vickie mutter something under her breath about calling in some favors, but his attention wasn't on her at this moment. This was going to take some doing to get right. Even with the map of the layout, they wouldn't know if the buildings would have the same purpose as they did in the

plans. There were a lot of unknowns, and they were about to dive
right into the middle of them.

"Vix, how many Kriegers could this place house, hypothetically?"

*"Millions. The stadium that was supposed to be there was sup-
posed to hold four hundred thousand. Eight million? Ten million?"*

"Let's hope they're underpopulated, then. Molotok, y'mind if
I take the lead on this? I've got some experience gettin' in an'
out of places quietly."

"I am experienced in making a great deal of noise. Lead us, Murdock." The two Russians looked grim. This had to be a nightmare
come true for Untermensch; John knew that he had been held in
Nazi captivity during WWII, and that the Nazis weren't exactly
the most humane captors. It was anyone's guess what Molotok was
thinking; having been raised by parents that fought in the war, in a
country that had been personally hit hard by it, it was a testament
that he was keeping it together as well as he was.

"All right, stay low and behind me. We want a small signature
on this one. We don't engage unless there's an unavoidable risk
of discovery otherwise. An' once we're done, we're gettin' the hell
out of here, fast. Stick together, no matter what; we don't want to
get lost in this godforsaken place." With a final nod, John took
a breath . . . and stepped through the portal.

Just like that, the entire team was through. It was just like stepping through an open doorway. No fanfare, no special effects. Save
for the temperature and the air; the interior was completely climate
controlled. Where it had been damned cold and the air was thin
outside, inside it was only mildly cool, with crisp, dry sea-level air-
pressure. The power requirements to keep a space like that perfectly
conditioned was staggering in and of itself, not to mention all of
the other wonders that the Kriegers had to be powering.

The area of the entrance looked like a small gate, definitely off
the beaten path from the main thoroughfares, at least according
to Vickie's map in the HUD. John quickly got the team to cover
in the doorway for a squat building to the left; the doorway itself
was easily large enough for three sets of powered armor to walk
through abreast. The ground itself was . . . strange. Pale gray, it
contrasted slightly with the pure white structures around them.
It wasn't stone or asphalt, though. It felt different, like some sort
of hardened rubber. If nothing else, it helped to mute their steps.

It also helped to mute the steps of the Kriegers. John was just about to give the team the signal to move out when Vickie came in over the comm.

"Take cover. Try the door behind you and get into the building if you can. Now!"

Molotok and John both put their shoulders into the massive doors; after a second of straining, both of the massive doors swung inward. Unter and Sera followed them in, and shut the doors behind them. Everyone immediately leveled their weapons... on a completely empty room.

White floor, walls and ceiling. No windows. The entire ceiling glowed softly, with an indirect light just like daylight. No furniture. Nothing on the walls, or the floor.

"The hell?" The building looked like it had never been used... for anything. There would be time to figure out what that meant later. "Vic, what's the sitch? Why are we camped out in here?"

"Patrol."

"Patch video of it through the HUD?"

"Was already on it. This area is uninhabited but they must patrol it regularly."

An image formed underneath the map in the upper right of John's HUD. Three Krieger troopers in armor, they were marching down the street towards the gate. Three corresponding dots appeared on the map, matching their progress. The middle trooper advanced ahead of the other two, looking somewhat confused as he approached the open portal. He punched a series of commands into a control panel on his gauntlet, and the portal irised shut. The Krieger then turned back to his two subordinates, and began conversing with them in German.

"We could take them..." John glanced back; it was Unter. He had steel in his voice, and his desire to kill the Thulians was palpable.

"Yeah, and alert the rest of the freaking city. You die, then they accelerate whatever plans they have to march over the world and everybody else dies."

"Witch is being right, *tovarisch*. We are here to observe, no more, unless absolutely necessary." Molotok fixed Untermensch with a stare until the other relented, sniffing and fiddling with his rifle.

"I have seen this," Sera said in a low voice that vibrated with emotion. "I have seen this world ending in fire and death, and only the Thulians and their slaves left. I did not know how such a thing came to be—but—I can see it now. This is one of the paths that can end in fire and death. We must not be detected, or..." She didn't need to complete the sentence. And when John turned in surprise to look at her, he saw that her blue eyes had turned gold again, that same featureless gold that had marked those features when—

The world faded out from around him, and he *saw* it. Saw Untermensch dash out, whether before Moji had issued his orders or after, he couldn't tell. Saw Georgi take out all three of the Thulians, and then they were running, running through the streets of the city with Vickie trying in vain to find a bolt-hole for them. He watched as all of them were cut down, himself and Sera last. And then watched in accelerated time as the Thulians boiled out of their city, watched Bella try in vain to ready the world for an onslaught more terrible than anything they had seen yet. And saw it all end, as Sera had said, with the world in ruins, the survivors in slave camps, and the Kriegers triumphant—

John was snapped out of the vision by Molotok's voice. "They are moving out." John shook his head, then focused on the image from the HUD; the three troopers were going back the way they had come, apparently joking with each other judging by the way the shoulders on their armor was heaving.

"Sure as shit hope that the gizmo can open up that portal from the inside, otherwise we're here for the duration." John took stock of their situation. They had walked into way more than they had intended to. They didn't have the supplies or the support to stay much longer; Vickie could only keep her technomagical eyes going for so long before she ran out of juice, the eyes did, or both. The longer they stayed and the deeper they went into the city, the higher their chances of being detected were. If they were found out, it would completely negate the entire purpose of their mission...and if the vision was true, a whole lot worse than that.

"Look, I can take the eyes up just under the 'ceiling' of that force field and get a general gander. Collect as much data as I can in a single sweep. I think the force field itself will mask the presence of the eyes."

"Do it. The more time we spend on site, the higher our chances of discovery are." John looked to Molotok for confirmation.

"*Da.* We will wait, in position, until witch's toys complete their sweep. Then we shall exfiltrate."

"*Poke around in that building and see if you can learn anything? Johnny, if you see something that needs to be scanned or recorded, you've got some stuff onboard. Just say 'Overwatch: command: full scan on visual target.'*"

John started moving around the empty room. It was largely featureless save for a couple of protrusions in opposite corners. One looked like a water hook-up, with a sort of temperature control panel above it. It didn't actually have any sort of controls that John could fathom, however. On the other side, however, was an alien looking power outlet; a flat metal plate that he confirmed was magnetized after accidentally pressing his rifle against it, with three different orange lights circling it. He spoke the command Vickie had told him, and recorded everything he could about the feature; it might come in handy, at some point.

"*Lichten aus?*" Unter said tentatively. And suddenly they were plunged into complete darkness.

John immediately switched his HUD over to night vision, swinging around with the rifle. Everyone was looking at Unter, who was holding his hands up placatingly and grinning.

"*Izvineniya.* Apologies. Since I could not see controls, I wondered if the lights answered to voice. *Lichten auf.*" The lights came back up. Gradually, so they weren't blinded.

"Next time you are having bright idea, *dedushka* . . . don't. Being patrol partner with Old Man Bear is rubbing off on you." Molotok shook his head. "Witch-girl, how much longer?"

"*Not much. There's only so much equipment Verd could pack in those balls.*" There was strain in her voice. She sounded tired. "*Basic fly-by is the best I can do. Ten minutes more, I think.*"

It was one of the longest ten minutes of John's life.

When the four "eyes" had returned, it was with bad news.

"*Comrades, we've got a problem. Someone's camping the gate. He came from inside the city, so if you whack him, he'll be missed.*"

"Camping the gate?" Moji said, perplexed.

The video feed from one of the technomagical eyes appeared in the team's HUDs. A single lone Thulian, unarmored, was waiting by the section of barrier holding the gate that they had entered the city through. He was looking around furtively, his eyes darting around the streets and buildings. One moment, he was there; then his eyes grew wide, and he was running as if the Devil himself were chasing the Krieger. Seconds later, everyone saw why; another patrol of troopers, five this time, came up to the barrier. After a few barked orders, the troopers took up positions around the exact spot that the team needed to get through.

"*Der'mo* . . . Day continues to improve, does it not?" Unter spat on the ground to punctuate his remark.

"Victrix, we will be needing to find alternate means of leaving city. Can you find us an alternate route?"

"Let's settle for getting you out first. I need to look at that gate dingus in more depth. Try not to attract attention while I do."

John retrieved the Thulian device from the dump pouch on his belt. "Got the gizmo ready. Whatcha need me to do?"

"Don't turn it on, for God's sake. I don't want to take the chance it sends out some sort of tell-tale. Just hold it bare-handed, I might be able to get a good read on it through you."

"A-ffirmative." John tucked the device under his arm while he stripped off his gloves with his teeth. Sera already had her hand out for them, and brushed the back of one of his hands with a gentle finger when she took them. Calm seemed to come to him through the touch; he grinned, reciprocating the emotions as much as he could. He held it gingerly, and had the oddest sensation that Vickie was doing more than just "looking" through the camera magically integrated with his eyes. She was employing some other means of examining the device that felt like a feather tickling the back of his mind.

"It's not set to open a particular gate, it's a general-purpose gate-opener. So we just follow the same protocol around the rim of this joint, and if you find another one of those back doors, you can open it. But of course, that means turning it on, which means someone might notice."

"Unavoidable, if we wish to ever leave this decadent monstrosity. Murdock, lead us out; we will be on cover for you." With a curt nod, Molotok turned to converse with Unter in rapid-fire Russian. John noticed Unter's demeanor change ever so slightly; whereas before he had looked ready to kill every Krieger he could see, now he was back to his usual stony-faced self. *There'll be time enough for blood later, old man.* That seemed to be the gist of what Molotok had told their comrade, at any rate. Within moments, the team had their weapons ready and the rest of their gear squared away.

"Vix," Murdock said from the front of the team, "let me know when I've got a window of opportunity."

"*I know, waiting's the worst part. On the other hand, since these bricks don't have windows, no one can see in, either.*" The wait seemed interminable. "*Remember, people, the first bullet that flies means you're made. And if you're made, well, remember what Sera said. It's all over.*"

"Don't worry; with you on Overwatch an' me leadin' the way, they'll never have a chance t'see us. You an' I've had some practice at this," John said with a slight chuckle.

"*Stack up. I'm gonna give you a countdown to move out.*" The team was already in formation, ready and waiting, an easy tension that came from training and experience. "*And...five. Four. Three. Two. One. Move out and move fast. Follow the HUD.*"

With one fluid motion, John swept the door open just enough to allow the team to squeeze out through it. He kept low, almost in a half-crouch, and moved at a very brisk pace. His senses were working overtime as he took the team to the right, following the path outlined on his HUD by Vickie. He double checked every corner and street before taking the team out into the open at crossings. From what Vickie said on Overwatch, it seemed as if the outskirts of the city were largely deserted; as far as he could tell, all of the buildings they passed were as empty as the one they had hidden in. All of this was very fortunate; John did *not* want to see the vision he and Sera had shared come to pass, not one fraction of it. In ten minutes time of sneaking and running around the outer edge of the city, there hadn't been a single blip on the Thulian gizmo. Then the gauges redlined all at once, and the device started to vibrate in pulses again.

"Looks like we're at another backdoor." This part of the city wasn't composed of buildings, but rather, of a series of arches and steles. There was writing carved into them, but it was nothing John could read. It all looked somber though—in a uniquely unsettling and Thulian way, at least—and he got the impression that it all served some symbolic purpose rather than a practical one.

He pointed the gizmo at the end of the avenue of steles, and the door irised open in front of them. It was dark on the other side, too dark to see what was there, but it didn't matter. If Vix was right, just using the gizmo was giving the Thulians a signal and something to track, and they needed to be gone. Unter was the first one through, with a final scornful look back at the city.

"You've attracted attention. You've got about five minutes, max."

"Hurry, we must not be in area on other side!" Molotok allowed Sera to jump through first, then followed closely behind her. John was the last man through, just in case the gizmo were to click off suddenly. He stepped through, and felt the breeze part his hair as all of Vickie's "eyes" rushed over the top of his head through the portal like a miniature swarm of bees. He immediately keyed the Thulian device, and the portal closed behind them.

If the city-side of the portal had been spooky, this side pegged the gauge. They were in a narrow, steep-sided valley, probably more accurately termed a defile, that had been scoured clean of vegetation. From where they were, it was clear that niches had been carved into the sides of the valley. Orange letters glowed above each one, but it was too dark and too far away to see what was in them.

"Patrol behind you just missed seeing the door close."

"Too damned close. We need to *didi* the hell outta this place, 'fore someone gets the bright idea to open up the portal behind us." John replaced the Thulian device in his dump pouch, bringing his rifle up.

"Ravine makes a twist ahead, that'll get you out of immediate line of sight. Uh, do you want to know where you are?"

"I am having feeling you will tell us, whether we are wanting to hear or not." Molotok sighed. "How far from where we should be?"

"Too damn far to make the pickup. You'll have to follow this thing for about five miles until you get to a place you can, maybe, climb out. And it's all the wrong way. Oh, and you're in what I think is an alien cemetery. Boo."

John moved a few steps closer to the niches had been cleanly carved into the rock. The glowing orange letters were definitely Thulian; some of the inscriptions, however, had prominent swastikas at the end of them. *Creepy as all hell.*

"Let's get moving. We can find alternate route on way. Move out, *tovarischii*." The team set off at a steady jog; right now getting distance from the back door into the city was more important than stealth. With Vickie's eyes in the sky and John on point, they had decent chances of being able to avoid any potential entanglements, besides. The team covered the five miles in good time, though all of them were winded by the elevation and the exertion. The path, if you could call the barely-there goat trail they had been running along a path, terminated suddenly at a sheer rock face. Everyone stopped, circling up to catch their breath and drink some of the water they had brought with them while keeping a 360-degree watch.

"This is the end of the line, Vic. I think we're outta the immediate danger zone, but we need to get clear of this entire valley. And we're outta road." John gulped greedily from his canteen, then passed it to Sera; she finished off the other half of it. Empty canteens don't have their contents slosh around, after all.

"The only way out is up."

Molotok and Unter both slung their rifles. "We will have to be scaling the wall, then. We have ropes, climbing harnesses... is long climb, though." Molotok stroked his chin as he sized up the rock face in front of them.

John and Sera shared a look. Positioning herself behind and a little distance away from the oblivious CCCP team leader, Sera spread her wings and made a run at Molotok, catching him just under both armpits and launching herself—and him—into the sky. "Flying is faster," she said, her voice fading as they arced up into the distance. John could hear Molotok protesting, and did his best to suppress his laughter, with only moderate success.

Unter glanced at Murdock, then his shoulders slumped. *"Da, da.* Time for *svinya*-back ride." He threw his arms over John's shoulders from behind.

"Hold on tight, and kick your feet up after we're off the ground. Don't want to toast your boots." Concentrating—though not nearly as much as he had to previously—John lifted off the ground on a plume of flame, rocketing straight up with Untermensch on his back. Fortunately, like the missile he resembled, the beginning of the ride was relatively slow, and acceleration was gradual, or Unter might well have lost his grip. He cut the "thrust" a dozen feet from the edge of the rock face; their momentum carried them up and past the edge; Unter instinctively released his grip, and both of them landed easily on their feet as they came down from the apex of their arc.

Molotok didn't look quite shaken, but he wasn't very happy,

either. "Never again, without my permission. Or excoriation all around." He fumed for a moment, then clicked his tongue at them. "Victrix, where to now? And nowhere that is needing flying to. Enough for one day."

Two hours later the team had arrived at their new destination. Vickie had been silent for most of their trek; she said that she had a lot of things to prepare in order to get them the hell out of Dodge. But when she got them over what she said was the last of the hills and on another goat-path into a valley ... all they could see was the valley.

"*Borzhe moi*," Molotok said, wearily, as the last light of the sunset painted the mountains red. Ahead of them was a valley filled with a thin mist. No sign of life. "I thought you said we were almost there, witch! Are we trekking up mountain faces now?"

"*Do you really think I would do that to you? Just wait a moment, and let them turn the lights on.*"

It was like something out of a movie that John vaguely remembered. *Lost Horizon?* There was a shimmering effect on the mist, and then ... it was there. Perched like a flock of birds on the cliff on their side of the valley was a series of beautiful buildings, with the swooping red and gold roofs and pristine white walls of what could *only* be a Buddhist monastery of some sort. It looked like a movie set. John let out a low whistle. "They sure picked a nice spot. Welcome mat rolled out for us?"

"*If it wasn't, you wouldn't see it. Full speed ahead, comrades. Davay davay. They don't like leaving the lights on for very long.*"

John saw the path before them; you had to look for it, but it was there, and led to a small rope and wooden slat bridge. The bridge looked ancient, but after a few test steps, seemed sturdy enough. John and Sera were the first across, with the two Russians close behind. Everyone slung their weapons, though the two Russians continued to be alert and wary.

When they reached the end of the bridge, John spotted a small group of red-and-saffron-robed monks waiting for them. It didn't seem possible that they weren't freezing to death in what amounted to a couple of sheets wrapped around them, but they seemed perfectly comfortable....

... until they spotted Sera and JM emerging from the mist. Their eyes went wide, and they seemed startled and even a bit confused for a moment. Then as one, they bowed to Sera, deeply—turned a little, and bowed to John, only a little less deeply.

"Um, Vickie…what's this 'bout?" The two Russians shared a look, both just as confused as the one plastered on John's face.

Vickie didn't answer. Sera, however, murmured something to the monks, who bowed again, then held out their hands in what was clearly a welcoming gesture. She took their hands, smiling slightly, made a tender little gesture, bowed over their hands and murmured something else. Then she looked back over her shoulder. "It's all right, beloved. I explained." Without another word, the monks led her up a set of steps and into the monastery; John could feel the warmth and smell incense coming from the open doors.

"Right." He turned to Untermensch and Molotok, shrugged, and followed Sera inside. The Russians did the same. Their guides took them past a large group of more monks deep in some kind of meditation that also involved a droning chant, then out the other side of the first building, across another little wooden bridge, and into a second building, much smaller than the first. All the monks but one left them.

"Okay, folks, I know you are hungry and thirsty, but trust me, you don't want to eat right now." Vickie said as the monk waited patiently, as if he knew, somehow, that she was talking to them. *"Hold hands, and try to clear your minds. You ought to have an easy time of that, Murdock."*

"Har har, Teen Witch." The group clasped their hands together, forming a circle. The Russians looked uncertain and very uncomfortable.

"Victrix, what is meaning of this?"

Before she could answer, the monk patted John on the shoulder and said something, then walked out and closed the door.

Since Sera seemed to have understood the monks before, John looked to her. "Love?"

"He offered us his blessing," she said, serenely. "And told us he would pray for our souls."

"Wait, pray for our souls? What the hell—"

The room vanished, or rather, it felt and looked as if they were in the heart of an explosion. Every sense was pummeled, and it seemed that for an eternity they were in free fall.

And then they tumbled, nauseous to the point of vomiting and disoriented, onto the floor of—

Another room.

This one was round. There was an enormous, complicated diagram inlaid into the floor in what looked like semi-precious gems and several different kinds of stone. The ceiling overhead was a dome, inlaid with yet more diagrams, this time in many different kinds of wood. The dome matched the walls. The only illumination came from a chandelier full of candles that hung from the center of the dome, and four free-standing torches placed at equal intervals around the room.

Even Sera had been affected; she lay half on her side, panting with exertion. John was not in terribly good shape himself; it felt as if he had been running a marathon, all uphill. He was utterly drained as well as nauseous.

A door opened in the wall, a door he hadn't even seen for all the carvings and diagrams. There was brighter light out there, so he could see only that the person who had opened the door was female.

"What...the hell, Victrix..." John was able to choke down enough air to keep his gorge from rising. Everyone else was recovering slowly, as well. "A little warning next time might be nice."

For a moment, all he could hear in his ear was harsh panting. *"Sorry. This shit has to be timed to the nanosecond. I could explain, or I could juggle nitroglycerine. Pick one."*

Untermensch lifted himself off the floor, coming up to a knee. "Where in the name of Lenin's ghost are we?"

"Sorry, *tovarisch*," the woman who had entered the room said, brusquely. "That's on a need-to-know basis, and you don't need to know. In the US, eastern seaboard. That's all you get. Take this." She held out four pills on her hand. "Helps with the nausea."

Another person—a man this time—came in with four incongruously ordinary bottles of water—liter bottles. He handed one to each of them.

John downed the pill and half of the bottle of water. After spending a few more moments regulating his breathing, he had started to feel somewhat better. "Did we just get fuckin' *teleported*? Like, across the goddamn world?"

"You would not believe the number of favors Victrix called in and now owes for that, but yes, except we call it *apporting* when it's done by magic." The woman held out her hand to John, clearly to assist him to his feet.

"You're all mages?" He took her hand, which was surprisingly strong, and lifted himself up to standing. Then he helped Sera up.

The woman, iron-eyed and iron-haired, cracked just a little bit of a smile. "Since this is Victrix's first school, that would be a logical assumption, yes. And in the interest of saving the world, at least half our instructors are prostrate with nosebleeds and migraines right now."

Molotok stood up, unassisted, and only swayed for a moment before finding his feet. "And witches do this, zipping across the globe in blink of eye?"

"Actually, no. Rarely, and never with a group; the last time we tried retrieving more than one person at a time, Tunguska suffered a . . . critical failure." The entire team turned pale. She shrugged, then smiled a little more. "But, you are all here, you are all in one piece, no body parts have been mixed up, Victrix's math worked, and everyone survived at both ends with no explosions. Well done, us."

"Headmistress," the man said, clearly unable to contain himself any longer. "We really *must* publish this in *Apportation Quarterly*. It's a major breakthrough! Why, you and I could easily get tenured positions out of it!" The two moved away from the team, talking excitedly with each other.

John chose that moment to lean against Sera and ignore the two mages. "Vickie, how do we get home? I think I've had just 'bout as much magic as I can stomach for one day."

"That's all the magic you get, stud. Blacked-out van, so you don't see where you're going, as far as a little private airport. Private plane to Hartsfield, Atlanta. People's Transport to your bunk."

"Roger that. Murdock out; we'll see you on the flip side. Give Nat the heads-up that the mission was a success . . . and that we have a lot of talkin' to do." With that, John spoke the commands to key off the comm and Overwatch.

Sera took off her headset and stowed it in its pouch on her belt. "Well," she said, finally. "That was . . . a new thing."

"Lot of that goin' around lately, it seems." He wrapped his arm around her. "I think we deserve a break, quite honestly. Gimme some boring old normal things."

She held him tight, and said, sadly, "If only I could, beloved. If only I could. . . ."

CHAPTER TWENTY-THREE

Penny Black

MERCEDES LACKEY AND DENNIS LEE

Carefully, Penny shook Lacey's shoulder. This wasn't the first time that Penny had tried to wake the woman, but it was the first time Penny had actually touched her, other than to feed her. It was almost suppertime, by the feeling in her tummy, and Lacey's Guy had suggested that whatever the Dark Man was giving Lacey to make her sleep, it might be wearing off about that time.

"Miss," Penny said, quietly, while the other children watched her covertly, waiting to see what might happen to her if she woke the crazy lady. "Miss. Miss. Miss. You gotta wake up, Miss. There's a guy here, Miss. He wants to talk to you."

The woman batted at Penny's hand, and moaned. Penny noticed that she'd lost the tip of her little finger on that hand without any surprise. The Devil took bits of the children. Sometimes he would cut off some hair, other times he would jab a large needle into the belly and take something from inside. And sometimes, he took bits of finger, usually the tip. No one knew why. "Miss," she persisted, shaking gently. "The guy wants to talk to you, Miss."

Lacey muttered something. Penny thought she might be asking, *"Who is it? What do you want?"* Penny looked to the ghost. He shrugged, as if he couldn't figure out what she'd said, either.

"Miss Lacey," Penny said, "You've got to wake up."

"Her name isn't Lacey."

Penny blinked in surprise and turned her head again to look at the ghost. "Well, what is it, then?" she demanded.

To her surprise, the ghost looked unhappy at first, and then

327

screwed up his face in concentration. He sat that way for some time, before sagging in defeat. "I don't remember," he said, sadly.

That didn't make any sense! "How can you not remember if you know her?" Penny demanded, loudly enough that the other kids gave her one of those *looks*.

The ghost looked so sad that Penny felt horrible for asking the question. "When you die," he said, quietly, and with deep unhappiness, "The first thing you start to forget is names. First people you only ever heard about, then people you sort of know...then friends...then family...then..." He shrugged. "Then you forget your own name."

Penny's mouth dropped open in astonishment. "But...but... how can you forget your own name? Why would you?"

"Someone told me...I don't remember her name either. She was a magician, or at least she said she was. She said names were power. When you know someone's name, you have power over them, she said." He looked down at his hands, curled like petals over his knees. "Maybe we forget names so no one can call us back."

"Huh." She glanced over at Lacey-who-wasn't-Lacey, who had dropped back into oblivion.

"After a while, you forget more than your name," the ghost continued. "You forget who people were, or that you ever knew them. The only thing that anchors you is anger, hate, all the bad stuff. You start to fade, and you start to go to pieces. It makes you crazy. That's why all those other ghosts I chased away were crazy."

Penny felt her eyes widening. "But I thought...I thought when you died, you went to the good place, or the bad place," she whispered.

"I dunno." The ghost shrugged. "When I still remembered my name, I talked to another one that wasn't crazy yet, who said most people go...somewhere else. But some of us get stuck. He said there were three kinds that got stuck. Some were scared to move on. Some were stuck because of something they still needed to do. And some were stuck because someone needed *them*." His shoulders heaved a little, as if he had sighed. "I don't remember which kind I am."

He looked so sad again that Penny wanted to hug him. "I *bet*," she said, instead, "It's 'cause Lacey needs you. I bet once you help her, you'll go where you're s'posed to."

"You think?" he looked a little more cheerful at that.

"I bet!" Penny repeated, firmly.

He managed a smile. "I bet you're right, then," he agreed. "And the sooner we can wake her up and get her head fixed, the better."

"Right!" Penny said, as cheerfully as she could, and went back to shaking Lacey's shoulder. "Miss! Miss! You gotta wake up now, Miss!"

CHAPTER TWENTY-FOUR

Ice Cold

MERCEDES LACKEY AND VERONICA GIGUERE

Bella listened to Red Saviour describe her worst nightmare. She felt her temper boiling, as Natalya all but crowed over her team's uncovering of the main Thulian headquarters. And the only thing that kept it from exploding was the chilling effect of the videos of that headquarters: not a building, not a hollowed-out mountain. A city. A city of millions. And not a city of millions of civilians mixed in with a much smaller population of fighters. This was a city designed and planned to support a vast army, equipped with the latest of Thulian technology, which very likely was worse than anything they had already thrown at the rest of the world. The mere fact that every technological and magic trick in the world's arsenal had been deployed to find this city, and had failed, proved that.

"And your team killed one Thulian, and alerted the rest to their portals being opened off-schedule," she said flatly, interrupting Saviour's glee.

"*Shto?*" the Commissar replied, frowning. "They were not detected."

"But *something* was," Bella pointed out sharply. "One of their personnel has gone missing. Someone opened and closed their doors. These are *Kriegers,* Red Saviour! The mindset of the German technician attached to a society with the goal of world conquest! If they haven't yet leapt to the conclusion that we found them, they very soon will *deduce* that conclusion, which is *exactly* the scenario I didn't want to have happen!" She realized she had gotten to her feet and was shouting those last words only when she had hit the desk with the flat of her hand. She took a deep breath, and sat down, slowly.

Natalya watched her, eyes narrowed, but said nothing.

Bella wanted badly to . . . hit her. Throw things. Scream and rage. All of which would accomplish nothing, and the clock, started by the actions of Red Saviour, was ticking.

"Overwatch," she ordered. "Priority Command. Contact all on War List. Call emergency meeting. Override all other priorities."

She saw, with grim satisfaction, Red Saviour's head snap up as the *extremely* unpleasant tone of the War List alert rang through her skull at a volume intended to wake anyone even out of a drunken or drugged stupor. While Saviour was still reacting, *she* stepped from behind her desk and past Saviour, right out the door, headed for the conference room. Overwatch would be informing the Commissar of where that room was about now . . . and yes, this was a calculated insult, which Bella hoped would put Red Saviour in her place and make her understand that she and the CCCP were no more than one part of a vast machine which was now, thanks to her, lurching into unbalanced motion.

Bella could only pray that the Thulians were denser, or more self-confident, than she feared. *Lurching* was not the way to win a war.

The meeting was still going on, but despite all the recriminations, chest-thumping, arguments about who was to blame and who was to take precedence over someone else, the conclusion was foregone. Bella excused herself, ceding the chair to Yankee Pride gratefully. Pride was better at negotiating than she was, anyway. She wanted to get to the Quantator without Saviour around, and right now, Saviour was up to her eyeballs in recriminations and self-defense. If she tried one of her patented "storm out in a cream-colored huff" exits, she'd probably be arrested at the door by the agents of three global military powers, ECHO, and a Supernaut.

Time was of the essence, and rank hath its privileges. Bella ordered a jetpack brought to the nearest entrance (*"Now,* please.") and someone from Quartermaster Corps was waiting right there with it. He helped her don it, and she was moving while fastening the last buckle. Minutes later, rather than the half to three-quarters of an hour it would have taken by ground, she touched down at CCCP HQ.

The guard on duty was Untermensch, who clearly had realized by this point that CCCP in general and Red Saviour in particular had screwed the pooch. He ducked his head slightly, then shrugged and waved her in.

She marched straight to the door of the Quantator room with barely a nod at Chug. "Overwatch: open: Ramona," she ordered, and as soon as the slight carrier wave sound told her Ramona was live, began speaking even as she was powering up the Quantator. "Ramona, we have a shitstorm here. Get yourself and Merc on the main line, pronto. I need you to sell *icebergs* to Eskimos, and I need it yesterday."

The image faded, the bits of color disappearing from the screen. Ramona passed her hand over her forehead and scratched at a small flake of metal. "Well, that changes things. Not everything, just the general timetable."

"Timetable?" Mercurye shook his head, still stunned by the report from Bella. He hadn't known her ever to swear so profusely or vehemently. "Timetable for what?"

"For getting your amazing and remarkably absent benefactors into the game and onto the winning side. I thought we'd have a week or two, given how slowly they like to move and what you've told me about their tendencies to vote on everything." She offered him a rueful smile. "We can now blame the Russians and their illustrious 'Saviour' for compressing a few weeks of coordination into little more than a day, and months of prep into a week or so."

That assessment brought Merc to his feet. He waved both hands in front of him, blond surfer locks swaying back and forth with his protest. "No. No, I don't think you understand, Ramona. They won't. They can't, it goes against their idea of a true democracy. The arguments and counterarguments in the primary debate alone would take three days, and that's without breaks." He thought back to his initial requests for television shows and blue-box macaroni and cheese dinners; the latter had taken six days because someone's concern about the sodium content had sparked a secondary discussion. "You won't be able to rush them."

Ramona pushed herself up from the white microfiber sofa. She was every bit the person he remembered from their conversations via the quantator and their admittedly brief time together before he had arrived in Metis. She met his 'no' with a frown and folded her arms across her chest. "Not if their inaction could be what ultimately brings them down? If their desire for this pure 'democracy' is what winds up eradicating every last bit of freedom and humanity that they've loved to watch like some primetime sitcom for decades?"

"Well, when you put it that way..."

"That's what it's going to be, Rick. Bella's not one for exaggeration. She knows the difference between 'not so bad' and 'holy shit, *fire*' when it comes to situations, and right now, the Thulians are ready to burn everything that we know to the ground if we don't act." Ramona started to pace, movement that Rick found more soothing than unnerving.

As she went from one wall to another and circled the sofa, he padded to his favorite spot on the white carpet and sat cross-legged. Palms resting lightly on his knees, Rick closed his eyes. "Asking permission isn't going to get us anywhere. You might be able to clue in Marconi as to what needs to be done, but Tesla won't go along with it."

"Because," she prompted. Her tone said that she suspected the answer, but she wanted him to acknowledge it before she put it out in the open.

"Because he's Tesla? Because he wants proof?"

"Because he's scared." That statement surprised Mercurye; he opened his eyes to find Ramona leaning over the sofa, watching him. Slowly, her eyes lit up and one corner of her mouth stretched back into a sly smile. "Think about it. This is all he's known for how long? He and Marconi, if this goes, then they're gone. If they don't get canned in some huge data wipe, then they'd be held hostage by the Thulians."

"Maybe two in a series. Like a battery of captured geniuses, locked up to power something bigger." The idea awed Mercurye for a split second before the horror of his suggestion caught up to him. "Wait, you don't think they could actually do that, do you?"

"Gigantic floating spheres, enormous armored aliens, and I'm bleeding out metal. I've got a pretty big imagination these days." Ramona licked her lips and glanced to the door. "Do these guys have any kind of schedule for their proceedings? Is there a good time or a bad time to bring up these kinds of things in committees or whatever they use?"

Mercurye thought for a moment, trying to remember what Trina had told him during their conversations and the questions that he had asked. "Well, they don't like surprises. Everything has to go through the proper committees, and nothing is ever brought directly to the Assembly. Like, you couldn't just walk in there and bring it up."

"Perfect." With a speed that he didn't think Ramona possessed, she grabbed his wrist and pulled him up to a standing position. "Let's call Trina and figure out how to get there. Nothing like the element of surprise, right?"

For his part, Mercurye was too stunned to answer. The new Ramona was remarkably strong.

Trina agreed to go as far as the antechamber to the room that housed the Metisian Assembly. She led Mercurye and Ramona in front of the enormous double doors and offered them a weak smile. "If everything that you've said is true, then this is the right choice and I don't regret it."

"Don't worry, it's true." Bella had sent Ramona a "highlights tape" of what the CCCP team had seen of what they were now calling Ultima Thule. It fit; better than the original concept's name of "Germania" fit. When Marconi had figured out how to download it to the Metis systems; he'd been properly horrified by the vast size of the place, and the implication that there were *millions* of waiting warriors lurking there, ready to deploy at any moment. "Convincing them of the truth isn't going to be the problem."

Trina nodded in uncertain agreement. "Just be careful. No one has ever been banned from the Assembly, but that doesn't mean they won't try to remove you from the proceedings." She rose up on her toes and gave Mercurye a chaste kiss on the cheek. "Good luck."

To Ramona's surprise, the speedster blushed at the attention. He didn't return the kiss. "Won't be luck that we'll need. Just watch the door and let her talk. They won't be able to say no once Ramona starts talking."

"We hope." Ramona ran through the key information that Bella had sent. Marconi had his cue, and he had assured her that the Metisians would not be able to shut him out of the system easily. "You head clockwise once the doors open, Rick. I'll go center. Ready?"

He exhaled and shook out his hands and feet. "Call it."

Ramona flexed her fingers, her eyes fixed on the door. They would only have one opportunity. "Go."

Trina yanked on the door to allow a blur of white to rush in. The cries of indignation and protest came in seconds, and the noise grew to a roar in less than a minute. Ramona slipped through the door and allowed her eyes to adjust to the dim light. Like the room where she had stood face to gigantic face with Tesla and Marconi, she could not make out a ceiling or walls beyond the door she had just passed through. Air rushed behind her, proof of Mercurye's distraction while she made her way to what she hoped was the center of the room. Small blue-white lights illuminated frantic figures at long white tables. They gestured at her, motioning her back toward the double doors. Ramona ignored them and climbed on top of a table. She brought her foot down twice, the sharp crack of boot on marble reminiscent of a gavel. Immediately, the noise stopped.

"I wish to call the Assembly's attention to a matter of grave importance," Ramona began in a clear voice. She counted to five silently, hoping that someone would respond.

"On what grounds and for what purpose?" The clear and cultured tone came from somewhere above her left shoulder. Ramona guessed there was some kind of raised dais for speakers or key members to offer arguments.

"Survival. And, survival," she added with a touch of sarcasm. "Survival of Metis, I mean."

The room roared again in protest. "Out of order! This is not the proper procedure for the petition of the assembly!"

"This isn't a petition," Ramona shot into the darkness. "It's a warning. The Thulians are coming for you, the same way that they came for the rest of the Earth."

Those words silenced the room. Mercurye came to a stop next to her and rested a hand on her shoulder. "It's true," he called. "I've seen the proof, and you're all in danger. We're all in danger," he corrected.

The sonorous voice over her left shoulder asked the first question, one that Ramona had expected. "Why would you think that the Thulians are coming for us? We are not in the battle, and the Assembly has deemed there to be no need to join the conflict." Murmurs of approval followed his words. "We have not seen danger."

"Danger doesn't walk up to the front door and knock, and if you're doing your best to ignore all of the signs, then you're definitely not going to see it." Ramona cracked the heel of her boot twice against the marble, and Marconi answered with a slowly visible image of the Thulian city above the heads of the Assembly. Like the visages of the two elder scientists, the faint outline of the taller buildings and the perimeter sketched across the air. Pale blue lines darkened as the intricacies of the city filled in with more lines. White and silver shading gave depth and detail while symbols that Ramona guessed to be Metisian characters labeled the larger structure. Finally, a second, much smaller city outlined in yellow appeared beneath the outline. From the gasps and murmurs in the half-light, Ramona could only guess that the smaller city was Metis.

"The Thulians aren't idle or passive. Their attacks on Earth, on the metahumans of Earth and the innovations that Metis has generously provided them over the decades, have been calculated from the very beginning. Just like their city, which is far bigger and more complex than any of us could have imagined." Ramona snapped her fingers twice to bring the most prominent Thulian buildings to the foreground. "This isn't a city built for peace. This is a city designed to train soldiers and sustain a brutal war."

"But we are not at war with the Thulians." The voice behind Ramona reminded her with equal parts annoyance and condescension. "Earth is at war with them, and your ECHO is presently engaged in that conflict. We have not agreed to take any part in this conflict, Ms. Ferrari."

The fact that some holier-than-thou Metisian knew her name and used it in the same simpering tone as everyone who'd ever ignored her detective credentials during a critical investigation made Ramona's blood boil. She stepped back and craned her neck up to look at the speaker. A smooth-faced man in a white jacket that would have been fashionable in the seventies glared down at her, his mouth drawn tight. "First of all, it's Steel Maiden. I had these meta factors triggered without the help of any of your fancy technology or tweaking, so you can show some respect by using my callsign."

As soon as Ramona said "meta factors," murmured discussions sprang up around the room. Mercurye chuckled softly at her ear. "Now you've got 'em. Don't stop."

"That's right. Now we are able to trigger meta factors. There are metahumans on both sides of the fight, and plenty who are left in the middle, waiting for a side to choose them." Ramona returned her attention to the floating wireframe. She brought both index fingers together above her head and stretched them out to shoulder width. In response, the city grew and the central areas gained definition. "Based upon the information gathered—"

"Gathered by whom?" Another voice, mellifluous and light, came from the same balcony where the sour-faced representative stood. "How did you come by this very detailed map of the Thulian city?"

Ramona allowed herself a very small smirk. "We made it from the spy-scan of our infiltration team. We aren't limited to the technology that you, in your intermittent wisdom and benevolence, decide to give to us poor ordinary humans. When I say that we in ECHO have seen the city, I'm not exaggerating." The murmurs of surprise rippled around the room at that bit of news, encouraging her to continue. "We infiltrated, but there is a very high chance that the Thulians either know, or will realize soon, that we did. And when they do, they will escalate. This is a very real threat, and you cannot afford to sit up here and debate if you need to enter this conflict."

"The fabric of our society thrives on debate and innovation, my dear." The woman's simpering tone was more irritating than the man's sharp dismissal. "We have a process by which to arrive at these choices. A process that reflects a progressive and truly democratic society."

"Progressive, my metallic ass," Ramona spat. "It reflects a society of indecisive cowards who would rather watch some so-called lesser creatures fight for them so they never have to take responsibility for their downfall or the murder of one of their closest allies, Alex Tesla."

The mention of Alex Tesla brought the entire Assembly to a roar of accusations and arguments. Several of them screamed at Ramona, their gestures made more ghostly in the blue half-light. She stood silent and defiant and waved her left hand to dismiss the Thulian city, and the room plunged into darkness. Startled by the change from light to dark, the voices cut off.

She spoke into the darkness. "The Thulians can control meta factors. They have soldiers with metahuman traits, leaders in massive armies and allies on Earth. A choice to remain neutral is a choice for the death of your precious society." Ramona drew a deep breath, ready to drive in the final coffin nail. "The next time they mount a major attack, and it will be *soon*, they won't hold back. We destroyed their North American base. They hit us back and we drove them off. But they were holding back. We know that now, although we don't know why, now that we've seen this city. The next time, they'll throw *everything* at us, and they'll roll right over the top of us, and your only line of defense will be gone. If they don't *already* know about your existence, and you would be wise to assume that they *do*, they'll imply it from what they can pull out of the wreckage. And then they will be coming for you. They won't allow you to stand. Your choices will be simple: die, or be assimilated." She took a second long breath. Now to pull the reveal. "But now we know where they are, and what they have. We are going to have to attack them, now, when they are not expecting it and we stand a chance of succeeding. Remaining neutral is a choice to die yourselves, to murder Misters Tesla and Marconi, and destroy everything they have created in the name of your progress."

No one spoke. Ramona could feel Mercurye breathing next to her, little puffs of air just behind her ear. As the silence stretched on, he laced his fingers with hers. She squeezed his hand gently and took a deep breath. Icebergs never seemed that big at first sight, but Ramona had explained everything beneath the proverbial waves, and the Metisians had finally realized what that collision would mean for them.

In the space where the wireframe city had hung, the image of Tesla came to life in stunning three-dimensional clarity. Rather than simply an enormous talking head, a full figure stood on an imaginary platform above the Metisian Assembly in severe and fastidious dress. Hands clasped behind his back, he seemed to survey the stunned representatives with an expression equal parts disdain and disappointment. "It would seem obvious that Signore Marconi and I would prefer a choice that keeps us among the living, but the reason goes further. There are brilliant minds contained within ECHO, shrewd negotiators and accomplished tacticians who have ensured survival this far. Our allies seek collaboration, not protection."

"But they are still so young," the woman protested. "They lack a mature understanding of this particular conflict."

"I disagree." Tesla raised one finger to point at the ceiling. "For an organization thrust into new responsibilities among both the metahuman and arcane, their leadership is quite mature, and they are willing to explore new alternatives. Quite progressive."

Ramona pivoted so she could see both Tesla and the two Metisian leaders at the same time. The man and woman appeared perplexed by Tesla's presence. The man fiddled with the high collar of his jacket and stole a glance at Ramona. His mouth twisted in the manner of someone smelling manure, and she decided she really did not like the man. At least his counterpart had the decency to maintain a somewhat neutral expression. "And their technology, then? Do they have the advancement neces- sary to support the innovations that only we can provide? You yourself have expressed frustration over humanity's inability to fully appreciate the gifts of science when tempted with capitalism and sociological hierarchy."

It was tempting to remind this woman that she was part of this so-called sociological hierarchy, but Ramona pressed her lips together and resisted the urge to speak. Tesla gestured with a open palm to her and Mercurye, his normally severe express- ing softening the smallest bit. "And these representatives of that humanity have not only recognized our role as benefactors but have extended an offer of alliance. A symbiotic relationship. Was that not part of the Metisian intent when we founded this city? To find and foster equals?"

The room hummed with discussion. Mercurye leaned over. "I've never seen him with feet. I didn't think he had them."

"Special occasion," she replied. "I guess bringing argument for a vote to engage in war alongside ECHO is worthy of pants."

"I guess."

Discussion and debate continued among the various tiers of the Assembly, with the two lead representatives and Tesla remaining quiet. None of them addressed Ramona or Mercurye, although plenty of them stared and pointed. Ramona craned her neck up to see the woman frowning down at Mercurye with clear disap- proval. She elbowed him and pointed with her chin. "She's not happy with us."

"Mabel isn't happy with a lot of this. Trina says she's led a lot of the resistance to any additional involvement. She was also one of the people who came for Eisenfaust's body, which doesn't make any sense to me," he said. "With all that knowledge, why wouldn't they want help?"

She didn't want to answer him out loud, but Ramona could think of plenty of reasons for a prominent figure in a supposedly superior society to plead neutrality instead of alliance. She let go of Mercurye's hand and approached the full figure of Tesla. In a rather pedestrian fashion, he made as if to walk down a spiral staircase and came to stand in front of her. Ramona giggled when she realized that she had to look up to speak with the thin, refined man. "You're taller than I expected, sir."

"It is as I have always been. Sometimes, one's appearance in matters of diplomacy requires a certain presentation." He smoothed the front of his jacket and studied Ramona. "You are very direct in your negotiations. It would be difficult for those of the Assembly to tell you no."

She couldn't tell if he had intended the words as a compliment or just as an odd bit of conversation. "Yankee Pride and Belladonna Blue find that quality to be useful at times. Infuriating at others, but it's been pretty useful as of late."

"Indeed. Your choice of words was a bit sharp, but . . . appreciated," he finished. "My nephew believed wholeheartedly in an alliance of ECHO and Metis. He attempted an earlier alliance, but was never able to move beyond initial negotiations." Tesla sighed and shook his head, the outline blurring with the movement. "At least we are no longer at a stalemate. Either they will vote to assist, or not."

Ramona found the man's pessimism bothersome. She had managed to convince him to participate in a complex magical endeavor for the sake of unlocking the charter; compared to that, reminding the Metisians that their self-preservation demanded an alliance with ECHO seemed easy. "Let's strike the 'or not' from the sentence, sir. The vote's not final yet."

A single bell chimed in the hall from somewhere near the lead representatives. Tesla gave Ramona a curt nod and climbed the invisible staircase to stand next to Mabel. She didn't appear too unnerved by the wireframe man at her side. Mabel rang the small handbell a second time. The crisp tone was answered by all of the lights along the balconies going dark.

"In spite of the unorthodox presentation of this issue to the Assembly," the man on the dais began. He did not bother to hide his disdain for the two standing in the center of the room. "We call for a vote on the alliance of Metis with ECHO to unite in defense against the Thulians and their allies. We acknowledge that this course may result in conflict, but we bring this to the Assembly for a single and final vote." He stressed the last two words without looking at Ramona and Mercurye.

Ramona remained still and strained to see the members of the Assembly. Above her, the bell chimed a third time. "Final vote," Mercurye repeated next to her. "But what if something happens? What if they say no? Can't we petition a second time?" She wanted to point out that they hadn't exactly petitioned a first time. Mercurye shifted from one foot to the other with nervous energy. The room remained pitch black. "And what about us? If this fails, do we go on trial? I don't think they'd kill us, but I don't want to go back to that white room. Might as well give me a straitjacket."

"Rick..." Ramona became aware of small chimes from around the Assembly. She reached back to place a finger over his lips to stem the stream of worry. "Wait."

A single blue light shone near the door, Trina's face illuminated by the glowing disc in the palm of her hand. She stared up at Mabel in defiance, all traces of fear gone. Across the cavernous hall, another pinprick of blue light appeared, but Ramona could not make out the face of the owner. She held her breath as more dots of light appeared in the blackness, like so many stars in the Georgia sky. At some point, Mercurye took her hand from his lips and placed it flat against his chest. Ramona fought down the rising hope, not wanting to acknowledge any measure of victory should one person vote against the alliance of ECHO and Metis.

Light continued to spread through the Assembly, surrounding them and stretching up until Ramona could see the soft blue reflected on the mirrored ceiling. Now the pinpoints of lights became ribbons of blue, circling the Assembly and illuminating the solemn faces of thousands of Metisians. Unable to resist, she turned to check the pair on the dais.

The man held a blue disc. Mabel's disc glowed white, and Ramona clamped down on her anger. One vote would leave ECHO to fend for themselves, because of this so-called superior democracy. She resisted the urge to use Overwatch to notify Vickie or Bella to let them know of the decision; it made no sense to provide them with only part of the information. Mercurye let out a ragged breath; he must have seen Mabel as well.

Looks like it's white walls and Star Trek for me, too, she thought. Ramona hoped they would have the original series, at least. She had a soft spot for McCoy.

The bell chimed one last time. Ramona glanced to the door, wondering if Trina would be able to speak with them before the Metisian authorities hurried them off to separate cells for a superiorly intellectual reprimand. At the very least, Ramona owed the young woman a thank-you and an apology. She hoped that they wouldn't punish Trina too severely for her part in their plan.

To her surprise, Trina beamed at them, both hands cupped around her glowing disk. Ramona stared back, puzzled. She craned her neck back up to see Mabel, who now held no disk. The man next to her raised his blue disk above his head. "With one abstention, the petition is passed. The alliance is approved."

Mercurye grabbed her around the waist and hugged her. None in the Assembly applauded or offered congratulations. Ramona had enough sense of mind to smile up at Tesla; he gave her a crisp nod and the wireframe of his body faded in a thoroughly Cheshire manner. She thought she caught a wink as his head disappeared, but she couldn't be sure.

Outside of the Assembly, Trina pulled the doors shut, her cheeks flushed pink with excitement. She hugged each of them in turn before racing down the hallway. Mercurye caught Ramona in a tight hug and moved as if to kiss her, but Ramona held up a finger to his lips. "Overwatch, get me Parker," she murmured, her eyes locked on the speedster. "And tell them to send in those icebergs."

CHAPTER TWENTY-FIVE

Penny for Your Thoughts

MERCEDES LACKEY AND DENNIS LEE

"Miss. Miss. Miss," Penny repeated, wearily. They'd been at this, before breakfast and before supper, for days now. Three at least, maybe more. Penny had lost count. Poor Lacey-who-wasn't never came out of the drug fog. In a lot of ways, Penny envied her. She wouldn't have minded being able to sleep all day and all night too. It would be a sort of escape from here.

She hadn't expected any response this time, either, but her stomach was growling, and she thought that the Dark Man might be late today. The Devil had gotten some kids from one of the other cells; several, this time, she'd thought. Maybe that was why the Dark Man was late. And maybe that was why the shot on Lacey started to wear off.

All Penny knew for certain was that the woman's shoulder began to move under her gentle shaking, and for the first time, she raised her head to look, blearily, at Penny.

"Wha—" she said, mushily. "Wha—"

Penny still had her hand on Lacey's shoulder, and the woman didn't scream, or lunge at her, or start acting crazy as she tried to focus on Penny. But in the rest of the room, Penny could feel the other kids holding their breath, waiting to see what would happen.

"She's awake!" the ghost said, and ran a few steps to sit on his heels at her side, staring eagerly at Lacey's face. "She's awake! Now you can—"

But the moment the ghost dropped down beside Penny— everything changed.

343

Instead of looking at Penny, the woman's gaze snapped instantly to the ghost. Her face went dead white and she stared at the spirit in mixed horror and disbelief.

"You...died!" she rasped, going tense all over, her voice rising with every word. "I sent you off—if I hadn't sent you off, you'd still be alive, but I did and you died!"

The ghost nodded eagerly, but his face fell as Lacey started trying to back away from him.

"You died!" she shrilled, hysteria building. "I sent you, and you died!"

"Wait!" the ghost said, reaching out to her. "You don't understand! It's okay! I forgave you! I forgive you! I—"

But by now, Lacey was in full-throated hysterics, and any sense that had been in her eyes was gone. She was shrieking wordlessly at the top of her lungs, and had plastered herself tightly against the wall behind her, still scrabbling backwards to get away.

And that was when the door to the cell slammed open, and the Dark Man stormed it. "What is going on here?" he roared, his eyes fixed on Penny for a moment. But Lacey, who had fallen into shocked silence at his entrance, began screaming again and his gaze snapped to her.

He muttered something angrily, something Penny couldn't understand, and strode towards Lacey, shoving Penny aside to get at her, and stabbing her viciously with the hypodermic. Moments later, Lacey was unconscious again, head lolling, as the Dark Man unshackled her and threw her over his shoulder.

"Time to put you in your own kennel, *Hündin*," he growled, as Penny scuttled back to her bed. He moved heavily towards the door, only once pausing, as he began to close it, to rake the room with his glare.

But then, he stopped for a moment, and stared at Penny, his gaze sharpening as his brows furrowed in concentration.

"Eh..." he said, licking his lips in a way that made her skin crawl. "Fresh. So fresh..."

And then he was gone, taking Lacey with him.

CHAPTER TWENTY-SIX

Hurricane: Storm Surge

MERCEDES LACKEY AND DENNIS LEE

"Well, Red, I was wondering when you were going to get around to visiting me."

Harmony rose up from her cot and crossed her arms as the Djinni closed the door behind him. He turned, leaned back against the door, and faced her through the layers of her reinforced glass cell.

"Heard you were finally talking to people, darlin'," he said. "Figured I might have a go."

"Well, one does get dreadfully bored when ECHO locks them up. I'm sure you remember."

"Oh, it wasn't so bad," the Djinni said with a shrug. "Especially with what was happening on the outside. In here, all safe and tucked away, all I needed was some tele and it would have been a vacation."

"Television," Harmony scoffed. "I can't say I was ever a fan. Two-dimensional lands inhabited by characters of similar depth. Yet another modern marvel that serves to feed the imagination but only bleeds it dry. No, even in here I'm witness to things much more entertaining, much more satisfying."

"You're behind the times then," Red said. "Seriously, you never watched *Lost*?"

Harmony cocked her head, and strolled forward to the limit of her space, pressing her hands to the glass. Her eyes bore into Red.

"You play him well," she said, finally. "But you're not the Djinni."

Red sighed, and came to attention. Harmony watched as he removed his scarf, revealing a horribly scarred neck thick with knotted flesh. The bottom half of his face hung in tattered ropes of skin, obscene against the pristine nature of his flawless lips.

"You sure about that?" the Djinni asked.

"Oh, I know you've come in contact with him," Harmony said. "Enough to get a full lay of the land, but it's not the look you need to worry about. The Djinni has a certain swagger to him, and it's subtle enough to hide the little, little boy he's got trapped inside. What you're doing is passable, I suppose, but not to me. My senses go a little deeper. But you knew that, didn't you? I suppose that's why you're here. Either to test how good your impersonation is, or to see what I know, to get into his head even further. How am I doing?"

"You were always a tricky one, Else, and far too clever for your own good." The voice was still the Djinni's but the accent... very, very faintly Germanic.

She snickered, and made a little faux-curtsey. "Thank you, but I go by Harm now."

"Harm," Doppelgaenger laughed. "How appropriate."

"So I've heard," Harmony said. "Repeatedly, in fact. It's getting a bit old, I think. So to what do I owe the pleasure? I can't remember the last time you actually sought me out. If memory serves, we've done our best to avoid one another."

"Yes," Doppelgaenger said. "Ever since that unfortunate misunderstanding in Riga. I believe you referred to it as professional courtesy."

"Well, no," Harmony disagreed. "My exact words were 'cross me again and I'll hoist your shapeshifting head on a poleax.' Is that why you're here? Old transgressions? You're not really thinking to address past wrongs while I'm caged and helpless, are you?"

"Of course not, my dear," he said. "Even in that cell, I know better than to underestimate you. And you, me, I suppose. We both know where our true gifts lie, and not in anything as obvious as our powers."

"Information, then," Harmony smiled. "I take it we're free to talk?"

"I've found that conversations with you are seldom without a price, but if you're referring to the security feeds, then yes. For all their bluster about advanced technology, ECHO is still vulnerable to rather archaic countermeasures."

Doppelgaenger stepped forward. His face seemed to collapse on itself, then settled in place. He smiled at her, his features now handsome, with blue eyes twinkling under a shock of well-coiffed blond hair.

"There, proof," he said. "You know I would not expose this face unless I was certain of privacy. I've heard what you have been doing here with your time. It seems a little out of place for you, but I'm sure you wear benevolence well. Is it everything you wish it to be?"

"You know? Why I am not surprised?" Harmony said. "Still up to your old ways, Rune, with your fingers in too many pies. Who is it, I wonder, that you're wearing as you wander freely around the ECHO campus? I haven't sensed anything of you at all. Surely not one of my immediate captors then."

"Don't be so sure, Harm," Doppelgaenger smirked. "I have gotten so much better since we last met."

"Your self-confidence was always a weakness, Rune. I felt your sadistic heart beating beneath Red Djinni's within moments of... ah, I understand. The Djinni is a complicated sort of fellow, isn't he? Not the sort you would easily hide beneath, as you have so many others."

"And you know the Djinni so well?" Doppelgaenger raised an eyebrow. "I should like to put that to the test. And yes, I know the rules. Information for information. I'll even go first. Someone was in the Vault doing a job when our forces hit Atlanta. Bulwark's wife Amethist was killed there, trying to stop whomever it was, I assume. You might feed this to Jensen, who will get it back to Bulwark. I strongly suspect that at least some of the security camera footage survived the explosion; the footage was stored in hardened, EMP-proof canisters of flash memory at a distance from the cameras themselves. You should be able to barter that information for something."

"I'll keep that in mind," Harmony said dryly. "All right. I'll give you a memory. Something to show you a side of the Djinni I doubt you've seen."

Scope was still under orders not to use her eyes, which left Harmony without her gunnery instructor. Not that Harmony actually needed the instruction, of course, but the ruse needed to be kept up, and the poor, traumatized, guilty creature that Harmony should be after her failure in the Catacombs would be trying to make up for her panic by obsessive target practice.

Harmony was mostly there just for show, and mainly hoped to register her presence with Bulwark, but it was the Djinni who turned up. Well, he would do. He was wearing a face she vaguely recognized from entertainment news, although she couldn't have said who it was. Harmony didn't pay much attention to movies and television.

She was deliberately doing badly, and had schooled her face into an expression of despair, but otherwise was not overtly attempting to draw attention to herself and her failure. This was a delicate balancing act—she had to look guilty, she had to look as if she was trying to the best of her ability, she had to look as if she was not fishing for sympathy. So she pretended to concentrate on her targets to the extent that she "didn't notice" the Djinni in the next stall, until all her magazines were empty and she pulled off her ear protection to reload.

"Darlin'," the Djinni drawled. "I hate to point this out, but you're more of a danger to me than you are to your target."

She allowed a couple of tears to well up. "I know," she replied, with frustration and despair in her voice. "I . . . I don't know what I'm doing wrong!"

"You're choking up," the Djinni replied, immediately. "Tensing when you fire, instead of relaxing. I can show you—"

"Please!" she begged, and of course, given the chance to put his arms around an attractive woman to show her how to properly hold her weapon, he seized it, as she knew he would. And she was grateful, but not too grateful, since the Djinni was the black sheep of the group, and Harmony should know to be careful around him. And she allowed herself to "improve," but not so much he might get suspicious. A careful, skillful dance.

"You know, this might be why you choked in the Catacombs," Djinni continued, stepping back to let her fire the next set of rounds unassisted. "You're thinking too much, you're letting your imagination paint everything that can go wrong, and then you tense up instead of letting go. Once you've got all the information you're going to get, act on your first impulse. And if you fail, don't let failure tie you in knots. Keep moving. Keep trying something else. Throw enough out there, something *is going to stick, and as long as you keep moving, you're harder to hit."*

"Like Acrobat?" she hazarded.

He rolled his eyes, but agreed. "Boy's constantly off-balance, but he stays loose, and as long as he keeps moving, he never faceplants."

They worked without speaking for a good long while, she allowing herself to continue to improve, he coming in to make tiny corrections to her grip, aim and stance. And finally, he called a halt. "That's enough for the day," he said, and she returned the weapons to the armory and picked up her Overwatch headset, cam and mic from her locker. And he made a face.

"Nannycam," he scoffed. "Don't you go anywhere without it?"

"What if we get a call?" she responded. "It's better to have it on *me*." Since he was still making a sour face, she put out a little probe of her own, to see if some information could be pried out of him. "Why are you so down on Victrix? She's useful. We would never have survived that trip to the Catacombs without her!"

"Or we might have gotten through them without incident," he countered, immediately, harshly. Then he held up a hand. "It was her magic that triggered that trap—"

"And it was her magic that got us out," Harmony pointed out, delighted to have gotten an emotional response out of him. "Her magic that got us past other traps...."

"Magic," he muttered in disgust. By this time they were out in the open, with no one to overhear. He looked as if he was considering something. She kept her expression encouraging. "Let me tell you about magic," he said, after a moment. "It's dangerous. It's unpredictable. It killed someone I ... cared about. And I'm not talking out of inexperience here, the opposite. I was stupid enough to play around with magic, and it bit me and everyone else in the ass." She could sense something she hadn't expected from him. Fear! He truly was afraid of magic! "Victrix will give you all kinds of blather about probability and math, but I know. You can't predict what the outcome is going to be when you mess with it. When we first started working with it, I thought we could. I thought we had a handle on everything. I'm susceptible to the stuff, and the way it worked through me was I stabilized and strengthened it. And then ... the rules changed, for no reason that any of us could see, and suddenly I destabilized what was going through me. And ... somebody died. Died in the most horrible, painful way you could possibly imagine." His voice faltered a moment, then hardened. "So no matter what Victrix tells you, don't believe her. It's crazy and unpredictable, you can't depend on it, and anyone who does is an idiot."

The emotions seething in him delighted her. This had really

*struck a nerve! Fear, doubt, guilt . . . strong, strong enough to crack
his famous facade for a moment.*

"I'll accept the nanny-cam," *he said, after a long moment, as
she sensed him getting himself back under tight control.* "You're
right, it's useful. But damn if I am ever going to depend on *magic.*
And you'd be smart to do the same."

Harmony cut off the memory, and watched as Doppelgaenger
came back into the present time. He was . . . grinning. And when
he was fully back, he gave her an ironic little bow.

"As ever, you live up to your reputation, fraulein," he said,
without a trace of mockery. "This is exceedingly useful to me. So
nice to see the Djinni in a vulnerable state, at last. I can use that."

"You're playing with fire," Harmony warned him, knowing he
wouldn't listen, or believe her. And he didn't. He just rearranged
his features into the Djinni's again without another word, donned
the scarf, and sauntered out again.

Leaving her to wonder if she had given him . . . *too* much.

CHAPTER TWENTY-SEVEN

Collision

CODY MARTIN, DENNIS LEE AND MERCEDES LACKEY

Victoria Victrix: Overwatch Suite

Vickie was beginning to feel as if she hadn't left the chair in her Overwatch suite for a year. She'd certainly been sleeping in it the last couple of days, waking up to whoever was pinging her, stumbling into the bathroom for showers, the kitchen for whatever passed for food, and for coffee. Her eyes were sore, her back hurt despite her special chair, and her mouth was always dry. She couldn't keep this up forever... but there was no one else who could do what she was doing. If there had been, she would have gladly handed it off. Or would she? The old Vickie would have packed her bags and gone somewhere no one would ever find her. There were plenty of places she knew where the Thulians (or anyone else for that matter) were unlikely to look for decades. Well, the monastery, for one. It had been there for hundreds of years, and the Thulians had no idea they had built their super-city on *its* doorstep.

But she couldn't do that anymore. And she couldn't hand off a job she knew she was uniquely qualified to handle. She couldn't ignore what was at stake.

And she could not abandon her friends. People she loved.

It had been—how long? Longer than a week, but not more than two, since she'd coordinated pulling the team out of the Himalayas. If it hadn't been for the implants and the headsets, she didn't think she could have done it without scattering their molecules across half the world, and even then, she'd had the distinct and frighteningly powerful jolt of *something else* lending a helping hand at the last minute. *I'm going to be owing favors for the next three lifetimes, if I have them,* she thought ruefully, as she made contact with the Indian Army yet again, assuring them that everything was on schedule. They were nervous to the point of hysteria, and she didn't blame them. It couldn't have been easy, finding out what was on your proverbial front lawn.

If it hadn't been for Grey and Herb, she probably wouldn't have lasted this long. Herb fetched what he could carry and had learned how to use the microwave...though there had been some early missteps. Grey did what a familiar always did at times of great need; he kept her steady, he supplied arcane energy, and he told off-color jokes. Sometimes she thought the last might even be the most important.

This was it. The armies of the world were massed in India for "war games"—although as far as the world knew there were not nearly as many troops as actually were out there now, so far as the public was concerned, it was only small portions of the armies of the Pacific Alliance. ECHO, CCCP, and the Supernaut Corps had been moving in surreptitiously since everything had gotten put on the accelerated schedule. The US military and Russia had had large forces on standby for just such an assault; while many had tried to shuffle off the responsibility onto ECHO to deal with the Thulians, there were enough prudent and forward-thinking planners to figure out that eventually some real firepower would need to be called in. Pop-up attacks and flare-ups were one thing; taking the fight to the enemy, where their strength was...that's how you won wars.

Vickie just hoped that the Thulians' hubris and the disinformation that she and her counterparts throughout the world had helped spread would keep the enemy from guessing what the good guys were actually up to.

It was a damned good thing those forces had been prepared and ready to go, too. If they hadn't been, there wouldn't have been any chance to assemble them and have them where they needed to be in time. Now, there were no less than three US Navy battlegroups in the Bay of Bengal. Tens of thousands of ground troops, entire fighter wings and combat aviation brigades, and what looked like an all-star collection of Special Operations forces from around the globe were all gathered at a staging area in the northeastern corner of Uttar Pradesh where India, Nepal and Tibet all met. It was impressive, to say the least. The government of Pakistan was overtly making saber-rattling noises at India and its allies, and covertly sending in troops of their own. Pakistan knew damn well that if the Thulians started marching, Pakistan would become pavement. Maybe a giant airstrip....

Today was the day, and the clock was counting down the last couple of hours.

Would I have tattled on Saviour instead of helping her if I'd known then how freaking big Ultima Thule was? Hindsight was always twenty-twenty, and Vickie often woke up from her uneasy naps feeling wracked with guilt. *I don't know.* How long would it have been before the Thulians launched another huge attack? Weeks? Months? Never? *I can't predict these bastards. It's like they're following contradictory orders.* Well, they *were* freaking aliens. *I suppose it's fruitless to try and figure out how they think. For all I know this is how they make war on their planet, wherever that is. Maybe they're just as puzzled by us.*

Vickie hadn't been in on much of the planning. That wasn't her forte. And she figured she had her hands full, first, in contacting anyone and everyone who could spread obfuscation and disinformation and convincing them that they needed to do so, and second, in making sure all the key players were wired up, and knew how to use their rigs. She *had* designed the mobile Command and Control center, which was in a supersonic bomber. If she'd had a choice, it would have been in something with vertical take-off ability, but this was at least inconspicuous among all the other bombers. There was nothing on the outside to distinguish it as different from the rest. She'd created a resonance rig for it that worked with her magic-communications relay. *Wish I'd had time to get all the comm on magic freqs,* she thought unhappily. The best she'd been able to manage was magic scrambling. Hopefully if the Thulians picked up anything, it would only sound like static.

As for the disinformation...well, often enough "the enemy of my enemy..." held true, and even some of the worst warlords and crime figures were not at all keen on becoming Thulian paste. Working through her parents at the FBI, clandestine and downright illegal lines of communication had been worked, and worked hard. She was glad she hadn't had to do most of that.

She'd probably have been throwing up at the thought of who was going to be briefly "on their side."

A lot of her special headsets had gone out too, and she hadn't been told to whom, yet, other than that the infil teams... and others... would get them. They told her how many were needed—which had been about five times more than she could actually make in the short time she was allotted, and she had said so in no uncertain terms. They hadn't liked that. But she'd made an analogy with the first atomic bombs that at least had been understood. *"I've only got so much inobtanium,"* she'd said sharply. *"So you get that many and no more, and right now, the elves mining the stuff are on strike."* There had been grumbling, but acceptance. A shortage of a supply, they understood. That she and only *she* could *make* the things—they would never have accepted that.

The only loose end was Khanjar, but the assassin was involved in a project of her own with a handpicked group. Bella had no orders about her, and Vickie was content to leave Khanji out of the loop for now.

There were new monitors in here as a consequence of having all the new teams, and they were starting to come up live. The Supernauts had refused a direct link; they were autonomous as far as she was concerned. She assumed they'd answer the orders of whoever was in the hot seat, but maybe not. Like a barbarian horde, probably they'd just do what they wanted to, and you'd have to work around that. They were under Worker's Champion's purview, so hopefully he'd keep their destructive tendencies focused.

There was a quick beeping chime from one of her monitors. *Ah, the infil teams are coming up.* This was where she was going to do most of her work, when it all came down to cases. *"Team Red, up."* That was Molotok, Marx bless him. Playboy off the field, steady as a rock on it, and after the experience in the first infil, she knew that he trusted her. He probably would never say as much, at least to her face, but he didn't second-guess her anymore. Progress was progress. "Reading you clear, Team Red," she said. She had them *all* implanted now, except for the Seraphym. There were no spares left. But Molotok greatly appreciated the tech, now that he had it. Team Red's mission was to find and disable whatever it was that was keeping the force field and illusion up over the valley.

"Team Blue, we are go." That was Bulwark. They had the same mission. Both Red and Blue would use the same cemetery-port that the CCCP had left by; Red would, predictably, go left, Blue would go right.

"Team Earth, go." That was another ECHO team, led by Corbie, but holding people from ECHO Europe. *"Team Fire, we are ready."* A Red Chinese meta team. They'd follow Red and Blue in a half an hour. There were a total of eight metahuman teams, all tasked with taking down the field, and when the field went down, penetrating Ultima Thule and sabotaging anything that looked important. Nothing had been left to chance. If they lost Red and Blue, there was Earth and Fire, North and South, Lion and Tiger. Someone was going to get those fields down. *Please, oh gods, let us not lose anyone. Or at least, not anyone I know...* She felt briefly guilty for the thought, but couldn't dwell on it now.

The first metahuman teams would also be supported by a collection of the best SOF teams the world had to offer. By allied agreement, the first to go in would be from the United States; Army Rangers, Green Berets, 1st SFOD-D (popularly known as Delta Force) and several detachments of SEALs. From around the globe, there were both the UK and Australian SAS, Canadian JTF2, Chinese PLA SOF, German GSG9 that had asked specifically to be included, Spetznaz and VDV from Russia, and naturally Indian Ghatak Force troops. Initially there had been a huge fear about the conflicting command structures involved with so many disparate forces, but somehow it had all fallen together. Apparently the "head honcho" for this entire operation had been able to rope everything together, put the organization in place, and get everyone to nod their heads north and south on it. It was a feat that impressed her. In any other context, she would have called it "miraculous." Then again...she knew all about this guy. He had a metahuman ability that had never been identified before, although she strongly suspected that Alex Tesla's father'd had it, given how quickly he had been able to form ECHO after WWII. The "mystery man" was a supreme tactician; that didn't seem to adequately cover his metahuman ability, but it was the core of it. Moves and countermoves, strategy, all of it came more than naturally to the man in charge; he seemed to be able to read people, realize their strengths and weaknesses, when they would need help and in what instances, how to best utilize them. What really made it all work was...well, him. He was never an overbearing commander, but instead knew just the right amount and kind of pressure needed to get his subordinates to not only follow his commands, but trust in him implicitly. It didn't hurt that he was a natural charmer, to boot. Confident, and humble without being overly self-deprecating. And one more thing. Something intangible. Something quite possibly metahuman. Something, oddly, Dominic Verdigris had. An amazing charisma that drew people to him and brought a level of automatic trust. It even seemed to work over comm links.

The dingus that opened the portal was staying outside the field. The portal would be opened for no longer than it took the teams to dash across. It would close immediately. Thirty-one minutes later, it would be opened again. Then twenty-eight minutes after that. Then fifteen. Nothing predictable. The last team through would take the dingus with them, and leave it concealed near the first "grave" they encountered. Tesla Generator pulses would be timed to match the portal openings out there where the "war games" were being held. Hopefully the Thulians would think that was causing a glitch in their system.

She ran through all the "away team" feeds, at least, the ones that were hard-wired with implants into Overwatch Two, and paused when she checked John and Sera's. Sera was still on a headset. Vickie still didn't dare try and interface with whatever it was that made her tick. But the feeds she *did* get from Sera were eerily in sync with the ones she was getting from Murdock. Heart-rate, respiration, bio feeds...nearly identical. *The hell is going on with those two?* She hadn't dared probe the "magic" (if you could call it that) the two shared, either. Celestial in origin, that was all she could, or dared to, verify. As for the Overwatch Two implants Johnny still had...something was going on with those, too, but at least they weren't cutting themselves off from the network. More like...something there was filtering what she got. She was still getting exactly the same data, but she sensed something "hovering" over the link, watchfully. *Not going there. Don't need a guide or a road map. You just stay over there, and feed me what I need, and we'll be fine.*

She did have to wonder what was going to happen when John met Delta, *if* he did. He had been Special Operations himself; first Rangers, then Delta. Did *they* know him, or about him? Would he run into someone he knew? It was a pretty closed community. And what was the meeting going to do to him, even if there was no recognition by either side?

Well, he knew Delta was going to be there. He was a big boy. Still....

"Overwatch: open: John Murdock," she commanded. "Bluebird of Happiness to Ural Smasher. You read?"

Red Team: Forward Staging Area

"Murdock here," John said with a chuckle. "The Commissar put you up to callin' me that, or is this your bright idea?"

"We're not on the clock yet. I'm being my cheerful and sarcastic self. How goes?"

John glanced around the glorified barn. It was hard to even call it that; stacked stone walls, dirt floor and a corrugated steel roof completed the picture. It wasn't nearly big enough for their purposes, but then again, the "coalition" had commandeered several of them. The entire room was filled with tables, whiteboards and charts, with people squeezed in between them all. And weapons; assault rifles and battle rifles, grenades, grenade launchers, RPGs, enough ammunition outside under tarps and camo nets to *start* and *finish* WWIII. The entire room was a flurry of activity, despite the cramped conditions. Team leaders gathering up their squads, aides running around to update maps and pass on messages, and then of course all of the various metas gearing up. Each individual team seemed to be running mostly the same weapons, for those that carried them. There were several individuals with some more exotic offerings, but for the most part things were kept standardized. John himself was wearing web gear to hold all of the magazines, grenades, and medical supplies that he would need, not to mention mission-specific gear, like explosive charges to use on whatever was powering the Krieger shields. It seemed like the rest of the CCCP was traveling as light as he was; ammo was the heaviest thing all of them were carrying, since they figured they'd need a lot of it. But their main goal was infiltration; getting in, breaking what needed breaking and then helping the main forces in taking the city.

It was going to be goddamned bloody.

"It's kickin' right along. I figure we ought to be ready to roll in fifteen, judgin' by everyone's progress." He took a moment to move off to the side, out of everyone's way. "How're you holdin' up?"

"Don't worry about me, I have caffeine."

"I worry 'bout everyone. It's one of my hobbies." John looked up, noticing that Molotok was calling together the "Red" team. "Time for me to go. I'll check back in soon. Copy?"

There was a moment of hesitation on the line. *"Any issues with you and Delta I should know about?"*

John paused, thinking. "Shouldn't be. Everyone's a professional, here. Afterwards...I just don't know. We'll have to see how it plays out." He had noticed a large group of Delta operators when everyone was first arriving. It had given him a start, even though he had known they would be there. A lot of different feelings had surfaced because of that; fear, longing for the familiar, a certain loneliness that he hadn't felt in a long time. Long forgotten things. John had done his best to tamp them down for the moment. The job had to come first; they wouldn't have a second shot at this.

"Do me a favor and just...fly the hell out of there if you get a hint of trouble out of them, all right?"

"Roger that. I don't anticipate it, but I'll keep my head on a swivel. Murdock out." John turned in time to see Red Saviour II duck through the low entrance, bee-lining for her people. No one from the CCCP called for attention, but everyone straightened up and faced her anyway. When she was sure that she had everyone's gaze, she began speaking.

"You will be having briefing from Operations Commander soon. This is my briefing to *you,* my wolves." She showed her teeth in something that was not a smile. It was altogether too vicious and gleeful for that. "I have met Operations Commander. He is to be having my confidence. But he does not know you as I know you." She met each of their eyes in turn. "This is to being our Stalingrad. No more, no less. We win here, or we lose all."

Soviet Bear, in a rare show of soberness, muttered. "Will not be like Stalingrad, Commissar. *Should* not be, if we are wanting to live through it. Should never again be." Just the quiet way that Pavel had spoken was enough to cause the rest of the team to share looks.

"If we do not win here, it will be Stalingrad as if *fascista* won, Old Bear," Natalya corrected, but without rebuke. "There is no other option. We win, or we lose all. Not just lose here—we lose the world. This is our chance to drive *them* back! We will seize it!"

Again, she looked around at them, meeting their eyes, each in turn, with a fierce glare as if she was trying to instill in them the fire that she felt. "There is no one better here than you. No one! You are more than a *nekulturny* 'team.' You are brothers and sisters. You are my wolf pack!" She narrowed her eyes. "And I will to be *wery* disappointed if you do not pull down the *fascista* jackal!"

Untermensch turned towards his fellow CCCPers, and began pumping his fist into the air, crying, *"Ura, ura, ura!"* Several of the older Soviet metas, then the younger ones, and finally some of the Spetznaz and VDV in the barn began to echo the cry. John could almost feel how charged the atmosphere was with emotion, the raw current of everyone's will. The other teams in the crowded building turned to stare; John thought he saw just a moment of envy in the Chinese team's eyes. It was heady, to say the least. Finally the shouts died down when Natalya put her hand up.

"That is all. I will not be giving you orders, except for that. You already have all the orders you need. Strike for the throat, my wolves, and come back with the blood of the *fascista* hot in your belly!" With a final nod, the Commissar turned on her heel and walked to the entrance of the barn, leaving the teams to finish their preparations.

Molotok was the first to break the relative silence in the barn. "We lift in ten, *tovarischi*. Final inspection and then we are moving out. Get to it!"

John felt Sera's eyes on him; it was an actual sensation, like the gentle caress of a hand on his cheek. He turned to meet her gaze. Her eyes were . . . different. Not the pupilless gold of her former self, nor the "ordinary human" deep blue, but blue with a flicker of gold deep inside. The rest of the team dispersed, doing their final checks on their gear and making sure that everything was ready before the team stepped off. John approached Sera at the same time that she stepped towards him.

"We are not wolves," she said, softly. "Not in the way she means it."

John thought for a moment, taking her hand into his. "No, we're not. But we're not sheep, either. An' this is war, darlin'. We've got lives dependin' on us. A whole world, if not worlds." He held her hand up to where they could both see it. "I'll never let anythin' happen to you again. Y'know that, right?"

She didn't smile. But she did hold his hand tighter. "And I will never let anything happen to you." She paused in thought. "We must do what we must. But we must not be...*vengeful*. Yes? Looking for revenge...what is it that the Chinese sage said? You must dig *two* graves."

"You're right. Darlin', you know me. Who I was, what I did. There are a lot of guys like me here today, 'bout to help us on this job. That's a good thing. It's not 'bout emotion; it can't be. It's 'bout the job. If it starts gettin' away from that, people start gettin' hurt. So..." He sighed deeply. "We do the job. We make sure everyone else can do their job. But, it ain't gonna be easy."

She held his hand to her lips. "We must do what we must, beloved. Trust in me, as I trust in you."

He grinned lopsidedly. "That's the easiest thing in the world for me, love."

"No, I mean *trust* me. Completely. There are things you are holding from me." Her eyes searched his. "There is not much time, and we *must* be as one, if we are to succeed in this undertaking...."

John's breath caught. She knew. *Shit, of course she knows, grunt. After what both of you have been through, how couldn't she?* "You're right again, darlin'." He took her by the elbow, leading her to the only quiet corner of the barn, a spot where a forlorn little table stood with now-drained and cold coffee urns, where they wouldn't be run over by all of the commotion. "I've been gettin' new...I don't know what to call them. Senses? I've been able to read people better, see things more clearly. I've never been one to miss details, but now...this is somethin' else. I mean, like *beyond*, even with my enhancements."

Her eyes continued to search his. "Are you anticipating actions? Not as in, something you *think* others will do, but something you *know* they will do? And then, they do it?"

John became animated. "Yes! It's...it's not even anticipation. I mean, with trainin', you get a feel for what'll happen, because of cause an' effect. This was *more*. Surety, almost. Like y'know what to do, how to do it, and when."

She nodded. "I no longer see the futures as I did, as the great tapestry of all that has been and everything that might be. But... when someone suggests something, or I think of an act...I can see the consequences. Can you?"

John thought back, specifically to their first incursion into Ultima Thule. "It's not … always on. Uncontrollable; it'll happen when it happens. What is it, d'ya think?"

"I do not know what to call it. But I know I have shared some of my powers with you, and some with Bella." Now a faint ghost of a smile crossed her lips. "I think some of it happened when you came back to us, the first time, though you were not then yourself. And then the second time, when *you* reawakened, divided the remaining powers equally between us. But do not fear, my heart is wholly yours, beloved."

"Never a doubt in my mind, love." John noticed that everyone was starting to move towards the entrance. "Looks like it's time to go. Y'ready?"

"As are you." She squeezed his hand but did not let it go. "Trust. I think that trust will carry us through."

They held hands tightly a moment longer, then shouldered their packs and walked through the entrance. It was past three A.M., local time. The lack of nearby light sources from cities meant that the entire starscape was laid out above them and the sky was so full of stars that it would make you dizzy to stare at them for too long; the Milky Way was clearly visible, not as a mere band of stars, but a great wash of star-filled light across the sky. The beauty of it was enough to momentarily distract him from what was to come; he could feel Sera's silent awe at the sight as well.

Ahead of them, on a hastily constructed airfield, were easily dozens of ECHO Swifts, spooled up and ready to take off. They were in a valley among the mountains; their staging area was a goat and sheep farm, gladly given up for the effort by the owners, who might have *looked* as if they were unchanged from their herding ancestors of centuries past, but who knew all about the Invasion, the second attempt, and did not want to see a third. The airfield had been laid out, rather than constructed, John now saw as he approached more closely; the Swifts were VTOL craft, and they were about to fly nape-of-the-earth plots to get the infil teams to within an easy hike of that cemetery-valley.

Nape-of-the-earth. In the Himalayas. This was not going to be a comfortable trip. On the other hand, at least the Swifts were unlikely to fall apart in midair.

Each of the Swifts had a hastily-made paper sign next to the loading door, with the name of the infil team prominently on it.

John scanned the field, spotted "Red" with a Red Star on the side of one Swift off to the—inevitably—far left of the field. He spoke softly. "Overwatch: open: Team Red," waited a moment, and said, "Comrades, spotted our ride. Far left, front." Sera was already beside him, but the rest of the team soon fell in behind. Molotok, like any good team leader, made sure his entire team was on the bird before he boarded. *Every op. Last on, first off.* Despite his limited contact with the Russian, he liked the man immensely; he had the qualities that people looked for and needed in a leader.

Once the entire team was on, Molotok looked toward the pilot of the craft; he made a spinning motion with the index and middle finger on his right hand. The pilot gave a nod, and shortly after the pilot had spoken into his mic the craft began to lift off. It was going to be a long and bumpy ride to their drop zone, but John felt ready for it.

"Rock an' roll," he said quietly to himself. As if in answer to that, Overwatch began to play CCR in his ear. He couldn't help himself. Despite the hazard and the danger, John Murdock reached over and squeezed the hand of the strange and beautiful creature he loved, and smiled.

Belladonna Blue: Command and Control Center

Bella waited in the Command and Control center trying not to fidget. She was waiting for the operations commander . . . who was not *her.* She felt the eyes of everyone else in the cramped quarters surreptitiously watching her. She was head of ECHO. But command had been bestowed upon someone else. And they wondered how she was going to take that.

Gairdner had been with her when she'd been told. They'd sent a four-star general to deliver the edict. He had come at the worst possible time, of course. It wasn't often that Bella and Bull argued, and the general had stepped into a doozy of a fight.

". . . I don't see why we are arguing about this," Bull said. "It's my team, my call. Scope is a liability in the field right now. I'm grounding her for this one. She simply isn't ready."

"If you don't clear her for your team, I'll just put her on another," Bella snapped. "We don't have the luxury of holding back anyone. Hell, I've conscripted Spoonbender and re-upped some retirees for this! If Saviour hadn't screwed the pooch and we'd done this

on our *schedule and not scrambling to catch the Thulians before they catch us, then sure, fine, you could have done whatever you wanted to with her. But Saviour did, and we field every living meta we can get."*

"It's a mistake to just field anyone you can get your hands on," Bull insisted. *"More bodies doesn't mean squat if you have to watch over them like..."*

"She goes!" Bella barked. "That's it, soldier! You have your orders!"

And that was when the four-star had turned up at the door and the argument stopped dead and had never really been resolved.

So now Gairdner was about to get on an ECHO Swift with his team, Scope included, and she was about to hand over command of this whole enchilada to someone she had never met. Someone who didn't know her people the way she knew them. Someone who—

The door opened, and the entire complement inside the plane stood—no, leapt—to attention. But the Chinese-American who entered had no insignia whatsoever on his uniform. No rank. No ribbons. Just a name tag. *A. Chang.*

"Arthur Chang?" Gairdner had exclaimed, before Bella could say anything. "Arthur Chang from—"

The General had nodded. "He told me he knew you, Bulwark."

Bella stood, but slowly, as the gentleman with the face of a Buddhist monk and the eyes of a sage approached her. He paused before her, and offered her his hand. She took it. The handshake was neither weak nor aggressive. "Arthur Chang," he said, with a touch of formality. "Callsign *Art of War.*"

She couldn't help it. Her lips twitched a little. "I hope you bitchslapped the idiot that landed you with that callsign into next week. That is a *terrible* pun."

He smiled, fleetingly. "Yes," he said, simply. "It is."

Bella had listened carefully as Bulwark described the metahuman they called "Art of War." How they had both discovered their abilities while serving together in the Marines...Bulwark first, because his was obvious. But then...Art...discovered that he had something that must have been the military equivalent of Verdigris's genius. For him, strategy, tactics, the ebb and flow of battle, it was all instinctive. There was nothing for him to learn, nothing to study, it was all right in there, in his head, without picking up a single book.

According to Gairdner, Arthur had been tested by every simulation, had been put in charge of one side of war games time and time again, and at greater levels of complexity, and nothing had been much of a challenge for him. Then he'd come one day to say goodbye. Now here he was again. And every single military leader had agreed; this was the man who would lead in this battle.

And Gairdner...

She stood aside and made a slight gesture towards the command chair, then picked up the headset—wired to Overwatch One, not Two—that had been hanging off the arm, and handed it to him. "To be absolutely honest, sir, under any other circumstances, I'd be fighting you tooth and nail for the hotseat," she said quietly, for his ears only, although she knew that those closest to them could probably hear her. "But the one person whose judgment I trust most in the world trusts *you*. And that's enough for me. Take care of this fight. I'm going now to take care of my people."

He took the headset from her with his left hand, and slowly saluted her with his right. "I will take care of all of our people, Ms. Parker. And will do my best to deliver yours back to you." He paused for a moment, looking to the floor before meeting her eyes again. "Thank you for your trust. I know it couldn't have come easily; it wouldn't for me, at least."

Bella nodded, as the tension that had been in the air faded. Without another word, she made her way through the cramped command center, and back out the door, to the Swift that was going to take her to the forward medical station, which was where she calculated she could do the most good. It wasn't as if she didn't have her Overwatch implants; whatever she needed to do for her ECHO people, she could do from anywhere. But the only place she could *heal* them was there.

And Vickie and her secrets are secret still. No matter how much Gairdner trusts Chang...I am not trusting him with that.

Behind her, as the door closed, she heard Art of War speaking. "All right, gentlemen, ladies," he said in a firm, commanding voice. "We've trained for this long enough. Time to go to work."

Red Saviour: Forward Command Center

Natalya felt the cool morning air on her face as she walked briskly to where the secondary observation and control center was located, in a squat communal building a distance from the barns where the teams had been preparing. As much as she wanted to be in the thick of the fighting, her place was here; receiving directives from the operations center and then ordering her people how to best carry them out. She knew that this made sense, tactically, but she still couldn't help but feel resentful of it all the same. She did her level best to completely inhale the smoke from her cigarette during her walk. It didn't help to calm her, but it gave her something to do besides look for something to punch. Just before entering the building at her destination she stamped out the butt, much to the disdain of the door sentries.

"*Overwatch to Red Leader.*"

"*Da. Speak.*"

"*Away teams are within ten minutes of the touchdown point. Teams Red and Blue will probably land within five seconds of each other or less.*"

"*Horosho.* I will be in position, ready to act as man of middle, barking into microphone like a good *devushka*." Taking a deep breath to steady herself, Natalya confidently strode forward, through the doors and into the building. It was awash with activity, just like the buildings she had come from. Instead of weapons and the people that would use them, however, this place was full of tactical displays, communications equipment, and more of the highest-ranking military men than she had ever seen in one place in her entire life. Everyone was moving, talking, reading, typing on PDAs and the like. And on a side table, the ubiquitous urns of coffee, though from the aromatic odor, the coffee was of considerably higher quality than what the infil teams had been granted, and from the bustle of underlings around the table, said coffee was never allowed to grow scorched or stale. And for the Indian, Japanese, Chinese... who knows, even Arabic leaders, who liked their tea as well as their coffee, the urns of coffee had been joined by urns of tea. Presumably also of high quality.

Rank hath its privileges.

In deference to the Russians, she even spotted a samovar.

The Commissar spied her position; each of the command stations was clearly marked for each team or element of the assault. She walked towards it, but was suddenly obstructed. Worker's Champion—how had she not noticed his massive frame when she first walked in?—blocked her way.

"Natalya Shostakovaya," he said by way of a greeting. Instantly she felt small and young—again. "It seems your CCCP is of use." Unspoken, but not unfelt, were the words *"after all..."* She hadn't seen or spoken with him at length since she had been demoted and disgraced in Red Square, at the beginning of the Invasion. More than a year later, and yet she continued to feel intimidated by her "Uncle Boryets."

She set her shoulders, crossing her arms as she looked up at the giant of a man. *Steel in your voice!* "Sturdy comrades will always be of use. I would not have any others than those in my command."

"Art of War asked specifically that CCCP and the best of ECHO be the first teams in." That was Victrix in her ear. And there was an evil little chuckle. *"He said the Supernauts would probably blunder around like unweaned bull-calves and throw the entire plan into ruins within the first five minutes."* Now *that* brought a tiny smile to Natalya's face, whether it was true or not, curling her lips. Worker's Champion's frown deepened at the sight of it.

"Something amuses you, *devushka?* I would not have thought sending your 'sturdy comrades' into a killing zone would be something to cause you amusement."

His comment killed Natalya's smile instantly. "Without my comrades, we would not know about the enemy stronghold in the first place," she replied, an edge to her voice. "And they got in and out without detection the first time, despite what Blue Girl says. Could your tin-suited men boast of such things, busy as they were with protecting oil refineries, train stations, border crossings and airports?"

A shadow of anger crossed Boryets' face, but he repressed it. *One point scored.* "The Supernauts go where they are commanded, and are obedient to their orders, which, I fear, is not always the case with the CCCP," he retorted smoothly. "If you value the lives of your comrades, Natalya Shostakovaya, you would learn the folly of this. Or perhaps their lives only matter as a way for you to slake your thirst for violence." Without another word, he stepped from in front of her, moving to the other side of the building where his own command station was.

Natalya's jaw hung open for the barest fraction of a second before she snapped it shut, gritting her teeth and marching for her command station. She stood behind it, gripping the edges of the desk unit...and wanting nothing more than to tear it from its moorings and throw it as hard as she could at the wall. At first all she could think about was how Boryets could have the gall to speak to her that way, about her own people. Then her anger cooled, and it was replaced by something... worse, and insidious. Doubt. This was supposed to be her war, as her father and Boryets had had their Great Patriotic War. Was she making grave missteps in how she was fighting it? She had always been hot-tempered, and had long ago decided that she would rather have spirit and the ability to drive ahead while others pondered and dithered, trying to decide. But was her anger blinding her? Did she let it guide her decisions, even to the detriment of her comrades?

This entire operation started due to her unwillingness to wait for the plans of her adopted *sestra*, Belladonna Parker, to come to fruition. Would things have been better if she had waited, had listened to her friend and ally? Not only were the billions of lives of the planet were at stake, but more immediately, those of her last friends and family.

"Commissar, Boryets may be trying to goad you into revealing how the CCCP team managed to get in, get out and stay in communication without revealing themselves. Not even Art of War knows about Overwatch Two, only Overwatch One."

"Worker's Champion has even less use and even more disdain of magic than I do. What would his motive behind this being, besides?" It seemed unlikely to her... but the little *vedma* had uncanny insights into people and their behavior. More than once, since creating Overwatch, Victrix had warned her about people's actions or motivations that seemed unlikely, but had proven true.

"He doesn't know it's magic. He doesn't know how you did it. But you can bet your favorite bust of Lenin that he wants to find out, so he can use it with his Supernauts. He probably assumes it's a technical breakthrough one of your tinkerers did, something you got from Bella and ECHO, or a powerful psion you discovered. The first two, he probably thinks he can steal if he knows what it is, and the third—he can take from you directly, if it's a Russian. Don't let him trick you into saying something before you speak. He knows how to push your buttons; after all, he installed most of them."

"Da, da." The witch-girl was right. It did little to soothe the pain of having incurred Boryets' disappointment and disdain, however. As much as her "uncle" frustrated her and her plans... there had been a time, once, when he had been a second father figure in her life. Stern, but the height of what it meant to be Russian at the same time. He had taught her much, had been the one person outside of Molotok whom she could confide in when she had displeased her father. Even though that time had ended long ago, she still could feel its echoes when she spoke with him.

"Commissar, he's angry because you did something he couldn't. He's angry because you have something he doesn't." There was an audible snort. *"More than that, your people have a devotion to you he hasn't seen since the Great Patriotic War. Do you think any of his tin soldiers have the kind of loyalty to him that you do from CCCP? You heard him."* The imitation was uncanny. *"'They go where they are ordered and do what they are commanded.' That sounds like a lapdog to me, not a wolf pack. That's training and brainwashing, not loyalty."*

She allowed herself a small laugh. "Loyalty requires brains. Something their forebear and namesake only possessed when it came to posturing, his tinkering, and securing political position."

"Don't let him guilt you or goad you into showing your hand. Remember, Overwatch Two is effective only as long as it remains a secret. As long as I remain a secret. There never was a secret yet that Worker's Champion didn't want to know. And remember who he was in bed with, back in the bad old days. Ask Pavel or Georgi."

Now *that* suggestion brought an unpleasant taste to her mouth. But the girl did have a point...didn't she? "...perhaps, Daughter of Rasputin. First, we are having jobs to do. I with commanding my people. And you are not having time to hold hand of Commissar, *da?*"

"Damn right. My down-time is just about up." There was a brief pause. *"Teams Red and Blue at the LZ now. Touching down in... three...two...one. Op is go."*

Natalya focused on the command console in front of her, and with a murmured command, brought up her internal HUD. She was directly linked to all of the information concerning her people, ready to wield them to their fullest. Her doubts all vanished to the back of her mind. This is what they had been preparing for, searching the world for, fighting and dying for. A chance to destroy the *fascista* where *he* lived. She wouldn't waste this opportunity.

What is it, the Victrix says? Ah yes. It is go-time.

Blue Team: Ultima Thule

As they made their way up the sheltered mountain pass, Bulwark noted with satisfaction how little noise eight full squads of Earth's deadliest combatants could make. As was his custom, he had placed himself in the vanguard, and he found it rather unnerving as he slowly guided them up the slope to hear little more than the blustering wind whipping around the tops of the mountains that towered above them, and then to look back from time to time and see dozens of them, right at his back, matching his every step.

"Ow! Sonuvabitch..."

He paused, and held a fist high, motioning them all to stop. In his ear he heard Victrix echo his command; in English, but every one of the mixed group behind him had been drilled to understand a half a dozen simple commands in English. Only ECHO, ECHO Euro, and CCCP had implants, but every one of the other teams was wired directly into Overwatch Two as well as Overwatch One and the Colt Brothers via Victrix's original gear. Earpieces, throat mics, wristbands for vital sign monitoring and lapel cameras—though some, like the Chinese team, had mounted their cameras on the front of their helmets.

He shot a wary sideways glance at Scope.

"Sorry," Scope whispered. "Sharp rock."

Bull shook his head and opened his fingers wide. He heard Victrix give the go command, and they returned to their silent march up the pass. Just hours before, he had been arguing with Bella over Scope's involvement in this mission. She wasn't ready; she was far from ready, but Bella had overruled him. Back with the main force surrounding the mountain city, perhaps, but Scope simply had no business being here with the infiltrators. Every man and woman here was at the top of his or her game, each ready to strike swiftly and without pause, knowing what was at stake. Win all, or lose all. Victrix had given him a translation of Saviour's "pep talk" to her group, and as insane as Natalya Shostakovaya was, most of the time, she was dead right this time. Win now, or lose all. Scope had not seen anything approaching real field duty for months. But Bella had overruled him, and he had been forced to admit his squad lacked a sniper. For all her faults, Scope could still shoot better than any of them, even with her now-shaky hands.

He frowned as he navigated a tricky ledge, strewn with jagged pebbles, and thought of his other questionable squad member. Under normal circumstances, he wouldn't have even considered taking Mel along. Without her illusions, she was only as good as her training and current health, physical and otherwise. She had surprised them all, especially him, when she had come out on top in the demolitions crash course. Perhaps he shouldn't have been surprised. She had certainly taken herself to task at her rehabilitation, pushing herself harder with each passing day to returning to fighting form. He watched as she glided up the pass with ease, despite wearing a heavy rucksack filled with explosives. She moved with practiced grace and confidence. As for her mental state, well, she was with the Djinni. That was a lunacy of its own kind, yet somehow their relationship was oddly calming for both of them. He took a few more steps before realizing that he had not counted the Djinni as yet another risky choice of squad member. At some point during their own rather rocky relationship, Bulwark had come to see Red Djinni as a valued member of his team. He wondered when that had happened. It seemed significant, somehow. He glanced back at Red, who scampered silently behind him. From time to time, the Djinni nodded to Mel, who flashed him subtle smiles in response. For the past few weeks, Red Djinni and Mel had grown stronger together, steadier; and dare he say it, almost reliable? And reliable was something he very much needed right now.

He groaned inwardly as Scope nearly tripped, and he heard the detonators in her pack clink loudly as she righted herself.

"You were supposed to strap those down," he murmured.

"Yeah," Scope muttered. "My bad. Sorry."

"Keep them quiet," he whispered. "We're almost at the rendezvous."

"Five hundred yards, Bulwark. Just around that bend past the clearing ahead." The map in his HUD flashed an update.

At a small clearing, just two hundred feet shy of their destination, Bull signaled a halt. As one, his troops knelt down and waited. He scanned the bushes and nodded in satisfaction as a figure garbed in complete black emerged from them. She was the smallest soldier he had ever met in his life. If he hadn't known better, he would have sworn the Chinese had erroneously enlisted a ten-year-old child. An undersized ten-year-old child, at that.

"Report, *Shŏushú* Shuma," he said.

The girl reached up, pulled off her mask, and greeted him with an impish grin.

"A-OK, USA," she said. "No baddy bads, no sensors, no nothing. Green light."

"Good," Bull grunted. "Fall in with your squad."

Shuma came to attention at her full height, which barely cleared his knees, saluted him smartly, and tumbled down the pass to join her comrades.

"Freaky little ninja," Scope muttered, as Bull ordered them forward.

Around the bend that Victrix had described, the valley—now more properly termed a "defile"—changed. The vegetation had been scoured from the rocks to either side, and sealed niches had been cut into the rock. Orange letters glowed above each one. At the end of the defile, was...apparently...a huge, empty valley sweeping away before them. That was the illusion that the protective bubble over the whole valley projected. It was not a hospitable-looking valley and did not contain a water source; no herder, looking for a place to graze sheep, goats, or yaks, would give it a second glance.

"That's far enough, folks," Bull said, and called for a halt. "No one approach that opening, unless you want to lose any limbs. Our scouts say it's an illusion." He gestured, signaling the approximate estimation of the disintegration field and motioned for Murdock to come forward. John obliged, reaching into his pocket and removed a round, smoothly dimpled object.

"You sure you know how to work that thing?" Bull asked.

"Give me a second here, Bulwark," John said. "Vix is feedin' me instructions right now. Might need a moment to get this right."

Bull nodded and watched patiently as John's attention turned to the voice in his ear. He took a moment to scan the troops, who were taking advantage of the brief period of respite to check over their equipment. Even though the defile was wide enough to accommodate them comfortably, the prudent squadrons pressed together, wary of disturbing the glowing walls, which shone with an eerie light.

All except Scope, of course.

With the casual air of a bemused sightseer, she strolled to one side and lit up a cigarette, feigning mild interest in the glowing glyphs that illuminated the passageway. They were incomprehensible, and she shrugged in indifference until Bulwark snatched the cigarette from her mouth and firmly put it out under his boot.

"What's your damage, Bull?" she demanded.

"You are," Bull said. He pointed at the rest of the infiltrators. "They are doing what they should, preparing themselves for the mission ahead while being mindful of their surroundings." He pointed at Scope, his finger nearly poking her eye. "You are being a space cadet and endangering us all by wandering from the path. Mind telling me what's going through that empty cavity between your ears?" At this moment he was as angry with Bella as he was with Scope. How could she *not* have seen how unready Scope was for this? He would rather have had the old Scope, the one who made mistakes because of trying too hard, than this one.

"I'm prepping too," Scope shrugged. "This is the first real stop we've had in ages, and I was jonesing. And you know how some people are about cigarettes. Get one going anywhere near them and they act like you're vomiting tumors into their mouths."

"You should be inspecting your weapons." Why did he need to tell her this? The old Scope would have already field-stripped them, inspected the parts, and put them back together again. Twice.

"My guns are always ready." This Scope didn't seem to care that there was a streak of tarnish on the barrel of her rifle. The old Scope not only would have had that off, she'd have made sure there wasn't a reflective centimeter on any of them. Bull had a nightmare moment of imagining his sniper being blown away because everything in the valley had homed in on the twinkle of light off her weapon.

Surely she hadn't been that careless. *Yet she was careless enough to wander off the known path.* "You shouldn't leave your group. We don't have any intel on what to expect here."

"What *is* all this, anyway?" Scope asked, jerking her head towards the glyph-lined walls.

If he told her, would she at least go back to the others? "Our best approximation from Victrix is that this is where they bury their dead."

"Oh," Scope said, exaggerating her surprise. "So we're talking dead Kriegers behind these glowy symbols."

Well, that didn't work. "That's right."

"Jesus, Scope," Victrix said with alarm, in both their ears. *"This isn't the scenic tour of Krieger-land!"*

"You ask me, Bull, I'd say this is a great place to start our run," Scope laughed, ignoring her. "We haven't fired a single shot, and we've already got a body count." She chuckled as she lit up another cigarette and leaned back against the passage wall.

"Scope, no, *don't . . .*"

Behind her, a glyph blazed to life, accompanied by a shrill whistle of alarm. Scope jerked away from the wall, her cigarette tumbling from her lips. She looked up. Following her gaze, Bull watched as debris erupted high above them from a series of detonations along the cliff face.

"Huddle up!" Bull roared as he raced back to his startled infiltrators. "On me, double time!"

And in his ear, Victrix repeated the order.

Above them, enormous slabs of rock seemed to detach themselves from the walls in eerie slow-motion, then hurtled down. A horrific sound accompanied them, the thunder of gods, as the slabs tore apart and rained certain death upon them. The squads came together, scrambling without a word, much less any screams of fright, and froze in place as an enormous nimbus of light erupted above them, catching the first jagged boulders that plunged down on them in an onslaught of stone. In the canopy of light, giant stalactites appeared to grow downward towards them, some reaching so close as to almost touch them. With a sudden and elastic release, Bull's kinetic shield sprang back, hurling the rocky debris up, up and away. The infiltrators watched in awe as some of the boulders careened forwards, only to be atomized in the now visible disintegration field, while most of the falling rock was hurled back towards the mountain pass they had just spent hours climbing. And then darkness, as the shield dissipated and a harsh cloud of heavy dust and rubble settled around them.

Victoria Victrix: Overwatch Suite

As total disaster unfolded before her "eyes," Vickie was snapping orders at Grey. She was going to need a shit-ton of help. "Overwatch: Bulwark on monitor one. Grey, watch everyone else's vitals that we've got. Send red alerts to the handlers for the other teams." *Oh gods, if anything happens to Bull, Bella will never . . .* Even as the rocks were vaulting back in all directions, it was obvious that Bull had taken a massive, massive hit. Everything was redlining.

No, he was crashing.

Oh no you don't! With a savage curse and a surge of power that burned out four of her reserve-energy crystals, sending Grey scrambling to replace them, Vickie did the only thing she could do, since she was not a healer. She put Bull's body in "temporary hold." It made everything in his body *stay* the way it was when she fired it off, and would only last for about as long as it would take to get him to the forward med station. This was one of those "Heisenberg uncertainty" things; she knew the minimum time it would probably hold, but not the maximum.

Please, let it last that long....

"Overwatch: open: Moji! *Moji!*" she cried, her voice cracking. "Bulwark's down!"

"Not to worry, little sestra. Am taking command." Somehow, some way, Molotok sounded as cool as if he were flirting with some coed in a bar. That was one thing less to worry about. With a scattershot of contacts, she made sure all the team handlers knew what was up, while Molotok bellowed over the last sounds of falling rock and the shocked responses of the infiltrators.

"Comrades! Too late for stealth, we go, all of us, now. *Murdock, get portal open, leave it open! All teams, stage at field, get in* fast and hard. *Team Blue, Red Djinni is now leader!"* John must have gotten the portal open in double-time because the next thing she heard was—*"Now! Davay, davay, davay! Go, go, go!"*

She checked back in with the other team handlers, who were on the ball so far as she could tell, and went back to Bull. Her spell was holding. *"Moji, we need two flyers to evac Bull back to the Swifts. Make it the SFO for Corbie's Euro team; they've got jetpacks."*

"Da, vedma."

She listened with one ear while she checked on Bulwark again. His brain activity spiked. *Don't you* dare *try to move, you...* "Bulwark!" she said, sharply. "I need you to stay completely quiet. Don't move, don't speak. I've lost one of you guys already, and I—" her voice broke and she quickly steadied it. "I'm not losing you."

Since Corbie was a natural flier, his entire team and their non-metahuman SFO support had been outfitted with the ECHO jetpacks, in case the field generator turned out to be someplace that was otherwise inaccessible. Now the biggest two, with the beefiest packs, separated from the SFO team and eased Bulwark onto a stretcher as the rest of their team piled through the portal. A moment later, and they were in the air.

Through Molotok's eye-cam, Vickie got a glimpse of Scope, silent, seemingly numb, watching as Bulwark was carried off, strapped to the stretcher between the two fliers. Then she ducked her head and followed the rest of her team, the last of them to charge through the hole in the field. Then Molotok followed, and there was nothing left for her to do but keep Bull's vitals on her monitor and follow the teams in her charge.

Red Team: Ultima Thule

John made sure that he was the first person from Red Team, and consequently the first person of the entire infiltration section, through the portal and into Ultima Thule. His rifle shouldered, he scanned for threats as he sprinted left to the nearest cover; he knew that everyone else would be right on his ass. *So much for a covert entry; there's no way in hell the Kriegers didn't notice that.* In moments, Sera, Molotok, Untermensch, Soviet Bear and Mamona were all against the same cover with him. John glanced back towards the portal; all of the other infil teams were through, and were quickly spreading out on their assigned routes. With any luck, at least some of them would get to their targets and get the shield down so that the main assault could begin.

Vix swore creatively in his ear. *"There's no way the Kriegers missed that,"* she said, echoing his thoughts. *"Speed is your best friend, comrades. Johnny, throw all your eyes in the air."* John let his rifle hang by the sling for a moment as he opened a pouch, shoved his hand in to retrieve all of the sensor eyes, and chucked them hard into the air. Vix must have been practicing, and practicing hard; they vanished almost as soon as they left his hand, and he just heard the faint *whoosh* of displaced air as they flew up and away. There were easily dozens of other such magical eyes being used by the other infiltration teams. *Witch girl is gettin' good.*

"Victrix, bringing up route on HUDs." Molotok also had his rifle up and out, scanning his sector. They couldn't sit here much longer if they wanted a chance.

There was a pause. *"Overhead view from eyes,"* she said. *"Partial map overlay."* She said it in English; probably meant this was going out to all the teams. Overwatch was "smart" enough that the Red Team members showed as bright blue dots, all the others as a grayed-out blue with abbreviated team designations above them. The same would hold for the other teams. It was also "smart" enough to center the HUD map on them. Worryingly, there were some red dots starting to appear as Vickie's "eyes" spotted Thulians. *Getting crowded on the playing field.*

"Move," Molotok said in a harsh whisper. He hit John on the shoulder once for emphasis; he was going to be the point man for the team. With a nod, John set off, moving quickly in a half-crouch along the route that Vickie had marked for them. He had memorized it prior to stepping off for the mission, but the visual cue gave him one less thing he had to worry about messing up. Due to all of the marked enemy units starting to show up on the HUD map, though, they'd have to alter their route. John whispered, engaging his subvocal mic. "We've got the lead elements of the welcomin' committee up ahead. Adjustin' route."

John lead the team down a side alley between two of the pristine white buildings, keeping his rifle directed to the front. If anything popped out at them, he'd have to take it down, and silently; the suppressor, while not perfectly silent, would keep any "unfriendlies" from getting a good fix on the direction that the rifle fire was coming from. The sound bouncing off of all of the buildings would help with that, too. Once they came to the end of the alley, John flattened himself against the wall on his right side, then slowly and deliberately edged himself towards the corner. Peeking only one eye around the corner, he checked both ways down the street. "Clear." He swung around to the right, bringing his rifle back up. He was starting to hear sporadic gunfire off in the distance...followed closely by the unmistakable sound of Thulian energy cannons.

"*Overwatch to Team Red.*"

Moji replied. "Go, Overwatch."

"*All teams except Blue, so far, are encountering hostiles. More hostiles on the way. Cat's out of the bag.*"

"Copy, Overwatch. Proceeding with mission." Moji muttered something under his breath in Russian. Vix replied the same way. John thought he made out the names "Scope" and "Bulwark" from both of them. "Double time, Murdock. We are being on accelerated schedule, now."

John nodded his assent. No point in worrying about Bulwark;

that was way out of his hands. He picked up the pace moderately, but there was only so fast you could go while being anything resembling stealthy. They were making good progress, though; so far as John could see on his HUD map, they had gotten further than any of the other infiltration teams in their immediate area, save for Blue Team.

"Bull was frikking right. Scope wasn't—SHIT, contact front! Coming out of the building, three right!"

The team was out in the open, right in front of a building but not near any sort of cover that they could get to in time. Three Kriegers, all in trooper armor, exited a building about one hundred meters in front of the team. They seemed to turn as one, facing the group of metas, and went statue-still, as if they were stunned, for a second. Then, belatedly, they raised their arm cannons. John was the first to act; his enhancements were already keyed up, and the movement of the Kriegers seemed exaggerated and slow to him. He quickly stepped into the street, clearing some obstructing pillars from his line of sight. He dropped his rifle to his side, thrusting out both hands, he...

He didn't concentrate. It was more that he *let go*. His hands flared white-hot for a moment, surrounded by plasma that didn't so much as scorch a hair—and then the plasma erupted away from him, to engulf the three Kriegers in a white inferno. Sera leapt into the air and over his head, half flying, half jumping, and came down ahead of him and to his right. She manifested her spear of fire and threw it, all in a single motion, then leapt back again, alighting beside him, another spear already in her hand, as the Krieger on the right, impaled, slowly toppled over. John, focusing on the Krieger on the left, concentrated the fire on his hands for a second before loosing it; it flashed out in a solid beam, hitting the trooper square in the chest and burning a hole through him. The rest of the team raised their rifles in almost perfect sync, stitching the remaining disoriented and weakened trooper with suppressed rounds, starting at the joints and working their way up until he was dead.

"Pooch officially screwed. They know where you are. Three groups converging. Watch your HUDs. Sec, gotta juggle."

Vickie was right. They were officially on the radar of the Kriegers. Unless they could break free and slip the net the Kriegers were trying to envelop them with, they'd be stuck.

"Keep moving!" Unter elbowed Molotok, nodding down the street. Some three hundred yards away, more Kriegers were appearing, making their way to the team.

"You heard the man. Move out!" Molotok shouldered his rifle again, keeping it trained on the approaching enemies. John decided to take the team closer to the center of the city, cutting to the right through a boulevard. He could see that the Kriegers were still closing in; at least seven teams, now. *This is goin' to be tight, no two ways about it.* John kept their pace as fast as he dared. They hadn't gone more than two blocks when he got the strangest tingle at the back of his brain. He had the presence of mind to look back at Sera for a moment.

Her eyes were blazing blue and gold, and he knew, though he could not see them, that his were doing the same. He felt the bond between them in a way he had not felt it before. They were not *one,* but yin and yang, two planets orbiting the same sun, aware, acutely aware, of what the other was doing at every moment. Not only the present...but briefly into the future as well. They anticipated each other perfectly, intent and action blurring into each other.

"Contact right," John breathed, letting his rifle hang as his hands were sheathed in flame. Sera manifested both spear and sword. Molotok didn't have time to protest before the pair sprinted forward and turned a corner, facing four bewildered Krieger troopers who had been waiting in ambush. John bathed the entire group with nearly white-hot fire in one quick burst. Sera launched herself straight up into the air and came down between two of the Kriegers, impaling one helmet-to-toes with her spear as she landed, and half-turning instantly to bisect the other with her sword.

Before the other two could react, she was in the air again. While they were trying to track her, John moved forward. With a flick of his wrist, he sent a beam of plasma to blast the helmeted head off of the Krieger on the left. The remaining one noticed his presence, and was about to bring his arm cannons to bear. John ducked under the Krieger's aim, manifesting his own, much larger fire-sword. Some part of his mind not occupied with fighting thought again that it might pass for a Scottish claymore. With a backhanded sweep John hamstrung the trooper as he stepped past him, then turned and plunged the sword through the Krieger's back as he fell to his knees. The sword dissipated as soon as the trooper was dead. John snapped his head up, looking past the team, then unholstered his 1911 and fired once. The single round hit an unarmored Thulian, who was coming from behind Mamona, in the throat, sending the creature gurgling to the ground as he dropped the knife he had meant to plant in her back. Sera landed beside him at that same moment, and the two of them went into identical postures of readiness.

Moji stared at them for a long moment. *"Borze moi...."*

"Behind!" Sera called, in a high, clear voice. Moji, Unter, Bear and Mamona were suddenly in the thick of a Thulian squad; most of them were unarmored, but there was a single one in Krieger armor. The one John had dropped had only been the first. Unter lashed out with precise Systema strikes against the enemy nearest to him, breaking bones and destroying organs with each blow. Mamona ducked under a shot from a Thulian energy pistol, then stepped next to her attacker; almost casually, she stabbed the man, first in his kidneys, then his liver, then above his clavicle and down into his heart, forcing him to the ground. Bear pulled the Krieger who was focusing on him into the barrel of his PPSh while firing it before sending the man flaming down the street with a burst of plasma from his gauntlets.

Molotok grabbed the final unarmored Thulian by the throat. The creature clawed at the team leader's forearm fruitlessly. Then Molotok *squeezed*. The Thulian went limp, very dead, before Molotok threw him for the entire length of the next block. Spinning his head around, he dropped to the ground to leg sweep the armored trooper before it could bring its cannons to bear on his comrades. Molotok pinned it to the ground as Unter, Bear, and Mamona began to methodically shoot all of the Krieger's joints, sending sparks and spurts of blood onto the ground. Satisfied, he finally stood up, looking directly into the armored Krieger's visor.

"Die slow, *svinya*."

"Moji," John said, after a glance at his HUD showed him this was just the first of far too many Kriegers bearing down on them. "We need to move, an' right now. We're at risk of gettin' enveloped, here. They've got our number, just 'bout."

Molotok nodded, then signaled for the team to head out. Things were going to start to get really interesting in this part of the city. John just hoped they could live through it.

Belladonna Blue: Forward Medical Unit

For agonizing minutes, all Bella could do was watch Bull's vital signs in her HUD, and wait for the Swift to reach the med unit. And curse herself and Scope. Herself, most of all. *I'm the one who put her in the field. I'm the one who overrode Bull. If I hadn't . . .*

In snatches, Vickie had told her what she'd done. *"This is like a body-tourniquet. I basically froze everything at the moment I set the spell. If blood vessels were about to rupture, that stopped them, like that. It's a dumb spell, it doesn't tell me anything and I wouldn't know what to do if it did tell me anything. We* hope *it lasts 'til it gets there and he's in your hands. If it lasts longer, then you get that many more seconds to fix things before it wears off. It's . . . he's pretty bad, Bella. Prepare yourself."*

The entire team was waiting for the Swift to come in hot and offload their precious cargo. Herself, Soviette, Gilead, Panacea, Einhorn. There were other healers, another half dozen she'd recruited and trained, and others from the other nations, ECHO Euro, and conventional doctors, but these four were the ones she trusted, who'd worked with her hand in hand. And Upyr . . . Upyr who had, in the fifteen minutes that had passed since the disaster in the pass, recruited (or dragooned) a full thirty Marines to serve as living "batteries." Bella might not have "angel juice" for this, but she was going to have the next best thing. Upyr would stand right at her back with one hand on her and one hand on the Marine she was siphoning energy from, and when he flagged, the next would step up, and the next. . . .

And then they heard the Swift, its noise suppressors off, screaming in to a hot landing.

"Still holding," Vickie said in her ear, and then was off again. The HUD showed that the Thulian city was a maelstrom of blue and red dots, with the red converging on the blue. For the first time, Bella was grateful that someone else was in the hot seat instead of her. But there was only a second to feel that gratitude, because at that exact moment, she and the team were running out the door to get Bull into the shelter of the med unit tent with the assistance of the medics on the Swift.

As soon as they got him inside, Bella tore off the blanket that covered him, and witnessed one of her nightmares spring to life. He was . . . mangled. The arms and legs seemed bent in obscene places. What skin was exposed looked like one big bruise, and his face . . .

Oh god, his entire face is swollen shut.

She gave herself a second, just one, to take a breath and pull herself together.

"Einhorn, right arm and leg. Gilead, left arm and leg. Sovie, head. Panacea, pain." She fired off instructions as they all raced beside the gurney. It was just dawn . . . pale, pearly light streaming over the improvised airfield. It would still be dark in the mountains. The room was already prepped, with a regular surgeon and team waiting, just in case, but she shook her head at them as they all shoved through the curtains. There was nothing a conventional doctor could do here. Under any other circumstances—

—dear God, he'd be liquified goo inside.

Only two things had prevented that; the work she had done strengthening his bones and muscles and organs, and Vickie's spell, which had stopped *everything* mere fractions of a second after the avalanche. There were microruptures everywhere, and he'd have been bleeding out internally in seconds if it had not been for that spell. Which was still holding, giving her more precious time.

"Sovie?"

"Severe concussion, *sestra,* and micro-ruptures." Sovie sounded clinical and calm. "Nothing I cannot handle."

"The *bones!*" Einhorn wailed, appalled. "The bones are *bent!*"

Of course they were bent; Bulwark's bones were as much metal as bone now, so instead of breaking under the terrible strain they had held until they bent . . . and she could feel, though she walled it away, just how terrible the pain was. "What the hell can we—" she bit off, feeling a horrible surge of despair for a moment. A broken bone could be set, but how would you *straighten* something like this without doing even more irreparable damage to his muscles?

"Spoonbender!" Panacea all but shouted. And Bella's despair cleared. The shy, innocuous OpOne, barely a meta by most peoples' standards, had been along brought to aid with equipment repairs. With Spoonbender around, you often didn't need to disassemble equipment to repair it . . .

And he can bend Bull's bones back without hurting the rest of him!

"Overwatch!" she commanded. "Open Spoonbender. Bender, this is Bella. We need you at Bay One of the med unit five minutes ago. STAT!"

"*Uh . . . what? Uh, Roger!*" Spoonbender stammered.

"Get to work, Blue. I'll explain when he gets here. That spell could give out at any moment," Gilead grated, her voice rough as it always was when she was working.

At that moment, Bella felt a familiar presence behind her, and a warm hand planted on the back of her neck. *Upyr.* "Go to work, *sestra*. I am to being petrol station." The Russian girl chuckled a little. "We can do this. I know. It is Bulwark and we do not fail him."

Doctors were always told never to work on family members or loved ones . . . emotions would inevitably complicate matters.

Screw that. She would use her emotions to fuel her healing. She would use *everything* to fuel her healing. As she felt energy coursing into her from the hand at the back of her neck, she sank into that semi-trance where she could somehow see and feel everything that was wrong, everything that was broken. And she did not allow herself a moment of despair over it. Vickie's spell, somehow, was still holding, granting her yet a little more grace time to mend the worst.

Heart first. Oh, the irony! . . . *here we go.*

Blue Team: Ultima Thule

They had been on the move, ever since they had broken through John's portal and into the city. The plan had been simple. Each squad had been given a path to take. Get in, avoid detection if possible, and get to your target. Take energy readings; if it's big enough, then it's probably a generator. Blow it up.

Red Djinni swore under his breath as he led his squad through the alleys of Ultima Thule. It was the only plan they had, the best they could do under the rushed circumstances, but there were so many things that could go wrong, so many uncertainties, that he had cringed each time someone had suggested contingency measures. Call it what you wanted, even with an advance wave of infiltrators to knock out the defensive shield, this was still a kick-in-the-door approach. This was merely a prelude to a full-out assault, and he had never, ever seen one go off without a hitch.

Still, it was the best they had, and during the frantic planning stages, he had kept his mouth shut.

Maybe I should have raised just one or two suggestions...

For one, he might have personally requested a pro-parkour team. He glanced up at the closely packed architecture of the streets. The rooftops were close enough to allow for at least one group of freerunners to race to their objective above the chaotic battles that now raged in the streets below. Mel and Scope had just begun their training, relatively speaking, and the clunky suit of armor that Silent Knight had to wear to safely contain him and his sonic weapons made him about as agile as an arthritic turtle. And there was Bull, of course. The man was as strong and stubborn as an ox, but mobility had never really been his strong suit even *before* Blue had worked her voodoo on him and turned him into someone you didn't want sitting on your couch.

Not that it mattered, of course. Bull wasn't with them anymore, not after Scope had blown their entry and ruined the element of surprise, their one advantage in this whole mess of a plan. Perhaps he should have spoken up about that one too. Bull had benched Scope, with good reason, and had been overruled by Bella. Would it have made a difference if Red had spoken up, if he had tried to scream some sense into her? Hindsight, twenty-twenty, and all he could do now was deal.

And he had to deal. With Bull gone, Moji had yanked Red up to a leadership role. Who else in their squad could lead? This, he told himself, was not good. History had taught him that Red Djinni calling the shots had seldom, if ever, worked out well. Insanity was defined as repeating the same act, with the expectation of different results; and even *knowing* that, he was somehow forced to repeat history. History, he had decided, was a bitch.

Still, his squad had one thing going for them. Despite the bulk and plodding limitations of his armor, Silent Knight had provided them something invaluable. They were able to move at good speed without a sound. The armor soaked it all up, masking their footsteps and its own clatter by simply absorbing all nearby sonic energy. Scope's eyes warned them of danger, Red was adept at finding concealment and could easily herd them under cover, and when they needed to move at a dead and silent run, Knight would make it happen.

"Overwatch to Djinni."

Red brought his squad to a halt and ushered them from sight under a nearby alcove. He signaled Knight to turn off the sound dampening.

"What is it, Vix?" he whispered. "We're on the run here."

"Tell me what you need. Other than a miracle. And throw my eyes in the air, please."

"What we need is a do-over," he muttered as he released the latch on his rucksack and let the eyes fly up and vanish.

"No can do. Map on HUD, you guys are blue, Kriegers are red. You've gotten behind them. You're the only ones who have. Everyone else has been spotted. Do you see your objective?"

"Yeah, about that..." Red popped his head out of hiding and gave his surroundings a quick once-over. "You realize now that your secret Nazi Utopia schematics were...incomplete, right?"

"I realized that from the get-go. I didn't have a lot of data-mining time on the first pass. I'm map-correcting on the fly."

"Don't be too hard on yourself," Red said. "Looks like the overall layout's about right. The city's sectioned off like you said, but they've made a few changes to Hitler's wet dream."

"Hence, eyes. Keep checking your HUD, I've got them spread out in a cone along your probable route. Alleys. Hitler didn't think of them, these guys did, good place for sneaking. See here and here? Guess is that's what alleys are usually for, which means low traffic." The map in the HUD was changing even as he looked at it. *"If we figure efficiency, I'm thinking these buildings here are probably combined waste handling and warehouses. Maybe they've got something that can take waste and recycle it into food and parts."*

"Okay, those make sense, but what do you make of the giant towers they've got circling the middle ring?" Red could actually see one, rising over the rooftops, from where he and the others were huddled under an overhang. A tower, not unlike an elongated pyramid shape, surmounted with a half-globe. It looked rather like a mushroom. The half-globe itself was covered with a skin of something...white. Matte, rather than shiny.

"They could be anything," Vix said. *"Their spacing suggests communication towers, defensive centers, or..."*

Red heard her gasp.

"I'm afraid to ask," he said. "You know you tend to squeak when you give me bad news."

"Then I better show you," Vix answered.

The video sprang up on his HUD, and Red watched in horror as the video feed from one of Vickie's eyes, now high above the city, gave him a startling aerial view of one section of the ring of towers. From the base of each, dozens of Thulian foot soldiers and robot wolves came streaming out and began to fill the streets. And from the tops, giant robotic eagles took flight high above, directing the ground troops towards the various skirmishes that raged around the city.

"Defensive centers," Red muttered, grimly. "Barracks, by the looks of them. Okay, how about we avoid the giant structures that are spitting out robots and other assorted Nazi-flavored bits of trash?"

"Good plan," Mel whispered, her eyes wide with fear.

Scope looked . . . well, utterly unlike herself. Stricken, sick, and very, very guilty. Red couldn't blame her for feeling guilty; hell, she *should* feel guilty! If it hadn't been for her, none of them would be in the situation they were now. If Bull died . . .

Bella won't let him die, he told himself. And he told himself that if Bull hadn't made it, Vix would have said something, so every minute that went by meant that Bella and her team were fixing things, and every minute that went by meant Bulwark was that much closer to being healed up.

If Bull was gone . . . Vix would have told at least *him,* wouldn't she?

Mind on the job.

Knight, on the other hand, had that *stance* that said he was ready to kick ass and take names. And maybe do without the name-taking part.

"Juggling. Back later. Watch HUDs." The silence in his ear was deafening, and he suddenly felt . . .

. . . alone. And not in a good way.

Dammit, she's got dozens of people to handle, she can't hold your hand through this one. Suck it up, Red.

"Watch your HUDs, people," he said, through the link, rather than loud enough to actually hear. Mel and Scope weren't hard-wired, because Vix had run out of sets before she got to the two people who had been last on the "need to wire" list, but Vickie had given them special headsets that projected something really close to his own in-eye HUD into their left eyes. "Knight, keep up the good work. Looks like we have the best chance. We're going in deeper."

Belladonna Blue: Forward Medical Unit

The spell let go, eventually, but not before Bella had healed the worst of the worst. Then it was a race not unlike one she had run before—the race to save him from what she had triggered when she'd tried to strengthen his bones and nearly killed him. Once again, she tasted the metallic flavor of terror, knew in a place outside of what she was concentrating on that her hands were shaking, felt the agony of what losing him would mean. Only it was worse, now because now she knew they really were a couple and... *oh God, if I lose him...*

This time, it was a race to stop all the hundreds, the thousands of places where he was bleeding. The mending would come later, when the battle was over, if they all survived, if she and he got somewhere safe, if there were no more dying demanding her skills.

If it hadn't been for Upyr and her volunteers, it would never have been possible.

She finished just as Spoonbender was starting on Bull's left leg. For whatever reason, it had been only the leg and arm bones that had bent. Maybe he'd instinctively taken the weight, the hideous pressure, on his arms and legs, as if he had been physically holding the rock from the teams. She still wasn't sure how his force-field ability worked. As she leaned on the operating table, panting and sweating as much as if she had been running a marathon, she felt how much this was hurting him, even with Panacea doing pain management. She grabbed a towel and mopped her face and neck with it, as Upyr transferred her attentions to Spoonbender, who was sweating, himself.

"You can do this, Axel," she said, quietly, putting confidence in her voice. He looked up at her, and she saw the bewilderment in his pale gray eyes, the fear in his thin, angular, Middle-Eastern face. She was struck by how young he was.

"But—"

"It's just like working with metal inside something else where you can't see it. Here," she moved over to his side of the table, put one hand on Bull's leg and the other on Axel's forehead. "I'll show you. Upyr will give you all the energy you need."

She *showed* him; showed him what she "saw." Felt his bewilderment turn to sudden understanding. Understood at that moment, herself, what part of his meta gift was; not only did he shape metal, gently, with his mind and will...he understood at an instinctive level when something was *not right* with that metal, and made it be *right* again. Micro-fractures, impurities in the metal; he didn't just bend metal, but acted as a sort of self-corrective cold forge for what he was working on, as well. She couldn't do that...but she could guide him. And Upyr could give him the energy he didn't have on his own.

Slowly at first, then faster as he gained confidence, the bones went...back. Back to the shapes they should have been. This was easier for her; she didn't need the boost from Upyr to guide him. And Mary Ann and Gilead had already been doing the same work on Bull's arms and legs that she had done on his torso, his organs. As she had done, they had been forced to prioritize; Bull was going to feel as if someone had been doing extensive surgery to his entire body, as well as feeling as if he had been beaten to within an inch of his life. He'd be feeling that way for some time while he healed naturally. And he would probably have to heal naturally for a while. There would be other casualties besides Bulwark. They all knew this. Had he not been the first...had the med unit not been empty...

Triage. I'd have black-tagged him myself. There were only the healers they had, and no way to recruit more. To take *four* of them out for a single patient, plus Upyr, at a time when there would have been casualties pouring in, would not have been *right,* and Bull himself would have told her so. They had to save as many as they could. Bulwark would have had to wait until they had taken care of the worst they could do fastest. He would never have made it....

She let none of that leak over to Spoonbender, who now was riding on a wave of elation that he was doing something *important.* For the first time ever in his life, he was the *only* person in all of ECHO, maybe in the whole world, who could have done what he was doing. She was not going to do anything to spoil that euphoria. Among other things, it was boosting *his* ability, and she needed every bit he could do.

And when he backed away from the table, having put everything to rights, she took his head in both her hands and kissed him. "Axel Nadir, you are *my* hero," she said, and meant it. And he blushed, and stammered, and the waves of happiness and—for the first time ever for him, a sense of real pride and accomplishment—buoyed every one of the healers with her. Even Einhorn stopped looking panicked.

She sent Spoonbender off, and they finished the job, as much as it could be finished. Because there was still a war going on out there, and she had left the well-being of her teams solely in Vickie and Arthur Chang's hands. This wasn't over. This had barely begun. Soon more casualties would come in. She would have liked to pray *no one I know, please,* but she knew that was impossible.

"Are we done here?" she asked, looking at her team, each in turn. And each in turn nodded.

"Overwatch: ping standard med team on standby for Bulwark," she said. They must have been waiting just outside the curtains, for they came in immediately. "There's going to be some internal bleeding," she told them. "At this point the only thing that isn't bruised is his hair. Treat him as if he just rolled down a mile of mountain cliff."

"Good God, Blue, he's almost the same color you are," said one of the physicians, Dr. Shahid, half in horror and half in amusement.

She wanted to touch him. And she didn't dare. For a while, any touch was just going to make the pain worse. "Sovie?" she said instead.

"I am being put him in twilight sleep for now. There will to being no brain swelling, but there will to be some effects of concussion. Am thinking he will wake in half an hour, no more than hour." The beautiful Russian, who was an actual physician as well as a healer, explained to the conventional medical team what they had done, as Bella caught up on the status of the infiltration.

Because Gairdner was only one man. The man she loved with a passion that hurt, sometimes, but only one man. The rest of her people were still out there. And they needed her too. *If he had died . . .*

If he had died, she would have buried her heart with him and carried on. He would expect no less. And he deserved no less.

Red Team: Ultima Thule

John was getting worried. Red Team's luck fully ran out after three more blocks. They had easily taken out another small group of Thulians while on the move, but quickly became involved in a running battle with first one, then, in rapid succession, three more groups. According to Vix's technomagical eyes and the map on their HUDs, more Kriegers were coming to join the party. All of the approaching enemies were blocking escape routes that the team could use. John and Sera could fly, but that would leave the rest of their comrades stranded, not to mention the possibility of being shot out of the sky. *Naw, we're goin' to stick together. Only way any of us are gettin' out of this.*

"Hey, boss," John said as he blasted a running Krieger once with a burst of plasma, sending the man crashing to the ground. "I don't mean to worry you, but we're surrounded."

"*Da*, poor bastards. They have nowhere to be hiding from us now." Molotok paused for a moment, apparently reviewing their options. "Up ahead, one block over. Hardpoint; looks to be a wall. We will hold up there, attempt to punch through the Kriegers when their line thins out."

Mamona cleared her throat as she finished reloading her rifle with a fresh magazine. "How do you know for sure their line is gonna thin out?"

"Because we are going to kill every *neschastnyy* one we see, *tovarisch*." He grinned. "Also because if they do not, we will die where we stand." Mamona gulped hard, but didn't have anything to add to that. The team moved out again, John in the lead. They wouldn't have much time once they reached the square with the wall; the Kriegers definitely had a fix on their position now, and it wouldn't be long before ground troops reached them, even with the slow Krieger armor.

The "wall" that Moji had spotted turned out to be a monument of some sort in the middle of a square. On both sides, it was carved with a relief sculpture of a beefy-looking woman holding a wreath over her head, flanked on either side by an equally beefy-looking man holding a sword and a shield, with two chunky horses framing the lot. There were obelisks at either end of the wall. As a hardpoint it would certainly do, at least better than the open street. It would take even the energy cannons of the Krieger Death Spheres a while to burn down that much marble.

"Even this may not be enough," Sera said, her voice pitched so low that the only reason they heard it was because it came in through their Overwatch link. "We will soon be attacked on all sides."

"She's got a point, Moji." John looked around; all of the buildings nearby seemed to only have one entrance; while that'd mean they'd only have to cover one way in, it also meant that they wouldn't have a way out. Molotok must have surmised the same.

"No other options, and we are running out of time. There's nothing more to do at—"

Bear brushed past John and Molotok, letting his PPSh hang on its sling. John could faintly pick up the sound as the old Soviet's gyroscopic heart ramped up as it pumped plasma from his internal chamber into his gauntlets. The first blast he fired hit the base of the obelisk on the left, obliterating a chunk of it. The obelisk began to lean, then completely toppled over. Bear took a moment to judge the position of the first obelisk, then adjusted his angle before firing on the second. With a tremendous crash and a huge cloud of dust, the second obelisk fell to the ground. The result was that they now had additional cover on their previously unprotected flanks.

"So much for *fascista* erections!" the old man cackled. John noticed Bear wince at the end; whenever he used his internal reserves for such a powerful blast, it weakened him a little, until he would have no more plasma left except what was needed to power his mechanical body. The rest of the team, silent and internally face-palming, ran to the wall. Molotok positioned each of them in such a way that they were covering all of the avenues of approach. John's job was to focus on armor; wherever trooper armor popped up, he was to flame it down so that the others' weapons would have better effect on target. Still, even with the cover... this looked like it was going to turn into a shit sandwich fast, and they'd all have to take a bite.

John checked his rifle, making sure his magazine was full and that he had a round chambered. "Vix," he said, "What's the disposition of the other teams? Anyone nearby who can link up with us, help get us outta this jam?"

"*Negative. No one nearby, everyone's getting pinned down except Team Blue. We're taking casualties.*" He heard her spout off something that sounded French. "*Sec.*"

Though she said nothing else, his HUD lit up with new information, none of it good. Moji, who must have been getting the same thing, swore. "We should have aborted missions when *idiotskiy Amerikanski* made rocks to fall!" he spat.

But Sera shook her head. "Red Saviour was right," was all she answered, but John—and surely everyone else—knew what she meant. They'd had *no* other choice. Red Saviour, for all of her faults, and they were many, was right. Their only chance was now, win all, or lose all. If they had aborted, the Kriegers would have still been alerted, and the battle would have been on *their* terms. If they could just get the field down—

"Heads up, comrades! We've got company." That was Mamona. John turned to look at her sector just in time to see four Kriegers, all in trooper armor, come around a corner. They took a second to orient on the memorial wall and fallen obelisks, then started firing. Chunks of the obelisks were blown away by the actinic beams, sending shards of marble and dust flying and filling the air with the stink of burnt ozone. John sent a burst of fire in their direction, engulfing all of the armor at once. After letting them burn for a moment, the rest of the team opened up with their rifles, starting with the joints and moving on to center-of-mass shots as the armor weakened.

Things became a blur of fire, energy beams, explosions and gunshots after that first squad. John was only able to keep up because of his connection with Sera; able to anticipate where the armored troopers would show up, combined with his Overwatch HUD, he kept his fires going and their enemies weakened. Occasionally he would send a blast of plasma to take out a few targets completely, but for the most part he was busy augmenting the team's firepower. Mamona was deep in concentration, pausing in between volleys to direct her powers outward, extending them further than she had ever attempted before. The closer groups of Kriegers were disoriented by her meta ability, some vomiting violently, others knocked off of their feet as their equilibrium was lost. All of this served to make easy targets for the rest of the team, especially against the unarmored Kriegers. Bear fired his PPSh in long bursts, laughing and cursing in Russian, only pausing long enough to charge up his gauntlets and send a concussive plasma burst to destroy whatever the enemy was using for cover, or sometimes to take down a vulnerable trooper. It was starting to wear on him, though; he couldn't keep it up forever.

Sera's "rate of fire" was much slower; it took her longer to manifest a fire spear than it did to level a volley of bullets. But once she did so, she cast the weapon with all the effectiveness

392 Lackey, Martin, Lee, & Giguere

of Zeus's lightning bolts, unerringly hitting her target. Usually she struck for the throat of the armored Kriegers; that seemed to hit some extremely weak spot, for they would suddenly seize up and shake in place before dropping to the street, unmoving. But twice or three times she pinned two or more together, sometimes to a wall or the ground, making them easy prey for the rest of the team.

"*Overwatch to Red Team.*"

"Overwatch, go," Moji answered, coolly finishing off a Krieger with a burst from his rifle.

"*Reinforcements for Kriegers headed your way. You're in a hot spot, with three big groups converging.*" There was a pause; she was undoubtedly juggling a lot, even with help from Gamayun and the Colt brothers. "*Update: a sphere and two wolves incoming. Two minutes.*"

"Copy. Position is untenable. Let us be hoping Blue Team gets through, and soon. Will hold as long as we can. Red Team, over and out." Molotok dropped down behind cover to reload. "Things are becoming more complicated. Ammo check; make your rounds count." To punctuate his sentence, he leaned around the edge of the cover he was behind, drilling two unarmored Thulian infantry with center-of-mass shots; he ducked back in time to avoid an energy bolt that was close enough to blacken the marble it passed over before impacting on the far side of the square.

"One minute," said Sera. Somehow John knew she was right. He felt the unmistakable bone-shaking *hum* of the Death Sphere propulsion units, and sixty seconds later, the thing itself appeared over the rooftops. About half its tentacles were out, waving menacingly, and the whine of the energy cannons as they ramped up to fire was enough to set John's teeth on edge. *One good blast from that thing, and we're toast.* John knew what he had to do, and knew that Sera was in sync with him. He planted his feet, focusing on the underside of the ship, letting his fires build in his hands before snapping them out; a thick beam of plasma impacted the underbelly of the ship, cutting a gaping hole through it. He then had to shut the beam off to blast more fire at the oncoming sets of troopers, lest they be overrun. Even so, the Kriegers had taken advantage of the momentary opportunity to advance closer.

But Sera was already flinging her fire-spear with all her might at the hole he had blasted. Before anyone in the ship had time to react to John's blast, her spear shot through the opening. And whatever it hit in there, whether it was an operator or control mechanism, the effect was immediate. The entire sphere canted over sideways and began spinning crazily, tentacles whipping wildly, before it lurched back the way it had come, steadily losing height. It got just out of sight behind the rooftops when there was a tremendous explosion, and a plume of orange flame and thick, billowing black smoke from somewhere near enough that the ground shook with the impact.

That'll give us a little breathing room. Will it be enough?

Victoria Victrix: Overwatch Suite

To say that Vickie had her hands full was rather like saying that the surface of the Sun was just a little warm.

From the moment when Scope had created a fuck-up so monumental that there were no words for it, she'd been keeping so many balls in the air—some of them the *literal* balls that were her flying, invisible eyes—that she had lost count. But she hadn't lost *track*. She knew exactly where everyone was, and how they were faring. Gamayun and the Colts, stationed in a second Overwatch plane alongside the Command and Control center, were handling the non-meta SFO teams; Gamayun had all the Russians, the Germans and the Chinese, while the Colts had everyone else. Working under *them* were the Euro, Eurasian, and Pan-Pacific ECHO Overwatch One leads that the Colts had been training. Herb and Grey handled her eyes, moving them as swarms rather than individually. That, at least, allowed Vickie to concentrate on the metas.

The Chinese had taken the first casualty; their sniper, who'd gotten sniped himself. So far there were no actual deaths ... yet. But there were a good dozen people out of the action unless someone on their teams happened to be a healer along with his or her primary talent. All the teams were pinned down but Djinni's; most had managed to take cover inside those windowless buildings. That gave them a limited port to defend, but also a limited port to fire from. Only Red Team was out in the open; she wasn't sure if that was brilliant or suicidal.

Her planning for this had included a backup magical power supply; she wasn't going to rely on a single circle of mages this time. She'd been collecting boxes of "batteries" shipped to her by overnight messenger since long before Red Saviour had blown the sitch; crystals stuffed so full of magical energy that they glowed to normal sight. She had these arrayed in a bank of holders, and when one burned out and went dark, Grey or Herb replaced it.

There *were* some magical things she *could* have done even at this distance, if she'd just had the time... but she didn't have the time. This wasn't two teams of infiltrators, this was eight, plus their supporting SFO teams, and all of the eyes that JM and Djinni could carry. It was so crazy she didn't even have time to think about how crazy it was.

All she could do was try to keep up. Which was becoming increasingly harder by the moment.

Blue Team: Ultima Thule

Within the massive circle of tower barracks, the members of Blue Team were able to make better time. It had taken some precise timing, Knight's silencing abilities and a lot of luck, but they had crossed the threshold without detection. Now, with the bulk of the fighting happening outside the circle's perimeter, they met little resistance, just the occasional pair of sentries that regularly patrolled the city streets. Some they simply avoided, but in a few instances they had been forced to take steps. Their ambushes were silent. With Knight taking point, they descended on their victims, his armor soaking up the thunder of incendiaries, gunfire and the short-lived screams of their marks. Occasionally, Knight discharged the buildup of energy into a subsonic blast himself.

They were nearing their target zone. From their HUDs, it was clear they were the only ones who were. Perhaps just one squad fulfilling their bombing run would suffice. Red Djinni certainly hoped so.

They took shelter in another alley, and Red signaled for Knight to lift his sonic cloak and motioned them together for a brief huddle.

"We're really close," Red whispered. "Keep it tight. I don't need to tell you how bad it would be to mess up now. Scope, you've got the sensors. Pass them to Mel to fire up."

Scope scowled at him.

"I know, I know," Red said. "Bull made them your responsibility. I'm making them hers."

"You going to fill me in on *why*?" Scope asked.

"Because I don't trust you to do anything more than shoot things in the head right now!" Red snapped. "You can complain to Bull later, when we get back, *if* we get back, and if Bull's still alive. I gave you an order, soldier. Give Operative Reverie the sensors. Now."

"Red, please..." Scope said, blanching. "I can do this, please, I need to do something now, something..." She grimaced and clamped a shaking hand to her mouth to steady herself. She shuddered and took a few breaths.

"I need to do something right," she finished, and fixed Red with a pleading look.

"Fine, get it running." Red sighed, rising to his feet. "On me, we move in bursts. When I take cover, be right behind me. Send a ping through the comms if you pick up anything, Scope." And that was another complication. Scope and Mel were not hardwired; Vickie had run out of implants before they'd been certified for this cluster. They were on earpieces and throat mics, with little projector HUDs on stalks they had to tuck out of the way when they weren't looking at them. At least they were on the sets tied into the magic freqs, not the conventional ones. "Start it up again, Knight. On three, two, one..."

Red took a glimpse out of the alley, scanned their immediate surroundings and dashed across the empty street. He led them closer to the center of the city, under cover through more alleyways, making sure they surfaced on larger avenues only when necessary. Their progress was agonizingly slow, necessitated by the absolute need for stealth. Finally, after what seemed like an eternity of this, he called for another huddle.

"We're almost out of our target zone," he whispered, and gave Scope a questioning look.

"Nothing," Scope sighed as she rechecked the scanner readings. "Nothing big enough, anyway, not by the way Vix had these calibrated. Something big enough to power that"—she pointed up at the energy field that blanketed the city—"is going to spike almost off the charts on this thing. I've been getting blips, that's all."

"Could the source be shielded?" Mel asked. "I mean, I know intel said it wasn't likely, but still..."

"It might be," Red answered, but shook his head. "But not enough. To project the field, our guys say each point of generation has to have at least one strong, open focal point. The scanners should pick that up from within a few hundred feet, easy. If we passed it, the readings should have spiked."

"May I?" Silent Knight asked, and reached out his hand.

Scope gave him an angry look in protest, thought better of it, and cast her eyes down as she passed him the scanner. Knight took the device and opened the readout, expanding the timeline. He grunted, and held it up for all to see. Red took one look, and cursed.

"What?" Scope demanded. "What is it?"

"The readings," Red scowled. "Look at the trend. No major spikes, but the baseline's been dropping from the moment you turned it on."

"What...what does that mean?" Scope asked, her voice now very small.

"It means, whatever we're looking for, we've been moving away from it this entire time."

From beneath his scarf, Red shot Scope a furious glare while Mel and Silent Knight shared a quick, uneasy look. No one said it, but it was obviously on everyone's mind. Scope had been too eager to prove herself, had been so focused on seeing that telltale energy spike that she had not been paying attention to the big picture. Another rookie mistake, one that had cost them precious time. The infiltrators, spread so thin now, were depending on them, the one team that had made it passed the bulk of the Thulian defenses, the one team that had a clear shot at lowering the defensive field to allow the rest of the allied nations to join the assault on the Thulian city. It shouldn't have been this way. Her earlier mistake had cost them their one advantage, stealth, and now her carelessness had led them in the wrong direction. And she obviously knew it. Her look was one of shock, then horror and then a remorse so pure and naked that it forced Mel and Knight to look away in shame.

But Red didn't let her go. His eyes remained fixed on hers and when he spoke, the strain in his voice to keep his composure was palpable.

"Let's think this through a moment," he said. "Before things really go tits-up. We passed it, we must have, if the readings are growing weaker. Nothing we passed by really stood out."

"Unless it was underground," Knight said.

"Even then," Red growled, shaking his head. "Even then, it would need a focus, something to direct the energy out. Out and..."

He stopped, and looked to the sky.

"And up." Mel said, finishing his thought. Together, they looked at the ring of towers that circled the inner city.

"But those are the defensive towers," Knight said. "We saw all those Thulians and their robo-pets pouring out of them. They obviously house the majority of the troops in this city. Why would they ring the inner city, if they're not meant to protect it?"

"No," Red muttered. "Their positioning isn't to protect the inner city, but to anchor the *shield*. Look, they make a perfect ring, and each can channel energy up. They're forming a keystone above us, and the rest of the shield cascades down from it."

"Why would they house so many troops then?" Mel asked.

"Because the shield's the main defense of this place," Scope offered in a shaky voice, her head bobbing in mournful understanding. "And protecting the shield would be the priority."

"Right," Red agreed. "They're shield generators first, barracks second. It's our best guess, but there's only one way to be sure."

He reached out, firmly took the scanner from Scope's hands and passed it to Mel. Scope closed her eyes, her hands falling to her sides.

"Let me know when we've got confirmation," Red grunted, and motioned them up for the arduous trek back.

Mel hesitated, then nodded. "Okay, I'll signal when we're close. But, Red, each of those towers is in the open and they're protected by multiple squads of armored Kriegers and God knows how many wolves and eagles... how are we going to get close to them? There's nowhere to hide."

"I guess I'll have to think of something on the way," Red muttered. "Let's focus on getting there first."

Red Team: Ultima Thule

The Death Sphere had only been the beginning of the push the Kriegers had made to overrun Red Team. Luckily, they hadn't sent out any more air support in the form of spheres; apparently, they had a lot on their plates with all of the scattered teams. John hoped that the losses for their side weren't too bad so far, but he didn't count on it. There were just too many Kriegers, and not enough people on the meta teams who could tangle with them effectively. The teams that didn't have a meta with fire powers of some sort were all issued at least one of the modified RPG systems, or grenade launchers with similar munitions. Still, it wasn't going to be enough when the teams had the entire city full of Nazis coming down on their heads.

Probably all that had saved them so far was the simple fact that there was only so much room in the streets to funnel mayhem towards them.

John had just flash-cooked an unarmored fire team of Kriegers who were setting up on a rooftop, when the Robo-Wolves arrived. They came from two different streets simultaneously, crossing paths as they charged around the square. The team shot at them, but the bullets pinged off of their metal hides. John tried a fire-blast, but the one he shot was unaffected; evidently this was a newer model, hardened against fire. Even one of Bear's more powerful concussive plasma blasts was deflected, splashing off like so much water.

Or maybe not....

John noticed that some of its armored hide had peeled away, exposing some wires and mechanics, maybe hydraulics. It might be immune to his fire, but not completely to Bear's concussive energy blasts!

"Bear, hit it again! Same location!" Beside John, Sera had manifested a spear without prompting, weighing it in one hand as she waited for Bear to give her a weaker target. Bear nodded wearily, then turned, plasma collecting in his gauntlets. His eyes tracked the wolf that he had damaged as it ran through the square. Spotting his chance, he raised his gauntlets and fired off a precisely aimed, but much more powerful burst. It caught the wolf in the exact same spot, sending it tumbling along the ground, crushing an armored suit and its accompanying unarmored infantry. The wolf's entire shoulder was ripped open, one leg missing and its "ribs" showing, showering sparks. Sera seized the moment and raced forward out of cover a few steps, flinging her spear like an Olympic javelin-thrower. It impaled the wolf, sending a shuddering spasm through it, not unlike a seizure, which had the effect of sending its flailing limbs tearing at more of its allies who had the misfortune to be within range. By the time the seizure was over and the wolf "dead," Sera was back under cover again.

Bear sagged to the pavement, groaning and panting. He didn't even try for a quip; it was clear that the effort had depleted his reserves; he only had enough plasma left to power his mechanical body and heart. "Here, Old Bear," Unter grunted, handing the old man a metal flask. Bear tasted it, then gulped it greedily. John got the harsh whiff of vodka. "Sorry, did *nyet* pack Chef Oh Boy."

Pavel perked up slightly after downing the entire flask, enough to shoulder his rifle again. "Next time, will not have oversight, *da?*"

Before Untermensch could answer, the remaining wolf charged directly at their cover. It was followed by a large number of infantry, all of them firing energy weapons.

Molotok scowled, focusing his fire on the infantry instead of the wolf. "Prepare to be defending yourselves!" The infantry was advancing from three directions; this was the push, where they'd try to overwhelm Red Team and finish them off.

Let's see what we can do 'bout *that.* John concentrated for a moment, then shouted to the team. "Get down!" Everyone ducked instinctively. Once he was sure no one was in danger, he released a gigantic, explosive cloud of fire from his hands. The cloud raced out, almost instantly engulfing the wolf and the infantry that followed it. Several of the infantry were *Panzershreck*-like two man teams; the munitions they were carrying immediately cooked off, causing secondary explosions inside the cloud of flame. John could "feel" the wolf getting knocked down, its sensors confused by the blasts. He continued to pour on the fire for another second. The infantry from the other two directions were just about to reach them, and he'd be open to getting shot in the back if he didn't start paying attention. *Hope that was enough.*

After that, John didn't have any more time to think. The Krieger infantry stormed over the barriers and were amongst the team. The trooper armor was still advancing slowly, but they were no longer firing for fear of hitting their own. The first thing John did was to bring his rifle up, dropping five Kriegers with short bursts in quick succession. With his rifle empty, he let go of it, transitioning to his 1911. Firing almost as fast as he could pull the trigger and switch targets, three more Kriegers were dead for sure, with a fourth down on the ground. In the back of his mind he felt a chill of . . . something too detached to be awe, and a little akin to fear. He knew how good his senses were with his enhancements keyed, but this was a magnitude past that. Anticipating *exactly* what his foes were going to do and where they were going to be, even when he couldn't actually *see* them.

He ducked under an energy bolt from a Krieger pistol, reloading his own pistol, turning and aiming all at once. He emptied the gun again at his attacker and two more Kriegers. The fighting was too close for more shooting, so he holstered his pistol. Three Kriegers rushed him all at once, one of them armed with a knife. He stood his ground, waiting for them to get closer. With the first one finally in range, John kicked out his knee, hyperextending it backwards with a gut-churning crack, causing the Thulian to fall to the ground screaming. The other two reached him at the same time; he dodged the wide-arced swipe from the one with the knife, parrying the kick of the second one with an open-handed slap that complemented the Thulian's momentum. Knowing he had a second until that one was back in the fight, he turned to the knife-wielding Krieger in time to catch the man's wrist mid-lunge with both hands. He squeezed and felt the bones in the man's arm give way. With a sharp tug, John carried the man and his knife past himself, planting the knife in the shoulder of the second Thulian as he recovered. Releasing the Krieger's arm, he finished him off with a vicious punch to the Krieger's throat, resulting in an audible crunch and a spray of blood from the man's mouth. The second Krieger had pulled the knife from his shoulder when John simply turned to him, raised a hand, and set the Thulian on fire; the man stumbled backwards over the barrier, still clawing fruitlessly at the flames. John had a scant moment to survey the fighting.

The oddest thing struck him now; the *smell.* It made his hackles rise with the instinctive reaction to *alien.* He vaguely remembered that same smell back in the North American headquarters, and again from that pop-up cell he and Sera had caught in the old school, but it hadn't been that strong, perhaps because there had been so many humans among the creatures they had called Thulians. But these Kriegers were *all* "Thulians," and . . . their bodies smelled wrong, their blood smelled wrong. Even though the scent was "like" several things—orange, burned cinnamon, musk—his body recognized that it was not actually those things, it was *other,* and reacted accordingly.

He was aware of Sera even though he couldn't actually see

her, only the wash of fire that showed where she stood, or leapt, or flew. Surrounded by fire, she was a dervish with a sword of flame, spinning like a deadly top, leaping over the heads of her opponents, aided by powerful thrusts of her wings, to land behind them and take them out from the rear. He was also aware how she mourned each and every death, *feeling* that grief with a depth even he couldn't fathom; and yet, she did not allow that sorrow to stop her.

Unter and Bear were working together, fighting back to back; Unter's nearly indestructible hands lashed out with precision and fury, blocking both knives and unarmed blows from the Kriegers or striking with deadly accuracy. Bear, who was still flagging, took several blows to his metallic body, but wasn't nearly as affected as he should have been, to the dismay of his attackers. With buttstrokes from his PPSh he would clear the space immediately in front of him, then hose down several Kriegers at once with bullets. Neither joked nor chided the other.

Mamona was frantically trying to keep up with the stream of enemies that kept attacking her. She had begun to run out of knives, so she resorted to moving from body to body, fighting as she went; when she reached one with a knife stuck in it, she would yank it out and immediately plant it in another Krieger. She was saved several times by her ability to interfere with the equilibrium of her enemies; right before a Krieger could land a killing blow, she would interrupt him, causing him to stagger, fall to the ground and convulse, vomiting or clawing at his ears. Even so, she had suffered a few gashes, a black eye and a bloodied nose.

Molotok shone in this kind of fight. Super-strong and resilient, he was engaging nearly half of the Kriegers inside of the barriers. With an almost casual backhand he would send two or more Kriegers flying, necks broken. A kick turned another into a ragdoll projectile, knocking down several of his allies. He would even use individual Thulians as weapons, swinging them around to bludgeon others, or as shields to take incoming energy blasts. It was like watching a god swatting defiant mortals, scattering them like toys.

But this didn't seem to do more than put a dent in the oncoming horde of Thulians. *I'm about sick of this shit.* If they were occupied with the infantry for much longer, the trooper armor would reach them. And sooner or later, someone was going to miss his mark and get killed, even with Sera and John trying to be everywhere at once in the fight. *Time to get some breathin' room.* John saw in his mind what he needed to do, and knew that Sera understood as well.

"Everyone drop!" he shouted as loudly as he could, hoping it was enough to reach over the din of the fighting, or that at least they'd hear through their ear-implants. Unter responded immediately, but had to drag a cursing Bear down. Molotok dove for the ground as well, but while sweeping and breaking the legs of half a dozen Kriegers.

Mamona stood with her back to him; either she hadn't heard him, or was a bit groggy from whatever had blacked her eye. John was already building up his fires, and there was nothing he could do, they didn't have any time left—

But again, Sera anticipated him; as she leapt back over the barrier to take cover, one enormous wing swept out and pulled in with a flash of fire-feathers, sweeping Mamona back in towards Sera with it. With the wing curled around her comrade, Sera went to the ground, taking Mamona with her, the wing over her like a sheltering umbrella.

He'd done this twice before, once, back in that warehouse, and once at the North American HQ, but both times wildly out of control. This time...the control came to him as if he had practiced this very maneuver a hundred times. The release of his fires would not be chaotic and random, but precise. As precise as Sera's strikes. With the rest of the team clear, John released the pent-up fires in one burst; a plasma wave, traveling at roughly neck level, issued in all directions, centered on him. It caught the majority of the Kriegers in the upper chest, neck or face; it was a grisly sight as their newly "shortened" bodies fell burning to the ground. The monument wall was scarred in one thick line, not quite enough to cut completely through the heavy marble and bronze. The rest of the team quickly regained their positions, shoving aside the bodies. Movement to their left caught John's attention. In the conflagration he had created earlier, he saw the stunned Robo-Wolf begin to regain its footing.

"We've got problems." He checked his rifle, making sure it was topped off, then did the same with his pistol. With Pavel's energy levels so low, he couldn't possibly pull off another plasma shot.

Also, due to the way these new wolves were hardened to fire, his own powers wouldn't have much effect. If that Robo-Wolf led another charge, the team would be in real trouble; they had only barely managed to survive the last one.

Molotok seemed to size up the entire situation at the same time as John. Looking around their barrier, he bent down and grabbed one of the last living Kriegers; one of the ones that he had broken the legs of with his last leg sweep. He headbutted the Thulian, either killing it or knocking it unconscious. Setting it on the barrier, he then shrugged off his patrol pack, dug around in it for a second, and then retrieved one of their mission-specific ordnance packs; essentially a demolition charge, to be used on one of the Krieger shield generators. Grabbing the dead or unconscious Krieger, he first primed the bomb, then stuffed it down the front of the Krieger's field blouse. Looking to the now standing Robo-Wolf, he paused, judging the distance, and then *threw* the Krieger in a fastball pitch at the wolf.

The wolf had time to look up right before the Krieger messily impacted its neck. In a moment of revulsion it reminded John of a really big, juicy bug hitting a windshield on the interstate.

"Down," Molotok said calmly. The team dropped behind the barrier again. John glanced over at the team leader, and saw that he had a detonator in his hand. Smiling, he flipped up the activation latch and then thumbed the trigger.

It sounded like two tectonic plates had decided to slam together in an earthy high five right in front of them. The ground bucked and the entire team was bathed in a too-hot pressure wave. When they had regained enough of their senses to look, John saw that one of the wolf's claws was embedded in the wall just above his head, still smoking. Peeking over the top of the cover, he saw there was a sizable crater and nothing else where the Robo-Wolf had been. All of the trooper armor in the square had been knocked down, with several of them obviously dead from the explosion or the debris it had sent flying out.

"You guys sure know how to get my attention." Vix sounded exhausted. *"Good job, Moji. Passing the word to the rest that the dogs can get blowed up real good. Might as well use those bombs on something."*

"Kriegers were being out of neon signs to get little witch's attention. Bomb seemed good alternative."

"You do know those are special payloads, right? Lotsa nuvo-thermite. Or whatever the hell the hot stuff ECHO packed in there is. I didn't get details. Probably why the wolf went—sec—"

The Krieger troopers had begun to recover; most of those that were able to, began shooting as soon as they could stand, while others dragged some of their fallen comrades away. Soon, the energy beams were constant, slamming into the obelisk barriers and the wall again. The relief carvings were almost unrecognizable now. Whatever the stone was, it might look like marble, but it was holding up better against the beams than John had thought it would. Still, their cover was wearing down, slowly but surely. For some reason, the Krieger troopers weren't advancing, just firing and pinning the team in place. John did his best to blast several with fire so that the team could whittle away at them with their rifles, taking out the odd one with his plasma while Sera did the same with her spears. But the Kriegers refused to advance.

"They're up to somethin'. We need to figure out an exit strategy, and soon—"

John's words were drowned out when the first of the artillery hit. The artillery was some sort of weird type that John had never seen before. When the shell impacted, it also seemed to release a burst of the same energy that Thulian arm cannons fired. It fell short of their position, but it was utterly devastating where it did land. Apparently the Kriegers weren't worried about creating a few potholes, or even taking down some buildings, so long as they took out Red Team. Slowly, but methodically, the impacts started to march forward, coming closer and closer to the team.

"I'm really not likin' this, fellas!" Mamona huddled beneath the cover, wincing with every explosion.

The team had nowhere to go; the troopers were keeping them pinned, and the artillery was still homing in on them. John's mind searched for alternatives, something that they could do. He and Sera could grab some of the team, maybe fly, but they couldn't hold everyone, and they'd surely be cut to ribbons by the troopers. Could Vix make them a hole deep enough to hide in?

If she could have, she would have already.

Everyone on the team looked to each other, hoping someone had some idea to save them. They all realized that there was nothing to be done; they were stuck. John heart sank, and he took Sera's hand, dust falling onto the back of his glove from the shaking monument. *We've had a damned good run, and made the bastards pay for it. I just hope that we beat 'em in the end.*

His eyes met Sera's, and he felt a sense of calm as she met his gaze solemnly; he wouldn't be alone this time. He never would be alone again.

He was about to tell her that he loved her when something tickled the back of his mind, causing him to look over his shoulder. For the briefest moment, he thought he saw dark figures running on the rooftop. He was almost convinced that he was just seeing things.

Then the artillery stopped abruptly. The troopers' energy cannons slackened in their firing, then stopped completely.

"*Chto' yebat?*" Unter looked more annoyed than surprised. The team collectively peered over the barriers. The troopers were looking around, shouting to each other in confusion. The artillery started up again suddenly... but this time it was much closer to the Krieger lines than it was to the team. And it started moving *towards* the Kriegers. Some of them broke and ran, but others weren't as lucky. The blasts demolished entire sections of buildings, bursting trooper armor or simply obliterating it in an explosive wash of energy. Once it became clear that the team's demise wasn't so certain, all of the CCCP infiltrators resumed shooting again, many times at fleeing targets.

Soon the entire square was a burning ring of destroyed buildings and dead Thulians. The artillery stopped once again. After several seconds there were multiple explosions in the distance, at different points in the city.

"Stay on guard. No knowing what is coming next. Be prepared to move out." Molotok couldn't help but let some measure of being impressed at the destruction creep into his voice.

Vix was swearing softly under her breath. "Âleechaa'itsa'ii biyaazh. *Someone just bought a bunch of our people some breathing room,*" she said, after a moment. "*It wasn't just you. Fire, Earth, North and Sky were all pinned down, like you. Now... they're not. And those artillery pieces just blowed the hell up.*"

"And it wasn't our people, Vic?" John asked, surveying the damage. He could still hear fighting off in the distance, but for the moment it looked like their area was clear of any threats. He couldn't "feel" any hostile presences, as weird as it was to think about. *Gotta talk with Sera more about this hoodoo stuff. I'm not complaining, but damn if it isn't strange as all get out.*

"Contact front!" That was Mamona. The team all snapped their attention in the direction she was looking, rifles raised, or in Sera's case, a spear. Through the dust and smoke from the burning trooper armor, John could see that there was a sizable group moving towards them. And they were moving professionally; all sectors covered, good spacing, keeping their footfalls light. Another one of the infil teams? They weren't showing up on Vic's radar—some sort of Krieger trick? Reviving the old stormtrooper infiltration methods, maybe? Wait . . . there was one blip, marked as friendly . . . but there were still too many moving figures to account for.

As soon as the first of them cleared the smoke, John knew it wasn't a Krieger trick. The uniform, the patches and especially the woman leading the group clearly identified who they were.

Blacksnake; with Khanjar, kitted up in full combat gear, NVGs perched up on the top of her head, leading the way. They must have come in at close to the same time that the teams had, in the pre-dawn.

"Do not be letting your guards down. No telling what these snakes are to be playing at," Bear muttered. Unter nodded agreement, lightly elbowing Mamona to remind her to bring her rifle back to her shoulder.

But Sera leapt lightly over the barrier and approached them, empty-handed, bee-lining for Khanjar. Molotok and the other Russians all tried to protest, but she was already there by the time any of them realized what she intended to do. John held up his hand, then lowered his rifle to a low ready.

"She knows what she's doin', gents." John vaulted over the barrier, walking to meet with his wife. He turned back to face the team briefly. "All the same, cover me, will ya?"

Unter nodded. John arrived by Sera's side just as she started talking; Molotok had decided to move up with him, so that they were both flanking Sera.

Sera was already holding out her hand. "Khanjar. So we have you to thank?"

Khanjar looked at the outstretched hand as if it was a cobra, and took it gingerly for a moment. "Dom is . . . indisposed, not paying any attention to this part of the world nor to what I was doing in it. And I had a contingent that was loyal only to me." She let go of the hand and looked up. "Belladonna and I have had an understanding for some little while. It seemed a good moment to exercise my option to aid. We followed on your teams, after they had already drawn away most of the fire."

"And Bella does not know you are here?" Sera cocked her head to one side, inviting an answer.

"*She does now,*" Vix said in their ears. "*I thought only I could swear like that.*"

Khanjar shook her head. "It seemed prudent not to divulge anything to anyone. Not even my group knew what I intended other than that we were going to strike at a Thulian stronghold, nor where we were going, until we arrived."

Now John spoke up. "Why? What's your play in all of this?" he asked, his voice maybe harder and sharper than he had intended. But Blacksnake had tried to kill him—personally—twice. Dominick Verdigris had tortured and nearly killed Sera. And right at this moment, he damn well *was* going to look this particular gift horse in the mouth.

"Because I have no intention of destroying my karma by being involved with the murder of a Celestial," Khanjar replied, also sharply, then did a double-take in John's direction, and amended, "*Celestials.*" She took a deep, deep breath, and then shook her head slightly, as if she had been taken quite entirely by surprise, and didn't like the sensation.

Now how in the hell does she know about that? More to talk to Sera about . . . later. We've got work to do right now.

"And I intend to enjoy the world," she continued. "I do not think it would be nearly so pleasant with these dogs ruling it." She glanced slightly to her right as the man there nodded. "Neither do these men. I chose them with care. They have not been pleased that we have been combating things other than Nazis."

"So, you are to be helping us. *Horosho.*" Molotok paused. "Overwatch, what is best course of action at this point in mission?"

Without any prompting that John could hear, Sera unhooked her earpiece and held it out. Vickie's amplified voice came through loud enough to be heard by all of them.

"*Since we've blown any chance of secrecy, I'm told by Command to relay that Red, Earth, Fire, North, South, Sky and Sea are directed to link up and make a concerted push. Directions on your HUDs for linkup. Objective to be selected at that time.*"

Molotok pointed towards the direction that the HUD outlined

to the nearest infiltration team. "You and your forces will being accompanying us. Once joined with our comrades, we will destroy the *fascista*."

Khanjar ignored him, looking directly at John and Sera instead. Sera glanced at John. "Covering fire for our movements?" she murmured.

John shook his head. "Naw, Moji is right. We can't afford to get pinned down like that again. We'll stick together, move in concert. Fire an' maneuver warfare."

"Operative Khanjar, I now have your Blacksnake team freqs. Patching in now. I won't be giving orders, just warning and directions, some info on your HUDs. Orders will be up to you and Molotok. My feed to your HUDs will be blue."

Khanjar's eyes widened for a moment. "That was better than military-grade rolling encryption on our comm systems. You are a useful one."

"And you're a damn useful ally. Thanks."

Khanjar licked her lips as if they had gone dry. "*This* cannot be Celestial? She is not, so what is—" she said, but immediately shook her head. "No. I do not wish to know. We will take left flank." With that, she whistled shrilly, and her team formed up.

John turned to Sera, cocking his head to the side. "After this is all over, remind me to ask you what the hell that was all 'bout sometime."

"Trust, beloved," Sera replied, her gaze bathing him in warmth. "It is all about trust." She hurried after Molotok. "Quickly! We must go!"

Belladonna Blue: Forward Medical Unit

Bella sagged forward, holding herself up against the cold steel of the medical table, sweating and shaking from the things she had witnessed. And it hadn't only been Red Team that had nearly been destroyed, it had been ECHO Europe and Corbie as well. If it hadn't been for Khanjar...

That...had been close. Too close. How in hell Khanjar had managed to sneak her forces in through that open portal...

When we were moving into place, everyone was concentrating on what was ahead, not what was behind? No, that can't have been it. Blacksnake must have some stealth tech we don't know about.

That stood to reason, they were a PMC that often did covert operations anyway. But how had Khanji managed to distract Verdigris long enough to get a force of *any* size put together, much less infiltrate them behind ECHO?

I must have been kidding myself when I thought Verdigris wasn't paying attention. I bet he is, but right now, he's figuring to let us and the Thulians butt heads, then cozy up to whoever starts to win. That would make perfect sense. *Except for Sera. He wanted Sera, and I doubt he's given up on getting her. Dominic Verdigris never gives up on what he wants.*

She wrenched her thoughts away, and concentrated on the images being projected in her vision by her implanted HUD. Blue Team was still on the move, still undetected, and still behind the main Thulian forces. Somehow Red Djinni was keeping them safe.

But all of the teams had been cut off from the portal now; she could see the concentration of red dots at that spot, and if the Thulians hadn't closed it down, they'd certainly booby-trapped it, or were waiting in ambush. If it was still open, maybe the SFO troops in reserve could—

Stop it. That's not your job now.

"Bella..."

The only reason she heard that thread of a whisper was because his mouth-mic picked it up. Bull was awake.

"Overwatch: Bull, private," she said quietly, shoving herself away from the table and taking a few unsteady steps towards the curtained-off section of the recovery tent where he'd been left. Lucky Bulwark; as the first casualty, he'd gotten the corner spot, where two of the walls of the inflated forward medical unit met. He'd have a tiny amount of privacy. "Gairdner, don't move. Don't even try, or I'll sedate you, if your conventional team doesn't beat me to it and do it first."

"Yes'm." This is what passed for humor with Bulwark. She wasn't sure whether to laugh or cry. At least he was feeling "good" enough in a relative sense to make a stab at humor.

"Did you playback yet?" she asked, hurrying past the airlock in the middle of the structure. Positive airflow kept the "building" inflated, and at the same time, would keep chemical or biological agents out. Probably....

It was surreal in here, all the empty cots, everything white or steel. Overhead was the inflated fabric of the "building" itself, also white, to let in the most light. Like a scene from a 1960s science fiction movie.

"*Yes.*" She was almost to his spot, easy to see by the curtains pulled shut around it.

"Good." She was through the curtains, eyes only for him, ignoring all the gear that was hooked up to him, quietly doing its monitoring. Everything was green, but she already knew that.

He still looked like hell, but Sovie had gotten the swelling down on his face somewhat. It only looked blue and puffy and his eyes weren't swollen shut anymore. No surprise, they were also so bloodshot, the whites were veined like marble. His eyes tracked her sensibly as she checked his chart, checked the IVs to make sure they matched the chart, then went down on her knees beside the cot and laid her hand as lightly as a feather on his. *Please, let me not have triggered something else. Please...*

"Got me...on the good drugs..." he rasped. *Good, then the pain isn't unbearable right now.*

"Well, you earned them," she retorted, after a quick check revealed nothing more going on than metahealing. Not quite Untermensch-level, but faster than she had dared hope. The relief nearly made her faint.

"Art's doing...all right." So, he was tracking the teams himself. She'd been biting her thumb most of the time, second-guessing Art of War, and not knowing if what she would have done would have been better, worse, or made no difference at all.

"So's Molotok," she replied. "Putting Djinni in charge of Blue seems to have worked out."

Bulwark's swollen lips twitched downward a little. "In spite..."

"You were right. I was wrong." *And it almost cost us everything.* "I am never going to countermand your..."

"Stop." Bull's hand stirred a little under hers. "Done. Over. She's...Red's problem now."

"Yes," she said, her heart alternately aching and rejoicing. "And now, you're mine."

Blue Team: Ultima Thule

In the open square surrounding one of the tall, dome-capped towers, five full squads of Thulian guards stood at attention, scanning their immediate perimeter for any sign of intruders. In the distance, sounds of combat raged throughout the city, though they had yet to see any of it. Orders were orders. Their tower could not be compromised and they were to defend it with their lives. Beside them, dozens of robotic wolves sat on their metallic haunches, still, but ready to leap into the fray with a single command. High overhead, the eagles continued to soar and act as aerial scouts. This part of city was secure, and with ample time to dig in, nothing short of a legion of invaders would unearth them from this spot.

So they were taken completely by surprise when three invaders emerged around a nearby building and were marched unceremoniously into the square, herded by a lone figure, at gunpoint. As one, the wolves came to their feet while each guardsman turned and raised an energy cannon in their direction. It was an impressive sight, and coupled with the synchronized sound of hydraulic legs and the heavy stomp of armored boots, along with the eerie hum of each cannon ramping up with deadly intention, it was intimidating enough to stop the three captives in their tracks. They looked hesitantly back at their captor.

"Did I say you could stop marching, ECHO *schwein*?" he snarled. "Into the tower with you! Our, how do you *schwach, erbärmlich Narren* say it, 'play date,' will have to wait. I must be elsewhere and see to our other unwanted guests."

From one of the Thulian's squads, one trooper detached himself from the ranks, motioned to two of the wolves, and approached the newcomers. He kept his cannon raised, and barked at them in German.

"*Unglaublich*," the captor muttered. "*Das trottel* . . . Does he honestly not recognize me?"

He stepped forward past his prisoners, glared at the Thulian, and let loose a blistering barrage of contempt in German, enough to give the Thulian pause and lower his cannon, slightly.

"Doppelgaenger?" The Thulian said, and looked down at the wolves. The wolves rose up, bared their teeth, and bathed the newcomers with a probing red light from their eyes. After a moment the light faded, they relaxed, and they turned to pad their way back to their place in the guard formation.

The lone Thulian watched them go and turned back to the stranger. Seemingly satisfied, he came to attention and saluted smartly.

"*Herr Doppelgaenger!*" he barked.

Doppelgaenger approached him slowly, his lips parting into a sadistic grin.

"Was hast du mich nennen?"

The Thulian faltered, bewildered, then snapped to attention again.

"Verzeihen Sie mir, Herr! Ich wollte sagen, Meister Doppelgaenger!"

"Besser," Doppelgaenger snarled. He pointed his rifle at his prisoners. *"Diese ECHO Abschaum sind meine Gefangenen, ich will..."*

"Excuse me," Mel said, interrupting. "Would y'all mind speaking English? If you're planning on just killing us here, least you could do is let us see it coming."

Doppelgaenger stiffened up, turned on his heel, marched quickly up to Mel and gave her a vicious backhand. Mel gasped, her head flying back, and spat blood. Silent Knight gave an angry cry and lunged forward, only to meet the barrel of Doppelgaenger's rifle firmly pressed into his neck. There followed a tense pause, but Doppelgaenger merely chuckled and let the rifle drop to his side.

"You are right, of course," he said. "Please, excuse my manners. I was just about to tell my subordinate here that I am taking you to the holding cells, until I have such time to deal with you properly. We seem to be in the midst of an assault on our fair city, if you haven't noticed, and I am needed elsewhere. But do not worry, I will make it a priority to see that you are personally and properly bled dry and gutted like the sub-humans you are."

He glanced back at the Thulians standing in formation, chose one at random and and gestured with a flick of his head.

"Du, da," Doppelgaenger barked. *"Diese drei sind unter meiner Kontrolle. Führe uns zu den Zellen."*

The Thulian stepped forward, gave a quick salute and marched back to the tower.

Doppelgaenger bowed to his captives with a grandiose wave of his hand. "After you, my honored playthings."

Mel glared at him, wiped the blood from her lips, and started after the dispatched Thulian guard. Knight and Scope fell into step behind her. Doppelgaenger trained his rifle on them again, and whistled a jaunty marching tune as he brought up the rear. Ahead, the guard had already opened the gate and was waiting in small antechamber inside. Once they had all entered, the guard keyed in a passcode and signaled the heavy door to close behind them.

That's when they jumped him.

The guard screamed as Knight barreled into him. Not that it

did any good; no sound escaped from his lips, or from anywhere at all, as the armored man's suit absorbed it all. They fell to the floor, grappling, when the guard noticed the muzzle of a heavy revolver just inches from his face. Scope's expression was dispassionate and cold as she squeezed off a few rounds point-blank in complete silence. The bullets pierced the thin mesh just under the nose guard and bounced around inside the otherwise impervious helmet. The Thulian's body stiffened up, then relaxed as Knight released his grip and picked himself up off the floor. He looked about, gave the thumbs-up, and turned off his sonic dampening so they could speak normally.

"I can't believe that worked," Scope said, shaking her head.

"I admit, I got a little worried when those wolves started probing us," Doppelgaenger shrugged. "Wonder what that was about...?" He turned away, took a deep breath and grunted as he shed his face. Scope reached into her sack and threw him a long, red scarf. The Djinni reached out, caught it blindly, and wrapped it around his head.

"That's better," he said, turning back to them. "That's not a face I want to wear any longer than I have to."

"You wore him well," Mel said in congratulations. "Well enough to convince those goons, anyway."

"I've seen him in front of his men," Red offered. "He's not much more than bluster and snarls to them. He saves the poetry for his enemies, not to mention the true depths of his sadism." He swore, reminded of something. "Listen, Mel, about that slap..."

"It was a good touch," Mel interrupted, smiling. "I mean, not a *good* touch, *cher*, and we both know just how good you can be..."

"Get a darn room," Knight muttered.

"... but it worked," Mel finished. "I think it got us where we needed to be."

"We're not there yet," Red disagreed. "We need a new reading."

Mel nodded and pulled out the scanner. She studied it for a moment, and smiled. "Confirmation," she crowed. "Two hundred feet, give or take, right below us."

Red looked up. Of course, all he saw was the ceiling, but it didn't take any imagination for the rest of them to know he was thinking of that mushroom shape up there. "So...the generator is down under us, but the operational end is up there...field projector?"

He looked back down and straight at Silent Knight, who was

the closest thing they had to a techie. "Seems likely," Knight agreed in his synthesized voice. "But why not ask—"

"Vix!" Red interrupted, slapping his head. "Overwatch: open—"

"*Never left you, bonehead. Nice job with the impersonation. Sec while I make all of your sensors do what I never intended them to do. . . .*" Red could have sworn he heard the tapping of keys . . . tapping that sounded far too fast to be strictly human. "*Roger that. It's . . . and this is kinda unnerving . . . a variation on the Tesla energy projector. So, yeah, my guess is these towers are doing two things, powering everything in the city and powering the field generator up above. Since there's a ring of these, they gotta be working together. Take one down, the whole shield'll fall apart. Exactly as you said, Red; they form a keystone, and the shield cascades from that. I take back the bonehead part.*"

"Let's go then," the Djinni said. "Double-time. Our guys are fighting for their lives out there, so we're going to need to throw the sneaky playbook out and up the risk factor here for speed. We might meet resistance. If it moves and isn't us, take it out. Knight, make with the quiet."

Silent Knight nodded, and together they moved deeper into the tower, weapons drawn. From the antechamber, they found their way into a short corridor lined with recessed doors. Red noted the banners above each, shook his head and motioned them forward until they arrived at a solid security portal at the end. He studied the console for a moment. With a grimace, he shook one hand free from a glove, sprouted his claws and pried the console face loose from the wall. He noted the tangle of wires beneath, selected a few seemingly at random and neatly snipped them with his fingertips. He was rewarded with an small shower of sparks, and then darkness as all the lights in the hallway powered down. One by one, they lit up their shoulder-mounted flashlights—tiny, but ridiculously powerful LEDs—and went to work. Red reached into his satchel and pulled out a number of small, sticky rubber spheres. He handed them to Scope, who pressed them in place at regular intervals along the edge of the door while Mel emptied the contents from her hip sack over the floor. Red threw a detonator to Knight and they retreated back, finding cover in the door recesses that lined the hallway.

A countdown flared up in their HUDs, and they braced for detonation.

Each silent explosion fired off in turn, a series of sharp flares of light accompanied by the vibration underfoot of broken steel pistons as the door supports shattered and collapsed. They emerged in time to see the security door collapse inward and a squad of Kriegers rush out towards them, weapons drawn. The Thulians opened fire and Red ducked back behind cover, barely dodging a lethal blast from an energy cannon. Pinned down, he looked across the narrow hall to see Mel, also pressed back against a door. She held up her hand, flashed him a grin, and pressed down firmly on her own detonator.

The Kriegers, eager to press their advantage, didn't notice the tiny red LEDs that sprang to life under their feet, not until they were engulfed by sudden jets of fire, goo and plasma that shot up from the floor beneath them.

"*Thank you, Dominic Verdigris,*" Red heard Vix mutter under her breath.

As one, Red Djinni's infiltrators flew out from their nests and riddled their foes with bullets. The Krieger armor, suddenly caked with ECHO incendiary gel and superheated to a fragile state, cracked and shattered under the rain of gunfire. Confused and silently screaming, they succumbed to the onslaught and fell in place, charred, smoking and bleeding out.

Red's squad rushed forward, pausing only to plug a few rounds definitively into the head of each Krieger, and dashed to the inner well of the tower. They arrived at a well-lit, open shaft, ringed with grated walkways and a circular staircase leading down around an enormous pillar of steel. Extinguishing their shoulder LEDs, they raced down the stairs, with only a few stops to scan for opposition, above or below. When they reached the bottom, they hesitated and peered cautiously through an open security door. The remaining guards, in their haste, had left the portal open, and as Red's group entered a cavernous chamber they were met with near-blinding light from beneath them. They found themselves on another grated, circular walk-way, with open stairs spiraling down the outer walls of a large, bulbous room. In the center, an enormous Tesla generator rose up and disappeared into the steel pillar lining the open shaft. Red motioned to Knight, who nodded and turned off his noise dampener, releasing the crackle and electrical hum of the Tesla generator. They peered down into the room. Aside from the coil and a few large monitoring instruments, the chamber appeared to be empty.

"Clear," Red said with satisfaction. "Overwatch, we are at target. Ladies, let's get those bombs set."

Mel and Scope nodded and raced down the stairs to the chamber floor while Red and Silent Knight stood guard at the door. Mel ran ahead and began planting explosives around the base of the Tesla coil, while Scope struggled to remove the detonators from her rucksack. She knelt down to set the first, and cursed as the display scolded her with an error message. Frowning, she tried another detonator, but was met with the same error message. Her expression turned to panic as she removed yet another detonator, then another, only to be met with that accursed error message. She scooped the detonators up and went down the line of explosives. None of the bomb connections registered correctly.

"Djinni!" Scope yelled, as Mel ran over to check her work. "We got a problem!"

"Of course we do!" Red snarled as he leaned over the railing above them. "God forbid things ever go smoothly with this outfit!"

"The detonators aren't registering!" Scope cried. "They're all reading connection errors!"

"What, did you get the contacts dirty?" Red asked.

"Of course not!"

"Your pack's been clanking ever since we left base camp!" Red scolded her. "You should have secured them better; we haven't been out for a gentle stroll, y'know. They probably got messed up in transit."

"A little jostling wouldn't have done this, Red, and you know it!" Scope shouted.

"She's right," Mel said. "This shouldn't be happening."

"Then what's causing it?" Red demanded.

"*I don't know!*" Scope screamed. "*And we really don't have time to suss it out!*"

"We're going to have to make time," Red replied, grimly. "Unless we get the timers going, there's no way to get them to blow in sync unless it's manually."

"Even that's a long shot, Red," Mel warned. "If you're off by even a millisecond, you risk only partial detonation. Might not be enough to bring this baby down."

"I know," the Djinni said. "I'm open to other..."

"There's someone moving up there," Silent Knight interrupted from the door. "I'm seeing shadows milling around at the top."

"Oh, perfect," Djinni muttered as he joined the armored man. He snuck a peek up the shaft. Sure enough, he caught a glimpse of armored Kriegers at the top, heard a few shouts of alarm, and the telltale echo of clattering boots slamming down on the grated staircase. Slowly, he crept out into the open shaft to get a better look, doing his best to keep hidden under the circular stairs.

"Can't get a decent count," he hissed. "More than one, can't be more than ten."

Knight joined him and extended a hand out towards the center of the shaft. After a moment, he shook his armored head regretfully. "We're too far away," he whispered. "My readings can't make out how many footsteps, sorry."

"Too much interference from the generator," Mel agreed as she slipped in behind them, her scanner in hand. "They're moving together, can't pick out the individual energy signatures."

"There's only two of them."

Red Djinni turned. Scope stood in the doorway, her features almost indiscernible as the bright light of the chamber at her back cast the rest of her in shadow. She glanced up again, nodded in confirmation, and looked back at Red. She sighed, and her shoulders sagged a bit as she stepped back through the portal.

"Scope, what are you...?"

"I'll give you fifteen minutes," she said. "Fifteen minutes to fight your way out. After that, I'm going to blow it."

"Don't be an idiot," Red snarled. "We can..."

"No," she interrupted. "This has to happen, and now. There's too much at stake. Our guys are being picked off up there without the cavalry. There's enough on my head already, it's time to get this assault moving." She sighed again, then straightened up. "What's Bull always say? *Rise up.* Tell him for me, won't you? Tell him I'm sorry. Tell him I know what a colossal screw-up I've been. Tell him what I did. I think he'd want to know."

And before Red could say another word, Scope reached for the door and slammed it shut. The security panel lit up, and a stream of red LEDs flashed before turning a bright, steady green.

"Scope!" Red hissed. "Scope, open that goddamn door and you..."

She appeared at a small eye slit in the door. She blinked slowly, and appeared utterly calm.

"Fifteen minutes," she repeated. "You'd better get moving."

And then she was gone.

Red Team: Ultima Thule

With Blacksnake acting as support, Red Team was starting to make real progress. They had continued to encounter Krieger resistance, but with the added firepower from the private contractors the team was able to push through. Blacksnake had their own version of the CCCP/ECHO incendiary rounds; theirs required two separate shells, each containing a different gel-like substance. The Blacksnake versions were just as effective, though it was tricky getting the two shells to hit at nearly the same place. Several of the other teams had already linked up, including some of the SOF groups. Despite the breathing room bought by Blacksnake taking over and then taking out the strange Thulian artillery, there had been multiple casualties suffered on several of the teams. No names were mentioned, but John Murdock didn't like the tones he was hearing over the comm. *Can't focus on that now. We gotta drive on.*

They were about four blocks away from the main contingent of meta teams when the ambush came. The Kriegers had found some way to be partially shielded from the eyes overhead; they didn't show up on the HUDs until they sprang from their ambush positions to attack. Three Blacksnake operatives were instantly taken out by energy blasts. Immediately the mercs and Red Team scattered, assaulting through the ambush positions on the sides of the street; the Kriegers, all unarmored, fell quickly. Molotok, who was in the lead, took a burst of machine-gun fire to the chest. Confused and staggered for only a moment, he raised his rifle and shot the offending Krieger dead, causing him to fall from a roof onto the street before.

"What was that? I thought Kriegers only were using energy weapons?" He rubbed his chest, noting the holes the bullets and their splatter had ripped in his load-bearing equipment; otherwise, due to his resiliency and the nanoweave shirt he was wearing, he was unharmed.

Unter, peeking his head around the corner where the team

had formed up, looked at the body of the dead Krieger, then grunted. "MP40. Before your time, *tovarisch*, but I became... well acquainted with it. Must being an antique."

Bear clicked his tongue, firing off a burst from his PPSh. "Inferior *fascista* garbage. Still no match for superior Soviet persuader. They used to try to capture these from the battlefield, recognizing—"

"*Be quiet, Old Bear,*" came a chorus, not only from the CCCP comrades, but from three or four of the Blacksnake who were near enough both to hear Bear begin and to have picked up on the phrase by now.

Molotok threw a grenade, waiting for the explosion and attendant Krieger shouts before he called into Overwatch. "Open: Khanjar. Khanjar, what is your disposition?"

Vix had seamlessly integrated the Blacksnake comm with the Overwatch system. "*Other side of the street. We have a total of three down, two injured. Trooper armor is advancing down the street.*" John saw four Blacksnake mercs suddenly emerge from side alleys, shouldering RPGs, aiming, and firing in quick succession. "*Correction. Trooper armor neutralized. Resistance should fold shortly.*" He had to give the Blacksnake operatives their due. They were good.

Khanjar, however, was a cut above. With the trooper armor down, she rushed a Thulian position; three of them were crouched behind a fallen column of that same marble-like substance, where they had been taking potshots at the Red Team's side of the street. Efficiently, she vaulted over the cover the Kriegers had been using, landing among them in a low crouch. Before any of them could react with more than a gasp, she started to punch them in some sort of martial arts form he didn't recognize; it reminded John of Untermensch fighting, the way that bones gave way with every impact. Her style was very circular, and she did something he had never seen anyone do quite this way before, she actually *dove* past her opponents several times, landed in a somersault, and came up fighting. The last Krieger she actually *stabbed* in the chest with her bare hand; the Thulian shrieked once as he died, slipping off of her hand. She shook the gore off of it, then motioned for the rest of her operatives to move up.

"*Got more incoming, check your HUDs. Most from city center, some are between you and the rest of the teams. Seem to be trying to keep you from hooking up.*" John saw on his HUD that Vickie was right; two fairly large groups of Kriegers were homing in on their position. *"They know exactly where you are. Probably got the city wired up with cams we can't see, or it's the Robo-Eagles, or both."* John saw several of the Robo-Eagles wheeling in the sky overhead, and half-thought about blasting one of them; not enough value for the kill, seeing as it would be like turning on a spotlight, highlighting their position.

During the pause in the fighting, the Blacksnake operatives recovered their dead and wounded. John figured that they'd have to dig in for the moment, take care of the oncoming Kriegers, and then try to link up with the other teams, or have the teams link up with them. He trusted in Vickie and the commanders back at the base to make the right call; his job right now was to be a trigger-puller and fire-chucker. Molotok and Khanjar went about getting everyone set up in defensive positions; several Black-snake squads were put on the rooftops, especially those armed with the RPGs with specialty warheads. Red Team's job—along with Khanjar and a couple of squads of mercs—would be on the ground, providing a base of fire. *Also means we'll be taking the brunt of the attack.* John decided to check on Bear and Mamona; both of them had had a rough time during this mission so far. Mamona was fine for the most part; a little shaken up from her injuries and getting pinned by the artillery, but she was keeping it together. Bear ... looked ragged. He actually pushed away a proffered flask, his face gone pale and his eyes tired.

John looked up from his survey of the team feeling grim about Bear's chances—then caught Sera's gaze. He felt something unspo-ken pass between them and bind them together again, suddenly heard *that music* well up gently in his mind. A great calm came over him, and he found himself moving towards Bear, as Sera mirrored his every step coming from the other direction. They met at the old man, who looked up at them, startled.

"Shto—" Bear began, but they had eyes only for each other. Still moving in mirror-fashion, and as if in a kind of dream, with the music swelling inside him, John rested his left hand on Bear's right shoulder. And an instant later, Sera placed her right hand atop his. Then they matched their free hands, palm to palm, his right facing her left. He felt the need to concentrate, and closed his eyes, the better to do so, aware as he did so that she was doing the same.

Then he felt a jolt of—something—pass from them to Bear. The music faded.

He opened his eyes, stepping back, hands falling away from Sera's, glancing down at Bear.

Bear looked, if not like a new man, certainly a revived one. There was color in his face again, and when Unter, looking a little rattled, absently held out the flask, Bear seized it and drained it. His plasma chamber was still barely visible, obviously still drained, but he seemed to have been somewhat invigorated.

"Next time am having hung over, will be calling you two."

"On yer feet, Pavel. We've got some more Nazis for you to cuss out." John and Unter both helped the old Soviet to his feet, steadying him for a moment.

"I will destroy many of them!" Bear declared, grandly waving in the general direction of the enemy.

Unter waved a hand under his nose. "Perhaps you only need breathe on them, Old Bear."

"Get into positions; they are coming." Molotok didn't need to say anything more; the rest of the team found where they should be, preparing for the oncoming Thulians. The Blacksnake teams and Red Team were all relatively well concealed, behind good cover. The Kriegers knew what area they were in, but hopefully didn't have pinpoint positions nailed down. If they could just get the Kriegers drawn in a little before the opening shots of the attack, they had a chance of throwing them into disarray, maybe even breaking the back of the attackers enough so that they could link up with the other infiltration teams.

"*Contact, front. Scouting element.*" A less-natural voice, probably because of electronic scrambling and de-scrambling. That was one of the Blacksnake operatives. Using one of the connected camera views from one of Vickie's technomagical "eyes," John had a bird's-eye view of the oncoming force without having to risk breaking cover. He saw three unarmored Kriegers, moving quickly and low, come around the corner of a building at the end of the street. They used hand signals, advancing forward in bounds. *They're gettin' cautious.* Once they had surveyed the street, they signaled for the rest of the force to start moving up. It was comprised mostly of armored troopers, with flanking elements of unarmored Kriegers moving parallel via alleys and side streets. The second force, the one between the team and their comrades, was almost completely made up of trooper armor; they couldn't maneuver through the alleys, so they stayed on the main street, slowly advancing.

Molotok waited until the bulk of the trooper armor was in the street, with most of them past the furthest Blacksnake team on the rooftops.

"Now. Rooftop teams, engage at will."

"*Roof. Engage.*" That was a female voice; probably—no, without a doubt—Khanjar, confirming the order.

From both sides of the street contrails from rockets streaked down into the back of the Krieger formation. Two troopers were taken out instantly, and messily. The rest initially were caught by surprise, but soon started firing at the edges of the rooftops from where the offending RPGs came from.

"Ground team, fire now!" "*Engage all.*" Khanjar's order overran the second half of Moji's.

John leaned around the corner, judged the distance and the spread of the Kriegers, then released a lethal blast of fire. The stream of fire impacted one of the lead troopers at the center of their formation; from there, it blossomed, spreading until it had engulfed most of the powered armor. He was immediately answered by a hail of Thulian energy cannon fire, ducking out of the way at the last second before chunks of the corner he was taking cover behind disappeared in a wash of actinic energy. The rest of the team and the Blacksnake mercs all began the main body of gunfire, targeting individual trooper armor while they were still out in the open. Several more fell, but the Kriegers had begun to take cover, firing and moving. John held back in cover a moment; for this little while, there was nothing he could do.

"Love...I want to try something. Make a little flame in your hand for me?" Sera huddled up against his side, as he let the others lay down a withering barrage of fire. John, moving his rifle out of the way, held up his right hand, palm up, and ignited a small sphere of flame. Sera gingerly moved her finger near it... then into it. John started, his jaw dropping, thinking he was about to burn her. Her face lit up with a smile. "Your fires do not harm me any more than my own do!" she exclaimed. "We can use this, I think. At the least, you need not be concerned about striking me."

John grinned, then nodded. "Let's wait for the right moment. Don't want to blow our shot with the trick until we need to."

He and Sera rejoined their comrades, John alternately blasting troopers with his fires or shooting them with his rifle, while Sera was occupied with manifesting and throwing her fire spears with deadly accuracy. The Kriegers had taken some losses, but they were starting to coordinate better. One of the rooftop RPG teams, followed shortly by another, were killed when the Kriegers began to lob grenades onto the rooftops; the grenades would land, going off not with an explosion, but a sphere of Thulian energy. Nearly anything within its blast radius would be reduced to dust and vapor.

"Second group, advancing on right flank!" That was Untermensch, shouting over the gunfire and explosions. This group was almost entirely trooper armor. They reached the junction between the street the team was on and the one they had been traveling along, oriented to the teams, and began firing immediately. One of the Blacksnake teams on the ground was blindsided, a withering volley of energy blasts cutting down all but one of the operatives. John whirled around to face the new enemy; he could tell that Sera was already moving, anticipating what he was going to do. Again, the music faded into the back of his mind, and all his senses became keener, sharper. He thought he knew that music, now—what it was. But there was no time to think about it. Concentrating, visualizing what he wanted to happen, he willed fire into his hands, then immediately raised his arms, the flames shooting out to meet the Kriegers.

John felt everything happening in a double-vision, seeing it and also *seeing it before;* it was like a form of instant déjà vu, intense and almost perfect. Sera dashed from cover, causing some of the rest of the squad to shout or gasp as she ran in front of John's hands, disappearing within the torrent of fire. The front wave of the flames had crashed into the first troopers, heating their armor and obscuring their vision. They continued firing as their allies behind them found cover to the sides of the street, not daring to venture into the inferno.

And then, though it was difficult to see through the fire, *something* began cutting the Kriegers down. John knew what it was, though. That *something* was Sera, whirling and dancing within his fires and her own, her firesword nothing but a deadly flicker among the greater flames, until the last of the Thulians toppled to the pavement. Then *something* almost too bright to see flashed up and into the air out of the inferno, flames trailing it.

And Sera landed, breathless, behind him. John shut off his fires all at once, the last wisps of flame dissipating into the air. With no small amount of satisfaction, he noticed that the remaining Kriegers were visibly unnerved when they saw the front ranks of trooper armor had been both burned and cut to smoking pieces. Two troopers actually tried to plod away, and were shot in the back by what John figured was a commanding officer. Concentrating, he fired off a plasma blast, hitting the leader in the back of the head and killing him instantly. The rest of the troopers tried to regain their composure, returning fire, but John could tell their hearts weren't into it. Their shots were wild, panicked, with only a few coming close to John's cover. Several other Kriegers retreated, not even bothering to shoot; no one stopped them.

"*Borzhe moi,*" Molotok breathed. "When are you learning to do *that?*"

"Just now," Sera said, still catching her breath. "I do not believe that they will fall for our trick again so easily, however."

"Well, be coming up with more. The *fascista* are giving us many problems." An explosion, followed by screams, punctuated his words. The Kriegers, despite taking heavy losses, were still advancing from the city square. The Blacksnake mercs and Red Team were making them pay for every inch, but that didn't change the fact that they were an isolated group fighting against what amounted to an army.

"*Red Team Leader, do you read me?*" That was Khanjar; John couldn't see where she was, and he had other things to worry about at the moment. Spotting a group of unarmored Kriegers coming out from an alley across from their position, John charged his fires and blasted the entire group, sending them to the ground flaming.

"This is Red Team Leader," Molotok said, pausing to aim his rifle and fire a burst into the chest of a trooper that had been weakened by an RPG. "Go ahead."

"*Position is untenable. We have multiple casualties, and the enemy is still advancing. Advising that we make a push for the other teams, or withdraw.*"

"Check your HUDs. Pullback is a big no-can-do," Vix replied, before Molotok could. *"You're being rear-flanked. Exit's about to be cut off. The other teams are still bogged down, so you're on your own for now."*

Molotok uttered a long string of expletives in Russian. "Copy, Overwatch. Khanjar; we will have to be regrouping and making push for other teams. Only option. Prepare to join our position. We will provide covering fire." He turned to the rest of the team. "This will be getting messy."

Red Team: Generator Tower

"Do you really think she can do it?" Knight asked.

"She's not leaving us with much choice but to trust her reflexes," Mel said. "We don't have time to figure a way past this door. We already used most of our security countermeasures upstairs."

Above them, the sound of footsteps were growing louder.

"And there's that too," she said. "We're going to have company pretty soon now."

"Damn her," Red cursed. "All right, she made the call. We're going to have to play it out. Only two, we might be able to take on two. But not if they know we're coming. Those damn energy cannons might pick us off at a distance, and if they're smart they would just destroy the staircase around us. We need a distraction from up top. Knight, can you throw sound?"

Silent Knight shook his head. "No, I just channel it in concentrated beams. I can make a ruckus above them, but they'll see the blast and know it came from down here."

"So much for that," Red muttered, and snuck another peek up the shaft. They had descended about halfway. At least their descent had slowed. As they neared the bottom, they were being more cautious. "Mel, got any ideas?"

She didn't answer. She appeared to be lost in thought.

"Mel?" Red nudged her.

"What? Oh, sorry," she apologized. She reached into her pocket, and withdrew her remaining incendiary mini-bombs. She passed them to Red. "If you're going to get in close, you'll need these, the last of the fire-bangs. We don't have the luxury of an ambush this time, so forget the fancier settings. Just press here to set them to explode, then here to activate the magnet and countdown. If you plant it right, you'll get a nice searing detonation right on their armor. Try not to get any on you."

"Still have to get in close, though." Red frowned. "I suppose we could try the Doppelgaenger disguise again. It'll be tight though, dunno if I can grow it in time, or what our cover story's going to be. We left a lot of dead Kriegers up there to explain our way out of this."

"No, too risky," Mel agreed. She bit her lip in indecision. "Risky...oh Lord, I don't know if I'm ready to try something this big. It hurts to even think about it."

"What are you talking about?" Red asked.

"Something I've been working on," Mel sighed. "Something I lost before."

"Since when do you make with the cryptic?" Djinni asked. "If you've got something, share with the class, please."

She rewarded him with a soft chuckle. Reaching out, she caressed his face through his thick scarf. "Do you trust me?" she asked.

Red Djinni stared at her. Did he trust her? In the short time they had been together, Red found he had been relying on her more and more. What had begun simply as two lonely people finding solace together in bed had grown into . . . into what, exactly? He had shared more with her than anyone, even Victrix and Bulwark, ever since he had joined ECHO. When he needed support, comfort or just a steady someone to bounce ideas off of, his first instinct was now to go to her. She had a way of cutting through the emotional baggage that could cloud anyone's judgment and get to the heart of the matter. What was important? Looking past pride and fear, past the mundane day-to-day trivialities that seemed to have a chokehold on most people, Mel's outlook on life had a way of bringing clarity to all of Red's insecurities. The lady had obviously seen a lot in her time, had suffered through most of it, but she was still here, still kicking, still *fighting*. She was a part of him now and if he didn't have her, he simply didn't know what he would do.

"Do I trust you?" the Djinni said, and marveled as he was struck with the answer. "Yeah, I do."

"Then maybe that'll be enough," she said as she gazed upwards. "Haven't really been myself lately. Haven't been able to get things to work right. Maybe all I needed was you. Maybe that's all I've ever needed."

She took a breath, held it, and exhaled slowly. Above them, the sounds of footsteps stopped and were replaced by surprised cries of alarm, followed by a barrage of energy-cannon fire. Red and Knight exchanged a surprised look and peeked out to witness an impossible sight. High above them, at the very top, ECHO forces came streaming into the open shaft and began thundering down the stairs. The descending Kriegers had thrown themselves against the wall, their cannons trained upwards, trying their best to snipe the ECHO troops as they came into view without destroying the stairs, their only exit from what was essentially a very deep, smooth pit. The first few shots seemed to find their mark, felling the ECHO soldiers in place. One soldier screamed as the blast evaporated half of his chest. He fell over the railing and plummeted straight down the shaft, past the startled Kriegers, only to fade out of existence before hitting the bottom.

"I'll be damned," Red breathed. "You got your illusions back!"

"For a while, actually," Mel grunted, as beads of perspiration began to form on her brow. "Only small stuff, so I kept it quiet. Haven't tried anything quite this...big yet. You better get moving. Don't know how long I can keep this going."

"What are you talking about, I'm not leaving you down..."

"Go!" Mel hissed, her eyes locked on her illusion high above. "You and Knight, close the distance before they realize we're here, before they figure out they're shooting at figments of my imagination! I can't move with you and concentrate. I'll follow when you take them out. Go!"

Red hesitated, and clutched her hand. "You start climbing the minute, the *minute*, it's clear. You got it?"

She nodded, but kept her eyes firmly set on the combat above. Red let go of her hand, and turned to Silent Knight.

"You ready?" he asked. The armored man nodded as Red pulled off his gloves, and then his nanoweave shirt, exposing his arms and torso.

"Then let's make this quick," Red grunted, and sprouted his claws.

With his sonic dampeners at full power, Knight followed the Djinni as they dashed up the stairs. Red kept his eyes firmly set on the Kriegers, trusting his radial awareness to lead him to sure footing on the treacherous stairway. Mel's illusion was keeping them busy, and more importantly, focusing their attention up at the top of the open shaft. Her phantom ECHO warriors screamed at each other, and kept out of line of sight of the Kriegers and their deadly energy cannons, firing the occasional blind shot over the railing. They appeared to be pinned down, but their cover fire managed to hold the Kriegers' interest. At full speed, Red and Silent Knight closed the distance in seconds, and they fell upon the first Krieger before he could even register their presence.

Knight put on a burst of speed and hit the Thulian low around the knees, knocking him to the ground. The guard fell in surprise, his legs swept out from under him. Before he could raise his arm cannon, Red leapt over Knight and came down on the Krieger's helmet. The Djinni reared back, noting a thin cleft where the nose guard met the helmet's visor, and struck. His claws tore through the slim opening, and he fought down a surge of revulsion as his fingertips tore through bone, flesh and gray matter.

The other Krieger, noting the sudden silence, looked back at them and staggered back in alarm. Red ripped his claws loose from the now limp Thulian guard, and as he shot forward he heard a buzzing crescendo behind him as Knight ceased his noise dampening and ramped up his sonic blast. The second Thulian was now clearly audible, spewing curses as he too raised his energy cannon and leveled a blast directly at Red's heart.

With a shout, Knight battered Red to the side with his free hand and caught the energy blast high on his shoulder as his own sonic discharge slammed into the guard, throwing the Krieger back against the wall, where he bounced with a clatter of metal against stone and fell to his knees on the narrow stairway.

Red caught himself against the wall, righted himself, and continued his advance, risking a quick look back at Silent Knight. The big man had fallen backwards, exposed circuitry sizzling and spewing out sparks from his damaged shoulder. He flailed like a turtle on its back, but at least he was moving. He waved Red on, struggling to remove his more traditional ECHO sidearm from its holster at his side. Red flew forward, pressing his advantage, but the Krieger had recovered from Knight's concussive bolt and was ready for him. Despite the bulk of his armor, the Thulian proved nimble and moved with surprising speed. He deflected Red's attack with a quick sweep of his cannon arm, and countered with a brutal jab that caught the Djinni a solid blow to the stomach. Red grunted, fell back a moment, and groaned as he felt a building pain in his abdomen.

Oh man, that's really going to hurt in a minute...

It had been a mistake to assume all the armored Kriegers had traded agility for near invulnerability. Apparently, it was still possible to dodge and weave while wearing all that metal. For the most part, they didn't need to. Their energy cannons were enough to take down most opposition from a distance. And the energy cannon was still Red's biggest concern, so he advanced again, albeit warily, and struggled with the concept of keeping close enough to prevent the guard from simply gunning him down and somehow getting through his defenses with his bare hands.

He opted for misdirection. He led with his right, which was immediately parried by the guard's cannon arm, and followed with a piercing strike with his left hand claws with unerring precision at the cleft in the Thulian's nosepiece. The Thulian deflected the blow with a contemptuous head bob, let the claws deflect down and away from his face and immediately caught Red's wrist with his free hand. He turned, twisting Red's arm, and the Djinni was forced to follow with a sideways somersault or risk the Krieger simply snapping the bones in his forearm. Red landed on his feet and flailed instinctively at the armored hand that held his wrist in a vice-like grip. The Krieger howled in pain as Red's claws pierced their way through the flexible fabric at the wrist, and let the Djinni go.

Got 'im, he's not going to be grabbing me any time soon. Still, he's damn quick, and if I'm not careful he can still bash me to death...

Red cursed as he leapt back, dodging two massive overhand strikes. The Krieger had apparently read his mind, accepting his obvious advantages of strength and a near-impervious shell, opting to simply crush his foe with his arms. He raised his arms again, his murderous intentions clear, when a few rounds from Knight's sidearm ricocheted harmlessly off his torso. Red looked back. Silent Knight held the gun with a shaky hand. Now sitting upright, his whole body actually twitched, and it was clear that the damage to his suit was more severe than Red had previously thought. Knight tried to come to his feet, but his arm jerked again, one knee buckled at the joint, and he fell with a clatter to his side.

The Thulian watched Knight thrash and struggle, and leveled the barrel of his cannon at Silent Knight's head.

"Hello!" Red snarled, knocking the cannon to the side. The deflected energy blast tore away at the guardrail, leaving an enormous gap. Red slapped at the side of the Krieger's helmet. "Rude!" he mocked. "You've already got a dance partner! Dance with the one that brung you, moron!"

That drew the Krieger's attention away from Silent Knight. Red was still too close for the Krieger to use his arm cannon as a blasting weapon...but not too close for him to use it as a club. Red ducked under the first swing, but couldn't dodge the second; he managed to catch it on the shoulder instead of his head, but it still hurt like hell, and the follow-up to his ribs wasn't any better. Red backed down a couple of steps, taking him out of range of a third blow, then went for broke.

He made a diving tackle at the Krieger; the Thulian dodged it easily, but Red had been expecting that. He shot past, his hands already up in front of him. As soon as they touched the wall, Red folded his body up, turning his head to spot the Krieger; shoving with all of his might, he sprung from the wall. His legs hit the Krieger in the lower back before he was even fully extended, throwing his entire body weight and as much strength as he could muster into the blow.

It worked. The Thulian's legs buckled, he overbalanced, and went through the missing section of the guardrail into the pit.

The momentum *also* drove Red over the side of the stairs, but he managed to grab the broken railing with both hands—

—at about the same time that he felt an armored hand clamp down on his leg.

"Well, that's just great!" Red hissed, his hands struggling to keep a grip on the walkway. He glanced down, and saw the Krieger holding onto him for dear life with his injured hand, blood now flowing freely from the tear Red had made with his claws. The other hand, fully enveloped in the cannon's chassis, was a blunt instrument, lacking even simple articulation necessary to maintain a grip. The Krieger looked around, and flinched when he noticed the drop, easily a hundred feet to the bottom of the shaft. Desperately, he began to rock back and forth...

"Oh, no you don't!" Red snarled, and fought the Krieger's movements by flailing his legs. The Krieger screamed, his grip on Red's leg slipping as pain erupted in his slashed wrist. *"Wenn Sie nur schwingen für die Treppe zu denken, werde ich gehen lassen."*

The Thulian looked up, growling.

"*Du bluffst.*"

"No bluff," Red croaked. He took a deep breath, and let his right hand fall away from the walkway. He gasped as he tightened his grip with his left, stifling a scream as the weight of both of them threatened to tear his arm from its socket. He held his right arm tight against his chest, his fingers gripping his scarf as a child might clutch a security blanket. He glared down at the Krieger defiantly. "Your move, shithead."

"*Bist du verrückt?*" the Thulian demanded, his body now still, his visor locked in horror on Red's furious eyes.

Despite the pain, and the brutal strain of keeping his fingers locked on the metal walkway, Red erupted in shaky laughter.

"Seriously, I have to get that printed on some business cards..." he chuckled.

"*Genug. Sehr gut. Dann sterben wir beide.*" the Krieger said, raising his cannon.

Red stopped laughing, and pulled his free hand away from the folds of his scarf, now clutching one of Mel's blinking incendiary bombs. He flicked his wrist and let the button-sized explosive drop and latch onto the Krieger's helmet with a magnetic hum. The guard hissed in surprise, and shouted in alarm as he realized what Red had done. He raised his cannon higher, leveling it at the Djinni's chest. Red saw a blue light begin to glow down the length of the barrel and heard a dull voltaic whine as the cannon ramped up.

He kicked at the gun, in reflex, as the bomb detonated in a flash of light and an eruption of condensed plasma.

The Krieger was killed instantly as his face seemed to simply implode, his grip on Red's leg falling away and his cannon, knocked away by Red's boot, discharging its payload into the wall. He didn't even have the opportunity to scream. So Red screamed instead as searing hot plasma splashed onto his legs, immediately burning away several layers of skin and gouging divots into his flesh. The Krieger's lifeless, smoking body flew back with tremendous force from the cannon blast, shot down the pit and collided with the fragile stairwell, neatly shearing an entire section of the stairs from the wall. Together, the Krieger and a good thirty feet of the stairway fell the remainder of the shaft to the bottom...

...where they had left Mel.

"Mel, take cover!" Red screamed.

She didn't answer, and before Red could shout again, the bottom of the shaft erupted in an enormous flash of light and the ear-splitting boom of an explosion. Red averted his eyes, and when he opened them he saw the base of the pit now awash in flames and thick black smoke starting to climb up the pit towards them.

"Mel!" Red screamed.

Red Team: Ultima Thule

Red Team had lost all but two of the Blacksnake RPG teams after the Kriegers had made a renewed push to isolate them. The last two RPG teams were pinned down, unable to effectively employ their munitions—unless they wanted to die, that is. Untermensch was down; a grenade that had been armed by one of the Black-snake operatives, who had died mid-throw after his head was taken off by an energy blast, had rolled next to Red Team's position. Untermensch had been the first to spot the danger; he had shoved Mamona behind him, then took nearly the entire blast to his body, shielding his comrades. At first glance he looked like he was dead; the nanoweave had stopped some of the fragments, but not all of them. Blood flowed from the holes in his uniform, and his face was in tatters. A quick check for his pulse revealed that he was in fact *not* dead; his visible wounds were already starting to close, his healing factor kicking in. Since the Kriegers were too far down the street for her powers to affect them, Mamona was put in charge of guarding Georgi and checking on his status.

Bear was no longer cursing or laughing, only firing his PPSh in short bursts or throwing a grenade. Molotok was similarly grim. Their advance had stalled. And there were more and more Kriegers piling in to take their lives.

"Khanjar. Molotok. Get your teams in under the spot I've high-lighted. Move, now!" The "spot" Vix had highlighted was a building that had had its front facade blown off, but was otherwise intact. It actually looked as if the front *had* been a facade; the sides and the roof were massive, but the rubble in front showed the wall now gone had been a quarter of the thickness of the rest.

"Murdock, Bear; smoke." Molotok let his rifle hang by his side as he fished around in one of the pouches of his vest, retrieving a smoke grenade; John and Pavel did the same. "Murdock, northern side of the street. Bear, you and I towards the other group of *fascista*." Nodding, John pulled the pin on his grenade. He leaned out around the corner of their cover only long enough to throw the grenade. As he watched it arc through the air, it started to deploy dense white smoke before it landed in front of the group of Kriegers coming from the center of the city. Blue streaks shot through the growing cloud as it thickened. Some unarmored Kriegers, growing bold, tried to dash through the smoke; John dropped all three with quick bursts from his rifle.

"Khanjar, we have deployed a screen. When it has set, we will be moving to the rally point. Cover us, we will cover you."

"*Understood.*"

Once the smoke had completely blocked any sight of the attacking Kriegers, Molotok signaled for the team to move out. As Mamona gaped in shock, Sera picked up Unter in her arms, as if he weighed nothing, and began her run at Molotok's signal. They kept their spacing, making sure no one on the team was closer than five paces; actinic bolts of energy sliced through the air around them, scorching the street and surrounding buildings in narrow misses. After doing a quick visual check to make sure his team had made it, Molotok contacted Khanjar.

"We are being in place. Be bringing the wounded."

"Moji," Sera said, as she laid Unter down gently. "I can bring one, perhaps more." She looked around... and John saw that her eyes blazed that featureless gold. "I know where they are."

"Go, and quickly." Molotok turned from her, raising his rifle in the direction of the enemy. "Khanjar, we have angel coming to assist you with transporting casualties. Hold fire, repeat, hold fire."

Sera spread her wings, and was gone before John could say anything. Red Team started firing steadily into the smoke at either end of the street, making sure that the Kriegers were keeping their heads down. No more than thirty seconds later, and she was back, with a Blacksnake merc cradled in her arms. John was already waiting; she transferred the young man to John and was away again, back with a second in the time it took him to put his burden down towards the back of the room. A second transfer, and she was away for the third time just as the first of Khanjar's men came stumbling into their cover. She managed two more by the time all of the mercs had joined them.

She was panting at this point, winded, but smiled a little at

John. "They were foolish enough to use their...their heat-seeing? When the smoke came up. They will be quite blinded for a little while longer."

Her eyes had gone back to blue, with that gold flickering in the depths.

"Overwatch," Molotok said. "We are in position, those of us still alive. Please advise."

"John. Hand on ground. Chop chop." John complied immediately, stripping off a glove and pressing his palm to the floor.

"Everybody else stand away from the front. And three. Two. One."

It was not unlike an earthquake. The pavement split as the rock of the mountains erupted in a ragged but climbable slope, shaking everyone who happened to be standing right off his or her feet, and filling in the front of the building where the wall had once been. Vickie didn't *quite* send it all the way to the roof; there were still firing-ports, or places that could be used as firing-ports. But the Thulians were going to have the devil's own time getting at them.

"Oh...kay." There was no doubt Vickie was exhausted. *"Overwatch to all teams. That's all the magic you get today."*

"Thanks for the Alamo, Vic. Let's hope it turns out better this time around." John glanced around. They had perhaps thirty people, all together, Blacksnake and CCCP. Almost everyone was wounded in some way, ranging from the minor to the severe. One bit of good news was that Unter was starting to come around; his face was still covered in blood, but the underlying wounds were mostly gone.

"Shit's gonna break loose any minute. I just needed to get you guys under cover until it does."

"Kutte ki olad," Khanjar swore, her eyes huge at the sight of the earthen barrier. "I do not wish to know where in the many hells or heavens you people recruit."

"I should say our friend is very good at miracles," Sera said, mildly, as she helped one of the Blacksnake mercs bandage another. "And I know you have seen this—" she waved her hand at the earth-and-rock barrier "—before."

"How did you—" Khanjar cut off what she was going to say. "Never mind. I should know better than to question a Deva. It is one thing to see such a thing. It is another to be knocked off the feet by it."

They ran out of time to discuss it any further. The smoke had begun to clear, and the Kriegers were advancing. The next few minutes were filled with gunfire, explosions, shouted orders and . . . occasionally screams. John was startled while changing his magazine for his rifle when Unter thumped against the barrier next to him; most of the blood had been cleaned off of his face, but he still looked like ten miles of bad road.

Georgi grunted, spitting into the dirt. "No time for napping when there are still *fascista* to kill."

John pulled back on the charging handle for his rifle, chambering a round. "You have your pick of 'em, old man. More than enough to go around."

Blue Team: Generator Tower

Silent Knight heaved, and pulled Red up to safety on what was left of the stairway. Red peered down the open shaft, but the smoke continued to rise around them, obscuring their vision. He screamed down to Mel again, but she didn't answer.

"You're hurt," Knight said.

Red glanced at the armored man. His open chestplate was now a mess of loose wires. Red nodded in understanding. Knight had disconnected his power source. It had stopped the malfunctioning armor from spasming, allowing Knight to regain his footing, but had rendered it useless in the process. Without power running to the mechanized chassis, Silent Knight had not only lost his sonic abilities, but was now burdened with about seventy pounds of clunky steel.

"You're one to talk," Red scoffed, and winced as his scorched legs continued to burn in pain. "Don't worry about me, the heat cauterized the wounds. I'm healing up as we speak. You're the one who's leaking. Here, take this."

Red reached up and unwrapped the scarf around his head. Silent Knight shuddered. Well, the Djinni couldn't blame him; he knew that his face was smooth, hairless, *alien*, lacking anything even remotely human except for a thin slit for a mouth, a pair of nostrils at the end of a brief stub for a nose, and lidless eyes.

"Is that . . . is that your real face?"

"Of course not," Red replied, binding his scarf around Knight's injured shoulder. "You're looking at my base foundation, don't have time for anything more right now. Try not to think about it. Think of something else, like how we're going to get down there and get Mel."

"Djinni, we've got minutes left to get out of here before Scope blows the place. Do you really think we have time to . . . ?"

"Yeah, minutes," Red interrupted. "So I'm not going to waste time arguing with you. I'm not leaving without her. You can stay and help, or you can go. Make up your mind, right now."

Knight stared at him for a brief moment, then sighed with a reluctant shake of his head. He reached inside his chest plate and tugged at a latch. His armor fell apart, the pieces dropping to the parapet with a clatter. Underneath, he was clad in nanoweave, his only concession to the standard ECHO uniform a bright yellow and red crest emblazoned on his shoulder. It depicted a lionized coat of arms under a simple fist pulsing within concentric circles of power, perhaps a keepsake from his previous time as an independent street vigilante. Knight removed his helmet and let it fall with the rest of his armor. Red had never seen him out of the armor. He looked . . . normal. Average height, with a slightly athletic build; he wasn't as ripped and wolf-lean as Murdock, or as buff as Bulwark. His skin was paler than it should have been, too; a byproduct of spending so much time in his armor, probably. A boyish if plain face; messy blond hair and brown eyes. The only thing unusual about him was his cheekbones; they looked as if they belonged on a Grecian statue. He looked young, but the eyes told a different story. Those were a pair of eyes that had seen—too much.

Then again, Red reflected, at this point, they probably all had eyes like that.

Now he was left only with the implanted tech/magic hybrid equipment Vickie had given him. Not an in-ear speaker but a direct implant to his auditory nerve, modified so that he could turn it on and off. And not one but two, one in each ear. Silent Knight was deaf, which was the only reason why he could operate that suit of his, which would have *made* a normal person deaf within moments. Thanks to Overwatch Two, he could hear again.

"It was a good suit," he said, his voice having that odd, flat cast to it that the speech of the deaf (or formerly deaf) tended to have. "It lasted longer than my previous upgrades, but it's toast now. Be able to move faster without it." Knight reached down to retrieve his sidearm and gunbelt from the suit, and strapped them in place. "So what's your plan?"

Red Djinni peered down the shaft again but the rising smoke was, if anything, even thicker now. He hissed as the smoke and soot struck his eyes, making them water, and took a second to grow some eyelids.

"We need some rope," he said.

"Don't have any."

"Seriously?" Red scoffed. "What kind of armored adventuring hero doesn't carry rope, a grappling hook and a ten-foot-pole with him?" He gave their surroundings a quick once-over. There was nothing in sight, nothing they could use to lower themselves down to Mel.

"You'd think anal-retentive Nazis would have some sense of safety regulations," Knight said. "Rolled-up fire hoses at regular intervals in the walls or something like that."

"You see the size of this city?" Red asked, still looking about desperately for anything resembling rope. "You gotta figure they ran out of funds somewhere. Probably blew their wad on heroic monuments, or..." He paused.

"You just thought of something, didn't you?"

"I did," the Djinni said, biting his lip.

"From the look on your face, I'm not going to like it, am I?"

"It's a little weird, and I've never tried it before," the Djinni admitted. He took a breath to calm himself and extended his left hand out to Silent Knight. "Just go with it."

Red grew a new set of claws, and Knight took a step back in apprehension as they slowly flowed out towards him, razor-tips first.

"I don't see how jabbing me in the face with your finger knives is going to help," Knight stammered.

"Wait for it," Red seethed, and grunted as the claws suddenly went limp and dangled from his fingertips. They continued to grow and Knight, seizing on the idea, grasped them gingerly. He wound them around the exposed railing and anchored the growing rope around his waist.

"Flesh rope," Knight said, and chuckled. "Brilliant. And...eww."

"Yeah," Red agreed, and looked over the side again. "You got me?"

Knight pressed himself back to the wall and nodded. "Go. But are you sure this will hold?"

"Like I said, first time. Say a prayer, will you?"

Knight nodded, and Red rolled off the exposed stairway. He swung in place for a moment, testing the tensile strength of his skin. He was putting it through tremendous strain, no doubt about it. He relaxed, willed it to be thicker, tougher, and after another calming breath, willed it to grow.

He started to descend, surprised at how easy it was, and gambled with a few fast growth spurts. The skin held, and soon Red was rappelling down the shaft, screaming Mel's name again. He closed his eyes and took a deep breath just before piercing the heart of the smoke. While his eyes were useless here, he concentrated with his other senses, especially his radial awareness. He swung about, probing around him for any movement, anything that suggested Mel was trapped there in the billowing heat. And the heat was intense; coupled with the rising soot, it was like navigating through a sauna in a blackout. He could barely "see" more than a foot in any direction. It only got worse as he descended closer to the flames; the blaze was masking more and more of his surroundings. He was getting too close, it was getting too hot, and he didn't dare open his mouth to scream out to Mel again. He needed to find her soon, before he ran out of breath, before he fell too far into the flames to pull himself out, before he taxed his rope of skin beyond itself, where the heat and tension would eventually singe and tear away his lifeline.

He was getting dizzy. His lungs began to burn; he needed to take a breath. And it wasn't just his lungs. His feet felt like they were now dancing just inches above the flames. He was swimming in grit, and every pore in his skin was screaming, clogged with grime and burnt ashes. It was playing havoc with his radial awareness. Pretty soon, it would impossible to sense anything around him. He hadn't considered that before, trusting in his senses to make his way through the smoke. He had simply jumped in, to save the girl, to be the hero.

To be the hero. I'm really doing this again, the hero thing. Guess I have been, for a while now. Guess it's time to stop denying it. Maybe it'll stick this time. Maybe I want it to. Maybe I should get my head out of my ass, get Mel, and get out of here before I die.

He was honest enough with himself to admit he was starting to panic. He tried to tell himself it was perfectly reasonable to panic, seeing as he was suffocating in extreme heat over a bonfire while swinging on a fragile rope made from his own epidermis, but it didn't seem to help. Instead, it was the final push, and just as he prepared to swing up and start climbing up himself back to Silent Knight, he felt a hand grasp his and then thin, shaking legs wrap themselves around his waist.

It was Mel. Without opening his eyes, without saying a word, he knew it was her, just the touch of her.

There wasn't time for anything that would have done that moment justice. The relief of knowing she was alive, the sheer joy of feeling her against him, they didn't have the luxury of words or even a simple kiss. So he stole a moment, just a moment, to give her a quick squeeze before motioning her up. She seemed to understand, and began climbing up his rope. He felt her feet release from his shoulders, and he began to climb up after her. There was a strange and growing disconnect in his mind, which Red understood to be one of the final stages of asphyxiation before losing consciousness. He was on the verge of blacking out when he realized the heat wasn't as alarming, the smoke wasn't as dense or tenacious, and he drew in a sudden desperate breath. Opening his eyes, he saw Mel climbing above him and he felt a surge in his arms, a need to be next to her, that drove him forwards. They dragged themselves onto the broken stairway, hauled up by Silent Knight, and took a few moments to cough uncontrollably, lying precariously close to the edge.

"I'm sure you two could use a breather," Silent Knight said, "but really, I think we're pressing our luck with that..."

"Bomb!" Mel screamed, nodding in agreement. She coughed again and sprang to her feet. "How much time?"

"A minute, maybe less..." Red croaked. "I think this would be..."

"Less talking, more running!" Mel screamed and darted up the stairs. Red and Silent Knight ran after her. There was no grace in their flight, just the certainty that if they stumbled and fell, they were lost. There was some concern in the planning stages, Red remembered, that the explosives were too small. No matter what the engineers said, no one could quite grasp how the slim charges could possibly deliver the punch they needed to take out a power generator, much less the safety margin of an entire building.

Red recalled how he had examined one of the charges, had thoughtfully turned it over in his hands, and the only question he had asked the technicians.

"What's this bomb called again?"

"The Inferno II," one of the technicians had answered. "We lost the first prototype, and it's specs, during the Invasion. We were able to reverse engineer this model. It's not as compact as the first, and you'll need to place multiple charges, but our simulations suggest an equal payload as the first, assuming you get the detonator sequence sync right."

Red had nodded, feigning only a passing interest in the device.

"Good name," was all he had said, before handing it carefully back.

So they ran, and while Mel and Silent Knight probably didn't realize the extent of the Inferno's blast radius, Red didn't think it was something he was ever likely to forget. He urged them on, and as they arrived at the top landing, they heard a shrill alarm ring out beneath them.

"Go!" Red shouted. "Countdown's started!"

They barreled through the portal, through the connecting hall, and skidded to a stop by the outer door. Red slammed into the portal lock and was rewarded with a steely hiss as the round portal slowly rolled open. He ushered Mel and Knight out first, and they ran back out onto the streets of Ultima Thule, right through the surprised ranks of the assembled Thulians stationed outside.

"Was . . . ?"

"Look out, coming through!" Red yelled as they broke through the ranks and ran screaming for cover. The battalion guards watched them go, stunned, until their leader recovered his wits and barked an order. As one, the Thulians raised their cannons and took aim at the fleeing ECHO operatives.

"*Schießen!*"

"Dive!" Red screamed, and shoved Mel and Silent Knight into a recessed stairwell at the top of a nearby alley. As they rolled and banged down the concrete steps, they heard the whine and *whoomph* as a few arm cannons went off, but they were drowned out as the earth itself seemed to buckle and groan from a massive detonation from beneath them.

Red Team: Ultima Thule

A flash and a scream caused John to flinch, turning away from the barrier momentarily. When he looked back, he saw that a fourth of it had been decimated on the left corner; one of the Thulian grenades, more than likely. *That's going to be a problem.* With a weakness in their cover, the Kriegers could just chip away at it until they had nothing left keeping them from storming in the building.

"Shit. Incoming!"

One of the Blacksnake operatives pointed; it was unnecessary, however. Several squads of Kriegers were moving quickly through the smoke; armored troopers leading with energy shields, while unarmored infantry followed behind them. More troopers were still firing from the rear, trying to pin Red Team and the Blacksnake mercs down while their comrades advanced. Everyone was firing as fast and as accurately as they could; John was doing his best to hit the troopers with his flames, but there was just too much incoming fire for him to line up a good shot. A single grenade bounced through the broken section of the barrier; scooping it up before anyone else could react, Molotok threw it out the door as hard as he could. Chance had it that it landed next to one of the advancing Thulian squads. The explosion of Thulian energy ripped the lead trooper in half, while also killing most of the rest behind him.

"They're goin' to make it inside." John looked over at Unter. The old Soviet returned the look, then shrugged.

"I would be feeling sorry for them, if they weren't such *svinya*. Let us make them reconsider joining us."

And then Vix shouted a warning. *"Holy* shit, *it's coming down!"*

At that moment, there was a deep, distant *thud,* one that shook the pavement and the rocks of Vickie's barrier exactly like an earthquake, as well as being a sound.

And then, the sky exploded, silently.

If you had taken the Northern Lights, hooked them up to the average rock concert's effects rig, and then juiced it with Niagara Falls, you'd have gotten something that was, perhaps, a tenth of the light show going on in the sky for the next minute or so. The reddish curtain that had arced over the top of this valley rippled and heaved and danced; meanwhile, there was a clear, wedge-shaped section that had just disappeared, letting the blue of the normal sky shine through, the edges of the wedge wavering and surging, and sending tendrils out, as if they were trying to join up again. Everyone was transfixed by the mayhem going on above them, even the Kriegers. That went on silently for a minute, maybe two, but not more than three... and then the fun started. The entire canopy roiled, as massive bolts of electricity began to arc across the sky for thirty seconds more. There were several more explosions. And then . . .

The shield vanished. The reddish hue that had fallen over everything was replaced by the normal, clear light of the Himalayas, with a beautiful cloudless sky overhead. And a chill wind swept through the entire valley in a brief hurricane rush, dropping the ambient temperature by at least sixty degrees all at once.

The fighting started up again, once the impact of what had happened sank in for everyone; the Kriegers weren't looking as sure of themselves, however. Many weren't acting as coordinated as before, nowhere near as bold. John briefly saw some of the commanders at the back cajoling and even striking their subordinates, urging them forward.

"Overwatch to all teams. Well done. Objective achieved. Dig in, danger close fire missions commencing now."

"The Alamo didn't have that. But I'm sure as hell glad we have it." John then did his best to make himself as small as possible behind the barrier as the artillery shells began impacting among the Kriegers.

Belladonna Blue: Forward Medical Unit

Bella remained at Bulwark's side, occasionally adding to his own inherent healing as she had extra energy to spare. But both of them were preoccupied with the information coming in on their HUDs. And neither of them bothered Vickie; it was crystal clear that even with Gamayun and the Colts to help, she was pushing herself to the mental and physical limit to keep up with the needs of the teams. Vickie herself was fully wired into Overwatch, even more than anyone else, because she experimented on herself before she added anything to Overwatch packages. Bella could call up Vickie's vitals in a heartbeat, and when she did, it looked as if the tiny mage was running full out on the parkour course, even though Bella knew she was in her chair in her Overwatch suite. Bella could only hope she wasn't going to burn out before it was all over. After all, she'd already passed out cold from her efforts on the North American HQ attack; this looked to be . . . much, much worse. And Bella was half a world away this time, with no "angel airlift" to help her get back to the mage.

Mostly, though, she kept her eyes and ears glued to Blue Team.

She knew without saying anything that Bulwark was doing the same. She cursed herself again when Scope fumbled the sensors, losing the team precious time. And again when the detonators failed to work, despite Vickie's desperate attempts at a long-distance diagnostic. Unfortunately, the bombs, and the detonators, had never been anywhere near the little mage. She had not done the design work on them (and why should she have?) and they weren't "smart," so she couldn't hack into them.

But when Scope slammed the door on the rest of the team, to sacrifice herself by blowing the bombs manually, she nearly broke.

"Overwatch: Vix. *Vickie!*" she cried, her fingernails cutting bloody crescents in her palms. *"Get me—"*

"No can do," Vickie said, her voice raspy with strain. *"She's off Overwatch; turned off her comm. She was never hardwired because she was never cleared before I ran out of sets."*

"Dammit!" Bella cried, slamming her hand down on the table beside her so hard she left a dent in the metal top. She couldn't look at Bull; she couldn't meet his eyes. This was her fault. From beginning to end, this was her fault.

"Bella," came the whisper inside her ear, overlaying the fainter whisper from outside. Tears burning her eyes, she met his. "Her choice, Bella," Gairdner said.

And maybe her redemption. "Still my fault," she said, bitterly, angrily, wishing there was some way she could punish herself enough. . . .

She listened to and watched the fight in the tower, silent witness as Mel was first lost, then miraculously rescued, the frantic flight to escape, then—

"Holy shit, *it's coming down!"* Vix exclaimed on wide-broadcast.

From where they were, there was no way to see the field, much less the field coming down, but Bella had to restrain herself to keep from dashing outside to look anyway. There was no mistaking the fact that *something* big had happened, however, as the ground trembled beneath them, rattling the chair she was sitting on and the cot Bulwark was lying on. But she could see it all through Vix's little magical "eyes," and it was . . . spectacular.

But not spectacular enough to make her forget that Scope was somewhere under that pile of stone and metal.

"Begin danger close fire missions," Art ordered before the last of the fireworks had faded from the sky. *"Paint us targets."*

"Beginning danger close fire missions. Painting targets," Vickie responded instantly, and the distant thunder of the artillery, positioned even further away than the Forward Medical Base, began. Bella listened as Art of War directed troops, Apaches, and fighter-bombers into the air.

But almost immediately, the Kriegers began countermeasures. Bella groaned wordlessly on seeing the defenses that the Thulians were throwing up, now that the field was down. Of course they were, they'd had all that time to get ready once stealth had been blown. They weren't stupid, and they weren't overconfident. While they'd tried to take down the strike teams, they'd also been manning up the main defenses *assuming* the shield would come down . . .

The casualties! "Overwatch: battlemap," she ordered, and checked the exit points. The two that they already knew of, what she supposed was the main entrance, and that entrance at the graveyard, were thick with red dots. Those could be fought through, but . . . with those air defenses, they'd *never* be able to airlift casualties from the city itself.

"Clear entry one and two," she heard Art of War say, even as she thought of that herself. *"Get me evac Swifts on the ground there, prepare to take on casualties."*

"But we need a healer out there!" she exclaimed aloud. Some of the ones that would die otherwise could be saved if there was a healer to do what the conventional med teams couldn't—

She hadn't realized that Einhorn was beside her until the girl spoke. "Bella, I'll go!" she said instantly. "I'll be safer than any of you, I can make even the Thulians like me!"

And she was right of course; her empathic projection worked on anything with an organic brain. A quick glance at Bulwark, a little nod from him, and she agreed, even before she thought. "Go!" she exclaimed. "Overwatch: MedEvac Swifts. MedEvac, we have healer Einhorn heading your way. Save a Swift for her."

"Roger, Blue," came the short reply, and Einhorn vanished before Bella could have second thoughts.

But now things were rapidly spooling up, as Red Saviour bulled her way onto the freqs. *"Art of War: Red Saviour on air. I will be to leading my CCCP in at Entry One to come to relief of Team Red and Spearhead."* Her tone brooked absolutely no argument, and Art of War must either have prepared himself for this eventuality, or was resigned to it.

"*Understood, Red Saviour,*" he said. "*Good luck,*" and he went on to continue directing the larger battle.

All that Bella could do was wait, watch for the Swifts returning with the first of the casualties, and mourn. Because once the casualties started pouring in, there would be no time for grief.

Red Team: Ultima Thule

The massive bombardment of Ultima Thule had started off strong, catching the Kriegers completely flat-footed, but had since lost steam. It appeared that, after all, the barrier had not been the only defense of the city. John realized, belatedly, that this was only logical. After all, the planners had been Nazis, who had watched their cities turned into smoking piles of rubble during the last world war, and were not going to rely on a single-point-of-failure defensive system.

Hell, maybe they watched Star Wars.

After the initial battery of fire, the Kriegers pulled another trick out of their sleeves; at several points around the city, particularly on the edges and then spaced out evenly in the main body of buildings, were anti-missile defense systems. They sprouted from rooftops and dedicated pads concealed underground, and looked like multibarreled turrets; torrents of energy shot out from each one, filling the air with hundreds of streams of energy. That had immediately lessened the effectiveness of the artillery and missile strikes that were coming from the staging areas and designated artillery points. The turrets also seemed to act as ad-hoc anti-aircraft systems, tracking and attempting to destroy the attack helicopters and fighter jets that were supporting the allied infantry.

The fighting had become a largely conventional slugfest. The allies had quickly flooded into the city, on the ground and by helicopter, setting up landing zones and rally points from which troops could deploy. ECHO energy broadcasters were dropped into the city at these rally points, and started up almost as soon as they hit the ground; any Krieger troopers, and even the Death Spheres to an extent, within the portable broadcasters' range would have their armor become vulnerable without it needing to be heated up first. With the artillery, MLRS barrages and precision missile strikes, along with the Apache gunships and jets dropping munitions wherever they found targets, it was no longer stranded units fighting for survival. It was army against army. The Thulians recognized this, and seemed to have pulled out all of the stops. Death Spheres, troopers, Robo-wolves and eagles all flooded the sky and streets of Ultima Thule, rushing to meet the attackers in small unit action.

The attackers were still outnumbered. When attacking a defensive position, you wanted to greatly outnumber the defenders... because you were going to more than likely lose quite a few people in taking down the defenders.

Red Team and the surviving Blacksnake operatives had finally linked up with the other beleaguered infiltration teams and several of the SOF units. Since the infiltration teams were deeper into the city than most of the conventional forces, they were tasked with holding the ground they had gained until reinforcements could arrive for a concerted push. Ammunition and a small, man-portable ECHO broadcast generator had been rushed to the infiltration teams, now collectively designated as Spearhead Group, to help with the fighting. The Kriegers threw everything they had at the group, but so far each attack had been repelled. For the first time since the botched entry into Ultima Thule, and the following ambushes, there was hope that the strike would be successful.

And for the first time since the botched entry, Red Team had some breathing room. John ran to the fighting position that Sera was crouched behind; it was the remnant of one of the walls that Vickie had constructed with her geomancy, shored up with debris from some of the damaged buildings and, in a grisly display, some of the downed trooper armor. He shouldered into the cover next to her, reloading his rifle as he crouched down.

"Having fun yet, darlin'?" He was slightly out of breath, but still managed a genuine lopsided grin. The two of them had been trying to be everywhere at once again, John setting his fires and shooting, Sera helping to recover wounded and throwing her spears.

She put her forehead against his chest, and her shoulders shook with barely audible sobs. "I want to go home," she choked out. "I want this to be over. So much pain...so much death...all of it so useless..."

John let go of his rifle, letting it hang by its sling. He realized that he should have expected this; she *felt* every death, even those of their enemies, and grieved for every single one. How long could anyone, even an angel, bear that sort of emotional barrage before breaking down? He took her shoulders into his hands, pulling her to him. "It's not useless, darlin'. It's horrible, bloody and unspeakably awful. But it's not useless. What we're doin' here today isn't for some sorta bloodlust or revenge, at least not for us. It's to make sure that no one has to fight these bastards again, or to suffer another catastrophe like the Invasion. These monsters won't stop until we're all dead or enslaved; you saw that, and you said so yourself. Remember? This is why you chose to be here, on Earth, as an Instrument. If we fight them here, an' now, we can prevent that." He pulled her back so that he could look into her eyes. They were glassy with tears, but still fierce under the pain. He could actually *feel* her pain, her sense of loss, through their connection. He did his best to send his love for her, his strength and determination through that link. "This is necessary. You an' I are here t'make sure that it's done right."

She rested her head against his chest again. "How can you bear such pain?"

"Not easily. But I do it because I have to. *We* have to, darlin'." He lifted her chin with his right hand. "Don't worry; we're together in this, an' we always will be."

She searched his eyes, earnestly. Whatever she found there seemed to satisfy her. But what she said surprised him. "And so you rightly remind me. *'Death shall have no dominion.'*"

At that moment Bear thumped into the cover behind Sera, breathing hard. "Not to interrupt, but if lovebirds are being done cooing to each other, there is a war to fight."

"Old Bear, you should take a moment to rest," Sera said, turning a gaze full of concern on him.

He waved her off, leaning around the cover to fire another burst from his PPSh. "*Nyet.* Will rest when dead."

Before Sera or John could respond, there were shouts coming in over the comms.

"*Urgent traffic, Overwatch! We got something new here, love! It's big, pissed off and got way too many bloody teeth!*" That was Corbie; he and Earth Team, the European ECHO metas, were still isolated, harrying the enemy in hit-and-run attacks behind their lines. John immediately pulled up a map overview on his HUD, showing him the entire city and the position of friendly units. *There!*

It was almost unnecessary. Seconds after Corbie's message on the comm, there was a deep, rumbling *roar* that seemed to fill the entire city. It was answered by two more similar roars, both further away. Looking in the direction where Corbie's team was, John saw something that almost made him wonder if he was hallucinating. Corbie was flying erratically, trying to dodge and weave through the air like a sparrow evading a falcon...from below him, there was a gigantic crash, with a cloud of dust and pieces of buildings flying up into the air. John could see something *moving* within that cloud of debris, thrashing about. Was it some sort of ground version of a Death Sphere, a Thulian tank? Whatever it was, by the size of the debris cloud, it was huge! And it seemed perfectly willing to wreck everything in its path to get at Corbie. But why didn't he fly higher?

A glance further upward solved that question. There were three Robo-Eagles circling overhead, making sure the Brit couldn't escape further skywards.

Just as John noted that, and as Sera tensed up and half-spread her wings, clearly getting ready to fly to Corbie's aid, the thing that was chasing the Brit showed itself.

Something the size of a football field *reared* into the air just beneath the Brit, who barely managed to evade the swipe of an enormous claw trying to smash him to the earth, a plume of fire that actually scorched some of his wing-feathers, and the flash of a couple of energy-beams that only cut off because they were sweeping towards the Thulian troops below.

"It's a goddamned dragon," John said in disbelief.

Dragon was the first thing that flashed into his head when John saw it. Everyone was stunned, watching the behemoth chasing the diminutive Corbie through the sky. It looked like someone from the 1930s had designed it; black-chromed, streamlined, segmented armor running its entire length. It didn't have any horns or other ornamentation on it; it didn't need it. Its chest was as wide as a semi-truck with attached trailer, from end to end. Four beefy legs, all ending in talons as big as a man. It didn't have wings, but that didn't make it look any smaller or diminished. Its tail lashed in huge arcs, sweeping away the tops of several buildings as casually as if they had been made of toothpicks. It leapt into the air, trying to catch Corbie in mid-dodge. John braced himself, waiting for the thing to fall back to earth, and Sera ducked back behind the shelter of the wall, anticipating debris flying in all directions when it did.

But it didn't fall back to earth. As it reached the top of its jump, the bone-vibrating *hum* of Thulian propulsion units shook John so hard he felt it from his hair to the soles of his feet, and that all-too-familiar sullen orange glow traced the edges of every segment of the dragon's armor.

"*Ah, bloody* Hell! *Come on!*" Corbie groaned. "*How is that even possible?*"

The thing had a relatively short neck, but it was still able to snake its head around and belch a plume of fire at the flying meta. Corbie just folded his wings and dropped right out from under the danger, then snapped them open again, and dove under the right leg before it could make a snatch at him. Once under the chest, he changed directions, coming up around the side of the torso until he was just over the backbone.

The dragon seemed to have lost sight of him for the moment, and turned its attention to nearby ground troops who had pushed further into the city than Spearhead, some of whom were trying to hit it with ECHO special-issue RPGs. The rounds impacted with the dragon's underbelly, but the patches of burning material didn't seem to affect it at all. Roaring with annoyance, the dragon craned its neck down, issuing a massive, roiling fireball from its mouth. The ground troops were completely lost in the flames, no time for any of them to even scream before they were consumed.

Cursing hoarsely over the comm, Corbie folded his wings and made a dive towards a building just a couple of hundred yards up the street from the spot where the CCCP team had taken shelter. The dragon was still engaged in polishing off the last of the ground troops, and didn't spot him in the smoke from the fires it was setting. The Brit landed hard, stumbled, and got in under cover. There was movement immediately behind him, as more figures ran into the building. John heaved a sigh of relief. At least now the dragon couldn't see him. . . .

"*This is Earth Team. We're all cozy in a Krieger building. Bastard seems to have lost track of us for the moment, but we can't exactly put the kettle on yet. Some . . . complications in here.*"

"*Team Earth, shelter in place. Apaches incoming. Corbie, hand on ground, please. Good, map of structure uploaded to you; follow your HUD, I found the strongest spot in the building.*"

Three AH-64 Apaches in tight formation screamed overhead at that moment, their rotors beating through the air as they started a gun run on the dragon. All three opened up with their chainguns at the same time, followed by the ear-splitting shriek of Hydra 70 unguided rockets being launched. All of the rounds from the chaingun and nearly all of the rockets impacted with the main trunk of the dragon, the *thwock* of the 30mm rounds and the low-pitched rumble of the explosives drowning out all other sound for a moment.

Nothing can take that much punishment and keep moving. John had personally seen what an Apache could do against armored transports and tanks; they were the kings of the sky on whatever battlefield they flew over, providing close air support and generally ruining the day of anyone that had the misfortune to get in the gunners' sights. And that was *without* the new ordnance that had been developed to handle Krieger armor. Thick black smoke and orange flame covered the body of the dragon, obscuring it from view. A cheer went through the infiltration teams and SOF around John.

All of the cheering died when the dragon *surged* through the smoke from the explosives, roaring straight at the oncoming helos. They tried to break off, but it was too late. The middle chopper was torn to pieces as the dragon's massive jaws closed around it, a fireball and an explosion enveloping the head for a moment. The Apache on the left, still firing its chaingun at the behemoth's head, had its tail rotor sheared off by a lazy swipe of one of the dragon's claws, sending it spinning to the ground to a crash landing, coming apart and exploding after rolling on the ground. The third Apache was able to swing around the dragon, climbing as fast as it could to get away from the danger. Seemingly as an afterthought, the dragon turned its massive head, opening its jaws. From something embedded there, it fired the largest Thulian energy-cannon beam that John had ever seen; the helo disappeared in the rush of blue energy, as if it had never been.

The dragon roared into the silence, and its head swiveled downwards as it looked for more victims.

John felt Sera's eyes on him and turned his head slightly. Her eyes were blazing gold again, and there was sheer fury in her gaze. The *music* washed over him; nothing subtle or fading about it this time. It sounded as angry as Sera looked. He knew what she was thinking, because he had been thinking the exact same thing. *Let's kill that big bastard.*

They nodded to each other simultaneously; she spread her wings and launched straight upwards, already blazing in fire. John swung his rifle's sling off of his shoulders and back, leaving the gun leaning against cover. Without a word, he vaulted over the barrier; he could vaguely hear shouting and cursing behind him, but he wasn't focusing on that. His enhancements already keyed up, he moved with blinding speed. The Krieger troops in front of him were momentarily caught off guard, but quickly recovered; blasts from their energy cannons split the air around him, impacting with the ground and buildings but never touching him. As he sprinted past their positions, he took the time to turn at the waist and blast four with plasma as a parting gift, never stopping his forward motion. He looked up, seeing that Sera was directly above him. With a final kick off of the ground, he launched himself into the air; his fires blazed a second later from his lower legs and feet, rocketing him upward.

"All troops, all troops, hold your fire on the dragon! Dammit, you two, what the hell do you think you're doing? If three Apaches couldn't dent that thing, then—"

"Find us weaknesses, little sister." There was fury in Sera's voice, something he had *never* heard in it before. *"And while you do, we shall prevent it from touching those below."*

Vix cursed in more languages than John had time to count, because at that moment...he had his hands full. In his right he manifested his own fire-sword, collecting and building up his fires in the other hand. The air around them was filled with energy blasts, both from ground troopers and the missile-defense turrets. Sera was pulling aerial maneuvers that looked impossible, and certainly defied, if not broke, several laws of physics. As she flew and dodged and evaded, she was manifesting fire-spears, aiming them at the thing's "eyes."

She was also leading it away from where Spearhead had dug in, and towards the center of the Thulian City. *Good. Anything that gets wrecked or dead in there is less we have to deal with later.* While the dragon was focusing on Sera, John did his best to probe its defenses; he fired blast after blast of fire and plasma, trying to hit it in the joints or the spots between its segmented armor plates. Nothing penetrated, all of the fire simply splashing against its hide harmlessly. He didn't have time to hold still and charge up a truly powerful blast; between the energy turrets and the dragon, it was everything he and Sera could do to keep mobile and not be shot or swatted from the sky. The dragon snapped its jaws, narrowly missing Sera. She spun and whirled just out of its reach, continuously throwing fiery spears at it.

"Where the neck meets the shoulders!" Vix rasped.

John saw his chance; he knew through their connection that Sera would keep it distracted and off balance. Putting a burst of speed on, he dove for the dragon's back where the neck connected with the main trunk of its body, while Sera arrowed up, then came down literally *on* its head. She clung there with arms and legs, wings tightly folded, and as she did, she washed the head over with fire that cascaded and dripped from her body, temporarily blinding it. Gripping his sword in both hands, John killed his speed at the last second, spinning the sword in his grip so that it was point down. As he landed, he thrust the sword down with all of his enhanced might, hitting the dragon right between two of its armor plates. Sawing and prying the sword back and forth and sending up a shower of sparks, he saw that a small opening had formed. He withdrew his sword, turning it back in his hands so that he was gripping it normally, and then began slashing at the breach in the robotic beast's armor. He could sense *something* deep within the dragon. A...presence? It was the mind of something, strange and alien, hooked directly into the beast with wires; it was visceral body horror, and John mentally recoiled from it. John knew that Sera sensed it as well; it was an abomination, the evil fusion of flesh and Krieger technology. Pain and hatred and insanity emanated from it in staggering waves.

He understood that he had made as big a breach in the thing's armor as he could in the little time he and Sera had before it would shake her off. He felt Sera's assent, and as he blasted off the thing's back, knew she had leapt from the head and was half-running, half-flying down the neck. The trick now was for *him* to keep it occupied. He could feel its malice; it knew *he* had hurt it, and it wanted to hurt him in return. He put as much speed into his flying as he could, twisting and turning through the sky, narrowly dodging energy cannons from the dragon as well as from the ground. He was glad that he had brought goggles this time; the wind would have been blinding otherwise, as he could feel the skin on his face being dragged back from the force. He had no idea how Sera ever managed to see while flying.

Sera reached the spot where he had made the breach in the dragon's armor. Manifesting another spear, she slammed it down through the hole, then clung to it while the dragon bucked and rolled ... John felt its pain through her senses. Felt how Sera had *hurt* it, a creature that never expected to be hurt. How could it be? It was invincible! The surprise and shock were almost as great as the pain, and the wrath it felt at such a *betrayal* was even greater.

She withdrew the spear a little, then slammed it down again, somehow lengthening it as she did so until the point burst through the dragon's chest, transfixing the entire cybernetic beast with a needle of fire. The dragon roared and twisted and rolled; she used the pain she caused it to goad it further away from the allied forces, twisting and pulling her spear to direct it. It had never felt this much agony, ever, in its entire lifetime, and all it could do now was mindlessly try to escape. It twisted and rolled through the air, clawing fruitlessly at its own back, unable to reach her because of its construction, sending shards of its own armor falling to the ground.

Beloved, he heard in his mind. And then, communication that went deeper than words, intermingled with the music. He understood, he *saw* what they needed to do, and exactly when. And at precisely the right moment when she needed to act, Sera gathered all the fire that was within her, and funneled it into her spear. And when every bit of energy that she could muster had passed into the weapon—

—she released it.

Muffled explosions began to rock the dragon from *inside*. The armor containing its mechanisms bulged and gave way; flames and black, oily smoke shooting out in long streams as the armor split. The entire dragon spasmed, its limbs curved in agony with each explosion.

And the sense of *presence* from within ended, cut off abruptly in a mental shriek of unbearable agony. What had been connected to that living mind, however, was still functioning. The head thrashed around, shooting gouts of flame, and the mouth and eye energy cannons fired simultaneously; wherever the mouth cannon's beam struck, even the sturdiest looking Krieger buildings were reduced to rubble. It was still dangerous, even without the malevolent presence buried deep within it. John, pausing in the air ahead of the oncoming dragon, focused all of his energy into his sword, tapping his deepest reserves. The fire sword went from orange to yellow to blinding white. When he didn't think he could hold it any longer, John took the sword in both hands, raising it above his head and behind his back before throwing it as hard as he could at the dragon. He and Sera both knew what would happen; she took to the sky, springing from its back, letting the air catch in her wings before turning sharply and flying in the opposite direction. John rocketed straight upwards, climbing as fast as he could. The sword, which looked like a new miniature sun flying through the air, impacted the dragon's head dead center, lodging there; a split second later, the head detonated in a blinding flash as an expanding sphere of superheated plasma completely engulfed the dragon's head and shoulders. The explosion was deafening as the air displaced, sounding as if God himself had split the sky in a hundred pieces. Chancing a look down, John saw that the upper body of the dragon was a smoking ruin; the rest of the body rolled downward until it hit the streets, destroying dozens of buildings and carving a huge furrow in the ground before it exploded, less brilliantly than John's sword, but still with a massive fireball.

John could feel his energy flagging; glancing down and to the right, he could immediately tell that Sera was spent as well. There was no sign of the Robo-Eagles that had been overhead. *Knocked for a loop? Knocked out of the sky?* His question was answered moments later; several jets had been diverted, and with their improved munitions had turned all but one of the Robo-Eagles to slag.

Good hunting, fellas.

Still dodging through the sky to avoid the energy turrets and the odd trooper arm cannon, John and Sera made their way back to the sky overhead of the Spearhead Group. In concert they both dove for the ground, landing next to each other among the other infiltrators and soldiers. Both of them were completely out of breath, and Sera sagged to her knees, wings drooping to either side; John knew that it would be a good while before either of them could do anything like that again.

There was absolute silence all around them, save for the

occasional weapons-fire exchange between an element of the allied forces and the Kriegers. John moved closer to Sera, helping her to stand. They both glanced around, reading the expressions of their comrades. Some were visibly frightened, others still awestruck.

"I... didn't know you could do that," Vickie said in their ears, sounded three parts awed and one part terrified.

"Neither did we, Vic. An' I don't think we'll be able to pull a stunt like that anytime in the near future. Damn near took everythin' out of us."

Sera sagged even further, looking—and to John's senses, feeling—as if she very much needed to lie down. Her breathing was labored, and her hair hung about her face in tangled, sweat-soaked strands. John felt as if he had run seven marathons back to back while humping a three-hundred-pound ruck on his back; nevertheless he did his best to send some of his strength to her through their connection.

Molotok had sprinted over to them, keeping low so as not to present a target for the Kriegers down the street. He stopped short of them, his face neutral and appraising both of them. After several very long moments, he spoke slowly. "Next time... do not be doing that without orders. Is that understood, tovarischii?"

"Y'got it, boss." John looked around, then retrieved his rifle from the ground, shrugging the sling back over his shoulder.

Wordlessly, Soviet Bear came to their side, and silently offered them his precious flask. From the odor emanating from it, it had obviously been refilled, somehow. John took it, uncapped the flask and took a swig, grimacing as he swallowed and handed it back to Bear.

"Much obliged. Now," he said, checking the chamber of his rifle to make sure that a round was chambered before looking back at the rest of the team. "Shall we get to kickin' some more ass?"

Earth Team: Ultima Thule

Corbie was damned glad that little witch had fixed him up with her fancy gear, the internal everything, the HUD, all of that. He'd have been going crazy, otherwise. Earth Team, comprised of himself and several metas from the ECHO Europe contingent, had been the first to suffer a casualty. Initially, the team had attempted to fly straight to their target, staying low over the rooftops. It had worked for a few blocks; Corbie had been on point, while the rest of the team followed with jetpacks; Earth Team had been able to get further, faster than the other teams because of it. Corbie's hope had been that, since the element of surprise had ruined the prospect of a stealthy entrance and approach to their target, that by making a mad dash for it that they would be able to catch the Kriegers with their knickers down.

It hadn't been a bad plan. It just didn't work, is all.

The team's fire specialty—a younger lad the name of Fernand, Corbie couldn't remember his callsign for the life of him—had been right behind Corbie in the flying formation. Things were going well; it looked like the team was going to be able to slip past the Kriegers before they knew what was going on.

The energy blast came from below them on the street. Corbie knew that it had been meant for him, but the shooter hadn't led him enough with his aim. The blast had clipped Fernand in the shoulder, with part of it carrying through to the jetpack, destroying both. The meta dropped like a stone, bouncing off the corner of a building before he landed, hard, on the street below. Corbie had immediately pulled up, calling the rest of the team to circle around. But the air had already started to fill with more Thulian energy-cannon blasts. Fernand had landed right in the center of a Krieger platoon. Several had begun to advance on him, barking orders. Corbie knew that they had to get to him, somehow, and also knew that it was hopeless. He saw Fernand look up at him and give him a little salute, and felt pierced by his gaze. *Bloody hell . . . he knows. He knows we can't get to him.* Everything inside of Corbie screamed against that thought, willing reality to change to something less horrible. It was his fault, his plan, that had caused this.

The young Frenchman dragged himself off of the ground with only one arm, the other barely attached to his body. He spat blood on the nearest trooper. *"Ta mere suce des bites en enfer."* Before any of the Kriegers could react, Fernand exhaled forcefully, sending a fine cloud of barely visible gas into the immediate area. He had retrieved an antique lighter from his pocket while he had been talking; now, he ignited it. Instantly, there was a massive explosion. Fernand's metapower was that he was able to create a fuel-air explosive with his breath; those Kriegers that weren't immediately set ablaze or disintegrated by the explosion were knocked off of their feet, some of the nearer ones actually sent rolling down the street. Corbie and the rest of the team, despite having climbed higher in the air, were buffeted by the tremendous shockwave. Corbie was barely able to recover, and the rest of the team would have been sent tumbling through the air if it weren't for the gyroscopic stabilization of their jetpacks. Usually, Fernand kept his breath weapon small and manageable. This time...he hadn't. Upon surveying the site of the explosion, Corbie saw that there was nothing left where the meta had been. Against the objections of his team, he ordered that they push on.

Earth Team stayed on the ground after that point. This had demoralized them, on top of the emotional crash that had followed Scope's spectacular screw-up; Fernand had been well liked by the rest of the Europeans. Corbie, their team leader, was an outsider. He had been doing his best to keep them moving, to harass the Kriegers; with their fire specialist gone, they only had the ECHO RPG warheads to take down trooper armor.

So they avoided the armored troops. Instead, they decided to go after unarmored Krieger groups, doing hit and run attacks. The German on the team, Carl Rheinhardt, callsign *Fledermaus,* had the ability to cloud the vision of enemies and also see through the eyes of those around him; helpful, considering he had been born without a set of his own. He had helped to keep the team from getting overwhelmed; blinding Kriegers before a strike, seeing through the eyes of any who were coming before anyone else on the team had a chance of knowing they were there, and covering their retreat through more judicious blinding.

But this strategy only brought temporary respites, so the team had to continually displace, keeping their direction random so that the Thulians couldn't predict where they had gone. Which meant that even trying for their original target was out of the question. Corbie was the only one completely wired to Overwatch Two, although the others could hear and talk to Vickie via their earpieces and throat mics, and they all had the little boom-HUDs. But none of them knew her and knew what she could do, and trusted her the way that Corbie did.

And anyway, she was dividing her attention among eight teams. He was feeling the lack.

Buck up, old lad. At least she's got her eyes in the air for us.

In fact, if it hadn't been for her "eyes," and the constantly updated HUD, they'd have been seriously hosed. He couldn't imagine how she was doing this for eight teams—but then, she was a computer wizard and a computer *wizard,* so maybe the magic stuff had something to do with all of this.

But I wish to hell she could magical-port us out of here. We're arse-deep in the gutter and heading for the sewer.

When the shield had fallen, Corbie used the small victory to spur his team forward; they'd be scouts, helping to keep the Kriegers from overwhelming the main body of the infiltration teams. There were still a few sullen looks, but everyone obeyed. When the call came, Earth Team was just a little over four hundred meters from Spearhead Group.

"Overwatch to Earth-leader. Corbie, you look relatively clear. I need a pair of live eyeballs on something I don't like."

"Roger that, love. I'll hunker down the team and take a recce. What do you need?"

"Lemme paint you a good stash-point for the team. Your guys need some breathing space or you're gonna faceplant."

Corbie's HUD lit up; roughly one hundred and fifty meters to the northwest was a structure that was doing...something. It seemed like it was opening, but there was some interference with the eye cam. The building that Vic had highlighted was halfway between their current position and the structure; all the Kriegers in the immediate area were focusing on Spearhead Group, so they had a clear approach for the moment.

"Let's mount up, chaps. Got a mission from on high." Carl nodded his assent, moving up to be on point; he took a bearing off of Corbie's HUD, then started off at an easy trot. The other Brit in the group, their super-strength meta who went by the name "Guvnor," followed. It was only the Italian, Pietro, that hung back. He was the group's speedster; he could move at a blur, and had been responsible for most of the few armored kills they had made, speeding up to a set of armor and planting a bomb on it before anyone could react. He had also been the best friend of Fernand. Instead of following the rest of the team, he simply stood, staring hard at Corbie.

"Got to get a move on, Pietro. Don't want Vic or, heaven forbid, Bella on our asses about lollygagging." There was a very tense moment; Corbie could feel how angry Pietro was, and how instead of focusing that emotion on the enemy, he was laying it square on Corbie's shoulders. After a few heartbeats, Pietro started to follow the others without saying a word. *That's going to be a problem. If we live long enough for it to be, that is.*

"Earth team, I need crow-boy's eyes in the sky. Command wants you four to make a safe-zone for casualties until we can get some pickup out or medics in. Spearhead will start funneling them in as soon as you've got the building secure, reinforced and as invisible as you can make it." Vix was making no effort to hide her strain or her exhaustion. *"We're getting hammered out here."*

Everyone keyed an affirmative on their comms. Once his team was in place and performing their tasks, Corbie decided it was time to take to the sky. It was going to be tricky, no doubt; with all of the anti-missile and anti-air turrets firing constantly, not to mention the Robo-Eagles in the sky, he was going to have a time of it. *That's just the job; time to get a move on.*

Then again, the buildings around here were all big; four stories and more tall. If he flew at about the three-story level, there was a good chance he wouldn't be spotted by ground troops, and he'd definitely be under the level where the turrets could get a bead on him.

Just like chasing down runners in downtown Atlanta, he told himself, and suited action to thoughts.

It seemed to work, too! And thanks to the map-overlay of the HUD, he could detour around hot spots.

As he got near his goal, which was some sort of big, domed structure, he began hunting for a spot where he could land and still observe with some semblance of fragile safety. He spotted a place where something had taken a big bite out of a structure just below the roofline, and he dodged in there. It was a tight squeeze of a landing, but he made it, and turned his attention and the cameras embedded in his eyes on his target.

Which...was definitely moving.

"Cor...that thing's opening up like a kid's surprise-egg!" he exclaimed.

"I am not liking this, Limey," Vix replied. *"Nothing that is going to be opening up around here is going to have anything good for us inside."*

"Then I better get closer." Before Vix could object, he took to the air again. Scanning around, he could see the Krieger forces moving to engage Spearhead Group; all of them were already tagged by Vix's eye cams, so he ignored them for now. A few powerful wingbeats later, and he had enough elevation to get a look down into the structure.

But great clouds of steam billowing out of the opening dome frustrated his attempts to make out what was in there as he approached it. Well, other than what looked like...a gantry, or other support structure, with something inside it. The others—and he could see two more from where he was flying—looked to be opening up at the same rate. They were both further away, and seemed to be spaced equidistant from each other.

"Rockets?" he thought out loud for Vix's benefit. "But why would they need rockets or missiles when they've got their bloody spheres? Some sort of super-sphere?"

"There was one of those at the North American HQ."

"Didn'tcha bury that big ugly, too?"

"Yeah, but I can't do that here without burying our peeps. And that assumes I got the juice. Not sure I do, Limey. I'm a yard of cheesecloth stretched over a football pitch right now."

"Figured a repeat performance was a bit much to ask for. Going to maneuver a bit closer, see if I can see anything more." Before Vix could object again, he eyed his angle of attack and picked a trajectory that would let him shoot past it without (he hoped) attracting the notice of who or whatever was manning those turrets.

And he was just about halfway to his goal when the smoke or steam suddenly blew away in another of those icy wind-gusts, as the gantry fell away, just like at a rocket launch, and he saw—

"Holy mother of God!" he shouted, starting to backwing. *"It's a bleeding* dragon!" There was the unmistakable shriek of Robo-Eagles above him, and he knew he had made a grievous mistake. Three of them were wheeling in the sky above him, acting as spotters; they clearly had seen him, and weren't being quiet about it.

The sleek, black-chromed monster swung its head towards him, eyes blazing, and opened its mouth. He didn't wait around to find out what was going to come out of that mouth. Doing a fast wing-over so hard it hurt, he dove down among the buildings to try to hide from the thing.

But he heard it crashing down to the ground *much* too close behind him. It didn't seem to care what it wrecked, as long as it could catch him, either.

At least the bloody bastard doesn't have wings!

With Vix frantically highlighting a path for him on his HUD, and the monster painted as a big—*much* too big—red dot on the map behind him, he dodged among the buildings, weaving between the rooftops while trying to put as much distance between himself and the dragon as possible.

"Urgent traffic, Overwatch!" he called out on the all-freqs band, for the benefit of Spearhead as well as Vickie. "We got something new here, love! It's big, pissed off, and got way too many bloody teeth!" Behind him the thing was thrashing its way through the city, sending pieces of stone and steel half the size of cars flying with every move it made. And he couldn't go *up* to evade it, because those bloody Robo-Eagles were overhead, ready to dive on him the minute he tried to climb above the level of the rooftops.

And then, as if all of that wasn't bad enough, the thing jumped at him.

He evaded it only by the luck of the gods themselves. He braced himself for the flying debris when it crashed back to earth again.

Only, it didn't. "Ah, bloody *Hell! Come on!*" Corbie groaned. "How is that even possible?"

The hum of Thulian drives was the answer to that; it was vibrating him so hard his feathers rattled. But how could *anything,* even alien tech, keep something the size of several football pitches in the air like that?

It was coming straight for him, and the *only* chance he could see was a desperation move. Rather than flying away from it, he flew *towards* it, ducking under a clawed hand the size of three lorries that tried to swat him out of the air, and evading a gout of flame so closely he could hear and smell his feathers scorching. Then he got under it, and did a quick direction change, coming up around its torso and into what he fervently hoped was its blind spot, at its shoulder blades. He had never, in his entire life, been so utterly and completely terrified. Not even on the day of the Invasion or the MARTA attack.

His ploy worked. It lost track of him. But while he hovered for a moment, looking for a chance to get clear of the damned thing, it turned its attention to the ground troops. And to his horror, not only were they completely unable to so much as dent it...

...he watched the thing immolate them.

Cursing in despair, he saw his opportunity and grabbed it, diving down into the tangle of wrecked and unwrecked buildings, darting through the smoke to further cover his flight, and finally landing hard enough to send him stumbling and somehow making it inside the building where the rest of his team was heading for.

By the time he got in where the rest of the team had been running to, and finally stopped moving, Corbie was breathing hard, bent over and his wings quivering. "Now that was too bloody close." He took a moment to steady himself. Then he noticed that they all had their weapons raised, aiming at the back of the room. His entire body immediately felt the alert, and he raised his own sidearm, scanning in the darkness of the room.

"Eyes. Watching us. False partition, back of the wall." Fledermaus thrust his chin forward, indicating the wall he was referring to. "They do not seem to be armed . . . that I can see."

Corbie licked his lips, brushing the sweat off of his brow with his off hand. "Order them out, real slow." Carl complied, barking out commands in guttural German. Slowly, almost a dozen Kriegers came out from behind a breakaway panel; it blended fairly well in with the rest of the furnishings in the room. If it hadn't been for Carl, Corbie doubted they would have ever known that the Kriegers were there; somehow he had been able to connect with the Kriegers hiding behind that false wall and see through their eyes. The German was right; none of them were carrying weapons, but . . . something was off about them. They all wore similar uniforms; something like coveralls, slate gray, with pockets and—tool belts?

The most disconcerting thing was their faces. Some of them were obviously Thulian; the slit noses, the skin texture, their eyes. Others were plainly human; just as normal, though very Aryan, as anyone else. And mixed in . . . were creatures that seemed to be a blend of both; part Thulian, part human. How in *hell* was that even possible? He'd had long arguments during his nerdier moments with Merc about how bloody insane *Star Trek* was for even *going* there; anyone with any glimmer of understanding of biology knew it would be impossible for aliens and humans to cross. Their biology wouldn't just be different, it *had* to be incompatible!

And yet . . . there they were, bold as brass. They had more hair than the full-Thulians, slightly more developed noses and different eye colors. It was disturbing, and Corbie didn't like the implications. And all of them, Thulians, humans, and the hybrids were looking at him with fear and hatred.

Corbie motioned with his pistol, keeping it trained on the Kriegers. "Guvnor, Pietro, search them. Make sure they don't have anything hidden on them, look for intel, anything. Then flex-cuff them and sit them down." The two metas complied, with Carl barking more orders to the Kriegers. The search didn't turn up anything particularly useful; more tools, what appeared to be some technical manuals and printed orders, a few devices that looked like data-pads of some sort. Pietro was ... more than a little rough with some of the prisoners, going so far as to gut-punch one of the Thulians who dared to meet his eyes.

"Ease off, mate. We've got them dead to rights." Guvnor put a hand on Pietro's shoulder, but the Italian angrily shook it off.

"Interesting choice of words."

"Stow it. I've gotta report this." Corbie didn't holster his pistol, but he did lower it as he spoke on the comm.

"This is Earth Team. We're all cozy in a Krieger building. The big bastard seems to have lost track of us for the moment, but we can't exactly put the kettle on yet. Some ... complications in here."

"Team Earth, shelter in place. Apaches incoming. Corbie, hand on ground, please." Slowly, cautiously, he knelt to give Vix what she needed, never taking his eyes off the Kriegers. *"Good, map of structure uploaded to you; follow your HUD, I found the strongest spot in the building."*

"Will do, love. Gotta handle something first." *And how, pray tell, do you plan on handling it, bird-brain?* There hadn't been much talk about taking prisoners when the planning for this mission went on. No one thought that there would be much need for it; Krieger troopers fought to the death or withdrew; any wounded or dead they couldn't retrieve they remotely immolated, turning the suits and anyone inside to slag. It was gruesome, but effective; there weren't Thulian prisoners to interrogate, ever. Why should this city be any different?

Of course it *was* different; nothing about this operation had gone to plan so far, so why should a little detail like dealing with non-combatants go the way it should have?

Guvnor must have sensed what was going through Corbie's mind. "Corb, what do we do with this lot? We can't stay here forever, not with that bloody great big beasty outside."

"I'm thinking," came Corbie's reply. What *could* the team do with them? March them at gunpoint all the way back to the staging area? They simply weren't equipped to deal with prisoners.

"I will tell you what we will do." Pietro stepped forward, placing the muzzle of his sidearm on the forehead of one of the Thulian captives. "The Kriegers do not take prisoners. Neither shall we."

"Fuck's sake, point that thing away, Pietro!" Corbie started forward, pulling at the Italian's arm, but was brushed off. "They're civilians, non-combatants! We can't kill—"

"Civilians," Pietro interrupted, "non-combatants? Look at them." He stared down into the eyes of the Krieger he had his pistol pointed at. "They hate us. They want to kill us, even now. And besides, killing civilians has never been a problem for the Kriegers. These—these *abominations* wouldn't hesitate to shoot us if the situation were reversed."

Fledermaus stepped forward, his hands held up placatingly. "Pietro, I do not think we should disobey Corbie. He is the team leader, and—"

"Shut it, Carl. You're going to let this Americanized outsider tell you what to do? Look how well it turned out for Fernand. The boy wasn't even twenty, and trusting this soft *idiota* killed him." Corbie was staring at the ground now, his sidearm holstered and his hands at his sides. "Look, he's having himself a sook right now." Pietro spat in disgust before turning back to the Kriegers. "I say we shoot them all, and any others we find..."

"Pietro..." Corbie said, softly.

"They didn't hesitate to shoot Fernand, and I can swear to you by God they won't show us any mercy if they get us on our knees..."

"Pietro..." he repeated.

Finally, Pietro whirled around, snarling, to face Corbie. "What?"

The punch hit the Italian squarely in the nose, sending the man reeling back into the arms of the Guvnor. A trickle of blood leaked from both nostrils, and Pietro's eyes immediately began to darken; his nose was probably broken. Wiping some of the blood off with the back of his hand, then seeing it, his eyes went wide. Everyone, especially Pietro, was stunned. The Kriegers didn't dare move, since Fledermaus was still holding a pistol on them.

"Here's how it's going to be, chaps." Corbie was no longer looking at the ground. Though he was short, he seemed to fill the room right then; his anger was bubbling underneath the surface, and he had to work hard to keep his voice even. "We are *not* killing any bloody civilians, Thulian, Krieger or anything in-between. We are going to tie this lot up, lock them in here, and mark the building on the map. We'll have Vix start extrapolating which other buildings might have non-combatants in them, based on this one. And then we'll carry on with our mission, taking the fight to the *enemy*. You know, those blokes out there with the energy cannons who are shooting at our friends right now."

He raised his hand, leveling a finger at Pietro. "And if anyone tries to hurt someone who doesn't have a weapon, I'll shoot the bastard down myself. Is that clear?"

The Guvnor and Fledermaus both nodded. "*Ja* . . . team leader." Corbie saw the barest hint of a smile at the corners of Carl's mouth.

"You've got it, boss." The Guvnor stood Pietro up, then trained his pistol back on the captive Kriegers. Pietro stood there, hand on his ruined nose, looking at the ground.

"What's it going to be, Pietro? Team player, or are you staying on the bench?"

There was a flash of anger from the Italian, his eyes blazing for a moment . . . and then, defeated, his shoulders slumped forward and he reluctantly nodded.

"Good. All right, make sure they're secured. Then we're locking this place up tight. I'm calling it in to Vix."

Corbie turned from the group, and when he was sure they were all occupied with the Kriegers, let out one shuddering long breath. *Jesus on a crutch, I never want to have to do something like that again.*

"*Vic's already got it, mate. Good job. You missed the excitement outside. Go join Spearhead and secure us a spot for casualties.*" That was Sam Colt. Vickie must have been up to her chin in fires.

"Roge-o, Sam. We'll rally up soon enough. Earth Team out."

Red Saviour: Ultima Thule

Red Saviour II would be prepared for a fight when she landed at Entry One. She couldn't sit on the sidelines any longer, relaying commands for her teams and watching as they were put into conflict with the enemy, again and again, while she was safe. Her every instinct had screamed at her that she needed to be there. Once the shield over Ultima Thule was brought down, she had her opening; she had barely finished stating that she was going to join the main assault before she left her Command and Control desk, sprinting for the door. Art of War, the masterful tactician and strategist that he was, must have seen the move coming somehow; he had already made allowances for her specifically to do what she had done, before she even knew she was going to do it.

Her team was ready and waiting for her; Rusalka, the WWII-era water manipulator, was originally going to lead the team, but immediately deferred to the Commissar. Formed around her were the rest; Upyr with her trusty KS-23 shotgun, her pale face contrasting with the black and red CCCP uniform she wore. Chug stood by Thea's side, scratching a crude drawing in the dirt with the tip of one of his rocky toes. He was particularly reserved right now. Natalya noted that he was keeping his distance from the last two members of the team, keeping Thea and Rusalka between himself and them.

The last two were Flins and Marowit; they were twins, both psionicists transferred from Russia by Worker's Champion. Flins was a "lethal" psionicist; the tall, thin man with sharp features hardly ever spoke, but could kill with a thought, shutting down the central nervous system of a person if he concentrated hard enough. Next to him was his sister, Marowit; she seemed to be able to keep her brother, who was somewhat...disturbed...in line. Her metapowers seemed to be similar to her brother's; she was able to influence dreams or nightmares, some such thing. She did the talking for both of them, reading his mind and then relaying his thoughts. Natalya knew that Marowit had previously been KGB, and at some unspecified point had left the organization, returning with her brother in tow shortly after the Invasion. It was heavily implied in rumors that Flins had been used in a covert assassination program during the Cold War and even after, but none of it was substantiated. Natalya didn't have very many dealings with the pair; they did their duties satisfactorily, were up to date on all of their reports, and otherwise kept to themselves. Understaffed as she was in Atlanta, each warm body she could procure was welcome.

The ride with the mass of other Swifts was spent mostly in

silence; occasionally Thea would talk with Chug, calming him; he didn't like aerial rides very much, preferring to stay on the ground whenever possible. As they neared Ultima Thule, the Commissar could see the thick columns of smoke rising from all areas of the city. There were constant explosions in the sky over the city, as well as on the ground; incoming missiles and artillery, many being intercepted by the defense grid of energy turrets that the Kriegers had set up. Still, some were getting through, smashing the enemy and helping her comrades where they did.

When Natalya's Swift landed at Entry One, it was amidst chaos. There were hundreds of troops and vehicles moving, unloading equipment, personnel and more vehicles. Armored personnel carriers were being dropped in on specially outfitted Swifts; some were mounted with mobile ECHO broadcast units, while others ferried men to the front lines of the fighting. There were also the wounded; so many dozens of them, being loaded up into the Swifts just as soon as there was room for them. Natalya spotted the ECHO healer Einhorn running in the direction of the wounded soldiers after she had dismounted one of the other Swifts.

"Davay, davay! There are *fascistas* spilling our comrades' blood!" She was the first one off of the Swift, leading the way. Her personal HUD already had the location of Spearhead Group and Red Team pulled up, with a route that would get her team there the fastest. She calculated the distance in her head. *Still not fast enough.* She scanned the forward staging area, then settled quickly on an alternative. "Follow me." Running, she lead her team to a group of VDV—elite Russian airborne troopers—who were assembling around a pair of APCs.

"I am Commissar Natalya Shostakovaya, callsign Red Saviour II, leader of the CCCP. I will be commandeering this vehicle and all of you men," she said forcefully in rapid-fire Russian. The non-commissioned officer that was in charge of the squad conferred with his men, then nodded. With some shouting and jostling, the airborne troopers and Natalya's team piled into a BMP-3; a sturdy Russian armored personnel carrier. Everyone that couldn't fit into that one was put into a BMD-2, a specialized version that the VDV often used. Once the hatches were secure, the heavy diesel engines roared to life, and both vehicles cruised out of the ready area and towards the fighting, the BMD in the lead.

The interiors were cramped, with very little room for anyone to so much as scratch themselves. Chug was very nervous at this point, rocking back and forth gently. Thea was still trying to keep him calm, telling him that soon they would be outside and that he could protect his friends from the "bad mans," but this did little to ease him. He seemed to be very shy, not looking at any of the airborne soldiers.

"Chug," Thea said. "These are being sturdy Russians, just like you. They will protect you, and you will protect them. *Da?*"

Chug, still looking bashful, managed a craggy smile. "Okay. Chug can do that."

"*Overwatch: Vix to Red Saviour.*"

"*Da*, Red Saviour here, over."

"*I just juggled things so you get Gamayun all to yourself. If you need me, shout.*"

"*Horosho.* We will need her." She paused for a moment, then said more quietly. "Thank you. Red Saviour, over and out."

"*Gamayun here, Commissar. I am following you on the map.*" Unlike Victrix, who was still back in Atlanta, Gamayun was physically on the ground here in the Himalayas—with the Command and Control Unit, in fact, the nearest area they thought was safe. Her talent was a limited-area remote viewing; holding an inverted shot glass over a map, she had an almost prescient view of what was going on there. The range of her ability was only about ten miles; while she had been first tagged for use in espionage, the limits of her powers and the utility of spy satellites kept her shelved...until the CCCP found her to be the perfect coordinator for patrols. Now she would apply her skills here, in full combat, utilizing the lessons she had learned sitting in the CIC of the CCCP in Atlanta. So she would be a second set of "eyes" on their path, watching for ambush, besides Vickie's flying cameras. Natalya was more than grateful to Victrix for this; there were only so many of those cameras, and they could not be everywhere. To have arranged for Gamayun to be assigned only to her group—*Boryets may well be spluttering into his helmet right now. Surely it took magic to accomplish this. Perhaps she gave him a camera of his own. He always did trust technology over people.*

It didn't take long before the two APCs came into contact. The explosions were constant outside of the metal skin of the vehicles, and were growing closer the further into the city they went. Several times the vehicles would be rocked on their tracks.

The Russians within remained stoic, or did their best to appear that way.

"*Gamayun to Red Team Two! Commissar, ambush—!*" The woman was unable to get any other words through before explosions—this time right next to the vehicles—rocked the earth.

"*B'lyad'!*" The driver of the lead BMD was shouting over the comms; immediately, both vehicles began firing their main guns and the coaxial machine guns in long, ragged bursts. Both vehicles continued to speed forward, trying to clear the kill zone of the ambush. Some of the soldiers around Natalya began praying, others clutching their AK-74s in death grips. *Dammit! This route was supposed to be cleared.* There was a tremendous explosion, and the BMP that they were riding in skidded to a halt, causing everyone to slide into each other. The crew was shouting for everyone to dismount; they were still firing the chain gun and the main cannon as quickly as they could, the gunner frantically turning the coaxial weapons as the turret ponderously rotated between each shot.

The VDV troops were the first out, followed by Natalya and her team. She charged her fists, ready to fight. She was almost staggered by what she saw as she rounded the side of the BMP. The BMD that had been in the lead was a smoking ruin, its cannon canted wildly into the air. Three VDV troopers ran to the hatch at the back, prying it open to try to get any survivors out; the only thing that came out was a wash of flame and black smoke. Their commander shouted for them to clear away from it before the munitions cooked off. Natalya could barely hear anything over the sound of the remaining APC's weapons. The VDV soon added their own weapons fire to the cacophony.

"*Commissar, you have ambushers on both sides; rooftops and streets. Mostly unarmored, with four troopers that I can see. The street is blocked by the downed BMD; you will have to proceed on foot. Calling in close air support, but they are up to their ears in it already.*"

Natalya glanced at the map overview of her area; she saw the positions that the enemy had chosen. It was a good ambush spot, with plenty of shooting positions and not much cover for her people. She decided to act immediately, before they could become bogged down.

"Chug! Get the tin soldier-men! Upyr, Rusalka, the left flank! Flins, Marowit, with me on the right! Support the VDV!" She didn't have to wait to see what her people would do; she knew that they were already starting to carry out her orders. Thea's shotgun immediately began to bark a response, and Chug let out a gravelly roar as he charged forward. Natalya searched for her own targets. *There!* A group of four Kriegers were on a rooftop, shooting down with energy weapons and throwing grenades at the VDV. Kicking off the ground on a plume of her metahuman energy, she flew to the side of the building, staying close to it so that she wouldn't be a target for them. Once she was past the edge of the rooftop, she spun around, then killed her flight. She had timed it right at the apex of her momentum, and came down on the roof as if she had simply stepped down a foot. As soon as her feet touched down, she went into a forward roll; her position was right behind the Kriegers, and none of them had seen her. Coming up in a crouch, she added extra power to her charged fists; her first punch broke the back of one of the Kriegers, almost folding him in half before he was catapulted forward over the ledge of the building. Belatedly, the others turned to face her, but she was already among them. She kicked the energy pistol of the nearest Krieger, causing it to discharge into the rooftop before it could be brought to bear on her. She spun around, snapping her head with the movement so that she could keep eyes on her target. An energy-charged backhand decimated the Krieger's face, leaving it in smoking ruins and breaking the creature's neck. The second-to-last Krieger screamed, pulling out a knife and lunging for her; she juked to the left, then the right, pushing him in the back and causing him to go flying past her in a dive, landing face-first on the roof. The other Krieger was fumbling with one of his grenades; Natalya dissipated the energy in her right hand, unholstered her Makarov, and shot the Thulian three times in the face before holstering her pistol again. He fell to the roof, the unarmed grenade still in hand.

The Krieger with the knife had recovered, spitting blood. He ran at her again, all reckless abandon. Natalya smiled wolfishly, waiting for him. When he was near enough, she charged her fists, then dashed forward to meet the Krieger. He was caught off-guard, and faltered at the last second. A flurry of energy-charged punches pummeled his body, pulping bone and organs. Finally, she grabbed the barely living Thulian by the throat, and delivered a final uppercut blow, sending him through the air.

She glanced around herself, looking for more targets, momentarily forgetting that she could find them in her HUD. And a burst of fire in the distance caught her attention.

She did a double-take as she focused on it, her jaw dropping open a little. *"Borzhe moi..."* Surely that was not a—dragon? A dragon the size of—what? A soccer field? Easily!

And what was that, flying about it, harassing it like a pair of overly ambitious fireflies?

Fireflies? *Fire?*

"Gamayun!" she barked, but got no response. Cursing silently, she tried another. *"Overwatch! Victrix!"*

"Busy with dragon, JM and Sera!" the little mage rasped back. Well, that was what she wanted to know, wasn't it? *"Nechevo, spasibo,"* she replied. "Overwatch, Gamay—" But she didn't get a chance to finish the word, as the sizzle of an energy-weapon bolt passed within a foot of her head. Now cursing not at all silently, she dove for cover. She inched towards the edge of the roof then, turning her head sideways to present as small a target as possible, and peeked over it. She saw where the energy blasts were coming from; another group of Kriegers on a rooftop across the street. She cursed... and then her hand bumped into something small and cylindrical; the Thulian grenade. Natalya studied the device for a moment; it was exceedingly simple, evidently modeled on the old Nazi "potato masher" grenades, but with a different arming mechanism. Instead of untwisting a cap on the bottom and yanking on a pull cord, it came with a safety cap and an activation stud. She ripped the safety cap off—the part the dead Thulian had been having trouble with—and mashed down on the stud before throwing it across the street. It landed among the Kriegers firing at her, and went off a split-second later; the sphere of energy engulfed all four of them, as well as part of the building they were stationed on; everything the sphere touched disintegrated. *Fitting, using the scum's own foul weapons against them.*

She leaned over the edge, still careful not to expose herself as she surveyed the street below. The rest of the Krieger ambush was folding. Upyr and Rusalka had been able to put down a squad of unarmored Kriegers with the assistance of the VDV; Natalya watched as Rusalka ordered all of the airborne troopers to empty their canteens, then used her meta ability to weaponize the spilled water. It flew through the air, controlled by Rusalka, to blind and smother the Kriegers as she concentrated it on their faces. It was quick work for Thea to rush in with her shotgun and put each of the Thulians down judiciously. The VDV had taken some more injuries while assaulting the other positions, but thankfully no one else looked critical.

None of the VDV had assisted Flins and Marowit; from the way the normally unflappable troopers were moving and talking with each other, Natalya got the impression that none of them wanted to go *near* the two metas. Both of them had stayed behind cover, eyes closed for concentration. Within moments, the screams started. One Thulian was clutching his head as blood streamed from his eyes, ears and nose before he fell to the ground, dead. Another began shouting, unholstered his pistol, and started shooting several of his compatriots before he was put down by them. The survivors all then began to claw at their own flesh; some were crying, others were screaming, and most disturbing of all . . . some were laughing hysterically. The horrific chaos lasted only a few moments before all of them had found appropriately large veins, torn them open with their own hands, and collapsed, bleeding out, onto the pavement.

Finally, there was Chug. He had rushed the Krieger troopers headlong, bellowing at them. Several energy blasts had impacted directly with his squat, rocky body, one blast even catching him full in the face. His pace never slowed; the actinic energy only left his stony exterior slightly smoking on the surface. He crashed into the troopers, knocking them down like bowling pins. He had kept them off balance, knocking each one down as they attempted to get up. The VDV soon saw the opportunity that the CCCPer was creating; the chain gun and coaxial gun opened up, targeting the joints of the Kriegers. The gunners didn't have to check their fire too much; any stray rounds that happened to hit Chug simply ricocheted off or splattered against his hide. Soon, all but one of the troopers were immobilized, their joints destroyed, and blood and other fluids oozing from the mutilated metal. The final one was able to snap a blast off; it took a single VDV soldier directly in the chest, killing him instantly. Chug plodded up behind the remaining Krieger, gripping its helmet with both hands.

"Bad mans!" Mineral tears were streaming down his face as he grunted once, pulling with all of his strength. The Krieger

flailed its arms for a moment, and then stopped moving altogether when the helmet—head still inside—came free. With a wordless, angry shout, Chug threw the gory trophy; it embedded, faceplate facing outward, in the side of a building, like a twisted piece of modern sculpture. Chug sniffled, wiping some of the tears away with the back of his hand. "Bad mans don't hurt Chug's friends."

Upyr started forward to go to Chug's side, apparently to comfort him...but immediately staggered backwards a step. Natalya's head snapped up in the direction that Thea was looking, and understood why her comrade had been so taken aback.

It was *another* dragon. This one was longer and thinner than the one she had seen Murdock and Sera engaging. It didn't have arms or legs, only a sleek and continuous snake-like body after the massive head. It was flying through the air like the other dragon, baleful Thulian-orange light showing past its segmented armor as it twisted and turned in the air. Its head turned, focusing on Chug; he was easily one hundred meters away from the rest of the team. Everyone began shouting to him at once, telling him to run, but he only looked confused, still sniffling in the middle of the street. The dragon surged forward, the trunk of its body filling the wide street as it barreled towards Chug. When it was within twenty meters of the short metahuman, it loosed an ear-splitting shriek; only then did Chug turn...just in time to disappear within the gaping maw of the dragon.

Natalya screamed with inexpressible fury and anguish. For the first time in this entire war, she felt herself frozen, unable to move, riveted in place by a needle of emotional agony. She wanted to charge the unnatural construction, to pummel it to pieces, and yet, she could not move. It was not only pain that held her in vice-like jaws. It was guilt.

She had thought that she could never hurt as much as when Petrograd, one of her oldest, dearest friends, had sacrificed himself to save them all from Sarin gas in the Invasion. But no. This was worse, so much worse. Poor, innocent, devoted Chug—

And it was her fault. She should never have brought him on this mission. She should have ordered him to *stay* with the rest of them. Or left him to guard Soviette. This was her fault, another comrade gone senselessly, and it was her fault. Boryets was right. Her recklessness was what had killed them all, every friend that had ever depended upon her.

The BMP began firing all of its weapons a moment later, focusing on the head of the dragon. Nearly all of the VDV opened up with their individual weapons as well; AK-74s and Pecheneg machine guns filled the air with a storm of lead, all of which was completely ineffective against the armored hide of the dragon.

"*. . . air support en route, Commissar. Jets will distract the dragon while your force retreats.*" Gamayun's voice was quiet; with her ability, she would have seen what had happened to Chug better than if she had been there herself. Natalya wished that her Overwatch rig was like any other comm device, right then; that way she could tear it off and smash it beneath her boot. Instead she simply acknowledged the message, and was about to issue the order for everyone to retreat—

—until the dragon roared again, focusing on her contingent. It had coiled upon itself, like a rattlesnake, ready to spring forward and attack. Natalya watched as it began to uncoil, using that stored energy to launch itself at her and her comrades . . . but the dragon hesitated at the last moment. Its "face" was mechanical, and betrayed no emotion other than the feral hatred that had been etched into its features by its creators to strike terror into the hearts of its enemies. But its body language was a different matter. There was apprehension there. *What is the damnable beast waiting for? Does it toy with us?* The dragon looked as if it were going to start its attack again, when it paused . . . and then reared up, an unmistakable shriek of agony issuing from its head. The dragon thrashed back and forth, destroying entire buildings in its pain and sending showers of rubble flying through the air.

"To the BMP! Take cover!" Natalya was too far away, but she could at least make sure that her comrades were safe. They were too spread out, and there was far too much debris falling to earth, some of it already crashing to the ground and exploding; someone was bound to be in the wrong spot at the wrong time.

Not if I can be helping it.

She kicked off of the roof on a plume of her meta energy, flying into the air. She judged that even with her fists fully charged with energy, she wouldn't be able to break some of the bigger pieces without being crushed herself. For those, she focused on redirecting them, pushing them out of the way with a meta-powered shove. The smaller pieces she was able to pulverize, discharging the energy from her fists in devastating blows. It was like trying to swat rain as it fell, however; there was so much rubble flying through the air, and she couldn't keep up. A soccer-ball-sized chunk of stone clipped her in the shoulder, spinning her like a top and breaking her concentration; even with the ECHO nanoweave stiffening and absorbing some of the kinetic energy, Natalya felt as if her entire shoulder were on fire. The next chunk caught her square in the back, knocking the wind out of her and causing the edges of her vision to go black. She fought for consciousness, seeing the ground rushing up to meet her. *Falling, falling!* At the last moment she was able to release her meta energy from the bottom of her feet, breaking her fall. She still landed hard, knocking her head against the cobble street; a cool, silent darkness engulfed her, and she stopped thinking.

She didn't know how long she had been out; she came to sputtering for breath, fighting with her spasming diaphragm to force air into her lungs. She felt hands loop under her arms, dragging her forward. She struggled for a moment, until she saw that the uniforms attached to those arms were in covered in VDV pattern camo. Two of the airborne soldiers were carrying her to the back of the BMP; there, Thea was waiting, her gloves off and her face glowing. Several of the soldiers already in the BMP, as well as Rusalka, were looking noticeably paler. As soon as she reached them, Thea pressed her hands to Natalya's face; immediately she felt more clear-headed, and her breathing more under control. Standing under her own power, she rushed to the side of the BMP, looking down the street. The dragon was still out there, and still thrashing.

The dragon spasmed a final time, shrieking futilely into the air before it collapsed to the ground, like a long rope dropped from a height. Its head fell to the east, crushing a row of buildings; the tail doing the same in the west. It rolled along towards the BMP; Natalya thought that it would actually reach them, crushing the APC like the buildings, when it skidded to a halt, throwing up cobbles and blocks of stone. The middle of the seemingly dead dragon lay draped in the street. *Could it be the firebombers, Murdock and Sera? What brought it down?* Slowly, the rest of her team and the VDV dismounted from the back of the BMP. Everyone kept their weapons trained on the body of the dragon, wary about what new horror might visit them. There was a . . . thumping noise coming from the section in front of them. Natalya charged her fists; whatever happened, she would be ready for it.

Or so she thought. A section of the armored plates, orange light no longer shining between them, started to shake and bulge outwards. With a final thunderous crash, the plates split outwards, a cloud of smoke pouring from the hole. Everyone trained their weapons on the opening... and a short, craggy figure stepped out, looking anxious. He had a handful of sputtering machinery in his right hand, a black and viscous liquid seeping from the ends of torn cables.

Within moments, he had spotted the Commissar and his comrades, and with a bellow of joy, he began lumbering towards them. Upyr gave a choked cry and ran past Saviour, to fling her arms about the rocky creature's neck.

It was Chug. For all of his terrible strength, he was always gentle with those that he cared for. Even the smallest of creatures had nothing to fear from him; he could cradle his pet squirrels with a gentleness that was in direct opposition to his brawn, and his comrades knew his embraces were as safe as a child's. He patted Thea's back comfortingly, as if he understood that they had all been devastated when the dragon "ate" him. Maybe he did. He seemed to understand, even sense, emotions at a deeply instinctive level. It was a mistake to deem him as simple; he might not grasp complicated situations, but his ability to cut through complications to the heart of a matter was profound.

It appeared he had "cut to the heart of the matter" this time, as well.

Natalya walked towards them, slowly, fighting to get her emotions under control. Relief and elation were the two uppermost, but there were plenty of others churning her insides and making her feel light-headed and just a little sick. Rusalka was on the comm already, calling off the airstrikes.

"Chug found this. Bad monster not know Chug is *tuff*." He held up his hand. The box he had was black, with cables and wires covering it. Through the narrowest slit at the front, Natalya could see what appeared to be a human brain—or rather, *a* brain, since whether it was human or not was not apparent—with wires running through it, floating in an amber liquid.

"*Borzhe moi*," one of the VDV soldiers said. "He ripped the damn thing's brain out." The assembled troopers began to cheer, crowding around Chug and patting him on the shoulder. Chug, initially apprehensive, smiled, beaming with pride.

"You did very well, Chuggy," Thea said, wiping away her tears with the back of her hands. "You are *bolshoi geroi*. Comrade Untermensch will be to giving you medal."

Chug rumbled uncertainly. "Instead of medal...Chug have cookies...?"

"I will bake you many, many cookies," Thea promised. Chug's smile broadened at that.

More figures stumbled through the opening that Chug had created in the dragon; after a moment of confusion and fear that it was Kriegers, everyone relaxed upon recognizing that the uniforms were that of other coalition forces. One man, an American army captain, stepped forward, shaking his head to clear it.

"Sumbitch must've been some sort of way for them to capture prisoners. Swallowed up my entire platoon; soon as we were in it, it put us in some sort of stasis. We could see and hear, but couldn't move. Scared the bejeesus outta me." He looked over at Chug. "If it weren't for your rocky buddy there...I don't want to think about what the Kriegers would have done with us. The stasis field didn't even hardly affect him; just seemed to have pissed him off." The captain turned to face Natalya. "We owe y'all one, ma'am. How can we help?"

Saviour straightened. Mere minutes ago, she might have arrogantly told the *Amerikanski* that she had no need of him or his men. An hour ago, she would have done so with a sneer. Now...

"We are needing to rendezvous with Spearhead, and the rest of my CCCP in Red Team," she said. "And I do not think we can be getting there alone. Your assistance would be welcome and appreciated."

Do not kick gift horse, Natalya Shostakovaya, she told herself. *You cannot being to afford such stupidity, ever again.*

Red Team: Ultima Thule

Spearhead Group, and consequently Red Team, were in trouble again. John knew that the advance had stalled; his HUD hookup through Overwatch gave him a pretty decent battlefield awareness, and the situation was rapidly deteriorating. Every time they made a push, the Kriegers pushed back just as hard. Sometimes harder; without the ECHO broadcasters that were being brought up from the rear, he knew that the line would have folded. Even with all of the artillery, the air strikes, the guided missiles and every available fire-chucker like him, they just couldn't hit enough targets fast enough. The Kriegers were flooding this area of the city with troopers, Robo-Eagles and Wolves, and Death Spheres. At one point he saw a squadron streaking away from the city; he came to the sickening realization that they were on a heading that would lead directly to the staging area. There was nothing he could do about it at the moment, other than report it on the comm; he had his hands full as it was.

Sera touched his arm to get his attention, and looked at him, her face furrowed with anxiety, her blue eyes flickering with gold. "They are going to target the broadcasters," she said, her voice trembling with fear and exhaustion. Their fight with the cyborg dragon had taken nearly everything out of them, for a time. That had been followed by some of the most intense fighting that John had ever seen, and they hadn't had a chance to truly recover.

"I know. When those are toast, our combat effectiveness is goin' to get cut by a whole bunch. We gotta protect those as much as we can, otherwise we're gonna get steamrolled." John leaned around the barrier they were using for cover, firing off a blast of plasma. "This can't last forever, though. We need somethin' to start drivin' for the center of the city again."

Another contingent of troops from the rear came to reinforce Spearhead Group; leading them was none other than Red Saviour, her Red Team Two and a mixed force of VDV and American soldiers behind her. Almost immediately they started lending their firepower to the battle; welcome as they were, it seemed like just another drop in the bucket. The Kriegers weren't simply rushing headlong into combat anymore; they were using cover, the personal and directional shields that the trooper armor could generate, and air support in the form of the Death Spheres and Robo-Eagles. *At least there aren't any more of those damned dragons.*

But that was only one blessing amid the mayhem. And the Kriegers knew this city; the best that the allied forces had were the maps Vickie was generating, and only those lucky enough to be wired into Overwatch Two—and Command and Control—had the benefit of those.

To answer the reinforcements for the allies, the Kriegers sent some of their own. The ground troops began advancing, first throwing a volley of grenades to soften up the defensive positions; an ECHO telekinetic was able to deflect the majority of the grenades, but enough got through. Anyone caught in the blasts didn't have a chance to scream before they simply ceased to exist as anything more than a cloud of ash. Then the shielded Kriegers started trudging forward; the shields prevented them from firing and slowed them down, but essentially made them invulnerable to any conventional weapons—fired from in front of them, at least. A massed group of more trooper armor and unarmored Thulians followed behind the shield wall, throwing grenades and taking potshots around the sides of the wall.

"Fire units; execute."

That was John's signal. He and the other fire-chuckers ramped up and let loose with a blast of fire at the same moment, washing the entire street in front of them with flames. The unarmored Thulians were taken out, not as neatly and cleanly as their own people had been evaporated by the energy grenades. These Kriegers screamed, some of them for quite some time. The armored troopers continued to march forward, undeterred. The Kriegers were also trying something new. John—and Sera as well—got a sense of it before it happened. Robo-Eagles swarmed over the rooftops behind the Krieger lines; each of them was carrying a Krieger, energy shields up from the arm cannons. But these Kriegers were also strapped with ... something. The forces of Spearhead Group fired at the Kriegers and Eagles, but the shields kept them largely protected.

It wasn't until the first trooper dropped straight from the claws of an eagle behind the Spearhead lines that John knew what they had been hooked up with. The trooper hit the ground next to one of the forwardmost ECHO broadcaster units; its shields dropped, and it began firing at the surrounding soldiers. It was only able to kill a few before it was taken out ... but as soon as the dead Krieger fell to the ground, an explosion like those generated by Thulian grenades, but much larger, enveloped the immediate area. The generator, two squads of soldiers and part of a building were completely gone when the blast subsided. And the line of Kriegers surged forward, their armor no longer weakened.

"Goddamn suicide troopers," John cursed, spitting on the ground. "They're goin' for the broadcasters."

"Focus all fire on the Eagles carrying troopers! We must be defending the ECHO broadcasters!" Molotok was doing his best to rally those around him, but it seemed to be too little, too late.

The entire force shifted their fire upwards, attempting to take out the troopers or their eagles. The Apaches and "zoomies" weren't able to get close enough to engage the suicide troopers; they were currently committed in a gigantic "furball"—aerial dogfight—above the city, doing their best to survive.

Sera had manifested a spear and was weighing it in her hand, then John felt her eyes on him again. He shut off his fires for a moment, and turned to her. "If we combine our powers—" she said, tentatively.

John nodded, knowing through their connection what her intent was. He grasped her spear in both hands while she still held it. Concentrating for a moment, he wreathed his hands in flame, funneling his own fires into the spear. When he didn't think he could bear it for another moment, he let go, stepping back from her.

She didn't hesitate for an instant; in the blink of an eye, she was throwing the incandescent spear as hard as she could. It flashed across the distance between them and the airborne Kriegers like a comet. And then it struck. The spear pierced straight through the energy shield of one of the lead troopers; it seemed to slow as it *pushed* through the shield, until it had gone completely through and lodged in the chest of the trooper. Then there was the detonation; the suicide trooper's payload went off in a dazzling explosion of actinic energy, the sphere expanding and swallowing several of the other Eagles.

There were no cheers from the other soldiers, not now; there was no time, and no energy to spare. Everyone continued firing, shouting orders, retrieving the wounded. They were saved, but only for the moment.

Sera dropped her hand on John's shoulder; he turned to look at her, through a haze of golden light, and saw her eyes blazing with that same light. The music swelled within him. And he knew—and she knew—

They turned as one, and left the forward line, racing together, dodging energy blasts and leaping over debris, knowing there were mere moments to spare before—

✧   ✧   ✧

The last Robo-Eagle carrying one of the suicide troopers was diving, hard and fast, for the last ECHO broadcast generator. John and Sera were both too exhausted to take it out before it would reach its target; the battle with the dragon, and the subsequent non-stop fighting, had left them both utterly drained, pushing forward through sheer willpower. The Kriegers had kept coming, wave after wave. If this broadcast generator went down, then the offensive would fold; they'd be driven back.

And that was if they were lucky. If they weren't lucky—If the Kriegers had another wave staged, waiting for the generator to go down...they would be slaughtered.

A Robo-Eagle was coming, carrying a deadly payload.

Bear and Untermensch were stationed at the last generator. Both of them had seen the threat, and were firing their weapons at the threat, but none of it was having any effect; the submachine-gun and rifle rounds simply pinged off of the shield of the Krieger and the metal hide of the Eagle. RPGs streaked up from the ground, but the Eagle was too fast, dodging around them, even with its burden. John watched in his mind's eye—that's the best way he could describe it—and then watched it play out in reality as Bear, glancing over to Unter quickly, dropped his rifle, and raised his gauntlets. John put on a little more speed, racing through and dodging around the troops. Next to him, but in the air, Sera flew like the wind itself, so low to the heads of their comrades that they ducked reflexively.

Pavel, using the last of the energy from the plasma chamber in his chest, fired off a thunderous bolt of concussive plasma from his energy gauntlets. The blast struck true; the Eagle didn't have time to dodge around it, catching the shot full in the chest. Knocked for a loop, the Eagle and the trooper it was carrying both plummeted to the ground, landing in the Krieger ranks; less than a second later the trooper detonated, either accidentally triggering its payload, or the impact having set the charges off. Dozens of Thulians were instantly vaporized, scattering their front lines. This time a ragged cry did rise amongst the coalition forces; the advancing trooper armor was scattered and disorganized, opening many of them up as targets for more conventional weapons. The advance was halted, at least for the moment.

When Sera and John reached the last broadcast generator, they found Georgi kneeling next to Pavel. The old Soviet was using a gloved hand to gently close Pavel's eyes. His gyroscopic heart, normally spinning with stored plasma, lay inert in his chest. Georgi was stony-faced, looking up to John and Sera slowly.

"He ran out. The last shot . . . it was all he was having left."

Red Saviour arrived next, skidding to a halt after a dead run. She looked as if she had hit a brick wall. At first she had looked ecstatic . . . until she saw Bear on the ground, unmoving. Now she looked stricken, stunned, her hands closed into fists as if she wanted to pummel something, but there was nothing to hit.

John felt both shock and a moment of sudden, absolute resolution. *Not like Perun. I'm not losin' another comrade. Never again, if I can goddamned help it.*

But the music was still sounding in his mind, and John started to move; almost unconsciously, he took Sera's hand, leading her over to Bear. Unter looked to them, suddenly suspicious; John didn't pay any attention to him. Sera looked at John blankly for a moment, and then an understanding sprang up between them, at a level too deep for words. They knelt down on either side of Pavel; as one, they placed their hands on his chest, Sera's on top of John's. He concentrated, reaching deep into his reserves of energy; he could feel Sera feeding him more, helping to direct and concentrate it all. He wreathed his hands in flame. *It's not quite right . . . there.* The music in his mind swelled to full, resonant chords. The fires turned from orange-yellow to white-hot, plasma; then the plasma took on the same red hue as Bear's concussive blasts. John was sweating, and yet freezing at the same time, and Sera's face was wracked with the strain of what they were doing. This wasn't a blast. This was . . . something else. Delicate. Precise as a laser-scalpel. Attuned as a violin at perfect pitch. It had to go from *here* to *there* without . . . hurting anything. Slowly, the plasma faded from John's hands . . . somehow passing through Pavel's chestplate without harming it, into the cavity with his gyroscopic heart. The empty space filled, and then flooded the heart.

The heart moved. Just a little, at first, as if it had been flicked with a finger. Then again. Then, it made a single rotation, slowly. Another. It picked up a little speed, slowed until he was afraid it was going to stop again, picked up speed, spun in starts, before the heart finally got momentum, kept it, and started spinning in earnest. John pulled his and Sera's hands away, extinguishing the plasma coming from them; the edges of his vision went dark, and he was barely able to catch Sera as she fainted. She felt as light as if she was made of nothing but bones and feathers.

Pavel's eyes flew open, and he sucked in one shuddering breath. "*Shto?*" He looked around, confused at everyone staring at him, at Sera's unconscious form and John. It felt to John as if he was breathing air that was too thin. He struggled to regain his composure, but couldn't seem to stop panting.

Georgi was the first to speak. "You were being...gone, Old Bear."

"Was being the best nap I've had since before the fall of Berlin. What happened?"

Everyone turned to look at John and Sera. Saviour in particular stared at both of them as if she didn't recognize them, as if they were *dangerous,* as if she wasn't sure whether they were on her side. Unter simply stared at them, his face still emotionless. Bear, seeing the way the others were reacting, was confused and unsettled. The Commissar looked like she was about to speak—when an energy bolt whizzed past her head, causing everyone to flinch and duck down.

The Commissar started again, then checked herself. "We are still having enemies to deal with. Old Bear, get off ass and start shooting. Georgi, keep him from taking nap again. Murdock... deal with your woman, then get back to fighting. We need your fire." What was left unsaid was that there would most certainly be a...discussion, later, about John and Sera, and what they had done. John wasn't looking forward to that, but he couldn't worry about it for now.

Victoria Victrix: Overwatch Suite

The rack of energy-storage crystals on Vickie's desk had been refilled four times. Or so she thought; she had lost an accurate count early on, too busy dealing with the infiltration teams and then later the entire assault force. Grey and Herb had just tossed the blackened, sometimes cracked, depleted crystals aside, and there was a pile of the rocks spilling over the side of the desk and onto the floor. Vickie felt like one of those crystals; overheated, cracking and just about spent. But she couldn't stop. She was needed everywhere. With Grey and Herb flying her "eyes" for her, she could spare her attention for what they were actually showing her; her hands flew over the keyboard as she moved from group to group—from Djinni to Corbie to Murdock, to those who were kitted up with the headsets like the Chinese. She'd damn near passed out getting up the rock barriers that had saved a couple of the groups before the Thulian Shield came down. The only reason she hadn't fallen down was that she *couldn't*. Passing out was not an option. But by now she was running on sheer force of will and not much else.

From her vantage of the entire battlefield she could see the overall pattern that was emerging, and she knew that Art of War could see it too. More and more Thulians were pouring into the battle zone from the farther side of Ultima Thule, and there weren't enough allied troops to handle them. They couldn't get enough troops in there fast enough, not without more of the Tesla generators than they had to soften up the defending forces. And those generators were clearly the primary targets for the Thulians, who knew very well how vulnerable the devices made them. One by one, they were going down.

She could tell by the spike in Bella's vitals that she saw it too.

But there was no time, and no energy, to *feel* anything. Not when people were relying on her battlefield data, on her warning voice in their ear, on her guidance, and on the tiny dregs of magic she could still manage to throw out there. Emotion was a luxury right now, and she was pared down to bone and sinew.

Then a new voice, someone she didn't recognize, pierced through the iron of her concentration. *"Jesus—Incoming! Incoming!"*

Jolted out of her near-trance, she scanned the banks of monitors frantically, trying to spot what that meant—and felt a gut-punch as she saw the mass of dots streaking from the far side of Ultima Thule towards Base Camp, moving as fast or faster than any jet fighter. The color, the aura of orange light, told her what they were.

Death Spheres. And there wasn't a damn thing she could do about them. Even if she'd had the resource of the Hammer available to her, it couldn't have taken out more than one or two. The now-depleted orbital platform took hours to get into position; pre-selected targets could have tungsten rods dropped on them in minutes, if you had a good idea where they would be, and with her magic "eyes" she had painted a bulls-eye right on top of the weapon that had threatened to turn the tide against them. But the station had exhausted its ammunition during the battle of the Thulian North American HQ, against the gigantic, possibly prototype Death Sphere—and hadn't been resupplied. That would have taken either a metahuman who could fly in vacuum—which, so far as she was aware, didn't exist—or some form of conventional space vehicle and a spacewalk, which had not exactly been a priority. And that had been only a single target, Now, there were...hundreds.

Before any jets or attack helicopters could be diverted to intercept them, the Death Spheres had arrived at the staging area. Bolts of energy razed the ground, destroying entire buildings or ripping vehicles and heavy equipment apart. A pair of spheres stopped in the air, hovering for a moment; then the thermite jets shot out from beneath them, burning everything they touched. Several ground troops began to fire back immediately; those closest to any of the Death Spheres were snatched into the air or impaled by the mass of mechanical tentacles that each sphere possessed.

All of this carnage passed on Vickie's screens in utter silence, save for the radio chatter. She watched, frozen, caught in the paralysis of utter helplessness. Slowly, too slowly, the defense rallied; jets and attack choppers made attack runs—all "danger close"—and soldiers began using surface-to-air rockets with ECHO payloads. The ECHO broadcasters at the staging area enabled the coalition forces to damage and destroy the Death Spheres with conventional weapons, but it all seemed like too little, too late. The damage was done by the time the last Death Sphere was destroyed, intentionally crashing itself into one of the few standing farm buildings before exploding. The staging area was a ruin; vehicles, ordnance and troops meant to be funneled to the fighting, destroyed. Hundreds, thousands of people...all dead or dying, in the span of mere minutes. Bella and her healers were spreading out among the downed troops, but the numbers that could be saved were vastly outweighed by the numbers of those past saving.

Then she heard it, the order from Art of War. *"Activate the Glass option,"* the man said grimly, from his command chair. *"We may have to use it."*

Vickie thought her heart stopped the moment she heard those words. She couldn't breathe, couldn't think, because she *knew* what that meant. The nuclear option. Not just one, but...well.

she didn't know how many, exactly, but at least a dozen nuclear missiles had been reprogrammed and aimed for Ultima Thule. And Art of War had just ordered them armed. If they were used, they would be launched and detonated sequentially; once started, there would be no stopping the sequence. Each nuke would launch, detonate over the city, and then several minutes later the next would do the same, until there were no warheads left. With the staging area being as close as it was to Ultima Thule, it was likely that they wouldn't get out unscathed if nukes started going off. Art of War knew that, of course...and yet he was still willing to detonate them. As for the people still in that valley...

"Sir... is that even going to work?" someone asked.

"We're out of options. Our people on the ground are going to be overrun and crushed, and soon. We need to get as many out as possible." There was a long, quiet pause over the comms. "The offensive has failed."

Somehow, Vickie's hands were moving over her keyboard without her consciously ordering them. For everyone wired into Overwatch Two, their HUDS were now flashing the evacuation order and showing the quickest way out of the city. For everyone wired into Overwatch One, a pre-recorded message was repeating in their left ears.

And that was all she could do. From thousands of miles away, that was all she could do. No earthen barrier that she could throw up would protect her friends, the people she loved, from the hell that was going to fall on them. All her magic, all her skill...none of it mattered.

Her hands fell limply onto the keys, and her eyes welled up with helpless tears, blurring the scenes of carnage on her monitors.

And yet...they kept fighting.

The wounded were being evacuated the hard way, largely not by vehicle, but by being carried, or half-supported, by fellow soldiers. She caught sight of a flash of black wings—Corbie, following the route on his HUD, directing the others. And, as her "eye" turned, there was another flash, of white this time—Einhorn, moving among the wounded, a touch here, a touch there, giving just enough healing, just enough strength to keep a faltering man moving.

Vickie watched as Einhorn dashed into the open and knelt to tend to one large group of wounded at the edge of the landing zone. All too suddenly, there was an explosion, followed by another and then another. A Death Sphere streaked overhead; it was quickly engaged by ground troops and air assets, but not before it had dropped a deadly payload.

Krieger armored troopers, an even dozen of them, all landed at the edge of the landing zone . . . right next to Einhorn and the wounded. Vickie did not expect what happened next.

The pearly little horn that gave the girl her call-sign began to glow, casting a gentle radiance on the wounded. Somehow, they struggled to their feet and began to move, with others rushing in to assist them when it was obvious that—for some unknown reason—the Kriegers were not moving. Einhorn's eyes were fixed on the armored Thulians—and they were not moving.

In fact . . . one after another, they began to droop, or bow their heads. One of them even began to shake. And that was when Vickie understood what she was doing.

Projective empathy. It was part of the meta's powers, and was usually more of an annoyance than anything due to her emotional outbursts. Somehow, Einhorn had gotten into even the Thulians' alien heads, and was bombarding them with—what? Grief? Remorse? Whatever it was, she had them in her emotional clutches, and she was not letting them go. Vickie found her hands clutching the armrests of her chair, willing more strength into the girl, as behind her, the men she had been healing and guarding were getting away, out of sight, out of range. Just a little more . . .

A single, thin beam of energy lanced out from a distant rooftop. The beam struck Einhorn in the back, just to the left of her spine. She turned, confused, looking for what had hit her. Then it seemed as if she grew too tired to stand any longer, collapsing to the ground. It looked unreal; even falling to the ground, she looked graceful and beautiful. It was almost theatrical, a movie death scene rather than the brutal reality of war. Vickie didn't need to check her monitors, but did so anyway, mostly out of habit. The readings confirmed what she already knew; Einhorn was dead. The soldiers around her immediately responded; first venting their rage upon the Krieger troopers that Einhorn had been entrancing, just now coming out of their stupor. Then upon the sniper, calling in artillery and using crew-served weapons to completely flatten the entire building the Thulian had been perched on.

Vickie swore, scrubbing tears of rage out of her eyes with the back of her hand. There wasn't time for grief; she had too many others that she had to try to save. She flung herself back into the frantic effort to get as many of her friends out of that valley as she could. Maybe the mountains would protect them. Maybe they wouldn't—but if she didn't at least try...

She was sending Djinni's team out the opposite direction of everyone else. He didn't understand, but he was following her directions anyway. From where he and the remains of the Misfits were, there was no way they'd get to the "right" exit point anyway. There were too many Kriegers between them and the original LZ. Maybe, just maybe, with the Thulians focused on the main assault, Blue Team could sneak out.

Spearhead wasn't retreating. They couldn't even if they wanted to; if they tried to run, they'd be cut down in the streets by the Kriegers who were pressing in from nearly all sides. So instead, they stayed to fight. Holding the line there meant that the rest of the forces would have more time to get clear. Their position was no longer the leading edge of an assault, but a "die in place" holdout; they'd occupy the Kriegers, and take down as many of them as they could. Even from the high elevation of the eye she was currently using, she could clearly pick out where Sera and John were. It would've been hard not to see them; great torrents of fire and spears made of flame were constantly assaulting the Kriegers, keeping them at bay. She didn't know where the two of them were getting the energy; after everything they had already done, and how much it had taken out of them...

She didn't want to watch Djinni. She couldn't. After the shield had gone down, Red and the remaining members of his team had opted to remain in the city and fight. Not the wisest of decisions, given that Silent Knight had lost his armor and between the three of them they only had a handful of magazines of ammunition left. It hadn't taken them long to go through them, and they had been forced to retreat to the city limits for evac. Of all the infiltrators, the survivors of Blue Team had the best chance of getting out of the blast zone, but that was a slender chance at best. And even if they got out of the immediate blast zone... the radiation, the fallout, the blast-wave...

There was a sound coming from her chest, a sound she hadn't even been conscious of making until this moment. It was the dull moan of a dying animal. Because there wasn't a chance. Not a chance in hell—no one was getting out of there alive. *We failed. And the world is about to fall.* In the novels that she wrote, the good guys won out in the end. Sure, there might be a long, hard road before they reached the end, and there would be loss... but the main character always found her true love, conquered evil and lived happily ever after. That's the way things were supposed to work.

The Thulians did not care about any of that. Once they had finished killing here, the rest of the world would be next. They couldn't leave this assault unanswered; it would be the Invasion all over again, but worse, so much worse. The only thing that would stop them would be for Art of War to call in the nukes and turn this part of the Himalayas into glass. And that would still leave everyone dead. A literal Pyrrhic victory... if it even stayed a victory. Because if the Thulians had forces concealed elsewhere... there would be nothing left to counter them.

"Unidentified contacts coming in from the south. It's... they're huge!" Vickie's heart went from *stopped* to *racing.* For no purpose, of course, what could she do about it? More Thulians... would just make Art of War call in the Glass Strike all the sooner. The staging area couldn't take another hit. If this was a wave of reinforcements for the Thulians...

Reflexively, she focused on Red. He and the others were nearly to the edge of the city. Now that the Barrier was down, there was a clear exit ahead of them. She couldn't tell him goodbye, couldn't paralyze them by telling them what was coming. After everything they had gone through, all of it, she couldn't even tell him goodbye....

"Red," she said, urgently. *"Move like you're on fire.* Please! Don't stop, don't think, and don't look behind you until you have a mountain between you and that city!"

He didn't answer right away. From his mic she heard heavy breathing, the rushing of wind, he was running.

"I read you," he said, finally. "It's bad, isn't it?"

She couldn't lie. Not to him. "It's bad."

"There really any point for us to keep running?"

"If you can get enough rock between you and what's coming? Maybe."

"We'll see what we can find," he panted. "But if this goes tits-up, I need you to..."

"*Shut up!*" Vickie screamed. "*Shut up and run! Whatever you're going to say, tell me later! When you're back, when you're…back…*"

"Victrix, listen to me. In case I don't make it, in case I'm not there to remind you, I need to do it now. Remember what you promised me."

"What I promised you?"

"Right, what you promised me," Red said. "Tell me, right now, what you promised."

"That…I won't give up. I'll keep fighting to the bitter end.…" She choked on a sob.

"That's my girl. Give Herb a tickle and Grey a kick for me. With a little luck, I'll see you soon. Red out."

<Vic. Heads up. Corbie needs an alternate route,> Grey said in her head, and she dashed tears out of her eyes and yanked her attention back to Team Earth and the stream of wounded they were trying to get out of the blast zone.

"*Bella…*" she heard from Bulwark—and then silence as he switched to private mode. He knew this was the end. And now, so did she. Vickie saw it in their readouts; the sudden hammering of the hearts…then the acceptance…then the monitors going dark as both of them closed their eyes. What were they saying to each other? What could they say?

She squeezed her own eyes shut, tears leaking out from both corners, painful sobs wracking her chest. It couldn't be more than a few moments now.

The Kriegers made their push. Their numbers had reached critical mass; they had enough troopers, Robo-Eagles and Wolves, and Death Spheres to steamroll through the city. Many of them had been building up near Spearhead Group. Even watching through the monitors, Vickie couldn't help but jump at Spearhead's response to the Thulian offensive; a titanic cloud of flame erupted from a pinpoint on the front lines for Spearhead Group, racing toward the Thulian lines. *Murdock's arc-light routine.* She'd seen it twice before now, and this was the third. Each time, it got.… bigger. She saw the reason; one of her eyes, keyed to Spearhead's location, showed Sera and John standing together in front of the defensive positions. Sera stood behind him, a hand on either shoulder; she…glowed, glowed white-hot, her fires pulsing like a heartbeat, and that energy was passing into John with every pulse.

Even with all of that fire, the Kriegers moved forward. She watched as the light blinked out, and John and Sera both collapsed to the ground, the last of their energy spent. Much of what wasn't on fire in that part of the city before had been ignited in a cone-shaped swath leading from the front of Spearhead Group's position. Everyone kept fighting, even as the Kriegers marched forward, and the unidentified readings on the radar reached the edge of the valley.

At first Vickie thought it was an explosion, some sort of impact with the edge of the mountains. Torrents of fire and cloud roiled there, menacing... but also as if the force that created the inferno was, inexplicably, holding back. Then the first edge of a craft pushed through the periphery of the clouds, fire and smoke streaking off it. That leading edge was followed by more, and more... *ship.* An immense craft, easily more than four times the size of the gigantic Death Sphere that Vickie had helped bury back in New Mexico. Four of the dragons like the one that Sera and John had ended could have stretched along its diameter and still had room before they reached the edge. Vickie's first reaction was that it was a new type of Death Sphere, a world-ender of some sort, come to wipe them all from existence. But... it wasn't a sphere at all. As it pushed out through the clouds of smoke and fire at the edge of the valley, its shape became clearer.

It was a saucer. An enormous, silvery, featureless saucer. There was no sign of the orange glare that was the signature of the Thulian propulsion. This craft merely hung in the sky, brilliant against the black smoke, the fires of the city reflected, distorted, in the chrome of its underside.

An even dozen craft seemed to peel off of the ship; all of them were identical, smaller versions of the mothership, about the size of a normal Death Sphere. They streaked over the city, faster and with almost sickening acceleration; they literally went from stopped to full speed instantly. They kept formation, a perfect "flying V," and were over Spearhead Group in mere moments. Vickie spotted John and Sera, feebly stirring, Sera trying to get John to his feet; some of the CCCP were trying to fight their way to them, but enemy fire kept them pinned down. Trooper armor was closing in; they were almost upon the couple...

The lead saucer opened fire. A single concentrated lance of what looked like blue-white lightning erupted from the edge of the craft, and hit the trooper closest to John and Sera. The Krieger exploded as soon as the beam touched him, sending smoking pieces flying, and the arc of—electricity? plasma?—passed on to the next, who suffered a similar fate. A heartbeat later, all of the dozen saucers began firing; through the sensors on the eyes she could hear a continuous roll of thunder from the blasts, all of which targeted the Thulians. Then she recognized it: TDRs, "Tesla Death Rays," only hundreds of times more powerful than the experimental models deployed at New Mexico. Armored troopers were completely destroyed, Robo-Wolves and Eagles left dead with smoking holes in their hides, and Death Spheres were sent flaming to the ground below. All from single, precise shots. The mothership started adding to the destruction, hundreds of blasts of deadly but focused lightning finding targets within the city, slowly marching from south to north ahead of the coalition forces.

And a frequency that Vickie had not heard from in weeks lit up on both Overwatch One and Two, in "broadcast all" mode.

"Steel Maiden and Mercurye to ECHO and allies. Are we too late for the party?"

Before Vickie could respond, Art of War had opened his comm. *"Welcome, Steel Maiden and Mercurye. I think we saved you a few."*

And that, that was when Vickie knew she might have one last, little trick to pull out of the bag, one ally she hadn't yet called on. It wouldn't save everyone. It wouldn't bring back the dead. But it would make a little difference.

Belladonna Blue: Forward Medical Base

It was like a miracle. It *was* a miracle. The huge Metisian mothership, and the squadron of smaller vessels it had brought piggyback, had materialized in the nick of time, before Art of War began the Glass Strike. It was like something out of a book.

And Bella had absolutely no time to revel in it. There were too many victims on the ground, and she was the *only* one of the metahuman healers with the ability and capacity to pull the worst of the worst back from the brink.

Bull understood that. *"Go to work, Bella,"* he said, as soon as they both realized they were saved. *"Do your job."* Which was his way of saying "I love you, but they need you. I can wait."

She wished, dearly, for Sera and her "angel juice," or Thea and her line of volunteers, but she had what she had, and she was going to make it stretch as far, and for as long, as she could. And try not to despair at the numbers of those yet to be tended whom she would not be able to help.

She had lost count of the men and women who had passed under her hands, and was on the verge of blacking out when... out of nowhere, a hand fell on her shoulder, and new strength flooded into her. Renewed, she finished knitting up the ruptured insides of a young medic, and turned, expecting to see Thea, only to look into the wise and wizened face of a Tibetan in a saffron robe.

She blinked, completely at a loss for words... and saw that the monk was only one of at least two dozen more, politely queued up behind him. Fortunately, she didn't have to say anything, for the monk spoke first, in British-accented English.

"Your magician friend sent us," he said, with a little smile that reminded her of the Dalai Lama. "We are not healers, but we have the means to give you the strength to heal. Carry on, my child."

Tears of gratitude sprang into her eyes, and the monk wiped them from her cheeks with a gentle thumb and an understanding nod. Then he put his hand back on her shoulder... and Belladonna Blue went back to work, the work that she alone could do.

Belladonna Blue: Forward Medical Base

"Overwatch to Bells. Kali wants to pay her respects. And I think you two need some face-time palaver."

Vickie's voice was flat, but that wasn't because she didn't approve of Khanjar paying a little call, it was probably because she didn't have the energy to do more than mumble right now. "I'm good with that," Bella replied. "Give me a second, I'll flit to somewhere that she can ghost into so we won't be interrupted."

Now where would that be... ah. Behind the ruins of the Coalition Command and Control building, that barn the allies took over. All the bodies had been cleared out, and there was still plenty of smoke and small fires burning. That should give Khanji plenty of cover.

Without looking as if she were in a hurry, but also walking purposefully, she made her way to the remains of the farm buildings. Vickie was tracking her, of course, and would be feeding her location to Khanji via the Kali rig.

"I have to apologize, Bells. I had too many balls in the air and I wasn't watching for Kali. I should have been. That she got in under our radar is my fault."

"Oh, for God's sake, Vix, who do you think you are?" Bella snapped. "Sauron's all-seeing eye? I have it on good authority that *he* missed a couple of hobbits!"

"...okay."

By this time she had reached what she considered to be a good spot, a niche in a tumbled-down wall where the view was restricted. She tested the stone to make sure it wasn't going to collapse on her, and leaned against it, waiting. She didn't have to wait long.

"Incoming," Vickie warned her.

Khanjar seemed to materialize out of the smoke, appearing before Bella. She was still wearing her Blacksnake gear; it was covered in grime and burns. She looked almost imperious, haughty as she coldly appraised Bella.

But the empathic vibes she got off the Indian meta weren't haughty at all. Just...controlled. Very controlled. Khanjar reminded her of Nat, actually. Both women were driven, both were extremely conscious that they needed to *appear* as well as *be* strong. Both were...unappreciated by those who should have given them more credit. *One of these days...especially if she joins our side... I should introduce them. They'll either love or hate each other.* "Khanjar," she said, with a nod. "Glad you requested this meet. I was going to ask, but you beat me to it."

The operative merely nodded her head. "It seemed prudent that we talk, given the way things have...progressed." She peered around momentarily. "You were not followed, I take it?"

"Well, as you know yourself, it's hard to sneak up on an empath. Were you?" She raised an eyebrow, to show she meant it ironically.

This time Bella was surprised; Khanjar smiled, ever so slightly. "No, I do not believe I was. Also with your...friend, Victrix, watching our every move, I doubt we shall be surprised by anyone. Correct?"

Bella nodded. "Let me cut to the chase for you. Maybe Verd is not paying your whereabouts any attention, but I think we need some plausible deniability for you. I've come up with some."

"Dom—Verdigris, for all of his faults, is a man of many resources.

If he was unaware of my departure, he's surely aware of my presence here now." Khanjar nodded, and relaxed against the other wall, mirroring Bella's pose. Deliberate? Probably. Bella doubted that Khanjar ever did anything by accident.

"So . . . I have one idea. Have you any?" she asked.

Khanjar nodded once. "Indeed, I do. First, what is your idea?"

"You got wind of the operation and came for the looting. I'm going to arrange for some duplicate Thulian equipment to be left where you and yours can make off with it. I figure Verd would try to do this anyway, and this way I control what he gets. What's yours?" Bella knew that there were plenty of people who would be appalled by this plan, but the way she saw it, Verdigris was going to get the tech one way or another. He had enough officials bribed in enough governments to ensure that. But once he had *some* shinies, he probably would concentrate on those, and not try for more. Vix flashed a green light in her HUD, showing she liked the plan.

"Simple. Dom is a man of singular purpose; when he wants something, he's rarely dissuaded. I was going to tell him that, despite my earlier reservations, I came here to capture the Deva— the one you call the Seraphym."

Bella blinked. "Huh. That's . . . interesting." *Surely, given what she's said so far, she wasn't* really *going to try for Sera . . . was she?* "Could you have pulled that off?"

Khanjar was silent for a moment, thinking. "Could I, at the time that the . . . other agent was sent after her? Perhaps. The better question is; would I have tried, if Verdigris had asked me to in the first place? I believe your friend, the Seraphym, has the answer." She turned her head to the side. "I believe that, together, both of these reasons will be sufficient to deflect Verdigris' suspicions."

"So, came for the—what did you call her?—the Deva, stayed for the looting." Bella nodded. "I'll make sure you get what looks choice. Small, portable, not obviously broken, melted or otherwise crapped up. It'll be left in that graveyard area; I'll have my people make a phony tomb if you don't want it left in the open. And I'll have *in-situ* snapshots of each piece so Verd can make a reasonable guess at what it's for." She inclined her head at Khanjar. "I'll try and make it look as thorough as I know you are."

"Her vitals spike every time she even talks about tackling Sera. No worries, Bells." The little whisper from Vickie made her relax

a bit more, as did the strong sense of *not going there* she got
from the Blacksnake op.

"I appreciate your ... candor, Ms. Parker. Continue doing what
you must, and I shall do the same."

"Oh, one more thing. What do you want me to do if we find
any of your people hurt?" That was the last loose end. There
were enough different uniforms in the coalition that Bella was
pretty sure no one would think twice about seeing one of the
Blacksnake ops, but Vickie had them all tagged at this point,
and Bella was pretty sure she could spirit a wounded Snake out
to where Khanjar could pick him up.

"All of my people are already accounted for. In one fashion
or another." Khanjar paused for a moment, turning to go ... and
then turning back. "I thank you for your concern. Blacksnake is
not evil, not entirely. Nor are the men working for it. Many of
them fought and died today, for the same ends that you seek."

"You relieve me." Bella was absolutely certain, given what she
felt from Khanjar, that "accounted for" did *not* mean "eliminated."
"Your men were heroes, today, Khanjar. So were you. I wish
people could know that."

Another smile, but this one was much sadder. "It does not
matter that people know we are fighting for them, Ms. Parker.
It only matters that we fight. We shall be in touch."

"You can bet on it." Bella waited until Khanjar had faded into
the smoke before leaving the niche herself. She took the long
way back.

Belladonna Blue: Command and Control Center

Bella felt as if she shouldn't be there. It was not the first time,
and probably would not be the last, but never had she felt less
prepared and more overwhelmed by her position as CEO of ECHO.

It was three days after the assault on Ultima Thule. Three days
since they had almost failed, and been saved at the last moment.
The Metisian mothership was gone, leaving behind Merc and
Ramona and a single ship with a couple of highly excitable female
pilots who looked like something out of a 1960s Sci-fi show. So
was Khanjar, which as much high-tech Thulian loot as a chopper
could carry. There was still so much work to do, it was difficult
to fathom where she should even start. So many wounded ... *too*

many. She had been working triple shifts, only kept awake now by caffeine and an energy boost from Thea a few minutes earlier.

At the moment she was lined up with generals, colonels and other military officials, headed by Arthur Chang, who was resplendent in a uniform with more medals and ribbons than Bella had ever seen in person before. And general's stars. Which, really, did not surprise her. Everyone was run ragged, but all of the uniforms were pressed and clean for this press conference. It was being held aboard the Command and Control plane, with video feeds for the viewers and for the interviewees. She felt horribly out of place, despite several other metahumans scattered among the ranks. There was Natalya, her CCCP dress uniform looking crisp; she had flatly refused any makeup to cover up the cuts and bruises on her face and neck. An... interesting distance away from her was Worker's Champion; as predicted, his Supernauts had basically refused all orders save for those from Boryets, and had simply rampaged their way through the city. As a result, they'd suffered tremendous losses. Which probably didn't matter to Boryets; there were more fools to fill the Supernaut suits where the last lot had come from. Ramona Ferrari had placed herself between Bella and Nat, reflecting her position as the intermediary between CCCP and ECHO. The commanders of the metahuman forces from the Chinese and other non-western contingents were also here, but none of *them* were under the spotlight the way Bella was. She was the CEO of ECHO, and the most visible place to start placing blame. And oh, there would be blame... for starters, blame that the attack had been kept secret, and blame that it hadn't happened sooner. Never mind the reality of the situation and what had led up to this point.

The monitors lit up, each one originally meant to hold a battle-field situation, a map, or information, and each one now holding a face. Reporters, representatives of government...

The questions started all at once, blaring over the speakers connected to the monitor of the press room back in the USA. The most predictable thing was that many of the reporters were directing their questions to Bella. After all, it had been ECHO that had been holding the line against the Thulians; it had been ECHO that was the focus of the Thulian attacks. And she was the head, the "warleader," of ECHO; the last offensive that had been mounted, in New Mexico, had been under her command. They naturally assumed she was the one in command here.

It was a cacophony. She could barely make out some of the questions, pitched more shrilly than others. *"Why have we only just now heard of this?" "Why did ECHO keep the location of this Thulian city a secret?" "Why wasn't the city attacked sooner?" "Is this the end of the Thulian threat?" "What is the nature of ECHO's involvement with this international force?"*

The questions felt like an artillery barrage. She kept her head high, even though she half wanted to scream at them all to *shut up,* and half wanted to slap her hand down on the kill switch. Where was Spin Doctor? Why didn't Vickie have him murmuring advice in her ear?

Arthur held up a hand; whether it was his presence even through a monitor screen or something else, all of the reporters and varied representatives fell silent. "First, ladies and gentlemen, I'd like to thank you all for taking the time to assemble for this conference. We don't have much time to speak, since there's quite a bit of work yet to be done, so I'm going to be as brief as possible while trying to answer the most pertinent questions." He paused for a moment, then continued. "My name is General Arthur Chang of the United States Marine Corps, leader of the coalition forces here in the Himalayas. Three days ago, at four-thirty A.M. local time, a coalition of troops from militaries from every corner of the planet came together and mounted an attack on what we believed to be the heart of the Krieger menace, a city called Ultima Thule. The city was located in a remote stretch of the Himalayan mountains, and was concealed in such a way that it was not able to be located by conventional means. This attack was conducted in secrecy so as not to alert our mutual enemy. The attack was a success. Through the courageous and valiant actions of the best that our world has to offer, we were able to capture the city." Arthur stopped again, allowing his words to sink in. "To accomplish this task, we enlisted the help of ECHO, the CCCP, the Supernaut Corps, and several other national metahuman organizations. Despite the extraordinary forces we arrayed against the enemy, we suffered significant losses, and are still processing the prisoners that surrendered to our forces. Until we have finished with that, and fully taking control of the city, there are not many details that can be furnished. Now, I believe that the President's press conference, and those of other national leaders, are going to start soon, so I'm going to sign off. Thank you, and good night."

Before the assembled body could begin their questions anew, the screens and microphones were switched off. Everyone in the room gradually relaxed, shuffling around and talking quietly amongst each other. Bella felt dizzy with relief, and actually had to put her hand on the back of a chair for a moment to steady herself.

Then, before he got caught up in something else, she crossed the few steps between them, and lightly touched Chang's elbow. He broke off what he was saying to an aide to turn his attention towards her. "I want to thank you, General. Twice. Both times for pulling my fat out of the fire. Here and now, and when you took over the job of commanding in the first place."

He smiled. "Don't thank me just yet, ma'am. We're not done yet. Still have a meeting to attend, and I have a feeling that this one will not be nearly as quick or pleasant as the press conference." Arthur swept an arm out in front of himself. "Will you accompany me, ma'am?"

"'Once more unto the breach,'" she said dryly.

He shook his head. "No, don't quote Boudicca. She ultimately lost."

Bella raised an eyebrow. "I thought I was quoting Henry the Fifth. All right, then. 'Damn the torpedoes. Full speed ahead.'"

The entire group was slowly shuffling out of the cramped C and C plane, and when Bella ducked out of the fuselage door, she saw they were heading towards another one of the same sort of inflatable shelters that the medic units were in. Well, at least they wouldn't be elbow-to-ear in there. The warmth once they got inside was very welcome; it probably wasn't more than a degree or two above freezing out in the open.

The setup resembled the auxiliary command center—now a heap of smoking stone and corrugated tin, and only quick thinking by everyone concerned had gotten all but a couple of staff out before one of the Thulian spheres had blasted it. There were several concentric rings of seats and desks, networked laptops on each, and a name plate. She spotted hers and headed for it, wincing as she sat down. She hadn't realized she had strained so many muscles....

She noticed as she sat down that there was one other thing on the desk. A little light, currently off, but with a button beside it. She smiled to herself. Well, that was one way to handle what was likely to be another barrage of questions. Whether or not Boryets and Nat would consider themselves required to *use* the light, however, rather than just shouting over the top of anyone who was trying to speak, was another thing altogether.

Arthur Chang took his place at the center seat, looked around to be sure that everyone had at least gotten to the right desk, and sat down. "All right. We have . . . a lot of business to deal with. Does anyone—"

Having already recognized what the little light was for, Bella had already slapped her button before he finished the sentence. She thought she saw a hint of amusement in his eye as he acknowledged her. "ECHO Lead Parker, go ahead."

"Prisoners," she said succinctly. "There are . . . thousands. We didn't make any plans for them, since we've never had Kriegers actually surrender before, and we can't exactly turn them loose. Hell, we don't even know what they *eat*. What are we going to do with them?"

At the far end of the room the representative for the Chinese Red Army metahuman team, a diminutive man wearing a face wrap and dark shades, pressed the button at his desk, the small light coming on. Arthur nodded to him.

"Is simple. They are still the enemy. They signed no Geneva Convention. Many are not even human, and those who are, are clearly in compact with the enemy. So, we deal with them like traitors; line them up and shoot them. Simple."

The room immediately erupted into roaring argument. Bella thought about trying to interject something into it, then thought better of the idea. Boryets and Nat seemed to be in almost-perfect agreement with the Chinese, with one little difference: they both wanted to torture a few dozen just to see if anything useful about the wrecked tech of the city could be gotten out of them. Bella only wished that Murdock were here; he'd managed to get some sense into Nat's head—

Hmm. Murdock gambit. . . .

"Overwatch," she murmured. "Open Red Saviour private. Nat. Boryets is trying to goad you into looking like a barbarian. Five minutes more, and he'll ramp up your temper and then he'll abandon the position of torture and execution, leaving you standing there holding the baby. Remember what Murdock said about torture when we interrogated Bad Bowie. Beat Boryets at his own game."

The Commissar shot a glance over to Bella, looking more

annoyed than anything. Instead of using the light on her desk to signal her desire to speak, Natalya charged her fist with energy and brought it down—lightly for her—with a clang against the metal desk. Everyone in the room turned to look at her, some of the closer military officials visibly startled.

"Perhaps summary execution after . . . enhanced interrogation is too quick for these dogs. There is being much to learn from them, if time is taken. Catching more flies with sugar, da? There may being other cells of *fascista* still scattered out in world, waiting to launch attacks anew. Then, there is matter of the . . . hybrids. The Thulian-human mixes. How such thing is even being possible . . . may be good to question them on it." She shrugged. "Nuremberg is being working once, and the world will be wanting to see these dogs face justice."

Worker's Champion looked at the Commissar coolly, and was about to speak before Arthur cut him and everyone else in the room off.

"The United States military already has a system in place for processing prisoners of war. I assure all of you that any intelligence we might be able to glean from the detainees will be shared—equally, I might add—with everyone's intelligence services and governments. At the same time, we are extremely visible right now; we're on the world stage, and any mistreatment of these prisoners will echo through history, tainting what we've accomplished here. It's not our job to determine their ultimate fate; our job is to make sure that there are no more threats out there, and to handle any that are. After all, as the Commissar rightly pointed out, their predecessors faced justice at Nuremberg, and there is no reason why such trials cannot take place again. In fact, there is every reason that they should. Agreed?" Before he was half finished, Red Saviour was nodding vigorously, and the more she nodded, the more Worker's Champion glowered.

One by one, everyone gave their assent. It was the combination of the Commissar's and Art's force of personality that ensured the argument ended, and right there. Bella couldn't help but notice a tiny smirk on the Commissar's face. She'd won over Worker's Champion, in front of *everyone,* and had used the ploy he'd potentially intended to use on her to boot.

That set the tone for the rest of the meeting. Some more ridiculous solutions were proposed, but for the most part Natalya and

Arthur remained in agreement...sometimes with some gentle persuasion from Bella for the Commissar. Once more, Bella was overwhelmingly grateful for the Overwatch system. She could rein in Nat without anything overt and potentially embarrassing. The occupation of the city was determined to be a multinational affair with NATO oversight, much to the chagrin of the Indian military, who wanted the whole nine yards for themselves. Other important matters, such as airlift evacs for wounded to military hospitals, where to house the Krieger detainees, priority of study of the remains of the Thulian city and technology, and so on, were dealt with more expeditiously. Before the city capitulated, it seemed that many of the support personnel and some of the troopers had slagged as much tech and equipment that they could, to keep it from falling into the coalition's hands. Bella had seen pictures and video feed of some of the wreckage; only guessing at the purpose of some of the machines, she was still unsettled. All sorts of obscure devices and mechanisms, manufacturing centers...even chambers that clearly were meant to hold living beings.

Finally there was a long moment of silence. And when the light at the desk of the German delegate came on, it almost made Bella start. "Just one small operational question," the officer said, with crisp politeness and not even a trace of an accent. "Why was CCCP fielding OpFours without informing the rest of the coalition?"

All eyes turned towards the Commissar, whose expression froze. Bella decided to bail her out and give her time to think. "ECHO and the CCCP have worked very closely since CCCP headquartered in Atlanta," she said into the tense silence. "I can tell you that to my certain and very personal knowledge, at least one of the individuals you refer to was certainly not displaying OpFour characteristics until today. As for the Seraphym..." She shrugged eloquently. "I'm not sure what she is. And neither is anyone else, although there's been plenty of speculation about it. She appeared, working on our side, in the first Invasion and has never officially been with ECHO *or* the CCCP, although the CCCP accepted her as an ally-combatant when she volunteered. All I know is she's still on our side." She lifted an eyebrow at the German. "Of course, if you want to question her yourself..."

The German army representative shifted uncomfortably. The Commissar took this opportunity to interject.

"Metahuman powers have being known to fluctuate, especially in times of stress. We did not willfully withhold information about the capabilities of our comrades; to do so would have been foolish, since planning could take such a factor into account. I assure all of you, however; my people are not being ones that you need to worry about. The situation with the two comrades in question is under control."

Bella understood the apprehension, and she couldn't help but feel some herself. There were very, very few OpFour's around, and for good reason. Even someone like Worker's Champion or Chug, whose superstrength and invulnerability were the stuff of modern legends, only qualified as OpThree. Many of the OpFours still in existence were forces of nature; where they went, things *changed*. And not necessarily for the better; nearly all of the most powerful metahumans had some sort of mental instability. For the most part, whenever they were used they were channeled as best as was possible, but sometimes... attempts to control them just didn't work. The incident with the Mountain was still the matter of a lot of controversy back in Atlanta. So far, it didn't seem as if John and Sera were a danger to anyone; the level of power that they evidenced during the attack was the most frightening aspect of the two of them, not the way they used it. Once they were all back stateside, she hoped she would get the opportunity to talk with both of them again, get a better read on them. Though, really, if she got a chance *now*... she'd feel a lot more comfortable.

The Commissar was saved from further questioning about the couple. There was an LCD screen hanging on the wall behind Arthur Chang that had been dark until this moment. Now it came to life. Vickie's weary face appeared in it. "Permission to speak, sir," she said into the silence. "I... uh... don't have a light to flash at you."

Taken by surprise at the hijacking of his own equipment, Chang turned to stare at Vickie in surprise. "Who—" he began.

Bella interjected smoothly. "One of my electronic intel techs back in Atlanta, sir. You interfaced with her during the battle. She wouldn't be interrupting if she hadn't discovered something."

Chang nodded. "Very well then, please speak, miss—"

"Been going through camera footage, and got this, sir," Vickie said, *not* identifying herself as Overwatch, much less as the operator of Overwatch Two. The screen switched to what Bella recognized as the moment right after the Metisian ship appeared. This was a relatively undamaged part of the city, and there was something in the middle of the picture that riveted everyone's attention.

A metal dragon.

By now, everyone was familiar with the images of the flying fire-breather that Murdock and the Seraphym had destroyed, and the serpentine troop-devourer that Chug had literally punched his way out of. This was not either one of those.

It was hard to tell for certain, but Bella got the impression that this beast was larger than either of the other two. There were a couple hundred armored Kriegers attached to the sides for transport, as they did with the Death Spheres. The thing had its neck stretched out and its mouth open, and more unarmored Kriegers were running in through the mouth, some with their arms full of equipment or things unidentifiable.

The focus zoomed in. Bella gasped, and so did anyone else who recognized who the two figures running for the dragon were.

Ubermensch, in his full armor, being pulled along by Valkyria. He was gesticulating, clearly objecting to retreat. She was not taking "no" for an answer. The focus zoomed in even tighter; and Valkyria paused.

Then she turned her head and stared. Right at the camera. Which should not have been possible, Bella knew, since Vickie's little spy-eyes were invisible. But what happened the next moment confirmed that somehow, not only was Valkyria aware that she was being filmed, she could *see* what was doing the spying. Because she frowned, pulled out a pistol of some kind—and pointed it at the camera.

And the screen went blank.

But before anyone could react to that, a new view, from farther away, came up. The camera zoomed in again, but it was so far away that the only thing that could be determined was that the two figures running into the dragon's mouth were indeed Ubermensch and Valkyria. And once they were aboard, the mouth snapped shut, the head lifted up, and the dragon rose into the air, scales outlined in the orange glow of Thulian propulsion. Taking advantage of the billowing clouds of black smoke, it disappeared into them, only to reappear in the distance. Then it rose over the side of the mountain, and was gone.

"That was an evac, sirs, ladies," said Vickie. "And an evac generally has a place to evac *to.*"

A light came on at a desk at the back. "I know some people who might be able to help with that," said a welcome and familiar voice, and Ramona Ferrari stood up so that people would be better able to see her.

It looked as if she'd gotten better control over her rebellious epidermis; there was just enough metal showing along the edges of her cheeks and jawline to make it obvious she was metahuman. She was wearing a standard ECHO nanoweave uniform rather than the armor-and-nanoweave suit Bella had had made for her, and had a lit cigarette in one hand.

"Steel Maiden?" Arthur Chang said.

Ramona nodded. "Yes, sir. Also former ECHO detective Ramona Ferrari," she added. "And the time has come to tell you all about a group of people who call themselves *Metis.*"

CHAPTER TWENTY-EIGHT

Soul of a Man

MERCEDES LACKEY AND CODY MARTIN

John never thought he could be so bodily tired as he was after the assault on Ultima Thule. After the Metisians had come riding to the rescue at the last possible second, it had still been a day and a half of bloody fighting against the remnants of the Krieger forces before they finally caved. Once that happened, nearly the entire complement of CCCP personnel—save for the Commissar, Molotok and a few others as security—were shipped back to Atlanta, with Untermensch in charge. The city needed a CCCP presence, for public relations as much as for keeping the peace. The same went for ECHO; anyone who wasn't part of the leadership council was on a C-130 back stateside. The conventional military forces were to be in charge of the prisoners captured and were holding what remained of the ruined city. That suited John just fine; they had gone in, done what needed to be done, and then they got to go home.

Even though he and Sera had slept, for the most part, the entire way back, the flight had been somewhat tense. No one seemed to want to sit too close to them, and there were lots of glances and whispers directed their way. John was sure that he could actually *feel* the apprehension and fear that everyone was experiencing, though he still didn't know how. Initially, it had been no better once they were back at the CCCP HQ, unloading and inventorying equipment, running through post-operation medicals, and the like. What there was of equipment to bring back, that is; there hadn't been a lot to haul home. What hadn't been used had, more often than not, been destroyed in the

506

fighting. Much of the equipment had been borrowed from ECHO, so it wasn't that much of a net loss, but in true Russian fashion, everything had to be double-checked, with paperwork filled out in triplicate, by hand.

Everyone around the base was walking on eggshells when it came to John and Sera, none of them willing to break the silence to talk about the obvious questions; just how powerful were John and Sera, now, and could they still be trusted with all of that power? John had heard talk that they were thinking of classifying him and Sera as OpFours, now. It was unfathomable for him. It didn't feel like he was all that powerful, or drastically changed. Well, besides his health; he hadn't realized how tired he had always been when he was still dying. The new ... senses were what really bothered him the most. But he still felt like the same man; not insane, not vested with terrible power. Just ... same ol' John Murdock, who liked a few brews after a long day on patrol, would tear into a good steak like a tiger, and had a healthily carnal interest in the love of his life.

It was Pavel who saved him and Sera, in the end. Most of the team was assembled in one of the larger storage rooms, moving and logging crates. Bear had been shifting uncomfortably on his feet; he was watching everyone else, how they were reacting to John and Sera, still keeping their distance. Finally, it seemed that he was fed up.

"*Eto smeshno,*" he muttered, uncrossing his arms and standing up. He clomped loudly over to John and Sera with everyone's eyes on him. There was a pause that seemed to go on too long as everyone was quiet and still.

"So, Murdock. Are you planning on being exploding any time soon? If is being so, give warning so I may relocate stock of Chef Oh Boy cans. A bear can get hungry. No? Good. Help with welding job in motorpool after we finish chore here."

And just like that, the tension snapped like an overstretched rubber band. The others began treating John and Sera like part of the team again. Georgi was his usual gruff and stoic self, Thea began calling him "Chonny" again, and Jadwiga badgered him about getting an updated medical.

He hadn't realized how much he had come to depend on all that, until it was gone. After having been on the run from the Program for so many years, and being completely alone, he now had friends, family even. First with the neighborhood that he had helped to rebuild and defend. Next with the CCCP, his teammates who accepted him even now when others feared or shunned him. And finally, Sera, his beloved. That was surely a mystery to top all others; that he had found love again. It all added up, and gave him a full heart. *I haven't felt home in a long, long time. But I think this is what it's like.*

It wasn't until later that night, after their shift had ended and they were able to retreat back to his squat, that John and Sera had a few moments alone. They were both still exhausted from the work of the day and their exertions during the battle in the Himalayan mountains. Instead of flying—which he was starting to really enjoy, now that he was getting better at it—they walked quietly, taking in the cooler night air and the quiet sounds of the neighborhood settling down for the evening. They took their time, arm in arm, each with their thoughts. They didn't need to talk right then, it seemed; enjoying each other's company was enough.

Sera waited until both of them had cleaned up and become comfortable before she approached John. He was on the roof of the squat, where they had so often talked, sipping a cold beer.

She waited a moment, poised in the entrance to the roof, regarding him from behind. How often she had watched him like this, and him not aware of it! But now—

"Someone tell you to keep the door propped open with your-self, darlin'?" he chuckled, not turning his head. She laughed a little, and joined him, arms crossed on the edge of the parapet that surrounded the flat roof.

"You knew I was there."

He grinned lopsidedly. "I knew. Can't help knowin' anymore, it seems. We're stuck together." He leaned over, brushing his shoulder against hers.

"Does this trouble you? It is...a symptom of how things have changed, for both of us." She turned her gaze on him; at the moment, her eyes were human, a beautiful blue.

"That part won't ever trouble me, I don't think, darlin'. But the other stuff...it's given me a lot to think 'bout, that's for sure. I can feel others' emotions if they're close enough, now; it isn't quite mind-readin', thank goodness. I don't know if I could handle bein' in anyone's head but my own."

"Then I will take that burden upon myself," she said, gravely.

"I shall shield you from it. But...the emotions, I do not think I can shield you from. It is something you...I...*we* need. We must always know the cost of what we do to those around us."

"Well...hell, darlin'. I can't ask you to do that on your own. We'll handle it together; it's how we've come this far." He took her hand. "I just want to know what the hell it *is*, first. This may be old hat to you an' other angels, but it's fairly new for lil' ol' me, y'know." He softened his words by grinning at the end.

She smiled, and lifted his hand to her lips to kiss it. "No magic, nothing you have not heard of before. Just what Bella does. Telepathy, and empathy. I shared both with her, when you... changed. So the power of both is divided by three, and the power itself is lessened from what it once was, as all my powers are. Empathy, that is simple. You feel what others feel. *We* need that, you and I, so we are always aware of the impact of our power. Telepathy, you can, indeed, read at least the surface thoughts of others. Bella is more powerful than either of us, there, now. She can read deeply, deeply beneath the surface, as deep as she cares to go. I began sharing power with her before you and I came to know each other well."

"Maybe I ought to start takin' lessons from her to get a handle on this. Think she'd go for it? I don't feel comfortable with it as it stands; I sure as shit wouldn't want a baby telepath traipsin' around my noggin."

She took his hand in both of hers. "You can trust Bella as you can trust me. And it would relieve her greatly. She is concerned about us."

"We'll have t'do somethin' 'bout that. Havin' Bella on our side can only help when it comes to Natalya." He thought for a few moments, sipping from his beer before continuing. "As far as the new...abilities go, there's also how we are when somethin' needs doin'. Like fightin'."

She nodded. "We frighten people. We are...we are very, very powerful together. Much more so than the two of us separately. I think perhaps even you are frightened."

John shrugged, pondering for a moment. "No, it's not quite that. I mean, that's somethin' else that we *are* gonna have to deal with. I'm used to bein' one of the things that goes bump in the night for bad guys, so bein' feared isn't...new. Bein' feared like *this* is. We've both been dangerous people for a long while; hell, all of our friends are dangerous. It's that now we're bein' seen as dangerous to the wrong sort of folks. Our people. Ol' Man Bear saved our bacon earlier, that's for certain. Not quite sure how things are gonna play out with the Commissar, though. You saw her face when we . . . well, when we brought Pavel back."

Sera shook her head. "We did not bring Pavel back. He had not left. We merely made it possible for him to continue."

"Y'see, that's the thing, though. Did you know that we could do that, before we did it? It was like one moment he was gone . . . but then we started movin', not needin' to say a single word, and we did what we did. I sure as hell didn't know."

"How do you think Bella saved the Commissar?" She laid one hand lightly over his. "How do you think Bella saved *you?* That was once one of *my* powers. Now it is *ours,* shared. We know, without knowing how we know, when it is Permitted to assist others to live, and we make it so." She turned her gaze skyward. "It is not everyone we may assist, and only rarely, but we will know when Permission is given. If you were to listen closely, you would hear it, the Voice that tells you these things, but in the midst of chaos it is not possible to listen, and so the Infinite makes it known within us and shows us the way."

"That's pretty spooky, y'know. At least for a dumb grunt like me." He took another swig of his beer. "Somethin' like that happens when we're fightin', too, doesn't it? But different, I think. We're more in control, we decide what to do . . . but it's like it's all laid out for us beforehand. What movements to make, where to strike, when to dodge."

"Together, we can see the futures. Not as much as I once could, alone, but that truly *would* drive us both mad." She shook her hair back, so that it fell between her wings and down her back. "We see what our enemies will do, and so we can move to counter them."

"So, it's kind of a . . . battle-sense, or something. Does that sound right?" He turned to look her in the eyes, setting his beer on the ledge. She turned her gaze from the heavens to meet his eyes.

"That is a very good thing to call it," she said gravely. "The sense of how the battle will flow. I . . . think . . . if we were to be quiet together, we would see more of the futures. How much, I do not know, and I know it would be limited. Mathew March could not bear the sight. I am not altogether sure how much we could."

"Heh. I'm not sure that I want t'see much of the future; the present is complicated enough as is."

She smiled, and brushed the side of his face with her fingers. "It must be done together if it is done at all, beloved."

"Let's hold off on all the divination an' spooky stuff. I've got a better idea of how we can spend our time for the evenin'."

She chuckled, low and happily. "One does not need to see the futures to predict what you have in mind."

"What can I say?" He grinned again. "I'm a simple man, sometimes."

This was not a call Vickie was even *remotely* comfortable with making. But it had to be done. Bella was counting on her.

"Overwatch: open: JM: private. Johnny?"

It took a few moments before she heard a reply. "Murdock here. What's the sitch, Vick?" It sounded like he was still waking up. Given the last few days that everyone had gone through, she wasn't surprised that he was resting up. Last few days? Bloody hell, this last *month* had been a roller coaster, and most of it had been utterly terrifying. If there were any justice, they would all be on a beach in Tahiti right now.

It's such a magical place, and Lord knows that Thea could use some sun. . . .

"Listen, big guy, I am gonna cut straight to the chase. You guys are scaring the bejeezus out of anyone who knows anything about metas, and it is a *damn* good thing no one has released footage of you two to the press yet. Bella promised everyone to give you a once-over, she can't because she's ass-deep in VIPs and Metisian crap, so she asked me to. So . . . you got time to come over and get magically vetted as sound and sane?"

"Give us fifteen to get decent an' get over there?"

"Sure. Shall I send a cab?" she asked, not entirely in jest. *How are they going to get dressed and over here in fifteen minutes? Are they materializing clothing now? Is he going to pick her up and carry her while he sprints? It'd take a Ural at least half an hour to get here.*

Then again . . . maybe there aren't any Urals left. Still . . . how the hell are they going to get here so fast?

"Naw, save the fare. We'll manage. See you in fifteen; Murdock out." She went to put on a pot of green tea.

Fifteen minutes later to the dot, there was a knock on the same window Red Djinni had plunged through to save her life. She had had it replaced with a kind of miniature metal French door, a metal gate that opened inward, glass that slid up, and screen that opened outward so she could open it to fresh air, and, yes, let aerialists like the Djinni in, but still have the security of bars on it. And there was a tiny faux-balcony out there, just enough for a foothold.

Sera and JM were hovering outside the window. Thankfully, they were both fully dressed. John was balanced on what looked for all the world like *rocket motors* on his feet. Well, the flames of rocket motors, anyway. She threw the window open, staring at him. Okay, sure, she knew thanks to his ocular camera that he flew, but this was the first time she'd seen it in person.

"Mornin', comrade. Got a pot of tea ready?"

"Uh, yeah, come on in." She backed away from the window, wondering how they were going to manage the maneuver of getting inside without falling or getting wings hung up on the window. Or, in his case, *setting fire to the building*.

Sera accomplished it by backing up a bit, getting higher than the window, touching down on the balcony with her feet, grasping the upper ledge of the window and swinging inside with wings tucked in to her body and tightly closed.

John dropped down a few feet below the bottom of the window, until only the top of his head was showing. Then, with a loud pop, he ramped up and then turned off the fires around his feet, propelling him up and in just enough to clear the window and land at his full height on the floor.

"Know how to make an entrance, for sure," she said, closing the window again.

"I'm gettin' better. Sera can still fly circles 'round me anytime she feels like it." To Vickie's surprise, Sera's response to that sally was a low chuckle and a happy smile. A smile! Vickie tried to think if there had been *any* time that she had ever seen the angel smile, and couldn't. There was nothing wistful or sad about the smile; it was full of joy and contentment. She was changing. No, she *had changed*.

And so had John Murdock. The ease and relaxation of the "new" John, the surety of the old John, and a quiet joy that matched the Seraphym's. In fact...

In fact, they were no longer, in several senses, *two* beings. They were two halves of a greater whole. Yin and yang, twin stars, two living flames intermingling to be brighter together than they would be apart. The Seraphym—the old Seraphym—had made Vickie's knees melt with awe. These two, together, only filled her with wonder. *Nothing will ever separate them. Nothing. Not death, not time, nothing known to this reality.* It was...perfection.

Her mouth was dry and she went to pour three mugs of tea, downing one before handing the other two off. "Well, so..." She swallowed hard again. "Sera, I am going to take a pass on vetting you. First of all, you were an OpFour quadruple Lutz combination with a triple toe loop, a double Salchow and a half flip, and a ten-point-zero from the Soviet judge *before,* and you didn't wig out on anyone. I think we can count on you not going postal now."

Sera hid a smile behind the tea mug, but Vickie saw her raise an amused eyebrow.

"On the other hand, Johnny, you were just a garden-variety fire-chucker before you turned into Vulcan, God of Fire, though maybe Perun would be more appropriate..."

She stopped short when she noticed John wince ever so slightly, and watched Sera gently place a hand on his forearm. He feigned mock hurt to cover for himself, but she could tell that she had struck a nerve. "Garden variety? I figured I was at least mid-shelf."

Oh, shit. Wasn't there a CCCP meta who died next to him by that name? Yeah, during the Reb attack that Ubermensch showed up for. Way to stick your foot in it, Vix.

She swallowed nervously, and continued her train of thought. "So..."

"So. You want to perform rites over me, with incense an' athames an' all sorts of other mystical implements, to insure that I won't turn inside out and set everythin' on fire. Well, unless I'm asked to, right?" John sipped his mug of green tea quietly, his eyes watching her with a sort of bemused intensity over the edge of the cup.

"Asked to? Or told to?" she asked soberly. *Is he going to insist on being asked politely or is he still willing to follow orders? Because...we really don't need an arrogant godlet right now....*

John waved his free hand outward, placatingly. "Just a turn of phrase, comrade. All the same," he said, folding the hand under his arm as he sipped from the mug. "You invited us here for a reason. We came here, right?"

If this had been either of the old JMs, she wouldn't have

hesitated. The words would have had no extra weight behind them, they would have been simple, and simply interpreted. But this was a man who had done impossible things. He had all of the lethal skills of the old man, and far more power.

And he killed, and did not hesitate. That was the problem. Before, angered, he could have killed . . . several people, if he had to, bare-handed, without his fires. But it would have been precise and surgical, and there would have been no overkill. People would be dead, but only if it was necessary.

This was a . . . man? . . . with the same calm ability to kill. But was he a man with the same control, the same judgment, the same *restraint?*

And that last strike before the Kriegers had made their final push, when Sera had been boosting him . . . before they collapsed, he had fried *blocks*-worth of the city, and the two of them weren't even at full power when they'd done it; they'd been exhausted by their earlier efforts. What could they do if they *were* at full power? What had Michael March said? "The world in flames"? Had she been wrong in her interpretation all this time? Was this what he had seen?

But did that jive with what she knew about John as a man, as a human—well, metahuman—being? Would that much power have made that much difference? Other OpFours had come fully into their powers, from nothing, and that much change over that short time period *had* made them all crazy. A lot crazy, like some, or only a little crazy, thinking you were a goddess, or drowning yourself in the middle of the ocean because you were suicidally depressed. . . .

Maybe coming into your power slowly . . . you stayed yourself. Maybe when you had someone who loved you, who completed you, and who, herself, was preternaturally *stable,* you would be stable too?

Only one way to find out. "Let's do this," she said, putting her mug down. "I promise it won't hurt you." *Me? Well . . . remains to be seen.*

John shrugged, finishing his mug before setting it on a kitchen counter. "Lead on, Teenage Witch."

The little rock-creature that Vickie called Herb came toddling into the living room, spotted Sera, and made a beeline for her. Vickie's enormous familiar sauntered up to John and looked up at him, then gave him a brief brush of his head and followed Herb.

That steadied her. If Herb—who was still an Earth Elemental—and

Grey, who was far more attuned to the preternatural than she was, were comfortable with John . . .

"After you," she said, opening the door to her workroom.

She'd put away the cot that Sera had used here for so long, and it was back to being the magical workroom that she was used to. Well, sort of. There was still a boost in her wards and shields that seemed to be permanent and could *only* be attributed to the presence of the Seraphym. Even at reduced power, she had had Celestial protections, and that seemed to have "rubbed off" on Vickie's own protections. As John took his place in the center of her magical circle . . . without her direction . . . she raised the wards and strengthened the shields with a brief invocation and a triggering thought.

"All right. Like I said, this won't hurt you," she told him, and began the process that would reduce him to the mathemagical formulas that would, she hoped, tell her everything she needed to know. "You can talk if you like."

All right, Johnny Murdock. How much of "you" is still in there? She knew exactly what "he" used to look like . . . from her old sample, she had a mathemagical model that described him in every possible way . . . from the simple physical structure, through the enhancements and powers, to his personality. Now she had to build a new model to compare the old one to.

Simple physical structure. That was the "least complicated." And already there were differences, positive ones. The thing that had been killing him was gone. But not at the expense of losing his old powers. Now . . . enhancements and powers . . .

Oh, new things there. Without asking him what they were, she couldn't actually *know* what they were. But there was something she recognized from Bella as *Empathy and Telepathy.* There was something else in the mix too . . . something she couldn't ID. But it was linked in with what she knew were mental/psionic powers, and she wasn't going to have to worry about that. If he were going to have problems with being a psion, he'd have shown it by now.

Fires . . . her eyes widened as she realized how amped up they were. Oh, she'd known that, but here it was, quantified. *But he's not the powerhouse the original Seraphym was . . . thanks be to the gods.* People were *not* meant to handle that kind of power. Well, the instability of the OpFours pretty much proved that. And . . . she looked closer . . . closer . . . was that a Celest—

There was no warning. There was a shrill of visceral alarm and suddenly she found herself propelled into the wall, as if she had been backhanded by a giant. She didn't even have the chance to prepare herself for a better fall; she hit the wall and slid down it, seeing stars.

"Jesus!" Johnny was instantly by her side. "Are you all right, kiddo?"

Her brain wasn't working. She looked up at him, dazed. "What… happened?" she managed.

"I…I don't know. I felt somethin' buildin', so I…I guess I kinda shut off the connection? Are you okay?" He looked concerned, crouching over her but careful not to touch her, as if he was afraid he would give off static electricity, or worse.

She laughed shakily. "Show me on the doll where the bad magician touched your angel-parts, Johnny," she said.

He cocked his head at her, then grinned lopsidedly. "You ain't right, mage. Y'know that, I hope."

"Let's try this another way. Out to the living room, with Sera there. No shields, no wards. I think whatever that was, it interpreted my looking as a threat. I think with Sera there, it might not. Or she'll keep it from zotting me." She started to try to get to her feet, but didn't get the chance. John picked her up bodily and set her down again, carefully.

Once out in the living room, she explained to Sera what she was going to do, who listened, nodding. "I believe I know what happened, and yes, I believe I can prevent it from hurting you again."

Vickie raised an eyebrow at John. "I *did* say that it wasn't going to hurt *you*." And without waiting for a reply, and with John sitting beside Sera on the sofa, she repeated her incantations, this time zeroing in on the fire-powers.

This time…rather than attacking her, the "Celestial" component did something she had never seen magic do before. It scrambled and blurred itself, changing the equations so rapidly she literally could not read them. "All righty then," she said aloud, satisfied that at least it wasn't going to constitute a threat. It just didn't want anyone who might be able to *use* it to *look* at it. That was fine. *I don't want to muck with Celestial magic anyway. Ever. Way above my pay grade.*

She dismissed everything with a sigh. "Short form, you two aren't going to go crazy, and you aren't going to hurt anything that doesn't deserve it, at least as long as you two are together.

John, the two of you are *insanely* powerful and dangerous in the right circumstances, you especially, given your personal experience combined with the new abilities and senses you have. Sera acts as . . . a channel for the power, and as your governor. And don't worry *what would happen if she were gone.* It won't matter. She could be *vaporized* and you would still be 'together' in all the senses that count. I *think* you are as powerful as you are going to get; from here on out, it's a matter of refining and honing what you can do. Better control, more precise application. Experience. Learning how to pace yourselves."

"I think we're all on the same page, Vic. This is all pretty new territory for me, but Sera said she's gonna help me get a handle on it. We were thinkin' of maybe askin' Bella for some help with some of the . . . new stuff, too." He looked down at the floor for a moment, intently studying the carpet for a beat before he raised his head and stared into Vickie's eyes. "Are we really *that* powerful, though? As much as everyone has been sayin'?"

"Off the charts," she replied. "Okay, there has never been a fire-powered OpFour before, so your potential for destruction really has people nervous. Since no two OpFours have been alike, it's kind of hard to compare you. But . . . have you guys even *seen* the footage of the two of you?"

Sera and John looked to each other, then back to Vickie as they shook their heads.

"Permit me." She picked up the wireless keyboard that she kept on the coffee table, woke up the TV, swapped it to be an Overwatch monitor. "Overwatch: play all footage living room: UT Seraphym/Murdock."

This was the first time she had reviewed *all* of the footage, and there were some sequences caught by "eyes" piloted by Grey and Herb, or following the pair on automatic, that even she hadn't seen. From the first lances and spears of fire to the final swath of destruction before they both collapsed and the Metisian ship showed up, it was . . . okay, she was getting that hair-on-the-back-of-the-neck scare she was sure a lot of military blokes were right now.

When the screen went blank, she turned to the two of them. "See what I mean?"

John was the first to speak. "Y'know, I didn't know how flattering nanoweave pants were. If'n I had any money, I'd buy up some ECHO stock for that alone."

Sera giggled and elbowed him in the ribs. *She giggled. The angel giggled. I didn't know they did that.* But the giggle had the odd effect of making that edge-of-the-cliff, waiting-for-lightning feeling ease up.

So she sighed with exaggeration. "Don't quit your day job, Murdock. No way you're replacing Craig Ferguson."

"All right, all right. Anyways." He turned to look at Vickie again. "I see your point. D'you think that you an' Bella vettin' us is gonna be enough to calm folks down? We just got done with one battle; I don't want to start fightin' a whole new sort any time soon, if'n it can be helped."

"Yes and no," she said honestly. "The people you actually have to worry about—all the military blokes—will stand down on the Condition Red where you two are concerned. But you know how this works, if they don't already have a firing solution to take you two out at need, they are going to start working on one. Just in case. Because that's how this works. Right?"

"I hate to say it, but you aren't wrong. We're potential threats now. We're on their radar, which is a bad place to be. That'll be somethin' we have to figure out how to deal with, long-term. Once Bella an' the Commissar are back from Metis."

"If they were not considering neutralizing us at need, I would consider them to be suicidally foolish," Sera put in. "How could they possibly trust us without *believing* in what I was? And belief… is not something one can force upon someone." She shrugged. "But what of ordinary folk? A mob is as dangerous as a missile."

"Spin Doctor," Vickie said succinctly. "Already working on it. Figuring out exactly how to release that footage, and he'll be ready when we get the go-ahead from the military mavens." She hesitated a moment. "One of the notions he broached was to doctor the footage, tone your destruction down a couple of notches. Maybe eliminate something, like the two of you duoing that dragon…."

"I'll leave all that to the specialist; public relations hasn't really been my strong point… like ever."

"I am indifferent. They may show whatever they please so long as they do not demand we hobble ourselves in reality," Sera said, shrugging. John nodded; Herb had brought more mugs of tea for them, and John took his immediately.

"We just want to keep doin' our jobs. Whatever we need to make happen for that, well, that's what needs to be done."

She had to smile a little. When she thought about the old,

pre-Invasion days, and even just afterwards, when it seemed as if half of the focus of every meta was...publicity. Autographs, action figures, fan clubs. So many of them would have had a meltdown at the very idea of having their footage doctored to portray *less* than what they could do. "You and Djinni," she murmured. "Different reasons, of course...."

And as always, there was pain when she thought of Djinni. She *had* reviewed every bit of his footage already. If there had been any shred of doubt in her mind about Red and Mel...well, the footage in the Tesla Tower, and their reaction when the Metisians saved everyone's bacon and they knew the Glass Strike had been called off, would have told her that Mel and Red were...

Right for each other. Give it up, Victrix. Give it up.

John and Sera shared a look, then turned to face Vickie. "Hey, kiddo...You all right? It's somethin' 'bout Red, isn't it?"

She started, and then recovered outwardly, if not inwardly. *Empathy and Telepathy. Hell.*

John held up his hands placatingly. "I wasn't tryin' to pry, honest. Like I said, still gettin' used to this new stuff. More of a case of 'couldn't help but hear,' y'know?"

She swallowed tears. "It doesn't matter. Whatever I feel, it doesn't matter. It won't change anything, and..." She couldn't complete the sentence.

"You can't know that, not for certain, kiddo." He set down his mug, moving forward to the edge of his seat on the couch. "You obviously feel pretty damn strongly for the Djinni; it's comin' off of you in waves. I've gotten to know him a bit better since the raid in the Superstition Mountains; he's an all right sort...for a reckless asshole. Reminds me of someone, now that I think 'bout it..." He punctuated his sentence with one of his grins. "I don't think that that would be somethin' he could ignore."

"It doesn't matter," she replied, with more force than she had intended...and tears she had *not* wanted to start, escaping to scald their way down her face. "He's with Reverie—Mel. It—I'm just a friend. Besides," she added, bitterly. "I'm an agoraphobic freak-show. And she's beautiful. The 'contest' was over before it ever started. First Bella, then Mel, it's not as if someone like me could ever get in the arena, much less compete." She couldn't continue, her throat closed and she scrubbed at the tears on her face with her gloved hands.

"Hey, listen. S'alright, kiddo. I didn't mean to dig all this up for you. We've all been through a helluva lot the last couple of years. Hell, the last few days, especially. But things are lookin' up; you gotta see that." He glanced over his shoulder at Sera quickly before continuing. "I ran from a lot of things, for years. You know 'bout the meat of it; the government, the Program, and so on. But I was also on the run from who I was as a person, an' what I wanted. I pushed people away, an' didn't allow myself to find love until it was almost too late. It might be a stretch to say that it was part of what was killin' me, but I don't think it'd be that much of a stretch."

Sera touched his hand, and that simple act made Vickie's eyes burn all over again. "I ... do not know what to advise you," the Seraphym said, humbly. "Only that you must not cut yourself off from emotion. That will destroy you. Perhaps you should tell the Djinni?"

But the uncertainty in the Seraphym's voice only hardened the resolve in Vickie. "Not an option," she said, harshly. "I will not destroy the trust he has in me just to indulge in a stupid fantasy. We're not done. We're not even close to being done. Some of the key Thulians and a lot of personnel escaped, and you don't escape unless you have a place to escape *to*." She took a deep breath, swallowed the last of her tears, and steeled her voice. "I won't jeopardize the team for emotion. It's only me, and what I feel doesn't matter; what I do, does."

"Y'gotta do what you think is best, of course. I'm not tryin' to say anythin' different. Just ... go for love, always. We don't have much time here, and love is always worth the effort, no matter what. That's one of the few things that I've learned in my short time on this spinning rock."

His words surprised her. This wasn't something she was used to hearing out of John, the self-described "dumb grunt." "Is it worth it ..." She thought she'd defeated her tears. "Is it worth it if it never goes any farther than you?" She couldn't hold it back anymore. "Because ... it hurts. It just hurts so much."

"You'll never know if'n you don't try, kiddo. I'm not sayin' now is the right time, but I do know that I don't like seein' you like this. Who else is goin' t' steer my dumb ass in the right direction on an operation?"

She closed her eyes, fought for and obtained control again. No point in arguing with them, and right now ... right now their very presence here was rubbing salt in the raw wound, though they couldn't have known that. "Thanks, Johnny. I appreciate the advice." Could they tell she was lying? *Magic shields work a lot like psionic shields ...* She threw up her own and hardened it. "I'll think about it. But please, don't tell anyone else about this, promise? I don't want this to go any further. Even Bella doesn't know." Around Bella, she kept her shields like diamond. It wasn't as if all her friends didn't have too much to worry about already without adding a soppy unrequited love to the mix.

"No problem, Vix. If'n you need anythin', y'know how to reach us. Just a call an' a short flight away." They stood up and headed for the window. She followed them. She got the feeling that they knew very well she was only paying lip service to their words, but they didn't seem inclined to press the point, and she ... well, she just wanted to get back to things she could do something about.

The more she worked, the less she had to feel.

She closed and locked up the window after them, and stood there for a moment, staring at her living room without seeing it. Then she started as Sam Colt opened her link.

"Overwatch: Sam to Vix."

"Go, Sam," she said, jumping over the coffee table and sprinting for the control room, heart hammering. What could have happened now? Some horror weapon rising out of the rubble? Poison gas? Neurotoxins?

"I think you need to hear this."

Her HUD switched on as she launched into her chair, and all her monitors lit up. *"... found her wandering around in the ruins,"* someone was saying as Sam Colt focused one of the eyes she had left behind on a search-and-rescue team. *"Looks like she's one of the infil team members. We're sending her back to Atlanta as soon as we can get her on a plane, but she's pretty disoriented. Can you ID her?"*

Sam zoomed the cam in on the woman on the stretcher, who was weakly protesting that she could walk on her own.

Vickie gasped in disbelief.

Filthy, bruised, uniform torn in several places, two black eyes, blond hair a snarled mess, she was still unmistakable.

It was Scope.

I need a little explanation here. I was not going to let my people go on a Metisian field trip without some backup. I got some of our Overwatch One contingent who were heading home to hand over their earpieces and throat mics to Bella, who in her turn handed them over to the three Metisian pilots we trusted and to Merc. Then I integrated Tesla and Marconi into the system. If for some reason the Metisians decided We Weren't Worthy, I wanted a way to communicate and maybe get them all out of there before the excrement hit the rotating blade.

Paranoid?

If they're really out to get you, you're not paranoid.

CHAPTER TWENTY-NINE

Ablivion

MERCEDES LACKEY, DENNIS LEE, CODY MARTIN AND VERONICA GIGUERE

The quarters that had been assigned to each of the delegates to Metis reminded Bella of the white rooms at the end of *2001: A Space Odyssey.* Everything was white; furniture, walls, floors and ceiling, with completely non-directional, soft light flooding everything. The only color was provided by the things they had brought with them. Except that, unlike the rooms in the movie, when you happened to lie down—or said "Lights out"—the rooms went to black, with a little lighted path that guided you to the bathroom.

Bella was still trying to process actually *being* here. Vickie's call was not helping that.

"Wait, *what?*" Bella said, clutching her hair with one hand. "It's..."

"*It's Scope,*" Vickie replied in her ear. "*It's definitely Scope. They're air-evacing her right back to Atlanta. The question is, what do you, Bull and Yank want to do with her when she gets there?*"

Thank God for Overwatch conference calls... "Guys?" Bella said, staring at the plain white wall of the guest quarters she shared with Bulwark... who was getting yet another of the Metis-style medical treatment sessions that were working along with her own healing powers to accelerate his recovery past everyone's expectations. "I...I'm still kind of in shock here, but...how in *hell* did she survive getting a tower dropped on her if..."

"*Forget the tower,*" Pride said. "*You saw the specs on that modular bomb. She should have been vaporized the moment it hit, her and*"

523

everything in a fifty-yard radius. I don't think we're going to get any answers here, not until we examine her. Is she even injured?"

"Nothing too bad," Vickie said. *"It all seems to be superficial cuts and bruises. She's weak though, dazed, dehydrated, doesn't seem to remember anything."*

Bella glanced at Bull, who was flat on his back, shirtless, on a special treatment "bed" that had been brought in for him, replacing one of the two couches. Whatever it did, it seemed to replicate some of her own abilities and add others. The Metisian physicians had explained it supplied additional nutrients directly through skin contact rather than IV. How the hell it managed *that* she had no idea. But it definitely was working as advertised. He certainly looked better, stronger, and he was back to his old stalwart poker face. The novelty of having a lover she couldn't read had worn off a bit. Sometimes, like right now, it was downright irritating. She wasn't picking up anything from him. There was nothing to suggest he was elated or suspicious or even *surprised* about Scope's return. He simply lay there, listening. She felt an irrational urge to bop him on the head, perhaps jar something resembling an emotion out of him.

"I don't like it," she said flatly. "Unless she somehow manifested a whole new power and teleported herself out in the nick of time..."

"Or someone else got her out," Pride said. *"Or she knew the layout of that tower beforehand, and managed to put some distance between herself and ground zero before it blew. Of course, for that to have happened, she would have had to keep some naughty secrets from us..."*

"I'm not sure I like where this line of thought is going," Bull interrupted. "I get it. Her appearance is highly suspicious, but before we get to the wild accusations, we'll need to talk to her."

"Bull, this is all about deciding what the hell we do with her when she gets here." replied Vickie. *"What if Harm wasn't the only mole we had in the works? You want that walking around on the campus without a minder with all of you gone?"*

"I'm not suggesting any such thing," Bull said. "I agree, she should be detained, but I want it made clear to her she is not, strictly speaking, a prisoner. We're just not in a position to take any chances. Trust me, she'll understand that."

"If it is, in fact, her," he added as an afterthought. "I think it best to run all the physical tests you can on her before we get back. Play it up as your standard suite of physicals."

"*Okay, then, what do we do with her? Slap one of those wristbands you put on Red on her? Want me to come up with something?*" Even over the comm, they could all hear Vickie's voice hardening. "*I've got some pretty interesting coercion spells in my arsenal.*"

"That's not going to cut it," Bella said. "She may not be a prisoner, but I want to be sure she's secure. Like Bull said, we're not taking any chances. Put her in Top Hold."

"*Okay, relaying that to the welcoming committee. Also, I don't have full Overwatch sets, but I can jury-rig a tag I can slap on her that will track her every move in case she manages to make a break for it.*"

"It will do," Bull said. He adjusted himself on his bed. "How is she, Victrix?"

"*I told you, she's dazed with minor injuries, and...*"

"I mean how *is* she?"

"*Oh,*" Vickie said. "*Couldn't tell you, seeing as I haven't spoken to her yet. Remember, she's not wired up with O-Two, and she lost or threw away her O-One mic and headset. From the reports, she's not speaking much, she stares off in space a lot, but she seems agitated. She trembles a lot.*"

"*Not surprising,*" Pride said. "*She's been through a lot.*"

"There's another explanation," Bella said, and shared a sad look with Bulwark. "Scope would probably be jonesing about now."

Bull nodded. "Please keep her under observation, Victrix. I'll need to have a long talk with her when we get back, after we look over her test results."

"*I'll see what I can jury-rig. I might be able to add a direct observational component to that tag. If I can, and I can feed it to tech rather than magic, you want me to add it to your Overwatch suite? Just the four of us.*"

"No," Bella said, firmly. "Unless something goes kablooey, just keep an eye on her. I have a feeling we're going to have our hands full here."

A soft, non-directional chime interrupted her. "*It is time for the Council meeting with the Delegates,*" said a pleasant (a little *too* pleasant) female voice with no discernable accent. "*All delegates and guests should make their way to the Marconi Grand Foyer.*"

"*Roger that. Will be monitoring and recording the discussion with the Metisians per orders. Victrix out.*"

"And on that note..." Bull sat up and swung his legs over the side of his bed, reaching for his uniform tunic, which was draped on the platform next to him.

"Hey, hey, whoa, whoa there, Mr. Stubborn Mule," Bella said, trying to press him back down. "Did I say you were fit to get out of that thing?"

"Bella," Bulwark said, resting his hand gently on hers. "I'm fine. I should be there, and are you really going to wheel me around in this contraption?"

"If that is what it will take to keep you from undoing everything Metis and I have done to you so far," she snapped. "Fortunately, our hosts have provided us with something better." She whistled, and what looked like a very comfortable, if somewhat skeletal, recliner on wheels obediently glided over to the side of the treatment bed.

"Please, I'm hardly an invalid."

"About a week ago you were hardly alive," she reminded him.

Bulwark glared at the wheelchair, then back to Bella.

"I know better than to get in that thing," he rumbled. "But then, I also know even better than to argue with you when your eyes start to flash like that."

"*Wise man,*" Pride chuckled.

Bull sat up again, pulled on his nanoweave uniform tunic, waved off Bella's attempts to assist him and eased himself into the wheelchair.

"Shall we?" he asked, motioning to the door. Bella led the way, the wheelchair following her like an eager puppy.

"*All delegates and guests should make their way to the Marconi Grand Foyer.*" Ramona recognized Mabel's saccharine politeness and made a face. She picked at a flake of metal on one knuckle while Pride finished his conversation with the voices between his ears. Tweaking her appearance took a bit of concentration and creativity, but Ramona enjoyed the effect it had on the Metisians as well as the newly-arrived ECHO leadership. Mercurye waited at the door for them expectantly, as if showing up late for the meeting was one of the last things he wanted to do.

"Well, looks like there's one less empty cell waiting when we get back." Pride leaned forward and let out a long breath. He did not have the appearance of a man willing to jump when

Mabel beckoned. "Victrix said that Scope's turned up in spite of the disaster at Ultima Thule. They're going to keep an eye on her, but..."

"But you think it's suspicious," Ramona finished. "Not finding a body would have made more sense."

Pride hesitated. "I'm not saying that she should have died, or that I'm not happy to see her whole. Losing anyone within the organization is never easy, and we've lost a lot of folks in the last few years. At the same time, the circumstances and the results just don't add up." He sighed heavily and pushed himself up from the pristine white couch. "And at this point, we can't afford blind optimism."

"Not arguing with you, boss." Ramona stretched and followed suit, her joints making metallic popping noises with the effort. Pride frowned, but she waved off his concern. "I'd like to believe that we can celebrate the little victories, but that's just too convenient."

Mercurye stepped aside to let them pass before falling in beside Ramona. The wide passageway would have allowed another to join them with plenty of shoulder space to spare. "That battle can't really fit the description of a little victory, can it? You had Chang there for the offensive, not to mention support from other affiliate organizations. The entire Thulian city crumbled, according to the reports that I got to see. That looks like a win for the good guys."

Ramona held back a smile, years of experience giving her the skills to temper her immediate emotions. Pride didn't show any amusement at Merc's words; on the contrary, they seemed to bother the usually easygoing metahuman. He narrowed his eyes and spoke tersely. "It was an enormous battle, and there were enormous casualties on both sides. It's a little too recent for me to consider it a victory when we're still contacting next of kin for the fallen." He clasped his hands behind his back and took a few steps ahead of the other two, apparently ready to end the conversation there.

Mercurye tried to catch up, but Ramona put a hand on his elbow. She held the speedster back a few paces to give Yankee Pride room for thought before they had to face the Metisians. Merc let out a long breath, the gesture deflating the poor guy like a kid's punching doll. "Sorry," he mumbled to the space between them. "I thought I was being helpful."

"I know. You've just been removed from a lot of it, and he's been thrown in the thick of it." Ramona slid her hand from his elbow to his palm and interlaced their fingers. "You're probably the only person in ECHO who isn't creeped out by the whitewash around here."

That made Merc snort. "I'm used to it. That doesn't mean that I'm not creeped out. I do like the clothes, though. Might be hard to give these up for nanoweave when they let us leave."

If, not when. Ramona had discussed her concerns about the Metisians' detainment of Mercurye with Bella, Bull and Pride as Vickie weighed in via Overwatch. Keeping someone in Metis afforded them a direct link to Tesla and Marconi that was not limited by the quantator, and the nature of war meant that they would need to rely more and more upon the collective experience and expertise of the two elder statesmen of the science city. If that meant that she would have to stay in Metis, she wanted to be ready to break that news to Merc. In spite of the thought-speed message relay of Overwatch, Ramona figured that Arthur Chang would want the speedster closer to the battle than here. Then again . . . that wasn't Chang's call. Disposition of ECHO personnel was strictly up to Bella and Pride. So maybe they could *both* stay.

And anyway, Vickie had made sure all three of the Metisian pilots who had struck up such a firm friendship with Rick had gotten Overwatch One sets. A commute via Metisian saucer was mere hours. They could work something out.

"Your seats are waiting." Mabel's false cheer resonated just around the corner. Ramona ground her teeth together as they caught up to Pride. *On the other hand . . . if I never saw Mabel again, I would consider myself lucky.* Mabel eyed Mercurye with a hungry smile and gestured to the doors. "Yankee Pride and, ah, Steel Maiden are expected with the ECHO delegation. Rick, if you would be a dear and escort me—"

Both Pride and Ramona tensed, but it was Mercurye who interrupted Mabel with charm so magnetic it would have put Spin Doctor to shame. He held up the hand clasped with Ramona. "I would, but it seems I'm already tagged for escort duty. Maybe next summit?"

Mercurye breezed past Mabel, tucking Ramona's hand into the crook of his elbow. Behind them, Ramona heard Pride rumble a genteel offer as replacement. She choked back a laugh at Mabel's offended refusal and waited for him to catch up to them. For his part, Yankee Pride didn't appear the least bit bothered by the Metisian representative's behavior.

"Must be a societal quirk. Bless her heart," he drawled loud enough for her to hear. "I guess we'll find our seats on our own."

Red Saviour was...unsettled. On the one hand, she was actually ahead in the little game of points she was playing in her mind with Worker's Champion. And...that was thanks to Bella, who had surreptitiously given her hints of how to handle the old man. From being contemptuous of the ECHO leader, Natalya was finding herself in the slightly uncomfortable position of feeling grateful to her. Even of...wanting to follow her advice. Once in a while.

On the other hand, she was where she had wanted to be, for months now, about to confront the Metisians...only to discover that she really didn't want to be here after all. Their hosts had given them all materials to peruse about the Metisian society, and it was...Marxian communism at its heart. Everything devoted to the good of the whole. Equal distribution of material goods. No one confined to a single role, unless that was something he preferred. All decisions requiring the consensus of all. Which should have made her elated. But this Marxian communism had resulted in an insular, arrogant society, sure of its superiority, cut off from the plight of the workers outside of Metis, and sure that it, and it alone, was wise enough to decide what might be dribbled down to the lesser masses.

This room should have pleased her. This society was oddly spartan (at least when it came to obvious things that could be considered luxuries), nothing excessive, at least on the surface. No wasted energy; everything efficient and practical for use. But Metis didn't please her, because of all of the hidden technology, so hidden as to seem magical. These wonders—the things like the miraculous "healing bed" that were so commonplace they could be wheeled into a bedroom!—could have truly led to freedom from capitalist oppression for the workers of the world. But the Metisians were hoarding them. It disgusted her. Especially when she thought about the comrades who had been lost...

Those who have the ability to act, should. Those who do not, only support the actions of those who are evil. These ivory-tower intellectuals are almost as culpable as the fascista *themselves.*

Decision by consensus had also lost its attraction for her. Decision by consensus was what had enabled the Metisians to hide behind the white walls of their city when they could have ended the conflict at the point of the first Invasion, or shortly thereafter. So many dead, so much loss...and every bit of it preventable.

She wanted this farce to be over as quickly as possible, so that she could return to her people in Atlanta and get back to doing something that actually *mattered*.

She wished Boryets had not been invited. She should have been sufficient to represent Russia's interests. After all, was that not the supposed, overt *reason* she had been sent to Atlanta in the first place? But it seemed that the Metisians were aware that in reality she had been disgraced and in exile. The only reason she was here in the first place was because Belladonna had not only argued strongly for her attendance, but had hinted that she and Bulwark would rethink their own attendance if the Metisians did not include CCCP. Strangely, Boryets had not objected. For some reason, that vexed her all the more. Intrigue and games; the sheen on the memories she held of him from her youth had tarnished considerably, and she saw him more and more for the politician he had become. More like the Metisians than he probably knew, he was a manipulator, not a creature of action anymore.

Well, just look at the way he had *manipulated* the Metisians themselves into allowing a coterie of his precious Supernauts to be included as "special security"! She wondered very strongly how he had managed that. None of the other delegates had been allowed such a large group of attendants. The one concession that Boryets seemed to have made was to leave the majority of the Supernauts outside of the proceedings.

Bluster and show. I have more in common with my blue capitalist sestra *than I do with the man who was my mentor.*

Well, at least she had her *bolshoi brat* at her side. Molotok; she could count on Moji and he could count on her. And he was more comfortable with people like the Metisians than she was. Honestly, he was comfortable with everyone he met; good looks to match any Hollywood leading man, but with a decidedly Russian cast to his jaw and his eyes, he was always quick to smile and offer a laconic joke. Moji had always been the more public-friendly of the two of them, which certainly didn't hurt him where the fairer sex was concerned. This held true even in

Metis, where Natalya had spied more than a few Metisian women eyeing her comrade appraisingly.

The other three of her contingent, she was not as certain of. Rusalka had proven to be a sturdy enough comrade, but she was of the same generation as Boryets, both of them fighting together in the Great Patriotic War. Ties like that didn't wither so easily, and Natalya kept the elementalist at arm's length. Flins and Marowit, the last two of their contingent, made her uneasy. For that matter, they seemed to make *everyone* uneasy, especially Chug. Their performance during the battle for Ultima Thule had been satisfactory, if disturbing, but in the wake of the fight, it was her unease that persisted. This didn't seem to bother the pair a whit. They largely stayed at the back of the group, Marowit occasionally whispering something to Flins, who would only nod in response, his face utterly blank.

Perhaps I should have asked for Murdock and his woman. But... not possible. There had been whispers and... less-than-diplomatic statements uttered about those two by many in the leadership council. Objectively, she understood. It wasn't every day that metahumans manifested that level of power, with little to no warning. There had been calls to take them into custody immediately after the fighting, to at least interrogate them, even to turn them over to the US military. The memory of what had happened with The Mountain was still very clear in all of their minds. Natalya had immediately shut down all such talk—at least out in the open—by stating it was a CCCP matter, and would be resolved by her and no one else. Again, there had been no objection from Boryets, and Bella had thrown in her, and consequently ECHO's, support for Natalya. That had relieved some fears held by the generals; perhaps they were just glad that the responsibility would fall on someone else's shoulders if the pair turned malicious. But Bella's support did little to quiet her own doubts. Murdock had been a sturdy comrade in the past, a reliable operator. But, with all of the drastic changes he and his strange woman had undergone... the couple were an unknown quantity, now. Were they going to be tools, weapons that she could wield... or time bombs, waiting to destroy her and those nearby?

"Victrix to Saviour."

"Da, witch girl. I am listening."

"Got the results of the Murdock exam. Clean bill of health, he's

not crazy. He's pretty much the same guy you recruited, but more...
stable, actually, if that's even possible. He's not going to crack, no
matter what. He might be the first completely sane OpFour, ever."

"And the woman?"

There was an odd chuckle. *"Has a personal message for you. Ya to,
shto ya, Natalya Shostakovaya. Pomnyu Rabochiye Ray, i schitayut."*

*I am what I am, Natalya Shostakovaya. Remember Worker's
Paradise, and believe.*

That caused her breath to catch for a moment. She did her
best to hide it, though. "*Da*, fine. We'll talk more of them later.
Must be going through tedious meetings so egg-shaped heads are
having time to make long speeches."

As if to underscore that, a soft chime punctuated the end of
her sentence. *"It is time for the Council meeting with the Delegates.
All delegates and guests should make their way to the Marconi
Grand Foyer."*

The door to her room slid open, and Molotok gestured to her
from the hallway. "Come, *sestra*. I think smoking section is this
way."

Natalya elbowed Moji in the ribs as she walked past him, eliciting an amused chuckle and mock pain as he rubbed the spot.
The Metisians had absolutely forbidden her from lighting up, but
had provided her with a cigarette-shaped device they said would
satisfy her cravings without "endangering those around her." She
had turned her nose up at it, muttering that she would rather
wait than pretend to smoke. By now, however, her cravings were
in such force she was starting to consider using it, and actually
had it in the breast pocket of her uniform.

Natalya marched at the front, following a lightly scintillating
pattern of lights that marked their path. Molotok, Rusalka, Flins
and Marowit all fell in behind her. Here and there along their
path they would see Metisians going about their lives, all wearing
the same white outfits and talking quietly. At some point they
were joined by Worker's Champion and a quartet of Supernaut
soldiers, all utterly silent as they followed. She wanted to turn
and confront Boryets, to scream and shout and curse at him
and all of the other old fools who had helped plunge the world
into ruin, but she kept herself in check—barely. Now was the
time to maintain composure, to show that he and the rest of the
dinosaurs in Moscow were wrong about her.

The door opened before they reached it, to reveal a—what else?—rectangle of white light. It seemed that the Metisians thought that the future had to be white...even though the inhabitants of Metis itself were a mix of every possible race she had been able to identify. They entered the Assembly Chamber, as it was called, and once past the door, the light dimmed to a pleasant overall glow. As if anything here in this city was *ever* anything but bathed in a pleasant overall glow...Natalya felt herself craving the harsh sodium streetlights and dirty streets of Moscow more than ever, for the first time in what seemed years. Even Atlanta was preferable to this. At least Atlanta was real.

It was a predictably circular chamber, with a dais in the middle, and successively higher levels of white tables with comfortable white chairs behind them. Each of those tables sported both a blue light and white sign with blue lettering, identifying at least the nationality of those who were sitting at the table. Her eyes went to the tiers above, and spotted RUSSIA: SUPERNAUTS on the third tier. So where was CCCP? She felt increasingly uneasy as she scanned tier after tier and saw nothing...

"Earth to Nat. You're down here, ground floor, table next to ECHO." Startled by Ramona Ferrari's voice in her ear, her gaze snapped down to the tables in front of the dais, and the one occupied by Belladonna, Bulwark, Yankee Pride, and Mercurye, with Ramona on the end. Catching her eye, Ramona nodded to the empty table immediately next to her.

She immediately stalked over there, her mind and body screaming for nicotine as she plopped down in the centermost chair, a chair which disconcertingly molded itself to her, *cradling* her rather than allowing her to sit. Molotok took the seat to her right, with Rusalka on her left. Flins and Marowit chose to stand in the back; Natalya was conscious that she didn't enjoy the feeling of having the pair behind her.

"Marconi and Tesla insisted on having you up front." That was Belladonna. *"Mind you, I was going to have you share our table if they hadn't."*

Natalya started to speak, then clamped her jaw shut. She looked over to where Belladonna sat, muttered to herself, and then stood up abruptly. She stomped over to the ECHO table, stopping in front of Bella's position at it. "Blue girl...*sestra*...thank you. I still am thinking this is unnecessary farce, and cannot be out of this bright children's model soon enough, but...thank you. For believing and standing by. You are truly a sturdy comrade, and will always be counted as such."

Bella blinked, but recovered quickly. "We don't always see eye to eye, Commissar, but at least we never try to deliberately sabotage each other. Or punch each other. I was mad as hops when you sent your people out looking for Ultima Thule, but believe me, *I understand* why you did it. I can't think of anything harder for someone who is used to action..." she glanced at Bulwark "...than to sit back and wait. Sometimes it's intolerable, not having anything to hit."

"You are having good point. Hand-to-hand practice, once back in Atlanta? CCCP HQ has adequate gym facilities. Few leaks, most lights work."

Bella smiled, and hid it behind her hand. "You'd win unless I cheated. But I'd appreciate some *Systema* lessons."

Bulwark barely cracked a smile. "You could use some *Systema* lessons," he rumbled.

"Is settled. Let us finish this...exercise, so that we may return all the sooner, *da*?" She nodded curtly, then went back to her seat. Moji arched an eyebrow, waiting until she was seated before he spoke.

"That was different. You didn't even break anything."

"Shut up, *brat,* or I shall start here." She could have been annoyed, but instead felt a smile of her own creep its way into her lips. *It is good to have friends, not just comrades.* Borzhei moi, *I'm turning soft and American!*

The last of the delegates filed into the chamber with its mirrored ceiling. They barely took up the first five tiers. There was room for thousands of people here...concrete proof that the Metisians did operate by consensus. The very last person to walk in was Arthur Chang, in full military regalia. While it would have been expected for a representative from the State Department or the President's cabinet to act as representative, there had been some sort of...agreement worked out with the President. Metis had insisted on his presence; that had settled the matter, in the end. He remained impassive as he made his way to his seat, at the table next to ECHO's. He looked eminently calm and capable; Natalya found herself liking the man for his strategic expertise and the care he showered his troops with, if nothing else. Once he was seated, the light chatter that had filled the chamber fell to a hush.

The two Metisians who had been standing to one side of the dais took the three steps up to it. There was already a table with a pair of plain white cubes on it. Once the two Metisians, a man and a woman, took their places on either side of the table, the two cubes glowed, and suddenly there were two projected men, one in front of each cube, joining them. It was clear that these were projections, because they were slightly transparent. The one on Natalya's right was shorter than the other, but she recognized them both from the wireframe versions of their heads that had appeared when she went to speak with them via the quantator currently residing in the secure room of CCCP headquarters. Tesla and Marconi, of course.

"Those of you who are unfamiliar with faces of history will not recognize our two . . . incorporeal associates," said the male Metisian, in a white suit that looked to Natalya as if it had been stolen from a state-sponsored science fiction film of the 1970s. "May I present to you Nikolai Tesla and Enrico Guglielmo Marconi." Each man nodded slightly at the sound of his name. Virtually everyone except those at the ECHO and CCCP tables gasped as the implications began to dawn on them. "Together they are the founders of what came to be known as Metis, where you find yourselves now, a city and a society based on science for the greatest possible good."

A murmur began, which Natalya predicted would become a roar if something was not done about it. The speaker stilled the sound with a raised hand. "When you return to your rooms, you will find documents waiting, which should answer every one of the questions that are occurring to you now. And if you have other questions, you have been given access to the universal terminals through which you may ask whatever you please."

Ah, but will you answer *those questions?* Nat thought to herself. While she trusted Tesla and Marconi—insofar as she could trust any of these people—she did *not* trust the openness and honesty of these Metisians. Her government, past and present, was no saint on the world stage. But she found that people professing to be working in the best interests of everyone often were able to justify the worst atrocities and evils to themselves. She saw no reason why these Metisians would be any different, so far.

The monopoly they had on their technology, and the immense power that granted them in relation to every other force on the planet...it gave her pause to think what they might do, with the power vacuum created by the Thulians and their weakening of even the strongest nations on the planet. A technocracy would be no better than slavery by oligarchs or fascists.

Art of War was the first to realize what the blue light was for...or perhaps was the first of those who had figured it out to decide to use it. He waved his hand over the top of it, and it went from a dim glow to a bright one.

"General Chang?" the Metisian said, acknowledging him.

"Thank you for the introduction to Masters Tesla and Marconi," Chang said smoothly. "But who might you and your companion be?"

The man smiled. "We are the delegated representatives of Metis, although every citizen is currently monitoring this conference," he replied. "I am Citizen Raymond Freiberg, and my fellow delegate is Citizen Mabel Aldante. She and I represent the opposing factions within Metis, insofar as our involvement with the rest of the world is concerned. I am in favor, and she is in opposition."

"Thank you for that clarification, Citizen Raymond," Chang said gravely. "I am relieved to discover I am not going to have to refer to you by, say, two sets of numbers."

There was a ripple of quiet laughter through the congregation, but it quickly subsided.

"But Citizens, gentlemen, ladies, the question that I think is paramount here is this. You elected to reveal yourselves and come to our aid at Ultima Thule—and believe me, we are grateful. But just exactly how much more are you going to supply to us now? You have to face facts; there are probably tens of thousands of you, and billions of us. The proverbial cat is out of the bag. I don't think you can go back into hiding again." He steepled his fingers just under his face. "I am sure that while *some* governments would be inclined to just quietly sit back and let you be, the majority are going to assume that if you are not forthcoming in sharing what you have, then you will be as much a threat as the Thulians. If not now, then in the future." There were shouts of agreement and some decidedly less agreeable shouting. Mabel looked triumphant, and cast a glance at Raymond as if to say "I told you so."

But Chang wasn't done. He raised his hand and the shouts quieted. "This is something that no government, especially the United States government, can abide. We need to know your intentions, and establish a means for disseminating the technology and the scientific grounding so that the world might protect itself against any future aggressors like the Thulians."

Natalya felt herself holding her breath. Art of War had beaten her to the punch with his questions, and she decided it was probably for the best. She would have certainly been less diplomatic with her tone and wording; it seemed that his ability for strategy not only extended to the battlefield, but also to wars of words. The assembled crowd erupted once Arthur had finished speaking again, each delegate wishing to have their say heard first. Natalya noticed that Belladonna and Worker's Champion each held back; Bella conferring with Bulwark, while Boryets simply watched.

"Gentlemen! Ladies!" Marconi boomed, voice amplified, over the growing tumult. "Is your very presence here not an indication that Metis has every intention of sharing our knowledge? If we had wanted to keep our wisdom to ourselves, would we have *brought* you here in the first place? In *our* vehicles? Vehicles which your own weapons' systems were unable to detect until we allowed them to?"

Tesla nodded as the voices subsided. "We could easily have made our appearance, dealt with the Thulians, and vanished, and you would have been none the wiser. Instead, you are here as our guests. Please calm your fears. Emotionalism will not win you allies among us, and you will have to convince *every* Metisian among us in order to achieve your goals. We are a true democracy."

Nat snorted a little. Tesla twitched an eyebrow in her direction, but continued on. "Each and every vote will be held where you can see it, and it will be *your* task, as representatives of your various governments, to convince us that you are prepared to use what we hold wisely." He raised his voice a little. "Furthermore, there will be no playing of favorites. What one receives, all will receive. You may wish to take that into consideration."

The room exploded into shouting again at that. Natalya decided to tune out as much of it as possible, as different nations loudly argued their cases for receiving the lion's share of technology due to their contributions during the war against the Kriegers. She and Art of War, Belladonna, and Worker's Champion were part of a small contingent that remained largely silent, allowing the more self-important delegates to blow as much hot air as they liked. The need for a cigarette grew more and more urgent as the puerile conjecture carried on.

"This, ladies and gentlemen," Marconi boomed over the top of them all, after the ones on the dais had let the cacophony continue for about ten minutes, "Is *not* your decision to make. It is ours. There may be billions of you, but you have no way of accessing our records without our cooperation. Each piece of information will be given to all, or none. That was our unilateral decision. As the Americans are so fond of saying, 'take it, or leave it.'"

Silence fell. Chang's light came on again.

"General Chang," said Raymond.

"It seems, Citizen, you have us over the proverbial barrel. As we Americans are so fond of saying." That actually got a weak laugh; that was all Arthur seemed to need to break some of the tension in the room, however. He spread his hands. "You're holding the cards and you are offering to share the pot, to use another Americanism. Shall we turn the discussion to what exactly is *in* that pot, then?" He straightened slightly. "I see this for what it is; an opportunity for global cooperation and enrichment on a level heretofore unknown. In fact, in my view, when this conference is over, we may well find ourselves with nothing to fight each other over, ever again. We've bested, with help, a tyrannical, aggressive military force bent on world domination. This is something that *should* unite us! We've survived against impossible odds, facing an enemy both old and new to the world. I think that gives us more to come together over than to divide further."

Nat heaved a silent sigh of relief, glad that she had not been called on to speak.

"*I feel like a minnow at a shark convention,*" Bella murmured covertly into her Overwatch mic.

"*I feel like a kid with fingerpaints watching Michelangelo,*" Vickie put in. "*Hell, watching Michelangelo taking my fingerpaints and recreating the Mona Lisa.*"

"I am being glad that this Art of War is with us. These piranha would tear each other apart for scraps, baubles and broken trinkets. He is keeping them from that . . . and maybe saving us all from ourselves. Not bad, for *Amerikanski.*" She appreciated the man all the more; one by one, she saw the delegates sway to his passionate rhetoric. She knew it would not be as simple as convincing one room of people to agree not to tear each others' throats out, but it was an important step. It appeared that he was the right man to help them take that first step.

As the silence reigned, Mabel and Raymond exchanged another look. Mabel looked sour, Raymond pleased. "In that case, perhaps you would care to take a small break in the debate to hear from our biology department? We will start at the last, a very recent discovery made possible by our fledgling relationship with ECHO. We trust the significance of our findings, and the vast potential it suggests for future endeavors, won't be lost on you. Ladies and gentlemen, at long last we have confirmed the origin of metapowers."

This time, instead of an uproar, there were only gasps and unvoiced questions as the delegates of the world rose to their feet. Mabel and Raymond approached the center of the dais in silence, collected the cubes projecting the images of Tesla and Marconi, and brought them down to an ornate pedestal at the foot of the steps. The room hushed as the lights dimmed and at the center, the dais began to rise up from the ground. Beneath the rising platform a round, brightly lit, glass-walled room came into view. It was bare, except for a tall, white-gowned man, who stood beside an open, stylized sarcophagus. Inside the ornate coffin was the body of a man who looked to be in his mid-thirties, with chiseled features, blond hair, and a build that could only be described as "heroic." In fact, he looked like something out of a Nazi propaganda poster, or commemorative statue.

"Good Lord!" Yankee Pride exclaimed, rising from his seat. "It's Eisenfaust!"

A tense murmur rose from the crowd, and was silenced as a voice boomed from unseen loud speakers, bringing the assembled delegates to a still.

"Ladies and gentlemen!"

Within the glass-lined room, the man in white held up his hand. He cast an arrogant look out into the crowd, his mouth bent in a perpetual sneer, and waited. Finally he let his hand drop, satisfied he had everyone's undivided attention, and continued.

"My name is Dr. Hermann Deimon Kestrel, and I suggest you remember it well, as I will be remembered as the man who has

deciphered one of the greatest mysteries of our time. Since the
appearance of the first metahumans during the second World War,
we have pondered the riddle behind meta-powered individuals.
Many have hypothesized foolish notions of higher beings, claimed
unfathomable machinations of magic, the common scapegoat in
paranormal occurrences, while other enlightened, logical think-
ers, such as myself, have delved deeper into the secrets contained
within the physiology of such beings. My contemporaries sought
answers in novel power sources, even going so far as to postulate
the existence of minute gateways to alternate realities. They were
fools. I now present to you irrefutable evidence that metapowers
are, in fact, encoded in our very genes. Once you hear my evidence, even the most skeptical amongst you will, I trust, agree
completely with my conclusions. Consider the natural evolution
of our species. Only an imbecile would fail to grasp that our
ever-changing genome is the natural genesis to any advances in
humanity as a whole..."

"*Oh, God,*" Bella muttered. "*He's one of* those. *He's actually
going to take one of the most amazing discoveries of all time and
put us to sleep with it.*"

"*Truly,*" Bull agreed.

"Is to be sounding like member of *Rossíiskaya Akadémiya
Núka,*" Saviour muttered. "Hours talking of self, minutes to
anything important. Head is to be pointed under that hair." It
was good to have the Overwatch system at all times, but at the
moment... the fact that she could complain to the like-minded
without the danger of being overheard was the only thing keeping her temper from snapping.

Above them all, a hologram sprang into existence depicting
a lifelike animation of two men pointing at a large-scale model
of DNA. Kestrel gestured to the hologram as it zoomed into the
model and panned out again as the point of view revealed a cellular nucleus, then an entire cell, a working heart, and finally a
stylized recreation of da Vinci's Vetruvian Man.

"Watson and Crick revolutionized the study of genetics in
1953 with their discovery of the molecular structure of nucleic
acids..." Kestrel began, and led his audience from the origins of
molecular biology to the first sequenced genes in the seventies
and the invention of PCR in the early eighties. By the time he
reached the birth of the Human Genome Project, the assembly

of delegates had begun to grumble, impatient to hear about the actual discovery and taken aback at the sheer magnitude of Kestrel's condescending tone.

"Please, Doctor," General Chang interrupted. "Most of us do have a passing familiarity with these great advances in our understanding of biology. In the interest of time, might we progress to the point where you might enlighten us on how you have come to the discovery of the metagene?"

He was met with a low murmur of agreement from the crowd. Dr. Kestrel cast him a withering look, then waved in annoyance, signaling the projectionist to skip ahead in the presentation.

"Fine," Kestrel said. "If you're so set on withholding the proper introduction that such an important discovery requires, no, *deserves*, to fully grasp the gravity of these findings, then I suppose I could ingratiate myself to you. I suppose I could modulate my vocabulary as well, so that the laymen in the room might better keep up with the material."

"That would be most gracious of you," Arthur said, without a hint of a smile. Bella hid her own behind her hand, but not before Natalya saw it.

"My work into discovering the metagene, as you call it, had met with many obstacles of late. While there was evidence it existed, it was all indirect, and could never be replicated. I kept encountering . . . let's call them *gene ghosts*. One moment I believed I had properly isolated a gene, only to have it vanish upon retesting, failing to meet the scientific requirement of replicating results. It was frustrating, to say the least. This changed last year, when ECHO retrieved the body of the man known as Eisenfaust"—he motioned to the body in the sarcophagus—"and had the good sense to send it here to Metis. We wanted it because he was what we called a Meta Prime—one of the first metahumans to have his powers triggered. As such, his body was invaluable. You will, of course, have noticed that we enclosed in it this sealed chamber. It is necessary. This specimen has proven vital to any recent advancements I have made, and so I must decline any requests to personally inspect the body until I am satisfied I have exhausted my own efforts. It has undergone many complex but fragile preservation treatments, and I fear outside exposure may contaminate it."

He paused to monitor readings on a handheld unit, and continued.

"My initial tests revealed an interesting observation. Someone, somewhere, had taken it upon themselves to perform repetitive invasive studies on this man. It seems I wasn't the first to cut into him. Our inspections revealed numerous and minute scabs and scars across most of his vital organs, suggesting any number of biopsies and even multiple open-heart surgeries. Our theories were varied on why, until DNA analysis managed to finally isolate a promising chromosomal contig that yielded markers we had previously thought to be metagene-associated. What's more, portions of the contig also contained very discrete markers identifying them as transposable elements, though somewhat muted in their activity."

Bella gasped.

"What is it?" Bulwark asked.

"I think he's about to tell us our powers come from jumping genes," Bella said. This time she wasn't bothering to keep her voice low so that only Overwatch picked it up.

"I beg your pardon?"

"A jumping gene is one that actually moves around in the genome," Bella explained, now painfully aware that the entire convocation had turned their attention to her. "Something Barbara McClintock discovered in corn in the early fifties, got her the Nobel Prize years later. Turns out a big chunk of the human genome is made up of transposable elements, but I haven't heard of them actually doing anything except taking up space."

"Very good," Kestrel nodded. "I couldn't have put it more simply or less elegantly myself. Of course, Miss Parker's rather crude explanation omits most of the complexities of dealing with transposable elements, but you get the general concept. Simply put, unlike other transposable elements, the fully evolved metagene does not seem to replicate itself, but physically leaves its location and moves to another."

"Why fully evolved?" Bella asked.

"In the case of Eisenfaust, I believe his genetic code has been grossly tampered with," Kestrel continued, his eyes flicking toward Bella in annoyance. "His metagene, or I should say metagenes—there can hardly be only one, after all, with the diversity of metapowers that exist in our metahuman population—these metagenes appear to have been altered, the relocation activity of the transposable elements dulled. In their natural state they would have a rapid rate of relocation, but in their current and muted" capacity I have been able to ascertain that in the past they arose from a replicative type of jumping gene. I see I am confusing you. Simply put, earlier progenitors of the metagenes would have multiplied, making copies of themselves. Given the voracity of the typical rate of activity of modern day metagenes, such a process couldn't be viable. Chromosomes would rapidly grow, overtake the confines of the cell nucleus, of the cell itself, and—"

He made an explosive gesture with his hands.

"So it makes sense that the fully evolved metagenes do not replicate, they simply reposition themselves in the genome. Not to say replication doesn't happen on occasion. It would even be necessary in the early evolution of the gene, to account for the diversity we see now in metapowers. You see—"

"I'm sorry," Ramona interrupted. "Why was the jumping activity of Eisenfaust's metagenes slowed down in the first place?"

"Interruptions, interruptions, interruptions . . ." Kestrel seethed. "I do not have conclusive evidence on that, at this particular moment. It is one of the many projects I would be working on right now, including, I might add, finalizing the actual sequencing of these genes, if I weren't forced to present my initial findings to a gaggle of outsiders . . ."

"Doctor, please," Raymond said. "A little respect for our esteemed guests."

"Of course," Kestrel said, and took a breath to calm himself. "My initial hypothesis was that the Thulians sought to understand the origin of metapowers, as we did, and devised a way to disrupt the function of all transposable elements in individuals such as Eisenfaust in order to study them in a consistent manner. However, upon closer inspection, I determined their methods were far too precise and orchestrated, requiring an in-depth knowledge of their targets of study beforehand."

"You think the Kriegers already know all about these metagenes?" General Chang asked.

"Assuming they were the ones to have altered him," Kestrel said, "it would be more than mere hypothesis. It would be fact."

"Then what were they after?"

"From the nature of their modifications, my first impression was that they were seeking a process to nullify metagenes, perhaps even eliminate their existence entirely. You must understand, after I delineated the existence of metagenes, I had to sift through their own modifications to Eisenfaust's genome before resuming my own work. While they had stabilized the chromosomal local- ization of his metagenes, they had also grossly corrupted them. I learned from their mistakes, you might say. There was clear tampering, obvious markings of attempts at gene silencing. I was able to piece together an abridged story of their futile efforts to stem the acceleration of metagene proliferation."

"So, just to summarize for us non-Metisians," Ramona said as the doctor paused a half-second for air. "You figured all of this out thanks to the dead meta supremacist on the slab. You've realized that they don't normally stay in one place, which makes them harder to pin down, even in the same person. And what's more, the Kriegers knew all about these metagenes before you did. That about right?"

The doctor managed to contort his mouth into an even more offended sneer at Ramona's short summary of his verbal disserta- tion. "A blunt and incomplete abstract, yes, but—"

"So if they could stop these genes from moving, could isolate them, why didn't the Kriegers take it further?" Ramona let the question fall heavy in the center of the conversation. "In terms of technology, we were clearly outgunned during the Invasion. The only thing that stood in their way was the number of metahumans across the world. You said it looked like they were working on obliterating the metagenes, obliterating *metapowers*..."

Ramona paused.

"Were they close?" she asked. "Were they ever close to deci- mating the metahuman population?"

"Young lady," Kestrel said, "if you would allow me to finish, you would learn that it is now my hypothesis that the Thulians were not, in fact, attempting to silence metagenes."

Kestrel paused for effect.

"They were seeking answers on empowering them."

"But you said they were shutting them down," Ramona said.

"That was my initial thought, yes," Kestrel admitted. "But the deeper I probed, the clearer it became that I was mistaken, and they were looking for the opposite—"

He was interrupted by a truly ghastly, bubbling laugh.

The eyes of the corpse in the "sarcophagus" didn't open. But the laugh was coming from Eisenfaust.

"Idiot," the thing said, in a thick, gluey voice. There was a hair-raising buzzing when it spoke. And it wasn't speaking in just English; it seemed as if it were speaking in dozens of languages, all at once. "You are all idiots. But thank you so much for taking down all of your defenses. We thought we would never be able to get past them to find out where you were without taking drastic and fatiguing measures."

The thing shoved the lid of its enclosure aside—eyes still closed all the while. "Did you *really* think you were done with us? We have only been playing with you until now." Kestrel stared in paralyzed horror as the body of Eisenfaust—puppeted by God only knew what!—turned its sightless face towards him. "You've become inconvenient, you little insects, in your secret city. Now the time has come to swat you."

The corpse, in two jerky but too-quick movements, simultaneously smashed the sarcophagus and grabbed Kestrel by the shoulder. The hand squeezed, and everyone was able to hear the sound of the man's collarbone snapping over the intercom.

"Get it off! Get it off *get it off getitooooff!*" Kestrel's voice spiraled up into the soprano range as the pain hit him. The corpse paid no heed as it pulled him closer; with the hand that had smashed the sarcophagus, it retrieved a wicked-looking shard of glass. With deliberate slowness, it plunged the shard into the scientist's chest and twisted. Kestrel's scream no longer had words, just a single animalistic howl. The entire room exploded into activity; several of those attending the scientists in the examination room attempted to flee, jamming together at the door and pounding their fists against it uselessly. A handful tried to free Kestrel from the corpse of Eisenfaust. On the delegate-side of the glass, there were screams and shouts, everyone either trying to be heard or watching in frozen horror.

Natalya marched forward, pushing through the teeming crowd. Her eyes were fixed on the corpse. It had started vibrating; subtly at first, but more and more pronounced. It wasn't until it was shaking violently that anyone else noticed.

"What in God's name is it doing now?" *"Fuck, someone get* IN *there already!"* *"Why isn't it dead?"*

Then she noticed that the body was changing. The skin was peeling and blackening in patches, splitting. It started to actually *smoke* . . . and then light was spilling from its mouth. *Like it's burning, from the inside out.* The light grew brighter, now coming from the ragged tears in the corpse's skin. The thought came to her like a lightning bolt; it wasn't just immolating itself, it was ramping up, gathering power for—

"Bulwark! Dead man is to be exploding!" She shoved her way through the crowd more violently this time, trying to find the American. "Bulwark!"

Bulwark had gotten to his feet along with everyone else, the wheeled chair that had brought him here discarded like a toy. He loomed over everyone, a good head or more taller than even Worker's Champion. His gaze snapped to Natalya at the sound of his name.

"Bulwark!" she screamed, pointing violently at the animated corpse. *"BOMB!"*

Bulwark's eyes widened. *"DOWN!"* he thundered, and *"Get DOWN!"* And as people around him hit the floor, he flung his arms wide, and with them, his shield, which sprang up as a visible and rapidly widening bubble with him and Bella at the center.

Natalya turned back to the examination room; the light there had become so bright that it seemed to completely fill the chamber. There were more screams; first from the chamber itself, then from the delegates as they realized the danger. She barely had time to drop to the floor before it happened. The light became even more intense, blinding her, and then the muffled *whump-BOOM* as the blast wave exploded from the examination room and over the delegates.

Natalya choked for a few moments on the smoke, and shook her head to try and get the ringing in her ears to stop; everyone in the room was on the floor, save for Bulwark; his shield had certainly saved all of them. Still, it appeared that the assembled group was dazed; people coughing and stumbling to their feet, calling for help and otherwise getting in the way. She glanced to her right; Moji was already on his feet, doing his best to help squawking generals and their aides. The rest of her party seemed to be intact; Rusalka was still on her knees, but otherwise unharmed, while Flins and Marowit were off on their own at the back, as always. *Belladonna! Where is the blue girl?*

"Vix! What the hell just happened?" That was Bella's voice, but where was Bella? Natalya began pushing her way through the people around her, looking for her friend. No one was seriously injured, but nearly all of them were severely disoriented.

"*Forget that! You've got Kriegers moving in on Metis en masse! Get yourselves the hell out of there and anyone you can drag with you! Ramona, is there anything like a bomb shelter?*"

Fascista? Her mind swam. *Here? How . . . did they follow us from Ultima Thule?*

She didn't see Bella. But she did see Worker's Champion. He didn't appear to have been staggered by the explosion like the rest of them. He strode forward, walking with purpose to the front of the congregation. She reached out to him, and was about to speak . . . but he ignored her completely, moving past her and stepping over the other coalition representatives. He was flanked by two of his Supernauts; two more stood, still at attention, at the entrance to the room. *He is taking charge. Typical of him, but at least someone is. We need to rally a defense, evacuate the city, possibly. Uncle Boryets will be able to whip these simpering fools into something approaching usefulness.*

"Everyone, please!" It was Raymond. His once-pristine white uniform was covered in dust and burns, and he had a slight cut on his eyebrow; he and Mabel had been far closer to the blast than the rest of them. "Please, try to remain calm! We have the situation perfectly under control—"

His words were choked off as Worker's Champion wrapped a single hand around the Metisian's throat, then lifted him into the air. Raymond flailed for a few moments, clawing at the massive fingers clamped around his windpipe. Mabel, and the rest of the people in the room, stared on in shock.

"*Nyet.*" With a twitch of his thumb against the side of Raymond's jaw, Worker's Champion snapped the man's neck, who went limp in the Russian's grasp. With a jerk of his arm, Worker's Champion used the dead man's body as a bludgeon. Mabel was knocked to the floor *hard*. Her right temple hit the marble floor with a wet *crack* that told Nat she was probably dead, her body skidding across the smooth surface for several meters. Natalya's mind spasmed; she couldn't believe what she had seen.

Boryets pointed at the boxes—the projections of Tesla and Marconi had vanished—and one of the Supernauts obediently picked them up. He waved vaguely at the rest of the room. "Retrieve the target. Then kill them all," he said, and headed for the door, with the burdened Supernaut following closely behind him.

Bulwark had, by far, the loudest unamplified voice of anyone in the room. "Sound the alarm! We've been compromised!" he thundered. "Noncombatants to me! The rest of you, form up and take them down!"

The room exploded into a flurry of activity. The Supernauts at the back of the room began to spray fire as soon as Worker's Champion was past them; several Metisians were instantly incinerated, along with a number of the coalition members. Gunshots rang out, deafening in the enclosed space. More Supernaut troopers marched into the room, spreading out and spraying fire as they moved. One of the Supernauts separated from the rest, batting aside anyone that got in his way; at one point he hosed down an Indian general with bullets from one of his mounted machine guns.

Victrix was on the comm with information. *"The Supernauts are set up with fire and projectile weaponry. Boryets has enhanced strength and is more or less invulnerable. Yank, Ramona, Moji, if you can dodge the fire, you can handle the bullets. Nat . . . do what you do."* Made visible by the smoke, a force-field sprang up to Nat's left. *Now* she could see Bella, on her knees, ministering to someone. Mercurye was helping her; Nat watched as he performed insane aerial acrobatics, running and flipping through the air to dodge fire and machine-gun rounds as he picked up the wounded and brought them back to be tended to by Belladonna.

To add to the chaos, a deafening alarm sounded, punctuating the cacophony every few seconds.

That finally shocked her back to reality. Rusalka had unholstered her sidearm, firing at the Supernauts and probably looking for a water source to exploit. Flins and Marowit, however, were nowhere to be seen; they weren't front-line fighters, after all. Natalya wouldn't count them as assets. *Moji . . . where are you?*

It took her a moment to spot him; he was no longer helping the wounded, but sprinting for the same exit that Boryets had taken. For the briefest moment, she thought that he might be in league with the traitor. That notion vanished almost immediately as he bowled over one of the Supernauts that attempted to block his path. The Supernaut's armored chestplate was caved in roughly in the shape of a splayed-out hand. And just like that, he was gone.

"Nasrat!" She needed him; even if these Supernauts were blowhard fools like their namesake, they would still be difficult opponents, with their armor and weapons. Natalya felt someone

bump into her right shoulder. She whirled, her fist sheathed with glowing energy... to find Yankee Pride, his pose an almost perfect mimic of her own, including his energy gauntlet being fully charged.

Yank recovered first. "Nat! Go after them! I'll lay down covering fire!" Suiting his actions to words quite literally, he laid his gauntleted arm over her shoulder and fired at someone behind her. She felt the slight recoil jolt her body, ducked under his arm, and sprinted for the exit, trusting him to do what he said he would. The Supernauts closed ranks in front of her; she spotted two who were specifically focusing on her, while the others seemed concerned with the rest of the room. Her fist still charged, she loosed the ball of energy at the feet of the one on the left. The armored man was taken off his feet as the marble beneath him shattered in a shower of sparks. As he fell, he caught the arm of the other Supernaut soldier, causing the machine-gun burst meant for Natalya to go wide. Kicking off on a plume of her energy, she charged both of her fists, screaming as she flew through the air. The Supernaut faltered, trying to bring one of his arms up at the last second as Natalya brought both of her fists crashing down. The pent-up energy released, crushing his arm and crumpling the helmet with a satisfying metallic *crunch* until it was almost level with the shoulder pauldrons.

Not as sturdy as fortified Krieger trooper armor. Good.

Natalya spun around, leveling an energy blast at the downed Supernaut just as he was about to release a torrent of flame. The nozzle on the man's emitter was destroyed and the weapon backfired; the entire suit became consumed with liquid fire, seeping in through the sections that Natalya had damaged. She heard the man scream through the grill on his helmet, but didn't have time to worry about the pathetic dog.

The rapid fire of the Supernauts' machine guns came in retaliation for their screaming comrade. A trio of shots whistled by Natalya's ear before Ramona threw herself into the path of the rest of them. The other woman's face contorted in pain, but she shoved Natalya down the hall. "Keep running!" Ramona spat a glob of what looked like metal onto the floor. Most of her exposed skin had taken on a dull gray sheen and she grunted as another volley of shots intended for Nat hit her squarely between the shoulder blades. "Pride and me, we've got you covered! *Davay*, right?"

She snarled and charged ahead. Two more of the Supernauts converged on her at once. She managed to knock the first aside with a Systema move and concentrated on destroying the face of the second, whirling to deal with the first—

But her intended target had already found himself in the crosshairs of someone else. Bella was staring at him with terrible intensity, and he was shaking.

Shto? Natalya decided to take advantage of his situation and moved in...unfortunately, just at the moment that he went into a full-out, spasming seizure. An actual attack she could have predicted and countered—this unpredictable flailing caught her off-guard, and his right arm, with all the unrestricted power of his servo-motors behind it, caught her across the stomach, drove all the air out of her, and sent her flying across the room. She felt her spine impact with the wall, and stars swam into her vision.

Everything looked surreal. The flames, the gunfire, the people running. Blasts from Pride's power gauntlet left rainbow streaks in her vision. She saw Bulwark holding a huge shield firm against bullets and keeping Supernauts beyond an effective distance for their flamethrowers, and Mercurye crawling past her on hands and knees after another victim. Finally, she focused on Art of War. Four of the Supernauts had him cornered, separated from the rest of the generals. They weren't firing at him, however; just advancing, arms spread wide. It occurred to her that they didn't want to kill him, though for the life of her she couldn't fathom why at that moment. *They are traitors. They are supposed to try to kill us. Why hold back?*

The Supernauts surged forward in concert. Arthur was ready for them, however. He rolled forward from the half-crouch that he had been positioned in, scooping up a shard of marble as he did so. He jammed it, *hard,* into the knee joint of the middle Supernaut soldier, sawing it back and forth until it found purchase—and blood. The soldier screamed in agony; Arthur swung his shoulder underneath the soldier's knee, then lifted with all of his might; the armored man fell backwards, his mounted machine guns and flame emitters firing at the ceiling of the chamber. Arthur swept his hand across the floor, never staying still; like magic, another shard of marble was in his hand. This time he shoved the jagged piece of rock through the armpit of the next Supernaut; the man cried out, and his arm went limp. Arthur positioned himself behind the disabled soldier, grabbing the dangling left arm in one hand. With the other hand, still holding the make-shift knife, he twisted. The soldier's weapons began discharging; flame and round after round of machine-gun fire issued forth, sweeping over the other two Supernauts.

One of the Supernauts went down quickly; the other only took grazing wounds, and waited until the soldier Arthur had control of wrenched his arm away, swiping the intact one in a brutal arc at Arthur's head. The general ducked underneath it, jamming the shard into a gap in the armor near the soldier's kidney. The injured Supernaut fell backwards, giving Arthur enough time to scuttle over the soldier's chest and jam the piece of marble into the man's unprotected throat, snapping it off in a sputter of blood. The final Supernaut took advantage of hav-ing Arthur's back turned to him; he ran forward, armored feet clanking against the marble, as he lifted up the metahuman in a bear hug from behind.

They want to kidnap him. He's one of their targets; they want his abilities! Natalya willed her limbs to move, but they were slug-gish and refused to obey her commands. She tried to summon energy to her fists, but produced only a weak flash of glowing sparks that dissipated as soon as they manifested. She watched, helplessly, as the scene played out before her.

Arthur wriggled and writhed, trying to slip from the rock-solid hold of the Supernaut. The soldier had begun marching towards the exit; the other Supernauts were providing covering fire for it. With Natalya out of action, there was no one between the armored soldier holding Arthur and the exit.

For the briefest moment, their eyes met. It wasn't a long moment, but it was clear he *saw* her, and could see she was clear of the fight. She felt paralyzed by his gaze.

Arthur was somehow able to slip an arm free from the bear hug the Supernaut soldier had him in. With a final shout, he thrust a fist backwards, still holding the shard of marble he had used so effectively earlier. The shard penetrated one of the feeder lines for the flamethrowers; the pressurized fuel ejected from the breach in a aerosolized plume . . . and then caught on the pilot flame at the end of the weapon emitters. The explosion enveloped the pair and two more Supernauts, leaving a blinding afterimage in front of Natalya's eyes. Blinking hard, it took her several moments before she could see anything coherently again. Where Arthur and the Supernaut had been standing...was only charred wreckage. The two other Supernauts caught in the blast were most certainly dead; both lay unmoving and smoldering near the exit.

She felt a hand under her arm, hauling her to her feet. "Dammit, Nat, *they're getting away!*" Yank shoved her out the door, then turned to face the developing carnage in the room, covering her escape. She almost fell onto her face, half falling and half running. *Find him, and kill him!* She didn't have time for any other thoughts. She had to stop Worker's Champion. He had the boxes that contained the consciousnesses of Tesla and Marconi; the traitor's masters could *not* be allowed to take possession of them. Her veins felt like they were pumping acid and her breath burned in her lungs as she ran, her arms and legs driving her forward like pistons.

Everything came into focus for her. She knew what she needed to do, then. *Kill Boryets. Get the boxes back.* She didn't allow herself to think too hard on it; that invited questions, even madness, at how her mentor, her adoptive uncle, could betray her and every ideal they had ever held. She just knew that she had to kill him; that was the only way to make sense of any of this. The rest was a blur; she saw thick, black smoke, in stark contrast to the white surroundings. Explosions in the distance, and the all too familiar shape of Thulian Death Spheres. There was lightning, as well; some product of the Metisian defensive measures. It was having an effect, but she couldn't gauge how much; that didn't concern her at the moment. Only vengeance and retribution. It was a craving that consumed her until there was nothing else in her mind.

Natalya turned a corner...and it felt as if the world lurched to the side, hard. She almost fell over, stopped in the hallway with her arms thrown out to catch herself. She shook her head...and then recoiled in horror. The ground in front of her was strewn with corpses, and she recognized all of their faces. Georgi, Pavel, Molotok, Thea and Gamayun, Jadwiga; all of them lay dead, burned, broken. Even Murdock and Sera were there, and Chug. Zmey and Perun were there, as well. Petrograd, his armor shattered and burning. Protestors from the day of the Invasion. All of them were looking at her, their eyes accusing her. *Your fault! Failure! Useless! Where were you when we needed you?*

She fell to her knees, a wordless cry on her lips. She felt the air catch in her lungs; she couldn't breathe, didn't want to, just wanted to die. The walls felt like they were closing in, and her vision grew dark. The accusations grew louder in her mind, and she couldn't look away from the eyes of the dead. She wanted to join them, she deserved to join them, nothing else would wash the stain of her failures away. They were right! Where *had* she been when they needed her? What did the Amerikanski call it? Grandstanding! Showing off....

A single gunshot sounded, and her world went stark white for a moment. She felt her body lurch forward, her arms barely able to catch her before she hit the ground. Natalya vomited. When her stomach was empty, she looked up. The hallway was empty; no bodies, just white floor and walls. The voices were gone; the only thing she heard were explosions and the wail of alarms. She turned...and saw Marowit, slumped to the floor and clutching a bullet wound in her throat, blood seeping through her fingers. Her eyes bulged as her stare met Natalya's gaze. She raised her hand, reaching for Natalya. *She's using her powers on me!* Natalya fumbled for her pistol, still disoriented. It took what seemed like years for her to remove it from her holster, disengage the safety, and raise it. She was close enough that she didn't use the sights; in her state, she wouldn't have been able to anyway. She fired, again and again, until the magazine was completely empty. Her point shooting was accurate enough; Marowit was *very* dead now; most of the rounds had hit her in the head and throat, where the nanoweave armor didn't offer any protection.

There was movement somewhere behind the dead metahuman; Natalya whirled, bringing her empty pistol to bear. Flins walked forward slowly; a Makarov, identical to Natalya's, was in his hand. He dropped it to the ground when he was over Marowit's body, his face still emotionless.

"No more dreams. No more control," he said in monotone Russian. Then he turned to look at Natalya, those dead eyes studying her for a moment before closing in concentration. She recognized what was happening; he was going to kill her, just like Marowits had tried. The scene during the battle in Ultima Thule played through her mind; Kriegers with blood streaming from their eyes and ears, dead before they could hit the ground. She pulled the trigger for her pistol—it clicked loudly on an empty chamber.

She knew that she was going to die; there was no time for her to reload, or to summon enough energy to her fists to blast at Flins with. Everything seemed to slow and take on unnaturally sharp detail. Was this part of his power, or merely her own reaction to imminent death?

A water fountain on the far side of the hallway from Flins exploded, breaking his concentration and causing him to open his eyes. The water, which had started spraying towards the ceiling...coalesced, gathering in on itself. In the space of a breath, the water launched itself towards Flins; it slammed into his chest, propelling the thin, tall Russian off of his feet and against the wall, pinning his back to it. The water flowed over his mouth and nose, a firehose blast still being continuously slammed into his chest. Natalya saw emotion in his eyes for the first time; fear and hatred. Those eyes locked onto her again.

"Not this time, you bastard!" With a shout, she gathered energy to her free hand, and flung it with all of her might and will towards Flins. It hit his body squarely, and the entire hallway rumbled as the energy discharged. The water abruptly stopped. She could see scorch marks against the dripping wall, and an unmistakable smear of red. Further down the hallway was Flins' body, crumpled. *There's only one person here who can manipulate water. I won't be caught unaware again.* Natalya collected energy to both of her fists, first holstering her Makarov.

"Rusalka! Come out!"

"They were going to kill you, Commissar." Rusalka walked out from behind an alcove, her hands at her sides and her head hanging, her entire posture one of defeat and grief. "I couldn't let them. I was supposed to watch, supposed to keep an eye on you. When I failed, they were sent to keep me in line."

Natalya shook her head, uncomprehending. The other Russian woman was openly weeping now. "Worker's Champion...Boryets... he said it was to be for the greater good. That you were too dangerous to leave to your own devices in Atlanta. That he trusted me. We had fought together for so long..." She looked up, her eyes red and brimming with tears. "How could I have known? What he would do?"

Natalya allowed the energy surrounding her fists to dissipate into the air. She opened her mouth to speak, even going so far as to reach for Rusalka...but held back. *I do not have time for this. I need to keep moving, to help Moji.* She did her best to keep her voice even, speaking in Russian, as Rusalka had. "Evacuate civilians. We will deal with you back in Atlanta. If you wish to redeem yourself and your shame, you will *not* be giving me reasons to regret allowing you to live." Without waiting for a response, Natalya turned and dashed down the hallway in the direction that Worker's Champion and Molotok had been going. *All this time...he had been a traitor, and had left more traitors in our midst. How many people have died because of their treason? How many more will die now?* Natalya clenched her teeth hard enough that she began to taste blood as she ran; she felt as if her rage would consume her and the world. *Let it destroy Boryets first, before he can do more harm.* It did not take her as long as she thought it would before she had caught up to her targets.

She stumbled over a shallow step and emerged into an open space; a landing of sorts, a cantilevered launch pad for the Metis craft. Natalya had arrived on one such port, but it had been far different from this. This one...was littered with bodies. Over a dozen Supernauts, all dead, covered nearly every inch of space on the launch pad and the ramp leading up to it. Most of them had been messily torn apart; arms, legs, heads all lain strewn about. She noticed one mostly intact Supernaut soldier with a bayonet handle sticking out of an eye slit; the body was still quivering on the ground. Natalya, hardened by her time as a detective and then a soldier in the war against the Kriegers, still felt her gorge rise at the scene of carnage in front of her. The structure itself had taken tremendous damage; it looked as if two titans had done battle here, the environment taking the punishment of their wrath.

There is so much blood.

It all stood in stark contrast to the white marble of the Meti- sian surroundings. Even against the red and black armor of the Supernauts, the blood was thick and shiny, catching the light of the setting sun.

At the very end of the landing stood Worker's Champion. Kneeling before him was Molotok. Natalya had known him since they were children; the most injured she had ever seen him was when he had had a bloody nose after having an entire factory collapsed on him by demolition explosives. Now...his face was pulped. His uniform was ripped in dozens of places, exposing the bruised and bleeding skin beneath. Her *bolshoi brat*, arms limp at his sides, allowed his head to loll to the side, his gaze falling upon her. Both eyes were blackened and hideously swollen, barely visible through the slits of his eyelids. Those pale blue dots bored into her, and she thought that she saw the barest hint of a smile creep onto his ruined lips, the red blood marring his white teeth.

Boryets picked Molotok up by the neck. He regarded his fellow Russian curiously, cocking his head to the side, his face still a stony mask. Then he *punched*. Aimed for the center of Moji's chest. The first blow was a deep thud. The second was a splintering *crack*. The third and final punch was a much more wet-sounding *rip*. This time, when Worker's Champion pulled back his fist, it was covered in gore. Unceremoniously, he dropped Moji at his feet. The younger meta landed on his knees, and stayed slumped there for a moment, before falling forward in a grotesque, boneless sort of way. When Moji's head hit the ground, his eyes were fixed upon Natalya again, sightless.

For a moment, Natalya couldn't move; she was shaking so terribly that she was vibrating in place, torn simultaneously by grief so terrible she wanted to scream it to the universe, rage so all-encompassing that she was literally seeing everything through a red haze, and guilt so deep she could not see the bottom of it. *His eyes...his EYES!* A sound began down in her chest; it started as a sob, but grew and grew until it burst out of her chest in a wordless howl, the cry of someone utterly betrayed, whose world has been destroyed before her eyes by the one she trusted most, leaving nothing but ashes. Now there was nothing. *Nothing!*

Nothing but revenge.

Natalya launched herself at Worker's Champion. Her vision had gone red, and dark around the edges. All she saw was a man she had once worshipped, now her most hated enemy, standing over the body of one she had loved dearly as a brother. She met him, her body fully extended in flight, her fists charged with all of the energy she could muster. She dove straight for his center, wishing to drive through his cancerous and traitorous heart, to do to him what he had done to her *bolshoi brat*. The explosion almost blinded her, sending her flipping through the air with the concussion at the last second. Boryets was staggered, for a moment, almost unbelieving, it seemed, that she would dare approach him, much less attack. She refused to recoil, however;

Natalya renewed her attack, charging her fists and pummeling every joint, every pressure point of her opponent with blows that would have leveled houses.

Boryets stood statue-still, taking all of the hits impassively. With inhuman calm, he reached out, grabbing Natalya by the shoulder. She continued to pound on him, charging her fists with enough energy to destroy entire buildings. She discharged all of this energy, fruitlessly, against Worker's Champion's shoulders, chest, neck and head, until she was utterly spent. Finally, she just beat her fists against him, unpowered, weeping and shouting hoarsely in Russian.

"Why? Why, uncle? Why would you betray us, everyone and everything you loved? Why, you bastard?"

Boryet's face remained utterly devoid of emotion. He set her down, gently, and then shoved her with two fingers. It was enough to send her flying back, tumbling over the bodies of the dead Supernauts.

He picked up the boxes, covered in the blood of one of the dead Supernaut soldiers. "You wouldn't understand, ignorant child." Natalya thought she almost heard a tinge of sadness in his words. Marshalling all of her remaining strength, she raised her head off of the platform. She spat at him, baring her teeth. It was all she could do. She was too exhausted to even raise a fist to shake at him.

"*Traitor!* Betrayer! *Murdering fucking bastard! I will kill you, and you will die screaming! Know this! Have no rest, because you will die alone, in pain, begging for mercy, you fucking coward!*"

Finally, Boryets showed some emotion. His countenance darkened, his lips turning down into a grim frown. Before he could speak, however, a Thulian Death Sphere rose behind him, huge against the backdrop of the city. A portal opened seamlessly on its side, bathing him in baleful orange light.

Boryets opened his mouth to speak—but was stopped short. "*Hinein mit du! Gerade jetzt!*" Harsh shouting in German sounded from inside of the Death Sphere. He looked over his shoulder, then back to Natalya. With a final sneer, he turned on his heel and stalked into the open portal, shrouded in that horrible orange light. The entrance into the Death Sphere closed behind him. With a bone-rattling hum, the Death Sphere rose into the sky, streaking away from the doomed city.

Natalya did her best to summon energy to her fists, to strike out at her traitorous uncle. All she could do was raise her fists uselessly, a plaintive cry escaping her lips before she fell unconscious in a pool of the blood of her enemies.

"Where's Nat?" Ramona shouted via Overwatch.

Yankee Pride answered. *"She went after Worker's Champion—he took Tesla and Marconi! We need—"*

"No, he didn't," Mercurye interrupted. *"Those were just projection cubes—"*

"Well, *if you know where they are, get them!"* Bella interrupted. *"Vix says the city is going down! We need to evac everyone five minutes ago!"*

"I've got your transport," Vickie appended. *"Get the ghosts!"*

That was all Rick needed. Mercurye flew down the hallway, a hand tight around Ramona's forearm. She kept chirping directions based upon the information that appeared in the heads-up display, directing him down one corridor and another. The structure shook, each explosion threatening to cave in a possible escape route. Ramona yelped as one of the walls buckled; she stumbled forward as Merc pulled her through one of the sheer gel curtains and into a small closet-sized space.

"Mr. Tesla? Mr. Marconi?" Mercurye called into the darkness. "We need to hurry, please!"

"Your urgency is noted, young man." Tesla's voice resonated from the floor, the walls crackling with the familiar blue wireframes. "Enrico and I share your concerns. Ms. Ferrari, I trust that you have coordinated transportation?"

"Already done. Your ticket out is warming up the saucer." Victrix barked in her ears. *"But you need to—"*

A violent explosion tore a hole in the ceiling of the closet and drowned out the rest of Overwatch's instructions. The tang of ozone mixed with a sulfuric odor seeped into the space. Ramona started to gag. Merc wrapped an arm around her waist and pulled her back through the blue gel curtain. The smooth composite floor had buckled, and the blue currents of consciousness raced over the broken edges frantically.

"Vic?" Ramona coughed and spat out a thin aluminum-tasting wad of gunk.

"The systems are going down. The Metisian infrastructure keeps

breaking off in pieces. We're losing whole sections of the city every second." More information flashed in the corner of Ramona's right eye; parts of the Metisian map dimmed and faded from blue to yellow to black in a flickering pattern of destruction.

"You will have to find a containment unit, *Signorina!*" Marconi's usually calm voice had risen to a frantic pitch. "Without some means of transport, you won't be able to bring us with you."

"Enrico is correct," Tesla's voice chimed in, more angry than frantic. "There should be a way to create something suitable from the composite tiles that remain."

"There's no time, Nikola," Marconi wailed. "We never planned for something of this magnitude, especially in such a short amount of time! In all of our years here, we never established any kind of protocol for this kind of evacuation!"

"*Calm down. You have two minutes, which is ninety seconds more than we can afford.*" Victrix rasped, hoarse from shouting orders over the cacophony of screams and explosions. "*We need another option, and more than that, we don't have the time to find a way to carry the gents in any containers. Gents, the only secure way to get you out is inside Ramona and Rick. Soul-transfer, just like we did to unlock the charter. Ramona, I'm going to transmit you some sigils. I need you to trace them exactly. Right hand blue, left hand yellow. Both hands green. A one means index finger, a two means index and middle finger. Zero means your thumb.*" She paused, and an intricate design not unlike a Kandinsky painting appeared in Ramona's left eye.

The blue currents along the walls crackled and flared as if in protest. Mercurye didn't appear much happier with the solution.

Ramona didn't blame them.

"*We have no choice. The Thulians are looking for people carrying Metisian objects; they have Worker's Champion, and I am pretty sure they know what Boryets stole is bogus. They are shooting to kill anyone holding anything, and recovering what they held from the body. We can't protect you the way you are.*"

Ramona added, "We can't lose you. We don't want to lose you. This is the best that we've got, and, well...if you've got to ride somebody out of this place, wouldn't you rather it be the two of us? At least you, uh, know what you're getting into."

The walls crackled azure again. Merc laughed nervously.

"*I've already done this with you once; that means all I am doing is a remote repeat of an established protocol. That makes it much easier. I'm setting things up so I take all the risk. If it doesn't work, it backfires on me and you stay where you are. And...you find some other 'containment,' I'll try and get you lot into what you guys have that passes for a fallout shelter and we hope there is a possibility of rescue."* Vickie didn't sound all that confident about the "possibility of rescue." But knowing Vickie as she did, Ramona had the distinct impression that what she was about to try was nothing like as easy as she was trying to make it out to be.

"Nat. Nat. Wake up, Nat. Nat. Wake up. Wake up, Nat. Come on, you need to wake up. Now. Nat."

There was nothing that Natalya wanted to do more than sleep, at that moment. It seemed...easier. She *deserved* some rest, *nyet*? Why did everyone keep bothering her, trying to wake her up? Hadn't she done enough?

"Nat! Come on, Nat, I can see your brainwaves stirring. Which is a terrible analogy. Wake up before I make a worse one!"

"Go away, Daughter of Rasputin. Am sleeping." She wanted to keep her eyes closed. She wouldn't have to see her dear Moji dead, to see all of the blood and death anymore. She could just sleep, to finally rest. She had failed everyone else already; Moji, her comrades, herself. Why shouldn't she sleep, accept what was to come?

"Are you going to lie there until someone comes along and kills you? You think that's going to make up for Moji's murder, you dumb bitch? Okay, go ahead, die. And the rest of CCCP is going to die shortly after that."

That woke Natalya from her stupor. She lifted her head from the pavement, tasting acid and blood in her mouth. She started cursing, lifting herself bodily off of the ground. "When I find you, witch girl, you'll never being—"

Victrix interrupted her. *"Good. You're alive and ready to fight. Goddamnit, Nat, we need you* now. *Get your commie ass moving!"*

"Plot me a course. We will be dealing with how I beat you to death for insults later."

"Everyone else is heading for Trina's saucer. I think it's here. The city's going down, Nat, the best we can do is get people out of it."

She started running, following the blinking directions on her

HUD. "Going down? What of the defenses? These technocratic bastards were able to decimate Kriegers? Why are they being steamrolled?"

"Because they caught Metis with the shields down and the defenses unmanned. Because the idiot Metisians figured we'd won, and no one paid any attention when I pointed out that there was some concerted evac, and to have an evacuation, you have to have a place to evacuate to. And because these don't seem to be the same Kriegers."

"*Pizdets,*" she swore. She ran; everywhere she went, she saw more death and destruction. Metisians were fleeing, with many bodies littering the walkways and corridors. Whenever she reached an open area, with a view to the skyline of the city, she saw Thulian ships, creeping ever forward towards the city center. From beneath each of them was an unbreaking stream of thermite, bathing the city below in white-hot flames. Where those flames didn't touch, actinic blazes from energy cannons streamed outwards. The Kriegers didn't wish to take this city; they wanted to utterly destroy it, to raze and incinerate it and have it forgotten forever. There would be no prisoners, no surrender; this was genocide.

Natalya ran into the remainder of the Atlanta contingent— literally—wholly by accident. She rounded a corner, and suddenly she was face-first with Rusalka, and missed crashing into her by dint only of sheer luck. Everyone stopped for a moment, their powers keying up until they realized that they were on the same side.

"We need to evacuate. The city is falling. Moji—Molotok is dead. Worker's Champion, the traitorous dog, killed him." The Commissar did her best to choke back her emotions as she spoke her dead friend's name. Rusalka kept her eyes cast to the ground.

"Jesus, Nat—" Bella shoved through the group of Metisians at the front of the group, and hugged her impulsively, ignoring the blood covering the Commissar...

Except that a moment later, as a flood of strength and reassurance poured into her, and a whispered voice in the back of her mind said :*Hold it together, Nat. You don't get to have a breakdown until we're out of here,*: she realized it was anything *but* impulsive. Bella was a projective and receptive empath at distance, but only a touch-telepath. :*Yes, I felt it all. Hang in there.*: Bella pulled back from her, staring into Natalya's eyes for a moment.

The Commissar took in a deep breath, then let it out, nodding. *There will be time to grieve later. Now, I am needed. If revenge is to be mine, I will need to live to exact it.*

With Bella were Bulwark, Yankee Pride, and a scattering of military leaders as well as the Metisians. Everyone looked as if they had seen some fighting; many were bloodied, even the Metisians with their white uniforms covered in dirt, blood and burns.

"Trina's ahead of you, at a saucer in a side-hanger. It's a medium-sized one; there should be room for all of you and anyone else you gather up. If we can get them all out of here, we should have about a dozen saucers of evacuees. Come on, people, move it!"

"You heard witch girl. We move, now!" The group didn't need any more encouragement than that; everyone began to run, or limp, in the direction of the saucer. Natalya dropped back long enough to pick up one of the Chinese military leaders bodily; his leg was a bloodied mess, and he was barely up to her chest in height, no burden at all to her to carry. He was in too much pain to protest. She began to run, following as closely behind Bulwark as she could, to take advantage of the shield for herself and her "passenger."

The walls remained dark, as if the two great minds sat in quiet conference. They finally flared to life and separated, one ribbon next to Mercurye and one next to Ramona. "That looks like a yes to me, Vic," Ramona said. She let out a long breath and focused on the design on the HUD, flexing her fingers.

"Follow the cursor. You can do this."

"Right. I can do this." *And if I can't, then I go down trying.*

There was no sign of the protections that Vickie had called "wards and shields," things she had insisted were absolutely necessary the last time. Ramona had the feeling this was Vickie's equivalent of walking a high-wire without a net, and she tried to keep every bit of her attention on the things Vickie was showing her how to trace in the air. As before, sometimes what she traced looked like a diagram, sometimes like an equation. *"You have to want this. You have to want this desperately, people,"* Vickie said, her voice tense with urgency. *"I am not going to pull any punches here. I'm pretty certain that if we can't get you out inside of Ramona and Rick, we are not going to get you out at all. I'm not sure the nearest fallout shelter is going to survive. The*

Thulians have wrecked the city between you and Trina, but Raina and Lyra have a family vehicle in a pretty secure place, and they told me that, hell or high water, they are going to wait for you."

The walls quivered, then went completely dark as the blue currents lifted from the wall and encircled them both. Rick had his eyes squeezed tightly shut; Ramona hoped he was concentrating on *wanting* his passenger very hard indeed.

As for herself, well...she did her best to get her terror to fuel the desire to get her familiar "tenant" back in the little efficiency apartment he'd once had in her head.

She felt the hair on the back of her neck rising involuntarily, and something like a charge building in the air, just before a lightning strike. Just like the last time. The tension began to ratchet up, and along with it...the sound of not-so-distant thunder. The Thulians were getting nearer. Just when she was ready to scream, the mage finally barked the word *"Fiat!"* and—

—*Thank God,* said Tesla in her head, as Rick's eyes snapped open and his mouth formed a little "o."

"Time to go! Rick, pick her up! RUN!"

She found herself scooped up in Mercurye's arms, as she had been that long-ago day when he ran her out to the Mountain. She ducked her head and made herself as small as possible, wishing it were also possible to shed some of the pounds and pounds of metal she had absorbed along the way. But he didn't seem to notice the extra weight.

But, Miss Ferrari! Tesla wailed, as they got another glimpse of the hideous destruction the Thulians were wreaking on Metis, *When we get free—where are we to go?*

"Vix, Tesla wants to know what you intend to—"

"Worry about what we download them into when you get the hell out of there intact!" Vickie interrupted. *"Now RUN!"*

Rick ran like a man possessed. They had no time left; the Thulians had reached the part of the city they were in, the Death Spheres above only pausing their thermite jets long enough for the armored troopers on the ground to sweep through any survivors. When Ramona dared to open her eyes, lifting her head from Rick's chest...she was confronted with snapshots of carnage. Several troopers lining Metisian men and women up against a wall to execute them. Explosions as entire buildings were ripped asunder by actinic energy beams. In a quick flash, she watched as a Robo-Eagle crashed through the glass dome ceiling of a building and emerged with the bleeding forms of two people in its talons, screeching as it lifted back into the sky. It was almost too much to bear; memories of the Invasion sprang fresh into her mind, a rising panic filling her. She tucked her head against Rick's chest again; he was like a machine, his legs pumping up and down, propelling them through the devastation and towards safety.

Following her instructions . . . with fire raging around them, and hell falling from the skies . . . Rick put on more speed and ran. He dodged falling debris, blurred past armored troopers, and just when Ramona was certain there was nowhere else to go, dashed into a courtyard—

—and there it was. A little saucer, about the size of two mini-vans put together, hovering just off the ground with the ramp down. Rick didn't hesitate for a second; he dashed inside. Raina didn't pause either; the saucer shot skyward with the ramp still down, and only Rick immediately leaping sideways into the body of the saucer kept them from tumbling down the same ramp they'd come up.

"Stealthing now!" Raina cried, as the ramp finally snapped shut. The entire saucer shuddered hard; the lights dimmed and then came up again. "We're hit!"

Ramona's heart was in her mouth. *We're going to die—*

"Stealth on!" exclaimed Lyra. The lights dimmed again, and the saucer made a whining sound, but there were no other ominous signs of impending doom.

Which could only mean—

They were safe. Unbelievably, they were safe. And going home.

Bella thought she had never seen anything as welcome as that Metisian saucer, hovering with the gangway an inch off the ground. There were other saucers in the air now—not just evacuees, but some Metisians evidently possessed spines and brains; these were all smaller saucers, but they seemed to be equipped with TDRs, and their pilots (or gunners) were using them to good effect. The giant saucer that had brought them all here was toast, however. With a sense of sick horror she saw it about five hundred yards away, sticking up out of the ground at a slant, its silver all blackened and tarnished and marred with blast holes. It looked as if it had gotten about a hundred yards up and had been shot down.

It was just pure luck it had crashed into an open space and not into buildings or what passed for a hanger.

But she knew she had to put her own feelings on hold for now. As she had told Saviour, no one had the luxury of emotion until after they were safe.

She dropped back, to make sure everyone made it in. It seemed impossible that she and Bulwark—who now cradled the German delegate in his powerful arms—had made it through that gauntlet of horror unscathed. It was a good thing she did; she spotted the Canadian general faltering and limping, about half a block back from the tail of their group. She sprinted back to him, draped his arm over her neck, and hauled him along in time to be right on the heels of the last one up the gangway.

Trina must have had some sort of camera watching; the gangway started to rise as soon as Bella got both feet on it, and the saucer started rising too. Trina wasn't being gentle, either, the momentum from the gangway practically propelled her into the crowd, and the hatch snapped shut.

Once inside, however, there was no sign that they were moving until she glanced up at the several viewscreens visible from where she stood, letting the Canadian gently down onto the floor.

Metis looked like a scene out a dystopian nightmare; a glimpse into hell, maybe. There were *hundreds* upon *hundreds* of Death Spheres. The entire outer two rings of the city had been completely destroyed; fires still burned nearly everywhere, but no buildings were standing in those sections of the city. Any time a spot of resistance rose up, in the form of a defensive battery of Tesla Death Rays or any other sort of fire, it was immediately beset and destroyed by a swarm of Death Spheres. They didn't seem to care how many casualties they were taking; formations of the deadly orbs whizzed through the air, raining burning thermite and energy blasts into the city below. Far in the distance, she saw the massive mechanical dragon that had escaped Ultima Thule; it was stomping through the city, ahead of a line of Death Spheres, completely impervious to any TDR fire that was directed at it. Wherever it went, death and destruction followed. With a sick feeling of familiarity, she was reminded of a Japanese monster movie brought to life. Instead of a man in a rubber suit, this monstrosity was real, ending lives with every movement and blast of fire or energy from its head.

Bella knelt beside the Canadian and laid her hand on his forehead, healing him without taking her attention from the screens. All over what was left of the city, saucers were arcing up—and vanishing. For a moment she wondered frantically if these Thulians had some new form of weapon that utterly obliterated their targets—but then, as she watched three Death Spheres converge on a spot where a saucer *had* been and mill around frantically, she realized that it was only the Metisian stealth-power, which evidently the Thulians couldn't crack.

The lights in their saucer dimmed as Trina kicked their vehicle into stealth mode, and then the view tilted alarmingly, although the deck stayed seemingly level. "We're going for altitude," the girl called out, and not only did the view tilt, but the carnage receded into the distance at an incredible rate.

"Overwatch: open Vix," Bella muttered quietly.

"*Vix, go.*"

"Ramona and Merc?"

"*Away, with cargo. Please do not ask me how I did that, I'd rather not think about how many chances I took.*"

"Have you updated home base?" Not that HQ could have done anything... but they needed to be told.

"*Was awaiting permission. Doing so now. Activate Spin Doctor?*"

"Might as well," Bella sighed. At least this was one disaster ECHO couldn't be blamed for.

But how CCCP was going to take the loss of Molotok, and the betrayal of Worker's Champion...

She glanced over at Red Saviour, who was slouched despondently in one of the saucer seating areas. *I'm going to have a lot of work to do.*

You couldn't tell from in here, but the saucer put on a huge boost of speed, and accelerated up into the stratosphere. The carnage below vanished into a white and black blot with flashes in it, and then disappeared under a layer of cloud as they moved even higher. Under other circumstances, she'd have watched the viewscreens and their panorama of near-space and the curve of the Earth hungrily, as she had on the trip in. It really was beautiful; perfect, even. Up here, you were so far away from all of the death, the misery, the loss.

But all around her she felt defeat, despair, grief and loss. She dropped her gaze to the other folks sharing the saucer. And aside from Gairdner—whom she couldn't read anyway—there was not one person here who was not sagging in hopelessness. Of the forty or so delegates and aides who had arrived in Metis, there were only eighteen left—unless somehow, someone had escaped in other saucers.

Except for Trina, there was not a single person in this vehicle who was unscathed. Scorches, cuts and bruises at the least, broken bones and serious wounds at the worst. But it wasn't the physical injuries that bothered her; it was the despair. It pressed down on everyone like a leaden weight. The Metisians were the worst; she felt they had given up entirely, and were just looking for an excuse to die—but the rest were nearly as despondent.

It was in their faces, the slack muscles, the complete lack of expression—these were Metisians and military men, after all, who were expected to repress at least any external signs of their emotions. It was in their body language, how they slumped in their seats, or lay on the floor, staring blankly at the ceiling. Some were in shock, but others clearly had descended into the stage of completely giving up all hope.

And when she considered what they had just lost . . . she stared into the abyss and considered plunging into it herself. After all, what *did* they have left? Without Metis, without Metisian backing . . . how could they ever beat back this entire *new* wave of Thulians? They didn't know *where* this lot had come from! They were all back to square one, but this time, their forces had been almost obliterated. Had the Thulians just been toying with them all this time? Where had the new force come from?

Their best commander . . . was gone. That might be the real death-blow. How could they hope to do anything without Arthur Chang? What did that leave them with? Herself? She felt torn between despair and sheer panic at the mere idea.

She remembered what Sera had described: the world dying in fire, going down under the boots of the enemy, to end in death and enslavement. And now . . . despite everything they had done, despite throwing *everything* they had at the enemy, they were still going down.

. . . *like hell we are.*

She had no idea where it came from, that little spark of defiance, like Hope in Pandora's Box, but suddenly it flared up, then caught fire, and burned with a growing anger.

"Vix," she said out loud. "Trina. Give me wide-open freqs. Full broadcast, unscrambled, to everyone you can reach. I don't care if the fucking Kriegers can hear me, hell, I *want* them to hear me!"

"*You got it, boss,*" Vickie replied immediately, as Trina gave her a startled look, but made some motions on her control board that Bella assumed gave her broadcast ability.

"Listen up, people," she said, her voice harsh with mixed emotions. "This is ECHO CEO Belladonna Blue."

Gairdner gave her a startled look, but didn't make any moves—or say anything—to make her think he disagreed with her going full broadcast.

"I won't sugar-coat this. We just got our asses handed to us. And you know what? We *deserved* that."

Now heads were coming up all over the saucer, staring at her in varying degrees of shock.

"We *deserved* that, because we have been fighting these rat bastards for over a year, and if there is one thing we should have learned by now, it's that you never, ever become complacent, and never, ever let your guard down. And what did we do? We got smug. We got complacent. We didn't listen to the couple of people warning us, and we let our guard down. *All of us.* We. Fucked. Up." Her voice hardened. "But we are, by God, not going to fuck up again."

She turned to Natalya. "Are we, Commissar Red Saviour?"

Nat's head snapped around and the Commissar stared at her blankly for a moment. Slowly, her face changed; the lines on her face disappeared, and the corners of her mouth turned up in a wolfish snarl.

"*Nyet, sestra!* These *nekulturny* running dogs are thinking that we are beaten, now. That we are weak, contemptible. We have been. But no more! They will bleed for this, and it is us who will be making them bleed!"

Those looks of shock were swiftly turning to something else. Hope, maybe? Certainly those around her had lost that despair, and she could feel the grief turning to anger.

"I know you're listening out there, you murdering bastards," she growled. "So you listen to this. We're *homo sapiens. One* race. *One* species. You've had it lucky up until now, because up until now, you've been fighting us piecemeal. Now, you're going to face us as a united force. Now we know what you are, and how you act. Now we *know* never to let our guard down."

"*Keep it up, Bells!*" Vickie exclaimed. "*You're on rebroadcast everywhere, and...*"

Instead of Vickie *telling* her, several views popped up in her HUD. ECHO HQ, and the metas gathered there were cheering. Crowds elsewhere, fists pumping, more cheering....

"You. Are. Dead. You just don't know it yet. And we are going to find you, and we are going to dig you out of whatever hole you popped out of, and we are going to tear you apart before we stuff you back into it." Her hands were clenched with anger, her face tight with it, and the Canadian general lying on the floor beside her was pounding the floor next to him with his uninjured hand, mouthing the word *yes!* over and over. "We are on fire with rage, and we *never* give up. We're not 'norms' and 'metas' and 'Metisians' anymore. We're *humanity,* and you have officially pissed us off." Gairdner was nodding encouragement at her, as the rest of the people in the saucer responded in their own way. Even the Metisians, who were showing the first signs of real fired-up emotion she had ever seen in them. "You'd better start feeling fear, you bastards, because you cannot imagine what we can do when we're united. And we are not going to stop gunning for you until either the last of us or the last of you lies broken and bleeding on the ground. *Our* ground. *Our* world. And if you've got a way off it, now might be the time to take it, because otherwise you are all going to end up with our boots in your teeth and our knives twisting in your guts."

She glanced at the viewscreens again. You could barely see the spot in the Andes where Metis had been.

"And as for Metis? Where you think you just got a big win?" Her lips lifted in a snarl. "You'd better think again, and think about running while you still have the chance. Because we're coming back. Count on it. We're coming. And we're coming for *you.*"

She signaled "wrap-up" with one finger in her visual field so Vickie would break off the broadcast. "*Broadcast off, Bells,*" Vickie confirmed.

She continued to stare at the viewscreen, as the others around her rallied, and those who were able began the scraps of plans, strategy, options. Calls were made to heads of state, the greatest military minds around the globe, to strategic reserves that had been preparing for a fight since the weeks after the Invasion. Trina and Vickie were kept busy opening comm links and fielding calls.

She'd weigh in when they actually had something. For now... for now she'd do what she did best. Because the Kriegers did not know humanity. And she did.

"Damn right," she whispered, clenching her jaw. "We're coming. And you will wish you had never been spawned."